# BONE WALKER

## AN ANASAZI MYSTERY

KATHLEEN O'NEAL GEAR
and
W. MICHAEL GEAR

**TOR®**

A TOM DOHERTY ASSOCIATES BOOK
NEW YORK

This is a work of fiction. All the characters and events portrayed in this book are either products of the author's imagination or are used fictitiously.

BONE WALKER

A Tor Book
Published by Tom Doherty Associates, LLC
175 Fifth Avenue
New York, NY 10010

www.tor.com

Tor® is a registered trademark of Tom Doherty Associates, LLC.

ISBN-13: 978-0-812-58982-5
ISBN-10: 0-812-58982-3
Library of Congress Catalog Card Number: 2001040496

First Edition: November 2001
First Mass Market Edition: October 2002

Printed in the United States of America

0  9  8  7  6  5  4  3  2

TO
Marv and Patricia Hatcher
with the greatest thanks
for having faith in us
when few others did

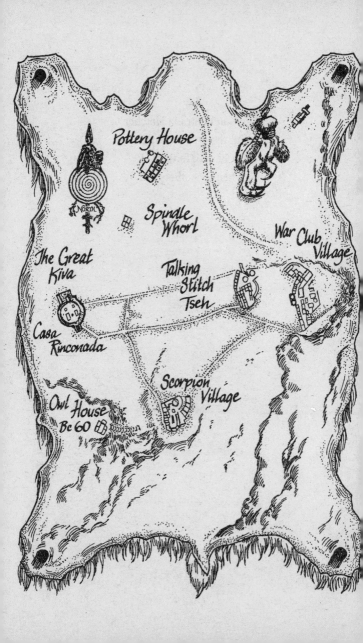

Center Place

Nikol

Chetro Ketl
Kettle Town

Pueblo Bonito

Talon Town

Casa Rinconada

Straight Path Wash

Singing Bird

High Sun House

# Acknowledgments

This novel would not have been possible without the support of our publisher, Tom Doherty; our editor, Bob Gleason; and the fine people at Forge Books. We would like to acknowledge the outstanding efforts of the field force, including the indefatigable Tom Espenschied, Bob Williams, Ellen Williams, Nancy Lindbloom, Larry Yoder, and Mark Janus. Katherine Cook read the manuscript for content and errors, and has provided her years of experience to make many of our books better. Our professional colleagues have spent their lives laboring under hot suns, in the rain and wind, to uncover the past of the Anasazi.

We sincerely thank all of you for your hard work.

# CHAPTER 1

Sun Cycle of the Great Horned Owl
The Falling River Moon

*FETID BREATH CARESSES my cheek as Death, the Blue God, leans over my shoulder to peer into my eyes.*

*I turn away to stare at this place where they have carried me. I lie in a rock-capped overhang where wind and water have undercut the dirty brown sandstone. To my right, against the wall, I see the piled litter of an old pack rat nest. Firelight flickers across the rough surface of the rock. Shadows leap. Shadows live on light.*

*The Blue God watches me, waiting, a hunger keening in her souls.*

*Five figures, wrapped in split-turkey-feather blankets, lie in a semicircle as if to protect me from the night and the bone-chilling wind.*

*The Blue God shifts, and I feel her need. Her craving flows through my bones and muscles like the tingling charge of a rubbed fur blanket. With each painful breath I take, she hunches like a starving coyote, waiting to leap on my breath-heart soul when it slips ever so lightly from my body.*

*The Blue God draws an expectant breath, and fear draws patterns along my age-withered muscles. I wait for her with anticipation; my loins tingle, the expectation of her caress as she devours me is like that of sexual release.*

*But I fear what comes after: the journey down the Trail of Sorrows where Spider Woman waits. There, beside her eternal fire, her nimble feet dance on the* ashes of evil . . . of those who have gone before me.

My hand still burns with the feel of the turquoise wolf—the Spirit amulet. He was my salvation. He would have led me through the maze, past the monsters, and down the correct trails to the Land of the Dead. The War Chief, Browser, tore the wolf from my hand. I searched for many sun cycles before I found the precious wolf and removed him from the dead Night Sun's mummified neck. May her soul mix with those tortured ashes under Spider Woman's feet. She brought the First People to this: Ruin. Pain. Death. She was the last great ruler of the Straight Path Nation. She gave up everything to marry one of the Made People: a lowly War Chief.

Her legacy to me should have been leadership of the Straight Path Nation. Instead all that she left me was hatred of all that was . . . and is. Most of all, hatred of myself and this world.

I have fought the new gods, the hideous half-human and half-animal katsinas. For that, Spider Woman should thank me, but her gratitude is as fickle as Wind Baby's when he sucks the last moisture from a parched cornfield.

Unlike Spider Woman, the Blue God cares not a whit for my actions. The Blue God, like me, is driven by an unwholesome appetite. She takes, sucking down the souls of the dying in an endless orgy of gluttony. I understand her desperate craving, for I have had my own.

The War Chief, Browser, asked, "How could you do it?" He does not know the ecstasy that thrilled every bone, muscle, and tissue, as I shot my hot seed into the flesh of my flesh. The gods, jealous as they are, forbid incest because it smacks of the immortal. Through it, a man can live forever.

I cough, and pain dances in my chest on feathery feet. Bright red blood seeps into my wounded lungs as broken ribs grate against each other.

The Blue God extends her muzzle, sniffing at my bloody mouth.

Is it time?

I struggle to maintain the hold on my breath-heart soul. I am drawn, lured forward by my wish to feel the Blue God's teeth, to know that ecstasy of release as I slide down her silky throat to the warmth of her stomach. I, too, have eaten souls, swallowed their meat, fusing their flesh with mine.

A tear forms on my eyelid, silvering the firelight and blurring my vision. Gods, I want this so much!

But the fear is stronger. Before I can experience that burst of relief, I must have the sacred turquoise wolf to lead me to salvation. He knows the way of the First People, when, after death, the breath-heart soul meets that forked trail. To the left lies the Sun Trail that leads to the Land of the Dead. There, I can spend eternity with my ancestors: the First People who climbed from the underworlds during the Age of Emergence and followed the Great North Road to the sunlight.

Without the turquoise wolf to guide me, I will be tricked into turning right, down the Trail of Sorrows. The smoke that I see—thinking it that of my ancestors' hearths—will rise from Spider Woman's piñon pine fire. As I approach, she will ensnare me and burn me into the ash she dances upon.

A wavering form detaches from the darkness beyond the sheltering rock. The Blue God moans in frustration as my daughter walks gracefully into the light of the fire. She stops, the wind teasing her long black hair. Wind Baby presses the yellow fabric of her dress against those full breasts and accents the sensual curve of her hip. As her eyes meet mine I see the question, the longing. She, too, is intimate with the Blue God. Is that the excitement I see reflected in her large dark eyes? Are they entwined like lovers in rapturous anticipation of my death?

I wet my bloody lips and say, "I will not die today."

*I see her carefully masked disappointment. Unlike me, she has never learned to curb her appetite. Her need frightens me. For all that I am, she is more, haunted, the sister of the Blue God. My daughter runs her tongue over her full red lips, wetting them sensually.*

*She says nothing as she steps gracefully to my side and lowers herself. I catch her scent, smoky, hot from running through the night to reach me. I close my eyes against the pain in my chest. Her breath is warm on my cheek; her tongue tickles my lips as she licks the clotted blood away.*

*The warmth of her body next to mine is a tonic.*

*It reminds me . . . there is much to live for.*

# CHAPTER 2

THEY CAME FROM the south, dressed in blue cotton tunics with red waist sashes. Eleven of them. Nine men and two women. They ran the old Great North Road. Years of sun had browned their lean bodies. They wore their hair in tight buns pinned with sharpened rabbit bone. All but one carried a bow and quiver slung over their left shoulders next to a ceramic canteen painted in geometric designs. Their right shoulders strained against the weight of thick packs woven from yucca leaves. In their hands, they held carefully crafted war clubs, stone-headed, with wooden, use-polished handles. They scanned their surroundings, eyes like obsidian beads, wary of ambush or the signs of passing warriors.

Onward they went, northward, their feet shuffling in

the distance-eating gait of practiced runners. Only one of them flagged from time to time, the old man who followed behind.

Unlike the others—who might have seen twenty-five sun cycles at most—he was old, an ancient man whose tunic looked more like a rag. He tended to bob and weave on his feet, his whip-thin legs like stalks, his withered arms sticklike under a skin that had the texture of old leather. He alone carried no weapons or pack. His brittle white hair had come loose from the bun, and haloed his old head in sun-graced wisps. His face was long, sharp, the gods having left him most of his teeth so that his lips didn't pucker over bare gums. Of them all, only the old man didn't cast wary glances to either side; he devoted his entire attention to the road.

They veered wide when they came upon stumbling parties of refugees: broken men, women, and children with threadbare packs on their backs who trudged disconsolately southward toward who knew what distant goal. At night, the eleven camped a half-hand's journey from the road, taking the high places, heedless of water or shelter from the prevailing winds.

Relentlessly, they pursued their way down from the timbered slopes of the mountains, past the ruined outposts of the Straight Path Nation and onto the Great South Road. They crossed the dune-stippled desert, barely glancing at the abandoned towers, the crumbling shrines, and the narrow earthworks that marked the roadway. They gave cursory inspection to South House where it hulked in ruin. Their feet whispered on the stone steps of the Corner Canyon stairway, and they spent the night beside the sagging remains of Corner Canyon kiva. The next morning they crossed the dry course of Straight Path Wash and followed the road between the ruins of Kettle Town and Talon Town. To their left they could see the rain-washed vacant doorways of Hillside village. One by one, taking their time to help the old man, they climbed up the dilapidated stairway where the Matrons of old had led glorious processions of the First People. They hardly glanced at Center Place Town. Broken potsherds crumbled under their feet as they trotted past the huge mounds of soul pots. Ancient priests had smashed the pots to release captured souls onto the Great North Road, where they could run to the sacred lake and the Land of the Dead.

Their pace never wavered as they trotted across the scrub sage and dune flats. At high sun, on the sixth day since passing Center Place, they wearily followed the trail down the bluffs, splashed across the shallow brown waters of the River of Souls, and passed the burned-out hulk of Northern Town. This time, tomorrow, they would reach their destination.

The future would be decided then. One way, or another.

*I SLIDE ACROSS the sandstone on my belly and sniff their tracks.*

*The hole in their leader's sandal left a thumb-sized space in the middle of the weave. When he passed by me earlier, his eyes gleamed with an unearthly light, as though he had seen the faces of the gods, and could no longer see this world. I touch the space and wonder at his foolishness.*

*"Mother?"*

*A chill breath blows my long hair as I gaze out at the dark hills.*

*"Mother, is Grandfather dying?" she asks.*

*I hear her in the rocks behind me, but I do not turn. Piper's Song has seen eight summers. She does not understand.*

*As Father Sun climbs into the morning sky, lavender*

*light spills across the land, chasing the Shadow People away. They hide in the crevices and beneath the ledges, trembling, thinning themselves to nothingness, hoping, he will not see them.*

"Is he dying, Mother?"

*I do not answer.*

*I am one of the Shadow People, afraid of the light, of things seen too clearly. It is only at night, when the sharp edges of life blur and go quiet, that I can think.*

"What's the matter with Grandfather, Mother?"

*She slithers forward and twines her dirty fists in my red sleeve. I am surprised by all this talking. More and more, of late, she is a mute. A child with no voice at all.*

"His heart is hurt."

*When I look at her, there's no one inside those eyes. They are black empty wells. She always looks past people, as though she's concentrating hard on some secret voice that only she can hear, and it occupies all of her attention.*

"Can't we fix it?"

"You've seen cloth that's been cut up? That's what Grandfather's heart looks like."

"Because that man bashed him with a stone-headed war club?"

"Yes."

*That man. That War Chief.*

*I flatten out on the ground again and sniff the tracks, but all I smell is old blood.*

*Strange. No matter how far I run, I smell his blood. It has an intoxicating taint, as though already rotten when it bubbles from Father's mouth. After he was first injured, I found myself sitting at his side for hands of time, just holding the scent in my lungs, like a starving wolf, waiting for the chance to feed.*

*Piper rolls to her back as though preparing to sit up.*

"Stay down," *I order.* "Be quiet."

*When I was younger than Piper, five summers, my clan abandoned me. They moved and left me behind. I was half mad when Father found me and took me into his arms.*

*How can I live without him? His blood is my blood and my daughter's blood. I fear we will die if he dies.*

*Yet I long for him to be dead. I hate him for what he did to me, to my sisters, to my daughter.*

*"Mother?"*

*She cups a hand and whispers in my ear. "I have some thread in my pack. Maybe we could sew the cuts back together, like we do cloth?" She fingers the rips in her own red-and-black cape as she says this.*

*"No, Piper. He needs a new heart."*

*Piper suddenly goes still. Her eyes are wide open, but they are looking inside, not out. For several long moments she stares as if frozen; then in a ferocious whisper she says, "Please, Mother, not my heart!"*

*She buries her face in my sleeve and I feel her warm breath on my arms. Her voice is muffled, but I know what she's saying, "Not my heart, not my heart."*

*I look out at the waking gray hills and murmur, "Not your heart. There is another."*

POWERED BY OCCASIONAL floods and spring runoff, Dry Creek had cut its slow way into the buff and gray uplands. As it neared the Spirit River, the valley widened out, leaving a broad floodplain nestled between cobble-strewn terraces. To either side lay broken hills stippled with juniper and piñon pine.

Stone Ghost followed a faint path across the greasewood-spotted flats. Wispy white hair clung to the aged skin of his brown scalp. His features seemed too large for the lean frame of his face: the nose a little too long and hooked, the mouth a bit too wide. Three spirals, faded now by age, had been tattooed on his chin. The sky reflected in the dark wells of his eyes. A battered turkey-feather cape hung from his thin, hunched shoulders. He stepped carefully in the darkening shadows, picking his way around the spiny branches of greasewood. Before him, sunset silhouetted the eroded terrace above the floodplain. Here and there rounded cobbles had rolled down the slopes to lodge in the sagebrush and clog the little rivulets that infrequent rains had etched into the hard gray dirt.

Stone Ghost watched the shadows as if they might be alive. He pressed a gnarled hand against the soft fabric of his tan shirt. The garment had been a gift, given to him by Rock Dove, Matron of Dry Creek village, to replace his old worn cotton shirt. Why the Matron had taken pity on him was beyond his understanding, but kindness always seemed more common when people were afraid.

He placed a sandaled foot into the shadows, felt carefully for purchase, and began to climb up the sloping terrace above the floodplain. What had his ancestors done to so turn the gods against them? He blinked up at the frayed clouds glowing against the silvered haze of sunset.

*A man has lived too long when he has lived to see the end of sanity.*

Too many revelations had been plucked from the safe warp and weft of lies spun about the last days of the First People and the fall of the Straight Path Nation. Now it was coming unraveled, and with it, his own complicity.

During the Age of Emergence, the First People had bravely climbed through a series of dark underworlds to get to this world of light. On the second day, the Creator decided the First People were too few and needed help to build the world, so he turned a variety of animals into humans: badgers, bears, buffaloes, ants, wolves, and other creatures. Hence they were Made People. The First People had always considered the Made People to be inferior—human on the outside but with animal souls and minds. They had enslaved and tortured the Made People. Fortunately, First People only married other First People and their blood weakened over time. When their Power began to wane, the Made People rose up and made war on the First People. One hundred sun cycles ago, the Made People hunted them down, and killed every last man, woman, and child. Or so they had believed until recently . . . when a group of White Moccasins had been seen roaming the forests of the northern mesas.

One hundred and ten sun cycles ago, Night Sun, the great Matron of Talon Town, abandoned her people to marry one of the Made People, her former War Chief, Ironwood. The aftermath of Night Sun's abdication of Power was disastrous. Night Sun and Ironwood fled Straight Path Canyon with their daughter, Cornsilk, and the man who would become Cornsilk's husband, and the greatest prophet in their history, the Blessed Poor Singer.

In the final scramble for power in a dying nation, the First People had grown suspicious of each other. They started hiring assassins to take each other's lives. They called them White Moccasins and considered them to be sacred warriors. The rulers selected their best warriors, groups of no more than ten, and sent them out to destroy anyone who might threaten them. They paid these assassins too handsomely to believe, showering them with baskets of coral, jet, turquoise, and rare seashells from the distant oceans. The fools did not realize what would happen next. When you give men such unrestrained power and wealth, it is like a Spirit plant in the veins. The assassins quickly amassed enough wealth so that they could adopt their own rules for who should live and who should die. Few escaped their wrath.

As Stone Ghost walked, a young man's face peered out from his memory. The ghostly eyes watched, unblinking, large and black, trying to measure his soul.

Is that what had happened twenty sun cycles ago? Stone Ghost had been fighting White Moccasins and hadn't known it?

Stone Ghost ignored the phantom's gaze and climbed step after step, feeling tightness in his withered leg muscles. The sandals on his age-thickened feet looked more like dark blobs against the ground. He had seen the like on the paintings his people did on sandstone cliffs.

*I am nothing more. A thin drawing. Colors dabbed on the stone face of life.* He could feel parts of himself flaking away, fading; just as paint made from flowers, fat, and charcoal did after too many searing suns.

The face in his memory nodded, the eyes large with sad anger.

*"Forgive me, I was as arrogant as my ancestors,"* he whispered to the hovering apparition. *"Two Hearts set the trap, but I was the weapon he wielded."*

What difference would it have made if Ocher—yes, that was the young warrior's name—had lived and sired children? With the coughing disease, the constant raids, with clans turning against their own, and drought, famine, and holy war broken loose in the land, would Ocher's life have meant anything? Or would he and his just be more moldering bodies lying in the bottom of some burned kiva? Had his death been such a tragedy, or only the difference of a couple of sun cycles?

Stone Ghost stepped over the crest of the terrace and gazed out at the sunset; it lay bruised against an indigo horizon of flat-topped buttes. To his right a pile of stones lay in a jumble: one of the First People's shrines, abandoned and collapsed.

"What are you doing out here?" a voice hissed from one side. His nephew, War Chief Browser, rose from behind a sagebrush. He had a round face with thick black brows and a flat nose. A gray blanket, the color of the soil, draped his shoulders. "Uncle Stone Ghost, didn't I tell you to stay in the village? Did you forget?"

Stone Ghost smiled. He did seem to be getting terribly forgetful of late, so his nephew's words didn't particularly bother him. He answered, "The only thing I forgot is how foolish you are."

Browser gave him an irritated look and hooked his war club to his belt again. In the twilight the angry red scar on Browser's forehead looked purple. A bandage swathed his arm.

Browser turned. "It's my uncle," he called in a soft voice.

"I know."

From several paces away, Catkin stood. A beautiful woman, she had cut her hair in mourning, and it hung about her oval face in irregular locks. Her long legs and slim figure made her appear taller than she was. She cast wary glances over the edge of the terrace.

"What are you doing out here, Uncle?" Browser demanded. "You, of all people, should know how dangerous it is. The White Moccasins might be anywhere."

"You and Catkin are not up here hunting White Moccasins, Nephew." Stone Ghost looked down the slope to the greasewood flat below. Did he feel *her* eyes on him even now?

Stone Ghost gazed back across the valley. The first fires cast their glow on Dry Creek village. The small rectangle of mud-plastered rooms nestled beneath an eroded sandstone ledge. In the forgotten past a basin had been dug into a seep below a crack in the sandstone. It provided a dribble of water. The supply had been consistent enough that over the years a settlement had sprung up. Room after room had been added to Dry Creek village until a block of twenty-six rooms stood beside the seep. Now, with refugees from Longtail village, every room was crowded. The overflow lived in brush shelters. The Katsinas' People couldn't stay here. Last summer's rains had been few and far between. The seep provided Dry Creek village with just enough water in times of drought to irrigate their pitiful crops. The process was laborious, plants watered one by one from a ceramic pot. The ditches that normally diverted runoff from Dry Creek had remained parched. Corn had withered, the harvest poor.

"Why did you pick this place to hunt for her?" Stone Ghost looked around at the low sage and the crumbled stone shrine.

"It has the best view of Dry Creek village," Catkin said, "and it's far enough away that the dogs wouldn't smell her and bark." Worry etched her delicate face. She served as War Chief Browser's deputy, one of the most blooded and skilled warriors in the world.

Browser nodded. "She's here, somewhere. Or was. Until you walked out here and announced our positions, Uncle. Now she knows we're hunting her."

Stone Ghost exhaled and his breath rose against the darkening lavender sky. "She didn't need me to know your positions, Nephew. She's been watching you all day. She is the most dedicated of all hunters, her mind twisted like a yucca rope, bent and kinked until it is no longer human but something animal. She hasn't taken her eyes from your movements all day, so she already knew you were here, waiting for her."

Browser did not respond. His gaze darted over every shadow.

Stone Ghost stared back at the lights twinkling in Dry Creek village. "I came to tell you that Matron Cloudblower has decided to take the Katsinas' People to Straight Path Canyon. She plans to rebuild the great kiva at Streambed Town. She thinks that perhaps that was the First People's kiva—the one where they climbed into this world."

"Why would she think that?" Browser's round face was gilded by the fading light.

"Because it might be," Stone Ghost said simply.

"And because Dry Creek village, despite Matron Rock Dove's warm welcome, cannot shelter us through the winter. Matron Cloudblower sent me to summon you that you might help her plan the move."

Browser nodded. "Very well. Tell her I will be there soon."

Stone Ghost dropped his voice to a whisper. "No. Now." He gripped Browser's sleeve. "You must never hunt her in the darkness, Nephew. She will kill you before you know it."

Catkin fingered her war club. "It is we who are hunting her, Elder."

"Is that truly what you think?" Stone Ghost laughed softly and began picking his way down the dark slope toward the flats below. "Do you remember that first night, Catkin, when you came to my house down at Smoking Mirror Butte? Do you remember what I told you?"

"You told me a great many things, Elder. As I recall, you even talked to a skull in a sack."

"Yes, my old friend, Crooked Nose. I wonder how he's doing down there. I miss his company." Stone Ghost took a breath. "Do you recall what I told you about the Blue God?"

Catkin put a hand on his elbow to steady him as they walked, and he patted her fingers in gratitude. "You said she was a bloody-headed woman, that she met the breath-heart soul as it climbed out of the grave. I told you I didn't believe in her."

"And I told you that your disbelief made you the rabbit in the brush, and she the cougar lying in wait." Stone Ghost wobbled when his foot snagged a root. "There is only one way to sneak up on a desperate predator."

"What is that, Uncle?" Browser asked from behind them. His voice sounded tired.

"You must find her weakness, and then use it against her. Do you know her weakness, Nephew?"

The silence stretched, and Stone Ghost concentrated on his feet.

Finally, Browser said, "No. Do you?"

"I think so."

Catkin turned to stare at Stone Ghost. "What is it?"

Stone Ghost navigated across a treacherous bed of loose rocks. "It is a place, not a thing. A place I am not even sure exists. A—"

"A place of legends," Browser whispered.

"Yes, I'm glad you remember, Nephew." He had told Browser this right after the kiva burned at Longtail village. "We should be going. Soon. It may take us several days to find it, if it can be found."

Browser came up beside Stone Ghost, and his face gleamed in the firelight cast by the village. "If it exists, we can find it."

Stone Ghost smiled sadly and looked down at the village. People sat before evening fires, wrapped in blankets. A few children ran across the plaza, strangely quiet.

"This is a witch's lair, Nephew. It may exist, but it will be surrounded by traps, and cloaked in darkness."

*I SLIP A hand from the darkness beneath the tumbled rocks of the First People's shrine and grasp the sandstone. One by one, I remove the stones until the gap is wide enough to raise my head and peer out into the night.*

*Old Stone Ghost is gone . . . and he has taken my prey with him.*

*I rise from the hollow like a Spirit from the earth, and turn toward the distant fires of Dry Creek village, watching the wavering shapes of three people move through the greasewood toward the light.*

*I sniff the air for their lingering scents. The breeze caresses my charcoal-smudged face.*

*I was so close! If the old man hadn't come . . .*

*I wait until they walk back into the village plaza; then a throaty laugh breaks from my full red lips. Browser will come to me again. It is inevitable.*

# CHAPTER 3

### Chaco Canyon, New Mexico

DR. DALE EMERSON Robertson froze in his tracks. He would have sworn he heard laughter, mocking and eerie. The faint sound seemed to dance on the cold desert night. As he cocked his head to listen, the sound faded. Moonlight washed the canyon with its pale brush, beaming whitely on the cracked rimrock, painting the rabbitbrush, chamisa, and sage.

"Must have been the wind," he whispered. Though no trace of a breeze could be felt in the chill air.

He shook off the dark premonition and resisted the urge to climb back into the warm safety of his pickup. Instead he locked the door and started down the path that led west from the Tseh So interpretive site toward the ruins of Casa Rinconada.

Chaco Canyon: a place of mystery. It spoke to every American archaeologist's soul. It had always spoken to Dale, but on this night he would have preferred to forget the past and what this half-baked Halloween journey might mean for him. His eyes drifted over the moonlit landscape.

Eons past, tectonic pressure, wind, and water had

carved the canyon through the Cretaceous Cliff House sandstone. People had come here, drawn by the alluvial soils in the canyon bottom where, as the rains came and went, corn, beans, and squash could be grown. Dale thought of the immense draw of Chaco Canyon, and how it had shaped men for thousands of years. It had reached a stunning climax over nine hundred years ago when the Anasazi charted the courses of the sun, moon, and stars. They had used that sophisticated astronomical information to lay out their enormous pueblos, schedule their complex ceremonies, and build hundreds of miles of roads.

He looked up at the star-patched sky. The late October chill ate into his bones, sending a shiver coursing through him. It was Halloween; he should have been home dropping candy into sacks as a means of placating little suburban ghosts and witches.

"This is a fool's errand," he murmured to himself in irritation.

He should have been in Santa Fe eating *pollo marengo* at the Pink Adobe with his adopted son, Dusty, and his friend of twenty years, Dr. Maureen Cole. Not out here. Not on a cold night like this.

Moonlight gilded the canyon rim a quarter mile to the south, and the weathered sandstone shone with a knuckle-white luminosity that mimicked freshly stripped bone. Cracks, fissures, and irregularities in the stone cast raven shadows.

Rains had washed little rivulets into the trail. Stones tried to roll under Dale's feet. He stopped, took a deep breath, and winced against the pain in his knees. His frosty breath rose pale in the cold night air. No wonder his knees hurt. Power and time were carnally entwined like two perverted lovers.

He was too old to be out here chasing a wild goose, but he had to find out if what he knew in his heart was the same truth his head had denied all these years.

*What happened to you that night, you old fool?*

The question rolled around in his mind like a polished stone. It had been a fool's errand—even back then. A dare that his "Western" mind had taken, and for which he now had no explanation except bad knees and an illusive but mocking memory. The problem was, he'd slipped that night, twenty-five years ago, fallen . . . and when he'd awakened the picture lodged in his mind had been so clear that he couldn't tell if it had been an artifact of the midnight fall, or a sight he'd seen with his eyes. He'd never known for sure.

The vision was of a sand painting on a cave floor. In the carefully poured grains of colored sand, he'd seen his image: a white man wearing a brown hat, with a trimmed beard, blue jeans, and western-style shirt. His hair had only been threaded with gray then. But it had been him. He'd known it.

Then he'd seen the three naked witches in the back of the cave, illuminated by firelight. One, a tall, pirouetting form, wore only a wolf katchina mask. Smooth muscles had rolled under sweat-shiny skin as the katchina dancer lifted his bow and shot a yucca-leaf arrow into the sand painting's knee. Dale had felt a terrible pain, like glassed fire, under his right knee-cap. As the macabre dancer shot a second arrow, Dale's left knee exploded in agony. He remembered crying out, falling into a gray abyss. Falling . . .

Hours later he'd come to, dazed, almost unable to walk, and practically had to crawl back to where he had left Dusty and the horses in a nearby arroyo.

For more than twenty-five years he had wondered what had happened to him that night. And then this morning, she had called. Was that why he'd come here, to this place? To the spot where he'd last seen her, where they had finally terminated what should never have been.

Power and time. Cycles of the sun and moon. They all came together in Chaco Canyon. After thirty-seven years, almost to the night, he was back. At this place.

It had been years since he had last heard from her. Her voice had been so clear over the phone line that morning that the intervening decades might not have been: *"You're not being funny, Dale."*

"Funny?" he had asked, confused not only by her call after so many years of mutual silence, but by the subject of the conversation.

*"The note says, 'We will meet at the center place where the ancestors climbed from the Shipapu into this world. In the corner house on the night when the dead live. Two cycles of the moon have come full. It is time to end what the four of us began. On the night of masks, at midnight, you shall make the journey. The wolf returns to its lair.' "*

"I didn't send you any note."

*"If you didn't, who did? Who else knows about this?"*

"I intend to find out. Can you fax it to me?"

*"Dale . . . you know what this means?"*

His knees hurt worse, as if someone had injected habanero pepper juice into the joints. A form of rheumatoid arthritis the doctors said, though they were a little hazy on the exact diagnosis.

He looked up at the gap where water had eaten into the sandstone rim to form Rinconada Canyon. To the east, in the gap just below the night-blackened horizon, was the stairway, a series of steps carved into the caprock where the ancient road led south to Tsin Kletsin. Here on the meridian line between Pueblo Bonito and Chetro Ketl, the high priests of Chaco had passed on the greatest of their ritual journeys. Now, he, too, followed it, seeking the end of a thirty-seven-year-old mystery.

"Is the note signed?" he had asked.

*"There is only one word: 'Kwewur.' Does that mean anything to you?"*

"Yes," he'd whispered.

It was old—a name from a long dead village called

Awatovi. Few whites outside of a handful of south-western archaeologists and a few folklorists had ever heard the name.

In the moon's glow he studied the bit of paper and crumbled it in his palm. His feet crunched loudly in the still darkness. To either side of the trail archaeo-logical sites—the so-called small houses—lay under low mounds of rubble. This part of the canyon was packed with archaeology. The irregular ground surface consisted of mounds—ruined pueblos—and depres-sions caused by collapsed pit houses. Speckled bits of pottery and flaked stone artifacts glinted in the moon-light.

Some investigators believed that while the Great Houses filled the north side of Chaco Wash, the south side had been reserved for the lower classes and itin-erant pilgrims who came to Chaco Canyon. It was here, some hypothesized, that the Chaco elite had provided a sort of "ceremonial circus" for the masses.

He strode past the interpretive marker that explained that fact to tourists, and made his way up the slight incline. Atop the knoll, he stopped. The desert was quiet, though in the distance the faint hooting of an owl could be heard. He exhaled again, his frosty breath rising toward the stars.

"Are you here?" he called out. "Kwewur? Is that what you call yourself?"

He looked up when dark wings moved through the moonlight above him. The owl hooted right over his head.

Dale looked down into the great kiva. Yes, he knew this place. Nearly nine hundred years ago the Chacoans had cut this huge hole through the sandstone cap of the knoll, down into the shale. The diameter measured sixty-three feet and five inches, an almost perfect circle. The sheer walls rose ten feet above the concentric stone bench. Thirty-four crypts pockmarked the curving wall.

Dale walked around the western side, looking down at the stone bench.

Had he been wrong? Was it all some elaborate hoax? Some irritating Halloween trick? He could feel the old Power rising in the air around him. Casa Rinconada's presence touched the soul. The Anasazi believed that kivas were doorways to the underworlds. Chacoans had used this place to impress the bucolic pilgrims who bore tribute from the far corners of the Southwest. Looking down, shadows seemed to move in the depths of the old Chacoan tunnel.

He walked around to the southern anteroom that led down into the interior. Park Service rules prohibited after-hours visits to the ruins. His mouth had gone dry as he stepped into the shadowed stairway. Stone grated underfoot; he lowered himself step by step into the gloom. At the bottom, cold stone rose around him, timeworn, silent, and ominous. He called out: "Hello?"

The faint scurrying of rodent feet on rock met his ears.

The pain in Dale's knees became excruciating. White moonlight sliced across the round room.

With growing unease, he looked around the huge kiva. The stone squares of the foot drums cast black shadows, and the central hearth, so many centuries dark, looked like an inky abyss. The square wall niches seemed to pulse, as though from vibrations coming from another realm. The eerie sensation of hidden eyes ate into him.

Dale nerved himself, and called out to the darkness. "If you're here, I've come to talk to you, to find out what this is all about."

This was madness. As he turned to leave he thought he heard . . . what? Fabric brushing stone?

Moonlight blazed on the northern wall, and a black slash, the old subterranean passageway, seemed to become a rip across the floor. There, 850 years ago, masked dancers would have magically appeared, rising, as if out of the very ground.

One hundred years after the fall of Chaco, the Anasazi returned to Casa Rinconada, filled in the tunnel, and refurbished this entire place. They had plastered over the old gods, and resanctified Casa Rinconada in the name of the katchinas.

Fear knotted his stomach. He felt sick.

Why had he been called here? Because of her? That had been thirty-seven years ago. He had found her here alone, on a moonlit night like this one. No one could have known what they had done here. And, after all these years, who would care?

The distant hoot of an owl carried on the still night. The death bird's lonely voice echoed off the stone walls.

"What do you want? Why bring *her* into this? She hasn't been part of my life for years. If this is a joke . . ."

Laughter seemed to come from everywhere; it reverberated off the ancient fitted stones.

Dale lifted a finger. "I warn you, if this is some student prank, you're going to regret ever—"

"Student?" a voice hissed.

A stone clattered behind Dale, and he spun, his heart stuttering in his chest. "Where are you? Come out and show yourself."

"Spider Woman awaits you, white man," the voice whispered. An acoustical trick, it seemed to issue from the stygian crypts on all sides.

"Who are you? Why did you want me to come here? What's this all about?" Dale swallowed hard.

"It's about you . . . me . . . and the past." The hollow voice sounded pained. "It's about love, Dale. Love is pain. And you hurt me so. You have hurt so many . . . and they don't even know how badly you wounded them." The echoing voice paused, as if listening. "Do you hear them crying?"

"What?"

"Forward . . . step forward."

Dale hesitantly walked out around the crumbled deflector wall and past the dark hearth. He squinted, seeing the design on the kiva floor. Moonlight washed out the colors, but he knew what he saw: a sand painting, carefully done—an effigy of an old man with bad knees, it wore a fedora hat. The expression on the drawing's face was one of terror.

Dale fought a sudden wave of nausea. Pressure, like constricting bands, tightened in his chest until he couldn't breathe.

"Are you afraid, Dr. Robertson?" the voice asked. "You, who terrorized so many? The ghosts of the ancestors are gathering around. Can you hear them? Sense them?"

Dale's mouth worked as he tried to form words.

An apparition rose from the gaping blackness of the subfloor tunnel. The creature wore a mask, a terrible mask in the shape of a wolf's head. Even in the moonlight, it looked ancient, battered and cracked with age.

"We have old business, you and I. It goes back . . . far back." He spread his black-painted arms like a bird preparing to soar, and in a voice as dry as sand, sang, "In Beauty it is begun. In Beauty it is begun." From his raised hands, a white moonlit haze fell.

"Sacred cornmeal," Dale whispered, and panicked.

His feet tangled as he turned to run, and the sudden intense pain in his right knee made him cry out. His leg collapsed under him. He hit the ground, hard, falling into the middle of the sand painting. Scrambling, he tried to get up, his knee burning in agony. His fingers clawed frantically through the sand, ruining the exquisitely detailed image.

A shadow blocked the moon. Dale looked up and could see the colors of the sacred mask: red, blue, and yellow. They encircled the gaping black pits of the eyeholes.

"Come," the hollow voice hissed, "let us go talk to the dead."

BROWSER FOLLOWED CATKIN and Stone Ghost across the plaza in Dry Creek village. Night had settled over the crowded village, and with it, the chill of late autumn. Low fires cast muted light on the knots of people who huddled under feather and cloth blankets, nursing the flames that cooked their evening suppers. Steam rose from pots of corn gruel on the coals.

The look of the people wounded his soul: vacant-eyed, listless, dwelling on the horrible memories locked in their heads. Two weeks ago they had abandoned their old home, Longtail village, and the tragedy they had left buried in the burned kiva. There, by the basket-load, they had carried dirt to bury the charred corpses of more than half of their children, torched by Two Hearts's rage.

What possessed a witch to hate so much that he would incinerate innocent children? Was it that they believed in different gods, or was there something so evil and twisted in Two Hearts's souls that he was nothing more than a malignant darkness that walked the land?

Browser touched the angry pink scar on his forehead. That scar, people could see. The one that had scabbed so poorly on his breath-heart soul remained invisible to all but him. From the moment he had married Ash Girl, he and the witch, Two Hearts, had been tied as tightly as a knotted cord. For that entire time he had unwittingly lived with the shadow of Two Hearts's evil. His wife, Ash Girl, had been Two Hearts's daughter. A woman tainted by incest, driven to madness by her father's crime until a monster soul had inhabited her.

*And I was too much of a fool to see what was right before my eyes, what shared my bed.*

Browser unknowingly had killed Ash Girl outside of a ruined house in Straight Path Canyon—and killed part of himself with that same arrow. For moons afterward, he had been lost, drowning in guilt and grief.

He studied Catkin from the corner of his eye. By killing Ash Girl, he had saved Catkin. He could finally admit to himself that had it been different, had he known what face lay beneath the wolf mask that Ash Girl wore, he would have still driven the arrow through Ash Girl's heart—through his wife's heart, the heart of the woman who had borne his dead son.

Gods, had he gone mad? Did the ancient crimes of the First People run in his blood?

Browser checked the position of his guards around the village. He nodded at Straighthorn, the young warrior who stood watch on the low line of rooftops overlooking the plaza, then turned to Jackrabbit, barely visible on the rim above the spring.

In the fires' glow, Dry Creek village looked peaceful, the cracked plaster-coated walls gilded by the light. Small windows reflected the warming fires within. How had it come to pass that this shabby little village could have become a beacon for the remnants of a people who had once lived in splendor?

As if to make the point, firelight gleamed on pendants of turquoise, copper bells, jet bracelets, and beaded breastplates.

The sight of it brought a twist to Browser's stomach. This broken people wore wealth looted from a hundred graves. Some of this same jewelry had been worn by his ancestors. Two Hearts had stolen it from the bones of the dead, and these people had stolen it from Two Hearts.

The weight of the little turquoise wolf in his belt

pouch tugged at him. It had belonged to Night Sun, his great-great-great-grandmother, the last of the powerful Matrons of Talon Town. She had been the first Matron to believe in the katsinas. For that, her people had hated her. After she'd left Talon Town, the First People had declared her an outcast and decreed that her traitorous name never be forgotten.

Browser grasped the wolf, feeling its shape through the fabric. He deserved to own it more than the man who had stolen it from her mummified corpse. At the touch of the wolf, a tingle ran through his fingers.

Stone Ghost hobbled over to the ladder that protruded from the kiva roof in the middle of the plaza. He grasped the gnarled wood with callused hands and carefully climbed down into the firelit interior.

At Catkin's questioning gaze, Browser smiled and indicated that she should follow.

Catkin led the way. He watched her take hold of the ladder, her muscular forearms rippling as her hands tightened on the wood, and she climbed down. Just before she disappeared into the interior, she looked up, and her eyes met his. The look touched his soul. Then her head vanished into the kiva.

Browser slipped his bow over his shoulder and followed her. His anxiety grew as he descended. At the bottom, he looked around. The underground chamber measured five paces across. The walls were plastered in white and painted with the dancing forms of the katsinas. One of the Blessed katsina masks lived in each of the square niches recessed into the wall. Browser's flesh prickled under their hollow-eyed gazes. Four honey-colored posts supported the cribbed roof. A low fire burned in the central hearth, the dry wood almost smokeless.

The new Matron of the Katsinas' People, Cloud-blower, sat to one side of the low fire. The sight of her reassured Browser. Her choice as Matron had been prophetic. If anyone could rally the people, it would be

Cloudblower. Touched by the gods, she was a *kok-wimu,* a woman's soul inhabiting a man's body. She had a reputation as one of the people's greatest Healers. Her knowledge of Spirit plants and the rituals that secured a person's breath-heart soul to their bones was unrivaled. Of all the living Katsinas' People, Cloudblower's fame alone could see them through the coming trials.

Behind her, Wading Bird crouched, one of the few elders they had left. He hunched under an old threadbare blanket, his bald head gleaming, and his lips sucked in over his toothless gums. He looked demented.

Matron Crossbill, of the Longtail Clan, sat opposite, her age-lined face reflecting the sorrow and strain of their current situation. Her village lay in ruins, and where she had once helped refugees, she now found herself one of them.

Rock Dove, Matron of Dry Creek village, reached out and laid a hand on the old woman's shoulder. Rock Dove had lost her mother in the fire at Longtail village. Now, unable to grieve when her people were looking to her for leadership, she had accepted responsibility for her own people as well as for the Katsinas' People. Browser could read the worry on her face. The simple truth was that Rock Dove had too many mouths to feed, too many bodies to shelter. And she had given her word that these people could share her hospitality.

Stone Ghost grunted as he seated himself on the split-willow matting. "It's getting cool out there."

"Drop a rock . . . and it falls. Change a sun cycle, and winter follows. Both are inevitable." Crossbill blinked her translucent eyes. "And now we must discuss another inevitability." She looked around, taking their measure. "If I've learned anything in my years, it's that stomachs will end up empty, no matter how much they are fed in the beginning."

"We have saved some of the corn we harvested from

Longtail village," Stone Ghost said. "All that wasn't burned."

Cloudblower nodded. "That's why I called this meeting. Crossbill and I have talked. We are going to move on."

Rock Dove gave her a sober appraisal. "The Katsinas' People and the Longtail Clan are welcome here. I have told you that. Somehow, we will manage. In the past, when we starved, Longtail Clan sent us food. When raiders prowled our hills, they sent us warriors. This will be difficult, but in my years I have survived many difficult things."

Cloudblower smiled, one hand twisting her long black hair, streaked as it was in gray. "Matron, I cannot allow the generosity of your heart to lead you to more suffering." Cloudblower leaned forward, beads of jet rattling where they lay on her chest. "We are the Katsinas' People. The Blessed Poor Singer prophesied that if we could find the First People's kiva and restore the opening to the underworlds, the wars would end, and the ancestors would restore their Blessing on this, the Fifth World. Our dead Matron believed Poor Singer's prophecy. We still believe it. It is our duty to continue our search."

Crossbill took a deep breath. "It is more than placing your village at risk, Rock Dove. Think about this world we are living in. About how we got here. In the time of our great-great-grandmothers, the katsinas came to give their vision to the Blessed Sternlight, the First People's Sunwatcher. They came to him in hopes of saving the world."

"And look where it got them," Wading Bird said bitterly. His bald head glowed yellow as he lowered his eyes to stare at the ground.

"I think the vision was altered," Crossbill continued, ignoring the outburst. "The Blessed Poor Singer told us the way: We must find the First People's kiva, the place where they emerged from the underworlds. It isn't just us, but the entire world that we have been tasked to save."

Cloudblower nodded. "Yes. Look around. What do we see? Villages abandoned, people fleeing to the east. Clans have turned upon themselves. Some, the old believers who cling to the Flute Player and his ways, make war on the Katsinas' People. The rains have failed. The coughing sickness spreads from village to village. The old roads of the First People are abandoned. Their great cities lie in ruins. We are like mice trapped in a pot who have turned on each other. We are eating each other when we need to work together to save our world."

A silence fell on the room.

Stone Ghost steepled his fingers. "We cannot forget that another element has been added."

People turned to look at him. Browser tensed, knowing where this was headed.

Stone Ghost smoothed the fabric on his new shirt. "When the Blessed Night Sun left Talon Town, and the earth was split, the Made People turned on the First People, hunting them down. Men, women, and children were mercilessly murdered by the hundreds. For years we have believed them all to be dead. Now we know that they are not. The White Moccasins are out there, and they are a force to be reckoned with."

"We only know of a handful," Rock Dove protested.

"Yes," Stone Ghost answered. "That's all that we know of. But they lived among us in Longtail village. And before that, in Hillside village, and who knows how many other places? Can you say for certain that none lives here among us in Dry Creek village?"

No one spoke, but people looked around uneasily.

Stone Ghost frowned as he rubbed his hands together. "They pose a unique challenge."

"How so, Elder?" Cloudblower had turned her soft brown eyes on Stone Ghost.

"You cannot hunt them down." Stone Ghost spread

his hands wide. "The Made People tried that more than one hundred sun cycles ago. If they did not succeed when most of the First People were known, how could we succeed now, when they are in hiding?"

Browser touched his stomach. Catkin's sudden piercing stare had a hawklike intensity. Gods, his flush wasn't obvious to anyone else, was it?

Crossbill said, "I suppose you know how to deal with them?"

"I do," Stone Ghost answered mildly.

"Tell us, Elder," Cloudblower said in a calm voice, her steady gaze on the old man's face. "Please."

Browser fought the urge to fidget. What did she suspect? Worse, what did she know? Only a fool underestimated Cloudblower.

Stone Ghost might have been discussing the milling of corn. "If you locate several of their warriors, and kill them, you might as well cut off an enemy's hair. It is but a matter of time before it will grow back."

"This isn't hair we're talking about," Wading Bird said. He looked irritated.

Talk concerning the First People struck close to Elder Wading Bird's heart. He was old enough to suspect—and probably to remember—what the tattooed spirals on Stone Ghost's chin meant.

"No, the White Moccasins are like a human body," Stone Ghost insisted. "One mind and heart runs everything else."

Cloudblower sat back, eyeing him curiously. "You mean if the heart is cut out the body will wither."

"Yes. It is their leader we must destroy, or the madness will go on and on. Not just with the remaining First People, but who do you think is stirring the hatred of the Flute Player's warriors? Why do you think they have begun killing Katsinas' People?"

"You think the poison comes from the White Moccasins?" Cloudblower asked thoughtfully.

"They have worked from the shadows for many

summers." Stone Ghost nodded. "Only now are they growing bolder, willing to strike openly. They are driven by the thirst for revenge, and seek only to make Made People kill each other."

Wading Bird's gaze locked on Stone Ghost's chin. "Why would you care?"

Browser held his breath, his fist tightening on his war club. His tension had cued Catkin, who rested her slim fingers on the handle of her club.

Stone Ghost frowned as though weighing his words carefully. "We are like a people bitten by a poisonous serpent. Unless the poison is driven out, we will continue to destroy ourselves until no one is left. Our villages will end up as vacant ruins, crumbling and forgotten. Someday another people will fill this land, and look at the weed-filled rubble and wonder who we were and why we vanished from the face of the earth."

"Do you think it will come to that?" Cloudblower asked in a pained voice.

"Think back, Matron," Stone Ghost told her. "When the Made People hunted down and killed the First People, it was to make the world better. Over one hundred sun cycles have passed since then. Are things better? Are the fields full of corn? Do our children grow up fat and happy? Are our towns flourishing?"

"What's the matter with you?" Crossbill snapped. "Do you want the First People back?"

Stone Ghost smiled. "What I meant is that we are destroying ourselves, Matron. Killing ourselves off faster than we can starve or die of the coughing disease. Our trade routes are cut and our clans—those that haven't fled—are dying. Who among you can name more among the living than the dead? At this rate, in another one hundred sun cycles, what will be left for our descendants? Will we *have* any descendants? It leaves me to wonder: When the last village is abandoned, will our hatred still linger there, tracing patterns in the dust?"

Browser felt a shiver run up his spine. Catkin swallowed hard and closed her eyes.

"What do you propose?" Cloudblower asked.

"As you continue your search for the First People's kiva, I will take my nephew and a small party and search out Two Hearts. We will destroy the poison that infects our world."

"Why you?" Wading Bird demanded suspiciously.

"It must be me," Stone Ghost insisted. "I have my reasons."

"But I need my War Chief," Cloudblower said, and gave Browser a worried look. "Browser—"

"I must go with my uncle," Browser replied evenly. It all began to make sense. Yes, it had to be him and Stone Ghost. No others would do. Dread gripped his heart with a stony fist.

# CHAPTER 4

THE ELEVEN TROTTED along the Great North Road, winding down its rain-rutted path to the river. Splashing through, they climbed up the gray, cobblestrewn bank. Their feet rustled through the weeds as they jogged across dry ditches and winter-fallow cornfields. Dust spiraled in their footsteps. Ahead of them, on the higher terrace, stood the cluster of massive buildings, one to either side of the road with the "Kiva of the Worlds" squatting between them like a fat drum. The Great North Road led to its low doorway.

The huge structure to the west, Dusk House, was reputed to have been built by the First People when they abandoned Straight Path Canyon over one hundred sun cycles ago. It was said that they had come here, to the Spirit River, where a constant supply of water was available to irrigate their cornfields. They had hoped to reestablish their control over the world in the aftermath of Night Sun's abdication of power. They had built Dusk House square, perfectly symmetrical; though somewhat dilapidated it stood as a stolid reminder of the First People's skills.

The eastern building, Sunrise House, had a more irregular appearance, the construction haphazard and unbalanced. The plaster had mottled where repair patches had been slapped onto the walls. Here and there, the underlying masonry could be seen. In comparison with its western counterpart, this town—a composite of three large and one small room blocks—was crudely built out of irregular and unfinished ashlars. Beyond this cluster, higher on the ridge and facing due south, stood North House, the gateway to the northern clans and the fabled Green Mesa villages.

As the eleven approached, a warning drum thumped and warriors gathered on the roofs, bows in their hands with arrows nocked. Other individuals converged from each side and called out to each other. Through the sporadic shouts, dogs could be heard barking.

The leader of the eleven, a tall young man with broad shoulders, veered from the road and drew up just beyond bow shot at Sunrise House. He shifted his pack on his back and squared his shoulders. A member of the Rattlesnake Clan of the Willow Stave Moiety, people called him Gray Thunder. After twenty-two summers, he was handsome, with wide cheekbones, a firm but mobile mouth, and straight nose. It was said that he had a special gift of the tongue, that he could talk birds down from the sky. His clan had chosen their best and bravest for this dangerous task. He took note of the head that peeked around the side of the town wall and realized that a flanking party waited just out of sight, hidden by the building's bulk. No fools, these.

He placed hands to the sides of his mouth and took a breath, calling in an accented voice: "I am Gray Thunder. I come from the south. I am here in peace. I and my party come in search of Matron Flame Carrier and the Katsinas' People. We have heard that they are here at Flowing Waters Town."

In the rear of the party, the old man propped his hands on his knees, gasping for breath. His straggling white hair flicked back and forth with the breeze.

On the wall before them, people bent their heads together, and finally a woman dressed in a red, white, and black dress stepped up to the edge of the roof. She wore her hair piled high and pinned. To Gray Thunder's eye, she had that look of command. Her voice confirmed it when she called: "You are not of the People. Not with that accent, Fire Dog. So, I am left to wonder, what business would a party of Fire Dogs have with Matron Flame Carrier?"

"To whom am I speaking? Are you Flame Carrier?"

Chuckles could be heard on the rooftops, as if this were high humor.

The woman called back, "No, warrior of the enemy, I am Blue Corn, of the Coyote Clan, Matron of Sunrise House and its territory. You still haven't answered my question about Flame Carrier. Why do you seek her? What do you and your warriors do in my country?"

Blue Corn? That was bad. He had been told that Flame Carrier could be found here. Blue Corn was noted for her allegiance to the old gods, the Flute Player and the Blue God.

"I am sent to speak with Matron Flame Carrier." Gray Thunder shifted, pointing to the corner of the wall. "Tell your warriors to stand down. I come in peace. We wish the Matron no harm." He smiled. "On the contrary, we would offer an alliance."

"What good has an alliance ever been with the Fire Dogs?"

Gray Thunder bit off a sharp retort and spread his

arms wide. "Look about you, Matron. I see the shabby
legacy of the Straight Path Nation. I have just passed
through the ruins of Straight Path Canyon. The great
white palaces are empty, the doorways gaping and
black. Ghosts walk among the flaking plaster walls. I
have seen the charred wreckage of Northern Town, its
ceilings fallen in ruin. Corn does not grow in the weed-
filled fields we have crossed coming here." He kicked
at the dry gray silt. "You have ditches here, Matron,
but in other parts of the country corn needs rain. Since
the fall of the First People, it has gone away. My clan,
my people, we believe that it is because we have failed
in Poor Singer's prophecy."

"A Fire Dog who cares about Poor Singer's prophecy?" Blue Corn said incredulously. "How can this
be?"

Gray Thunder cocked his head. "Have you lost so
much? Don't you know that Poor Singer was captured—"

Blue Corn replied, "We haven't lost our sense when
it comes to dealing with Fire Dogs! Do not tempt me
to kill you!"

Gray Thunder smiled. "Matron, I am already dead.
I have even seen the manner of it in a Dream. You
cannot frighten me by—"

"Then be good enough to tell us why you are here?"

"I *am* trying, Matron," Gray Thunder pleaded. "You
see, your people have apparently forgotten that Poor
Singer was taken captive by the Great War Chief, Jay
Bird. Many among my people heard and believed the
words of Poor Singer and Cornsilk."

"Why would a Fire Dog listen to anyone from the
Straight Path Nation?" The old woman sounded
slightly less certain of herself.

"May we talk to Matron Flame Carrier?" Gray Thunder asked plaintively. "We have come a long way at
great risk to ourselves. If, after we have talked to Flame

Carrier, you are dissatisfied, you may do with us as you will."

The warriors beside Gray Thunder shot him uneasy glances. He made a calming motion with his hand.

The old woman on the wall sighed. "Gray Thunder, that's what you are called?"

"I am."

"No matter what your motives, or how badly you would like to talk to Matron Flame Carrier, she will not hear you, and given your accent, that might be just as well."

"I do not understand, will you not even—"

The old woman raised an arm to cut him off. "You have come too late, Gray Thunder. Matron Flame Carrier is dead. She was murdered earlier this moon."

He cast a dispirited glance at the old man, who had finally caught his breath and straightened. A subtle communication passed between them, and Gray Thunder hesitated. "Matron, you claim that Flame Carrier is dead, yet you use her name. Does that not frighten you? Don't you fear that you will call her back from her journey to the Land of the Dead?"

Had he caught her in a lie? Was Flame Carrier really dead? The Straight Path People never spoke the names of their freshly dead for fear of drawing the ghosts back to this world.

"We only refrain from speaking the person's name for four days, Fire Dog, while the soul is on its journey to the Land of the Dead. Besides, there are those who say Flame Carrier did not die." Disbelieving humor laced Blue Corn's voice. "The story has come down from the north that, upon her death, she became a katsina and flew up to join the Cloud People."

Gray Thunder and the old man exchanged glances again. "Who told you this?"

"A Trader, a man who was there and saw it. His name is Old Pigeontail."

"Then . . ." Gray Thunder frowned. "What of the Katsinas' People? Do they still exist?"

"Until the Flute Player warriors manage to kill them off. And, from the looks of things, that might not be so long in coming."

Gray Thunder nodded, and said, "We would ask for your hospitality, Matron. In the name of the . . . of the katsinas. We would speak to the leader of the Katsinas' People, whoever she is."

"Why should I trust you?"

Frustrated, Gray Thunder said, "Matron, think! The First People are gone. War is everywhere. We have passed party after party of refugees. Drought lies upon the land like a curse and Wind Baby whines through desolate cornfields, whipping the dust into spirals. The wasting disease stalks your villages and ours, claiming us one by one. Where once children laughed, and young women smiled at youthful men, only silence and ruin remain. The bones of corpses litter empty kivas, their sightless skulls grinning in the darkness.

"I and my party believe in Poor Singer's prophecy. Because his promise is the only way to save our world, Matron. This war between the Flute Player's warriors and the Katsinas' People must be stopped or we will all be destroyed."

Blue Corn cocked her head. As the long moments passed, only the distant cry of the crows could be heard as they scavenged the refuse dumps behind the villages. Finally, she asked, "You know I do not approve of the katsinas. Why would you ask this of me?"

Gray Thunder lifted his chin. "You let the Katsinas' People come here, allowed them to rebuild the great kiva at Dusk House. Why would you do that if you were not at least tolerant of their beliefs?"

"To see if it worked, young Gray Thunder. It didn't. No opening to the underworlds appeared." She chuckled. "You know that we've been killing each other. Warriors loyal to the Blessed Flute Player have destroyed whole towns of Katsinas' People. If the Katsinas' People are defeated, dead, and but a memory, perhaps we can have peace again."

"Can you? With clans turning upon themselves and killing their own? Cousin against cousin? Brother against brother? How do you heal that kind of hatred?"

"How would you, Fire Dog?"

"By relating Poor Singer's vision as it truly was, Matron!" Gray Thunder tapped his muscular chest. "The truth must be spoken. I am here to speak it. In Poor Singer's words lie all of our salvations!"

"It is an age of madness." Blue Corn spread her arms. "And, that being the case, I am mad enough myself to see what would come of your silly mission. I will give you and your party shelter, Gray Thunder, and send a runner to find the new Matron of the Katsinas' People. If she will see you, I will grant safe passage. If not, you may go in peace. But a party of my warriors will follow you to make *sure* you leave our territory."

### Santa Fe, New Mexico

"So, what do you think?" Dusty Stewart asked as they walked out into the frosty Santa Fe evening. He buttoned his coat and exhaled to watch his breath.

"I think those are the best enchiladas I've ever eaten." Maureen tucked her coat tightly about her middle and watched a big Ford Expedition roll down the narrow street. Santa Fe, it seemed, favored either opulent and shiny SUVs or battered pickups. She tucked her bison-hide purse to her side with an elbow and sighed, breath frosting in the air. Across the street, two Halloween party-goers—dressed in costume as Bill Clinton and George W. Bush—staggered down the sidewalk, arm in arm.

She glanced back at the Pink Adobe restaurant. "All through supper I was thinking that this building was constructed at a time when my ancestors were still living in longhouses and had just met Europeans. Of all the North American cities I've ever been in, Santa Fe is the most remarkable."

"It is that," Stewart agreed as he led her to the Bronco. His blond hair and beard shone in the streetlights.

She opened the sprung passenger door, climbed in, and looked around at the packed truck, the back filled to the roof with screens, coolers, and carefully labeled boxes full of artifacts from their recently completed dig at Pueblo Animas. A smart person ignored the floor, covered as it was in empty beer bottles, fast-food wrappers, and the detritus of a field archaeologist's existence.

She had been called down from her physical anthropology lab at McMaster University in Hamilton, Ontario, by Dale Emerson Robertson. Dale needed her help to excavate a burned kiva filled with the charred skeletons of children and two butchered adults. Pueblo Animas would haunt her dreams, her mind's eye replaying what those last horrible moments must have been like for the victims when the place burned in A.D. 1263.

Dusty slid into the driver's seat and propped his arms on the steering wheel, only to stare out at the darkness in silence. She studied his hunched figure: a muscular cowboy-hatted shadow.

Hesitantly, he said, "It's Halloween. Trick or treat. I could set you up for the night. Save you the cost of a motel. My couch makes into a bed."

She watched him for a moment, the silence stretching. What was it about him that she had come to like? They were oil and water. She, the calculating Canadian scientist with impeccable credentials, he a footloose American dirt archaeologist with a clouded reputation. Yet they shared a love of antiquity—of people who

had lived long ago. In the beginning, when they'd first
met on a dig in upstate New York, they had hated each
other on sight.

"You sure you want to do that?" The words formed
easily, as if of their own volition.

"What's life for if you can't live dangerously?" He
reached for the ignition. Pulling away from the curb,
he drove toward the looming bulk of the Hotel Loretto,
its pueblo architecture outlined with glowing luminarias: plastic lights made to look like candles glowing in
paper bags. How Southwestern, totally in fitting with
Santa Fe's special charm. They crossed the river and
he took a right onto Alameda, turned again at Paseo de
Peralta, then took a left onto Canyon Road. A strip of
mellow adobe-walled galleries lined the way. She
peered at each, wondering at the interiors.

"You live close to here?"

"End of the road," he told her, and gestured at the
galleries. "None of this was here when Dad bought the
property in the fifties."

He said no more as they drove up the winding road
past painters', sculptors', and metalworkers' studios,
each illuminated by bright lights. Occasional pedestrians strode along the tree-lined sidewalks, their bodies
muffled in coats. Some walked dogs. They all looked
like the leisurely rich. At least, all but the children in
their costumes. They looked like kids anywhere, albeit,
when she looked more closely, they were really decked
out. No old sheets with holes cut in them, but slickly
tailored costumes that made them look like the real
thing. To her amusement, costumes of the American
president were vogue. It struck her that in the modern
world, politicians gave people more nightmares than
ghosts or goblins did.

"Your father must have been doing well. I heard that
he came from a rich family back East."

"Dad had a falling out with his family. They disin-
herited him when he ran off from the university to be-

come an archaeologist." He pointed to one of the huge Spanish-style houses. "Like I said, this wasn't here back in the fifties when Dad bought the place. I live in, well, more humble settings."

They took the jog in the road to Upper Canyon; she watched the million-dollar houses with glowing jack-o'-lanterns atop adobe walls pass by her window, and waited, unwilling to press him about the darkness in his voice. Anytime his father, Samuel Stewart, cropped into the conversation, Dusty grew morose.

At the end of the road, just before the curve that would take them back across the Santa Fe River, he pulled into a narrow dirt track that led down into the trees. The Bronco's lights illuminated a ratty-looking 1950s vintage trailer. Aluminum-sided, painted with what looked like flaking turquoise paint, it seemed to hunch in the night, a forlorn orphan dwarfed by high-dollar splendor.

Dusty stopped them before a plywood porch. A rusty metal barbecue stood to one side. After he shut off the truck, he sat for a moment in silence, then said, "Wait a minute. I'm out of my mind. You'd be a lot more comfortable in a—"

"I'll be fine, Dusty. Thank you."

She took matters into her own hands and stepped out into the late October night. She could smell damp soil and wood smoke in the air. Overhead, through the winter-bare branches of cottonwoods, she could see stars sparkling. A faint sighing came from the breeze through the piñons and juniper.

"If you're sure." Dusty sounded ominous as he led the way onto the porch, jingling his keys. She considered the warning note in his voice, remembering the various adventures she'd had with his vehicle: broken levers, mouse nests in the vent, nonfunctional air-conditioning, the missing seat belt he'd used for a tow strap. What on earth would his old battered trailer be like?

The porch sagged under her weight, reminding her of the "you might be a redneck" jokes told by that American comedian. Dusty had bent over a hasp and fiddled with a key in a padlock. The chrome door handle appeared more than a little bent, as if someone had used a pry bar on it.

When he stepped in and turned on the lights she followed him into a cramped living room. The front, under a louvered window, was dominated by a worn couch that supported two big pillows, several copies of *American Antiquity*, bound field reports, and a well-fingered copy of Steve LeBlanc's *Prehistoric Warfare in the American Southwest*. Age had given the lacquered-wood walls a honeyed glow. It didn't surprise her that a threadbare carpet covered the floor, cluttered here and there with books and a pile of clothing. A small black-and-white TV—a relic of the sixties—stood on a metal stand. Generous souls would call the kitchen "compact," with an ancient gas stove, a small refrigerator, and a chipped yellow porcelain sink. The linoleum-topped counter supported a dish drainer, several empty Guinness bottles, and a battered blender. Knowing Stewart, its sole use was probably for margaritas. Bound field reports were piled atop the two kitchen chairs. A broken screen—the wooden kind used by archaeologists to sift dirt—was propped next to the door. Stewart's idea of interior decorating, perhaps?

The photographs pinned to the wall showed archaeologists smiling at the camera while they perched on back-dirt piles and crumbling Anasazi walls. A framed picture, one cut from a *National Geographic* magazine, showed Dale Emerson Robertson, his battered fedora tipped back on his head to expose his wiry gray hair. His gentle brown eyes looked wistful, as if focused on a great distance.

Dale had left Pueblo Animas three days before, accompanying the site's owner, Moshe Alevy, to the airport at Farmington. From there, he should have driven back to his little house in the Albuquerque suburbs. He had probably had a delightful night dropping candy into bags.

"I'm sorry about the mess," Dusty said, hurrying to swipe a pile of papers from a plastic-upholstered chair. With the load cradled in his arms, he retreated down the narrow hallway behind the kitchen and ducked into a back room.

She smiled as she finished her inspection. The place looked just like Dusty's house ought to. Completely in fitting with his off-center personality.

"I turned the heat on." He emerged from the back, his blue eyes looking sheepish. "Want some coffee?"

"Sure." As he opened a wooden cabinet beside the sink and pulled a can of coffee from the shelf, she added, "It's homey."

He laughed at the humor in her voice. "Yeah, well, the neighbors really hate it. Especially the guy next door. He's got a one-point-four-million-dollar house perched to overlook my trailer. He's offered me an incredible amount of cash for the property."

She propped herself on a filing cabinet that snuggled between the TV and the kitchen counter. "Waiting for a recovery in the real estate market before you sell, Stewart?"

He measured coffee into an old blue enamel coffeepot. "It's just that, well, it's home, you know?" He gestured around with the red plastic measuring cup. "I mean, I like it here." A grin crossed his lips. "And I get the biggest kick out of driving the guy next door crazy. He's a lawyer, mind you, but he can't do a damned thing about me because this place was grandfathered long before covenants and zoning. Besides, what would I do with the money? I'd have to go find another place. Move all this stuff."

She arched her brow as she eyed the worn furniture. "You'd want to keep that old sofa?" Stuffing extruded from a hole in the arm. A pile of apparently dirty shirts made a mound beside it.

He shrugged. "Sure. No one else wants it. I'm gone a lot. This place has been broken into three times. The last time, they didn't take anything but the beer in the fridge and a bottle of tequila. I mean, what's to take?"

She noticed that the old black-and-white TV had a bent coat hanger for an antenna. "You've got a point there."

She turned to another of the pictures, this one a black-and-white of a tall young man in baggy trousers, a hat cocked on his head as he stood by a 1950s pickup. He had a handsome but vulnerable face. Hesitant eyes looked out over a straight nose and strong jaw. A shovel was propped insolently over his shoulder.

"That's my father," Dusty said as he walked up to stand behind her.

"Handsome man." Though she didn't think Dusty looked much like him.

"It runs in the family." He scooped another pile of books to clear a second kitchen chair. The table remained cluttered with stacks of index cards, Ziploc bags, and a crow quill pen that lay next to a bottle of ink, Liquid Paper, and clear fingernail polish.

"I was cataloging artifacts just before I left for Pueblo Animas," he told her on his return, and quickly piled the items into an old shoe box, looked around, and bent to shove it under the table. "Sorry. I'm a bit short on room here."

"Relax, Dusty." She slipped into a chair and sighed. "Save it for when *Good Housekeeping* comes to do a photo shoot."

Pulling a bottle of Guinness from the fridge, he uncapped it and seated himself next to her. "I'd offer you one, but I know better."

"Smart man." Maureen didn't drink. Ever.

A phone rang, the sound anachronistic, made with a real bell. Stewart muttered and stepped over to flip dirty shirts like a man turning compost. From the depths, he pulled out an old black dial telephone and removed the handset from the cradle. "It's your nickel," he said, then listened. "Hi, Sylvia. We just got in." He frowned. "Maureen and me." The frown deepened. "Not a chance. We're going to hang around for a couple of days and I'm going to play tourist guide. You know, do the restaurants and galleries. Walk around the Plaza. Eat on the balcony at the Ore House, and get the kind of culture we don't have to dig out of the ground." He listened for several seconds, then said, "No way." Another pause. "Well, if it takes two people, take Steve." Dusty's frown faded. "All right. Yeah, I'll tell Dale when I see him in Albuquerque tomorrow."

Stewart hung up and lowered the phone to the floor. "That was Sylvia. She checked the machine in the office. Dale left a message. One of our clients needs an archaeologist to boogie up to Colorado for a pipeline survey south of Mesa Verde tomorrow. Dale wanted you and me to go do the job."

"Just like that?"

"That's how contract archaeology works." He returned to the chair. "When you wake up in the morning, you never know where you're going to be sleeping that night, or in what state."

"Dale wanted me to go, too? That's strange."

Dusty gave her a deadpan look. "Doctor, you've been working with us for almost a month now. He thinks you're an employee just like the rest of us."

She wondered how she felt about that. It had been a long time since anyone had treated her like an employee. She gave the phone a hostile glance where it lay canted on the rumpled shirts and considered calling Dale back.

"Forget it," Dusty said. "Sylvia said he's not home. You can ream him out later."

Maureen gave it up with an ironic smile. Dale didn't

think of the world the way ordinary people did. "So, Sylvia's going?"

"That's the advantage of being boss. I can ruin her weekend instead." He glanced around. "I think I've got some wine here. Whoops, I mean . . ."

"Thanks. Coffee will be fine. I do miss it, though. It wasn't like I planned on becoming an alcoholic. After John died it was just easier than being alone."

He ran callused fingers through his blond hair and she watched the lines tighten around his blue eyes. "It still surprises me that you're not drowning in men. What's wrong with those guys in Canada? Are they uniques or something?"

"You mean eunuchs. And no, they're not." She could think of some Saskatchewan ranchers up in the bush that oozed more testosterone than a bulldozer. "Let's just say that I . . ." His blue-eyed stare was seeing right through her. "All right, honesty, eh? I couldn't stand the thought of touching some other man the way I did John. It would have been betrayal. Does that make sense?"

He fingered his bottle of Guinness as the coffeepot began to perk. "Yeah." He thought for a moment. "But . . . I mean, you still . . . well, don't you?"

"It would be like having sex on the altar, Stewart," she answered bluntly. "Breaking the covenant his body shared with mine. A betrayal of the man I loved."

He cocked his ear to listen to the coffeepot. "Maureen, it's your life. Live it the way you want to. Besides, relationships are all trouble. Every time a man and woman get involved, they make a mess of themselves."

She noticed the hardening of his mouth. "Not all men are John. And not all women are Ruth Ann Sullivan. Just because she left your father—"

"Coffee's ready." He rose on charged muscles and poured a cup for her. After he placed it on the table, he remained standing.

She cradled the cup and looked up at him. "Great, Stewart. I can talk about John, but you can't talk about your mother leaving your father? Do I detect a disparity here?"

He lowered himself into the chair. "It's all right when it's someone else's problem. Not so all right when it's your own." He stared absently into space, and in a moment of illumination, Maureen could see Samuel Stewart's ghost climbing up onto the sink in the mental institution to finally electrocute himself.

She peered down into her coffee and could see her reflection. Her Iroquoian blood showed in her straight nose and full lips and in her long black braid. "It's worse with men, I think. You're all supposed to be such stoic pillars. Baggage left over from the 'good old days' when men modeled themselves after the Industrial Revolution."

"I didn't follow that."

She propped her chin on a fist. "A cultural anthropologist once told me that culture reflects the age in which it functions. He said the Victorian age produced men like it did machines. Uniform, steel structures, mass-produced and unbendable. But when you looked inside, all you saw was the framework, girders, rivets, and nothing but empty space in between."

"You think I'm empty space in between?" He sounded offended.

"Not at all. You're just as fiercely protective about letting it out as I am about letting anyone in." She took a sip of coffee. "Your mother broke your father when she left him, and you can't allow yourself to take that same risk, no matter how miserable it makes you."

"And you, Doctor?" he asked in clipped tones.

"Me? I'm the one who had a perfect life with a man I loved. My trouble, Stewart"—she pointed at the Guinness in his hands—"and what led me to the bottle, is that I'd do anything to keep from admitting it's all over. That I've lost him."

She thought of her empty house overlooking Lake Ontario, its windows dark, the rooms quiet with the memories of John. When she finally returned, would she still feel him there, part of the wood, plaster, and walls? Or when Elder Walking Hawk had sent him north toward the Land of the Dead, had even that trace of him vanished?

"So," she asked softly, "just why did you ask me here, Stewart?"

He rolled the half-empty Guinness bottle between his thick thumb and forefinger. She watched the tendons in his hand, remembering how strong it was when it came to lifting broken rock out of a ruined pueblo, or how gentle and delicate it could be when he used a dental pick like a precision instrument to free a long-buried artifact.

"Thought you might need a place to sleep for the night." He shot her a worried glance. "Why did you say yes?"

She tried to look nonchalant. "How could I turn down the opportunity to sleep on a couch that was so important that not even three different thieves dared to steal it?"

Dusty laughed.

But why had she said yes? She was still thinking about that hours later as she lay on the foldout sofa bed. Dusty called this thing comfortable? It undulated like an accordion—each of its "ups" coinciding with her "downs." Beyond the louvered windows she could hear the wind in the trees, the pattering of little feet that she suspected were mice in the walls, and the creaking of the ancient trailer. Her gaze kept straying to the dark hallway that led back to his bedroom. This was lunacy. Tomorrow, she would have him drive her to Albuquerque where she would buy a ticket and fly home. She belonged in her little white house in Niagara-on-the-Lake, and she had work to do back in the physical anthropology lab at McMaster.

Yes, fly home tomorrow, and deal with the first day of the rest of her life.

# CHAPTER 5

CATKIN SWUNG HER battered war club as she walked. The sound of the stone head whistling through the air satisfied her, and lessened the turmoil in her chest. She had always been like this: driven to do something drastic when her emotions were frayed.

She had been there, in the cavern, when Browser confronted Elder Springbank; she had heard when the Elder was revealed as the legendary witch, Two Hearts. She had seen the old man, slumped against the stone, blood leaking from his lips. She had heard him calling to Browser: *"For the sake of the true gods, Browser! We shouldn't be fighting!* You are one of us! *Join us and we will let your Made People friends live."*

Browser had been told all of his life that he was one of the Made People. She knew him well enough to understand how disconcerting the old witch's words had been. But had he meant it, that Browser was one of the First People? Or had it been a trick, a means of distracting Browser so that the White Moccasins could kill him? How in the name of the gods could Browser pack up and go off to who knew where in search of the old beast—if he still lived?

It all smacked of lunacy. Gods knew, she'd lived enough lunacy in the last five sun cycles. Old Stone Ghost had been right about one thing, they were spiraling into a fiery pit. Every winter grew more desperate, every summer more violent and bloody. In the kiva, Stone Ghost had asked if they knew more living than dead. She knew far more dead people.

Her resolve stiffened as she stomped toward the little camp where Browser and Stone Ghost had retired after the council session in the kiva.

"Catkin?" a woman's voice called from one side. A dark shadow detached itself from one of the women's fires.

"Not now, Obsidian."

"Wait!" The woman hurried forward, her finely sewn fawn-leather cloak hanging around her. Long black hair cascaded over her shoulders. She wore high white moccasins decorated with antelope-hoof rattles that clattered with each step. Defiantly she matched Catkin's pace.

"I don't have time right now." Catkin looped her war club around on its thong in a suggestive manner.

"I have just heard," Obsidian said breathlessly. "The War Chief and Elder Stone Ghost are going after Springbank."

"You shouldn't listen to rumor." Catkin walked faster.

"Tell them not to go."

The pleading in Obsidian's voice brought Catkin to a stop. She turned, hefting the war club in her right hand. "What does it matter to you?"

"It matters!"

Catkin narrowed an eye, trying to read the woman's expression. Obsidian's normally superior demeanor had cracked. Desperation glittered in her large doelike eyes. Her full breasts rose and fell; shell-bead necklaces caught the light as if they rode on waves.

Catkin said, "Why did you come to me with this? Shouldn't you take it to your Matron?"

"You have influence with Browser and Elder Stone Ghost. They'll listen to you."

Against her better judgment, Catkin said, "If I tell them, they'll want a reason."

Obsidian hesitated, her triangular jaw cocked as she tried to weigh Catkin's worthiness. "They don't understand what they're walking into. This isn't some rogue War Chief, some petty raider, they are hunting. This is Two Hearts—the most dangerous witch in the world."

"They know that." Catkin lifted an eyebrow. "I take it you know quite a bit about the White Moccasins?"

Obsidian took a deep breath, voice controlled as though she were speaking to a child. "You must trust me on this. Catkin, they—"

"Trust you?" Catkin asked incredulously. "I'm still not sure that you weren't involved in our Matron's death back at Longtail village. I'd rather reach into a jar of scorpions than trust you."

Obsidian stiffened. "I had nothing to do with your Matron's death." She shook her head, the action flipping her silky black hair and rattling the turquoise beads she'd woven into her locks. "I can only tell you that you'll be doing them a favor by stopping them. It's up to you."

Obsidian turned and stalked away.

Catkin watched her go, and whispered, "Insect."

Taking a deep breath, she resumed her way toward Browser's fire. She could see him, his head bent close to Stone Ghost's as the War Chief fed sticks into the tiny blaze.

Her steps slowed as she approached, attention on Browser, on the familiar set of his broad shoulders. From long practice, she could read his expression: a deep-seated worry. Gods, how many times had he come to her with that look on his face? She had always listened, considered his words, and given him the wisest counsel a friend could give, despite the aching in her heart.

Three winters ago her husband, Wind Born, had died of the coughing sickness. Two winters had passed since she had joined the Katsinas' People. She had been lost in grief. Perhaps she had taken extra risks, or hadn't cared to live, but during a raid, the Fire Dogs had captured her when she took a foolish chance. That night had, in many ways, brought her back to life. She remembered the feeling of helplessness as they stripped her, the pain as they pried her legs apart. She had chewed through her lip, tasting blood as that first man thrust himself inside her. Something had made her open her eyes and look up past the grunting warrior's head. She had seen Browser appear there, magical as the katsinas, standing in the firelight, his war club raised. Like a hero from the old tales he had howled and laid about him with that bloody war club. The memory was of a blurred, fire-streaked phantom dancing through the dying warriors. The sounds had engraved themselves on her souls: the cries of the Fire Dogs; the howling torn from Browser's throat; and the smacking sounds as his club crushed their skulls.

Blood-smeared and spattered with gore, he'd lifted her from the ground, slung her across his shoulder, and pelted off into the night. Time had turned in on itself, her souls numb as she bounced on his shoulder like a sack of corn.

The next thing she remembered was the cool breeze on her hot cheek. His dark form hunched above her, silhouetted against the stars. At the first thought that had coalesced in her head, she had said, "A good War Chief doesn't risk himself or his party for the sake of one captive."

He had answered, "I could take you back."

In that moment, she had fallen in love with him. Never, in the intervening years, had she so much as laid a lover's finger on him. Despite the longing in his eyes, he had never encouraged her to be other than his best friend.

During the time he was married to Ash Girl, she had been his confidante and had ignored the knowledge that he had crept away to share Hophorn's bed. In the year since Hophorn's and Ash Girl's deaths, she had maintained her control, allowing him to grieve. Despite the craving she had for his touch, it was enough to be close to him.

Catkin forced herself forward, seeing him tense at the sound of gravel under her moccasin, his hand involuntarily gripping the handle of his war club. Then recognizing her familiar tread, his grip relaxed.

She stepped around and squatted opposite them, her war club on her knees as she glanced from Browser's face to Stone Ghost's. "I am ready when you are. Straighthorn and Jackrabbit are packing their few things."

Browser's face pinched. "You're not going. Neither are they. I need you here, to help Matron Flame . . . Matron Cloudblower to make the move to Streambed Town."

Catkin shook her head. "My duties as your deputy are over, War Chief. You are not my clansman and cannot order me. I joined the Katsinas' People of my own will. I leave them of my own will. When you go, you will need me. I will be there to watch your back. You will have to make your own way with Jackrabbit and Straighthorn."

Browser gave her a deadpan stare. The wrinkled corners of Stone Ghost's lips twitched with amusement.

"Obsidian just stopped me," Catkin continued. "You should know that she urged me to dissuade you from this mad scheme. She wouldn't give me a reason why."

"No," Browser said wearily. "I suppose she wouldn't. Catkin, I really don't want you to do this. It's not your fight."

"If it is yours, it is mine." She glanced out at the darkness, lowering her voice. "You don't know that he's still alive. I saw him, saw his color, the blood leaking from his mouth. When you struck, you broke his ribs and punctured a lung."

"He's alive," Stone Ghost said soberly. "Had he died, we would have heard."

"From whom? Obsidian?" Catkin asked pointedly. "She's one of them, isn't she?"

Browser's tightening jaw muscles betrayed him. "One of who?"

"A White Moccasin. One of the First People."

She had to give him credit, he kept his face straight when he said, "Probably."

Catkin pointed to the healing wound on his forehead. "If you hadn't taken a blow to the head and were thinking better, you would know the wisdom of taking Straighthorn and Jackrabbit with us. Straighthorn was there, in the cavern, when we faced the White Moccasins. He has told Jackrabbit everything he heard and saw. They are safer traveling with us than they would be here, where they could say anything they wished to anyone passing by."

Stone Ghost grunted in assent, his gaze measuring her.

"I cannot ask you—," Browser began stubbornly.

"That's why I have saved you the discomfort." Catkin met his eyes. "I am going with you, as you know I must."

Stone Ghost said, "I agree. I think Catkin's place is with us."

Browser looked bewildered. "You can't mean that. You know the risks as well as I do."

"Yes." Stone Ghost seemed unconcerned. "So does Catkin. I doubt she'd be offering to join us if she didn't. This is not just about us, Nephew, it is—"

"Hello the camp!" a voice called from the darkness.

Catkin leapt to her feet, her war club raised. Behind her, Browser jumped up, calling: "Who comes?"

"I am called Cricket Dancer, a man of the Coyote Clan. My Matron, Blue Corn, has sent me to find the Katsinas' People. I come with news for Matron Cloud-blower. A party of Fire Dogs has come to Flowing Waters Town. They come in search of the Katsinas' People. They wish a meeting."

Catkin saw Browser and Stone Ghost trade a look of surprise. Blue Corn? She was a staunch defender of the old gods, of the Flute Player.

"Come in!" Stone Ghost called to the darkness. "Tell us about this."

Catkin's spine tingled, remembering her last experience with the Fire Dogs.

MAGPIE WALKING HAWK Taylor, better known as "Maggie," sipped at a steaming cup of coffee as she drove her "puke-green" Park Service pickup truck over the Chaco Wash bridge. Frost left hoary patterns on the pickup's hood, the engine having warmed enough to outline the trellislike frame under the sheet metal.

*"Maggie! You're on dawn patrol!"* Her boss, Rupert Brown, the park superintendent, had sounded too cheery as he addressed his hungover staff at the morning meeting. The man seemed to have an unearthly glow, as though possessed of a great and powerful excitement. Everyone else looked like morgue specimens. Of course, Rupert had made only a token appearance at the Halloween party early on in the evening. He'd just made it back from business in the capital, and ducked out a little after seven. He couldn't even be found to give out the best costume prize.

Rupert was an interesting guy: one of the few Native Americans in a position of authority in the National Park Service. Tall, with a hawklike face, he was nearing retirement. His steely gray hair, long face, and probing brown eyes along with his unusual height gave him a commanding presence. As to how "Indian" he was, Maggie was unsure. Rupert looked like a typical southwestern mongrel: Anglo, Hispanic, and Indian, all rolled into one. Rumor had it that in the sixties he had been "White." The seventies and eighties had seen him promoted in the Park Service as a "Hispanic." Now, with Indians back in vogue, he was "Native American." Some said he was Navajo, others that he was of Puebloan stock. To Maggie, it didn't matter what he was. In her book, he'd proved to be a good-natured guy, and a capable boss, and that was what really counted.

The morning sun still hung below the eastern horizon, filling the sky with a purple luminosity that cast lavender across the high sandstone canyon walls. The sagebrush, greasewood, and chamisa were softened by the pastel colors and a dusting of frost that coated their branches.

She yawned, and faint tendrils of her breath hung in the cab's cold air. After the Halloween party last night, this was just way too early to be up and about. While Maggie didn't drink, she did like a good party. Not only that, Reggie Brown, the park superintendent's grandson, had been there. Reggie was tall, like Rupert, and good-looking.

She arched an eyebrow when she thought about his nice smile. He had a special power, a presence. People turned to look when he walked into a room. Maggie couldn't help but respond to that gleam in his eye when he looked at her. And while he did drink, he'd been moderate: only three bottles of beer spaced over the five hours she had been at the party. She was leery of alcohol. Her mother had been a drunk who had ended up dead in a car wreck when she passed out behind the wheel. Living with her on the spiral down had been the worst thing Maggie had ever endured. Lord knew, she'd have ended up badly, too, but for her grandmother, Slumber, and her two aunts.

She started, slamming a foot on the brake. Ahead in the road, right in the center of her lane, stood a great horned owl. She locked eyes with the bird as she slid to a stop. Her hands tightened on the steering wheel and a shiver wracked her.

"What do you want out here?" her voice cracked, barely more than a whisper.

As if he'd heard, the owl cocked his head. The large black pupils, swimming in yellow eyes, pierced her with their power. The universe might have narrowed to just the two of them. Time seemed to slow and stop . . . waiting.

As if slapped awake, she gasped and blinked. The road ahead of her was empty. Bare asphalt in the violet light of predawn. When had the bird taken wing? Why hadn't she seen it fly away?

Or, had it been there at all?

She clawed her coffee cup from the dash holder. Swigging the hot coffee in the thermal cup brought a grudging warmth to her chilled soul.

"My God," she whispered. "What did I see?"

She shook it off, and let off the brake, easing the truck forward. A wound had opened inside her, a sense of wrongness. She glanced at the truck phone and fought the desire to call her aunt. Sage Walking Hawk was the last of her beloved aunts—the women who had taken her under their wings and raised her after her mother's death. The old Keres blood ran thick in Aunt Sage's veins. She could see between the worlds. She would know what this owl wanted. The death bird wasn't known for bringing good news.

Magpie eased the truck around the curve in the road. Her heart was pounding like a powwow pot drum. On such a beautiful morning, what could possibly be wrong with the world?

She saw the truck as she pulled into the Casa Rinconada parking lot. The big Dodge diesel looked forlorn, the only vehicle in the lot. A thick coating of frost covered the candy-red paint. Dust tarnished the chrome wheels and bumpers.

Magpie pulled up behind it, her sense of premonition tingling after her encounter with the disappearing owl. And now, here was a truck in the lot? She growled to herself and checked her list of backcountry permits. Only one was outstanding, and that for a couple who had hiked into the Wijiji ruin yesterday. They would have parked in the lot miles to the east.

She looked at the truck, seeing the familiar lines, the amber clearance lights on the roof. She knew this vehicle. A glance at the New Mexico plates wasn't conclusive; but she knew those bumper stickers: AR-CHAEOLOGY—CAN YOU DIG IT? and ARCHAEOLOGIST FOR HIRE: HAVE TROWEL WILL TRAVEL.

"Dale?" Maggie asked the air. "What are you doing up here?"

Yes, she remembered this truck. She'd seen it the day he'd first driven it into Chaco Canyon. Over two years ago. They had been working at the 10K3 site in the western part of the canyon. Dale had traded in his ratty old International Scout for this opulent, chrome-plated four-wheel drive.

Maggie opened her door and stepped out, looking around. Nothing unusual could be seen. Her soul felt drawn to the Casa Rinconada trail, as if pulled by an invisible string. She ignored the impulse and walked over to the driver's side window. Dale wasn't inside, was he? From the frost the truck must have been here overnight.

With her ticket book, she scratched the frost away, and checked. To her immense relief no hunched body slumped there. The seat was empty but for a notebook, several cassettes from an audio book, and a thermos lying on its side.

She turned, staring around at the low sagebrush. "Dale? Are you here?"

The silence was broken by the faint roar of a jet somewhere in the stratosphere.

She trotted down the trail, past the Small House interpretive sign and up to the Casa Rinconada kiva. Cold burning her lungs, she stopped at the edge of the ruin and looked down into the gloomy interior. She'd had

a momentary image of Dale, facedown on the kiva
floor. But there, in the shadows, the vaguely human
outline just out from the firebox was only a dusting of
darker sand.

Placing a hand to her chest, Magpie took a moment
to catch her breath. A ghost of a breeze tugged at her
collar-length hair and seemed to caress her round
brown cheeks.

"Dale?" she asked plaintively, as if the touch might
have been his.

She blinked and, for an instant, could have sworn
that she saw him walking up the trail toward the Great
North Road, his fedora tipped back on wiry gray hair.
Then the image blurred and shifted, and an owl
swooped up from the spot where she'd last seen Dale.
Its yellow eyes burned like flames as it soared into the
dawn sky.

She closed her eyes and fought to still her heart. Her
aunts had all had the ability to see between the worlds.
Right here, not so many years ago, she had heard singing in the night. Thinking it was tourists out after dark
in violation of park regulations, she had come here,
ticket book in hand to write a citation, and found an
empty kiva bathed in white moonlight.

Chaco was a powerful place, and now, again, it
spoke to her. If only she could understand. She hurried
back toward her truck. Whatever had happened to Dale,
it wasn't good.

# CHAPTER 6

THE OLD-TIMEY JINGLE of Dusty's rotary phone blasted Maureen straight out of dreams. In them, Phil Morgan, her sycophantish colleague at McMaster University, had invited himself to dinner at her house in Niagara-on-the-Lake back in Ontario.

The nightmare of it was that she couldn't get him to leave. Phil just kept following her about the house, chattering incessantly about department trivia, the state of modern anthropology, and all the problems at the American Anthropological Association meetings. He was the Canadian liaison for the triple A.

Confused, but thankfully awake, she scrambled out from under the blankets and blinked at Dusty's living room—or at least the couple of inches of it left on either side of the foldout bed. It took her a moment to realize the jingling phone was buried underneath.

In the process of climbing off the foot of the bed she whacked her knee on the metal frame, then up-ended the whole show to paw through Dusty's dirty shirts for the phone.

"Hello?" she croaked, trying to clear the sleep from her throat.

"Maureen?" the curious voice asked on the other end.

It took her a second to place the caller, the young Chaco ranger: Magpie Walking Hawk Taylor. "Maggie?"

"Yes. Uh, have you heard from Dale?"

Maureen frowned at the concern in Maggie's voice as she said, "No, should I have?"

A hesitation, and then: "Look, I'm out at Chaco. I just did the rounds, you know, dawn patrol? Someone rides around and checks the loop before the park opens. Well, Dale's truck was in the Casa Rinconada parking lot. There's frost on the windshield . . . like it's been there all night."

"It's where?"

"Casa Rinconada. We have an interpretive trail that runs past a couple of small houses and the great kiva there. It's on the south side of Chaco Wash. Almost due south of Pueblo Bonito. You remember that place?"

Did she ever. Stewart had found her in Pueblo Bonito the morning after he'd shot off his mouth and told her point-blank that she was such a bitch it was no wonder she lived alone. Stewart had tracked her down the next morning, three miles from their Chaco Canyon dig. She had been sitting at the lip of a large kiva in the giant pueblo.

Maureen shook her head. "What was Dale doing out there?"

Maggie hesitated again. "We don't know. In fact, we didn't even know he was in the canyon. That's why I called. I thought maybe Dusty might know. Did Dale say anything about coming out here?"

Maureen frowned. "No. He wasn't home last night. Sylvia called saying she couldn't find him and she . . ." She glanced up.

Dusty stood where the narrow hallway opened into the cramped kitchen. He'd pulled on faded jeans, but his muscular chest was bare.

Maureen told him: "It's Maggie. She found Dale's truck in Chaco Canyon. Did Dale say he was going out there?"

Dusty crossed the floor and took the receiver from her hand. "What's wrong, Maggie?"

Maureen glanced down, horrified to realize she only wore a T-shirt and her panties. With unnatural haste, she shot a hand out and snagged up her pants. As she yanked them on, the pant leg was twisted and wouldn't pass her foot. Overbalanced, she toppled sideways into the wall.

"He's where?" Dusty asked, amusement in his eyes as he turned to watch Maureen claw for balance. In her fluster, she thought she caught the subtle rise of his eyebrows as he admired her long leg. After a moment, he added, "No. Not a word. I thought he was going from Farmington back to his house in Albuquerque after he dropped Alevy off at the airport. I expected to run into him at the lab today when we took in the Pueblo Animas stuff." Another long silence. "You tried him at home?" Dusty frowned as he listened to Maggie. "No, Maureen and I will drive down there and see if there's any kind of message or anything. You know Dale. He probably met some archaeologist and went out to look at Rinconada, or the stairway, or one of the small houses, got involved in the project and left with the other guy. He's probably planning to come back later and get his truck."

Maureen, having managed to pull her pants up, took a deep breath to settle her blush and read the mild concern on Stewart's face. Dale did do that sort of thing. He might have been one of the greatest archaeologists the world had ever known, but sometimes real-world concerns, things like National Park Service regulations, didn't compute.

"I'll be in touch as soon as I know," Dusty promised. "Thanks for calling." He bent down, hung up the phone, and turned puzzled eyes on Maureen. "When Dale left Pueblo Animas, he didn't say anything to you about going to Chaco Canyon, did he?"

Maureen shook her head and pulled back a fistful of unruly black hair that kept trying to tumble over her face. "No, but you know Dale. He rarely, if ever, gives you advance warning."

"Yeah, I know. He got carried away with petroglyphs in Tsegi Canyon one time and left a ten-person field crew abandoned on a mesa thirty miles south of Kayenta." Dusty slipped his hands into the back pockets of his jeans.

She saw concern line his forehead and asked, "Should we start to worry?"

He considered; then his expression cleared. "No. I've been doing this for years. It's just Dale. I go through this about once every six months. He doesn't show for a meeting, or vanishes without a trace, and he can't figure, for the life of him, why you were concerned."

Relieved, Maureen caught herself studying him: The morning light pouring through the windows gave his muscular body a golden glow. She was happy that she could ignore the way his flat belly tapered into a thin waist. A lesser woman would have caught herself outright admiring his broad shoulders and the swell of chest.

"So, what's the plan?" She used her casual voice just to demonstrate her nonchalance.

"I say we get showered, dressed, find some *huevos*, and drive down to the office in Albuquerque. We'll check and see if Dale left any messages, unload the artifacts, and if we still haven't found him, we'll drive by his house."

"What's the 'we' business?" she asked, crossing her arms.

"You don't want to come?"

"You said, and I quote, 'we get showered and dressed.'"

It took a half second before he grinned. "Well, you know, we do live in a desert environment; water, as the Anasazi knew, is something that you treat as a precious resource. It's not to be squandered lightly. Showering together is environmentally—"

"Not even in your most deluded dreams, Stewart." She picked up her suitcase, walked past him, and made her way through the kitchen and down the narrow hallway toward the cramped bathroom. Over her shoulder she called, "You do have clean towels, don't you?"

"That little cupboard to the right of the sink," he replied. She shot him one last glance, seeing him still in the cramped living room, his attention fixed on the phone where it lay in a nest of his rumpled shirts. She thought about his expression as she locked the door behind her.

Despite his cavalier words about Dale, he looked worried.

THE SCENT OF death fills this old kiva. My wounds have festered. Every time I take a breath, white-hot pain lances my body and I gag from the smell.

They have carried me here. To the wolf's lair. My fevered eyes drift around the circular chamber, noting the square wall crypts, the beautiful paintings on the plaster, the fire crackling in the middle of the floor. In the northern wall crypt, inside the painted rawhide box, I can feel the power of the mask. Despite the thin leather separating us, I can feel the mask's stare. I avert my eyes, looking up through the smokehole in the roof; I see the pink gleam of sunrise. One of the Cloud People hovers high above, as though watching me. I . . .

A sound. Fabric rustles.

It takes great effort to turn my head. She crouches to my left, across the fire, absolutely still. Her magnificent eyes glitter in the firelight. She is hunger itself, a black pit that must be filled.

"Shadow," I say. That is all I have breath for.

*She smiles, and I feel it across the chamber. Her need is overpowering. She is trembling, longing for the kill.*

*She rises like a dark ghost and floats toward me. Her icy hand smoothes gray hair from my brow and leisurely caresses its way down my face to my throat. The coolness feels so good I close my eyes and try to live in the movements of her hand. Her fingers lightly rub my chest, outlining each of my broken ribs; then they slide back up to my throat, and she delicately traces the shape of my windpipe.*

*Her fingers tighten, her nails digging in, as though to tear it from my flesh. She leans over and whispers in my ear, "I could, you know."*

*Her scent is musky, intoxicating. In my absence, it seems, she has been coupling with my warriors.*

*Laughter shakes me, and I cough from the pain.*

*Shadow's grip relaxes in confusion. "Why are you laughing?"*

*"Shadow," I say. "Where . . . is . . . Piper?"*

*A small dark form moves across the room. She has eyes like a wild dog's, large and unblinking, fixed on me, as though I am a mouse in the grass.*

*"Come here . . . child."*

*She remains as still as a newborn fawn when eagle's shadow passes over.*

*"Piper . . . I swear . . . if you do not . . . come, I will witch your breath-heart soul . . . and put it in a rock . . . so that it . . . never . . . finds its way to the Land of the Dead."*

*She trots across the chamber and stumbles in the bones beside the fire pit. She stops, her eyes huge. Her mouth quivers.*

*I laugh. "Someday . . . I will rename you . . . Bone Walker."*

*Piper runs forward and hides behind her mother. Shadow grabs her arm, drags her out, and shoves her toward me. "Your grandfather called you!"*

*Piper walks a step at a time, rubbing her arm where
her mother's fingers dug in. Her knees tremble. She is
a very beautiful child.*

*"Sit down," I order.*

*She kneels at my side and her long tangled hair falls
over my broken chest like a black cloud. Piper's eyes
go vacant, and she starts sucking on her lower lip, like
a newborn would a nipple.*

*"Here," I say. "Let me brush your hair."*

*I run my fingers through her hair, then let my hand
fall and slip it beneath her shirt. Her breasts are not
even tiny nubs.*

*A soothing wave tingles through me.*

*"Lie down."*

BROWSER LED HIS small vanguard of warriors
southward along the beaten trail that led to Flowing
Waters Town. They had left Dry Creek village when
the faint light of dawn first grayed the horizon. As the
sun slanted toward the west they topped the last rise,
passing the guard tower where sober-eyed warriors—
seeing Cricket Dancer—waved as they passed.

Browser's gut squirmed. They only had Cricket
Dancer's word that Blue Corn would honor a truce. It
had been less than a moon since Browser and Catkin
had found an entire village of Katsinas' People murdered, beheaded, and butchered, their corpses lying in
an abandoned kiva. Things had changed since the last
time they had been here. Then Blue Corn had simply
been disbelieving, now, he had heard, she was downright hostile to the Katsinas' People. Villages had been
attacked and burned by warriors faithful to the Flute
Player. How many of those raids had Blue Corn sanc-

tioned? Coming here might be akin to making camp in
a rattlesnake den.

Under the empty blue sky, the gray hills looked
dreary. They rose in lumpy layers above the pale cobble terraces that lined the river. Here and there, he
could see garden squares where people had planted
corn, beans, and squash last summer. The stalks and
vines had been collected for fuel as soon as they'd
dried enough to burn. Now the canals that watered
them drew forlorn lines across the dry soil.

The large three- and four-story buildings that made
up the core of Flowing Waters Town perched on the
terraces overlooking the river to the southeast. A thin
line of cottonwoods—so familiar to Browser from the
Katsinas' People's stay here almost two sun cycles
ago—stirred an ache in his heart. When they had lived
here, Hophorn, Ash Girl, Flame Carrier, Whiproot, and
Browser's young son, Grass Moon, had been alive. It
had been here in Flowing Waters Town that the boy
had first taken sick with the coughing disease and his
body had begun to waste away.

The lines around Browser's mouth deepened as he
looked down at the cluster of towns that dominated the
terrace. North House, situated at the terminus of the
Great North Road, hunched like one of the monsters
of the Beginning Time, its adobe brick walls gleaming
golden in the late fall sunlight. As Browser's party
passed, men, women, and children watched them from
the rooftops, and some even waved.

Rounding North House, they trotted down the raised
earthen causeway toward the lower terrace, where the
center of Flowing Waters Town hulked above the River
of Souls.

The larger, Dusk House, to the west of the road, had
been built by the First People back in the days when
their empire stretched across most of the world. They
had retreated to this location after the abandonment of
Straight Path Canyon. It was here that the Made People

exacted their vengeance for the lifetimes of domination they had endured at the hands of the First People.

Those of the First People who had not been killed outright had fled for their lives, dashing away into the hills to find their way to the few remaining towns that would take them in. In groups of twos and threes, they had been hunted down until the Made People had concluded that they had killed them all.

But they hadn't.

Browser raised a hand, bringing his party to a stop. He stood for a moment, panting from the long run from Dry Creek village. Search as he might, he could see no sign of danger in either of the two plastered towns before him.

"Looks peaceful," Catkin said from behind him. "If Blue Corn means treachery, she has been very clever. If the Fire Dogs are really here, so have they. Nothing's burning, no refugees came charging down the road in the middle of the night. I don't hear any screams or see any dead people lying around."

"I did not lie," Cricket Dancer said, a stiffness in his voice. "My Matron gave you her promise of safe passage." As he spoke, a young woman appeared on the roof of Sunrise House and began shaking the dust out of a blanket. A group of children burst from the corner of the building, laughing and chasing each other.

That more than anything reassured Browser. He looked back over his shoulder to see Cloudblower leading the long procession of Katsinas' People and the Longtail refugees that had joined them. Even some of Rock Dove's Dry Creek villagers had volunteered to make the trek to Flowing Waters Town to hear what the Fire Dogs had to say about Poor Singer's prophecy. The line of people looked like dots of color as they hurried along the earthen ramp leading down from North House. Their bright clothing contrasted to the somber gray of the surrounding hills.

"I hope this isn't a mistake. I'm not sure I trust Blue

Corn. She's shifted allegiances too often to suit me."
Catkin gave him a sidelong glance. "But you know her
better than I do."

Browser nodded. "I'm not sure what she really believes. Her mother and aunt were devout believers in
Poor Singer's prophecy. They thought it would bring
changes for the better. In the beginning Blue Corn was
skeptical. Whatever faith she had in the katsinas evaporated when Flame Carrier refurbished the great kiva
at Dusk House. When the doorway to the underworlds
didn't open, Blue Corn turned back to the old gods."

"Just so she doesn't turn on us, Browser." Catkin
shifted as she studied the two great houses. The round
curve of her hip was close to his. Despite the chill in
the mid-fall air he could feel her body heat. Strands of
her black hair gleamed bluish in the bright morning
sun. She, like he, had cut her hair short in mourning
for their recently murdered Matron. He need not look
back to know that none of the Katsinas' People except
Obsidian had long hair anymore. Why she hadn't cut
her hair, he couldn't guess.

"What are you thinking?" Catkin asked, glancing at
his serious expression.

"About Obsidian."

He could sense the sharpening of Catkin's interest.

"She still wears her hair long," Browser explained.

"And full of jewelry. We could buy a winter's food
for what she has hung on her body. She should be
grieving like the rest of us."

"I suppose it's because . . ." He didn't finish the
thought.

"Because it wasn't her Matron who died? You are
more charitable than I am, Browser." She lifted one of
her long legs and braced a sandaled foot on one knee
to stand storklike. "Every day I'm more inclined to
crack her skull with my war club."

She studied the two great houses and the World Kivas that sprinkled the earthworks around the houses,

then added, "Are we going in there to see what kind
of trap Blue Corn and these Fire Dogs have laid for
us? Or are we just going to let the Katsinas' People
walk into an ambush?"

Browser's thick black brows lifted. He turned to look
at her. "I do not think other War Chiefs have to put up
with such insolence."

Behind them, Jackrabbit chuckled nervously to relieve the tension. He was a young man of sixteen summers. Like so many of the warriors, he had seen more
life than his summers would have indicated. Beside
him, seventeen-summers-old Straighthorn showed no
hint of emotion. His heart was still numb over the loss
of his young love, Redcrop, another casualty of the
fighting around Longtail village. So many dead, so
much misery and grief. How, in the name of the gods,
did they stand it?

Browser carefully slipped his bow from his shoulder,
and with a practiced move, strummed the taut string.
War Chiefs in this day and age didn't travel with un-
strung bows. At least not the living ones.

He trotted out ahead of his party. If there was going
to be trouble, it would be best to learn of it before he
had to fight a retreating action.

Matron Blue Corn climbed up the ladder that led to her
roof. The rickety thing groaned under her weight. The
two upright poles were made of cottonwood—a brittle
and unpredictable wood. Pine would have made a good
solid ladder, but pine wasn't so easy to come by these
days, not when it might mean the lives of some of her
people were she to send them off to the distant hills to
get it.

The thirty-two sun cycles she had survived had used
her poorly. Never a particularly attractive woman,
years of worry and tragedy had taken a brutal toll. The
mantle of Matron had been passed from mother, to
aunt, to Blue Corn. After wavering, she had sided with

the Flute Player and the old gods. Faced with the re-
alities of an extended drought, and charges of witchcraft flying about like hardened rawhide shields, she
was no longer sure what she believed. With one exception: She desperately hoped each day that sunset
would find her people still alive and healthy.

And, now, Gray Thunder and his Fire Dogs had trotted up to her gated wall asking for sanctuary and to
speak to the freshly murdered Matron of the Katsinas'
People.

*I must have been mad to let them in here.*

She stepped out onto the pounded clay roof and
looked northward. A small party of warriors jogged
toward her. She knew that burly figure in front, his bow
at the ready. War Chief Browser wore a yellow shirt
these days. The only one he had, she assumed. At his
shoulder, reliable as Father Sun's rays after a summer
rain, came Deputy Catkin, her long lean body wrapped
in a red tunic. She ran with a bow over her shoulder,
and a war club in her right hand.

In the rear came Cricket Dancer, her most trusted
runner. Though he had been traveling for nearly a day
straight, he didn't stumble or weave.

Blue Corn winced when her knee sent a stabbing
pain up her leg. As a young girl, she had jammed that
knee jumping to the ground from a burning building
over in the canyon country west of the Green Mesas.
These days you were more likely to be killed by
Straight Path people, but on that long ago day it had
been a raid carried out by the Tower Builders. Odd,
you didn't hear so much about them anymore. The
story carried south by traders was that many of their
villages had turned to the katsinas, and they had their
own troubles with the Flute Player Believers.

She glanced up at the blue sky. Father Sun rode high,
his golden rays gleaming on the distant cloud people.
When Browser came within hailing distance, she
called, "Greetings, War Chief."

"Are you all right?" Browser asked, slowing to a stop just out of bow shot.

"We are fine," she returned. "Why, in the name of the Blessed Flute Player, wouldn't we be?"

If her appeal to the old god affected him, he gave no sign, answering, "We were concerned about the intentions of the Fire Dogs. Cricket Dancer told us that you had allowed them within your walls."

Did he think she was senile? She'd had them watched from the moment she gave them the narrow room block on the town's southern wall. "The Fire Dogs have been as good as their word. They have shared what little food they brought with them. A new kind of bread, a thinly patted corn cake they call 'piki.' And odd word, but it tastes good. Our gates are open; you may enter in safety."

She looked past him to the line of people who threaded their way down the causeway from North House. "Tell the rest they are welcome. Matron White Smoke cleaned up several rooms for you in Dusk House." She pointed to the huge square town three bow shots to the west. The towering image of the Flute Player adorned the east wall, and beside him, smaller and darker, stood the Blue God. She was a bloody-headed woman with enormous empty eyes.

"I will do so, Matron." Browser propped his hands on his hips and turned. He called, "Jackrabbit, Straighthorn, go and inform Matron White Smoke that our people are here; then inspect every room assigned to us. Many of those rooms have been walled up for sun cycles. I don't want any surprises. Catkin and I will go and pay our regards to Matron Blue Corn."

Browser's warriors split off, trotting warily toward the old ruin of the First People's last dream. White Smoke's Buffalo Clan occupied less than twenty of the hundred or so still-accessible rooms.

Blue Corn turned and started back for her ladder. Whatever the Fire Dogs were cooking up, it was time to stir the stew. She hoped that Cloudblower was no fool when it came to negotiations with canny characters like Gray Thunder.

# CHAPTER 7

### South of Bernalillo, New Mexico

TRAFFIC HAD BEEN desultory on the drive down I-25 from Santa Fe. The casino signs occupied Maureen's attention as she watched the countryside flash past the Bronco's window. To the east, the Sandia Mountains stood in silhouetted humps that shadowed the valley from the morning sun. The lingering taste of *huevos rancheros* titillated her taste buds. Something about the combination of eggs over-easy, hot corn tortillas fresh from the oven, *refritos*, cheddar, and chopped green chilis, with a rich seasoning of cumin, created ecstasy. She smiled; it was even better than the chocolate doughnuts and the rich black coffee in her favorite Tim Horton's off the QEW outside of Hamilton.

As they drove into the slanting morning sunlight, Dusty pulled his battered brown cowboy hat low and drove with one hand. He wore a thick denim coat and mirrored sunglasses.

"Why would Dale leave his truck sitting out there overnight and not tell anyone?" Dusty whispered, more to himself than to her. "It's just not like him."

She studied him as they passed the clutter of truck stops, industrial warehouses, and motels that introduced the southbound traveler to Albuquerque. "I thought you were the one who said not to worry about it."

Dusty let off the gas as he entered the speed zone, and the Bronco growled under compression. "I don't know. I mean, first the murder victims at the 10K3 site, then burned children in the kiva at Pueblo Animas. Too many peculiar things are happening." He shook his head.

"You're not thinking of *el basilisco*, are you?"

He glanced at her, then returned his attention to the road. "No."

Uh-huh, she thought, remembering the beautiful little coiled jet snake with the red coral eye that they'd dug up from a murdered woman's grave at the 10K3 site in Chaco Canyon. Dusty seemed to be plagued by Anasazi witchcraft.

"You think I'm crazy, Doctor?"

"I suspected that the moment I met you on that Proto-Iroquois site in New York, Stewart. All I can say is that after months of close exposure to your warm fuzzy personality, I'm convinced."

His mouth twisted. "Did I ever tell you what a charming person you are to be around? Always seeing the bright side, cheering a fellow up."

"That's my mission . . . *watch out!*" She threw a hand against the dash as Dusty jammed on the brakes to avoid rear-ending a little blue Toyota that swerved into their lane.

"Asshole!" Dusty yelled.

"Ouch!" She looked down at the big black revolver that slid out from under the seat and clunked into the back of her heel. "Stewart, I wish to God you'd get a seat belt for the passenger's seat!"

"Me? Why don't you wish some of these ostrich-headed idiots would drive like human beings? If it wasn't for lunatics like that, people wouldn't need seat belts!"

She grimaced down at the revolver. "There's a gun between my feet."

"Sounds Freudian."

Annoyed, she replied, "Of course, it does. You're a man."

"Maureen, it's just a pistol. Reach down and slide it back under the seat."

"Is it loaded?"

"You bet."

She stared at the gun. It seemed to ooze evil. "You know, you'd be in jail in Canada, and most of the civilized world."

"Yeah, yeah, Canada and Communist China have banned all the guns. Well, this is the United States of America. We're still mostly free to protect ourselves from bad guys. Just push the revolver back under the seat. It won't bite."

The sensation was like riding with a coiled rattlesnake between her boots. She used her heel to kick it back, glaring at him the whole time.

He wheeled them through the traffic to the exit onto I-40 eastbound. The Bronco thump-thumped over the cement overpass and merged into the line of shining autos that crept along at the post-rush-hour crawl.

Dusty took the exit onto Louisiana and hedged his way into the left lane. Maureen raised an eyebrow when they passed the Winrock Mall and its trendy stores. At the light on Independence, he waited for the arrow, passed the Marriott, and wound around to a small industrial building hidden behind the hotel and the glass and brick restaurants.

The white building sported a sign stating: ROBERTSON & STEWART, CULTURAL RESOURCES CONSULTANTS.

"So, this is it?" Maureen opened the door and stepped out onto the small asphalt parking lot. It held four spaces that apparently didn't get a lot of use. The paint defining the spaces still looked fresh.

"Home away from home," Dusty told her as he walked around, opened the passenger door, and jammed some empty bottles between the seat bottom and the floorboard to keep the revolver in place.

Maureen shook her head.

Dusty unlocked the office's aluminum-framed glass door, then reached down to retrieve a weathered metate, an ancient grinding stone. He used the artifact to prop open the door.

"We rent this by the year. It serves for an office, lab, and place to keep the paperwork. Sometimes when we have extra field crew in town, we crash them in the back room."

He led her into a spartan but functional front office. The light wood veneer walls gleamed under the fluorescent lights. The metal desk sported a telephone, typewriter, and pencil cup. On a stand to the right stood a copy machine with a case of paper visible behind the open cabinet door. The calendar on the wall had been turned to September; never mind that this was the first day of November. The opposite wall had been covered with contiguous 1-to-500,000-scale maps of Arizona, New Mexico, southern Utah, and Colorado. Pins were stuck here and there in the maps, some with tags that denoted sites and others marking project areas. The big wooden case blocking the plate-glass window held stacks of USGS quadrangles.

Dusty pushed the button on the combination phone/ answering machine/fax that promptly told him he had four messages. The first ran.

A man with an English accent said, *"Dale, you son of a bitch! I didn't think that even you could sink this low! I will not allow you to pour salt into old wounds. Keep this up, and you'll think my last rebuttal to your article was a joke. I'll be your worst nightmare."*

Dusty frowned as the next message played. *"Dale? It's Maggie. We found your truck this morning. If you get this, please call and let us know you're all right."*

Two more Maggie messages followed, each slightly more concerned than the last.

Dusty picked up the phone and punched the speed dial. He listened for a moment, meeting Maureen's concerned stare. Finally he said, "Dale? Dusty. Hey, we're getting a little worried about you. If you get to your place before I do, I don't want to play tag with you all day long. Just stay put. We'll be there as soon as we get the Pueblo Animas artifacts unloaded. And call Maggie to let her know you're okay."

He hung up and stared at the phone for several moments.

"Who was the Englishman?" Maureen asked. He didn't sound very friendly.

"I don't know. I didn't recognize his voice. Maybe that's what this is all about. Dale's engaged, once again, in an academic squabble."

Maureen folded her arms. "What rebuttal was he talking about?"

Dusty shrugged. "I don't know. Dale's last published article, however, was about the evidence for cannibalism in the Southwest. The Englishman was probably upset that his alabaster Anasazi turned out to be human beings."

He walked over, opened the wooden door in the back wall, and flipped a light switch. Maureen followed him into a spacious lab. Cinder-block walls were lined with wooden shelving made of two-by-fours and plywood. From floor to ceiling they were packed with cardboard boxes full of brown paper artifact bags, soil sample bags, portions of broken pottery, collections of animal bone, and thick slabs of ground stone. A stack of shovels cluttered the corner behind the door. Wooden screens stood in the back of the room, all propped up like an angular line of soldiers.

Maureen ran a finger along one of the dusty lab tables. It, like the three others that ran lengthwise down the center of the room, had been constructed of two-by-fours and covered with plywood. Each table was littered with microscopes, calipers, light tables, maps, and stacks of reference books on southwestern ceramics, geology, archaeology, botany, and a host of other subjects. Shoe boxes held stacks of three-by-five index cards in clear sandwich bags that identified individual artifacts for curation.

Through the open door to her left, she could see a small bathroom with sink, toilet, and shower. To her right, more shelves lined the wall, bursting with reference books, field reports, and the other exotica of report production.

"Dale?" Dusty called. "You here?"

Maureen leaned over to examine the mouse dung on the file cabinets and boxes. "Nobody here but us mice."

"Yeah, I need to bait the traps again."

Dusty stepped to the closest table and rolled up the maps there. Scrounging a rubber band, he secured them and used a whisk broom to bat a cloud of dust from the tabletop. "That should be enough room for the Pueblo Animas stuff, right there." He pointed.

Maureen spent the next half hour packing in boxes of human bone, pottery sherds, soil samples, and other cultural material from their dig at Pueblo Animas. This, as in her specialty in physical anthropology, was where the real work started. Contrary to popular opinion and the image created by *National Geographic*, most archaeology was done in the lab, perched on uncomfortable chairs, peering down at bits of human trash that opened dim windows into long-vanished worlds.

As he set down the last of the boxes, Dusty said, "Okay, there it is. That's the last of the field records." He thumped the cardboard box full of forms. "Sylvia took the photos into the processor, so that's taken care of."

"Right. Let's go see if Dale's home," Maureen said, and headed for the front door. "He and I are going to have a little talk about this employee complex he's developed."

"You're going to beard Dale in his own house?"

"Yep."

"This I gotta see."

## Casa Rinconada, Chaco Canyon

Magpie propped her hands on her hips. She stood just above the gaping circumference of the Casa Rinconada great kiva. A cold wind tugged at her green Park Service jacket, and teased the ends of her shoulder-length hair where it escaped her silver clasp. Looking to the east, she could see her vehicle parked beside Dale's gleaming red truck. It was supposed to be her lunch hour. She checked her watch. In fifteen minutes she had to be back at the Visitors Center, on guard at the main desk to accommodate the few tourists who passed through this late in the season.

Maggie couldn't shake the feeling that something terrible had happened to Dale.

She sighed and looked around. Maybe it was just the stress she'd been under lately. Her elderly aunt Sage was dying of cancer. She lived alone just off the road north of Grants. Despite Magpie taking every chance to drive down to see her, the old woman refused to leave her old trailer house. She wanted to die in her house, not among strangers at a hospice in Albuquerque or at the hospital in Gallup.

Her eyes fixed on his red truck, as though it could send her a message, some subtle clue as to where Dale might be.

"I wouldn't worry about it," Rupert Brown, the park superintendent, had told her when she'd reported the vehicle. "This is Dale we're talking about. I've known him since before you were born. He does things like this. I think I'll write him a citation personally, just to see the expression on his face when he roars in here to protest."

But Maggie's encounter with the vanishing owl, the faint hazy vision of Dale walking right up this path toward Casa Rinconada, had been eating at her all day. She'd had to return for a second look.

Turning, she looked off to the west, up the low gray ridge that humped out from the side of Rincon Canyon's buff-colored sandstone. The grasses and brush, stroked by the wings of the wind, might have been beckoning her. Why? She knew that ridgetop. Nothing was up there except an unexcavated ruin.

The flash of white caught her eye. Maggie frowned, shading her vision as she studied it. It looked like a piece of paper. Trash. People were such pigs. Reggie, who had been hired to do minor repairs as well as collect the park trash, spent most of his time picking up trash.

The sound of a vehicle caused her to look to the north. From here she could see straight across the canyon to the Pueblo Bonito ruins almost due north. Slightly to the east stood the once proud walls of Chetro Ketl. To the west she could see Pueblo del Arroyo, the location of the only tri-wall structure in the canyon.

The vehicle was Rupert's shiny Dodge pickup, the newest and nicest of the Park Service units. Being boss had perks.

Rupert's truck thumped over the Chaco Wash bridge and made the turn into the Rinconada parking lot. He pulled up beside Magpie's truck and killed the engine. She walked partway down the trail to meet him.

Sunlight drenched his tall body. He had a handsome brown face and powerful eyes. Something about him had always affected her, as if the man broadcast on a frequency that she could detect but not really hear. She never knew what to do with that sense of power that surrounded him. Was it just something that spoke to her subconscious?

"Hey, Magpie, I thought you'd be headed back to the front desk." He smiled. He wore sunglasses and a black cowboy hat. His green Park Service winter coat sported the official patch on the shoulder. His long legs were encased in slim brown slacks.

"I just thought I'd come back and check. You know, about Dale. Something's not right about his truck being out here." She shook her head. "He would have at least checked in."

Rupert stuffed his long fingers into his back pockets as he turned, looking back at the parking lot. Maggie watched him as he carefully searched the surrounding canyon bottom. "Well, you can never tell with Dale. Rules and regulations have never had much of an impact on his behavior."

Maggie checked her watch again. "Rupert, I have to get back." She pointed at the bit of white paper up on the ridge. "You might want Reggie to drop by with his trash truck. That looks like something that blew out of someone's car."

"I sent him into town on a 'gofer' run. If you wouldn't mind trotting up and getting that, I'd appreciate it." He made a face. "I need to look around here a little bit."

Maggie gave him a cautious look.

Rupert read her expression and laughed. "Probably just a nut call. You know, we get them. Yesterday was Halloween. Some woman just called, asked for the superintendent, then told me that a white guy had fallen through a hole in the past. And that his head was sticking down into the Fourth World where he could see the ancestors."

A surge of adrenaline tingled Maggie's veins. "What did she mean?"

"I don't know." Rupert squinted up at the sun. "I'll look around here and see you back at the barn."

"Right." Maggie walked back up the trail and spilt off, climbing up to the bit of white paper that the wind

had wedged under a saltbush branch. She crumpled it
in her hand and straightened, only to see another
twenty paces beyond. Climbing to it, she picked it up.
On a whim she plodded to the ridgetop and looked
around. Chaco Canyon unfolded before her. Rupert was
walking the last of the trail loop through the small
houses on the way back to his vehicle. The ruins under
the far northern wall gleamed. To the south the rim of
Chacra Mesa shone in the midday sun. She could see
the ancient Anasazi stairway that led to Tsin Kletsin
on the mesa top. At first the oddity didn't register as
she lowered her eyes to the crumbled stone piled on
the ridgetop. It was the color rather than the shape that
caught her eye. Dark red, wine color rather than buff.
Like two juniper stumps, except . . . then her stumbling
mind put it together.

Two bloody feet atop legs stuck out of the dirt.
She screamed, *"Rupert!"*

# CHAPTER 8

Casa Rinconada Parking Lot, Chaco Canyon

MAGPIE WATCHED AS the park law enforcement
people climbed through the sagebrush to the mound of
stone visible on the ridgetop. The afternoon sun had
drained the color from the buff canyon walls and
bleached the aqua tones of the brush to a sickly green.
A hollow had grown in Maggie's stomach.

Beside her, Rupert Brown bowed his head and took
a deep breath. "The FBI's on the way."

Maggie glanced at him. "I'm sorry, Rupert. You knew him a lot longer than I did."

"Forty-three years," Rupert said sadly.

They'd celebrated Rupert's sixty-third birthday last month at the Visitors Center, but few people would guess his age. Except for his steely gray hair, he might have been in his late forties. He had a lean smooth face, with a long nose and sharp cheekbones. His intense brown eyes reminded Maggie of an eagle's, probing and memorable. At six feet six, Rupert Brown cut an imposing figure. His green Park Service uniform, like always, was impeccably clean and pressed.

"Dale got me into archaeology," he said. "He gave me a chance and then kept me on track. He helped me get into the university. He was the chairman of my thesis committee. Back in the late sixties, he arranged a job for me with the government. Dale went to bat for me, said that it was about time that an Indian archaeologist was put in charge of Chaco Canyon. But more than that, without Dale, I doubt I'd be alive today." He smiled wearily. "Every time I fell, he was always there to pick me up and kick me in the butt to get me going again."

Maggie's heart ached. Dale had helped so many people. "He was proud of you, Rupert. You've done a good job. The staff likes you."

Voices sounded from the ridge to Maggie's right where the law enforcement officers climbed over the site.

"Rupert, I want to see Dale."

Rupert turned concerned eyes on her. "Magpie, trust me on this, all right? You don't want to. I wish I hadn't. It's going to affect my sleep for a long time. It wasn't pretty . . . what they did to him."

Maggie fought the sudden urge to cry. "Why? Who would do anything terrible to Dale? Who'd rob him? What would they take? He didn't have anything!" She clenched her fists.

Rupert's expression pained at the tears welling in her eyes. "All right, if you really need to see him. Go. You're going to find out eventually, but I want you to prepare yourself. It looks like Dale met a witch out here." He paused. "Do you understand?"

Maggie blinked her eyes clear. "You—you mean an 'Indian' witch? You can't be serious."

He nodded. "This isn't an Anglo crime, which means this is going to be a real circus for us. The press, the publicity. Not only do we have to bury an old friend, but the investigation is going to turn this park upside down. We're in for an unholy mess once word gets out." He squinted. "Thank God we're past the tourist season. By tonight, when people start to hear, this place is going to be empty." He rubbed his jaw. "Or full, who knows?"

"I can't believe it. What kind of witch? What tribe?"

"I'm not sure. It's complicated, Magpie. He's buried upside down in the dirt. You saw how his feet were sticking up. They were bloody because the soles of his feet had been skinned off."

Maggie's knees went weak. Rupert reached out and grabbed her arm to steady her. "Who would do that? Who would want to make sure he could not walk to the Land of the Dead?"

"All I can think of is that somewhere in his long and colorful life, our old friend got crosswise with a witch. But, why bring him here? Why on my watch?" Rupert seemed to be speaking to the wind. "Is this a message for me? Something I'm supposed to understand?"

"The only thing I understand," Magpie said, "is that I just lost an old friend. It's as if I can hear Dale calling to me, telling me to watch out."

She looked up at him, and Rupert said, "I want you to take the day off. Maybe the week. I don't care. Go home, Magpie. Grieve. I'll call you and let you know when the funeral is. I just . . . well, go home. Get out of here."

She nodded as tears blurred her eyes. "All right, but I have to see him first, to say good-bye. If I don't, it will never be right between us."

Rupert stared at her, as if seeing into her soul. "Go on. But I warned you."

She started forward, and stopped, looking back, seeing his stricken face. "Will you be all right?"

He gave her a wounded smile. "I'm the park superintendent. I have to be. It says so in the job description, but that doesn't mean that I'm not going to sneak away and spend some time alone with memories of Dale."

"You're a good man, Rupert."

He looked suddenly lost and alone.

Magpie left him standing there, a desolate look in his eyes as she followed the trail left by the law enforcement personnel. She'd look, see what they'd done, and say good-bye.

Then, dear God, someone had to call Dusty.

A LARGE FIRE blazed near the sheltering west wall of Sunrise House, but it did little to thwart the cold. Catkin pulled her gray blanket more tightly about her shoulders and studied the faces of the people who had gathered below. In the flickering firelight, they resembled statues carved from a fine pale wood. Sunrise House was the perfect place to hold this assembly. The plaza was bounded by a two-story room block on the west and north, while a wing of single-story rooms enclosed the south up to the curving wall of the kiva. Set back on the north was yet a third story of rooms that used the roofs of those below for balcony space. That area was now crowded with observers who had come in from Dusk House, North House, and the surrounding great houses where news of the historic visit had been carried. Even the roof of the kiva was crowded with people.

The mere sight of that many on a kiva roof gave Catkin a chill. But a half moon ago, she had seen almost forty children incinerated on the roof of the tower kiva at Longtail village. Pray to the gods that no skulking warriors lurked in the dusk to ply their havoc here.

She glanced at Browser, standing to the right of Stone Ghost. His eyes seemed fixed on some distant point, as if he were staring at something in the sky just beyond the looming bulk of the great kiva's crowded roof.

He seemed preoccupied these days. First it had been the deaths of his wife, his son, and his lover, Hophorn. Then had come the long journey from Straight Path Canyon north to Longtail village. After that, the stories of warfare came filtering to them, borne on the flood of refugees leaving the Green Mesa villages. They told of whole villages wiped out by warriors loyal to the Flute Player and the old gods. Then Browser and Catkin had responded to a call from Aspen village—and seen the horror with their own eyes. A heartbeat after that their Matron, Flame Carrier, had been murdered, and within days Two Hearts had set the fire that killed over half of their children and destroyed Longtail village. Browser had come within a whisper of being killed in the subsequent fighting with the White Moccasins, and heard the truth of his ancestry. No wonder he was reeling. It would have been more a miracle if he'd still been the clearheaded War Chief she had first known when she came to the Katsinas' People over two sun cycles ago.

Well, if Browser could not concentrate on his duty, she would. She considered the village layout. Matron Cloudblower stood just ahead of Browser and Stone Ghost. Old Wading Bird was to Cloudblower's right. Matron Crossbill and several of her surviving elders, many with bandaged burns, clustered to Cloudblower's left. The remaining Katsinas' People pressed in behind her, their backs to the western room block.

Matron Blue Corn stood on the north side of the fire with a beautiful red parrot-feather cloak spread about her shoulders. She had pinned her hair up with turkey-bone pins that gleamed with inlaid turquoise, jet, and coral. Her flat angular face remained emotionless, but her crossed arms and stern posture reflected disapproval. An old man, a frog-faced elder, stood just behind her. From time to time, he would whisper into Blue Corn's ear. Who was he? Catkin didn't remember him from her previous visits here, but with the comings and goings of refugees, she couldn't know everyone.

The Matron's large dark eyes scanned the crowd, studying the faces one by one. When she met Catkin's hard stare, she stopped, as if measuring. It was Blue Corn who severed the connection when she turned to whisper to Rain Crow, her War Chief. He was a blocky man with broad shoulders. Sometime in the past, his face had stopped a war club. That collision had left a flattened nose, heavily scarred upper lip, and misaligned cheekbones. The fellow wore his long black hair pulled into a bun on the left side of his head. He listened to Matron Blue Corn, glanced briefly at Catkin, and said something to the frog-faced elder before turning and ducking into the crowd of villagers that thronged the space behind Blue Corn.

What had all that been about?

Catkin took a half step back, gestured with her hand, and caught Jackrabbit's attention. When the young warrior sidled close, she said, "I want you to choose a handful of warriors, tell them to spread out, keep an eye on things. Quietly."

His jaw muscles knotted as he looked past her at Browser. "I'm glad someone besides me is a little worried about this."

"The order came straight from the War Chief," Catkin lied. "He's doing his best not to show his distrust of either the Fire Dogs or Matron Blue Corn."

"I am glad to hear that," Jackrabbit told her, clapping a reassuring hand to her shoulder. "Consider your spies to be out."

"Move carefully, Jackrabbit, quietly," she reminded. "We want to be wary, not provocative."

He nodded and slipped away, stopping to whisper into Straighthorn's ear before moving on to Wrapped Hand, Straw Shield, and Two Cones. One by one the youths eased into the crowd.

Catkin returned her attention to the empty space south of the crackling fire. The door curtain facing the beaten clay plaza stirred, and an athletic young man ducked out, followed by nine warriors who spread out to either side before advancing in a solid rank toward the fire.

They wore fine blue cotton shirts that Catkin could see under their split-turkey-feather blankets. Each of the warriors carried a small willow basket made from yellow stays woven with black to create zigzag patterns. Buffalo-leather leggings rose above their thick yucca trail sandals, and each had a bright red sash about his waist.

An old man emerged last and took a position to the rear. He lowered his eyes, as if in deep thought. Catkin examined his tattered gray tunic. He must be a slave. Dirty wisps of white hair had escaped the bun at the back of his head and fallen over his wrinkled face.

The young Fire Dog stepped forward and smiled. He was a handsome man; no, more, a beautiful man. The planes of his face were perfect. His nose, cheeks, the firm chin and strong mouth, they might have sprung from a god rather than a human mother. Even the sparkle in his large brown eyes had an appealing otherworldliness. He stopped several steps from the fire, lifted his hands, and began to sing. The rich tenor of his voice carried out over the suddenly silent crowd, rising to echo from the plastered walls.

Catkin felt her soul lift, and in spite of her suspicions, she smiled. Though he sang in the language of the Fire Dogs, she knew most of the words. She had learned the language from the slaves her people kept.

*"I rise from fire.*
*Hear me, wind and sky.*
*Hear my song and Bless me.*
*I rise from fire.*
*I rise from water.*
*I rise from earth.*
*When I live, you live within me.*
*When I die, I will rise and become*
    *one with the clouds, my ancestors.*
*I rise.*
*I rise to be with you."*

When the last strains faded, only Wind Baby's whimpering among the roof poles could be heard.

After a few instants of silence, people began to shuffle, and the young man raised his hands higher. "I am Gray Thunder, of the Rattlesnake Clan! You call my people Fire Dogs because of the way we came to this earth. Since the beginning of time, we have either traded or fought with each other. Sometimes we have even lived in villages in the same valley, shared the water, wood, plants, and animals. We have a history, your people and mine. Perhaps we have much more."

"What would that be?" the frog-faced elder asked derisively from behind Blue Corn's shoulder.

Gray Thunder lowered his hands, and the gleam in his eyes intensified. "For many generations, my people believed that one day a child would be born who would bring about the end of the Straight Path Nation."

Whispers greeted his statement.

"It happened, as our prophets said it would! The great Poor Singer, son of Young Fawn and Chief Crow Beard, marked the end of the First People's reign.

Within a sun cycle of Poor Singer's capture, the First People had left Straight Path Canyon and come here. It was here, in Flowing Waters Town, that the Made People declared war on the First People, and drove them from this place."

"Perhaps he should tell us something we don't already know," Blue Corn said just loudly enough that most of the front ranks could hear. People laughed and Frog Face nodded.

"But Poor Singer brought more than the destruction of the First People. His birth also marked the beginning of a new cycle, that of the thlatsinas!" Gray Thunder's face shone. "Whom your people call katsinas."

Blue Corn made a disgusted sound.

Gray Thunder continued, "We have come to tell you of Poor Singer's vision. Why it was true, and why the thlatsinas tie the Made People and my people, the Mogollon, together."

"What?" Blue Corn's expression went hard.

Catkin took a step forward, intrigued. Either Gray Thunder had been hit in the head too many times, or he was about to turn their world upside down.

"Go on, please, Gray Thunder," Matron Cloud-blower called out in a strong voice. She wore a beautiful white dress with red spirals. "You have traveled a great distance to find us. Share your words about the Blessed Poor Singer."

Gray Thunder tilted his face back and, as if speaking to the darkened sky, said, "The thlatsinas were there when the Blessed Poor Singer was cut from his mother's womb by the priest, Sternlight."

Derisive mutters broke out among Blue Corn's people. She raised a hand to quiet them. "What are you talking about?" she called. "I have never heard that story!"

"No, but it is true!" Gray Thunder cried. "Have the constant wars, and the droughts and illnesses, robbed you of so much? Have you no stories of the Blessed Sternlight?"

"I remember," Stone Ghost said in a voice almost too low to hear. The crowd turned to face him. "He was the Sunwatcher of Talon Town when Night Sun was the Matron of the First People. Sternlight was taken captive by Jay Bird, the great Mogollon War Chief. Jay Bird was the only man ever to sack Talon Town. Blessed Gods, Gray Thunder, what else do you know?" Stone Ghost stepped forward, his wispy white hair blowing in the breeze.

"I know a great deal, Elder. I know a story about him that was never told in the Straight Path Nation. Not to the First People, and not to the Made People. It was told in the village under the Gila Monster Cliffs. Of Crow Beard, and Sternlight, and Young Fawn, and the child she carried. It was told about how Crow Beard had ordered his child—conceived in the Mogollon slave girl's womb—to be destroyed lest it be the fulfillment of prophecy."

The old Mogollon slave smiled slightly, his eyes on Gray Thunder's back.

The young Fire Dog continued: "It was told how Sternlight had managed to talk Crow Beard into sparing one: Young Fawn, or the child, but not both. It was on the morning when the Blessed Sternlight was ordered to kill the child that the thaltsinas first appeared to him. At that time, the Wolf Thlatsina walked side by side with the Blessed Sternlight and told him to kill Young Fawn. To cut the living child from her womb no matter what Chief Crow Beard had ordered. The Wolf Thlatsina told him that the child would mark the beginning of a new age."

"And Sternlight did this?" Blue Corn asked, her eyes narrowing as she studied Gray Thunder.

"Yes. Sternlight saved, and then hid, the prophet Poor Singer. He paid for it with his life. Young Fawn, the Mogollon slave girl, was the great Jay Bird's daughter. When he found out who had killed her, he drove a stiletto through the Blessed Sternlight's heart."

Blue Corn shouted, "Just another in a long line of Fire Dog atrocities!"

"Oh, it was anything but that." Gray Thunder appeared oblivious to the tone in Blue Corn's voice. "It was the beginning, you see. When Jay Bird drove his stiletto through Sternlight's heart, something happened to Poor Singer. He ran from Gila Monster Cliffs and fled high into the mountains. It was there that he talked to the thlatsinas for the first time. It is said that they changed him into a coyote, and that he ran northward across the sky. Far to the north, high in the mountains, he found a cave, its walls glittering with turquoise. He talked to the thlatsina who keeps the Tortoise Bundle, and she gave him a vision."

Blue Corn lifted one skeptical eyebrow. Her people seemed to be looking to her for some response. Matron Cloudblower wore an indulgent smile, her attention fixed on Gray Thunder. For her own part, Catkin didn't know whether to believe this ludicrous story or if she were hearing the ramblings of a madman. She was surprised, however, at the shocked expression on Stone Ghost's wrinkled face.

"Poor Singer's Power," Gray Thunder said, "was made manifest to all when he came down from the clouds with Cornsilk. Jay Bird was in the process of torturing the great War Chief, Ironwood, to death. When Jay Bird refused to stop, Poor Singer raised a hand and called the thlatsinas to him. At his bidding, they shook the earth, split a mountain apart, and hurled huge fiery rocks across the land. The quakes awakened the Rainbow Serpent. She crawled from the underworlds and snaked across the earth in a molten river. Everything in her path burned. Whole forests were gone in a blink. Ash fell from the skies for days, coating the entire world. Only when Straight Path Canyon was abandoned did the rainbow serpent stop and slowly begin to cool, hardening into stone."

The muscles in Blue Corn's arms knotted, the angle of her jaw set, as if she were on the verge of anger, but Catkin would have sworn she saw fear in the depths of her eyes.

The Matron began to lift her hand, a breath filling her lungs to give an order, when Gray Thunder said, "The Blessed Poor Singer told Jay Bird: 'You must have the heart of a cloud to walk upon the wind.'" His smile beamed out at his silent audience. "And so, I have come to ask you, do you have the heart of a cloud? Can you walk upon the wind? Poor Singer did. He offered his life to save that of his enemy."

"What enemy?" Stone Ghost asked.

Blue Corn answered, "If Poor Singer was Young Fawn's son, his enemy was Ironwood. The boy belonged to his mother's clan."

"It was Jay Bird and his Fire Dogs!" Matron White Smoke cried. "Poor Singer was raised in the Straight Path Nation. No matter what his real clan, he would have thought as we do!"

"No," Stone Ghost said with a sad shake of his head. "You are both wrong."

"Yes, they are." Gray Thunder's smile broadened. "Because that same enemy is here, today, walking among us."

People shifted nervously as the first few flakes of snow began to tumble out of the gray sky. Catkin could see the agitation in Blue Corn's face.

"I am here to end this constant warring! When you are ready, I will tell you about the enemy, and what you must do to have the heart of a cloud, so that we may all walk upon the wind." Gray Thunder's gaze seemed to focus for the first time, his attention hawk-like on Blue Corn. "Some here have placed their own needs above those of their people. The savage heart hears not the frightened cries of the infant. If you do not hear me, there will be blood, and more blood, and our peoples will be as dust before the wind." A great sadness began to well behind his pool-like eyes.

"I don't like talk that scares people." Blue Corn crossed her arms. "Things are bad enough."

"Worse than you know, Matron," Gray Thunder murmured. "It all stems from what happened to Poor Singer that day in Gila Monster Cliffs. Secrets were born. Secrets that must be brought into the open. I will tell them all . . . when the time is right."

Catkin saw Blue Corn's face suddenly go pale. *Does she know what secrets he means?*

"I have heard enough!" Blue Corn turned on her heel and angrily stalked through the crowd.

People immediately began to argue and demand explanations. Catkin pushed forward, placing herself between her people and the Sunrise Town villagers. The Fire Dog warriors closed around Gray Thunder. Only the old Mogollon slave with the dirty white hair stood alone, his eyes on Blue Corn as she disappeared into the crowd.

Stone Ghost's gaze fixed on that old man, as though he suddenly understood something no one else did. His attention did not waver as the Fire Dogs escorted Gray Thunder into one of the rooms that lined the southern edge of the town. Two warriors, a man and a woman, remained outside the door with war clubs in their hands.

Catkin turned to make sure her own people were safe, and noticed Blue Corn's War Chief, Rain Crow, standing at the corner of the plaza. The old frog-faced man was gesturing with his withered arms, jabbing an emphatic finger into the palm of his hand. Rain Crow nodded, his hard gaze on the doorway guarded by the Fire Dogs.

# CHAPTER 9

WHILE DUSTY SPED through the bright Albuquerque afternoon toward Dale's house, he considered every person who might have traveled with Dale up to Chaco. In his preoccupation, he nearly rear-ended the battered yellow pickup with inoperative brake lights that slowed in front of him.

"Where's a cop when you need him?" he growled. "If it was me, and my taillights were out, I'd have a ticket in five minutes."

"I doubt it, Stewart. This vehicle is a rolling violation wherever it goes, and you haven't gotten a single ticket since I've known you."

Dusty waited for a gap in traffic, wheeled into the left lane, and gassed the Bronco around the yellow pickup. In deference to Maureen, and in an attempt to do the right thing for once, he avoided the inclination to flip the guy the bird.

"Easy," Maureen warned when Dusty blasted around a lumbering semi on the Rio Grande bridge. Dusty cut right, too close to the truck's bumper, took the northbound exit onto Coors and let the Bronco's exhaust rumble as he decelerated down the ramp.

"He couldn't have been meeting either Steve or Sylvia. So, maybe it was someone from the department? Maggie's up at Chaco," he said, more to himself than to Maureen, "but she called, so it wasn't her. Maybe Rupert?"

"Who's Rupert?"

"Rupert Brown Horse. He goes by Brown. He was made park superintendent up at Chaco just after we dug 10K3." Dusty smiled. "He's an old-timer. I've known Rupert since I was a kid. He used to hang around with Dale. Hell, he used to hang around with Dad. He goes back that far."

"Let it go, Dusty. I'm sure there's some simple explanation."

Dusty checked traffic before merging onto Coors Boulevard. Off to the right, the Rio Grande floodplain looked cool, the last yellow leaves clinging to the winter-gray cottonwoods in the Bosque.

Dusty shook his head. "I was half expecting a note from Dale. At least a message on the answering machine. It must be pretty fascinating."

"What?"

"Whatever dragged him up there in such a hurry he didn't even remember to tell me he'd be out of town."

"Just how often does he do this?"

"Once every six months or so. It always scares me half silly." He paused, thoughtfully. "I suppose it's because I don't know what I'd do without him."

"It's not like you hadn't been abandoned before," she reminded. "That's deep in your subconscious, Dusty. But you're grown, and Dale, well, he's Dale."

Dusty turned left onto Montano Road, then followed it into the Taylor Ranch subdivision. He pulled into Dale's driveway on Kachina Street and shut the truck off. For a moment he sat there, feeling uneasy as he stared at the little adobe house. It had fake vigas poking out of the roofline. The stucco was a buff color, almost an off pink that Dusty had hated from the moment he first saw it. Two big picture windows overlooked a yard filled with cactus and stone. A large chamisa bush grew under the bedroom window. The cement sidewalk still had that white glare that proclaimed it had just been poured.

"So this is Dale's new house?" Maureen hesitated before she stepped up onto the porch. The place had a lonely look. While Dusty fished through his keys, she said, "Was there ever anyone special in Dale's life? Why didn't he ever marry?"

"For one thing, he's had me around his neck for about thirty years. Most women don't like ready-made families." Dusty pulled open the storm door and unlocked the big oaken door. "Oh, he had female friends, but you know how that is. They'd come and go. Once in a great while, he'd disappear up to Taos for a weekend with someone, but his romances never lasted long."

He shoved the door open and looked around. A big Spanish leather couch sat against the back wall. Beige carpet covered the floor. Two hand-carved *trasteros*, hutches, faced each other from opposite walls, their shelves filled with pottery, stone, and bone artifacts. The place smelled musty.

"Dale?" Dusty called. "Hello?"

Dread clung to Dusty's soul as he walked back through the arched opening. On the breakfast bar that separated the dining room from the kitchen, a half-eaten TV dinner sat. The enchiladas had dried and curled. A fork sat in the triangular pocket of desiccated *refritos*. The Spanish rice looked untouched. Dusty peered into Dale's old UNM coffee cup; a ring had formed where a couple of millimeters of cold coffee had evaporated.

Maureen inspected the TV dinner. "Dale eats this stuff?"

"When he doesn't get takeout," he replied. "Dale's a great believer in corn, beans, and squash, with lots of chilis. He thinks if he eats Mex for the rest of his life, he'll live to be one hundred."

Maureen's skeptical eyebrow arched.

"It looks like Dale rushed off in the middle of dinner." Dusty shook his head. "Something really had him excited."

"The phone?" she asked, pointing a slim finger at the combination telephone and answering machine.

"Maybe." Dusty reached over and pushed the button below the blinking red light. The display told him that six messages were waiting.

The machine clicked and whirred, and then a woman's voice said, *"I'm not kidding. Stop it, Dale! If it's not you, who is it?"*

Dusty met Maureen's inquiring stare and shrugged, but something about that voice chilled him, deep down, as though . . .

The second message began: *"Dale, if it's not you, and I'm no longer sure it is . . . then who?"* A pause. *"It's after midnight here. I don't care what time it is. Call me."*

After the machine clicked to indicate another call, a voice said, *"Hey, Dale. It's Sylvia."* A long pause. *"You there? Pick up, O high and mighty chief and leader."* Another, longer pause. *"Okay, I'll get in touch with you later about this pipeline thing. If I don't hear from you, I'll call Dusty for directions. It's on your head, then, 'cause you never know what Dusty will let me get away with."*

Dusty smiled as the machine clicked and played the first of Maggie's messages, followed by a second, and finally Dusty's morning message.

Maureen leaned against the wall. "The first woman sounded really angry. Did you recognize her voice?"

"No. But she was calling from a different time zone, and had an East Coast accent."

Dusty pushed the replay button and listened to the woman's voice again. Wasn't that a nasal New England accent? "If I've ever heard that voice, I don't remember it."

*But there was something . . .*

His stomach muscles clenched as though his belly knew something his brain refused to believe.

"Do you have any idea the number of people from

different time zones who might call Dale? He's worked around the globe. Maybe she's another person who didn't like his last article in *American Antiquity*."

"Maybe, but she sounded mad on the first message, and frightened on the second."

Dusty made an airy gesture with his hand. "So? Since when are archaeologists stable personalities?"

Maureen fastened her black eyes on his, a faint smile on her full lips. "That's one argument you win hands down. Archaeologists only seem to be happy when they're indignant."

He pushed the repeat button to listen to the messages yet again. First the Englishman on the office phone, and now this woman. Both angry. Did it mean anything?

Maureen took a turn about the kitchen, opening the refrigerator, checking the sink, and looking out into the backyard with its little cement patio surrounded by squares of red rock. Two small piñon pines grew at either end of the yard, Dale's fervent hope being that they'd grow large enough in the Albuquerque heat to bear nut crops. Dale had always loved fresh piñones.

Dusty crossed the dining room to the hallway that led into the back. He glanced around Dale's study. Floor-to-ceiling bookcases covered every inch of available wall space. The shelves literally groaned under the weight of packed volumes. A wooden desk was piled with books, journals, and papers. The gristmill for Dale's latest article, no doubt. Dusty looked down at the material, and was surprised to see a journal opened to an article by Scott Ferris on Neanderthal genetics. Something about breaking their DNA code. Dusty thoughtfully smoothed his beard. Ferris. The name was familiar. Wasn't he up at Colorado State University?

Two Anasazi skulls sat on a shelf to the right of Dale's desk: a male and a female. The male, a fellow with heavy brow ridges and a wide frontal bone was positioned to stare thoughtfully toward Dale's chair.

The female rested to the right, her empty orbits gazing at the male's profile. She had delicate features. She must have been a beautiful girl when she was alive.

"They should be on pads," Maureen said, stopping behind Dusty.

"I grew up with them." Dusty said. "Dale found them in the trash years ago. There was no provenience, so someone in the department was going to throw them away. Can you imagine? They were special to him, though I've never really known why. I don't think he's ever written an article without them at hand. When no one's around, he talks to them."

Maureen gave the skulls a warm appraisal. "I think I understand that better than anyone. Hello," she told the skulls. "I'm Maureen. A friend of Dale's."

Dusty figured it wasn't his place to interrupt conversations with dead people, so he turned away, searching for some clue as to why Dale would have left dinner to drive hell-bent for Chaco Canyon. His gaze played over the four tall file cabinets that contained all of Dale's notes: a lifetime of research. Each of the files held a separate paper or monograph authored or co-authored by Dale Emerson Robertson.

On impulse Dusty pulled open the top drawer and glanced at the folders labeled in Dale's neatly lettered script. He pulled out the first. "An Analysis of George Pepper and Excavations at Pueblo Bonito." A paper written for Neil Judd in 1940. Dusty smiled, tapping the folder against his palm. They were all there, every one in chronological order. Why had he never looked at these before?

The doorbell startled both of them. Dusty replaced the folder and headed back down the hallway, Maureen on his heels. He rounded the corner, passed through the arch and into the living room. To his surprise, a uniformed police officer was standing at the front door. Dusty gave Maureen a sidelong glance and opened the door, saying, "Can I help you?"

The cop stared at him. "Is this the residence of Dale Emerson Robertson?"

"Yes." Dusty's throat tightened. "What's this about?"

"Are you William Samuel Stewart? The owner of the vehicle parked in the driveway?"

"Yes," he answered again. His heart had started to pound. "Dale's in trouble, isn't he?"

The cop turned his attention to Maureen, asking, "Who are you?"

"Dr. Maureen Cole." The professional tone in Maureen's voice chilled Dusty's blood. She hesitated a moment, then said, "Officer, if you're here, Dale is either injured or dead. Which is it?"

The cop hesitated only a moment, before replying, "He's dead, ma'am."

Dusty sagged against the doorjamb.

From a long way away, he heard Maureen say, "Oh, my God. How did it happen?"

MAGPIE SIGNALED AND took Exit 79 off of I-40 East. She followed the familiar blacktop through Milan, and then through Grants, passed the gas station, and took New Mexico 547 north as it wound its way through Grants Canyon. At the entrance to her aunt's drive she took a right, rattling across the rusty cattle guard and down the rutted two-track road.

Sage Walking Hawk lived in an alcove in the side of the canyon. Four rusty car bodies sat on blocks, their wheels and engines long gone. A pathetic-looking Ford tractor, the old kind with faded gray paint, hunched beside a sagging toolshed. The carcasses of old washing machines and a defunct kitchen stove rested to one side of the flat, surrounded by a sea of brown weeds.

Magpie pulled up in front of Sage's trailer and turned off the engine. Her dust-streaked blue Ford 150 made clinking noises as it cooled. For the moment, Magpie leaned her head forward onto the steering wheel, feeling as if her body had been emptied out like water poured from a boot.

When she looked up, Aunt Sage was standing in the doorway of the old mobile home, her gray head cocked. She wore a faded blue print dress, fuzzy slippers, and a smudged apron. Her ancient face, wrinkled and time-worn, looked puzzled. With a stick-thin arm, she braced herself on the trailer door, a tiny hunchbacked skeleton of a woman who blinked at the world with cataract-filmed eyes.

Magpie opened her door and stepped out. "Hello, Aunt."

"Magpie? Is that you? I can't see so well anymore. I thought that looked like your truck. At least, the color's right."

"It's me."

Sage Walking Hawk nodded soberly. "You don't sound too good."

"I'm not, Aunt. Something has happened. Up at the park. I need to talk to you."

Sage reached out with arthritic hands, wiping them on her apron as she stepped back from the door. "You know, girl, for centuries our people left that place alone. It's only these fool White people that don't have sense enough to let the White Houses be."

"I know, Aunt."

Magpie looked around as she stepped into the trailer. The battered old couch, the picture of a young white man in a brown World War II army uniform, the teapots and cups were in their familiar places. The kitchen table overflowed with magazines, letters, and open tin cans, which held pencils, screwdrivers, pliers, a ruler, knife handles, and scissors.

One entire living-room wall was covered with a huge

loom. Stretched across it, an intricately woven rug was half-finished, multicolored warp hung expectantly. A shuttle waited between the weft, ready for use. Magpie didn't have to step close to see the dust on it.

"You gonna finish that rug?" she asked.

Sage chuckled dryly. "Not in this lifetime. Maybe in the next."

"I wish you'd go to the hospital."

"I've been to the hospital." Sage wobbled her way to the kitchen table and seated herself in one of the plastic-covered kitchen chairs, breathing hard. "That last dose of chemo almost killed me. Your favorite doctor says there's nothing to be done." She winced. "Anyway, I'm ready to go. Nothing is worth enduring this pain. It's like giving birth. No, worse. It never ends."

"They can give you medicine for the pain. Morphine. They have something called a hospice in Albuquerque—"

"I'm gonna die here," Sage insisted. "The Shiwana know to look for me here. Besides, I've been talking to my sisters lately. That Slumber, she'd talk your ear off."

Sage paused for a moment, and said, "You said you wanted to talk, child."

"*Na'ya*, something happened at the park. Something bad. I need you to explain it to me. Not as my *na'ya*, but as 'Empty Eyes,' the woman who sees the dead." She took a breath to nerve herself for her aunt's answers. "I always thought the gift that you and your sisters shared had passed my generation. But last night Dale Emerson Robertson, the anthropologist . . . do you remember him?"

"Yes. We called him 'Sharp Nose.' Him and his students. Always trying to see into the past. To know more than we wanted him to know."

"He was murdered in the park last night, *Na'ya*. Someone cut the soles off of his feet and buried him upside down in the ground. I was there when they dug him out." Magpie rubbed her hands together. "And there were other things."

The old woman straightened, and the years seemed to retreat from her cancerous body. "Somebody didn't want him walking to the Land of the Dead. He was making sure old Sharp Nose would be a homeless ghost, wandering the earth forever. Go on. I have to know everything."

### Kachina Street, Albuquerque, New Mexico

Officer Warren sat in the recliner across from the over-stuffed Spanish leather sofa, a notebook in his hand. Dale's living room seemed oddly dark despite the bright sunshine pouring through the big picture window.

Dusty sat beside Maureen. An expression of either panic or rage sparkled in his eyes. She couldn't tell for sure. She leaned closer, her thigh pressing reassuringly against his.

Officer Warren asked, "Were you here last night?"

"No," Dusty answered. "We stayed at my place in Santa Fe."

"Did anyone call you there?"

Dusty didn't answer. He seemed to be lost in thought, or perhaps memories of Dale.

Maureen said, "Sylvia Rhone. One of Dale's employees. She told Dusty that she couldn't reach Dale. This morning, Maggie Walking Hawk Taylor—a park ranger—called from Chaco Canyon. She said Dale's truck had been in the parking lot overnight."

Maureen's mind had recovered enough from the shock to begin putting the pieces together. Officer Warren didn't ask where Chaco was. He already knew. From her experience working with various police forces in Ontario, she could see where this was going.

"Officer Warren," she said, "I'm a board-certified forensic anthropologist. You're obviously conducting an investigation, which means Dale's death is suspicious. Why?"

Warren gave her that bland look, the one cops use when they don't want their faces read. "He was found in Chaco Canyon."

Dusty looked up suddenly. "What part of the canyon?"

"I don't know that, sir." Warren seemed sincere. "Just that he was dug up in the canyon."

"Dug up?" Dusty and Maureen asked in unison. Dusty continued, "What do you mean, dug up? Someone buried him?"

"That's all I've been told, sir. I'm sure those details will be released as they are uncovered." His expression didn't change. "Did you come here for a reason this morning? I take it you have a key to Dr. Robertson's house?"

Grief tightened Dusty's eyes. "Dale raised me. I consider him to be my father. Yes, I have a key."

Warren seemed to weigh the words, his keen gaze taking in Dusty's gray pallor. "How much did Ms. Taylor tell you?"

"Only that Dale's truck had been located this morning in the Casa Rinconada parking lot. She's known Dale for many years. She was concerned."

"Did Dr. Robertson spend much time at Chaco Canyon?"

"He was a New Mexico archaeologist, for God's sake!" Dusty cried. "Of course, he did!"

Maureen calmly said, "And in anticipation of your next question, Officer, no, Dale didn't tell us he was going to Chaco, or what he intended to do there. The first we heard of it was when Maggie called this morning."

"Did he give you any indication that anyone had been bothering him? Maybe threats? Any hint that he was worried about anything or anyone?"

"No, he . . . wait a minute," Dusty said. He walked

over and pulled the tape out of the answering machine. "A woman called him a few nights ago. She sounded scared. And—and there was an angry message from a man with an English accent on our office machine."

"Could I have that?" Officer Warren held out his hand and Dusty put the tape in it. "I'll need the tape at your office, too."

Dusty nodded and wiped his palms on his jeans, as though they'd been somehow soiled by the woman's voice on the tape. "Tell me how he died. I take it he did not have a heart attack, or a stroke, or die from other natural causes. Is that right?"

Warren replied, "Mr. Stewart, if everything you say checks out, I'll refer you to the agent in charge."

"You mean you're not in charge?" Dusty looked suddenly hostile, as though the officer had been wasting his precious time.

"I'm local," Warren answered. "Dr. Robertson was found on a national monument. That's federal jurisdiction. I was asked to check the residence on a drive-by. When I saw a vehicle in the driveway, I called it in, and they asked me to check out why someone with a Sante Fe address would be in Dr. Robertson's house." He rose to his feet. "You'll need to talk to the FBI."

# CHAPTER 10

BROWSER THREW HIS blanket to one side and shivered. His white breath lingered, ghostlike in the cold air. Around him, the plastered walls of the room seemed to close in, pressing on his souls. Someone in the distant past had painted a row of interlinking black diamonds just below the ceiling poles. The design had faded over the sun cycles. A water stain marked one wall where rain had leaked down from the abandoned floors above. Like so much of his world, this place, too, was falling apart.

He hadn't slept well, preoccupied by the curious words Gray Thunder had spoken, and Stone Ghost's insistence that today they would seek the young man out and interrogate him thoroughly.

So many questions came tumbling out of Browser's mind. Poor Singer had been one of his ancestors. He had married the Blessed Cornsilk who had given birth to Browser's great-grandfather, Snowbird, who had given birth to Grandmother Painted Turtle, and then to Prairie Flower, Browser's mother. And last night, he had heard that Poor Singer and Cornsilk were both present when the Blessed Sternlight was killed by Jay Bird. This was *his* family history he was learning from the Fire Dogs.

But why should the Fire Dogs care if Poor Singer's prophecy had been mistaken by the Katsinas' People? It had been so long ago.

He rubbed his eyes and reached for his war shirt, pulling it over his shoulders as he stood and searched for his sandals. With his weapons in hand, he ducked out through the low, T-shaped doorway into the gray light of dawn. A thin white coating of snow had fallen to leave the battered town looking oddly frail.

The block of rooms they had been given lay along the upper story on the eastern wall of Dusk House. Wind and weather had eroded the plaster that had once covered the roof poles. The protruding ends had been laboriously sanded smooth by long dead slaves, but the wood had weathered and cracked anyway, as gray now as the surrounding soil. As he walked across the roof to the ladder that led down past a line of kivas to the plaza, he wondered why the First People had come to this drab place. The river provided a constant supply of water that Straight Path Canyon did not, but why hadn't they gone farther upriver where the country was more pleasing to the eye?

He was considering this as he climbed down the ice-slick ladder and crossed the snow in the plaza to where Stone Ghost hunched over a small fire. Browser massaged his hands and squatted beside him. Through a gap in the wall, he could see to the World Kiva that had been constructed astride the Great North Road, and on to Sunrise Town, its lines softened by the thin layer of snow. Blue tendrils of smoke rose to merge with the predawn light.

"You are up early, Uncle."

Stone Ghost added another twig to the blaze. "It wasn't a night for sleep, was it, Nephew?" Stone Ghost turned curious eyes his way. "If you are worried, Catkin has already seen to the guards."

Browser suffered a pang of guilt. After a moment, he said, "I'm not a good War Chief, Uncle. I haven't been since my son died. Perhaps I should relinquish that duty to Catkin. She is better suited to it."

Browser extended his hands to the fire, grateful for the heat. All he'd ever wanted was a quiet life with his family. "Do you believe this Gray Thunder? Was any of what he said true?"

Stone Ghost stared up at the gray clouds scudding to the east. "Yes, at least it matched what my grandmother told me. But I was more surprised by Blue Corn's reaction. I think the Matron is hiding something."

"We are all hiding something, Uncle. We live in a world of secrets."

He looked across at Sunrise Town and the curved line of rooms where the Fire Dogs stayed.

"A secret is kept for a reason, Nephew." Stone Ghost's brown age-lined face turned somber. "Everything seems to return to the First People, and the days when their world began to crumble." He raised a hand to the ruined walls around them. "Everything returns to the moment when they came here."

Browser grimaced at the town. "This is a dismal place, Uncle. Why did they come to these gray hills when they could have gone upriver to better soil and a nicer place to live?"

Stone Ghost pointed across to the World Kiva and the Great North Road. "Because this place has Power. It lies due north of Center Place. Their Sunwatcher led them here, guided by the North Star. This place was to be the rebirth of the First People's Straight Path Nation. From here, they would grow bigger and better than they had been in Straight Path Canyon."

Browser looked around at the winter-fallow fields, and the gray hills visible beyond the river. "I don't think it worked out the way they planned."

"They didn't anticipate the anger of the Made People. Or that the Blessed Ravenfire would betray them."

"Ravenfire was Cornsilk's firstborn son, wasn't he? He was the one who betrayed Night Sun to the Made People, didn't he?"

"Yes, they enslaved her and finally tortured her to death." Stone Ghost's gnarled hands clenched over the fire. "I had heard the story that Gray Thunder told last night, though with a different twist. My grandmother taught me that Poor Singer's anger was so great that he, with the help of the katsinas, built a fire that burned into the lower world. That the fire laid waste to the land, and with it, he destroyed the man who raped Cornsilk—Ravenfire's father. Only after he burned away the man's crime did he give his prophecy."

"I don't recall hearing stories about Poor Singer being an angry man." Browser didn't know if the shiver that stalked his shoulders was from the cold, or the implications of what that might mean about the Katsinas' People's greatest prophet.

After a moment, Stone Ghost asked, "Have you heard what they are saying about your recently murdered Matron? Some say that she became a katsina and flew to the clouds."

"Yes, I know. But you and I buried her, Uncle."

"But do not forget that her body was dug up," Stone Ghost reminded. "The grave was empty. We know that Shadow Woman and Two Hearts took her, but the rest of the world would rather believe that your Matron flew to the clouds."

Browser frowned. In a low voice, he said, "That's crazy."

Stone Ghost shrugged. "Come, Nephew, let us walk over to Sunrise Town and present ourselves to Gray Thunder. If we do, perhaps he will tell us how he plans to end this craziness, and maybe he will share some of that fine piki bread they brought. From the looks of things, their packs are fuller than ours."

"They must be, given that we have almost nothing." Browser watched the last of the twigs burn to white ash before he stood and gripped his uncle's elbow. "The snow is slick, Uncle. Let me help you."

As they walked, Browser noted the location of his warriors. Straw Shield huddled under a blanket on the corner of the roof where he could see down the line of rooms occupied by the Katsinas' People. He nodded to Browser.

As they passed out of the confines of Dusk House, Catkin appeared on the north wall, her face haggard from lack of sleep. At the sight of her lithe form, Browser felt his heart lift. Her slim body moved with a feline grace. She had wrapped her long legs in leggings made from twists of rabbit hide. A turkey-feather cloak draped loosely over her shoulders, allowing unhampered access to her war club and the bow slung over her back.

She walked to the edge of the roof above them, and called, "Are you well, War Chief?"

"Fine, Catkin. We are on the way to speak with Gray Thunder."

She hesitated, that familiar look in her eyes as she glanced toward the Fire Dog guards.

Browser told her, "We will not be gone long."

She went to the nearest ladder and climbed down. When she fell into step beside him, the tension went out of his shoulders. Why was it that when she was away he felt in danger? He studied her from the corner of his eye. Cold had reddened her beautiful face, especially the tip of her turned-up nose. Her dark eyes scanned the surroundings as she walked warily ahead.

She had saved his life back at the White Moccasin's caverns. But for her quick reflexes he would have been killed. And how many times had he saved her? From the Mogollon, from Ash Girl, and in countless battles. They were tied, somehow, their destinies bound together. So, why, he wondered, had he never surrendered to his manhood and shared her blankets?

A smarter man would have made her his wife. A hollow sensation spread in his stomach. His last marriage had been a disaster.

They passed just south of the World Kiva with its three concentric walls. The story was that the First People had built it that way to initiate the young. That unlike the usual kiva where the different benches represented the worlds through which their ancestors had come, this was more accurate, that each level had its own initiation.

They entered the gap between the western and southern walls of Sunrise Town. Browser waved a greeting to the vigilant warrior who perched on the wall above them. The young man gave a nod, barely acknowledging their presence. As Stone Ghost led them around the curved wall and into the plaza, a cry carried on the still air.

Browser stopped, listened, and said, "Stay here, Uncle," before he trotted down the line of rooms.

Another shout broke the stillness. As he and Catkin rushed toward Gray Thunder's room, one of the Fire

Dog warriors, a woman, stumbled out of Gray Thunder's doorway, ripping the hanging aside. Blood dripped from her hands.

It took Browser a moment to decipher the words spoken in the anguished Fire Dog's language: "We are betrayed! Betrayed!"

Browser broke into a run, his hands up as the woman spun on one foot, her war club raised. "Stay back!" she shouted.

"Who betrayed you?" he shouted back. "How?"

The woman hesitated at the confusion in his eyes, then cried, *"Gray Thunder has been murdered!"*

Warriors boiled out of the adjacent rooms, some half-dressed, their weapons lifted. Many blinked themselves awake as they searched for the threat, and their eyes settled hungrily on Browser and Catkin.

"Wait!" Stone Ghost cried in the Mogollon tongue. He rushed forward, hands up. "We did not do this thing! Stop! Or we are all dead!"

Catkin held her war club at the ready, prepared to strike.

"Stop this!" Browser called to the Fire Dog woman. "You know we didn't do this! We just arrived!"

She seemed to waver, unsure of whether to strike him down or not.

Instinctively Browser dropped to his knees before her and offered his war club. "We are not your enemies! Upon my life, you must believe that!"

The panic in her eyes began to ebb as her own warriors crowded around. Their confused mutters sounded like the babbling of a brook to Browser's ears.

"Gray Thunder is dead," she repeated, and her voice broke. "What they did to him . . . it's terrible." And then her eyes widened, mouth open in awe. "It is . . . as he said."

"Who?" Stone Ghost asked, his command of Mogollon better than Browser's. "Who said? Who did this?"

"I don't know!" Tears glittered in her eyes. "I didn't see them!" She swallowed hard. "It was as he said." Her stunned eyes fixed on Browser. "Are you the one?"

In confusion, Browser asked, "What one? Tell us what you know. What——?"

"Browser!"

Catkin's call brought him to his feet. He spun and saw warriors tumbling out of the rooms in Sunrise Town. Blue Corn's burly War Chief, Rain Crow, led them, a stone-headed war club in his hand.

The Fire Dogs began to line out for battle. This was madness. In the blink of an eye, an arrow would be loosed, or an insult called, and nothing would stop the ensuing massacre.

Browser pushed the grief-stricken woman behind him as he raised his arms. "Stop! Come no closer! Rain Crow, do not let this happen!"

"What is this?" Rain Crow had pulled up, a dark look on his ruined face. "I heard cries. Did I hear right? That we are betrayed?"

"No!" Stone Ghost stepped between the factions, his thin white hair shining in the predawn glow. "Gray Thunder is dead. Murdered."

"Not by us!" Rain Crow turned his head and spat on the ground. "Do they think we did it?"

Browser heard the whispers passing between the agitated Fire Dogs. "Murdered?" "We are betrayed!" "Straight Path dogs!" "They planned this!" "Kill them all!"

Browser hung his war club on his belt and opened his hands to them. "Matron Blue Corn promised you safety, and she has kept her promise! You can't——"

"Gray Thunder is *dead!*" A young man pointed the tip of his bow at Browser. "Just the way he said! Is that what you call safe, dung eater!"

A chorus of assent went up as the Fire Dogs strengthened their resolve.

"Please. Wait!" Browser pleaded. "Whoever killed

Gray Thunder wants us to kill each other. I, for one, wished to hear Gray Thunder's words. Do not let this happen!"

"Let's just kill them all and end this foolishness," Rain Crow growled. "This nonsense has gone far enough."

Stone Ghost strode to Rain Crow and looked up. "Don't be a fool, War Chief. Browser is right. We're being played with. Do you want to be like a little girl's doll? Dressed up, made to do what someone wishes you to? Kill these Fire Dogs and you will unleash a whirlwind of war like nothing we've seen in a hundred sun cycles."

Rain Crow's ruined face became a mass of conflicting emotions.

"Our prophet is dead!" one of the Fire Dogs called. "This must be paid for in blood! He told us the rest of us would live! I, for one, am not afraid!"

Another called, "If we die, we will take *twice* our number of these suckling weasels with us!"

Rain Crow's warriors started forward with fury in their eyes.

The fools wanted this! Browser knew he was about to die, but took a stand in front of the Mogollon. "Rain Crow! You will have to go through me if you want to start this madness!" He raised his war club and crouched, ready to defend the Fire Dogs from his own people. Catkin positioned herself slightly to his right, breathing hard, ready for the coming assault.

*"Enough!"* A thin reedy voice ordered in Mogollon. "Lay your weapons down! Now!"

Browser shot a look over his shoulder. The old Mogollon slave had stepped out ahead of the Fire Dog warriors. One by one, he pointed his finger at them. Browser couldn't believe it as the Fire Dogs, expressions tortured, placed their bows and war clubs on the ground.

Stone Ghost braced his knees and stood his ground

in front of Rain Crow. "Tell your warriors to drop their weapons, War Chief."

Rain Crow lifted his club as if to strike the old man down.

A surge of adrenaline pumped through Browser as he stepped in front of the defiant Stone Ghost.

"You know me, War Chief," Browser said calmly. "You have seen me in battle. If there is war here today, it will start with the two of us, old friend." He let that hang for half a heartbeat, then added, "But it doesn't have to, Rain Crow. Don't you wish to know who did this, and why they want you to kill these people? Let us end this madness and find out what truly happened here. These people are not your enemies!"

Rain Crow's lopsided face contorted with the barest of smiles. "You had better be right, Browser. A man who stands up for these murdering reptiles can't afford many mistakes."

"No, he can't." Browser turned to the Sunrise warriors. "Lower your weapons. There will be no fighting today."

They hesitated, waiting for Rain Crow's orders. He nodded to them, and bows and clubs were slowly lowered.

The old Mogollon man stepped forward, his demeanor different from the meek and mild facade he had assumed the day before. Head high, he took Browser's measure, and then cast a suspicious glance at Stone Ghost. "You are both most unusual for your kind." His voice held only the slightest trace of Mogollon accent. "For a moment, I thought they were going to kill us despite our surrender."

"They were supposed to." Browser took in the old man's worn cloak and the faded red blanket that hung from his shoulders. He didn't look like a revered elder. His face, lined and thin, had a prominent nose. Tangled strands of snowy white hair fell over his ears.

"Gray Thunder is dead," the young woman reminded

in a trembling voice, and sobbed when she asked, "It is just as he said! The prophecy—"

"Hush!" the old Mogollon barked, eyes blazing with fury. "Guard your tongues!"

Stone Ghost moved awkwardly through the crowd. Despite the cold, his wrinkled face had beaded with sweat. He stopped before the stricken young Mogollon woman. She might have seen twenty summers, a muscular and attractive woman, her blue war shirt barely hiding her female figure. She had a delicate face with a pointed nose. Her hair was pinned tightly in a warrior's bun. "What is your name, child?"

"Clay Frog, Elder."

"Clay Frog, may I look at Gray Thunder? Perhaps I can tell what happened."

She glared back and forth between him and the gathered Sunrise warriors who stood around talking in low voices.

When she did not answer, Stone Ghost turned to the old Mogollon man. "We wish to know who did this as much as you do. Gray Thunder brought us a message. If he is dead, it is because of what he wished to tell us."

The old man's hard brown eyes fixed on Stone Ghost. "I have heard of you, Stone Ghost. You have a reputation for investigating things like this. Let us look together."

The young woman grudgingly gave way at the old man's gesture. Her eyes were fastened on Browser again, looking at him as though in a special reverence. Why? Just because he had placed himself between the Mogollon and the Sunrise warriors?

Stone Ghost walked to the doorway, pointing at the scuffed snow. "Nephew? Come. Tell me what you see?"

Browser moved forward and knelt.

"The snow has been completely disturbed, as if dragged to hide tracks."

Stone Ghost turned to the young woman. "Clay Frog, was there no guard at the door?"

She swallowed hard. "Yes. Myself and Acorn. He's . . . in there." She gestured to the door with a tortured expression. "I had to leave, Elder. It is my time of the moon. I wasn't gone but maybe one finger of time. Just to my quarters. I came right back, I swear! But I—I found . . . found . . ."

Only then did Browser run a quick count and realize that only nine Fire Dogs clustered around them. He reached for the door hanging.

"Careful, Nephew," Stone Ghost said, pointing at the blood that had discolored the ground inside the doorway. To the woman, he said, "Did anyone else enter this room after you discovered the murders?"

"No, Elder. You arrived just after I called out."

Browser stepped inside and the odor nearly overwhelmed him. He knew what he would see before his eyes adjusted. Stone Ghost and the old Mogollon man stepped through behind him.

"The dark spots on the wall"—Browser pointed— "are blood and offal."

"That is Acorn," the Mogollon elder said and swallowed hard.

The corpse was naked. His head had been crushed with a war club, and a wide cut gaped across the hollow of the ribs under the sternum. When the assailant had removed Acorn's genitals, it was not the hacking of battlefield rage, but a precision cut, perhaps with an obsidian blade. Instead of a tongue, the tip of the man's penis protruded from between his bloody lips. Blood had been used to paint dots on the arms and legs, a mockery of the usual burial pattern of stars.

The old Mogollon man moved to the second body. Gray Thunder lay on his back in the center of the room. Terrified eyes stared sightlessly at the ceiling poles. Blood was everywhere.

A fist seemed to tighten in Browser's belly. "Uncle? Do you see what I do?"

"Yes. It's the same, isn't it?"

Browser nodded.

The Mogollon elder braced himself against the wall to keep from reeling. "What are you talking about? What's the same?"

"See those tracks?" Stone Ghost pointed to the dark smears where someone had circled the body, stepping in the blood. "We saw this in Talon Town nearly a sun cycle ago."

"Yes," Browser said, "and your prophet's belly was cut open, the intestines pulled out. I see them there, in the corner. The killer slung them around like a rope. The same way that 'The Two' did with my warrior's body in Talon Town."

Browser straightened. Even Gray Thunder's body was laid out the same, his right arm extended, his left bent behind him. "Uncle," he said softly. "How can this be happening again? I killed Ash Girl. I thought I killed Two Hearts."

Stone Ghost walked around the room for several moments, carefully studying the bodies, the bloody footprints on the floor, and the grisly streaks on the walls. He turned to Browser. "Nephew, how many people were allowed to see the room where Whiproot was killed before it was cleaned up? *Who* saw it?"

# CHAPTER 11

### Kachina Street, Albuquerque, New Mexico

MAUREEN WATCHED DUSTY'S face as he tried to sort through the conflicting emotions. They had to be similar to her own, that sense of loss, of anger, of denied grief.

Dusty paced up and down Dale's living-room floor. The afternoon sunlight through the picture window gleamed in his blond hair and beard. She could see the muscles bunching under his white T-shirt as he smacked a hard fist into his palm. "What are we supposed to do? Just sit here and wait?"

"That's traditional for victims' families," she told him. She couldn't seem to figure out what to do with her hands; they kept clenching and unclenching, so she clasped them in her lap. "But I know it's hard to do."

"What was he doing at Chaco?" Dusty demanded. His blue eyes blazed as he paced. "Did he go there to meet someone? I can't figure this out."

Maureen had called the FBI's Albuquerque Field Office and been shunted through several secretaries until one finally told her that they could give her no information at this time and that an agent would be in touch.

Maureen steeled herself. "Dusty, we're not going to know anything until they decide to tell us. Look at it from their perspective. Someone died at Chaco under suspicious circumstances. Would you give information to the first person who called your office?"

"We ought to go up there." Dusty stopped short, a

half-crazy gleam in his eye. "Come on. Get your purse."

Maureen stared at him. "Dusty, this isn't a movie where you can go off and involve yourself in an investigation. Real police work doesn't function that way. Believe me, you work through channels, or they arrest you and put you in jail. It's called interfering with an investigation."

Some of the crazy gleam faded from his eyes. Through gritted teeth he said, "I can't stand this, Maureen. I have to do something!"

She walked to him and searched his face. He seemed to be keeping his expression stoic by sheer force of will. "I'm so sorry, Dusty. He was my good friend, too. But be patient. We'll find out what this is all about." She placed a hand on his arm and discovered he was shaking. Maureen tightened her grip.

They stood like that for several seconds; then Dusty turned and put his arms around her. She didn't know if he was offering solace or seeking it. It didn't matter. She slipped her arms around his waist and held him. There was a good deal of comfort in the feel of his broad chest and the steady rhythm of his breathing.

The ringing of the telephone separated them. She followed Dusty through the arch and into the kitchen where he picked up the phone on the breakfast bar and said, "Hello." Then, "Maggie, thank God! What's this all about? What happened to Dale?"

He listened for a moment, and then grabbed for the notepad and pen that lay beside the phone. He said, "Uh-huh," several times as he scribbled furiously. "He was where?" More scribbling. "I don't get it."

Maureen watched his frown deepen.

"That's crazy," he said, but he sounded confused. "Upside down? His feet sticking out?" He wrote on the pad again. "No. I don't have the faintest idea." He gave Maureen a serious look. His blue eyes seemed to burn from an inner fire. "No, Maggie. I don't know. Who's in charge? I see. Can you spell that?" He carefully printed out letters on the notepad. "Maggie, give me the details again. Maureen is going to want to hear them." He propped the phone against his ear as the pen danced across the paper. "Should we come up there?" A pause. "Okay. Thanks, Maggie. We'll be here or at the office for the next couple of hours. If you can't get us there, try the cell phone. I'll make sure it's on."

He hung up and stared into emptiness for a moment before meeting Maureen's eyes. "Okay, here's what Maggie knows. Someone called the park superintendent, Rupert Brown, remember? I told you about him. The caller told Rupert that some white man had fallen through a hole in the past. That his head was sticking into the Fourth World."

Dusty frowned at his notes.

"The Fourth World?"

"I assume it has some allusion to the Pueblo Creation stories. Sometimes there are three underworlds, sometimes four. It depends on the tribe. Maggie had found Dale's truck earlier and was looking around on her lunch hour. Brown got the call and got worried, so he was doing the rounds. They were searching around the small houses out by Casa Rinconada, and Maggie saw human feet sticking out of the dirt."

Maureen's chest hurt. "His feet? I don't understand."

Dusty threw the pen down on the pad, and clenched his teeth, as though struggling with himself. "I don't either. Maggie was very explicit about this. Dale was buried upside down in a hole. Whoever did it left his feet sticking out. Someone . . . someone murdered Dale." He swallowed hard. "For a reason. This is a ritualistic killing."

The first sensations of suffocation, that dreaded constriction of the throat, began to rise, cutting off her air. "Why?"

Images of Dale flashed through her mind: John, Dale, and her, sitting on the porch of her house over-

looking Lake Ontario; Dale teasing them on their wed-
ding day; Dale at her dissertation defense at McGill,
and the celebratory bottle of LaBatt's he'd bought her
afterward in that little dingy pub run by that charming
Québecois couple.

For so much of her life, Dale had been there. If not
physically present, his influence had still permeated her
existence. Now, once again, she felt another huge hole
being torn in her soul. Another piece of her had been
ripped out. First John, then her mother, and now Dale.

She slid into one of the kitchen chairs and dropped
her head into her hands. She hadn't felt like this since
that terrible night when she had walked in to find
John's body sprawled lifelessly on the kitchen floor.

*"Nothing is forever, Maureen,"* she heard Dale's
soft voice speaking across time from that day when she
had met him at the Toronto airport. Dale had canceled
a meeting in Washington in order to attend John's funeral. Doing so had probably cost him an appointment
on a presidential advisory board. It had been rumored
that it would have been a springboard into the Smithsonian and from there perhaps to a political appointment high in the U.S. Department of the Interior. God
knows, the Americans needed some voice of sanity
when it came to their cultural resources.

No, nothing was forever. As a physical anthropologist specializing in human osteology and paleopathology, she, of all people, understood that. But to have
Dale murdered? That changed the equation from the
inevitable failure of a heart, or the potential of cancerous cells gone riotous, to the unnatural realization that
someone's act of will had snuffed Dale's life away and
discarded his body in a manner meant, no doubt, to
demean. And, as in all such cases, it led her to scream
out: Why?

*"Come on, Maureen,"* Dale's gentle voice came
from her memory. *"Humans have been killing other
humans for the last two million years. It's part of who*

*we are as a species. You know this, so stop fooling yourself, and get around to figuring out the problem."*

The problem.

She pushed up from the table and found her way to the bathroom to blow her nose. When she'd finished, she glanced at herself in the mirror. She looked as bad as Dusty. Her strain showed in the tight lines at the corners of her eyes and in her clenched jaw.

But standing here surrounded by Dale's things: a razor, shaving cream, a bottle of aspirin left open on the counter next to the sink, his toothbrush in a glass—she could feel the warmth of his soul clinging to them like the fingerprints she knew covered their surfaces, and it helped a little.

She washed her face. Time to get back. She had just lost a friend and mentor. Dusty, for the second time in his life, had lost a father.

Steeling herself, she dried and stepped out into the hallway. In the living room, she grabbed up her purse. "Come on. There is something we can do."

Dusty gave her the sort of look a pilgrim would a saint. He was fishing his keys from his pocket as he headed for the door. "Where are we going?"

"Downtown, Dusty, for answers," she told him soberly. "I want to know what happened to Dale."

It wasn't until they were seated inside the Bronco, and Dusty had jabbed the keys into the ignition that he saw it. Maureen watched him scowl, open the door, and bend through the gap between the pillar and door frame to pluck the little white card from under the wiper.

"What's that?" Maureen asked.

Dusty twisted back into the driver's seat, the card between his thumb and forefinger. "I don't know. It was just stuck in there. One side's blank and the other . . ." He turned it over and froze.

Maureen leaned over, seeing the blue drawing. There, in excellent detail, she could see the image of a snake curled inside a hen's egg. A single reptilian eye stared up from the image, as if to paralyze her soul.

Her stunned mind identified it immediately: *el basilisco!*

CATKIN SAT NEXT to Browser in the great kiva in Sunrise Town, watching the crowd, feeling her heart pound rhythmically against her chest wall. The huge kiva felt like a trap.

Matron Blue Corn hunched like an old woman on the lowest tier of the northern bench. She had a sour expression on her face. They all waited for Blue Corn to call the Blessing and begin the proceedings, but she had not yet stood. War Chief Rain Crow sat just behind her, whispering in her ear. White Smoke and the other elders were arrayed to either side of her. None of them looked happy.

Every seat on the three concentric benches had been taken, and still more people crowded in the doorway, blocking the steps that led up to the cold day beyond.

There would be no quick exit from this place. Catkin kept that in mind as her eyes surveyed the crowd. If something went wrong, if there was a panic, chaos would ensue, and several people would be trampled to death.

Blue Corn shifted and seemed to be listening to her own people's whispers. All day long, Catkin had heard the same things whispered throughout the towns:

*"Gray Thunder said he would die . . . said he'd seen it in a Dream. Perhaps he was a prophet."*

*". . . or one of the katsinas come to earth. Maybe we should have listened . . ."*

The fools were turning Gray Thunder into a god—and he was barely cold.

Blue Corn's face tensed as she looked around.

The great kiva's interior had been painted red, yellow, and white with black zigzags dividing the upper and lower walls. Wall niches held the sacred artifacts common to the old gods. In the northern niche, a representation of the Blue God stood, made of straw and leather. In the western niche, Spider Woman's sacred plants bristled. The southern niche held offerings of turquoise, polished shell, and carved jet for both the male and female Flute Players. Here and there, brightly decorated with black paint on their white surfaces, soul pots waited to be taken south to Center Place, where they would be smashed and the soul of the dead set free to run the Great North Road to the afterlife.

White plaster coated the four thick pillars that supported the roof. Catkin's grandmother had told her that the ancestors had sanctified every pillar by placing turquoise, shell, and cornmeal in the holes before huge stone disks had been set as foundations; then the pillars had been built atop the stones. Thick ponderosa pine beams spanned the pillars to support the roof cribbing. Strips of juniper bark acted as a roof sealer. Then earth—to the depth of a man's forearm—insulated and finished the roof. Catkin looked up. Through the thick coating of soot, she could just barely make out the shadowed poles.

Juniper popped and sparked in the sacred hearth in the middle of the kiva. The foot drums, utilized for special ceremonies and the great dances, were unoccupied, but the split-pine planks had been worn shiny by the stamping of bare feet. When dancers beat their cadence on the wood, the sound thundered down into the sounding chamber and resonated into the underworlds to the delight of the ancestors.

"This is going to be dangerous," Browser whispered to Catkin as he looked around the ceremonial chamber. Sweat already glistened in his short black hair and across his flat nose.

"Not if Blue Corn keeps her wits," Catkin answered. She couldn't help but notice that the Mogollon warriors, especially that woman, Clay Frog, kept looking at Browser, whispering to each other, as they studied him with speculative eyes. Why? Just because he had stood up for them that morning?

Stone Ghost sat to Browser's left, speaking with the old Mogollon man. Their conversation was a curious pidgin of words taken from the two languages.

Catkin leaned close to Browser and asked, "Why do you think someone wanted to kill their prophet?"

"He was murdered because he wished to tell us something about our past. The past is the most dangerous thing in the world. I told you once, Catkin, that it was all related. I am only now starting to understand just how much."

"You mean you think their prophet was murdered because of something our ancestors—"

"We are ready," Blue Corn called out as she rose and scanned the crowd. Silence fell. She lifted her arms and murmured the ancient prayer:

*"Great Flute Player*
*At the sound of your flute*
*we came. Rising from the worlds.*
*Rising we came.*
*Led by your enchanting music.*
*From the darkness, you led the way.*
*With seeds upon your back.*
*Here. In the Fourth World, you led the way.*
*South.*
*Down the great road from darkness to the sun.*
*South. We hear your flute. We Dance your road.*
*Your path is our garden.*
*Bless us. Raise your flute and call the rains.*
*Cast your seed upon our gardens.*

*Make us fruitful.*
*Hututu. Hututu. Hututu"*

Catkin surprised herself when she caught her tongue wrapping around the familiar words of the old song. For how many sun cycles had her people sung that prayer? This new belief, that of the katsinas, didn't deny the Flute Player. No one claimed that the katsinas were greater than the old god. So why were people killing each other over what they believed? Unable to help herself, she looked to the south, toward the sun, where the Flute Player's greatest gift of light and warmth originated. The offerings in the niches shimmered in the firelight, turquoise, shell, and cornmeal. It was old, that combination, from the time when the First People ventured out from the underworlds.

"So," Blue Corn said, irritation in her voice, "our Mogollon guests came to tell us of the Blessed Poor Singer's prophecy. Now two of them have been murdered. On *my* doorstep, while under *my* protection." She turned her eyes in the direction of the Katsinas' People. "My people were not responsible for this crime. Of that, I am certain."

Matron White Smoke muttered in assent, her old eyes burning as she glared at the Katsinas' People.

Matron Cloudblower rose from where she sat several places down, to Catkin's right. She wore a yellow tunic belted at the waist by a yucca sash; she had collected her long graying black hair in a bun at the nape of her neck. The gathering quieted.

Cloudblower spread her muscular arms wide. "I have spoken with my people. I assure you, none of us wished the Mogollon prophet dead. You know that our quest for the First People's kiva has not been easy. We truly wished to hear the prophet's words, believing he might be able to help us. We are few in number now. We need help. The coughing sickness has carried away many of our people over the last three summers—"

"Witchcraft," someone hissed loud enough that it carried to all parts of the kiva. "False gods!"

Catkin cocked her head in search of the culprit, but couldn't pick out the speaker in the sea of faces.

She remembered Two Hearts's assertion in the cave above Longtail village that the katsinas brought the coughing disease. The memory lingered of her husband wasting away before her, his body wracked by coughs that left his lips bright with blood. His fevered eyes still stared out from her nightmares.

"There is no witchcraft among the katsinas," Cloudblower replied in a soft voice.

"No?" Blue Corn asked. "Springbank was one of the Katsinas' People, was he not? Didn't you tell me that he is the legendary witch, Two Hearts?"

Catkin's nerves tingled at the undercurrent of threat that slipped through the room. Warriors whispered to each other and propped their hands on belted stilettos and war clubs.

"I said there is no witchcraft among the katsinas, Matron." Cloudblower's expression turned sad. "What people do is another thing. Witches have their own needs and their own ways of filling them. Springbank lived among us, yes, but he wished to destroy the Katsinas' People. He was not one of us. He didn't believe in Poor Singer's prophecy."

Blue Corn's lips twitched. "What of this rumor that the legendary White Moccasins are prowling about?"

Stone Ghost stood and walked over to take Cloudblower's arm. His mangy turkey-feather cape swayed with each step. "Great Matron, it is no rumor. They are indeed a threat and they are indeed among us."

"What proof have you?"

"I have seen them. It was White Moccasins who killed every man, woman, and child in Aspen village. War Chief Browser can tell you the details, but the people at Aspen village suffered the same fate as legions of Made People did a hundred sun cycles ago."

Stone Ghost turned slowly, scanning the faces. "Do any of you remember the punishment exacted by the Blessed Sun from those who disobeyed him? He sent his red-shirted warriors to burn your village and desecrate your dead! His warriors stripped the offender's flesh from his bones, boiled it, and ate it while the few wailing survivors watched in horror."

To the now silent room, he added, "There was a reason that the Made People hunted the First People down and killed them." His voice dropped. "They had to be punished for their misdeeds."

"But we have only your words that these White Moccasins still exist?" Blue Corn leaned forward and propped her elbow on her knee. "Where is the proof, Elder? I heard all kinds of stories from Old Pidgeontail. Exciting battle, a secret cave, the old witch, Two Hearts, disguised as Elder Springbank, and incredible wealth. But where, Elder, is one of these White Moccasins? Show me a body."

Stone Ghost bowed his head and his wispy white hair glistened. "I cannot. They carried their dead away before Catkin could return with a war party. But they exist, Matron, and they hate us."

Catkin's eyes narrowed when she saw Obsidian. The woman sat frozen, rigid, her long glossy black hair interwoven with turquoise beads and coral bangles. She sat two rows back and to the left. Her large dark eyes were almost swimming, and one hand had risen to cover her perfect mouth.

"So," Blue Corn countered dryly. "Elder Stone Ghost has seen White Moccasins. I can place my faith in the word of a hermit who, until one sun cycle ago, lived by himself out in the sagebrush at the foot of Smoking Mirror Butte.

"Tell me, Elder, have not people also claimed that *you* are a witch?"

Catkin reached down, fingers resting lightly on the wood of her war club handle.

Stone Ghost tipped his wrinkled face up and smiled. "I do not understand, Matron. Why would you allow the assertions of fools to occupy your attention when you have two dead Mogollon guests, and your own warriors almost massacred the rest less than a hand of time ago? Are you trying to distract us from finding the prophet's murderer?"

Blue Corn gave him a cold look and waved a hand dismissively. "You are supposed to be able to solve such crimes. Why don't you do it?"

Stone Ghost nodded. "That will be difficult. The killer was brilliant."

Blue Corn scoffed, "What does it take to sneak up in a snowstorm, brain a sleepy guard, club a prophet, and cut up two bodies?"

"Is that what you think happened last night?" Stone Ghost seemed genuinely amazed.

"Well, that makes the most sense. For all we know, it could have been anyone. Perhaps"—her gaze narrowed—"even one of the Mogollon."

Whispers of angry disbelief erupted before their elder silenced them. Catkin had to say this for the old man, he commanded instant respect from his fiery young warriors. It had been many summers since she had seen that kind of discipline.

"Well," Blue Corn maintained, "how do we know they didn't kill him? Perhaps they, too, have their reasons for disliking the katsinas, or thlatsinas, as they call them? We have nothing more than their prophet's word that he was here on behalf of Poor Singer's prophecy."

Stone Ghost waved the Mogollon elder down as he started to stand to answer the charge, and said, "Matron Blue Corn, you make a very good point, and to be sure, it is worthy of consideration—because you are clearly supposed to think that. Like I said, the murderer was brilliant. Might I tell you why?"

Blue Corn arched a skeptical eyebrow. "I would appreciate that, Elder."

Stone Ghost hobbled toward her, one hand at his chin as though in deep thought. "The person who murdered the prophet wanted to achieve many things. First, he wanted the prophet dead before he could reveal what he knew of Poor Singer's prophecy. But he also had to destroy anyone who might know it. How to do that? The most obvious way was to have Rain Crow's warriors kill every Mogollon in your village—which came very near to happening. Only by accident did my nephew, Catkin, and I arrive in time to avert such a catastrophe. The murderer wanted you involved in a major war with the Fire Dogs. Not just petty raiding like we all like to engage in from time to time, but a blood vendetta. The fourth goal, of course, was to cast suspicion upon the Katsinas' People. The last thing the murderer wants is for you, Matron, to develop any kind of sympathy for the katsinas' cause. The more the Made People fight each other, the less likely we are to worry about 'mythical' White Moccasins slipping around injecting their venom. And," he said, and took a deep breath, "the final goal was to create dissension among the Katsinas' People. We are weak right now. We have a new Matron. If the murderer could frighten us badly enough to splinter our people, maybe the problem of the Katsinas' People would simply go away."

Blue Corn's expression had grown thoughtful. "How does killing a Mogollon prophet split the Katsinas' People? What would you care?"

"When we lived near Talon Town, a young warrior named Whiproot was killed—in exactly the same way as the Mogollon prophet. We believed the murderers were dead, but now, none of us can be sure. Many of our people will be wondering if we are dealing with ordinary murderers, or witches so powerful that we cannot kill them. We all know that truly great witches have ways of extending their own lives."

"How do the White Moccasins, the legendary warriors of the First People, fit into this?"

Stone Ghost shook his head. "I'm not certain yet."

"But you think the prophet's message threatened the White Moccasins?" Blue Corn had propped her chin on her palm, as though considering that.

"I do."

"So, you must find out what his message was."

Stone Ghost shook his head again. "No, my nephew and I have more important concerns."

Blue Corn's interest sharpened. "And just what do you think is more important than the murder of two of my guests?"

Stone Ghost walked back and looked down into Browser's dark eyes, before saying, "The murderer. We must find the old witch before he can extend his life again."

Blue Corn's face twisted incredulously. "You think Two Hearts killed the Mogollon prophet?"

Laughter sprinkled the sudden din of voices.

Stone Ghost replied, "Two Hearts or one of his assassins, yes."

Catkin saw Rain Crow shift. It was a subtle movement, but a quick one. She turned to follow his gaze.

Obsidian's beautiful face had gone white as newfallen snow, and her huge black eyes sparkled with fear.

Catkin followed her gaze to the crowd that filled the great kiva's stairway. It took her a moment to identify the man who had locked eyes with Obsidian. She knew him from his old face and odd, light brown eyes. The renowned Trader, Old Pigeontail. He was nodding slightly. Obsidian looked petrified with terror. Catkin had never seen such fear—except on the battlefield.

From warriors about to die.

"PIPER, COME . . . COME here."

Piper sits before the fire, tending it, as Mother said to do.

"Piper!"

She pulls her blanket over her head so that only one eye sees him lying on the other side of the fire. Mother is gone. There's no one to make her. The blanket smells dusty, like a dead animal's fur.

"I said . . . come!"

Grandfather's reaching hand is a skeleton's, the fingernails are long and twisted and yellow. They click like a grasshopper. Piper dreams of summer, when the grasshoppers fill the brush and leap when she tries to catch them.

The worst bad thing would be if Grandfather gets up.

Piper uses a stick to prod the fire and sparks crackle up like stars falling backward. She watches them swirl and rise toward the smokehole in the roof. She watches until she can't see them anymore, just blue sky and drifting Cloud People.

"If you don't . . . come over here! . . ."

Piper tilts her head. The Cloud People are flying so high, they are freezing. Freezing to death. Piper shivers and tucks her hands under her armpits.

From somewhere far away, she hears a voice shouting, "Piper! Piper! Piper . . ."

The Cloud People swirl and crowd together for warmth, but Piper can't feel it. She shivers harder and wishes she could fly up there with them. They would wrap their fluffy bodies around her and hold her tight and fly away . . .

Piper blinks.

*It is nighttime.*

*The fire is dead.*

*Groans make Piper turn.*

*Grandfather is eating yesterday's soup from a clay bowl. He makes sounds like a den of coyote pups, squeaking and growling, but his mouth is a fish's mouth, opening and closing. She imagines she can see bubbles climbing up, going higher, until they can escape through the smokehole to fly free.*

*"Piper," he calls. "Bring me . . . the water jar."*

*But Piper's eyes are on the smokehole and the invisible bubbles. The other little girl who lives inside her hears, but Piper doesn't really hear.*

*"Piper . . . for the sake . . . of the gods! Look at me!"*

*Piper jerks and looks.*

*Grandfather has dead flying squirrel eyes, huge and black. They glow in the starlight falling through the smokehole.*

*He is talking to her, but the door curtains in Piper's ears have fallen closed. She stares at Grandfather's silent moving lips.*

*Then curls into a tight ball beside the warm embers of the fire and falls asleep.*

*Voices whisper. From the bottom of her heart. The words rise up through her chest and come out her own mouth like snake hisses:*

*"Run away, run away, run away."*

# CHAPTER 12

MAUREEN HAD BEEN in similar buildings before, but always as an observer or outside expert called in to offer a professional opinion. This was the first time she'd entered a medical examiner's office as a victim's friend. Dusty walked stiffly at her side. She'd warned him that they might want him to identify the corpse, and he seemed to be dreading it more with every step.

The Office of the Medical Investigator of the State of New Mexico, the OMI, filled the eastern side of the ground floor of the Tri-State Labs and was run through the University of New Mexico Medical School. Maureen had worked with this OMI before and knew that they maintained a staff of full-time pathologists, labs, offices, and the facility for processing corpses. That included an autopsy room, cold room, isolation area, and rear garage entrance, where gurneys could be rolled in and out unobtrusively from ambulances.

Maureen stopped at the reception desk. "We'd like to see Sid Malroun, please."

The slender black-haired woman behind the counter studied Maureen from over her bifocals. "Do you have an appointment?"

"No, but I'm Dr. Maureen Cole, with the Department of Anthropology, McMaster University in Hamilton, Ontario. And this is Dusty Stewart."

"Just a moment, please." She picked up the phone and dialed a number.

Dusty walked away and pretended to study a picture of the San Francisco Peaks that graced the wall to their left. The light of dawn had turned the snowy mountains pink.

She watched him. He didn't fidget or pace. He stood absolutely still. Every moment seemed to drag on eternally, as though time had turned in upon itself. Perhaps he knew, as she did, that if they didn't keep busy, do what their professional selves demanded, the realization that Dale was truly dead would claim them.

The receptionist said, "Please, have a seat. Dr. Malroun is in the lab. He'll be with you as soon as he can."

She indicated the chairs next to the small wooden coffee table and the potted plant. Dusty walked over and sat down.

Maureen said, "Sid Malroun is an old acquaintance. Forensic anthropology is like archaeology, a small world. Everyone knows everyone else."

She took the chair opposite Dusty.

For a long time, neither of them spoke. Then Dusty looked at her with eyes as hard and glittering as sapphires. "I keep imagining what his last moments must have been like. I can see it happening from inside Dale's head."

She'd done the same thing after John's death. She'd imagined that he must have called out to her, wanted her there, and known at the end that he'd never see her again.

"Do you think he called out to you?" she asked softly.

Dusty stared at his hands. "If he did, it was for help."

*And you weren't there.*

Modern people had trouble with death. Adding a terrible and senseless murder into the mix just made it that much worse. Dusty's words ate into her. What had Dale's last moments been like? She couldn't help but feel his horror and desperation.

Dusty had pulled the card from his jacket pocket. In

silence, he turned it so that he could stare at the drawing of the basilisk.

"I wonder how long that was under the wiper?"

Dusty shook his head. "It wasn't there this morning. And you can bet that cop didn't leave it there. No, this is something else."

"Maybe we just didn't see it on the drive down from Santa Fe."

"Doctor, this stuck out like a white potsherd in a scatter of Emery Gray ware."

"Sylvia?" Maureen asked. "Maybe it's a joke?"

Dusty shook his head. "You know Sylvia. She'd never do something like this. No, this is a warning. A message for me."

"But, who knows about *el basilisco*?" Maureen asked. "Maggie?"

"Never. She takes things like this too seriously."

At that moment, a thin, bespectacled man stepped through the door. He'd gone completely bald since the last time she'd seen him. He wore a white lab coat and a surgical mask hung from straps around his neck. "Maureen?" he asked. "My God, it's good to see you! What on earth are you doing down here in the sunny south?"

"Hello, Sid." She stood and hugged him as Dusty stuck the card in his pocket. "How are Marla and the kids?"

"Marla's great. United just made her a full pilot. She's somewhere between Denver and Cincinnati as we speak. Will's a freshman this year, taking music of all things, and Tina is a junior in high school." He glanced at Dusty.

Maureen said, "This is Dusty Stewart. He's an archaeologist."

The men shook hands, Sid apparently oblivious of why they had come.

"Sid? Could we talk to you for a moment?" Maureen asked.

"Sure, come on back. I think there's a little coffee left in the pot." He pushed the door open and led them back into a long hallway lined with offices. "We just had a really strange . . ."

He stopped short, glancing at her, worry reflected in his face for the first time. "This isn't just a friendly visit, is it?"

"No," Maureen returned grimly. "Dale Emerson Robertson. That's why we're here. He was Dusty's adopted father. We'd like to know what you've found."

Sid glanced back and forth between them, as though trying to decide, then said, "Come on back," and led them farther down the lighted hallway to a cramped office filled with bookcases, a desk, and two chairs piled with reports. "Sit down. Have you talked to the FBI?"

"No," Maureen answered, and sat next to Dusty. "We'll be talking to them this afternoon. But they brought the body into OMI didn't they? It's federal jurisdiction, and you get everything in the region when there is a suspicious death."

Sid lowered himself to the corner of the desk. "Yeah, he's here. We just finished the autopsy. Maureen, look, I'm not sure I should be talking to you."

"Relax, Sid. All we want to know is what you found. In a few days, your report is going to be available to anyone involved in the discovery phase of the trial. We just want to know what happened."

Sid folded his arms and considered. "All right, it's just that, well, this is the first time we've had one of our own come through the back door. It's a little spooky."

"Spooky, how?" Dusty's shoulders squared, as though preparing himself.

"Robertson was buried upside down in one of the archaeological sites out at Chaco Canyon. Bill Hendersen, my associate, flew up there in a chopper this morning to watch the fibbies record the crime scene.

He said that Dale's feet were sticking out of the sand. This is the strange part. The bottoms of his feet had been skinned."

"What?" Dusty looked ashen.

"Skinned, Dr. Stewart. The hide carefully peeled off." Sid raised an eyebrow, waiting for some explanation. "You're an archaeologist, right? What does that mean?"

Dusty stared unblinking at Sid, then leaned back in his chair. "It's Navajo."

"Navajo?"

"Navajo witchcraft. Skin walkers. What else did you find?"

"Well"—Sid gestured awkwardly—"things I don't understand. Someone had poked yucca leaves through his knees, through the ligaments and synovial membranes until the points penetrated the joint between the tibia and the femur."

Dusty gripped the arms of the chair hard, but his voice came out soft. "Was anything buried with him? Any artifacts?"

"Hendersen said they found a twisted yucca rope, well, more like a hoop, I'd guess you'd say. It had been laid around him and then buried in the dirt."

Dusty swallowed hard. "Dale was *inside* the hoop?"

Sid nodded. "Why?"

Dusty shook his head, more in denial than negation. "Witches jump through yucca hoops to change shapes."

"So," Sid said, fascinated. "What does that mean? What did the murderer want him to change into?"

"I don't know. Go on. Tell me the rest."

"Well, some kind of meat was stuffed in his mouth. It was held in by a little rock sculpture, a carved black stone." Sid was watching Dusty warily now. "We haven't run the precipitation tests on the meat yet—"

"It's human," Dusty said. "Probably boiled and slightly decomposed, because it was dug from a fresh grave."

Sid shifted uncomfortably. "Boy, I really don't like the direction this is going."

Dusty turned to Maureen. "The murderer has crossed all the lines. Navajo, Puebloan, Mexican witchcraft, who knows what else."

"I don't get it," Sid said. "What was Dale into?"

"Dale wasn't into it," Maureen said, a sinking sensation in her gut. "His killer was."

"Dale's head . . ." Dusty hesitated. "What did you find?"

"Dear God," Maureen whispered. "You're not thinking . . ."

Sid waited for her to finish. When she didn't, he told Dusty, "The scalp had been peeled back on the right side over the ear. Someone used a hole saw, the kind carpenters use to cut holes for doorknobs into doors, to saw a hole in Dale's right parietal. How did you know?"

Dusty closed his eyes as though struggling with himself. "That sick son of a bitch."

"What?" Sid demanded to know as he straightened from the desk. "Tell me what it means?"

Dusty leaned forward, propped his elbows on his knees, and squinted, as though fighting for control.

Maureen knew why. He'd told her the story just last month. An old medicine man named Ruff-legged Hawk had told Dusty that his ancestors believed a soul could not reach the Land of the Dead unless it began the journey from Pueblo Alto, in Chaco Canyon. But this belief posed a problem, because people often died far away, while out on raids, or hunting. To solve this problem, people carried "soul pots" with them to catch the last breath—the escaping soul—of the dying, which they took back to Pueblo Alto and had priests ritually break to release the soul. Unfortunately, some people didn't want to wait for the person to die, so they—

"The stone figure in Dale's mouth," Dusty pressed,

"it was a snake coiled inside a broken eggshell, wasn't it?"

Sid could only nod. After a moment, he asked, "Why? Is that some special artifact? What is it?"

Dusty's gaze bored into Maureen as he softly responded, "It's called *el basilisco*."

BROWSER PULLED HIS blanket tight against the chill as he hurried across the flats toward Dusk House. Night had fallen cold and windy, a harbinger of the bitter winter to come. What would the Katsinas' People do? Most of their corn supply had been burned. They had nowhere to live, and winter was rolling down from the north.

He felt torn as he tramped into the wind, half of him wanted to stay, to help his people. The other half chafed to be off with his uncle in search of Two Hearts and Shadow. How did he do both?

A shiver coursed his bones as Wind Baby slipped icy fingers past his twisted-rabbit-fur blanket. The Cloud People, as though angered, had obscured the night sky, turning the world as black as boiled pine pitch. The only way Browser could tell his destination was by the glow of a fire pot on the southeast corner of Dusk House. There, one of his guards, probably Wrapped Hand, was crouching for warmth.

"Has anyone passed?" Browser called in greeting.

Wrapped Hand leaned out, his form but a blot against the sky. "Not to my knowledge, War Chief, but the only way I will know is if they stumble over their own feet and I hear them."

"Be wary, my friend."

"Indeed, War Chief. I have no wish to end up as that Fire Dog, Acorn, did."

"Good. Trust no one."

"Your words are tied to my souls, War Chief. Have a safe and restful night."

Browser passed through the gap that led into Dusk House's plaza. He ran his fingers along the weathered mud plaster that coated the south wall to keep from losing his way. He rounded the corner and proceeded to the ladder that led up to the rooftop. Once on top, the red glows of warming bowls lit the doorways.

He made his way straight to Matron Cloudblower's and called out, "Matron?"

"Come, Browser."

He ducked inside a square room. Red spirals painted the white walls. Overhead, soot-coated poles supported the roof. Cobwebs hung down, indicating that until the arrival of the Katsinas' People, no one had stayed here.

To Browser's surprise, three people sat around a fire bowl filled with glowing coals. Matron Cloudblower, Uncle Stone Ghost, and White Cone, the Mogollon elder. White Cone wore a thick brown blanket that looked as if it had been spun from buffalo wool.

"Come, War Chief." Matron Cloudblower indicated a place for him to sit beside her.

Browser knelt to her left and extended his cold hands to the warmth. "Cold out there. I can smell snow in the air. It's no night to be out."

"We were just talking," Cloudblower said, and frowned, as though her mind had knotted around a particularly thorny problem. "With the prophet dead, there is little reason for us to stay here any longer. While White Smoke is willing to trade food for some of the ornaments we recovered from the White Moccasins, she is hesitant to allow us to remain. She fears the coughing disease, even though many here are already coughing blood and their flesh is shrinking around their bones."

"I know," Browser sighed.

"Flowing Waters has food only because they have

fertile ground and a river to water it. They are surrounded by others without these things. People with failed crops will do anything to fill their bellies. Even sell their children and husbands into slavery. Flowing Waters exists like a fortress. Each of the towns is bristling with warriors. Unless they guard their fields they will be plucked clean. Unless they turn away the refugees, they will be buried under a wall of people. We were asked here by invitation. We should not impose upon that invitation."

"So, what are we going to do?"

"I will take the Katsinas' People to Straight Path Canyon to rebuild the great kiva at Streambed Town."

"While you and I," Stone Ghost said, "go in search of Two Hearts."

"Where do you expect to find him, Uncle?" Browser noted the hooded look in Stone Ghost's eyes.

Stone Ghost steepled his fingers. "He, too, is a creature of habit, one influenced by his birth and lineage. To find his lair, one must follow the path of the spiral, Browser, and there, at its center, he will either find Two Hearts or his corpse."

Irritated, Browser said, "I don't know what that means, Uncle."

The Mogollon elder's face might have been carved of old cedar wood for all the emotion he displayed.

"What if the White Moccasins attack our people while we're gone?" Browser asked. "I'm worried about this. I assume that Straighthorn and Jackrabbit are still going with us. Wrapped Hand, Straw Shield, and Two Cones are the best of our remaining warriors, but I don't think either one of them is suited to be War Chief. They don't have the experience to lead a war party."

Cloudblower looked at him with soft brown eyes. "That is true, War Chief, but I do."

Browser nodded. No one who knew her would question Cloudblower's ability as either a warrior or a leader. Her male body, though aging, still exhibited incredible strength, and in past battles, Cloudblower had shown such a thorough understanding of war that Browser, himself, would have had no qualms going into battle under her leadership. But for her interest in Healing and studying the sacred, she would have made an excellent War Chief.

Browser squinted at the coals in the warming bowl. "We don't have the warriors we once did, Cloudblower, and you'll have fewer when I leave."

"This cannot be helped. Sometimes, War Chief, we must do what we must do."

White Cone had been listening; now he said, "Given enough time, I could send a runner to the south. I could have warriors sent. Upon my orders, they would obey Matron Cloudblower."

"I'm not sure that's a wise idea, Elder," Browser said. "When the word gets around, it will play straight into the hands of our enemies."

People would distrust the Katsinas' People even more. They would raid them just to break up such an unholy alliance. It would strengthen the Flute Player Believers, and even unite them against the Katsinas' People.

"Then consider this: We have room for you in the south," White Cone said simply. "Our prophet was waiting for the right time to give you the rest of Poor Singer's prophecy. As he told you last night, much has been lost. You have forgotten things during your wars and migrations. Or, perhaps, they were never told in your lands. We have had our own problems with the drought, with the failure of the fields. Many of our people, too, have lost their way. Now it is time to heal old wounds"—his expression turned weary and defeated—"and to teach the lessons the thlatsinas wish our people to learn."

"You are asking people to forget everything that has happened for a thousand sun cycles, Elder."

An unsettling wisdom filled White Cone's eyes as he asked, "Are we that different, War Chief?"

"Most people will say so, Elder. Our ancestors climbed up from the underworlds; yours fell from the sky as dogs of fire. We come from different origins."

"The thlatsinas didn't think so." The Mogollon smiled the way a man would if he were in possession of some special secret. "But I hear your words, War Chief. Our prophet came here believing that our task would not be easy, but that it was necessary. Sometimes, as I have so recently learned, it is unpleasant to do hard things. That doesn't lessen the fact that they must be done."

Browser had no answer for that. Either the old man was a fool, or he was as crazy as a fox that turns silly circles in front of a covey of quail. They get so engrossed with the fox's lunacy that they fail to realize when they are within distance of a quick leap.

"We will leave tomorrow for Straight Path Canyon," Cloudblower said with finality.

"And I shall leave with my party before first light," Stone Ghost replied. He looked at Browser. "I have sent Catkin to pack the things we will need. She has informed Straighthorn and Jackrabbit and sworn them to secrecy. Can you be ready?"

Browser nodded. "I will be ready."

# CHAPTER 13

Conference Room, OMI, Albuquerque, New Mexico

DUSTY SLUMPED IN the uncomfortable chair, one leg out, the other tucked under him. His left elbow rested on the wooden veneer of the conference table, and he cupped a can of Coke in his right hand. Maureen sat beside him, an empty and sad look on her face.

He didn't know what he felt; this was a nightmare. The initial shock of Dale's death had been numbed by the unfolding roll of revelations about how he'd died. Each atrocity had chipped away part of Dusty's soul until he had become a husk, like a tamale wrapper left dry and forgotten on a windswept plaza. It was as though he no longer had the strength to feel anything.

Agent Sam Nichols of the FBI sat across from them. When Sid had called him and started to explain what they had guessed about Dale's death, the agent had dropped everything to drive straight to the OMI. Nichols had a short chunky body, thick black hair, and wore horn-rimmed glasses. Dark stubble lined his square jaw, and his right eye had a slight squint to it, as if it had been injured some time in the past. As he took notes, his pen made fluid strokes across the notepad. A tape recorder ran silently on the table in front of Dusty and Maureen.

Sid Malroun and Bill Hendersen sat at the end of the table, expressions grim, as Dusty forced himself to go over the points one by one. Somehow he had to stay focused, do what they asked him, so he could get out of here and drive to Chaco. He had to see the place where Dale was found or he'd go stark raving mad.

From some deep dark corner of his mind, his dead father, Samuel Stewart, wept—just as he had right after Dusty's mother left them.

Dusty closed his eyes for a moment. Those same cries had wakened him once in the middle of the night when he'd been seven. He'd opened his eyes and seen his father standing over his bed with a gun to his temple.

"Dr. Robertson didn't give you any indication that he'd been threatened?" Nichols asked again. "No men-

tion of the peculiar phone calls he'd been getting?
Notes? Nothing out of the ordinary?"

Dusty shook his head. "No. We found out about the
phone calls this morning. We haven't seen Dale since
he left Pueblo Animas. He went into Aztec with the
new owner of the Pueblo Animas site."

"Who?"

"Alevy," Maureen said as she toyed with her thick
black braid. "Moshe Alevy. He bought the Animas site
after the original investor found out about the burned
children."

Nichols perked up, his one good eye widening.
"What burned children?"

"About forty of them," Maureen whispered. Dusty
thought she looked like warmed over hell. "We won't
have a final minimum number of individuals until we
do the lab work. That's why Dale called me down from
McMaster University in Ontario. I teach there. Dale
wanted me to do the osteological analysis on the children."

"Dr. Cole is one of the finest in the discipline," Sid
added from the side. "I don't think Dale would have
trusted anyone else with a bone bed."

"And these burned children? That's been reported to
the authorities?"

"Prehistoric," Dusty said. "It's an archaeological
site. They burned in A.D. 1263. Someone torched the
kiva." He gave Nichols a dull gaze. "Human beings
were no different then than now." His eyes turned to
Sid Malroun.

Sid said, "Don't look here for a rebuttal. Forensic
anthropologists as a rule tend to have skewed percep-
tions about human beings. It's not like we get to see
the better angels of human nature."

"Would this Alevy character have any reason to kill
Dr. Robertson?"

"No," Dusty said absently. "He's Jewish. A Holo-
caust survivor. His goal is to preserve sites where atroc-

ities took place. As reminders about just how close the beast is in all of us."

"I'll be checking him out. Now, let's get back to this witchcraft." Nichols studied Dusty through his good eye. "Do you have any idea who this witch might be?"

Dusty took a deep breath and shook his head. "No. The only run-in Dale ever had with witches was long ago. God, what, almost twenty-five years now. I was just a kid. Dale had heard that a bunch of witches were holding ceremonies in a cave in Tsegi Canyon. You couldn't get there by car so we borrowed horses from an old Navajo friend of ours."

Dusty frowned, looking back into the past. "We had to ride for nearly a day to even get close to the place. When we did, Dale made me hold the horses down in a piñon grove in a little cove at the bottom of the canyon while he hiked up."

"Did he see witches?" Nichols asked, as though ready to get up and leave if Dusty said yes.

Dusty nodded. "He said that he climbed up to where he could see into this hollow in the sandstone. There were three of them. One of them wore a wolf mask. They had a big fire so Dale could see the inside of the cave pretty well. The thing that caught his attention was the sand painting on the floor."

"Sand painting?" Nichols asked. "That's Navajo, isn't it?"

Dusty shrugged. "Hopi, Zuni, and the rest of the Pueblo peoples have made pictures for thousands of years. But, yeah, I suppose that in this case it was more of a Navajo utilization. Dale told me that they'd drawn a picture of a white man. He was sure it was him. That scared him, and he started back down the hill. He saw the Wolf Witch shoot an arrow into the picture's knee, and Dale's knee gave out. Then the witch shot the painting's other knee, and Dale went tumbling down the slope.

"He didn't reach where I was until well after mid-

night. By then I was cold, scared, and more than ready
to get the hell out of there. Dale was, too. We rode all
night. Really pushed those poor bone-rack ponies.
Dale's knees were never right after that."

"What about you?" Nichols asked. "You were there.
Do you believe that Dr. Robertson saw witches?"

Dusty studied him, not really giving a damn, and
asked, "How long have you been in this part of the
country, Agent Nichols?"

"Look," he said simply, "we handle law enforcement
on the reservations. It doesn't matter what I believe or
don't believe. I've been here long enough, talked to
enough tribal police, to know that witchcraft is something that other people take seriously. I just want to
know about you, what you believe."

"Then, yes, I think Dale saw witches up there, and
it's entirely possible that one of them lured him out to
Chaco Canyon and murdered him." He could see Bill
Hendersen squirming uncomfortably, and added, "It's
not what you believe that counts. The Wolf Witch, or
someone like him, killed Dale, and tried to suck his
soul out of his head."

Nichols gave Dusty a deadpan look. "You know, I'll
tell you the truth. I'm from Baltimore. I liked Baltimore. Someday, I want to go back, so I can work on
crimes that make sense. You know, mob violence, international drug murders, good old-fashioned crimes of
passion. That's my kind of thing. I *really* don't appreciate this witchcraft bullshit. Now, your turn. Tell me
the truth. You honestly believe that's why the murderer
drilled a hole in his head? To suck his soul out?"

Dusty could tell from Nichols's disgusted expression
that he didn't really want to hear what Dusty thought,
but Dusty was going to tell him anyway. "I do. It's part
of the Native folklore here. The yucca hoop that was
around the body? That's more folklore. Witches change
shape by jumping through hoops twisted out of yucca."

"So, they expected Robertson to do what? Jump through the hoop and change shape?"

Nichols's tone was almost belligerent. Dusty leaned forward in his chair about to say something he'd regret when he was saved by a knock at the door.

A white-coated lab technician stuck her head in. She was young, perhaps twenty-five, with short blond hair. "Dr. Malroun? The results are in on the tissue inside Dr. Robertson's mouth. It tested positive for human. Blood type O."

"Dale was AB positive," Dusty said. "As I'm sure you already know."

Maureen's shoulders slumped, and Dusty reached out for her hand. The bones of her fingers felt thin and frail in his grip. He held them tightly.

Nichols took a deep breath. "What about the little stone fetish?"

*"El basilisco,"* Dusty said, and suddenly gaped, as understanding dawned. A prickling like a thousand chills ran up and down his spine. He lurched to his feet.

"What?" Nichols asked.

"The card. The card under the wiper. Dear God, he was there this afternoon . . . watching us! He walked right up to the Bronco while we were inside!"

"Who did?"

"Dale's killer. The witch!" Dusty pulled the card from his shirt pocket and handed it to Nichols.

CATKIN UNFOLDED HER war shirt and checked the sun-bleached fabric. Woven from Hohokam cotton, it had been red once, many sun cycles ago, but the color had faded to the palest of pinks. The material was light and more suited for summer wear, but it had

no holes in it. She refolded it and stuffed it into the
bottom of her pack. She placed a pair of buffalo-hide
moccasins on top of it. She had traded a turquoise-
inlaid comb to one of the Sunrise Town Traders for
them. Next she packed small sacks of cornmeal and
finally a supply of venison jerky.

She pulled two copper bells out and held them. She
hadn't approved of taking the bells, and just having
them set her teeth on edge. This was plunder taken
from the graves of the First People. On the one hand,
it was, and remained, property of the dead. On the other
hand, her people needed them as trade goods far more
than the dead did.

Her mind went back to that night outside Aspen village. She remembered finding the first of the copper
bells wedged into a slit in a desiccated mummy's belly.
She had remained at the trailhead while Browser went
down to check the silent village. Shadow Woman had
lured him into a kiva and trapped him there among the
corpses of her victims, leading him like a bird with
crumbs, but her bait had been these little copper bells.

Catkin tucked them away and lifted her fingertips to
her nose, smelling the faint metallic odor. So much of
her life had been touched by the First People, their
places, and things. The Katsinas' People's troubles began when Browser found a little turquoise wolf on the
spot where his lover, Hophorn, had been attacked.
Since then, they had stumbled from one disaster to another.

Browser still had that wolf. Legends said it was a
Spirit Helper made by the First People. With the wolf
as a guide, the soul of the dead could navigate the
trails, traps, and tangles of the roads in the underworlds. The wolf would lead them past the monsters
that guarded the way, take them past the dead ends
where a soul could end up lost and howling through
eternity. For the wicked, the wolf was essential, for it
would ensure that he took the right fork in the trail and

avoided Spider Woman's judgment. That was the problem with the First People. They were tainted by a Power gone wrong.

She took her stack of died corn cakes and placed them on the top of the pack before pulling the drawstrings tight. She hefted it, feeling the weight. Not too bad. On the sleeping mat lay her blanket made of split turkey feathers, her bow and quiver of arrows, and her war club. That was the sum of her worldly possessions.

"Catkin?" a soft voice called from the doorway.

Catkin turned, her hand instinctively reaching for her war club. "What is it?"

Obsidian ducked past the door hanging, her long black hair glistening, freshly washed in yucca root soap. The odor still clung to her. She wore a wealth of turquoise necklaces that hung over the exposed tops of her full breasts. A long fur cloak draped her shoulders; it had been fashioned from hide cut into strips and twisted so that the fur stuck out inside as well as outside.

"What do you want?" Catkin turned back to her pack. "I have things to do."

"You are leaving?"

"We all are. Tomorrow. The Matron is taking us south. Away from here."

"To Streambed Town." Obsidian's voice dropped to almost a whisper. "I know."

Obsidian's eyes seemed to enlarge. She stepped closer to Catkin. What was it that men saw in her? Why did they lose themselves in that depthless stare? When Catkin looked into those eyes, she saw something feral and dangerous.

Which reminded her of how they had looked in the Sunrise great kiva that morning. "Tell me, Obsidian, what's between you and Old Pigeontail?"

"Between us?" Obsidian's manner changed yet again, this time to one of pensive speculation.

"I saw you in the kiva. You looked like he was about

to reach out and grab your breath-heart soul right out of your body."

"Oh, that." Obsidian smiled warily. "I owe him for some items he traded me. It's just a debt that I squared with him."

"Uh-huh." *Lying camp bitch.* "Sure. Just a debt. What are you doing here?"

Obsidian's voice softened. "I want to go with you."

Catkin stared at her.

"You and the War Chief aren't going with Matron Cloudblower to Streambed Town, are you?" Obsidian tilted her head, and the faintest frown etched her forehead. "Let me go with you."

Catkin braced her legs. "I don't know what you're talking about."

"If you won't tell me when you're leaving, I'll go to Browser."

Catkin picked up her war club and ran her fingers down the use-polished wood. Obsidian seemed to understand. She adopted a slight crouch, and Catkin felt the hairs on her neck prickle. She said, "The War Chief needs his sleep, Obsidian. Ask him tomorrow."

"Beware, Catkin. He is *my* War Chief, too. I will speak with him when and if I wish to," she said, and ducked beneath the door hanging.

Every muscle in Catkin's body tensed. She knotted her gray blanket around her shoulders, hung her club on her belt, and walked out into the night after Obsidian.

She didn't see her, which struck Catkin as odd. She looked down the third story toward Browser's chamber. Obsidian couldn't be inside. Browser would have deliberately kept her outside for a time while he dressed. Had she run back to her own chamber?

Catkin walked five rooms down the line and ripped the leather hanging to one side. "Obsidian?"

Obsidian raised herself from her blankets and blinked into the faint light cast by the embers in the warming bowl. Tangled hair hung around her face. "What?" Her voice sounded sleepy.

Three other women, widows from Longtail village, slept in the same chamber with Obsidian. They lifted their heads, muttered something confused, and stared at Catkin.

Catkin whirled to look down at the stair-stepped roofs to her left, then beyond them into the plaza far below. What room had she ducked into? *Whose* room?

"Catkin?" Obsidian sounded disoriented. "What's wrong?"

A cold lump settled in her gut. "May I speak with you?"

Obsidian nodded and rose. She wore only a cotton tunic against the cold. Obsidian fumbled for a rabbit-hide blanket and wrapped it around her shoulders, before following Catkin out into the cold.

"Let's go to my chamber where we may speak in private."

They walked in silence, Catkin leading the way. She held the hanging to one side and gestured for Obsidian to go inside. She ducked through. Catkin followed her, studying the woman's face in the better light cast by her warming bowl. The fabric in Obsidian's shirt had been bunched under her smooth cheek; the impression of it could still be seen.

"Who is she?" Catkin asked. "The woman who was just here, pretending she was you."

Obsidian shifted her bare feet against the cold floor. "I don't understand."

"A woman, I would have sworn it was you, was just here. She wanted to know the War Chief's plans. Who is she?"

"I don't—"

"Gods *curse* you!" Catkin thrust her club under Obsidian's nose and shook it. "She looks exactly like you, but harder, something dangerous in her eyes. She was just in here, her hair washed, draped in turquoise.

You'll tell me, Obsidian, or I'll beat it out of you."

Obsidian swallowed hard. "Catkin, truly, I don't—"

Catkin's hand shot out and clamped around Obsidian's throat. She pushed the woman back against the plastered wall, tightening her grip as she leaned close to stare into those frightened eyes. "You do know, Obsidian. And you *will* tell me."

"Browser . . . knows!" Obsidian choked and squirmed in panic as Catkin tightened her grip.

Finally, gasping and slamming her fists into Catkin, she nodded, and croaked, "Let go!"

Catkin released her.

Obsidian slumped against the wall, coughing and rubbing her throat. Tears leaked down her cheek as she sucked in relieved breaths. "Must have been . . . Shadow."

Catkin straightened. Browser knew that Obsidian had a—a what? A twin sister? And didn't tell her!

Obsidian saw the look on Catkin's face and laughed, the sound hollow, mocking. "Be glad you thought she was me. She can sense things about people. If you'd reached for your club, she would have killed you."

Catkin *had* reached for her club. "Killed me? With what? One of her turquoise necklaces?"

Obsidian watched her through glistening eyes. "You're as good as dead and in her stew pot."

Catkin brought up her club and briefly considered smacking the woman with the handle to beat some respect into her. "Why did she come to me?"

"She can't go to Browser anymore. He knows." Obsidian closed her eyes and just breathed for several instants. "Take care, Catkin. Everything you think about her is wrong."

"Like what?"

Obsidian chuckled hoarsely. "Just like that night on the trail outside Aspen village. Do you know why she let you live? It was a simple convenience to her. She needed you to let Browser out of the kiva, that, and they didn't want to take a chance of alienating Browser before they could recruit him. If she'd murdered the woman Browser loves—"

"That's what Springbank meant when he asked Browser to join them." Catkin's throat tightened. "How do they plan to recruit him?"

A flash of anger lit Obsidian's eyes. "I don't know! I think Shadow believes she can bring Browser to her bed, and once he's there, he'll never leave."

"Then she's a fool."

"No, Catkin. She just doesn't know Browser, and that's the danger. If she really comes to know him, she will kill him."

"Why do you care what happens to Browser?"

Obsidian stared up at her. "If you knew what he is, who he is, you could answer that yourself."

Catkin's eyes narrowed. She did know. In her dreams, she still heard Two Hearts shouting, *"For the sake of the gods, Browser! We shouldn't be fighting! You are one of us. Join us and we will let your Made People friends live!"* Two Hearts was one of the First People. That meant Browser must be, as well, though he'd never told her so.

Catkin said, "You are one of the First People, aren't you, Obsidian? That's why you care about him? There are so few of you left. Why are you still here sullying yourself among the Made People. You could have run away with the White Moccasins."

Obsidian lowered her hands and let them dangle at her sides. "I have my reasons."

"Yes, I'm sure you do. Someone has to tell the White Moccasins what we're doing, where we're going, what our weaknesses are."

Obsidian looked physically ill. "Gods, it was bad enough when you came trouping into our village. I had to see him every day. Why do you think I spent so much time locked away in my room? Why do you think that no one suspected when *she* walked through the village dressed in *my* clothes?"

"He?"

Obsidian shook her head miserably. "If I tell you, I want your silence. If they find out, they'll kill me."

"Tell me what?"

She clenched her fists. "I can keep you alive, Catkin. Let me help you!"

"How can you help me?"

"I—I know things. I saw Shadow earlier today. Two Hearts told her to come to me. He wants me. He has ordered Shadow to bring me to him." She sank against the door frame and started shivering. But was it cold, or fear?

"Is that why you looked so frightened in the kiva this morning?"

"I know that you and Browser are going after him. What if . . . what if I could take you to him?"

Catkin stepped back and eyed the woman. "Why would you do that?"

"Because it might be the only way I can stay alive! If I don't go to him, he'll have me killed here, or wherever I run to. It won't matter. There's no place I can hide."

"Why would Two Hearts want to kill you? You're one of the First People. One of his own."

Obsidian wet her lips, and inhaled a halting breath. "He wants my heart, Catkin. Now do you understand?"

### Marriott Hotel, Albuquerque, New Mexico

From the window of his twenty-second-floor room, Dusty could see his office. The parking lot was empty, but less than eight hours ago, he'd been ten feet from Dale's murderer. Ten feet. He couldn't get that out of his mind.

He turned and the afternoon sunlight cast his shadow across Agent Nichols, where he sat at the table examining his notebook. The man's horn-rimmed glasses sat low on his nose, as though he needed to peer over them when he read.

The only time Dusty got to stay in hotels this nice was at professional meetings when they gave him the conference rate. Tonight the federal government was buying the room. Agent Nichols didn't want him loose to roam the streets. Which was probably a wise choice, given that Dusty kept swinging between murderous rage and a sincere longing to crawl into a hole and fall to pieces. A good imagination was crucial for a competent field archaeologist, and Dusty kept imagining how Dale felt as the drill cut into his scalp and skull. If he closed his eyes, he could feel the vibrations and pain buzzing through Dale's head. But how did he comprehend the actual horror of having that happen?

He ran a hand through his blond hair. He could see Dale's soft brown eyes looking at him over the years. Dusty had never told Dale that he loved him. It had been forbidden to speak of love in their male bond of an adoptive father-and-son relationship. Another of the odious bits of baggage he owed Ruth Ann Sullivan. When she left Samuel Stewart and sent him on the one-way road to the mental ward and the final desperate act of killing himself, she hadn't even said good-bye to Dusty. For years, his little boy brain had been certain she still loved him and would come back for him someday. When she hadn't, the word "love" became synonymous with "betrayal."

*I'll never be able to tell you, Dale, how lucky I was to have you for a father.*

When he looked up, Agent Nichols was watching him with a guarded expression.

The card with *el basilisco* on it had been FedExed to the FBI lab in Virginia. Technicians would be poring over it first thing in the morning.

"You really are going to stay here, right?" Nichols asked.

Dusty glanced at the door to Maureen's adjoining room. "Are you absolutely positive this is necessary?"

Nichols shrugged. "You tell me. You insist that you don't have a clue who this Wolf Witch is? Fine, maybe you don't. But maybe the Wolf Witch doesn't want to take that chance. Maybe he's waiting for you up in Santa Fe with his battery-operated drill."

"Gee, thanks. I'll sleep better knowing that."

"Good. I just want you to wake up alive. Look, if everything checks out, we'll get you out of here tomorrow. Okay?"

"Sure," Dusty said as he sat down in the opposite chair. "Nichols, I really need to know exactly where Dale's body was found. Can you tell me that?"

"Chaco Culture National—"

"I mean *where* in Chaco?"

"I don't know. Some ruins. Why? Is that important?"

Dusty replied, "It might be."

"Well, I could take the time to look that up, but I think it's more important to get our profilers to work on the murderer. We need to know what type of personality we're dealing with here."

Dusty shook his head. "You're thinking Western, Nichols. You have to think Indian. Dale went to the Casa Rinconada parking lot for a reason, and he was buried near that ruin—I suppose in one of the Small House sites—for a reason."

"What reason?"

"I won't have a clue until you tell me which site." Dusty crossed his arms over his aching chest. "Do you have a number for the site?"

"All right, I'll play along. According to the crime scene report Dr. Robertson was found in a site called Bc60. Does that mean anything to you?"

"One of the old UNM sites?" Dusty looked at Nichols, confused. "What was Dale doing up there? Nobody's touched those sites since 1942. Him going up there, that just doesn't make sense."

Nichols was still giving him that evaluative look. "Mr. Stewart, who is Dr. Robertson's beneficiary?"

Dusty looked at him blankly, trying to shift mental gears. "I have no idea. I guess I am. I think there's a will in his records. I know that Dale has a sister still living back East. They used to talk occasionally." He cocked his head quizzically. "It just never came up. Why?"

"Did he have insurance?"

"I think so, I remember . . . wait a minute. What's that supposed to mean?"

"Nothing. Just asking." Nichols lowered his voice. "You knew Dale better than anyone alive. Who could have hated him enough to do this to him? Think about it."

For no apparent reason, tears tightened Dusty's throat, and he hated it. He had to swallow hard before he could speak. "I *have* been thinking! Nobody hated Dale enough to do this."

"Prominent men generally have enemies, and Dr. Robertson was one of the most prominent men in his field."

Dusty just shook his head. "This isn't about academics, Agent Nichols. I've racked my brain but I can't come up with anyone in the field who'd murder Dale in this way. This is something else."

Nichols picked up his notebook and rose to his feet. "Please, don't leave the room without letting us know. Lock the door after I leave. I'm one door down. If anyone knocks on your door, even if you order room service"—he pointed to the phone—"you call me ASAP. You don't open that door until you see me through the peephole. Understand?"

"Right. Yeah."

Nichols gave him a cold stare. "The person who left the basilisk note on your Bronco knew you'd be there. He did that specifically to send you a message. You know why he did that?"

"Why?"

Nichols peered at him over his glasses. "He's thinking maybe you know who he is, and he wants you to know he can find you anytime he wants to. Get it?"

Dusty drummed his fingers on the tabletop. "I get it."

"Good," Nichols said softly. "Have a nice night." He closed the door behind him.

# CHAPTER 14

CATKIN CLUTCHED HER war club as she hurried across the third story toward Browser's chamber. Cold sheathed the crumbling walls and chilled the faces of the guards she had posted. Snow drifted down from the dark sky to whiten the world. She lifted a hand to Straighthorn, who stood at the northeast corner of Dusk House. He lifted a hand in return and cocked his head when a baby began to whimper somewhere in the distance. The sound wavered on the icy gusts of wind, rising and falling like flute music.

"Browser?" Catkin crouched beside the T-shaped doorway that led into his sleeping quarters. Wind Baby tugged at the gray blanket over her shoulders, leaching away her warmth.

"Catkin? Come. Have we overslept?"

"No. It's barely midnight."

She stepped into the chamber and hooked the leather door hanging over its peg. A reddish glow from the warming bowl painted the room, but most of the chamber remained pitch black.

"Where are you?" she asked. "I can't see you."

"Over here," his voice called from the right. "What's wrong?"

Catkin knelt just inside the doorway and waited for her eyes to adjust. When she could see him propped on one elbow in the rear of the chamber, she said, "Why didn't you tell me that Shadow was Obsidian's twin sister?"

Browser sat up and used one hand to comb tangled black hair from his eyes. "How do you know that?"

"I just had a visit from her."

In one fluid movement, Browser grabbed his war club, threw his blankets aside, and was on his feet. "When? How long ago?"

"Less than a finger of time. I've already checked with our guards. No one saw her."

Browser ducked out into the night, warily looking around. They both surveyed the empty plaza below. Several people must still be awake because soft crimson glows haloed a number of roof entries and doorways.

Browser turned to her. "Where did she go after she left your chamber?"

"I don't know. I immediately walked out after her, and she was gone."

Breathing hard, his eyes wide, Browser asked, "Why did she come to you?"

"She told me she knows we're not going to Streambed Town. She asked to go with us, and wanted to know when we were leaving. I wouldn't tell her, so she said she was going to ask you."

Browser fingered his club. "No one has come to my chamber except you. You're sure it was Shadow?"

Catkin nodded and propped her war club over her shoulder. "I thought she was Obsidian, which is who she pretended to be, so I went to Obsidian's chamber and woke her from a sound sleep. Obsidian told me."

Wind Baby played in the snow at the edge of the plaza, spinning around, kicking up white whirlwinds.

Browser walked to the edge of roof to look down. The Great North Road had filled with snow and created a blazing white line between them and Sunrise House, where the Mogollon stayed. Sounds of coughing and low conversation carried.

Catkin ground her teeth for a moment, then walked to his side. "You haven't answered my question."

Browser studied her through half-lidded eyes. "As to why I didn't tell you, I have my reasons."

"*Your reasons!* Your reasons have endangered my life . . . and that of other Katsinas' People."

"Just the opposite." He sounded so sure of himself. "Had she thought you had known her true identity, she would have killed you tonight, Catkin. I had hoped that by keeping the secret that she would be less wary. Those who are less wary make mistakes."

Catkin narrowed her eyes, remembering the sudden sense of danger she'd felt when Obsidian—Shadow— had reacted to her war club. Catkin rubbed the back of her neck to contain her discomfort, and said, "Perhaps you were right. But you should know that Obsidian— the real one—wants to come with us. She says she can lead us to Two Hearts."

"Why would she do that?"

"I am not certain, but she says if we don't take her, she'll be killed."

"By whom?"

Catkin lowered her war club to her side. "Apparently, Two Hearts is dying. He wants her heart."

Browser stared blindly at the ladder that led down to the ground. "Then I did wound him badly."

"I saw him slumped against the rock, holding his chest. You certainly broke his ribs. Perhaps one of the bone splinters punctured his heart, as well as his lung. Frothy blood pooled on his lips every time he coughed. I figured him for dead."

Browser folded his arms and shivered. "Blessed gods, Catkin. I have heard the old stories, that a witch uses a spindle to extract his relative's heart, then puts it into his own chest, but I—I don't think I ever really believed it."

"Obsidian believes it. She's terrified."

"Terrified enough that she would truly lead us to Two Hearts?"

Catkin expelled a breath. "I don't know. I don't think we should trust her, but if there is a chance that she could lead us to him—"

"Yes. We should take her with us, especially if . . ."

They both went silent when they saw a hunched little man with white hair emerge from the walls of Sunrise House and start across the Great North Road, headed toward them. His tattered turkey-feather cape flapped around his bony shoulders.

Catkin whispered, "What was your uncle doing in the Mogollon quarter at this time of night?"

"I don't know," Browser answered softly.

## Marriott Hotel, Albuquerque

Dusty toyed with the lasagna on his plate. It had seemed like a good idea when he'd seen it on the room service menu. Sometime between his order and the arrival of the food, his appetite had vanished.

Maureen wasn't doing any better. She had nibbled a couple of forks full of salad and picked at a cheeseburger now for nearly an hour. She had showered and dressed in blue jeans and a black turtleneck. Her hair hung down her back in a long braid.

Dusty put his fork down and stared around the confined room. "I don't know what I'm doing here."

"You're staying safe, that's what."

"I know, but I should be out there, trying to figure out what happened. I can hear Dale in the back of my head, saying, 'William,' in that gruff voice, 'what are you doing? There are things to be done!' "

Maureen smiled. "The first time I met Dale he scared

me. I mean, my God, here I was, an insecure graduate student and the great Dr. Robertson handed me a box of bones to go through and catalog. I opened the box and there was most of a skeleton in it, the dirt still sticking to the bones. I looked up and said, 'How do you want me to do this, Dr. Robertson?' Dale answered, 'Why, perfectly, Maureen. How else would you do it?' "

Dusty smiled. "I've seen him do that to a lot of students. He wanted to know immediately if a student would fold, or have the guts to stand up to him."

They were silent for a while, each lost in grief.

Maureen asked, "Do you really think it was the Tsegi Canyon witch?"

Dusty rubbed his tired face. The high-pitched scream of a drill was vibrating through his imagination. What had it felt like as that keen bit cut into living bone? How did a man feel when someone placed a tube against his quivering brain and began to suck his soul out? "I don't know, Maureen. How in the hell will we ever find out if we're stuck here with . . ." He straightened.

"What?"

"Dale's files." He met Maureen's dark eyes. "Everything's in there. Dale's entire life. If he actually knew his murderer, I wager the guy's in those files somewhere."

"Tomorrow," Maureen promised. "After they let us out of here, we'll start at the beginning and work our way through every page."

As HE WALKED, Browser sniffed the west wind blowing down from the high country. The scents of wood smoke and frozen earth seemed to hang in the still air. It had just started to snow again, and tiny flakes tapped his cheeks.

Muffled figures lined out behind him. Catkin followed with a spring in her long legs. Stone Ghost walked beside Obsidian, and Jackrabbit and Straighthorn brought up the rear. Their moccasined feet whispered on the fresh snow as they entered the gap in the wall and headed diagonally toward the Great North Road. Browser followed it south, across the terraces and down to the river. As they neared the water, Browser slowed. The bank would be slick and treacherous, especially for Stone Ghost.

"Nephew?" Stone Ghost called from behind. "May we wait here a moment."

Browser turned, peering back into the predawn darkness. "Of course, Uncle. Let me help you." He started back.

"No, I'm fine, Nephew. I'm not certain, but I hope that we—"

"Hello!" an accented voice called from the darkness, and nine shadowy figures rose from the riverbank.

Browser cried, "Get down!" and swung his war club over his head, ready to charge.

Stone Ghost grabbed his arm. "Wait, Nephew! These are not enemies. They come as friends."

Breathing hard, prepared for battle, Browser looked at him dumbly. "Friends? Who are they?"

To his left, he saw Catkin silently move away, ready to flank the small party that approached.

"Uncle?" Browser repeated.

"It's the Mogollon," Stone Ghost said. "Forgive me for not telling you sooner, Nephew, but their elder, White Cone, asked me not to. He feared that if anyone else knew, they would be murdered in their sleep, as their prophet was."

Browser still did not relax. "Why are they here?"

"They have elected to accompany us to the south.

They have no more reason to stay here—and plenty to join us."

As the Mogollon appeared out of the darkness, Stone Ghost stepped forward and clasped the white-haired elder's hand. "You are welcome among us, White Cone. But time is short. Come, let us be off."

"The sooner the better," White Cone agreed. "I doubt Matron Blue Corn will be pleased by the hole we cut in her south wall. Wrath seems to be her constant companion."

"Nephew," Stone Ghost turned to Browser, "let us proceed."

Browser gripped his uncle by the arm, as though helping him down the steep bank, and leaned close enough to whisper, "I thought this journey was a secret. How many others have you invited to join us?"

Stone Ghost patted Browser's hand. "No more than necessary."

Browser stopped at the edge of the water and motioned to Catkin. "Take Straighthorn and scout the opposite bank. Let me know if it is safe."

She nodded and trotted toward Straighthorn. Once they entered the water, they became almost invisible.

Browser surveyed the Mogollon. They stood five paces behind him, speaking softly to each other. Their elder, White Cone, watched Catkin and Straighthorn like a hawk with fat mice in sight.

Curious. Yesterday, he'd looked like a slave. Today, though sadness strained his features, he had an air of command. He stood tall and straight, and wary.

The familiar cry of the flicker, *kee-ar kee-ar*, came from the opposite bank, and Browser lifted his hand to get everyone's attention. "My warriors say the other side is safe, but let's go over a few people at a time, just in case they're wrong. Elder White Cone, perhaps you would like to select five people and lead the way."

"Yes, War Chief," he answered, and pointed to the five people closest to him.

They crossed without a sound.

Browser said, "Obsidian and Jackrabbit, I would be grateful if you would take my uncle and go next."

Jackrabbit trotted up to Stone Ghost. "Elder, please, let me help you." He took Stone Ghost's right arm and started across, followed by Obsidian. This time of the sun cycle, just before winter deepened, the river rose to about knee deep, but the current could be swift and unpredictable.

As the Cloud People shifted, Browser saw them bobbing against the faintly silvered surface of the water; then they stepped out onto the opposite bank and Jackrabbit waved.

Browser turned and scanned the remaining three Mogollon warriors. He removed his moccasins and gestured for them to follow him.

They had topped the silty gray uplands south of Flowing Waters Town by the time the sun began to brighten the clouds. In the faint light, Browser glanced back to the blocky buildings of Dusk and Sunrise houses. Above them, higher on the terraces, North Town and the smaller villages squatted like black blocks. The first morning fires glittered.

"May the katsinas be with us," Browser whispered.

Catkin, he noticed, walked at Obsidian's side. She kept glancing at Obsidian, as if she knew the woman had betrayed them. Obsidian refused to meet her eyes. She walked with her head down, and the jewels in her hair glittered as though aflame.

Browser led them over the crest of the hill and into the uplands that divided the Flowing Waters drainage from the Squash Blossom River. As his party stopped to catch their breath, he went over to Obsidian. She wore a long black cloak with the hood pulled up, and the spicy scent of blazing star petals surrounded her like a strange mist.

"Walk with me," he said.

"Of course."

When he was certain they could not be overheard, he said, "You're sure this is the way?"

"Yes, south along the Great North Road."

She looked back wistfully. She, too, had lost everything. Her entire past—all that she had ever been—lay behind her. The future, what little of it might remain, awaited her at the end of this same road. As though she felt his hard gaze on her, she tucked a stray tendril of long hair behind her ear and let her cloak fall open to reveal her red dress and half-bared breasts. Necklaces of turquoise and coral beads flashed around her throat.

"It is time to tell me where we are going, Obsidian."

"Just follow the road south."

"South to where?"

Her delicate brows slanted down, accenting the dark beauty of her face. "Browser, if I tell you, you will no longer have a reason to keep me alive."

"But I will, Obsidian, if I can. No matter what is behind us, I give you my word."

She seemed to be thinking this over as her eyes examined his face. "Forgive me, I can trust no one, Browser. I must keep my knowledge until I am no longer at risk."

"You will be at risk until Two Hearts is dead. I cannot kill him until I know where he is. When will you tell me?"

"When I decide to, and not a moment before."

He stared at the frozen grass a moment, then nodded. "As you wish."

Jackrabbit stood at the edge of the group with Straighthorn.

"Jackrabbit," Browser called, "I want you to remain here for one half-hand of time. Make sure we're not being followed; then catch up."

"Yes, War Chief."

Browser waved to the group and headed down the incline at a slow trot. He didn't wish to exhaust Stone

Ghost and White Cone, but they had to keep moving.

Stone Ghost caught up with Browser and trotted at his side.

"Uncle, it won't take Shadow long to figure this out. We are gone. The Mogollon are gone. Obsidian is missing. She will know what we're about."

Stone Ghost panted, "But perhaps we have gained just enough time that we can catch her off guard."

"What of the Mogollon, Uncle?" He lowered his voice. "Why are they here?"

"For the most disagreeable of reasons." Stone Ghost lowered his eyes to watch his feet.

"Which is?"

"They are bait, Nephew."

## Kachina Street, Albuquerque

Maureen arched her back where she sat on Dale's office floor, a stack of folders piled to either side of her. She felt as if she were invading his personal space, and the monumental task of going through his records was just beginning to dawn on her. They'd been at this for four hours already, and barely made it through the first file drawer. Everything had to be read, and Dale had added notes in the margins over the years, correcting his early observations and interpretations of the archaeology based on later discoveries. More important still, he had mentioned people in the scrawled notations. Which left them wondering, if a witch were mentioned, how would they know?

Dusty sat at the desk with his elbows propped on two separate files. He stroked his beard thoughtfully as he read. "I can't believe Dale saved all this. I mean, look here. This is his first undergraduate paper at Harvard. Twenty pages on the history of Ramses II for Intro to Western Civilization."

"You know, there's a Ph.D. dissertation in these old reports," she said, closing another of the files. "It's like an education in anthropological theory. I just finished a critique on why Piltdown had to be real."

"That's the great hoax, right?"

"Correct, Dawson's 'Dawn Man' who turned out to have a thirteen-thousand-year-old skull atop a well-filed orangutan jawbone. It was debunked in the late fifties."

Dusty pulled open the next file and frowned at the papers. "I think these are his lecture notes from a class. Should I can them?"

"Better not." Maureen shook her head.

"You're right." Dusty flipped through them, scanning page after page.

Maureen opened another file and started down the page. This was a collection of field notes from an excavation in Maryland. She passed through a series of level records from a shell midden test pit dug in the fifties, and stopped short. "Dusty?"

"What did you find?"

"Listen to this: 'June seventh, 1957. Accokeek 3-A. Dr. Mason assigned a new girl to work with us today. Her name's Ruth Sullivan. What a dish! Blond, blue-eyed, a sailor would have pinned her picture to a locker and never looked twice at Marlene Dietrich.' "

Dusty reached for the folder and Maureen watched his forehead line as he read the entry. "Dale knew her before my father did?"

"I haven't seen a reference to Samuel yet." She picked up another of the folders. "What did Dale tell you?"

"Not much. He always said things like, 'When I first met your father,' or 'When your father and I were young.' You know, nothing really specific." He riffled through the notes . . . and abruptly stopped, his eyes glued to a page.

"What's wrong?" Maureen asked.

"Nothing, it's just . . . this is my mother's handwriting."

"You know her handwriting?"

His gaze remained on the page, but the lines around his mouth tightened. "When I was a boy, she used to write me letters. You know, when she was away working on a site. I read them over and over. I kept every one until my father committed suicide. Then I shoved them in Dale's barbecue and burned them."

Maureen shuffled through the mess of papers in front of her, as though organizing them. "What was she writing about?"

"On page thirty-seven, she started taking the field notes." He scowled. "Not much in her report, either. Just more cooked clam shells."

Maureen finished the last of the folders and began stacking them, thankful for the opportunity to stand up and circulate blood to her legs. Dusty was staring absently at the file, lost in thought.

"Did you ever try and contact her?" Maureen asked casually as she refiled the folders.

"No," he said through a taut exhalation and shrugged.

Maureen pulled open the next drawer and found another stack of manila folders, each packed with pages. Out of curiosity she closed it and opened another, and another of the drawers, just to get an idea of the amount of material they were going to have to sift through.

The bottom drawer defied her. "Dusty? This one's locked."

He looked up from the Accokeek file. "Locked? I didn't know any of them were locked."

She tugged at the drawer, but it wouldn't open. "Definitely locked. Have you even seen what's in here?"

Dusty shook his head. "No. These are Dale's personal files." He pointed down the line of file cabinets to a newer model. "I filed stuff, sure, but over there. You know, reports from the eighties and nineties."

"Where would he have left the key?"

Dusty thought for a moment, then pulled open the

desk drawer and rummaged through pencils, pens, note cards, isolated artifacts without provenience, and knickknacks. "No key here." He shoved out of his chair. "Wait. Come on."

He led the way down the hallway to Dale's bedroom. Maureen shot a sad glance at the rumpled bed, partially made, awaiting the return of a man who would never sleep there again. Had Dale known when he left for Chaco that everything was about to end? Did he have the slightest hint that he would never return to this bed?

Dusty stopped before the dresser and lifted down a little black-on-white Tusayan style pot from a high shelf. It rattled as he upended it on the dresser and spilled out the contents: coins, a couple of bullets, buttons, several perforated pottery disks, and a ring of keys. Dusty swept the rest into his palm and poured it back into the pot. "It might be here," he told Maureen, lifting the key ring.

She followed him back to the office and watched as Dusty tried each key, with no luck.

"Next idea?" she asked, studying the file drawer.

"Be right back," he said and trotted out of the room. She heard the front door slam. In less than a minute, Dusty returned carrying a polaski, a sort of pickax archaeologists used for digging in cemented soil.

"A bit of overkill, don't you think?"

He grinned. "Dale wouldn't approve, Doctor, but one of the rules of archaeology is to use the tool appropriate to the task. You don't use dental picks to remove several meters of overburden."

She backed up. She had to hand it to Dusty. His years of training stood him in good stead. Within three whacks, he had the door sprung. He laid the pickax to one side and bent down. She watched as his back muscles tensed, biceps swelling under his tanned skin. The buckled drawer screeched and gave, sliding open to the light.

She leaned forward to look over his shoulder. A line

of bound books were stacked in a neat row, spine up.
Each had a date pressed in the spine with gold leaf.
"What are they?"

Dusty pulled out the one marked "1976" and opened
it to the first page, reading: "God, what a hangover.
Arrived early for the Society for Historical Archaeology meetings and ended up partying with the people
from the Anthro dept at Missouri. What a bunch of
animals. These kids! Where did they learn to drink like
that? I will try to work on my paper for the Colonial
New Mexico session—and avoid the 'Missouri Mafia'
for the rest of the conference."

Dusty looked up. "Maureen, these are his diaries."

"I didn't know he kept diaries."

"Yeah. He said they made him think better." Dusty
stroked his beard thoughtfully. "He told me once that
it was his way of talking to himself. God, I was never
ever supposed to so much as touch them."

Dusty reached for the latest, marked "2001," and
was in the process of pulling it out when the phone
rang. He rose, the diary in hand. "Want to get that?"

She walked out into the hallway and picked up the
phone before the answering machine could get it. "Dr.
Robertson's. May I help you?"

*"Yes, is Dale there, please?"*

"No, he's not." Maureen caught herself before she
could gasp. She knew that voice, had heard it each time
Dusty had replayed the answering machine for her and
the FBI. The faintly New England accent, the perfectly
articulated words.

*"Could you tell me where I could reach him?"*

"Excuse me, but who is this?"

Maureen could hear the hesitation on the other end
of the line. *"I'm an old friend and colleague of his."*

"Your *name* please," Maureen added with emphasis.

The woman hung up.

Maureen was staring at the telephone, her stomach
churning, when she heard a car pull into the driveway.

Preoccupied, she crossed to the front door in time to admit FBI agent Sam Nichols, who carried several folded newspapers under his left arm. He studied her with his good eye, noting her expression. "Something wrong, Dr. Cole?"

"We just had a phone call. I think it was the same woman on Dale's answering machine."

Nichols paused thoughtfully, then looked up to nod at Dusty as he emerged from the hallway with one of the diaries in his hands.

"Agent Nichols," Dusty greeted. "What can we do for you?"

Nichols removed the folded newspapers from beneath his left arm and flipped the first one open. He tapped an underlined section. "Did you know about this?"

"What?" Dusty's brows lowered as he read.

Maureen walked over to Dusty's side. It was a copy of *Anthropology News*, the newsletter of the American Anthropological Association. Maureen knew the publication, but rarely read it.

Dusty closed the paper, handed it to Maureen, and stepped away. He ran a hand through his blond hair. He didn't say anything for a while. Finally, he turned to Nichols. "No, I—I didn't know about it."

Nichols's square jaw moved as though he were grinding his teeth, trying to decide whether or not to arrest Dusty. "I came over to tell you that we chased down the phone records for Dr. Robertson's house and for your office. The one hangup was from a pay phone out at the airport." He glanced back and forth between Dusty and Maureen.

"And the others?" Maureen asked.

"It's time you told me everything you know about Carter Hawsworth."

Nichols tapped the paper in Maureen's hand, and she shot a quick look to see if Dusty was about to self-destruct. He looked unnaturally pale.

"What about Hawsworth?" Maureen asked, quickly thumbing through the pages.

Nichols shifted to look at her. "Who is he? How did he know Dr. Robertson?"

Dusty leaned a shoulder against the door frame. "My mother ran off with Hawsworth when I was six. Hawsworth was a colleague of Dale's."

Nichols peered at Dusty over his glasses and his black hair shone in the light. "You didn't know *anything* about this squabble? Robertson *never* mentioned it?"

"No. I swear."

Maureen found the section Nichols had underlined. She folded the newsletter back and read, *"Dr. Robertson's article about cannibalism and witchcraft in the Southwest contains just the sort of ignorant allegations that make witches cast lethal spells. Perhaps that's what it will take to force such 'scholars' to realize the impact their blind assertions have on living peoples. I, for one, plan to contact every witch I know and beg them to 'witch' him. He deserves our professional disdain as well as . . ."*

Maureen lowered the newsletter and stared at the rug. "That's Carter Hawsworth's voice on the answering machine, isn't it?"

"Correct, Dr. Cole," Nichols replied. "He's the man with the English accent."

# CHAPTER 15

DUSTY PLACED THE diary on the couch beside him and nervously rubbed his hands together. Maureen had gone to the kitchen for a freshly brewed cup of coffee, and now stood, one hip propped against the arched entry to the dining room. Her long braid hung down over her right shoulder, and she had a worried expression, as though she expected the world to end in the next few minutes.

Agent Nichols, who sat at the opposite end of the couch, opened his notebook and adjusted his glasses.

"How is it possible that you didn't know about this academic squabble? Isn't this the biggest anthropological organization in the world?" He pointed to the AAA newsletter.

Dusty shrugged. "Maybe. I don't belong to it. I'm an archaeologist. I belong to the Society for American Archaeology. There are dozens of anthropological associations, Nichols. No one can afford to belong to all of them, or read all of the publications they produce."

Nichols jotted something down, then said, "I want to know everything you remember about Carter Hawsworth."

"I barely remember him at all," Dusty said. "Just the way he talked. That English accent was unusual in the Southwest back then. Especially in the professional community. In that day and age most English anthropologists went to Africa."

"You said he ran off with your mother?" Nichols asked.

Dusty nodded. "In the sixties. I was just a kid. Hawsworth was studying social structure at Zuni. Mom had worked there. She offered to introduce him to some of the elders and the influential people. At the time, Dad was up in Blanding, Utah, doing some kind of salvage work on a site that was going to be bulldozed by the Utah highway department."

Dusty paused. "I knew something was wrong. I heard a man's voice one night and thought it was Dad, home early."

"But it was Hawsworth?" Nichols asked.

Dusty nodded.

Nichols studied him, clearly aware of Dusty's sudden discomfort. "Stewart, I need to know whatever you do. Anything you can remember, or have heard over the years, might be helpful to this investigation. So far as we have determined, Robertson and Hawsworth had been writing bitter rebuttals to each other's articles for over a year, but they had no direct contact prior to three days ago. If you know something, no matter how trivial, I need to hear it."

Dusty took a deep breath. "Well, it's ugly stuff. It was late one night. The bedroom door to my folks' room didn't close all the way. The foundation had shifted and the door didn't latch. I stopped short when I heard that English accent. I knew it wasn't Dad, so I didn't push the door open. I just stood outside."

He hadn't thought it would be this hard to talk about it, but here he was, a grown man, blushing like he had when he'd been six years old. "I looked through the door slit and saw my mother. She was standing by the bed, her shirt off, and this man was . . . well, I ran away when he tossed her on the bed and crawled on top of her."

Maureen's eyes tightened.

"Did you ever tell anyone?" Nichols asked. "Your father? A teacher? Some friend?"

Dusty shook his head. "Not even Dale. But I think Dad knew. Maybe he could see it in my eyes. Maybe she told him. I remember them fighting the day she left. She told him she wanted a man in her life, not a boy."

Nichols scribbled notes. "Thanks. It's probably nothing, but it might be."

Dusty nodded. "Sure."

How strange that telling someone about it gave him an odd sense of relief.

Nichols stood. "There's one other thing. This probably isn't the time to tell you, but . . ."

When he hesitated, Dusty said, "What is it?"

Nichols tucked his notebook into his jacket pocket and gestured awkwardly with his hand. "The woman on Dr. Robertson's answering machine is your mother, Ruth Ann Sullivan, the famous Harvard anthropologist and author."

Dusty froze.

Nichols held up a hand. "Or at least someone placed several calls from her home in Boston to the phone on that table." He pointed to Dale's phone.

Dusty turned to look. "Why would she call Dale? After all these years? It doesn't make any sense."

Dusty remembered the tone in her voice, first angry, thinking Dale was playing some trick on her, then frightened. His gut twisted. What was going on here?

Nichols looked at Maureen. "You're sure the woman who called today was the same woman who called earlier?"

Maureen clutched her coffee cup in both hands. "It was the same New England accent, mature, educated. I'd bet it was the same woman."

For some unknown reason, Dusty had butterflies in his stomach. What was it about the past? Why did it keep creeping out of the hidden places in his mind where he'd buried it, and what, if anything, did it have to do with Dale's murder?

"Is there anything else you want me to know about Hawsworth?" Nichols asked.

Dusty paced to the window and looked out at the street beyond. Two children in matching red stocking caps ran by. Winter had claimed the trees, leaving them bare and gray.

Dusty said, "Hawsworth and Sullivan were together for a while in the South Pacific. I've heard it was a nasty split. Lots of acrimony. He went back to England. I've seen his name every now and then in the journals but could never make myself read the articles. I guess he's still in England."

Nichols paused for a moment. "To your knowledge—with the exception of recent phone calls—he's never tried to contact Dr. Robertson?"

"If he did, Dale never told me." He cocked his head. "I guess you'll have to ask Hawsworth."

Nichols shoved his hands in his pockets. "He's not home."

"What do you mean?" Maureen asked. "You checked his place in London?"

"He leased his London home to his cousin, Georgia Swanson. She told me that Dr. Hawsworth has spent the last several years studying Navajo witchcraft. Right here in New Mexico. But he has no address here."

Dusty peered at Nichols with hard unblinking eyes. "That's impossible. I know every anthropologist working on the Navajo reservation."

Nichols nodded. "I'm sure you do. Mrs. Swanson said he'd sworn her to secrecy. Apparently his work here is personal, not professional."

"Then why did she tell you?" Maureen asked.

Nichols's eyebrows lifted. "I'm the FBI. That scares people in foreign countries. Besides, I told her I was worried about his safety."

Dusty massaged his forehead. "Hawsworth's study of witchcraft is personal, not professional? I don't like the sound of that."

His memory replayed Hawsworth's angry voice on the phone: *"Dale, you son of a bitch! I didn't think even you could sink this low."* Then he heard his mother's voice, high and strained: *"I'm not kidding. Stop it, Dale!"* Both sounded like people who were afraid they were being witched. By Dale? What had happened to frighten them so much?

Dusty folded his arms. Was it possible that after Hawsworth's last rebuttal in the AAA newsletter, Dale had decided to turn the tables on Hawsworth? That he had, as a joke, "witched" Hawsworth, and Hawsworth had taken it seriously?

Dusty looked up. "Have you contacted my mother?"

Nichols smiled, but it was a grim expression. "I will as soon as I can find her."

MATRON BLUE CORN awoke to the sounds of shouts in the plaza below. She jerked upright on her sleeping pallet, tossed her warm blanket to one side, and clawed for her tunic.

Shoving her feet into her sandals, she tore her macaw-feather cloak from its peg and whipped it around her shoulders as she ducked past the door hanging into the cold morning.

The first tentative glow of dawn shimmered on the foothills east of the river. She could see her warriors milling before the Fire Dogs' room block, passing in and out of the doorways, cursing, swinging their war clubs in frustration.

"What is happening?" she shouted above the din. "Are we being attacked?"

People rushed out of their rooms in various states of dress. Most were shouting, weapons clasped in their hands.

Rain Crow glanced up from the knot of warriors who had formed around him in the plaza. He waved for silence and called, "The Fire Dogs, Matron. They are gone! They slipped away in the night!"

She shouted, "Where were the guards? I ordered them watched at all times!"

Rain Crow answered, "The Fire Dogs cut a hole in the wall and escaped out the back. For all we know, they have been gone since nightfall. They could be anywhere. Perhaps perpetrating some outrage on one of the outlying towns."

Blue Corn gripped her cape. What a fool she had

been. Of course they'd run. Their young prophet had been murdered, his body mutilated. She, too, would have slipped away at first chance.

Below her, warriors gathered around Rain Crow. All looked up, waiting for her orders. "Very well, send out our best trackers. Find out where they went. Meanwhile, send for Matron Cloudblower and that old fool, Stone Ghost. As soon as we discover where the Fire Dogs have gone we can decide what to do."

"Where do you think they've gone?" a man asked from behind her.

Blue Corn turned to look at the skinny old man who leaned against the wall. His dark face might have been rawhide left in the sun for too many seasons. The crisscrossing wrinkles wrapped a fleshy nose and a brown slit of a mouth, but he had sharp eyes, and considerable spring to his step as he came toward her. A flowing cloak made of winter-white weasel hide hung down to his waist. His gray locks had been drawn into a tight bun at the back of his head.

"Pigeontail?" she said. "No one told me you were here."

The old Trader stopped before her, his head cocked. "No, great Matron. You seem to have had your hands full of other concerns. I arrived yesterday, too late for all the excitement. But I have heard such tales since I have been here! Fire Dogs! A prophet talking of Poor Singer and Sternlight! Murder! Mutilation! And no idea who the culprit might be! Now what is this, the Fire Dogs, whom I traveled so far to see, have escaped?"

She studied him. Something about his eyes, a lighter brown than she had ever seen before, had always bothered her. "You came here to see the Fire Dogs?" Her voice dripped skepticism.

He shrugged, smiling disarmingly. "It would have saved me a trip far to the south. They could have carried the weight for me. I have pottery, precious stones, superbly tanned hides of elk and buffalo. Things the Fire Dogs could use in the south."

"I'm sure." She looked down as Rain Crow sent his scouts out to cut for tracks. "Isn't it amazing that you are always in the right place to take advantage of the unusual?"

"The Flute Player has always favored me," he replied. "Or perhaps it is the times, Matron. One cannot go anywhere these days without seeing and hearing the unusual. Just last night one of your people told me that the First People are not dead, and that their dreaded warriors, the White Moccasins, walk among us."

"Did you believe it? Have you seen these White Moccasins with your own eyes?" A tightness seized her throat, almost choking her speech.

His odd sandy eyes fixed on hers, and he lowered his voice to a whisper. "Yes. In fact, I came to warn you that they are hunting Made People for their stew pots and cooking fires, eating them as if they were deer or turkeys. Beware."

Her spine prickled, but she said, "I have no time for such silly tales."

She stepped onto the ladder, careful of the white coating of hoarfrost, and started down to the ground to talk to Rain Crow. As she climbed down, Old Pigeontail called, "Indeed, Matron, you have more important matters to attend to. The Rainbow Serpent might be sleeping, but her dreams still shake the four corners of the world."

"Doddering old fool," she said under her breath. What did he know of slumbering serpents? He should try walking in her sandals for a while.

When she stepped to the ground, she looked up and met his eyes. All it would take would be a word whispered in the right ear, and the old man could be dealt with, once and for all. She—

*"Gods! Help me! Help!"*

Blue Corn whirled, looking toward the last of the

low rooms where the Fire Dogs had quartered. "What is it?"

An ashen-faced boy burst from the doorway. Blood—appearing black in the filtered morning light—splotched his hands. "I fell on him!" the boy, a lad of no more than ten summers, screamed. "I fell over him! He's all wet with blood!"

Rain Crow pushed past and stepped into the dark room. Blue Corn hurried after him. She blinked, seeing the darker figure of a man sprawled on the dirt floor. "Bring us a torch! We need light in here!"

Blue Corn reached down to touch the icy blood that had leaked from the body.

Rain Crow felt the victim's face. "The body is cold. This happened some time ago."

Dancing yellow light preceded the torchbearer as he leaned into the doorway. Blue Corn stared into the terror-fixed eyes of the dead. "White Spark," she said. "Wasn't he—?"

"Yes," Rain Crow said. "He was the guard who watched the Fire Dogs last night."

Rain Crow stood, his blocky body bulging muscles. Rage twisted his crooked face. "It seems that now we have an explanation for the haste of their departure." His hands knotted to fists. "He is my sister's son, Matron. A member of my clan."

She straightened up, but her eyes remained on the dead youth. "Then I will leave it to you to make sure his killer pays for this."

BROWSER SAT ON a crumbling stone wall overlooking the ruins of Northern Town. He'd called a brief halt, and for their part, his small band had taken advantage of it. They sat or reclined, taking the moment to sip from their canteens, eat, and rest. Uncle Stone Ghost lay flat on his back on his gray blanket, snoring softly.

Browser's gaze drifted to the right and he studied the charred ruins of Northern Town. The First People had built this place as the northern boundary of their empire. That was before the construction of Flowing Waters Town, before the abandonment of Straight Path Canyon. Made People had reoccupied the place but twenty sun cycles past. Some had been believers in the katsinas. Then, earlier this cycle, all had been killed. Massacred. Rumors blamed Flute Player warriors. It was said that here, too, the children had been herded onto the tower kiva roof, and the town set ablaze.

Did the bodies of children lie down there? Charred and lonely like those they had left behind at Longtail village?

He tried to shake off the feeling of doom, but couldn't take his gaze from the dead town. The roofs had fallen in to expose soot-blackened walls. A reddish tinge of oxidation could be seen around the tower kiva at the spine of the E-shaped building. Several human skeletons lay in the plaza. Their tattered, sun-faded clothing flapped as Wind Baby played among the whitening bones. The flesh was long gone to the crows, coyotes, and insects.

How far had his people fallen that they could leave their dead unburied? What had happened to the last of these people's families? Had their relatives fled in such terror that they dared not return to care for their kin? Without the proper rituals, the soul was condemned to wander the earth forever, homeless and alone, always searching for loved ones it could never find.

Browser feared that would happen to him, as did most warriors who fought lonely battles far from home.

Beyond the silent wreckage of the town lay the brown waters of the Squash Blossom River. Riffles washed the muddy banks and curled around the winter-bare willows. Tan sandstone terraces cast shadows across the far floodplain. Only the buttes and stone pillars on the heights gleamed in the slanted sunlight.

Catkin climbed up beside Browser and handed him a corn cake. Browser took it and smiled his thanks.

"We made good time," she told him, and gazed at the burned town below. A faint moan rose from the wind echoing in the roofless rooms.

"We did," Browser agreed around a mouthful. "Especially considering the ages of Uncle Stone Ghost and that old Mogollon, White Cone. Even Obsidian is moving well."

"She's motivated," Catkin said. "Every time she starts to lag, I remind her of witches' spindles and skewered hearts."

Browser smothered a smile. Westward, Jackrabbit ran through an abandoned cornfield, checking to see that no one hid amid the old stalks. "It must be hard, knowing that a witch wishes to cut your heart out of your body."

A stone's throw away, Obsidian leaned back on a blanket, her beautiful face to the sun. Gleaming black hair spilled down her arms. Browser studied the woman, aware of how that posture stretched her light blue dress against her full breasts.

"I wouldn't be thinking of her beauty, if I were you." Catkin pointed to the dead who lay unburied in the plaza below them. "We don't want to end up like that."

"No." Browser squinted against the sun, turning his thoughts from Obsidian's voluptuous body to Catkin's oval face with its turned-up nose. Her dark eyes had a gleam. "Do you really think I'm so foolish?"

She took another bite of her corn cake and, as she ate it, said, "Yes."

Browser finished his cake and dusted his hands off on his leather pants. "Your confidence in me has always been a comfort, Catkin."

She continued gazing down at Obsidian. "I have

been thinking about what happened at Flowing Waters Town. About the prophet's death."

"Have you come to any conclusions?"

"Just one. I fear that whoever murdered the prophet did so with help from inside Flowing Waters Town."

Browser lifted a shoulder. "It's possible, though I doubt Matron Blue Corn knew about it."

"Why do you say that?" Catkin pulled up one of her long legs and squinted at him.

"It would be too risky. If the Fire Dogs found out, they would destroy her village and kill every member of her clan." Browser frowned at the gutted ruins below. A charred beam swung in the wind, creaking and groaning.

"Well, perhaps you are right that Blue Corn wasn't involved, but there are others in whom she places her trust. How else could the murderer sneak in, kill the guard, and then mutilate the prophet? Blue Corn had guards posted to watch the Mogollon. Yet, no one heard anything? No one saw anything?"

"It strikes me as even more odd that the Mogollon only posted two guards to protect their prophet," Browser said. "What could White Cone have been thinking?"

Catkin pulled her canteen from her shoulder and sipped at the cold water. "Obviously he wasn't thinking."

She wiped her mouth with the back of her hand and gave the canteen to Browser. "I have considered the possibility that Rain Crow was the traitor inside the walls."

"Why?"

She turned to the sandstone bluffs beyond the river and carefully scanned the tumbled boulders, the shadowed cracks, and the patches of brush. "He seems like a weak man to me, easily seduced."

The way she said the last word, and the fact that her gaze remained on Obsidian, made Browser sit up straighter. "You think he was seduced and, in exchange, he let the murderer in to kill the prophet?"

"I think it likely. Men are frail creatures, Browser."

Browser sipped from the canteen. He didn't wish to respond to that statement, mostly because he feared it was true. "But I would think the frog-faced elder a more likely traitor. I never heard his name, but he seemed to have Blue Corn's ear. Either of them could have ordered the guard away. It would have given the killer plenty of time."

"Especially if the killer was a woman." Her eyes narrowed as she gazed at Obsidian.

Browser looked, too. No man alive could resist looking at a woman like Obsidian. An aura of sexuality floated around her the way mist did a steaming body on a winter morning.

"You think Obsidian killed the Mogollon prophet?"

"No. I saw her face in the kiva afterward. She didn't look like a woman who had just committed murder. No, I think . . ." She absently sloshed her canteen, checking how much water remained. "I think her sister killed him. I think that after she finished with Rain Crow, she walked right up to the Mogollon guard, and her smile enchanted him the way a snake does a bird. Then she struck."

Browser dusted the blue corn crumbs from the hem of his war shirt. He didn't like this line of thought, but it had to be considered. "Then it is also possible that Rain Crow, or whoever the traitor is, is allied with the White Moccasins. In which case, they will certainly wish to stop us."

"You mean kill us. Well . . ." She paused, and rephrased her words. "They may not wish to kill you, Stone Ghost, or Obsidian, but the rest of us will not be so lucky."

Browser bowed his head and grimaced at the crumbling wall. He'd been meaning to discuss it with her. After all, she'd been in the cave when Two Hearts had

shouted that Browser had the blood of the First People
running in his veins. She wasn't a fool. She must have
known what it meant the instant the old witch said it.
"I should have told you myself, but I didn't know for
certain until Uncle Stone Ghost told me."

Catkin shrugged. "I'm not the only one worried
about hidden First People. You realize that, don't
you?"

He looked down at the Mogollon warriors and
heaved a sigh. "Yes. I have been worried about it for
some time."

"Good."

He brushed at his long shirt again. "Catkin, thank
you, for all you have done for me over the last sun
cycle. I have been a poor War Chief. Without you, I
would have made even more mistakes than I did."

Her eyes softened, and she gave him that calm af-
fectionate look reserved only for him. "You have lost
so much, Browser, your wife, your son. Everyone wob-
bles after such events. I'm glad I could help you."

He hesitated, then reached out and touched her
cheek. It felt cool and smooth. "You are my best friend,
Catkin. Without you . . . I'm sure I would fall on my
face."

Her smile warmed the cold place in his soul. "As I
would without you."

Neither of them said anything for a time.

Then Catkin said, "Well, we should be on our way."

Browser stood up and stretched his tired back muscles. "Yes, let's go wake our elders."

As he led the way down to the river, he tried not to
stare overly long at the unburied dead.

*PIPER HUNCHES OVER and walks deeper, away
from the sunlight. The darkness hurts her eyes a little,*

*like when she puts her hands on ice in the winter, but it is warm in here. The fitted stones under her feet whisper as she walks.*

*"Hello," she calls, just to see if anyone answers back.*

*Her own voice hisses around her.*

*She walks faster and the water jar clunks against her hip, making little stabs.*

*As she nears the circle of sunlight ahead, Piper breathes deep, taking the old smells of dust and people into her heart, letting them sit there awhile before she blows them out and away.*

*Then she runs out into the sunlight, and toward the water-filled sandstone cistern in the rock ten paces ahead.*

*She quickly unties the jar from her belt and sinks it below the icy water.*

*Wind Baby spins over the ridgetop, kicking up dust, and tugging at Piper's hair.*

*She ignores him, and looks back at the jar that's filling up.*

*From under the water, a little girl stares at her. An ugly little girl, with a dirty face and hair like a dead bear's, filled with grass and sticks.*

*Piper leans closer and glares into the little girl's eyes.*

*Wondering why she's locked underwater where she's always cold. Wondering why the little girl doesn't just leap up and run away through the warm sunlight.*

*Piper's mouth whispers, but she doesn't know whose voice it is:*

*"Because there are monsters on the trails. Big monsters with sharp teeth."*

*Piper frowns at the little girl and tries to figure out how the girl could use her mouth to speak.*

*Piper leans down until her lips touch the water and the little girl's eyes are shining black stars.*

*"Don't be such a little baby," she whispers. "You're*

*fast. You can run faster than any monster."*

*But the little girl's eyes say she doesn't believe this. They are wide and scared.*

*"Then you're stupid," Piper says and gets to her feet.*

*Piper pulls her jar from the pool, ties it to her belt, and bravely stalks back toward the dark hole.*

*But high up above her an owl "hoo-hoos."*

*Piper stops to look. It is strange to see an owl in the daylight.*

*The owl lazily spirals down and lands on a boulder to Piper's right.*

*He has huge blinking eyes.*

*"Hello," Piper whispers.*

*"Hello," the owl answers.*

# CHAPTER 16

GARDUNO'S BIG MEXICAN restaurant was packed. Dusty and Maureen sat at a booth with a basket of tortilla chips and a bowl of wonderfully spicy salsa between them. The place had real atmosphere with its gaudy piñatas, pictures of Mexican heroes and anti-heroes, bits of brightly painted furniture and knick-knacks. A Saltillo tile floor was immaculate. Melodic brassy mariachi music seemed to propel the busy staff as they bustled back and forth with drinks, orders, and plates of steaming food.

Maureen used a chip to scoop up salsa and studied Dusty's pinched expression. He kept stroking his blond beard as if for something to do. "Want to talk about it?"

"No." He took a long drink of his Negra Modelo, a rich Mexican dark beer. "I feel like screaming, throwing the furniture around, and breaking things. So, if I start baring my soul, everyone here will regret it."

"That's a healthy response. I'd be worried about you if you didn't feel that way."

He stared sadly down into his half-empty mug, and Maureen could see the lines around his blue eyes tighten, like a man bracing against an almost overpowering strain. He hadn't shed a tear, hadn't railed against life, hadn't gone somewhere alone to lick his wounds. He'd been the epitome of strength. All business. No emotion. She wondered how long he could last.

She reached across the table and grasped his hand. "I can't give you any answers. I don't know any. What I can do is share your grief. If you want to talk about Dale—"

"You may not have any answers," Dusty cut her off, "but somebody does. I have to find out who."

"Want to elaborate on that?" She released his hand and reached for another tortilla chip. When he was ready, he'd talk to her.

"Dale was murdered by a witch, Maureen, or someone wants us to think it was a witch. My mother and her old lover are tied up in it, and I heard their voices on the phone; they both thought Dale was doing something to them." His frown deepened. "Could he have been? I've seen him play some pretty tasteless jokes on people, but when he left Pueblo Animas the other day, he wasn't in combat mode. At least, I didn't see it, if he was."

"Combat mode?" she asked.

Dusty shoved his mug between his palms. "Like over the cannibalism thing. Tim White, Christy Turner, and others have proved that people were eating people eight hundred years ago in the Southwest, but it's politically incorrect. When Dale wrote an article supporting the idea, the archaeological community went berserk—including, it seems, Carter Hawsworth. How could Dale, one of the great southwestern archaeologists, say something so terrible about their darling Anasazi? Dale stomped around for days, writing comments to the journals, delivering professional papers, phoning radio talk shows. He was a man on a mission, and the mission was that where science took us, we had to follow—even if it was uncomfortable." A faint smile touched his lips. "I remember him saying, 'William, when are my colleagues going to drop this alabaster Anasazi crap? We're not talking about angels; they were human beings! No better or worse than any other people!' "

Maureen laughed, remembering the fire in Dale's eyes when he took up a cause. "But you didn't see that at Pueblo Animas?"

"No." Dusty stopped shoving his mug and gripped it in both hands. "If he'd done something to Hawsworth or Sullivan—some perverted joke—he'd have shown it. Especially when he was looking at me. This was my mother and the man she left my father for. He probably wouldn't have told me outright, but I'd have known something was bugging him, and that somehow I was involved. No, this thing surprised him."

"What do you mean?"

His blue eyes glittered when he looked up. "Think about his house. He obviously went home to Albuquerque, pulled a TV dinner out of the freezer, and sat down to eat it. Then, something happened, a phone call, a knock on the door, and Dale never finished his dinner. Instead he immediately drove to Chaco Canyon, parked at Casa Rinconada, and walked out into the ruins. Looking for what? Did he go there to meet someone? Who?"

Maureen paused to drink her coffee. When she set the cup down again, she said, "You think it was your mother?"

Maureen tried to imagine how she'd ever be able to

deal with Ruth Ann Sullivan if she should ever meet her at a conference.

Dusty shrugged. "I wouldn't put anything past her, but more likely it's Carter Hawsworth. After all, he's here in New Mexico studying Navajo witchcraft. And nobody that I know of—and I know *everyone*—even knows he's here. That's very strange, don't you think?"

Maureen reached out and dipped a chip into the salsa. "The skinned feet, that's Navajo, right?"

"Yes, but the yucca hoop and the human flesh in Dale's mouth," Dusty countered, "that's Puebloan witchcraft. Not that it matters. Hispanic, Puebloan, and Navajo witches have borrowed from each other until the traditional lines have been blurred. Witches take power where they find it."

"What about burying him upside down? Did you understand that part about 'a white guy with his head in the underworlds'?"

"Puebloan peoples believe they came to this world by climbing through a series of underworlds. Kivas are openings to the underworlds. Don't you see? Dale's death was specifically tailored to him. Buried? In an archaeological site? With his head in the ground? How metaphorical can you get?"

Maureen considered that. "But would Hawsworth think that way? What do you know about him?"

Dusty tugged at his beard. "Well, I may have refused to read his professional articles, but he was the low-rent that screwed my mother before he ran off with her. Call it a morbid fascination. I actually have paid attention to his career."

"And?"

"He finished his Ph.D. at Cambridge, writing about Zuni metaphysics. Within a year he and Ruth Ann were floating around the South Pacific, doing Polynesian ethnography. Crystal waters, white beaches, coconuts, and friendly brown natives, that kind of thing. Two years, and a couple of controversial articles later, they were in central Australia, based in Alice Springs, where they spent quite a bit of time involved in Aboriginal ethnology. When I was nine, I was leafing through a copy of Dale's *Anthropology News* and saw a picture of them sharing a witchetty grub."

"A what?" Maureen asked quizzically.

"A big worm. An insect larva with about the same amount of protein that you'd get from a pork chop. Aborigines eat them raw. They don't have fancy Mexican restaurants like this in the Outback." Dusty scooped salsa onto a chip before returning to his narrative. "Ruth and Carter broke up in New Zealand. They were doing something with the Maori. Scuttlebutt says it got ugly in a hotel room in Wellington with screaming and hitting, and policemen dragging them apart."

"Isn't that about when Ruth Ann started to publish her books?" Maureen asked, thinking back, trying to remember when that first big best-seller had hit the market. Maureen had been an undergraduate at McGill. The book had been all the rave in the cultural anthropology classes.

"Yeah." Dusty took another swig of his beer. "Rumor has it that she hated him so much she wanted to discredit his research. Rather than try and do it at the meetings and in the professional journals, she took it to a mainstream publisher. She put her arguments in a popular book that ordinary people could understand, and sold it. Most of her theories could be supported, too, which gave her professional recognition, and an entire generation of people thought in her terms about human culture. When you think about it, what's more powerful, a well-argued article in *American Anthropologist* that only your colleagues will read, or a popular book read by millions?"

Maureen glanced around the restaurant. "I saw her on CBC one time. She was talking about the single-mother households and how after so many generations we had created a traditional matrilineage—especially among black populations and lower economic classes. She was arguing that until the dominant society realized that, we would continue to stumble in initiating social programs."

"Right. Everybody in the world has seen her on the CBC, CNN, or PBS, and outside of a few cultural anthropologists, who's ever heard of Hawsworth?"

"I hadn't until Dale mentioned him out at the 10K3 site in Chaco." Maureen leaned back as the waitress deposited a heaping plate of blue corn enchiladas. Thick chunks of pork dotted a tomatillo sauce. Melted cheddar topped the creation while a fresh whole jalapeño acted as a not-so-subtle garnish. She took a deep breath, inhaling the aroma of cumin and refried beans.

Dusty picked up his fork and began thoughtfully whittling away at his giant burrito—the gut bomb sort that bulged with carne picadillo, beans, and peppers.

While Dusty ate, lost in thought, Maureen kept replaying Dusty's story of seeing Carter Hawsworth and Ruth Ann Sullivan through the bedroom door. No wonder Dusty had had so many problems with women. His mother had screwed another man in front of his eyes, then she'd left, his father had committed suicide, and Dusty had been raised by Dale Emerson Robertson, a confirmed bachelor who never formed a serious long-term relationship with a woman. What kind of role models had Dusty had? The deck had been stacked against him from the beginning.

"I like Sam Nichols," Dusty said as he pushed his empty plate back.

"So do I." As Maureen speared another forkful of refritos, her stomach felt like it would burst. This place didn't skimp on food, that was for certain.

"But he's not going to solve this," Dusty said solemnly.

Maureen arched an inquisitive eyebrow. "Why is that?"

Dusty wiped his mouth with his napkin and tossed it on the table. "Because he doesn't believe in witchcraft."

Maureen's fork hovered over her refritos. "You think that's a prerequisite?"

"It damn sure helps."

Maureen gave him a worried look. "He'll call it 'interfering with an investigation,' Dusty."

"Interfering, hell. I may be the *only* one who can solve Dale's murder. He can ride along in the back of the Bronco, for all I care."

"He might frown at that gun you keep under your seat."

"This is New Mexico, Doctor, unlike Canada, we—"

The cell phone rang. Dusty reached into his shirt pocket, flipped out the small phone, and held it to his ear. "This is Stewart." He listened for a moment. "Sure, Rupert." Dusty glanced up at Maureen and his eyes tightened. "No, they haven't released the body yet. They're awaiting test results." Dusty listened for a time, nodding; then there was a long pause where he didn't move. He didn't even blink. Finally, in a low voice, he answered, "Hell, yes. You give me a permit, and you damn betcha I'll dig it. Uh-huh. Saturday. Right. Bye."

He punched the END button and slipped the phone back into his pocket. "Remember Rupert Brown? The park superintendent at Chaco? He has a Ph.D. in archaeology."

"What does he want you to dig?"

Dusty finished his beer in three swallows and set the mug on the table. "The site where Dale was found. Rupert thinks there's a reason Dale was killed there."

BROWSER SAT UP in the darkness and reached for his war club. Through the doorway of the dilapidated room he could see the Evening People shining over the ruins of Twin Heroes village.

On the other side of the room, Catkin silently sat up in her blankets. Barely audible, she asked, "What's wrong?"

"Nothing." He paused. "Yet."

Fabric rustled as she looked around. "Something disturbed you?"

"By now our enemies know that we are traveling south on this road. Even if everyone in our party is trustworthy, others use this road. Someone will have seen our tracks." He shivered as he reached for his cape. "Roll your things and let's awaken the others. I want to be gone from here."

A half-hand of time later, Browser led them, blinking and yawning, out of the shadowed ruins and onto the road.

They marched in silence until just before dawn; then Browser took them off the road and headed west into the undulating hills above the Squash Blossom breaks. As they hiked up onto the sheer rimrock, he heard Obsidian's voice: "Browser? Where are you going? This isn't the way." She trotted up beside him, breathing hard. The pale blue light shimmered through her long hair and glinted in her black cotton cape.

"I know that, Obsidian," he answered, and turned to Catkin. "Take the others and continue on across the rimrock. Parallel the Great North Road, but do not set foot on it. I will stay here for a time, to watch our back trail."

Catkin glanced curiously at Obsidian, but said, "Yes, War Chief," and left at a trot.

Obsidian started to leave, but Browser grabbed her arm. "No, I want you to stay with me."

She glared at his hand. "Why?"

Browser watched Catkin speak briefly with Stone Ghost and White Cone; then she led the party due south. In less than five hundred heartbeats they had crossed over the ridge and disappeared.

Browser released Obsidian. "I think we are being followed. I want you to watch with me."

"Me? Why me?" Her eyes were like dark, shining pools.

Browser walked to a high point, a rounded knob of sandstone, and got down on his belly. Obsidian stretched out beside him, and her black hair spilled around her body like a silken cloak of darkness. Her spicy scent filled the air.

She whispered, "Why do you think we're being followed?"

"Because that is what I would do?"

"What you would do?"

"Yes, if I were Blue Corn, or Two Hearts, or anyone curious as to why our party left in the middle of the night."

As she turned to look at the road, the morning wind blew her hair around her beautiful face. "Why would Blue Corn follow us? We did nothing to her."

"We left at the same time as the Mogollon. She must be wondering if we left together, and if so, what we are up to."

They lay silently side by side, listening to the cold winter darkness, seeing the horizon brighten. Then Browser felt her move, and a warm hand brushed his. He shuddered and turned to her.

"Browser," she said, "I have only realized recently how Shadow has affected you. You hate her, and you should. But I am not her."

"No, you're not."

"I've been lonely," she told him. "It comes from guarding secrets, from knowing who I am, and not being able to just be a woman."

"You could change."

Her eyes were wide and dark, and she was very beautiful. "Could I, Browser? Could you?"

"Could I change how?"

"Could you find a new life? Step into the role the gods have prepared you for?"

"And what role is that?"

"The leader of a people."

"What are you talking about?"

She slid closer to him and smoothed her hand over the muscles in his arm. "I would help you, Browser. You're stronger than you know. More important than you know. I am offering my help, willing to work with you to rebuild our world."

The scent of her, the warmth of her body . . .

"We are both First People, you and I," she whispered. "Both alone . . . and, gods, it's cold out here."

Every time his heart beat, a fiery sting of longing surged in his veins. He hadn't been with a woman in almost a sun cycle and suddenly felt like a man dying of thirst who had just been offered water.

Obsidian smiled and lifted her face. Her full lips were moist and shining. "Do I not attract you at all?" she asked.

He swallowed hard, knowing full well that all he had to do was reach over and touch her, and she would fold him into her arms. After that her soft flesh would open to him and nothing would ever be the same again.

"You do, but I . . ." He pushed up on his elbows, prepared to rise, and froze.

Yes, there. Movement. Gray figures ghosted out of the predawn twilight. They looked like ants as they scurried purposely for the crumbling walls of Twin Heroes village. Browser knew those capes: White Moccasins.

"There." He pointed.

Obsidian shook her head, as though she didn't see them; then her eyes widened. "Are those white capes?"

"I think so."

She let out a small wretched cry and scrambled backward, trying to get away.

Browser grabbed hand, and she struggled against him.

"Let go!" she hissed. "We have to run! Hurry! Let me go!" Utter terror twisted her face as she clawed at his hand.

Browser jerked her closer, his grip hard, and whispered, "Quiet. We're well away from their trap. Now, follow me, on your belly."

MAUREEN SNUGGED HER coat around her, bracing against a cold gust of wind that blasted the mountaintop. Dusty had insisted that Dale's memorial be held high on Sandia Crest. Three thousand feet below lay Albuquerque and the undeveloped Sandia Indian Reservation. The Rio Grande cut a gray-brown line across the valley and, to the west, the knobby heights of the San Mateo Mountains rose eleven thousand feet to Mount Taylor's summit. What a vista. But for the biting wind, it would have been magnificent. Just what Dale would have wanted.

Fifty-eight people had come. Maureen knew Sylvia Rhone, Steve Sanders, Michall Jefferson, and Maggie Walking Hawk Taylor; she had worked with them in the past. Agent Nichols stood in the rear, wearing a puffy goose-down parka. He held a video camera to his eye, panning the crowd, but not to record the proceedings—though the guests would not know that. One by one, she studied the faces. Most of the attendees were archaeologists and faculty from the University of New Mexico. They had been introduced in such a rush, the names had slipped away with the wind. The others were strangers, people who'd come in response to the obituary in the newspaper. Not even Dusty knew them. Only Dale's sister, a frail gray-haired woman in her eighties, represented his family. She huddled in a wheelchair, covered by blankets and looking miserable.

Maureen's eyes kept drifting to a tall elderly man who stood slightly to the rear, as if to separate himself from the assembly. He watched with his eyes narrowed against the wind, a frightened look on his reddened face. When his gaze met hers, she saw how hard he'd clenched his jaw.

Maureen leaned sideways to whisper to Dusty, "Who's that man in the rear?"

"What man?" Dusty turned, and his freshly washed blond hair tousled beneath the brim of his battered cowboy hat. He wore a heavy denim coat with the fleece collar pulled up. In his hands, he clutched the ancient Anasazi pot that held Dale's ashes.

"That man . . ." Her voice faded.

He was gone. She searched the crowd and caught sight of him heading for the parking lot. "That man. Over there."

Dusty looked, then shook his head. "I can't tell, probably an old friend from before my time."

He turned back to the crowd and clutched the black-on-white pot to his chest like a precious child. It had rested on Dale's *trastero*. Dusty said it had been Dale's favorite.

Addressing the crowd, Dusty shouted, "Dale would be so pleased to see you here. He'd also be amazed that you'd come out in such cold circumstances. In fact, he'd probably think we were out of our minds to be

up here when we could be in a nice warm tavern somewhere toasting him."

Scattered laughter broke out among the archaeological contingent. Someone called, "Here's to Dale!"

Dusty smiled, but the gesture was forced, and everyone knew it. The crowd moved in closer, huddling together to listen.

Sylvia and Maggie had their arms around each other.
Steve Sanders, the tall black man to Maureen's left,
just closed his eyes.

"As most of you know, Dale raised me." Dusty held
the pot out in his hands. "So, I'm not just saying good-
bye to a friend and colleague, but to a father. After my
father's death, Dale took me into his heart and his
home and never looked back. I've spent most of my
life thanking the Great Spirit that he did."

Dusty looked around, searching the faces. "He was
a man who touched other people's lives. When you
were down, Dale was always there to pick you up, dust
you off, and shove you forward again. He insisted that
people exceed his expectations. Somehow, he always
knew we could do better than we thought we could.
He demanded that of his peers . . . of himself, and most
of all of me. I could not have asked for a better father."

Dusty smiled, and Maureen couldn't be sure if it was
the bitter wind or the moment that brought a tear out
of the corner of his eye.

He looked down at the pot. "Dale was taken from
us. Someone lured him out to Chaco Canyon and murdered him. I swear, no matter how long it takes, I will
find out who killed him and why, but . . ." His voice
broke. He took a few moments to collect himself, then
inhaled a deep breath. "But I have to let you go now,
Dale. Thank you for all the years you stood by me. For
all the lessons you taught. I'm going to miss you." He
paused. "As I was taught in my kiva initiation, *Yupa.
Angwu!* 'Be on your way.' " He reached into the pot,
took out a handful of the gray ash, and let the wind

blow it away. "If you will all repeat after me, *Yupa. Angwu!*"

*"Yupa! Angwu!"* Maureen repeated as Dusty turned the pot and let the fierce west wind carry the physical remains of Dale Emerson Robertson across the barren rock and scrub of Sandia Crest.

*Be on your way, Dale.* Another loved one had vanished from her life, and she felt the stitch of loss in her heart.

"Thank you for coming," Dusty called. "We're having a reception at the office in town. Most of you know the way. If you don't, see me, Sylvia, Steve, or Michall for directions."

People began to trickle away, taking the trail back to the parking lot. Others came to cluster around Dusty. This was the part Maureen hated: the platitudes and offering of condolences. God, how she'd suffered through that after John's death. People just had to say something and no matter how sincere they were, it always reopened the wound.

Maureen walked to the lip of the mountain, faced into the wind, and let it chill the ache in her soul. The mountain dropped away at her feet, falling in jagged outcrops of gray. Brush and scattered pines filled the drainages. To her left she could see the aerial tram line that descended to northeastern Albuquerque. In the deepening glow of evening, lights flickered on in Albuquerque, as though marking the city's arteries and skeleton.

*What am I doing here?* The question caught her off guard. Dale was dead. She had come to the Southwest because of him. Now, here she was, standing on the edge of the precipice. She could turn around, walk back to the Bronco, and have Dusty drop her off at the Albuquerque airport. United would take her back to Denver, and from there she could book a flight to Toronto. By this time tomorrow, she could be sitting in her overstuffed easy chair at home, a cup of tea at hand, as she looked out the French windows at Lake Ontario. They'd had snow in Niagara-on-the-Lake, assuming, of course, that she could trust CNN. Her yard would be white, an unmarred blanket trimmed by the silvering waves that washed the shoreline fifty steps from her back door.

"Dale would have appreciated this," a voice said behind her.

She turned, finding a tall, hawk-faced man in a thick gray Filson coat, jeans, and wearing polished western boots. His black felt cowboy hat was pulled low over his eyes. He had a brown face and steely gray hair. Maureen's practiced eye noted the lines around his mouth and eyes, and the leathery skin on his neck. He had to be around sixty.

"Yes, he would have," Maureen answered. "He wasn't the type for a service in a building."

"Unless it was a half-excavated pueblo," the man added, smiling wistfully. He offered his hand. "I haven't met you. I'm Rupert Brown. An old friend of Dale's."

"The park superintendent? Dusty mentioned you. I'm glad to meet you, I'm Maureen Cole." She took his hand and shook. His fingers were oddly warm.

"Ah." He smiled. "Dr. Cole. Yes. Magpie calls you Washais. I assume that's your tribal name?" She nodded and he continued, "I read your report on 10K3. That was a brilliant piece of work. I'm not used to that kind of thorough skeletal analysis from contract archaeology."

"Well, Dale had a hunch about that site. I'm glad he called me in. It was a unique opportunity."

Their conversation waned, and Maureen turned and started back across the rocky ground toward Dusty. A knot of people had surrounded him, and he looked a little overwhelmed. Rupert Brown walked at her side.

"Dale and his hunches," Brown said. "God, I'll miss

him. Did Dusty tell you that I took that first job with
Dale to learn how to rob sites?"

"No." She stumbled on a loose stone and had to
spread her arms to keep her balance. Brown caught her
hand, steadying her. "Sorry. You were saying?"

Brown laughed. "Hey, I was a screwed-up young
man. It was the start of the southwestern Indian craze.
I thought I could make enough digging up pots and
selling them to keep myself in booze and dope. What
better way to learn how than to get paid by an archaeologist at the same time?"

Maureen gave him a sidelong glance. "What did you
do with the artifacts you took?"

"Most of them I sold. A few I kept. Later, when I
realized what an ass I'd been, I curated the rest at the
University of New Mexico." He paused, and a strange
look entered his dark eyes. "Except for a couple of
things I threw away."

"Threw away?" Maureen sounded appalled because
she was. "You threw away prehistoric artifacts?"

Rupert nodded. "I did. And I don't regret it. Those
things scared the daylights out of me."

Dark clouds swelled on the southern horizon. Maureen studied them for a time before she said, "Well, I
guess not all career opportunities work out."

"No." He smiled, seeing into the past. "I was looking
for a way to gain power, wealth, and prestige. More
than anything, I wanted people to look up to me, to
respect me. I would have given anything for that. What
did I know about archaeology? And then, working with
Dale, I touched the past." He looked down at the
ground and his smile faded. "I heard the ancestors, Dr.
Cole. They showed me a better way."

She decided she liked Rupert Brown. "Dusty says
you want to dig the site where Dale was found."

"Yes. I think it's essential." He gave her a careful
inspection, as though weighing her reaction to his
words. "Witches live by two means. First, they terrify

people so badly that no one will dare take action against them. That worked especially well in the old days. Second, they survive by misdirection and subterfuge."

"Do you believe in witchcraft?"

"I believe it works," Brown said. "So did Dale. Oh, I know all the studies. Classic works by people like Clyde Kluckhohn, E. E. Evans-Pritchard, and others. Walter Cannon even gave us a nice, tidy physiological explanation of how people die from having a spell cast on them. But none of that matters. What matters is that people die."

"You think that's what happened to Dale?"

He watched Dusty shaking hands with somber well-wishers. "I think Dale met a witch out there, and I don't think the witch buried him in that site by accident. I want to know why."

A brown-skinned man in a gray cowboy hat walked up to Dusty and hugged him. The two patted each other on the back like old friends.

"My son, Lupe," Rupert said. "He and Dusty grew up together. They were also initiated into a kiva together." He smiled crookedly. "You'd be shocked by the amount of trouble they managed to get into."

"Knowing Dusty, I doubt it." She watched as a younger man with long shining black hair followed Lupe to shake Dusty's hand. He looked to be in his early twenties, tall and muscular. Very good-looking.

"My grandson, Reggie," Rupert said, and his smile turned wry. "You'd be shocked by the amount of trouble he's currently in."

She glanced up. "Do all of your offspring get into trouble?"

"It seems to run in the family," Rupert said. "Lupe has pretty much straightened himself out. Reggie, on the other hand, God, I don't know what to do with him. He's got so much potential. He's a wizard with a computer. I can't even find my toothbrush in the morning and he can find anything in cyberspace." Rupert's face softened. "But he just can't seem to find his way."

Maureen watched as Reggie walked down and stood by Maggie. He seemed to be trying to comfort her. Maggie was listening to him with wide eyes, and nodding.

Behind them, Maureen noticed a woman wearing a black fur hat and dark glasses. Classy. The wind whipped her long black wool coat around black suede boots. She had her arms wrapped around her—probably for warmth—but it looked like she was hugging herself. She stood apart, and Maureen was positive she hadn't been present earlier.

The woman bent down and ran her fingers through the gray streak of ash still visible on the ground. Her face twisted, as though struggling against tears. Then, abruptly, she rose and walked briskly away.

"You said the witch was a 'he.' What makes you think so?" Maureen asked.

"In this part of the world, most witches are," Brown replied, and his gaze followed Maureen's to the woman striding for the parking lot. "But, on the other hand," he added, "maybe that's just what we're supposed to think."

# CHAPTER 17

"LET US TALK of the death of nations," old White Cone said as the fire crackled and spat. Yellow light illuminated the ring of faces.

They had camped in a dry creek bed spotted with junipers. Fortune had smiled on them that day. As they

paralleled the Great North Road, they had stumbled on
a pack of coyotes bringing down an old antelope doe.
Not even the crafty coyotes could keep a kill from human predators. The smell of roasting meat added a
nearly festive atmosphere to their dry camp.

*The death of nations?* Browser studied the faces
around the fire. What an improbable party. Eight Mogollon warriors, Jackrabbit and Straighthorn, the beautiful Obsidian, and the two elders. Catkin had taken
first watch, positioning herself above them on an
eroded clay formation that poked up from the desert
like a sharpened nipple.

"To what do you refer?" Stone Ghost asked. He
picked strips of steaming brown meat from the section
of vertebra he'd been given and popped them into his
mouth. The most tender meat had been given to the
elders. It made it easier on their toothless jaws.

White Cone smiled as he licked greasy fingers and
motioned around. "Don't you wonder? How could the
Straight Path Nation have fallen? Look about you. Each
of these pinnacles once was topped with a fortification.
Just over there, to the east, on the Great North Road,
was a signal tower. Charcoal still runs down its sides
when the rains come. Charcoal from the great signal
fires that tied Straight Path Canyon to its northern hold-
ings. The Blessed Sun controlled the whole world,
sending out his red-shirted warriors to enforce the
slightest of his whims. How could such a powerful nation fall?"

Browser's gut twisted. He had heard the stories. All
of them blamed his great-great-great-grandmother,
Night Sun, because she had given birth to a child by
her War Chief, Ironwood. Browser had always accepted the account as just another legend. But after
discovering he was descended from the First People,
after having *seen* the mummified body of Night Sun,
and heard the story of how the White Moccasins had
tortured her to death, he believed the stories.

"It was the Matron, Night Sun," Jackrabbit interjected through a mouthful of meat. "She betrayed the Straight Path Nation."

Browser winced, and hoped that no one noticed. Obsidian, too, had stiffened.

"You are wrong, my young friend." White Cone carefully wiped grease from his wrinkled brown fingers. "It was betrayal, yes. But not on the part of Matron Night Sun."

"Then, who?" Obsidian demanded to know. Her beautiful face gleamed in the firelight.

"Ah, that is the story I would tell." The old Mogollon smiled. "Some would say it was the coming of the thlatsinas who wrought the destruction of the First People and the Straight Path Nation, but that is not so."

"No?" Obsidian's dark eyes flashed.

"No, it was the passions of a single man," White Cone continued, "that brought down the First People."

"Which man?" Obsidian demanded.

White Cone fingered his wrinkled chin. "The Straight Path Nation was destroyed by the Blessed Sun. Have you ever heard that?"

"You mean Crow Beard?" Obsidian cocked her head.

"No, though he played a most important role. It was Night Sun's boy: the Blessed Snake Head. He was the dry rot that caused the collapse of the Straight Path Nation. He was a witch and his evil had eaten into the fiber of their world. He was killed by the warrior, Cone, whom he had betrayed. They buried Snake Head in Talon Town, in a sealed room, with a rock over his head."

Stone Ghost cocked his white head and his eyes gleamed in the firelight. "How do you, of all people, know this?"

White Cone waved a finger back and forth. "There are always two faces to betrayal. The great Jay Bird, the mightiest of all the Mogollon chiefs, was the other face of evil. When Crow Beard died, Night Sun's boy, Snake Head, became the Blessed Sun. Under his command was a warrior named Cone. Cone carried messages between Jay Bird and Snake Head."

"Snake Head," Stone Ghost said, eyes unfocused. "I remember hearing that he was buried as a witch. That the Blessed Featherstone became the Matron." He frowned. "It is said that she had the habit of losing her breath-heart soul. When she did, she babbled incoherently."

"Yes. That's right. It was at one of those times that she ordered the abandonment of Straight Path Canyon." White Cone studied Browser thoughtfully. "Oh, we heard the stories firsthand. Not only did we have spies everywhere, but many of our people, who'd been kept as slaves, escaped in the aftermath. At the time we thought it was victory; we had no way of knowing it was change. Change for all of us. We had no way to know that by attacking Talon Town we would be the instruments of Poor Singer's vision."

"You mean Jay Bird shouldn't have raided Talon Town?" Browser asked; it had been the single most devastating blow to the Straight Path Nation. That act had broken the First People's power in a way that no uprising, drought, or natural calamity could. Within one sun cycle, the canyon had been abandoned, and the Made People had begun a war against the First People. The First People had but a few sun cycles to survive.

"Of course we should have!" White Cone grinned like a stealthy fox. "They were our enemies. We fought constantly. They took our people as slaves and forced us to build their Great Houses, to cut and carry huge stones for their kivas. They forced us to worship them and their ascent from the underworlds, when we knew our ancestors came from the heavens; they were fiery wolves made from gouts of Father Sun's fire!"

"Then why do you care about Poor Singer's vision?" Stone Ghost asked.

The old Mogollon leaned back, a look of satisfaction on his wrinkled face. "No matter what the origins of your people or mine, the thlatsinas came to both of us. They may have given their vision to Sternlight first, but Poor Singer, a man born of Mogollon blood—a joining of the Blessed Sun, Crow Beard, and Young Fawn—brought it to us. When even Jay Bird refused to believe, Poor Singer raised his hands and the earth shook. Rocks tumbled, buildings fell, and for the second time in one hundred sun cycles, the Rainbow Serpent rose into the sky where the earth had been breached." He arched an ancient eyebrow. "How could we ignore such a powerful Dreamer?"

"Elder," Browser quietly asked. "Do you know what message your prophet carried? Someone killed him to keep him from telling us. If you know—"

"He went to Flowing Waters Town to save the world." White Cone looked sadly down at his hands. The greasy skin shone in the firelight. "To do that, he knew he had to die."

"He knew?" Stone Ghost straightened.

The old man looked suddenly tired. "Do you think Blue Corn and her allies are alone? There are doubters among the Mogollon, too. I, myself, have fought against the coming of the thlatsinas. I was a priest, you see. I Sang the planting ceremonies, and danced the part of the Blessed Flute Player when I was a youth. When our young prophet came down from the mountains, he was a changed man. A shy boy had climbed the heights, but a strong man descended."

Murmurs of assent eddied among the Mogollon warriors.

"I remember that night," White Cone said reverently. "My kiva—we were in ritual council—was performing the Sacred Rites of the Bow. The young prophet climbed down the ladder into the midst of our most secret ritual, and there, I swear, he stood in the sacred fire, his flesh untouched, and said, 'The thlatsinas have shown me the way.' He pointed right at me. 'You are the one who must go with me. You, who have never believed in Poor Singer's prophecy. You must be my witness.' "

"Witness to what?" Obsidian asked, clearly taken in by the old man's hollow-eyed stare as he watched the fire.

"To his death," the elder said calmly. "The prophet told us that night that in order to save the world, he must die. That upon his death, his soul would rise to the night sky and when the sun rose the next morning, he would be among the thlatsinas. He told us that we would know him when he came to our villages, because he would have a single buffalo horn growing out of the side of his head."

Browser glared down into his teacup. Nothing good had ever come from believing in visions and gods. He wasn't about to start.

Obsidian pushed long black hair over her shoulder and said, "Then how do we know that he didn't plan his own murder? He might have hired someone to kill him to prove his vision. Or you, White Cone, might have murdered him to prove it."

Browser pulled himself upright as the Mogollon warriors shot hard glances her way, but White Cone waved them down, and said, "The young warrior who was killed was a member of my kiva, an initiate of the Bow. You people are outsiders. You do not understand the Bow Society. It is—"

"The most sacred of all Fire Dog societies," Browser said. "I know of your kiva, and have great admiration for it. Your warriors offer their lives in exchange for the safety of the people. They stand to the last, no matter the cost. When you give your word, you will not break it."

White Cone eyed Browser with more respect. "We are all made upon the Bow, War Chief. We gave our sacred vow that our prophet would die only after all of us had been killed. Do you understand?"

"Yes," Stone Ghost said, reaching his hands out to the warmth of the fire. "You meant to prove him wrong."

White Cone nodded. "I did not believe his vision."

"What else did he tell you?"

White Cone's old face turned somber. "He told us how he would die, and that all but two of us would live. He told us they would bury him in the Kiva of the Worlds, and said it would sanctify that place for the thlatsinas."

Obsidian's full lips pulled into a thin white line. "But only one other Fire Dog died. His vision was wrong."

The wrinkles around White Cone's mouth cut deeper as he frowned. "Only one of us has died so far, Obsidian."

She tipped her head and the jewels in her hair sparkled. "Is that all?"

White Cone rubbed his temples, as though an ache had started behind his eyes. "No, our prophet also told us to attach ourselves to the man who had spoken for us." He looked up. "You, War Chief Browser. The prophet said that if we did all of these things, that his purpose on earth would be fulfilled, and that, though it would take many sun cycles, the thlatsinas would win this terrible war."

"Then," Stone Ghost said, and deep sadness filled his voice, "your prophet knew he would never give us the message he carried."

Browser shook his head, as though to rid himself of a buzzing fly. "Uncle, do you really believe this? Why would he come to us if he knew he would never deliver his message?"

White Cone gazed up at him with haunted eyes. "When I left my home, it was with the certainty that I would return vindicated in my beliefs, and escorting a chastened young 'prophet.' He would be a broken man, mocked by Blue Corn and her warriors. But it happened exactly as he said it would. I—I could not keep him safe."

"I still don't understand," Browser said. "You knew he was at risk and only placed two guards at his door?"

White Cone stared unhappily into the fire. "It was a long run up from the south, War Chief. The first night I placed five guards. My warriors were weaving on their feet. When nothing happened, when no threat materialized, I cut the number. If we rotated in twos, being that close to his room, surely we could tumble out—as you saw the other morning—in time to fight off any attack or threat to his person."

"I might have made the same decision." Browser cradled his chin thoughtfully. "Without knowing the future, you give warriors any chance to rest."

"It was as the thlatsinas ordained," White Cone said humbly. "A mistake I will never make again."

"So," Obsidian said disdainfully, "you now believe in the katsinas?"

"I believe," White Cone said with a reverent nod. "What surprises me is that so many of your own Katsinas' People do not." He turned to look accusingly at Browser.

Browser's thick black brows drew together. "I am just a warrior, Elder. I fight for my people. That is all. The ways and wills of gods are beyond me. And I am glad—"

"Browser?" Catkin's voice called from the night.

At the tension in her voice, he turned, cursing himself for having night-blinded himself with the fire. "Catkin? What's wrong?"

She walked in from the darkness, half off balance, and then Browser saw why. She tugged a filthy little girl by the hand.

"There is no alarm," Catkin called. "I found a child out there in the dark."

Obsidian rose from the fire and shielded her eyes, trying to see the child's face.

"A child?" White Cone asked. "So far from the road?"

Stone Ghost's eyes were on Obsidian as she walked away from camp, but he said, "There are many orphans these days, White Cone, children whose villages have been destroyed, their families killed."

Browser peered curiously at the child. Her long black hair was a mass of tangles. Her parents must have been killed days ago. "Straighthorn. Take Catkin's place on guard."

"Yes, War Chief."

Straighthorn wiped his hands on his war shirt, collected his weapons, and trotted past Catkin, taking but a moment to glance at the girl. After several steps, he stopped and turned. He studied the girl hard, then shook his head and hurried on into the night.

The girl had seen seven or eight sun cycles and dirt and soot coated her face and tattered clothing. When she looked up at Browser, her large dark eyes might have been mirrors of midnight. Her gaze seemed to drink in his soul.

"Where did you find her?" Browser asked.

"Climbing around in the darkness." Catkin studied the little girl. "She hasn't spoken a word, and it looks like she hasn't eaten in a while. I couldn't just leave her out there, though catching her proved more difficult than I'd thought. She's fast for one so small."

Browser bent down and looked at the child's haunted expression. "Do you have a name? What is your clan?"

She pressed her body against Catkin's leg and pulled at the torn hem of her war shirt.

Browser drew his knife from his belt and cut a long strip of meat from the antelope haunch by the fire. He held it out to the girl. "I'll trade you this for your name."

The little girl sniffed, the action feral, like that of a

starved cat. With astonishing speed, she grabbed the meat and put the whole thing in her mouth. Juices leaked down her face as she rushed to chew it up and swallow it.

"You still owe me your name," he reminded gently.

She pointed at the antelope carcass with a grimy finger. "Hungwy."

Browser cut another strip of meat from the carcass and handed it to the little girl. When she looked at him, her eyes resembled holes through the world.

MAGGIE STEPPED OUT of the Robertson and Stewart office door and walked out into the cool night. Albuquerque, located as it was in the Rio Grande valley, stayed warmer than Chaco Canyon did; nevertheless, the chill felt good after the heat, noise, and crowd in the archaeology office. Behind her, Dale's wake sounded like a dull roar. Professors were telling stories, people were mingling and drinking, and of course it was getting loud.

What was it about people and drinking? She sighed as the wind chilled the perspiration on her arms and face. Around her the automobiles, SUVs, and trucks that filled the parking lot waited patiently for their owners. Lights shone off the paint, glass, and chrome. The overflow lined the sides of the street for some distance.

Just to the south traffic roared past on I-40, individuals headed about their evening business, unaware that a passing was being marked. A scattered mosaic of lights in the high Marriott marked rooms occupied by people ignorant of Dale Emerson Robertson and his contributions to people's lives.

Dusty's face lingered in Magpie's memory: pained, longing to collapse in grief. For the first time in her life, she'd been able to look beyond a person's skin and feel the howling ache down inside Dusty's ribs. It scared her a little.

*"You gotta let yourself see,"* Aunt Sage's voice reminded. *"It's there for you, Magpie. You just never trusted yourself before. Look . . . look past this world. It's like those pictures at the mall. If you look at all the bits of color, suddenly you'll see an image. But when you blink, all that's left is the little bits of color."*

Could she? Drawing her lungs full, she looked up at the night, smeared here by the city and its pulsing illumination.

"Hey, Mag?" a cautious voice called from behind.

She turned and saw Reggie. He stood several paces away, leaning against a red car, his fists shoved in the pockets of his black jacket.

"Hey, Reggie. I needed some air."

"Yeah. Me, too." He walked up, his smile shining in the night. He had a handsome face, like his grandfather's. Tall and muscular, he stood right at six feet. He wore his black hair long, usually in a braid, but tonight it was held in a sleek ponytail clasped with a Zuni silver clip. New jeans looked stiff on his long thin legs and a white western snap shirt could be seen behind the black jacket. "Too many people."

She cocked her head. "That makes you nervous?"

He shrugged. "Yeah. College people. You know? I just don't feel like I fit in with all those smart white guys."

Magpie frowned down at the parking lot. "You're part white. Most of us are these days."

He scuffed a worn western boot on the pavement. "Yeah, you're right. I'm just paranoid, I guess." He gave her a shy apologetic smile. "What's blood, huh? It's soul that counts." He tapped his heart. "Power's in here. In what you believe. Not in book learning."

She was silent, having her own ideas about that. Finally she said, "Your grandfather has a Ph.D., Reggie."

Reggie bowed his head. "I know, and I'm really proud of him." There was reverence in his voice when he talked about Rupert. "But *Nana*'s not so different as you think, Mag. You only see him at the office. He's a cunning old warrior. Just like the old ones, biding his time to take coup."

"That's a Plains Indian thing. You turning yourself into a Sioux?"

"Not me," he stated matter-of-factly, and smiled again. "What are you doing tonight? Got a place to stay? You're not gonna drive all the way back up to Chaco, are you?"

She shook her head. "No. I have to get back to Aunt Sage's tonight. She's out north of Grants."

He frowned. "That's a long drive. You sure you'll be okay? It's pretty late."

The genuine concern in his voice made her smile. "I'll be fine. I've done it before."

"Okay, but if you change your mind, I've got an apartment here in town. Nothing much, just a room I rent. But you'd be more than welcome to crash there."

She liked Reggie, but not that much. Not yet. "Uh-huh. Just crash?"

*. . . a voice, soft, indistinct.*

Maggie stopped breathing and her gaze scanned the cars in the parking lot, then searched the sky. It *had* been a voice, though she couldn't exactly hear it. Something was happening to her. Ever since she'd seen the owl and Dale up near Rinconada, she'd felt as though her body were changing, growing in some primordial way that she didn't understand. She could hear better, see better; her sense of touch had become acute.

He nodded his head judiciously. "Yes, Magpie. Just crash. Nothing else. Let's see if I can say this right. I like you a lot. My Spirit Helper says you're special. I don't want to make no mistakes. Don't want to rush nothing. I don't want to be like *Nana*, in there, growing old and choking on love for a woman who never loved me."

"Rupert choking on love? I thought he and Sandy had a pretty good thing."

Reggie stared out at the night. She could see the pain in his dark eyes. Sandy, his grandmother, had died four years ago from cancer. Her death had broken Reggie's heart. He'd gotten into a lot of trouble after she died. "Don't get me wrong. They loved each other more than any two people I've ever known. But Grandpa's got a lot of old pain left. I really want to be different. People are going to look up to me one day, Mag. Just watch me."

"Yeah, Reggie, I will." She smiled. "In the meantime, take care of Rupert, huh? He's seemed distracted the last couple of months. Not quite his old self. And this thing with Dale, well, it's going to take time for him to heal."

"I will. *Nana* sure came through for me enough times. But just remember that he's more than you think he is." His dark eyes were shining as he watched her. "You sure you don't need a place to sleep?"

"No. I really have to make it back to Aunt Sage's. But I appreciate the offer." She smiled, enjoying his attention. "Tonight's the first time I met your dad, Lupe. He seems nice."

"He is. Now. You shoulda seen him back a couple of years. He'd do anything to cage a bottle. It was disgusting. He was disgusting."

Maggie folded her arms. The words obviously weren't meant to demean his father, he was just stating a fact.

"I haven't seen Lupe touch a drop tonight. Which is hard when everyone around you is drinking. Even more so when you're mourning the death of a good friend." She let out a breath. The lights of thousands of houses cast a golden halo over the city. "But I know what you mean. My mother was an alcoholic. She was dead drunk when she drove off the road and killed herself. Drinking scares me."

"Yeah, booze is a thief. It'll steal your soul. I swear two years ago Dad had lost his soul. Then something happened. Something *Nana* did to him. A Power thing, you know? A Healing in the old way. Now Dad's got a good thing going. Making flutes. He sells them to the whites that go to the galleries."

"Lupe's been out at the park quite a bit. I've seen his truck at Rupert's on a lot of nights. I've never had the chance to really talk to him though. I guess, from the things he and Dusty said tonight, they were really close once."

"Yeah. They grew up together." Reggie leaned on a car beside her. "Did you know that Lupe and Dusty were initiated into a kiva together? A *Hopi* kiva of all things."

"Yeah, I did ... well, I knew Dusty was." She frowned. "It's a dead kiva, isn't it?"

"It is. The Hopi are matrilineal. The clan died when the last female died. I guess there's another initiate out there, another man who went through the ritual with Dad and Dusty. He's in jail someplace. After him it's just Dusty and Dad." Reggie paused and glanced back at the people in the office.

Reggie's voice turned tender. "Dad and I grew up apart. It's only been in the last year, when he's been coming out to see *Nana*, that I've finally had a chance to talk to him about the bad old days. It's nice to get to know him. He's really been trying, you know?" Reggie was watching her carefully, as if studying her face. "It seems he's in and out of the park these days more than I am. And I work there. Dad and *Nana* have been arguing about something. I've asked but they won't tell me what's wrong."

"So, what do you think it is?"

Reggie lifted a shoulder. "I don't know. But *Nana*'s

worried about it. I can tell. Something's really wiggling around under his skin."

"Well, I like Rupert. I hope he can solve his trouble with Lupe. Come on, you can walk me back inside. I've got to say good-bye to Dusty—boy, is he going to be sorry tomorrow morning—and then I've got to drive out to my aunt's."

"Sure, Mag." Reggie offered her his arm and when she took it, he placed a gentle hand on top of hers. "And maybe when this all settles down we can go out, huh? Maybe get some dinner? Go for a walk, hell, I don't care. I just want to spend some time with you."

"You do, huh?"

"Yeah, I gotta feeling about you."

They walked back inside holding on to each other, and Maggie felt a little better.

# CHAPTER 18

"OH, GOOD LORD," Dusty groaned and gingerly rolled to his side.

Gradually it came back to him. The memorial party at the office had turned out to be a classic wake. Dale would have approved. Copious amounts of alcohol had been drunk. Stories had been told. A life had been remembered and toasted. Venerable professors emeriti had related tales of digs long back-filled, of arguments they had won or lost with Dale. Neophytes, students on their first digs, told how Dale had, in his short time, touched their lives with the magic of archaeology.

Dusty ran his tongue around the inside of his mouth.

He was dying of thirst and his head felt like it might explode.

He opened one eye and looked around. He was lying across Dale's big bed. He didn't recall how he'd gotten here, but it was comforting, a link to the man he'd loved with all of his heart. Grief vied with the throbbing misery of the hangover. Trying to imagine the future, how it would be, added to his grief. Whom would he talk to? Dale had always been there to listen, and then give advice.

*I'm alone now.*

That knowledge grew like a yawning pit in his already rebellious stomach. From this day forward, anything that should have been said between them would never be said—and he knew it for the first time.

Dusty sat up and found himself fully dressed, but for his boots, which rested neatly side by side against the nightstand. He frowned at that, finding it terribly out of character for him.

The faint odor of eggs, cheese, beans, and chili carried to his nose. At the first watering of his mouth, his stomach squirmed.

"Oh, God," he whispered, and doggedly pulled on his boots.

He gingerly walked down the hall to the bathroom, where he washed his face, cupped a half gallon of water into his greedy mouth, and ran a comb through his blond hair. His eyes looked like misshapen cherries. He knew from long experience that they'd stay swollen and red for most of the day. He grabbed the aspirin bottle and choked down three pills, desperately hoping they'd cut the knifelike pain in his brain.

He squinted at himself, decided he was presentable, and headed for the kitchen.

"Welcome to the world of the living, Stewart," Maureen greeted. She stood before the stove with a spatula in her hand, wearing blue jeans and a red turtleneck.

Her long black braid fell down her back like a glistening snake.

Dusty eased onto one of the stools at the breakfast bar and whispered, "Coffee. Hot, black coffee."

"Coming right up."

She handed him a steaming cup, and Dusty cradled it in both hands. "Okay. How'd I get here?"

Maureen's brows lifted. "Well," she said as she shoveled eggs onto a tortilla and put the plate in front of him. They looked marvelous: dripping melted cheddar topped red salsa while green speckles of jalapeño peeked out at him. The *refritos* might have been from the can, but on a morning like this, who was complaining? "Let's say that you were not the life of the party last night. The more stories they told about Dale, the more morose you became. The more morose, the more beer you drank, and the whole thing bootstrapped you into a mess. Lupe, Steve, and I poured you into the Bronco a little before midnight and you insisted on coming here, because you just knew Dale would be waiting for you." Her expression softened. "And, when I got you here, Dusty, you knew. So I put you to bed where you'd be closest to Dale."

He picked up a fork, but waited until she'd fixed her own plate and came to sit beside him before he took the first bite.

Maureen spread her napkin over her lap. "I wanted to join you last night. You don't know how hard it was not to."

"Yes," he said, "I do." The eggs were wonderful. "Where'd you learn to cook *huevos* like this? These are great."

"I've been watching a master. Did I get the cumin right?"

"Perfect." He frowned. "Where'd we get fresh cilantro? I don't remember any of it in Dale's fridge."

"At the Safeway supermarket, down the road. I had plenty of time this morning."

They finished breakfast in silence. Dusty didn't have
the strength to eat and talk. It would have required too
much concentration. Besides, his aching heart needed
companionable silence more than it did conversation.

After wiping up the last of the salsa with a tortilla
and washing it down with coffee, he said, "I didn't
dance with any strippers last night, did I? Didn't get
into any dick-swinging contests or do anything else stupid?"

She took a drink of coffee, then answered, "No. I
thought it best to get you away before you could generate more archaeological legends. Besides, I was
pretty sure you'd want to do your crying in private."

Dusty lowered a hand to his rebelling stomach.
"You're not trying to tell me that I . . . did I?"

"No. Would that bother you so much? To show your
grief to others?"

He nodded stiffly, said, "Yes, it would," and sipped
his coffee. His stomach knotted and squealed, as
though preparing to make a break for it. He sat as still
as possible. *Please, God, if you let me live through this,
I swear I'll never do it again.*

His headache only seemed to get worse. Probably
because God knew he was a liar.

When he laughed at himself, Maureen smiled.

"What are you chuckling at?" she asked as she collected the plates and took them to the kitchen sink.

"I was just contemplating the fact that hangovers are
the greatest impetus for prayer in the modern world.
Maybe if I drank more, I would be a truly holy person."

"You'd be holey, all right, at least your liver would."

He liked the way her body moved as she scoured
the dishes and placed them into the dishwasher. On the
wall behind her, the clock said 10:04.

"Jeez, I didn't realize it was so late." He finished his
coffee and let out a sigh. "What have you been doing
all morning?"

She pointed. "Take a look. I left a note card on page twenty-two."

He frowned and realized that the bound book on the tile counter beside her coffee cup was one of Dale's journals. Reaching across, he picked it up. "Been doing a little reading this morning?"

"Not much else to do unless I wanted to watch you sleep, which sounded about as interesting as watching railroad tracks rust."

He opened the diary to the marked page and started skimming, then reading every word, once, and finally twice. Each was as pointed as a sword, and aimed right at his heart. "I don't believe it."

"But there it is in his own handwriting."

Maureen brought the coffeepot around and refilled their cups as she waited for Dusty to finish reading. "Did you know any of that?"

Dusty raised his eyes from the page, stunned. "No. I—I didn't. He never told me."

Maureen was watching him closely. "That's 1963, Dusty. Ruth Ann was working on her Ph.D."

He returned his gaze to the diary and silently reread the words: *"Ruth is coming! Thank God. I feel like a millionaire whose ship has come in. She always turns me into a beaming idiot. The question is, where do we go for the first weekend? Taos, or Santa Fe? Finances are short, but I'm going to bite the bullet for a suite at La Fonda in Santa Fe."*

"What's La Fonda?" Maureen asked. "Fancy?"

Dusty nodded, and his voice sounded strained even to him. "Yeah. Right on the square. I didn't have time to take you there." He swallowed hard. "Dale and my mother . . ."

"There's a lot more, Dusty, though I don't know if you want to read it. I didn't get all the way through that summer yet, but that suite isn't so she can sleep in the bed while he's sacked out on the couch."

The book in Dusty's hands felt unnaturally warm.

He closed it and set it to one side. Tugging on his beard, he tried to still his roiling gut. Finally, he put a hand on his belly and tried to breathe deeply. "You mean they were lovers?"

Maureen glanced at his hand. "Is that the bombshell that just exploded in your life or the hangover?"

"A little of both, I think."

"Well," she said, and tapped the diary with a finger. "We shouldn't jump to any conclusions. Not until we've read all of his diaries."

Dusty barely heard. A numbness had settled on his soul. The idea of Ruth Ann and Dale . . . it just didn't gel in his mind.

The doorbell gave him a start. He jerked around, breathing hard.

"I'll get it," she said, and sprang to her feet.

When Maureen opened the door, Agent Nichols stood there, wearing a brown canvas coat against the November chill. A gray stocking cap covered his thick black hair.

Nichols asked, "Any more messages on the machine?"

"No," Maureen answered. "Come in. I just brewed a fresh pot of coffee. Can I get you a cup?"

"No, thanks." Nichols stepped inside, took off his stocking cap, and glanced back and forth between them. "Is there anything I might need to know?"

Dusty hesitated, then answered, "Not that I'm aware of. What's up? What have you discovered?"

Nichols crushed his hat in his hands. "Not much. Just some odds and ends."

Dusty swiveled around on his stool. "Define 'odds and ends.' "

Nichols stuffed his hat in his coat pocket and shrugged. "Well, remember I told you that we couldn't find Carter Hawsworth? He seems to have just dropped off the face of the earth. The same is true for Dr. Sullivan. She called in and told the department secretary to either cancel her classes or cover them, because she had—" He pulled his notebook from his pocket and flipped through to the right page. "—an important opportunity." When Nichols looked up, he asked, "I thought maybe one of them might have been in contact with you."

Dusty shook his head and glanced at Maureen.

She walked closer to Nichols. "Agent Nichols, did you see the woman in the black coat at the memorial yesterday? The one with the fur hat and dark glasses?"

"I've been over that tape twenty times. We've got most of the people IDed. I didn't see any woman in a fur hat with dark glasses."

"She showed up late." Maureen frowned as though considering. "She looked to be in her thirties. It's just that . . ."

"Go on," Nichols urged.

"Well, she came late, and she reached down to touch Dale's ashes. The action was . . . I guess you'd call it reverential. It caught my attention. That's all."

Nichols looked at Dusty. "You've got some interesting friends. Did you know that both Lupe and Reggie Brown have criminal records?"

"Yeah." Dusty winced. "Look, as to Lupe, he's an alcoholic. He did some stuff when he was on booze that he shouldn't have. If you've been here for any length of time, you're familiar with the problem. It doesn't mean he's not a good man. And he's dried out. I was really afraid that he'd fall off the wagon last night, but he didn't."

"Uh-huh. Did Lupe ever have any problems with Dr. Robertson?"

"No. I mean, you know, just the usual stuff. Dale didn't approve of some of the things he used to get me into when we were kids."

Nichols glanced down at his notes. "Did you know that ten years ago Dr. Robertson informed the Albuquerque police that Lupe Brown had stolen a car? Subsequently, Mr. Brown did six months in the Albuquerque jail."

"Yeah." Dusty's misery wasn't just the hangover. "The thing is, they talked about that later. Dale told Lupe he turned him in so that he'd get help."

"And Lupe just smiled and thanked Dr. Robertson for ratting him out?"

"No, not exactly." Dusty felt like throwing up. "Come on, Lupe didn't kill Dale."

"I have it here"—Nichols glanced at his notes— "that the arresting officer heard Lupe Brown swear— and I quote—'I'm gonna kill that self-righteous son of a bitch.' "

"You've got to believe me, Lupe and Dale talked about it after Lupe got out. Sure, Lupe wasn't happy about Dale turning him in, but he understood that Dale was just trying to help."

"I see." Nichols narrowed his good eye. "What about the kid, Reggie?"

"He's got problems, too. Bad home. His mother used to beat him. Drugs, alcohol, some trouble with the police."

"Like burglary, grand theft auto—that seems to run in the family—dealing in controlled substances, and he's currently on parole. It seems that El Paso cut him loose on Rupert's word that he could keep the boy out of trouble. Did you know that Reggie's wages out at Chaco are currently garnered to pay back the people he robbed?"

"Rupert kept Reggie alive. Listen, if anyone can straighten Reggie out, it's Rupert. He's got some kind of threat he uses to keep him in line. As long as Reggie's not around his mother, he does okay."

"I see." Nichols's predatory stare didn't abate. "Anything else you want to tell me? Anything that struck you as odd about the memorial?"

Dusty sat down on the couch. He took a deep breath to ease his headache before he said, "Maureen, don't forget the man that you saw leave early."

"What man?" Nichols asked.

Maureen turned her attention to Nichols. "That's right. He was standing behind you, Agent Nichols, on that rocky point. It was like he took one look and left. He had gray hair and curious eyes, light blue."

"Behind me?" Nichols asked. "As though he didn't want to get caught in any photos?"

"I didn't think of that." Maureen rubbed her arms as though suddenly chilled.

Nichols reached into his pocket and handed Maureen a photo. "Does this look like him?"

Maureen's eyes widened. "That's him. Who is he?"

"Are you *sure*?" Nichols asked.

"Yes, no question about it." She handed the photo to Dusty.

He studied it. The silver-haired man had a narrow, almost predatory face. Dusty thought the guy looked like the actor, Willem Dafoe, but older.

"I wish I'd seen him," Nichols said. "I need to have a word with him."

"Why? Who is he?" Dusty asked and handed the photo back to Nichols.

Nichols returned it to his pocket. "That's your old friend, Carter Hawsworth."

CATKIN WALKED A few paces behind Browser, studying him from the corner of her eye. In the slanting morning light, he seemed truly alive for the first time in moons. It was as though the brooding man he'd been for the past sun cycle had died, and a new War Chief had been born in his place. That cunning glint had returned to his eye, and his steps had the light wary quality of a bobcat's.

Catkin followed as Browser led their party down the trail into Singing Bird Canyon, a deeply cut fissure that time, wind, and water had worn into the northern side of Straight Path Canyon. Normally they would have followed the Great North Road past the ruins of Center Place, then across the mounds of broken soul pots that remained as mute testimony to the departed dead that had been set free to follow their way northward to the Land of the Dead. Catkin hoped the White Moccasins had followed that trail. But she couldn't be sure. None of them could. Though they'd tried very hard to hide their tracks, a party this large left sign.

Catkin looked at Browser. His thick black brows had drawn together as his dark eyes searched the landscape. She smiled to herself. She had missed this man, this calculating War Chief she'd met two sun cycles ago. She had seen him diminished by the illness and death of his son, the loss of his long-time lover, Hophorn, and the betrayal and death of his hideously soul-diseased wife. Each blow had whittled away a piece of him. Then came the horrors they'd survived at Aspen village, and the destruction of Longtail village. He had watched those children burn to death, and it had damaged him deep down.

But, today, knowing they were being hunted, he seemed to have returned to his old self.

When the trail begin to narrow, Catkin dropped back and let everyone else go before her. She walked last in line, placing her feet carefully on the trail that clung tortuously to the frozen soil of the canyon side. She slipped her bow from her shoulder and pulled two arrows from her quiver. As they descended into the canyon, they became easy targets. Any pair of sharp eyes on the canyon rim could spot them.

She gazed up at the spindly chamisa and rabbitbrush that had taken hold since the old days when every scrap of brush had been plucked from within two days' walk of the canyon, and scanned for signs of ambush.

Ahead of her, Straighthorn walked beside the strange little girl. He was paying close attention to the child, closer than Catkin thought prudent.

"Keep your eyes on the canyon, warrior," Catkin reminded softly. "If the White Moccasins jump us here, we'll be spitted on their roasting fire before dusk."

Straighthorn turned, and his thin face tensed. Despite the cold morning wind, sweat shone on his hooked nose and beaded his short black hair. "It's the girl," he said over his shoulder. "I'm not sure but . . ." He hesitated, studied the child's filthy face, and shook his head. "Maybe if she were clean I would know where I've seen her before."

"Straighthorn," Catkin replied, "think of the number of refugees who passed through Longtail village, and after that, the orphans who ran into Dry Creek village, and the desperate children who flooded Flowing Waters Town. They've all been dirty, half starved, and ragged."

"Yes, but, this is different. There's something about her eyes," he answered. "They're not . . . human."

Catkin searched the sandstone ledges above them before answering. "I'm not sure mine are either. I suspect this child has seen some terrible things. If you think looking into her eyes is unsettling, imagine what she must see when she closes them."

Straighthorn pulled the front of his threadbare red cape closed and stared down at the girl. "Perhaps that's why she won't speak, except to ask for food. She can't trust anyone."

The girl bit her lower lip and watched her moccasins, but Catkin could tell she was listening intently to their conversation.

Catkin said, "Traitors like Springbank have taught us all valuable lessons, warrior."

Straighthorn looked over his shoulder again, and his crudely chopped-off hair fluttered in the wind. "Do you trust anyone, Catkin?"

"Oh, yes. I trust the four of us: Browser, me, you, and Jackrabbit. We can be sure of each other as no other four people in the world."

During the fight with the White Moccasins, the bond between them had hardened like rawhide in the desert sun. Only death could separate them now.

Straighthorn nodded somberly. "Yes, I believe that." Then he used his chin to gesture to the people ahead of them. "And Obsidian? What do you think of her? Is she truly leading us to the old witch's lair, or to our doom?"

The little girl's head tipped to the side, as if to hear better.

Catkin took a moment to carefully step around a rock in the trail. People often made the mistake of talking openly in front of children and were horrified later when the child repeated their words at exactly the wrong instant. She said, "I am certain of only one thing, Straighthorn; she is doing what is best for her."

As they rounded a curve in the trail, sunlight shone on the cliff wall to the right, and Catkin saw the images that had been carved into the tan sandstone. Four spirals, two handprints, and four geometric figures surrounded a worn image of the Flute Player. Catkin breathed in the cool morning air and wondered about them. The priests of the First People had used stone tools to peck them into the rock, but few of the Made People knew what the symbols meant. Thunderbird spread his wings on the rock high above Catkin's head. She looked up and could make out smaller images of lizards, a rattlesnake, and a frog.

An eerie presence filled Straight Path Canyon. Though it had been more than one hundred sun cycles since the First People left, echoes of their Power lingered.

The trail widened ahead, and the canyon bottom spread before them. Talon Town sat like a huge crescent moon at the base of the northern cliff. Catkin saw

Browser's shoulders tense, and her souls replayed the memories that he must be seeing behind his eyes: his dying son coughing up blood, a woman's corpse lying facedown in a grave with a stone crushing her head, Whiproot's mutilated body in a ruined room in Talon Town, and that fateful moment when Browser drove an arrow through his wife's spirit-possessed body.

As they emerged from Singing Bird Canyon, Browser kept them to the low ground, following the channel of the arroyo, moving in a half crouch.

Catkin could hear the wheezing breath of the two elders and Obsidian.

To Catkin's relief the arroyo deepened as it cut through the flats. By the time they had reached the main channel, the dry creek bed cut twice a man's height into the tan soil; they remained completely hidden.

Browser lifted a hand to halt the procession and waved to Jackrabbit and Straighthorn. The two young warriors ran forward, and Browser sent them scurrying up the sides of the arroyo to scout for pursuers.

Stone Ghost and White Cone whispered to each other as they sat down on the frosty sand under the south wall. Obsidian wearily sank to the ground two paces away and leaned her head against the cliff. Her beautiful face bore a coating of dust, but her dark eyes gleamed. One of the Mogollon, a youth named Yucca Whip, smiled and offered Obsidian his canteen. He flushed when Obsidian returned his smile and took it.

Browser walked to stand over Obsidian. "You brought us here. Now what?"

Obsidian handed the canteen back to Yucca Whip. "I don't know exactly, but their lair is here, hidden like a wolf's den. This was the center of the First People's world, and it's the place where they keep the old gods alive. Like the heroes of legend, they expect to rise from the very earth and reconquer the Made People." She shook her head. "It's foolishness. Only death remains for us, Browser. Nothing else. Our time is gone."

Catkin started. Browser shot a worried look at the Mogollon. Had Obsidian lost her wits to speak so candidly of the First People?

Catkin said, "This canyon is filled with abandoned towns, kivas, shrines, and old pit houses, Obsidian. There are caves and hidden recesses, piles of fallen boulders. Surely you must have some idea of where Two Hearts hides? Is his lair along the north wall of the canyon, or the south wall?"

Obsidian's cloak blew in the wind, revealing the bare tops of her breasts, and the wealth of sparkling jewels she wore on her wrists and around her throat. "All I know is that they brought him here, wounded and dying—and this is where Shadow was supposed to bring me."

"He is here," Stone Ghost said from where he slumped against the water-worn earth.

"How do you know, Uncle?" Browser asked.

Stone Ghost scanned the attentive faces of the Mogollon and replied, "If you listen closely enough you can almost hear the footsteps of the Blue God as she sniffs for us in the greasewood."

Catkin's eyes shifted to the little girl. The child had turned to stare absently at the arroyo wall.

"What about tonight?" White Cone asked. "Where will we sleep?"

Browser caught sight of Jackrabbit as he stuck his head over the lip of the arroyo. "I see no one," he said. "As far as I can tell, we haven't been observed."

"Good." Browser fingered his war club, considered, and said, "We will work our way downstream. The new moon won't rise until late. In the darkness between sunset and moonrise we will make our way across the flats to Kettle Town."

"Why Kettle Town?" Catkin asked.

The little girl moved up beside Catkin, gripped a handful of Catkin's cape, and began drawing in the dirt with the holey toe of her moccasin. She sketched the likeness of a clay cooking pot between her feet.

Browser started walking, but said, "If we are discovered and attacked, it is like a pack rat's warren, with escape holes running in all directions. It should be safe, if anywhere in this canyon is."

Stone Ghost grunted as he rose to his feet and offered a hand to White Cone. "Yes, assuming that Two Hearts isn't lying in wait for us there, precisely because it has many escape routes. He always has a back way out of his hole."

"Well, if he is there, Uncle," Browser said, "the element of surprise will be with us." He used his war club to point to the Mogollon warriors. "And perhaps numbers as well."

The Mogollon lined out behind Browser. Catkin and the girl waited to go last.

"Go on," Catkin said, and put a hand against the girl's back to urge her forward. "Follow the others."

The little girl gave Catkin a wide-eyed look, then opened her mouth and started to sing. The strains of an ancient lullaby rose, carried by her sweet little girl voice:

> *"The Creator calls you,*
> *The Divine Mother has seen you*
> *    on your journey,*
> *She has seen your worn moccasins,*
> *She offers her life-giving breath,*
> *    Her breath of birth,*
> *    Her breath of water,*
> *    Her breath of seeds,*
> *    Her breath of death,*
> *Asking for your breath,*
> *    To add to her own,*
> *That the one great life of all might*
> *    continue unbroken."*

Catkin remembered her grandmother singing it to her when she'd been a child. It was old, very old. No one sang it these days. At least no one Catkin knew.

The girl skipped down the trail, as if suddenly happy.

Catkin's heart pounded, wondering why.

# CHAPTER 19

MAUREEN REACHED BEHIND the seat for the thermos. It was a calculated risk: Her coffee mug had been empty for nearly an hour, but what were the chances that she could fill it without splashing coffee all over herself and the Bronco's interior? The road here, a crowned-and-ditched berm bladed across the desert, reminded her more of a motocross track than a thoroughfare.

The Bronco jounced over a rutted section.

"Do me a favor, Dusty, slow down just long enough for me to pour a cup of coffee."

"Sure." He slowed to a crawl.

Maureen unscrewed the thermos, pulled the top off of her travel mug, and poured hot black coffee. She recapped everything and pointed straight ahead. "Okay, hit it."

Dusty eased the Bronco forward across the flat wasteland. Or at least, that's how she classified this high desert with its rabbitbrush, sparse bunchgrasses, and patches of low prickly pear. Old snowdrifts filled the arroyos and cowered behind the low rises. Above, occasional snowflakes twirled down from the gray sky. The way had deteriorated since they'd left U.S. 44,

until they pitched and rolled along this feeble excuse
for a road.

She picked up Dale's diary and tried to synchronize
her reading with the bouncing of the book.

"What did you learn?" Dusty asked as he gripped
the steering wheel.

She almost chipped a tooth when she took a sip from
her coffee mug. She swallowed and answered, "Are
you sure you don't want to read this yourself?"

Dusty made a face. "Yes, I do, Maureen. But right
now, I'm driving. Tell me what you've discovered."

"All right, I'm most of the way through 1959. Remember, Dale meets Ruth Ann at a dig in Maryland in
'57, and is smitten by her. Their first date is that summer. He's worried because he's ten years older than
she is. They correspond after the field season. In '58,
she gets her B.A. and comes to work for him in Arizona at a salvage excavation near Phoenix. It's a Hohokam site that's going to be destroyed during canal
building. In mid-July they become lovers."

Dusty hesitated. "Is it—well, graphic—the way it's
written?"

She sipped her coffee. "No, all he says is 'Last night
it happened. I don't know whether to scream for joy,
or to shoot myself in the head. I'm in love. God knows
where this will end. Ruth is the woman of my dreams.
Can I marry her? Can I muster the courage to ask, and
if so, will she say yes?' "

He steered around a big puddle in the center of the
road. Recent traffic had broken the ice, and it had re-
frozen into a jagged surface. "Did he ask?"

"Not yet. He and Ruth work together on the site.
They go to other southwestern sites for fun. Tuzigoot
one weekend, Casa Grande the next. Dale's writing is
almost poetic, things like: 'Went to a restaurant on
Camelback. When we came out the sunset set fire to
my soul.' "

"Set fire to his soul? Dale said that?" Dusty gave her an incredulous look.

She braced herself as they bounded across a washout in the road. "Boy, Maggie drives this all the time. Her kidneys must be flat."

"Are you kidding?" Dusty's mirrored sunglasses glinted as he turned. "This is a good road. As good as the last time you were over it."

She braced one hand against the roof. "That was a long time ago, and it doesn't look like they've had a road grader on it since."

"It's winter," he told her. "There aren't any tourists here." Dusty waved as they passed a mud-spattered pickup headed the other way. "And the Navajo don't seem to mind."

"Dale might have had poetry in his soul, Stewart, but you seem gloomily pragmatic." She shook her head. "Anyway, back to the diary. Summer ends and Ruth Ann heads back East. Dale goes into a funk. His diary talks about how he can't work. He calls her every night." She noted how Dusty had clamped his jaw. "Is this bothering you?"

His gaze fixed on the road. "Finding out that the man who raised me was sleeping with my mother is a disconcerting thing. I wonder why he never told me?"

She considered that, unwilling to answer. Dale knew how much Dusty hated his mother. If she'd been Dale, she doubted she'd have told Dusty.

"Look," she finally told him, "it doesn't matter. This was long before your father came along. In the 1963 diary, they break up. She wrote to Dale that she was seeing someone else at school that semester."

"So how did Dad and Ruth Ann get together out here?" Dusty was flexing his grip on the steering wheel.

"I haven't read that far yet." Maureen lifted a foot to prop herself on the dash, wishing yet again that she had a seat belt.

"It's just so much to take in," Dusty said. "Dale's death . . . then finding all these things out. I feel like I've been pulled sideways through one of those machines that make hamburger."

They bounced across a cattle guard and onto the pavement past the Chaco Culture sign. Dusty slowed, rolling down his window as a battered old Chevy pickup approached. Dusty stuck his arm out as the pickup slowed.

"Hey, Lupe!"

"Hi, ya, Dusty," Lupe called, his elbow out the window. "Hey there, Maureen! Dad said you were going to be up here. He's waiting for you at the office." Lupe's face narrowed with concern. "You okay, man?"

"Yeah."

"You don't look so good."

Dusty pointed to the journal in Maureen's hands. "Been reading Dale's diaries. Some of the things I'm learning, well, it's like a whole different Dale than I ever knew."

Lupe pursed his lips, a frown incising his forehead under the brim of a black Stetson. "I think sometimes we forget that our folks are people, too, you know? Anything in there about me?"

"Not yet. I'm still back at the early years. I'll let you know if there's anything juicy after we get up to the times you and me got into trouble."

"Yeah, do." Lupe grinned. "You know that FBI guy really put the screws to me this morning. Wanted to know if I had it in for Dale. He brought up that thing with the car."

"What did you say?"

Lupe laughed. "I told him that ten years ago I could have been suspect number one on his list of suspects with motive." His expression sobered. "Dusty, you know that Dale and I worked it all out. I forgave him for that. He was just trying to help. He told me it was the two-by-four approach to get my attention. Hell, for all I know, maybe he actually did. I hadn't been sober that long for years."

"He loved you, Lupe."

"Yeah, and I loved him." He looked oddly stricken at that. "You can't take your folks for granted. Hey, I gotta go. I gotta get to Santa Fe. Got a couple of flutes to deliver. Take care, huh?"

"You, too." Dusty accelerated, face pensive as he rolled up the window.

"Lupe's worried about you." Maureen studied him thoughtfully. "He was your best friend?"

"We had a lot of fun when we were little. I think I told you about the kiva initiation. I did that with Lupe. Then things changed. I started digging and Lupe wasn't into it. He got married too young. It was a nasty divorce. Lupe was drunk half the time and in trouble the rest. The court refused to give the boy to either his mother or his father. Rupert and his wife, Sandy, took Reggie in and raised him. But by then the boy was pretty screwed up. He suffered a lot of depression, and was in and out of detention schools for about ten years, mostly for fighting. Lupe blamed himself and sank deeper and deeper into the bottle."

Maureen thought about child abuse and the toll it took on Indian children every year. "I'm glad Reggie was taken in by his grandparents. Most children like that wind up in foster homes being cared for by strangers. I knew I liked Rupert."

Dusty smiled. "He was a sort of second father to me when I was a teenager. Before that he and Dale had been on some kind of outs. I never knew what, but after Dad killed himself, Rupert started coming around. Lupe was there, he was my age, and well, things just happened, you know?"

"Where was Dale when you and Lupe were getting into trouble?"

"Home cataloging artifacts. Dale once told me that if I ever landed in jail I'd better learn to like the food, because I was staying there." He looked at Maureen through his mirrored sunglasses, and smiled. "He meant it."

Dusty's entire life had been upended, and yet he could still smile. It amazed her.

As they wound down through Mocking Bird Canyon, toward the scene of the crime, she studied him, curious that the "Madman of New Mexico," as he had been called so often, seemed to be holding himself together through sheer force of will. But she wondered what was going to happen when he stood over the place where Dale had spent his last moments.

*Would I be strong enough to deal with this if Dale had been my father?*

She doubted it.

"Dusty," she said as they rolled up to the stop sign, "we'll get through this. You know that, don't you?"

He gave her a tired smile. "Worried about me, Doctor?"

"I'm worried about both of us." She reached out and cupped her hand over his where it rested on the gearshift.

"You'll be all right, Maureen. I know you." Her hand on his, he shifted the Bronco into low and took the turn toward the headquarters building. "And I'm all right, too."

The simple words filled her breast with an unfamiliar warmth—mostly because she knew he wasn't. She smiled, and felt as if a part of her soul that had lain dormant for years was stirring, coming back to life.

BROWSER TUCKED HIS blanket around his shoulders and stared out at the night from one of the half-collapsed doorways on Kettle Town's ruined third floor. Behind him the roof had fallen in, the supporting poles rotted through and splintered. Rain had eroded the packed earth that had once covered it. Most of the plaster had cracked off to expose the stone wall beneath. What had once been a residence for the First People's elite now made a home for bats, pack rats, and wasps.

His ancestors had lived here. Crow Beard, Night Sun, and Sternlight had walked here. Perhaps they had stood in this very doorway and looked out across this same vista.

Was that the cold sensation at the back of his neck? Was it the faint caress of the lost souls of the dead?

*I am one of the First People.* The truth still left him eerily uncomfortable.

He worked his hand into a fist and watched the muscles and tendons flex. Where was the difference? A Made Person's hand looked and worked the same. He had seen Made People and First People die. The same arteries, bones, and nerves ceased to function. In death they looked the same, smelled the same, and rotted the same.

If the difference between First People and Made People were not a thing of the body, was it a thing of the souls?

High over his head, a sliver of new moon blazed amid the sparkling Evening People. He could see across the flats to Straight Path Wash, and still farther to the rimrock that hemmed the canyon on the south. Here and there humps of distant buildings marred the washed clay of the canyon floor. All were dark. Only ten moons ago when he'd lived here, the villages south of the wash had twinkled. Had even those few tenacious farmers given up and left?

In the pale light his breath fogged. Silence lay heavily upon the canyon's cold sandstone and clay.

Browser crouched in the doorway and propped his war club across his knees. He'd promised himself when

he'd left here a few moons ago that he would never
return. Just a short run to the west, on the other side
of Talon Town's ominous ruins, a shallow pit en-
tombed the remains of his son. Closing his eyes, he
could imagine the earth, cold and unforgiving, pressing
against the boy's body. Did the pain of watching a
child die ever go away? He could face the deaths of
adults. They had lived. They had loved. But a child . . .

Browser's chest ached.

He turned to look westward to the place where Matron Flame Carrier and Cloudblower had dropped a
heavy stone atop his wife's body, then shoved dirt over
her grave.

This place haunted him, as though he could feel the
eyes of the dead watching.

The soft rasp of a moccasin on rubble sent a quiver
down his nerves. He eased farther into the shadows,
turning.

"Browser?" Catkin slipped past the fallen wreckage
of the roof and knelt beside him.

"What did you see?" he whispered.

"The back wall is mostly intact. Through there"—
she gestured at a darkened doorway with her war
club—"is the anteroom to a tower kiva. Three rooms
back a doorway leads you out onto the long porch that
runs the length of the town. We'll need to look at it in
the light. I'm not sure it's safe to walk on it."

"How's the view?"

"Good. From that porch, you can see the stairs cut
into the cliff and monitor the abandoned houses at the
base of the slope. Everything seems quiet tonight. I
didn't see any sign of life."

He nodded, indicating the small houses across the
wash. "I haven't seen a single sign of life out there
either. Ten moons ago the towns on the opposite canyon wall were occupied." A sadness went through him.
"This place is dying."

She sank down and braced her back against the stone

door frame. "Maybe it's time to let it die."

Browser saw her eyes tighten. "What's wrong?"

She hesitated. "I was making my rounds, checking our guards, when I overheard that strange little girl talking to herself."

"I thought she was supposed to stay with White Cone tonight?"

"She must have sneaked out. I found her huddled inside a pile of fallen roof timbers with a cornhusk doll clutched to her chest."

"What was she saying?"

Catkin's sandals scritched against the dirt on the floor. "Strange things. It was as though she was speaking to someone beside her. She said, 'I won't tell. I'm being good. I'm a good girl.'"

Browser lifted a shoulder. "What did it mean?"

Catkin's eyes strayed to the stairs cut into the cliff and moonlight sheathed her dark eyes. "I tried to talk to her, but she just looked at me with huge black eyes. At the end, I said, 'Who were you talking to?' and she pointed at nothing and said, 'Can't you see him?'"

Browser shook his head. "She's an orphan, Catkin. Her souls have been wounded so many times they're like an arm that has been burned, sliced, and punctured. All that's left is ugly scar tissue."

Her sharp eyes searched the flats before Kettle Town. "Do you think her souls are loose?"

"Maybe."

Browser impulsively slipped an arm around her shoulder and pulled her close to share warmth. It was the first time he'd ever touched her so. A smile turned her lips as she settled against him.

"What next?" she whispered. "How do we go about finding Two Hearts? I suspect his lair will be well guarded."

"I'm going to send out small parties at night, to search for activity," he told her. "No matter how careful they are, one of our scouts will see the glow of a fire, or hear their voices. Then we will—"

"Do you trust the Mogollon?"

"A little," he answered. "They are warriors of the
Bow. One of their prophets has been killed. Probably
by one of Two Hearts's assassins. I think they know
how important this hunt is. Imagine the prestige it will
bring to their society if they are there when Two Hearts
is hunted down and killed."

"You are more forgiving than I. I remember their
insults too well."

Browser could still see the faces of the Fire Dog
warriors who'd been raping her, which meant their
faces must be burned into her souls.

"I think we must forgive, Catkin. We are like coyotes with the foaming-mouth disease, mad, tearing at
each other because of wrongs committed by people
long dead." He exhaled and a white cloud drifted before his face. "Their prophet was right. If we don't stop
this, many sun cycles from now a new people will
come here and find these ruins, and wonder who we
were and why we destroyed ourselves."

Out in the night, an owl hooted, as if it were the
assent of the dead.

"I'LL RIDE IN back," Rupert Brown said as he
shoved the passenger seat forward and climbed into the
back of the Bronco.

Dusty took one last look around the Visitors Center
parking lot, and got behind the wheel. An unearthly
gray shimmer lit the canyon today. Part of it was the
snowflakes pirouetting out the leaden sky, but there
was something else, too. Dusty couldn't identify it; it
was as though the ghosts were dancing. He could feel
them all around him.

Maureen slid into the passenger seat and turned around. "How are you doing back there, Rupert?"

He maneuvered his feet around the thermos and a wealth of travel junk. "Fine, thanks." Then he added, "What's this?" as he studied the bound journal.

"We've been reading Dale's diaries from the early years. It's fascinating."

"Yeah," Dusty muttered. "And really upsetting. God, Rupert, you wouldn't believe the things I'm learning."

"It was a different time back then," Rupert said softly, inspecting the date on the cover. "Just keep that in mind." He laid the book to one side.

The fact that he didn't seem uncomfortable back with all the junk spoke well for his continued humility—a rare trait among federal bureaucrats.

Rupert's olive-green down coat sported the official government patch on his left shoulder: UNITED STATES DEPARTMENT OF THE INTERIOR, NATIONAL PARK SERVICE. He had pulled the earflaps of his red Scotch cap down against the biting west wind. "Let's go."

"Saw Lupe on the way out. He says Nichols really ran him through the third degree."

"Yeah, well, the good old FBI seems to be drawing one blank after another. They wanted to see Reggie, too, but it's his day off so he's staying in town."

Dusty drove around the canyon loop, took the exit, and pulled into the Casa Rinconada parking lot. He killed the ignition. Looking up to the west, there, on the low ridge jutting from under South Chacra's rimrock, he could already see the site. Yellow police tape crisscrossed everything. Two men stood up there, waiting.

He got out of the Bronco and inhaled a deep breath to fortify himself. He felt light-headed, as though his soul had somehow lifted out of his body.

Rupert led the way up the path.

Dusty and Maureen followed, walking side by side.

When they passed the Tseh So interpretive site, panic gripped his heart.

He looked up at the cliffs that rose to the south. Winter shadows striped the ancient stairway that had been laboriously carved into the cliff face. It had eased prehistoric travel from the canyon bottom to the top of South Chacra Mesa. From the top of the stairs, the South Road led to the Tsin Kletzin ruin, which huddled on the lonely mesa top. Tsin Kletzin made up the southern tip of an imaginary cross created by Pueblo Alto on the north, Pueblo Bonito on the west, and Chetro Ketl to the east.

It helped that Maureen walked beside him. She had become his lifeline to sanity—and the one reason he couldn't allow himself to crumble, like he wanted to. Just before they reached the yellow tape barrier, Dusty reached out for her hand. She clutched his fingers tightly. Dale must have walked this same path only a few days ago. Had he known what waited for him? *Who* waited for him?

The graveled trail forked, one route leading south to the archaeological site Bc59, the other to the great kiva of Casa Rinconada. Rupert led them southwest through the rabbitbrush and shocks of wheatgrass, to the base of a low shale ridge that shouldered its way out from the tumbled rim of South Chacra Mesa.

Dusty climbed.

Yellow plastic crime-scene tap warbled in the wind. On the other side stood Agent Nichols, his hands thrust deeply into the pockets of a brown canvas coat. He had the furred hood pulled up over his head. Another man, older, with gray hair, stood beside Nichols, wearing a long black wool coat over a gray suit. He had a scarf wrapped around his neck.

Dusty walked up to the tape. To the untrained eye the site would have looked like a crumbled rock outcrop. To Dusty's eye, it was anything but that.

"Dr. Stewart, Dr. Cole," Nichols said, "I'd like you

to meet my supervisor, Special Agent in Charge Ed Hammond."

Dusty shook the suited man's hand, but his eyes were drawn magnetically to the site beyond. The FBI agents might not have existed as he stepped forward, ducked under the tape, and walked out onto the ridgetop site.

"Whoa! Wait a minute!" Hammond called.

Dusty ignored him. He had to shove the image of Dale's mangled body out of his mind and concentrate on the archaeology. "I'd say this is a five-room, single-story small house." He pointed at the fresh dirt falling into a conelike hole at the bottom of what was obviously a kiva. "Is that were Dale was found? That hole?"

"It is." Nichols stepped up with Maureen beside him. "Dr. Robertson's body was lying upside down."

Dusty clenched his fists and walked to the edge of the kiva. He knelt to stare across the rubble.

"What is it?" Rupert asked, following his gaze.

"Did you know about this?" Dusty asked.

Rupert ducked beneath the tape and came to kneel beside Dusty. "What?"

"What are you looking at?" Hammond asked. His polished black shoes slipped on the rock as he ducked beneath the tape and tottered toward them.

"It's been potted," Dusty said, and pointed. "These three rooms were dug up, vandalized. It's been a while, though. Maybe thirty or forty years."

"Or tested," Rupert suggested. "Most of these Hosta Phase small houses were dug between 1939 and 1942."

"I remember," Dusty agreed. "But this wasn't professionally excavated, Rupert. These are pot-hunter holes. They weren't backfilled."

"That was a long time ago, Dusty. Methodology—"

"Was poor," Dusty finished. "Still, the UNM teams that did the excavations out here made sure they stabilized the ruins they excavated, and backfilled the rest to protect them. Why would they have left this one?

Rupert, you're the living expert on these Hosta small houses. You did your master's thesis on them. You've reviewed the field notes. Was there any mention of vandalism out here?"

Rupert fingered his chin, staring thoughtfully into the depression, as though to see into the past. Absently he said, "It's been a long time since I've looked at that information, Dusty, but I don't recall a mention of vandalism. I do know that this site wasn't revisited until the Chaco Center survey in 1971. We don't have any records of testing, let alone excavation, up here dating from the UNM period."

"How could they have missed it?" Dusty gestured down at the circle of Casa Rinconada and the hivelike foundations of the excavated small houses on the flat below. "This is a city out here."

"Who knows? Maybe the records were lost." He paused. "Or someone removed them."

Maureen leaned over Dusty's shoulder. From her expression, she must have been imagining Dale's upside-down body. "What else did you find?"

"Not a thing," Nichols answered. "And that's puzzling. Whoever buried Dr. Robertson didn't drop anything. He didn't leave any tracks. It's a clean site."

Rupert stood and fixed the FBI agents with knowing eyes. "You won't find anything on top of the ground, gentlemen. That's why I asked for this meeting. Dale was buried here for a reason. To understand, we must dig."

"This is a federal crime scene," Hammond reminded. "Why should we allow you to dig it up? Doesn't excavation destroy the site?"

"It does." Rupert shoved his hands into his pockets. "But if you don't dig, you'll never solve this case."

"What makes you so sure?" Hammond asked defiantly. "Don't underestimate the Bureau's capacity for ferreting out enough pieces of the puzzle to fill in the blanks. Whoever did this to Dr. Robertson knew him.

Was close to him. This wasn't a random act. It was a well thought out murder. Someone contacted Dr. Roberston and called him to this place. Someone he knew and trusted. We'll find that person."

Rupert shook his head. "No, you won't. This wasn't a 'White' crime. Sure, you're going to follow out every little lead, interview every anthropologist that Dale ever squabbled with, interrogate every student he ever failed. You'll look up all of his old lovers and find out that none of them were spurned to the point they'd kill Dale. Dale backed a lot of controversial issues. Are you going to check out all the Native American activists who hated Dale because he believed in Anasazi cannibalism and warfare? How about the BLM archaeologists that Dale raked over the coals for turning the federal cultural resources program into a paper shuffle instead of actually doing archaeology? For that matter, he hammered the Park Service pretty hard for our half-assed implementation of the Native American Graves Protection and Repatriation Act. Dale burned every bureaucrat's butt clear up to the Secretary of the Interior. You gonna check her out, too?"

Dusty stood, and found it strange that the action took all of his effort. Reluctantly he walked over to Rupert's side, facing the agents. "Rupert's right. Dale always called it like he saw it, but the profession's full of people like that. Why would they have picked Dale and not some of the other controversial figures?"

"Look," Rupert said tiredly. "I'm just trying to save you from a wild goose chase. What happened to Dale wasn't the result of some petty professional squabble. Witches kill for personal reasons." He aimed a finger at the ruins. "The answer is here. I have the excavation permit already filled out in my office. I'll beg for rubber stamps from the Advisory Council on Historic Places and the New Mexico State Historic Preservation Office. And you can bet that, for Dale's sake, I'll get it in twenty-four hours."

Hammond shivered in the wind. "Who's going to do this digging? You?"

"I can't. Conflict of interest. Dale was a personal friend." Rupert turned away and stepped over to the tape line where he stared down at the empty circle of Casa Rinconada's great kiva one hundred yards to the south. A strangely haunted look entered his eyes.

"I'll dig it," Dusty said. "I have the people. They'll fall over themselves to get a shovel into the ground here. We all loved Dale."

Hammond's look might have pierced steel. "No, Dr. Stewart. I want someone who didn't know Dr. Robertson, and I want my ERT team here."

"Your what?"

"My Evidence Recovery Team."

"Ed?" Nichols asked. "Did I just hear you right? You're going to authorize them to dig?"

Hammond continued chewing his lip for a moment, then nodded. "Yeah, Sam. Hell, maybe Brown is right. I don't buy this witch bullshit, but maybe the answers are here. The one thing we're damn short on is motive. You told me that yourself." He cast a speculative glance at Dusty that sent a cold shiver down his back. "Sam, let's see where this leads. Find some archaeologist who didn't know Dr. Robertson and keep a sharp eye on him while he digs this thing."

The wind whipped Maureen's long braid over her shoulder as she stepped forward and cocked her head. "Excuse me, Agent Hammond, but where are you going to find an archaeologist who didn't know Dale Emerson Robertson?"

"Surely there are archaeologists in the world who didn't know him. Pull in somebody from England," Hammond replied.

"England!" Dusty objected. "What the hell would a European archaeologist know about southwestern witchcraft? That would be like dropping me into a ninth-century Christian church and telling me to find signs of ancient Christian magic. I wouldn't have the slightest idea what I was looking for!"

"Archaeology is a very, very small world," Maureen told Hammond. "First of all, you do need a southwestern specialist, somebody knowledgeable in local tribal religions. Secondly, Dale knew everybody. You couldn't even go to Africa to find someone who didn't know Dale. Think of it in terms of investigating one of your deputy directors: The man is a legend and known by everyone in your Bureau. You simply can't avoid the entanglements of reputation and personality."

Hammond stared at her. "Then who could do the best job?"

"Me," Dusty insisted doggedly. Anger had momentarily replaced his grief.

Maureen shook her head. "No, Dusty, you're too close to the case. I know you wouldn't bias the data, but there are people who would accuse you of it."

Rupert said, "Agent Hammond, I'll give you a list of qualified archaeologists who hold federal antiquities permits. You can choose whomever you wish."

"Good." Hammond headed for the tape, looking half frozen. "We'll run background checks and make our decision."

"Wait!" Dusty ducked under the tape and followed Hammond. "You can't just pick someone from a list. You might get a lab rat who's never had dirt under his fingernails, and who wouldn't know a feature if it—"

Hammond turned irritated eyes on Dusty, and asked in a cold, probing voice: "Is there a reason you don't want an objective scientist to dig this site?"

Dusty felt a keen stab of anger. "Dale *raised* me, Hammond. He took me in when I didn't have anyone else. I want to make sure the excavation is done correctly!"

"Dusty?" Maureen called worriedly from behind.

But it was Rupert who clamped a hard hand on Dusty's shoulder and yanked him back, saying calmly to Hammond, "Cut Dusty a break, Mr. Hammond. This is hard on all of us, hardest on Dusty."

Hammond's gaze still bored into Dusty in an attempt to dissect his soul for innocence or guilt. He didn't give an inch.

Maureen took Dusty's other arm, and with Rupert's help led him away. When they were ten paces down the gravel path, Maureen said, "Good Lord, Dusty, why did you do that?"

"They're never going to find the killer if they pick some idiot to excavate this site!"

But that wasn't it, and he knew, it. They thought he might have killed Dale, and the notion left him swimming in confusion, hurt, and anger.

Sam Nichols called from behind, "We're not paid to be nice, just to find the bad guy."

"You're not going to find him without my help, Nichols," Dusty insisted.

Nichols walked toward them, and turned to fix his good eye on Hammond, who picked his way down the slope on his slippery city shoes. "Don't underestimate the Bureau," he said. "We do have specialists in other cultures."

"Yeah?" Dusty countered and shook off Maureen's and Rupert's hands to turn around. "Do you have a specialist who knows exactly why Carter Hawsworth would want to *personally* study Navajo witchcraft? Does your expert understand the twisted psychology of a want-to-be witch?"

Nichols squinted his good eye. "Who said Hawsworth was a want-to-be witch?"

When Dusty just stood there breathing hard, Nichols turned to Rupert. "I'll be looking forward to that list, Mr. Brown."

"I'll have it to you within the hour," Rupert promised, and gave Dusty the same look he had when he'd bailed Dusty and Lupe out of jail at the ages of sixteen—that "I'll kill you later" look.

Nichols nodded and started back for Hammond.

Rupert said, "Come on, Dusty, drive me back to my office. I'll spring for a hot cup of coffee; then you can go out and piss off more FBI guys while I make some phone calls."

STONE GHOST PROPPED his walking stick and leaned against the cold stone wall to listen. Her voice was sweet and high. The words of the song drifted through the chambers like a soft summer wind, rising and falling.

He walked forward until he found the room where she hid, and peered inside. The child sat in the dark corner in the back with a tattered cornhusk doll clutched to her chest. She rocked back and forth, petting the doll fiercely, singing to it.

Stone Ghost said, "Hello, child. Are you all right?"

The little girl turned to stone. The only things that moved were her eyes. Through a veil of dirty tangled hair, he saw them lift. They focused on Stone Ghost, as though he were the predator and she the mouse hiding in the brush.

Stone Ghost hobbled into the room and looked around. Thick cobwebs filled the corners and hung from the wasp nests that covered the ceiling like tan cones. Old mats and baskets scattered the floor. Is that where she'd found the tattered doll? In one of the baskets? It looked ancient. Its faded red dress had been mouse-chewed and stained with water that had dripped down through the cracks in the roof, but two jet eyes still stared from the face.

Stone Ghost shuffled through a pile of disintegrating floor mats and lowered himself in front of the little girl. She still didn't move. She just watched him.

He grunted as he extended his legs and rubbed his aching knees. "You're lucky you aren't old enough to hurt this way. Age is a curse."

Stone Ghost rested his walking stick on the floor at his side and sighed. "That's a pretty doll. Where did you find it?"

The girl's lips moved, as though she were nursing, but no sound emerged.

Stone Ghost smiled. "You know, I remember when people still lived here. Oh, it was many sun cycles ago, when I was just a boy, but this was a beautiful place."

Two parallel lines of blue spirals had been painted on the white walls. They encircled the room like azure jewels. But the place smelled of ancient destruction.

In the softest voice, Stone Ghost continued, "You know those spirals were very important to the First People. They were symbols of the journey through the underworlds to get to this place of light and warmth. Some of the First People believed their ancestors had climbed through three underworlds, others believed there had been four. But whether they believed this was the Fourth World, or the Fifth, they were very happy to be here."

The girl seemed to perk up. Her gaze shifted to the spirals, then darted back to Stone Ghost and landed on the spirals on his chin.

He asked, "Do you know what they mean?"

He thought the girl nodded, but it was such a subtle dip of her head, he couldn't be sure.

Stone Ghost touched his chin. "What do you think they mean?"

The child shifted her doll to her left hand and lifted her dirty right hand to point at the spirals on the wall.

"That's right," Stone Ghost praised. "Very good. They are the same."

She lowered her right hand to clutch her doll again, and Stone Ghost noticed the bruises on her forearm. He looked more closely and saw other bruises, older ones, on her throat. Four of them, as though a careless stranger had grabbed her by the throat and left finger-prints on her flesh.

"What happened here?" Stone Ghost asked and pointed.

The girl dared to glance down, as if trying to see her throat, but quickly focused on Stone Ghost again.

"Did someone hurt you, child?"

She blinked a couple of times, then stammered, "G-Grandfather."

Stone Ghost just nodded, fearing that if he showed any excitement that she had spoken, she might become mute again. "I'm sorry he hurt you."

She gripped her doll in a stranglehold, her own fingers digging in the way her grandfather's must have around her throat.

Stone Ghost exhaled. "Sometimes grown-ups don't understand that things hurt. Your grandfather probably didn't mean to hurt you."

Tears filled the girl's eyes, and she sucked her lip so hard it made a desperate squeal. He thought she tilted her head in disagreement.

"Do you think he meant to harm you?" Stone Ghost asked gently.

The girl blinked at her doll.

"How did you feel when he did that?"

They sat in silence for perhaps ten heartbeats, then the girl said, "Dizzy. Sick."

She'd spoken so softly, Stone Ghost had barely heard her.

He asked, "Did you do something bad that made your grandfather hurt you? Something that he thought was bad?"

The girl's eyes rolled upward, as though the answer were somewhere high above her, in a place she couldn't reach.

Stone Ghost waited.

The child finally lowered her gaze and propped her

doll on her drawn-up knees. She bounced the doll back
and forth and went back to singing the same lullaby
he'd heard when he'd first arrived. After a few verses,
she suddenly stopped, shook her doll hard, and through
gritted teeth growled, "You don't run away, B-Bone
. . . Walker! You don't ever run away! Do you hear
me?"

She threw the doll to the floor and hit it with a tiny
fist, then slowly turned to glare at Stone Ghost from
beneath long dark lashes.

Bone Walker? What an odd name for a little girl. A
chill went through him. Her eyes were no longer those
of a child, but something old and evil. She might have
been a ghost that had walked the earth alone and wailing for a thousand sun cycles.

Stone Ghost reached out to tenderly pat the doll's
dry cornhusk back. "What happened after he hurt you
for running away, Bone Walker?"

The little girl jerked as though he'd startled her from
a dream, and her mouth trembled.

Stone Ghost picked up the doll and handed it back
to her. She held it tightly for a long time, then leaned
toward Stone Ghost, and stared up at him with eyes
like obsidian beads.

Her lips moved.

He had to lean very close before he could hear her
whisper, *"He told me the owl was bad."*

Stone Ghost thought about that. "Did the owl make
you run away?"

She stared past Stone Ghost at something far away,
then curled on her side on the floor, yawned a wide
long yawn, and closed her eyes.

"Bone Walker . . . Bone Walker?"

In less than twenty heartbeats, her chest rose and fell
in the rhythms of deep sleep.

Stone Ghost exhaled hard and rubbed his knees.

# CHAPTER 20

BROWSER STEPPED INTO a chamber filled with burned roof timbers and carefully walked across the cluttered floor. Broken pots and old baskets lay in the corner to his left. The stench of bat dung and pack rat urine filled the air, and he could hear soft voices coming from the chambers ahead.

Before he entered the next chamber, he called, "Uncle?"

"Yes, Nephew. We are here. Come."

Browser ducked through a T-shaped doorway into a dimly lit chamber. Stone Ghost and White Cone sat before a small fire they'd built in an old gray bowl. Stone Ghost straightened and the firelight rippled through the feathers of his cape. His sparse white hair had a translucent quality, as though made of spiderwebs. He held out a hand to the willow twig mat beside him. "Sit, Nephew."

Browser knelt on the mat and looked at White Cone. The elder had a red-and-black striped blanket pulled over his head. It fell around him in such thick folds that only his wrinkled face, and the hand holding the blanket closed beneath his chin, showed.

"Uncle, we are almost out of food. What little we have left in our packs, along with the remains of the antelope, will feed us for another day. After that, we must find food."

The little orphan girl lay curled on her side in the back corner of the room, her dirty thumb in her mouth.

Her huge black eyes fixed on Browser with an unsettling intensity.

"Are there people here that we can trade with?" White Cone asked.

"If there are, we will have to do it carefully. The White Moccasins will have ears in every wall," Browser said.

Stone Ghost leaned forward. "Perhaps, when some of the smaller villages were abandoned, they cached corn, beans, and squash. We may wish to search their old chambers."

"I will do that, Uncle, but from what I've seen, they may have abandoned the canyon because of starvation. I saw no stubble in the fields, did you? The ground looked fallow to me."

"Yes," Stone Ghost agreed. "It did, which means we may be forced to hunt pack rats for a meal."

"I see food," the little girl said, barely audible.

"What?" White Cone asked and cocked his head.

The girl just stared at him.

Stone Ghost studied her with sober eyes.

"It is almost dark," White Cone said. "You will be sending out scouts, yes?"

"Yes." Browser nodded. "I want small parties of two to work their way around the canyon. We don't wish to draw attention to ourselves. All our scouts need to do is watch for our enemy, and determine which houses, if any, are likely prospects for food caches."

"I shall order my people to prepare." White Cone looked at Stone Ghost. "Curious, is it not? One hundred sun cycles ago, a Mogollon chief came here in a rage to raid Talon Town. Today we return in friendship, working hand-in-hand with Straight Path people to find the most famous witch of all time. Perhaps we are the inheritors of Poor Singer's prophecy after all."

"Perhaps, Elder," Browser said, "but I—"

The little girl suddenly hunched down and her eyes grew huge. "Do you see him?" she whispered.

"Who?" Browser spun around. This chamber nestled in the inner heart of the town. It had no windows, but part of the roof had collapsed and starlight penetrated through a hole in front of Browser. He stared up at it, trying to see if anything moved.

"He's lost," the girl hissed and started trembling. "See his big eyes?" Utter terror twisted her face. She leaped up and ran to hide behind Stone Ghost.

The Mogollon elder peered at her over his shoulder. "Poor child. She must have witnessed terrible things to send her souls spiraling into madness."

Stone Ghost shifted to look at the girl, and firelight sheathed his long-beaked nose. The wrinkles around his wide mouth deepened. "Yes," he said softly.

Browser rose and walked to the doorway. "I must see to my duties. Thank you, Elders. I wish you a pleasant evening."

He stepped into the next room and passed the Mogollon warriors. They sat around pots of stew. The last of their water and corn cakes had been mixed with bits of meat cut from the antelope's bones.

Browser nodded to them and continued on through a series of empty, dusty chambers. In the last room, he found Jackrabbit and Catkin.

"Anything?" he said as he stepped into the chamber.

Jackrabbit squatted in the starlight watching the empty plaza below, and the line of rooms that made up Kettle Town's southern wall. Catkin leaned against the west wall, her cloak pulled tightly about her shoulders. She had a half-eaten corn cake in her hand.

"No," Jackrabbit said. "Not yet."

Browser looked out the window. Beyond Kettle Town, he could see snow-filled roads and abandoned fields.

"The only thing that has moved is a hare," Jackrabbit said. "And he looked lonely."

"Where is Straighthorn?"

Catkin pointed to the roof. "He's hidden under an

old blanket in case anyone looks down from the cliff. But he has a good view."

Browser lowered himself beside Catkin and gestured at the doorway leading to the interior rooms. "This is a good place to hide out. So long as we stay in the interior rooms, the smoke from our cooking fires is dissipated by the ceilings. This morning, I showed the Mogollon the best escape routes through the passageways. Except for food, we'd be set to stay here indefinitely."

Catkin finished her corn cake and dusted her hands off on her buffalo-leather leggings. "Except for food, and the fact that within a day or two they will know we're here."

The pale gray light turned her dark eyes into pools of silver. Browser said, "Then we must work quickly."

"What about tonight? How are we going to do this?"

Browser turned to Jackrabbit. "Jackrabbit, I want you and Straighthorn to work your way toward Talon Town. Go slowly, stick to the shadows. Take a good look at Hillside village and the ruins of Talon Town. You know the place so you'll be able to tell if anyone's been there since the Katsinas' People left ten moons ago."

"Yes, War Chief." Jackrabbit nodded. "Do you remember Peavine?"

Catkin had been attacked by Ash Girl just after finding Peavine's body atop the stairway that led up the cliff.

"What about her?" Browser asked.

Jackrabbit didn't take his eyes off the plaza. "She kept a cache of corn in one of the old abandoned rooms halfway between here and Talon Town. Not many people knew about it, just my friend and me. We left so soon after Peavine's death, it might still be there."

"Look, but be careful. You, of all people, know how dangerous this is, Jackrabbit."

"I do, War Chief."

Catkin said, "Do you wish me to scout—"

"No. I want you to come with me. We need to find a high place where we can see over most of the canyon. If Two Hearts is here, he will have lookouts posted. We must find them before they find us."

Catkin's hand tightened around her war club. "Yes, I understand."

As the Cloud People gathered over the canyon, the starlight dimmed, leaving them in darkness. "It's time." Browser got to his feet. "Jackrabbit, take Straighthorn and go. May the katsinas be with you."

"And with you, War Chief."

Browser motioned to Catkin, and they walked out into the evening and climbed down the ladder into Kettle Town's plaza.

"This way," Browser said and took the lead.

Catkin followed him as he rounded Kettle Town's east wall and trotted across the weed-filled flat toward the small house against the cliff. The roofs of the irregular rooms led to the cliff stairway. Browser started up slowly, feeling the weathered ceiling poles, wondering if they would still hold his weight. They creaked as he climbed, but he made it to the ancient steps cut into the sandstone, and hurried upward. Catkin followed in silence.

When he reached the rim, Wind Baby's cold breath sucked his warmth away. Browser tucked his cloak tightly about his shoulders and looked around.

"How are you?" he whispered to Catkin. The last time she'd been up here, she'd been ambushed.

"Well enough. Let's hurry. The White Moccasins could be on top of us before we have the first hint of their presence."

Browser bent low and trotted along the worn sandstone to an overlook point. He crawled out onto the cold stone ledge and got down on his belly. Catkin eased out beside him.

For long moments, they watched the dark valley below. As the Cloud People sailed to the south, their shadows roamed the starlit ground.

"Nothing," Browser whispered. "No fires. From up here, the canyon looks dead."

Wind Baby blew down from the northwest, and his icy breath penetrated every niche in Browser's clothing. He cocked his head, sniffing. "Do you smell that?"

"What?"

"Smoke. It's very faint."

She lifted her turned-up nose and her nostrils flared. "I don't smell anything, but it could be from our own fires in Kettle Town."

Browser shook his head. "The wind is wrong."

"But Wind Baby plays along the canyon rims, Browser. He whips back and forth. You never know where—"

"Trust me. The smoke is coming from the northwest."

He led the way, crossing the waterworn rock and climbing the eroded terraces that led to the mesa top. As they hiked up the last outcrop and stepped onto the flats, Wind Baby shoved them mercilessly.

Browser bent into the gale and started forward with his war club in hand. Catkin trotted behind him.

"The only shelter up here is Center Place," she called from behind.

"I know. We may just find a group of mourners with soul pots who've come to release their loved ones' souls onto the Great North Road."

Browser trotted along the old road that led straight to Center Place.

There, he smelled it again: smoke on the wind.

Gesturing to Catkin, he slowed. Ahead in the darkness he could see Center Place. The two-story town faced south. A single low wall curved across the front to enclose the plaza with its eleven internal kivas.

Browser stopped and crouched down.

"Someone is there," Catkin said.

"Yes. Stay low."

She nodded.

Browser bent over and started forward. How long did they have until moonrise? One hand of time? He tried to remember. He and Catkin had to be away before then or they'd stand out like towers on the wind-swept surface.

Step by step the looming bulk of Center Place grew to fill the sky. Legends said that once, long ago, it had been a gleaming white palace, visible for miles along the Great North Road, but the plaster had flaked and fallen to the ground. The detritus made for uneven footing as Browser trotted into the shadows cast by the wall.

Two paces behind, Catkin moved with ghostly silence.

Browser worked around to where a wing wall had collapsed and climbed onto the abutment. He reached up and grasped the roof pole. Catkin, from long practice, cupped a hand and boosted him onto the flat roof.

Silence.

Reaching down, he grasped Catkin's hand and she scrambled up beside him. They lay on their bellies listening to the darkness. The smell of smoke drifted past with greater regularity, and with it, the unmistakable aromas of boiling corn and turkey.

They exchanged glances; then Browser crept forward on all fours and peered down into the plaza. To his right, three circular kivas jutted from the plaza floor of the L-shaped town. Straight in front of him, a red gleam lit one of the doorways partway down the northern room block. As he watched, shadows moved within.

Browser eased down from the parapet to the plaza floor. Catkin seemed to flow over the wall. Her war club was in hand, her head turning as she searched the plaza.

Browser kept to the shadows at the base of the walls.

He crossed the darkened kiva roofs, and slipped slowly down the northern wall. There, where one of the kivas abutted the northern room block, he crouched. Catkin wedged herself in beside him.

". . . they are here?" a voice inside asked.

"Somewhere," Blue Corn responded gruffly. "My sources couldn't be mistaken about that."

Catkin's eyes widened, and Browser made a calming motion with his hand.

"We'll find them," Rain Crow answered. "There is no way the Mogollon could have beaten our scouts here. Not with two old men to slow them down. No, Matron, we have them. No matter what, the canyon is a trap for them. Their plight reminds me of a pine nut on a rock. We are the pestle that shall crack them."

"This alliance bothers me," Blue Corn said uncertainly. "That old witch, Stone Ghost, is no one's fool. Why would he put in with the Fire Dogs? And War Chief Browser, despite the reputation he has developed for ineptness, has no love for the Fire Dogs either."

"I say this prophet offered them some foul bargain. A trick no doubt, manufactured for the moment, but Stone Ghost took it in the hope that he could save the Katsinas' People from our wrath." The voice belonged to an old man; it was deep and frail.

Browser stilled his breathing to hear better. Catkin had clutched her war club so tightly her hand shook.

"Their false gods are dying, and they are desperate to save them by any means necessary," the old man finished.

"Why would Browser care?" Rain Crow asked. "He only joined the Katsinas' People because his demented wife did. You heard the stories about her, didn't you? That she was a monster? Browser killed her himself to save his lover, Catkin."

Catkin stiffened, and Browser placed a restraining hand on her forearm. Beneath her cool skin, hardened muscles rippled.

"I don't understand this," Blue Corn returned. "What could the Fire Dogs have offered either Browser or Stone Ghost that would have turned them against us? The Fire Dogs have been our enemies since the beginning of time. Browser made his reputation from the daring raids he carried out against them. Why would he side with them?"

"His·nerve is broken," the old man said. "It happens. As Rain Crow said, he had to kill his own wife in the service of false gods. Perhaps that was when his blood turned to water."

Browser shifted uncomfortably. Is that what people thought of him? That he was a coward?

"I disagree. The man I saw stand between the Fire Dogs and my warriors had more than water for blood, Elder," Rain Crow said.

"It makes no difference," the old man stated firmly. "He and his Fire Dog friends shall die in Straight Path Canyon tomorrow."

"You're sure we have them boxed?" Blue Corn asked.

"Every high point is guarded. They cannot pass without our scouts seeing them. After that, it is only a matter of hunting them down."

"I left half my forces to guard the Katsinas' People. I hope we—"

"They will be docile," the old man said. "Cloudblower is a peacemaker."

"Yes," Blue Corn said. "That is how she's keeping the katsina heresy alive. Not only is she *kokwimu*, a sacred man-woman, but her knowledge of Healing has elevated her status among many of the clans. She goes everywhere to Heal, even to her enemies. People who would normally think ill of the katsinas think highly of Cloudblower."

Fabric rustled, and the old man said, "Then she must never leave Flowing Waters Town. My people will deal with her when the time comes. No one will know."

Browser's heart thudded in his chest. He had to get Cloudblower out of there!

"No one will know, except you, me, and Rain Crow," Blue Corn answered suspiciously.

"You have nothing to fear from my Flute Player warriors," the old man said. "We save our venom for the false believers."

"Just make sure where you inject it," Rain Crow warned. "If the stories are correct, and First People do still walk the land, you may wish to save as much of your venom as you can for them."

"The White Moccasins are a myth conjured by the Katsinas' People to frighten us," the old man said.

"What of the wealth they say they found in Two Hearts's cave? All that turquoise? The copper beads? The shell?" Blue Corn asked. "Did the Katsinas' People just conjure that up as well?"

"So they found some graves and robbed them."

"I would not discount the stories," Blue Corn answered. "It would explain a great many things that have happened over the past few sun cycles. Elder, you and I both know that your warriors did not destroy Aspen village. I sent scouts to check the veracity of the claims. They climbed into the kiva—and saw the bodies. Your men didn't do that."

"No. But that's not to say the Katsinas' People didn't destroy Aspen village. It is just as logical to suggest that Matron Eagle Hunter and her people threw out the katsinas. Flame Carrier couldn't allow that to happen, not with people turning back to the Flute Player and the Blue God, so Flame Carrier and her warriors attacked Aspen village. They were greeted as friends, and turned on their hosts. Perhaps Matron Flame Carrier was killed in the fighting. Perhaps that's where Browser received his wounds. Perhaps this whole story of the burned kiva at Longtail village is the desperate work of the Katsinas' People trying to keep the last of their 'believers' from returning to the old gods."

Browser's grip tightened on his war club, every muscle in his body charged. He had half risen when Catkin pulled him down into the shadows.

Blue Corn's disdainful voice returned. "I am no fool, Horned Ram. I sent warriors to Longtail village, too. The tower kiva and the rest of the town was burned to the ground."

Catkin's grip on his arm turned brutal; she pointed.

He followed her finger to the dark shapes that emerged from the far doorway, their hands clutching weapons.

Blue Corn's next words caught him off guard when she said, "My people tell me that Browser's story is correct. The bodies at Aspen village were headless, and the meat had been stripped from the bones." She made a tsking sound. "No, say what you will about Browser. Rain Crow and I know him. No matter what he believes—and I'm still not sure that he really believes in the katsinas—Browser wouldn't defile the dead. He's a man of honor."

"Bah!" the old man spat. "What is this? One would almost believe you were on this Browser's side! Are you forgetting that his people murdered your young warrior, White Spark, the night they slipped away like cowardly dogs?"

Browser stared at Catkin and she shook her head in confusion. A warrior was killed the night they left?

"We're not forgetting anything," Rain Crow answered. "I intend to find Browser, and his Mogollon allies, and when I do, I will kill them. But we must deal with one problem at a time. After that, if the White Moccasins are really out there, I shall deal with them, too."

"Good," the old man growled with satisfaction. "Now, come, let us eat. This stew looks good and smells even better. In a half-hand of time, the moon will rise and we can walk to the canyon rim. If they're camped down there, we should be able to spot their fires. Who knows? By sunrise, we may have killed them all."

Browser glanced around, seeing the warriors who had begun to gather in the plaza. They had huddled together on the south side, talking among themselves. Waiting.

Browser took Catkin's hand and eased slowly onto the kiva roof. Sticking close to the wall, he snaked his way across and then scuttled along the base of the wall.

The only thing in their favor was that the Flute Player warriors considered themselves the hunters. Betting his life on that fact, Browser quietly lifted Catkin to the abutment, and followed her over the wall into the night beyond.

"DOESN'T THAT HURT?" Stone Ghost asked.

Bone Walker pounded her chest with her fist again, as if to show him that it didn't, and rolled onto her back on the old willow-twig mat.

Stone Ghost leaned against the wall. Through the gap in the roof he could see Evening People gleaming. The scents of night, of cold stone and earth, blew around him, fanning the red coals in his warming bowl.

Bone Walker drew up her knees, crossed her legs, and started kicking one foot.

Stone Ghost said, "The Evening People are beautiful, aren't they?"

She looked up and seemed to be trying to decide. "Do they have breath-heart souls?"

Stone Ghost's bushy white brows lowered. "That's a good question. They don't have human bodies any longer, so I don't think they need breath-heart souls to keep their lungs working and their hearts beating."

"Maybe they have Spirit hearts that need to beat."

"Yes, that's possible."

Bone Walker pounded her chest again, hard.

Stone Ghost winced. "I think I heard your ribs crack."

She tipped her head back to see him, and tangled black hair spread around her. "My breath-heart soul hurts. Like it's turning to rock."

"Is that why you keep hitting yourself? To make it stop hurting?"

She nodded and looked back at the Evening People again. They twinkled like frost crystals strewn across a soft buffalo robe.

He said, "Well, child, the soul is the place where the heart suffers. I'm not surprised you hurt."

Stone Ghost studied the little girl, wondering what had happened that made her hurt so much inside. Was it just the beatings her grandfather had given her for running away, or something more?

Bone Walker blinked at the Evening People.

"Would you like to hear a story about a heart?"

She sucked her lower lip for a time, then nodded.

Stone Ghost smiled, and said, "There was once a very powerful holy man, named Dune the Derelict. One day, a young man came to him and begged Dune to teach him how to be a great Singer, so that he could help his people. Dune eyed the young man suspiciously and said, 'So, you want to be a great Singer, do you? Do you know how much work it takes?' The young man assured him he was willing to study very hard. He told Dune he would do anything Dune asked him to. So Dune said, 'Good. Let's play hide-and-seek.' "

Stone Ghost clapped his hands together, and Bone Walker scrambled onto her stomach to watch him more closely, as though she feared he might leap upon her and gobble her up.

He whispered, "What the young man did not know was that Dune had a magical yucca hoop hidden behind his back. Dune jumped through the yucca hoop and disappeared."

Bone Walker stopped sucking her lip and stared at Stone Ghost. "What did the young man do?"

"Well, he tried to find Dune. He looked everywhere, under rocks, on top of cliffs, he crawled around on his belly searching the grains of sand, but he couldn't find Dune anywhere."

Bone Walker frowned. "What happened? Did he go home?"

"No. The young man finally fell on the ground, kicked his heels, and shouted, 'This isn't fair! I came here to learn to be holy, and you vanished without teaching me a thing!' "

Stone Ghost clapped his hands again, and Bone Walker jumped.

He said, "Right at that instant, Dune reappeared. The young man was astounded. He said, 'Where were you? I looked everywhere for you!'

"Dune said, 'I was hiding in your heart. If you don't search your own heart first, what kind of a Singer will you be?' "

Bone Walker smiled, and it was like Father Sun breaking through black clouds. Her eyes glistened. "I like that story."

"Do you know what the young man's name was?"

"No, what?"

"His name was Buckthorn, but later on Dune gave him a new name. He called him Poor Singer."

Bone Walker's eyes widened. "Poor Singer! My great-great-grandfather was the son of the Blessed Cornsilk! I know many stories about Poor Singer, but I've never heard that one."

"Well, now you have."

Stone Ghost smiled, but blood had started to surge in his ears. He examined the triangular shape of her face, her full lips and midnight eyes. *She's one of the*

*First People, and she knows it. Who would have risked telling her?*

Bone Walker tugged at Stone Ghost's turkey-feather cape. "Do you know more stories about the Blessed Poor Singer?"

"Oh, many more. Let me see. Did you know that Poor Singer carried a pebble under his tongue for several sun cycles? Have you heard that story?"

Bone Walker lifted herself on her elbows and propped her chin on her palms. "No. Why did he do that? Didn't he get dirt in his mouth?"

"Well, probably. But he did it because Dune told him that if he didn't stop waggling his tongue he'd never be able to hear the divine musician."

Bone Walker cocked her head. "The what?"

"The divine musician. But let's start at the beginning. Let me see . . ." Stone Ghost rubbed his wrinkled chin and pretended to be thinking as he asked, "By the way, who was the man you saw a few hours ago?"

"Man?" Bone Walker frowned.

"Yes, when my nephew came into the room, you said you saw someone who was lost and had big eyes."

Bone Walker flattened herself on the floor and rested her chin on her hands. "That was an owl."

"Oh," Stone Ghost answered as though that made everything clear. "I see. Is Owl your Spirit Helper?"

Bone Walker thoughtfully poked at a hole in her blue sleeve. "He tries to help me."

"Well, that's good. Owls are very Powerful Spirit Helpers, child. Listen to him."

Bone Walker appeared to be concentrating on a strange taste at the back of her throat.

"What are you thinking about?" he asked.

"Rocks have souls. Did it hurt when the pebble clacked on Poor Singer's teeth?"

"Ah." Stone Ghost lifted a finger. "You are already looking in your own heart to find answers. Good girl. Well, let me tell you the whole story. Are you ready?"

"Yes." She stretched out on her back again and stared up at the Evening People.

Stone Ghost used his best storytelling voice, deep and slow: "When Dune first mentioned the divine musician, Poor Singer thought he meant Wind Baby's voice or the roar of the Thunderbirds, but Dune told him that the divine musician was not outside, he was inside. Unfortunately because of all the chatter that filled Poor Singer's brain, he couldn't hear anything. So, one day, while he was fasting, he tripped over a rock. It made him very angry. He'd been tripping over that same rock for days. Poor Singer yelled, 'Look at this! My toe has a big bruise! Why can't you live somewhere else? You're ugly and have sharp edges! I hate you!' "

Stone Ghost paused to take a breath and noticed that Bone Walker was listening intently, as though his voice were the only thing in the world. "Well, needless to say, Poor Singer was very surprised when the rock said, 'Why do you insist on kicking me in the belly every day?' Poor Singer—"

Bone Walker interrupted, "Didn't he know rocks have souls?"

"Yes, but there's a difference between knowing it—" Stone Ghost tapped his head. "—and *knowing* it." He lowered his hand to his heart.

"Oh." Bone Walker nodded earnestly in understanding. "Then what happened? Did he pet the rock?"

"I don't recall that in the story, but I'm sure he must have. The rock forgave him."

Bone Walker shoved tangled hair from her eyes and rolled over to peer at Stone Ghost. "When did he find the pebble?"

"He found it on his way back to Dune's house; the pebble was shining in the trail at his feet. He picked it up and put it in his mouth—"

"And sucked off all the dirt."

"Yes, but he put it in his mouth to remind him that

if he kept his own tongue from waggling, he might hear some of the other voices that called to him from the world. And he did, of course. The very next day, he heard the voices of clouds Singing, and trees weeping."

Bone Walker's huge black eyes widened. She didn't say a word. She just rolled to her back again and stared up at the shining Evening People.

Stone Ghost gave her a few moments to absorb that, then bravely reached out to touch her tangled hair. She froze at his touch.

"Bone Walker? Would you like me to brush your hair for you? I could—"

She let out a high-pitched animal scream, scrambled to her feet, and ran away.

# CHAPTER 21

MAUREEN HADN'T FELT so tired in ages. She turned the Bronco into Dale's driveway, shut off the engine, and killed the lights.

Dusty stirred in the passenger seat, stretching and yawning in the darkness. "Are we there?"

"Home sweet home. Or at least Dale's port in the storm."

Dusty opened the door and stepped out. Maureen watched him move the seat forward and twist into the back of the Bronco. He pawed his way past an empty doughnut box, a half-full sack of Doritos, and found Dale's journal, Maureen's thermos, and his notebook. He carried them inside.

They'd been just south of Zia when he'd pulled over and asked her to drive. Now, as she walked wearily to the door, she wasn't sure that had been such a smart idea. That last half hour into Albuquerque, she'd been seeing things—strange images spun from caffeine, stress, and exhaustion. She'd seen Dale's face reflected in the afterimages of sleeplessness. His voice had spoken to her, sifted from the whine of the tires and the rumble of the motor.

What had he been trying to tell her?

She fumbled with Dusty's keys and managed to unlock the door. The house was delightfully warm after the chill November air. A faint hum from the heat system was all she could hear. Walking to the answering machine, she noted that two calls were waiting.

"I'm headed for the sack," Dusty told her. "Who wants first dibs on the john?"

"I do. My thermos of coffee outweighs the bottle of Guinness you found under the seat." Lord knew how long it had been there. When Dusty had pulled it out, it had been covered with dust, the label half worn off. Nevertheless Stewart had pried the cap off and drunk it down before leaning his head back and surrendering to sleep.

Maureen walked down the hall past Dale's office and closed the bathroom door behind her. She was in the process of washing her hands when Dusty burst in the door with Dale's journal in his hand.

"We've had a break-in!" He whirled on his heel and trotted down the hallway.

"What?" She hurried after him and into Dale's office.

Dusty stopped in front of the familiar file cabinet. The door hung open. Where the diaries had been packed side by side, the drawer was empty.

"You didn't move them?"

Dusty shook his head. "No."

She took a deep breath. "Thank God I took that journal"—she pointed to the one in Dusty's hand—"this morning."

Dusty lifted it. "I was going to replace it. Old field habit. All day long I bitched to myself about how much excavation data has vanished over the years because of carelessness. The UNM field notes taken during the recording of the Hosta Phase small house where Dale was murdered might have answered a lot of questions." He clutched the diary tightly. "So I was going to be conscientious and put this back before I went to bed."

Maureen glanced around, suddenly worried. She whispered, "You don't think he's still in here, do you?"

Dusty's blue eyes gleamed. "I sure as hell hope so."

He started for the door, and she feared he might be going to the Bronco for his pistol. Maureen grabbed him by the shoulder. "Dusty, we need to walk straight out to the Bronco and use the cell phone to call Agent Nichols. The best thing you can do right now is remember exactly where you went after we walked in the door. What you touched. Nichols is going to want to know."

Dusty's jaw muscles bunched. "I'll let you call. I have other priorities."

He pulled away from her and headed down the hall, and out the front door, at a fast pace.

When they slid into the Bronco, Dusty pulled his pistol from beneath the seat, opened it to see that it was fully loaded, then snapped it closed and leaned back with his eyes on Dale's front door. "Call Nichols, Maureen. Tell him he'd better hurry, because I'm going to shoot the first person to walk out Dale's door."

DUSTY AND MAUREEN sat at a window seat in the Ore House restaurant, a second-story affair overlooking the Sante Fe Plaza. The decor charmed Maureen. The whitewashed adobe walls contrasted beautifully with worn Saltillo floor tiles. To her right, French windows looked out onto a porch, empty this frigid November evening.

Dusty thoughtfully sipped at his cappuccino, his gaze on the bundled pedestrians scurrying across the plaza. He'd declined a beer, swearing that he'd fall face first into his plate after the first one. He looked unusually handsome tonight, wearing a gray-plaid shirt and new Levi's.

"I don't understand," he murmured, as if to himself. "Nichols's crack ERT team didn't find a jimmied lock. After a whole day of dusting and taking samples, they found nothing."

Maureen folded her arms across her cream-colored wool sweater and leaned back in her chair. "Unless, like Nichols said, we didn't lock the door when we left."

"The door was locked," Dusty said. "You don't live in Albuquerque without learning to lock your doors. Even in the nice neighborhoods. I was the last one out. Believe me, I locked it."

"Well," she said and tilted her head. "Then someone had a key."

"*I'm* the only one who has a key to Dale's new house."

She lifted a shoulder, remembering the long string of questions they'd answered. The problem was, no one really knew who had keys to Dale's house. Dale might have given a key to someone else and Dusty didn't know it. That possibility had forced them to return to Santa Fe and the safety of Dusty's dilapidated trailer.

"A loony for your thoughts?" she said.

He smiled tiredly, his bearded cheeks gleaming in the light. "Just thinking of La Fonda. That's where Dale took her that night in 1962. If we could step back in time, we'd see Dale and my mother walking right out there. Holding hands, laughing the way lovers do."

A waitress with a notepad in her hand scurried by,

leaving a trail of perfume. The musky scent seemed oddly out of place here.

Maureen said, "You sound sad."

"Oh, it's just that it's a part of them I never had. I guess I feel like I've been robbed." Dusty blew on his cappuccino and steam curled around his handsome face. "I wish Dale had told me."

Maureen propped her elbows on the table and leaned toward him. Her long black braid fell over her shoulder. "He knew you'd read the journals eventually, eh? Maybe he just did."

The lines around Dusty's blue eyes tightened. "Except for the part of the story I'll never know, because some son of a bitch took his other journals. Why would someone do that, Maureen?"

"Names, dates, places. Whoever stole them knew Dale kept a journal, and knew what he'd written there, or at least suspected. Someone took a big risk to break into Dale's house."

"A big risk?" He studied her. "We were out of town. All the thief had to do was case the place, make sure we weren't home, and break in."

Maureen smoothed her fingers over the cool tabletop. "Yes, but it was someone desperate, Dusty. Desperate enough to be very, very careful. He left no prints."

When the waiter arrived with a bowl of pumpkin soup, Maureen surrendered herself to culinary delight. That treat was followed by a succulent tenderloin, topped with a green chili, avocado, and almond sauce. Black bean *refritos* layered with jack cheese and garnished with cilantro added to the feast. Dessert consisted of a piñon pine-nut bread pudding in a honey glaze followed by a cup of black coffee.

"I think I've died and gone to heaven." She smiled and gazed out at the Plaza.

Lights had started to come on, splashing the sidewalks with gold. Across the way, at La Fonda, luminarias glowed with a festive abandon.

The little candle on their table cast a magical glow in Dusty's eyes as he watched her. "Once you get used to eating in Santa Fe, food in the rest of the world seems bland."

"Just think," she said, "you made sure that my first meal in New Mexico was a stale sandwich from a gas station cooler at Crownpoint."

"I didn't know you then. I thought you were going to be a pain in the ass."

She smiled warmly. "I am a pain in the ass. I'm also stuffed, and I haven't had a full night's sleep for days. If you don't take me home, I'm going to fall over and start snoring."

They walked out into the cold November evening.

Maureen kept an eye on Dusty, watching the expression on his face as they passed the corner of La Fonda. His mind was definitely on Dale and Ruth Ann. They crossed the street in front of the Terbush Gallery, and walked down to where Dusty had parked.

As they drove up Canyon Road, she asked, "Why does it bother you so much, Dusty? It was a long time ago. Dale and your mother were both consenting adults."

He took the turn that led down to his humble little trailer. "I know but I just can't see them together."

After he unlocked the trailer, he looked around at the shabby surroundings. "You're sure you wouldn't feel better in a hotel?"

"I'll be fine," she told him, but as she stepped over to the foldout couch, added: "I just wish I could go back in time. I'd pay those burglars to steal this thing."

She could see the exhaustion in his eyes as he arched a brow and bent a finger, pointing to the hallway leading to the rear. "Go on, Doctor. I'll sleep on the couch. I've developed a sense of chivalry that I never knew I had."

"You're all charm, but I can't—"

"Sure you can." He pushed her gently toward the hallway. "I'll let you have the bathroom first, too. And don't worry. I won't barge in. Not even if I find a body in the hallway."

"Don't even joke about it."

As she made her way to the bathroom, she heard Dusty open the trailer door and step outside. A moment later, he reentered. After she brushed her teeth, she made her way to his bedroom, and found Dusty changing the sheets. She helped him tuck the corners and looked around. She'd never seen his bedroom. It had a compact dresser, a twin bed, and a mirror. A sliding closet was built into the wall. Drapes covered the narrow windows.

Maureen stopped short. The ugly pistol rested on the nightstand.

"I thought it might be smart," he said.

"Just because somebody drilled a hole in Dale's head and cut pieces off of him?"

Dusty finished smoothing the sheets and said, "Don't worry. I'll take it up front with me."

She sat on the side of the bed and pulled off her boots. "I actually feel safer because you have it. You're apparently turning me into a barbarian. Lord alone knows what you'll do to me next."

His eyes were puffy from the long days, the stress, and no sleep. He sat down beside her. "This is a mess, isn't it?"

"Murder always is." She put a companionable arm around his shoulder. "I ache all over and I feel like every muscle in my body is made of wet yarn, eh?"

"You are tired. You sound more Canadian than ever."

She laughed at that and playfully pulled him backward until they were lying side by side, legs dangling over the edge of the bed. "We'll figure this thing out, you know."

"Yes," he said through a long exhalation. "I know."

"It's really all right, Dusty. Dale had a good life. He lived well. You just can't do any better than that."

He hugged her and they both stared at the ceiling. Maureen didn't remember falling asleep.

"HORNED RAM," STONE Ghost said distastefully. He sat cross-legged in front of a bowl of glowing coals. The red embers cast a gaudy light over the long-abandoned chamber; it sparkled from the cobwebs that draped the ceiling, and the single black eye of the little girl who lay in the far corner to his right. He'd spread his turkey-feather cape over her to keep her warm while she slept. But she'd wakened the instant Browser and Catkin stepped into the chamber. She had pulled his cape over her head, and peered at them through one of the holes.

"Do you think he was the frog-faced elder at Sunrise House?" Catkin asked. She knelt to his left with her hands extended to the coals. The white wolves and bears painted on her faded red war shirt seemed to move in the wavering light.

"Probably." Stone Ghost pulled a willow stick from the firewood and toyed with it. He'd found an old sleeping mat rolled and stowed in one of the abandoned rooms. Stick by stick, he fed it to his warming fire. "It has been a great many sun cycles since I've seen him."

"What do we know about him?" Browser asked. His round face had a faint crimson hue. "I've heard he's a very traditional elder from over in the Red Rim country to the west."

Stone Ghost nodded and placed the twig onto the coals. Bone Walker had not moved since Browser and Catkin arrived. Where had she learned that? Who had taught her to be afraid to move in the presence of adults?

Stone Ghost said, "He is of the Ant Clan. I met him once. We were just youths. It's no wonder I didn't recognize him. He was married to one of those Alkali Water women. He married her despite the fact she had already divorced four husbands in about as many summers. It was rumored that she could not bear children."

"Could she?" Catkin asked.

"Oh, yes. In the next seven sun cycles, she gave him five children." Stone Ghost's wrinkles rearranged into somber lines as he watched a single tendril of fire curl up around the willow stick. "Then the Tower Builders raided from the north. Horned Ram was away. Upon his return he found his wife and children butchered and rotting in his doorway. For the next five sun cycles he and a small band of warriors raided the Tower Builders. It is said that they lived off the land, always moving, raiding small farmsteads and settlements. They appeared out of nowhere when the men were away and left no one alive. The Tower Builders chased them, but Horned Ram's Spirit Power was so great the Tower Builders never caught him. The story is told that one day the Blue God appeared and told him that was enough. That he should go home. And he did. He went back to the Red Rim country and lived in the canyons there."

"I've heard that his souls are loose," Browser said.

Stone Ghost pulled another stick from the old mat and used it to contemplatively poke at the coals. "The Tower Builders blamed him for terrible atrocities. According to one story, he hung a pregnant woman from a tree and slit open her belly so that her womb dropped onto an ant pile. They say he ate corn cakes while she screamed and the ants swarmed her living fetus."

Browser closed his eyes for a long moment, and Stone Ghost glanced at Catkin. She stared at the fire, but her jaw had gone hard, as though she found this

display of emotion unpleasant. Stone Ghost wondered
at that. Catkin loved Browser, but she clearly could not
stand to see him appear vulnerable, at least not in front
of others.

The little girl lifted her head, and Stone Ghost
watched her from the corner of his eye. She peered at
Browser like Cougar spying Rabbit, as though she
could smell weakness, and the scent drew her like a
dying animal to water.

Browser said, "No wonder Horned Ram is so feared
by his enemies."

Stone Ghost nodded. "Yes. When he returned from
raiding, he immediately started moving towns up onto
the mesa tops, then he built line-of-sight signaling towers. His people use polished slate mirrors to send messages back and forth. It is almost impossible to attack
them. Most of those who have tried are dead."

"His warriors are said to be very loyal." Browser
absently looked at the line of black spirals that decorated the white wall.

"Of course," Stone Ghost replied. "Horned Ram
brought them victory."

Catkin said, "His Spirit Power is supposed to make
him invincible. I have heard that he spends days without food or water, lying facedown on the kiva floor
with his ear to the underworld. The Blue God suppos-
edly whispers things that only he can hear."

Browser glared at the fire bowl. He didn't say anything for a time; then he looked at Stone Ghost. "I wish
the things they said about you were true, Uncle. I
would appreciate it if you would jump through a yucca
hoop and go make Blue Corn and her allies sick."

Stone Ghost chuckled. "Me, too."

The girl jerked. It was a small movement, but quick.
She stared at Stone Ghost with dark unblinking eyes,
like a hunting wolf suddenly surprised to discover that
a bear had sneaked up behind him.

"For days we have been pursued by White Moccasins," Browser said. "Now Blue Corn and her warriors are at Center Place, and she's posted warriors all around the canyon." He gestured his frustration. "Forgive me, but we're not in a very good situation here."

Stone Ghost smiled at that. "No, but we're still alive."

Catkin propped her chin on her knee and stared down at the floor. "I wonder who was killed the night we left?"

Browser said, "I don't know, but I—"

Stone Ghost interrupted, "I should have anticipated that."

Catkin turned and short black hair glinted. "Why?"

"Only a direct affront to Blue Corn would have goaded her into following us. She's very frightened."

Browser scowled. "She is?"

"Of course." Stone Ghost reached for another willow stick and snapped it into hand-sized lengths. "Her people are hungry. It is no longer safe to work the fields for fear of being killed by raiders. Starving refugees pour into her village constantly. Whole towns, like Longtail village, have been destroyed." He added the sticks to his warming bowl and smoke spiraled up toward the ceiling. "Worse, she knows that she faces Two Hearts and the White Moccasins on one side"—the little girl covered her head with his turkey-feather cape—"and Horned Ram and his Flute Player warriors on the other. Both men are desperate to save their worlds no matter how much blood they spill in the process. Then"—he waved a hand—"a young Mogollon prophet appears. He is like a spark in dry grass. When he is murdered, her own people turn him into a god."

"But he was a man, Elder," Catkin pointed out.

"Yes. He would have remained a man but for the way he was mutilated. His words now ring with a greater authority. Even the doubters among the Bow are convinced. And"—he lifted a finger and aimed it at Browser—"the Mogollon conversion is so powerful that they freely submit to the command of a Straight Path War Chief. Think of that, Nephew. The warriors of the Bow Society follow you. Obey your orders. Can you think of another time, ever, when Fire Dogs followed a Straight Path War Chief?"

Browser shook head. "No, I can't, Uncle."

"Our grip is very tenuous. If we fail, Nephew, our people are doomed. Two Hearts and Horned Ram will turn us upon each other like mice trapped in a pot."

"But how do I defeat them, Uncle?" Browser was lost in thought. "We are less than twenty strong. How do we find and kill Two Hearts, avoid his White Moccasins, and avoid Blue Corn's warriors, too?"

The willow sticks burst into bright yellow flame, and Stone Ghost saw the little girl's eye peeking through the hole in his cape. It looked like the glistening eye of a wild dog. He wondered what she must be thinking about all this. Did it remind her of the days before her village was attacked and her family murdered? Was she afraid? She didn't appear to be, but it was hard to tell.

Stone Ghost turned back to Browser. "We defeat them, Nephew, by having the heart of a cloud, just as Poor Singer said."

WHEN BROWSER AND Catkin had gone, Stone Ghost shifted to look at Bone Walker. She lay absolutely still, peering through the same hole in his turkey-feather cape.

"Well, Bone Walker," he said, "what do you think of all this?"

Bone Walker's eyes glinted.

Stone Ghost added a handful of twigs to the warming bowl and shivered as flames crackled to life. Orange light flickered through the chamber and danced in her tangled hair like ghostly wings.

"We're in real trouble," he continued. "We are being hunted by Blue Corn's warriors, Flute Player warriors, and White Moccasins. They have us surrounded. How do we overcome this?"

Bone Walker tugged his cape down so that the top half of her pretty face showed. "You said by having the heart of a cloud."

"Yes, I did," he replied through a long exhalation, "but I'm not sure my nephew understood."

She toyed with the feathers in his cape. "I didn't understand, either."

He could see her thinking, trying to work it out.

"What do you think the heart of a cloud is?" he asked.

Bone Walker petted the feather for a time. "Rain?"

"Oh, very good. And what is human rain?"

Bone Walker's gaze darted around the room, absently landing on the old baskets to her left, then the dusty mats to her right. She chewed the inside of her cheek before looking back at him and venturing, "Tears?"

"Very good."

"What happens when bones cry?"

"Bones? Can they cry?"

"Mine do."

"Is that how you got the name Bone Walker?"

She was silent. Then, just as he was about to speak, she said, "I'm just bones. Walking bones."

"How is that?"

"Bones are all that's left." She looked up, eyes engulfing his souls. "When you're dead. All that's left is bones. Bones that cry." She paused. "Tears are the heart of a cloud."

Stone Ghost smiled. "Someday, if you work very hard, you will be a great Singer. There are holy people ten times your age who do not know how to answer that question. But that is exactly what Poor Singer meant. He meant that we only see clearly when we live inside the tears of other people."

*"Live inside the tears of other people,"* she repeated to herself and crushed and recrushed the feathers of his cape. "But"—she rolled her eyes as though the answer lay somewhere in the high corners of the room—"if I can live inside tears, why can't I live inside my breath-heart soul?"

"Hmm?" Stone Ghost swiveled around to face her. The logic of children always amazed him. He wondered where she had found a connection between tears and her afterlife soul?

"My breath-heart soul," she said, "the one that runs the road to the Land of the Dead, where does it live while I am alive?"

"Ah," Stone Ghost said with great seriousness, "that is a question I have wondered about my entire life. Where do you think it lives?"

Bone Walker sat up and his cape fell around her waist. She put her hand to her chest and clutched a handful of faded blue fabric. "I don't know. I can't feel it."

"But you can feel it filling your lungs with air and your heart with blood, can't you?"

She nodded. "So it lives in my heart and lungs?"

"Well, no. I don't think so. I used to think the breath-heart soul was like a hunting coyote, always tiptoeing in the shadows, but I no longer believe that's true."

Bone Walker frowned intently at something just past Stone Ghost. In a very soft voice, she said, "My mother cries."

Stone Ghost cocked his head. Her thoughts had returned to tears.

"Why does she cry?"

"She's afraid."

Stone Ghost shivered suddenly, and Bone Walker

picked up his cape and trotted across the chamber to hand it to him.

"Thank you, child," he said as he slipped it around his shoulders. This small kindness pleased him. She had shown so few normal emotions since she had been with them. It seemed to him a good sign.

The cape felt warm from her body. He shivered again, but with relief. His old bones just couldn't stand the cold the way they once had. "Where's your blanket, Bone Walker? You must fetch it or you will be cold, too."

She ran across the cluttered room and pulled it from the dark corner. As she ran back, she knotted it around her narrow shoulders, then squatted at Stone Ghost's side before the warming bowl. Long dirty black tangles fell over her shoulder. He longed to wash and brush her hair, but she had yet to allow anyone to touch her.

Bone Walker toyed with a stick that rested beside the warming bowl. "So, where does it live?"

Stone Ghost watched her play with the stick, tapping it on the ground, on the side of the warming bowl, as though to make light of a question that was very important to her.

Stone Ghost tied the laces of his cape beneath his chin. "The answer is complicated. Are you sure you wish to hear what I think?"

Her gaze fixed upon his eyes. She nodded once, with utter gravity. "Tell me."

"All right, I'll try." He resettled himself so that his aching left leg was extended. "I think there is a place where a person's inner world and the outer world touch. Can you feel that? Close your eyes and search for that place."

Bone Walker did, and he could see her eyes moving beneath her lids. When she opened them, she poked her stick into the twig pile and shook her head. "I don't know."

"It's easiest to feel when you're just about asleep.

Anyway, I think that every place where those worlds touch makes a kind of invisible skin. While we're alive, it protects everything inside, including our hearts and lungs, but it also allows us to be connected with the outside world. It's that 'skin' that I think travels to the afterlife."

"A skin," she whispered. "A hollow skin?"

"No." He shook his head. "I think it's full of who you were when you were alive."

"But not bones or fingernails?"

"Well, Spirit bones and Spirit fingernails."

Bone Walker used the stick to draw a spiral in the dust on the floor. "Do you think someone can witch your breath-heart soul and put it in a rock? So that it can't find its way to the Land of the Dead?"

A tiny tremor had laced her voice when she asked the question. She peered hard at her stick, waiting.

"Yes," he said, "I believe that witches can do that. Why? Did someone tell you that?"

Bone Walker drew a long wavy line with her stick. He noted how her hand shook.

Stone Ghost said, "I won't let anyone do that to your soul, Bone Walker. I know many ways to protect a person's souls."

She cocked her head as though she didn't believe him.

"I'm very Powerful," he whispered.

"He's Powerful, too."

"Is he?" Stone Ghost tried to decide how to do this. In the softest voice possible, he asked, "What's his name? Perhaps I know him?"

Bone Walker tipped her head to the side. Her mouth opened slightly and her eyes went vacant, peering at something far away, or deep inside, he didn't know which. The stick made a soft thud on the floor as it fell from her fingers.

"Bone Walker?" he said, but it was as if the entry-way to her souls had been walled up.

*At just the thought of his name?*

Stone Ghost kept talking as though nothing had changed. "Do you know the story of the Great Warriors of East and West?"

Bone Walker didn't appear to hear him.

"Oh, it's a wonderful story. During the Age of Emergence, just after the First People climbed through the underworlds to get to this world of light, the Great Warriors had to kill many monsters that roamed the face of the world. In the last horrifying battle, the mortally wounded monsters turned the Warriors to stone, but their heroism had earned them special places in the skyworld. Their souls soared into heaven, where they now sparkle on either side of Father Sun. But sometimes"—he lowered his voice to a whisper—"the Warriors return to earth as shooting stars and walk among men, advising and helping."

A deep breath filled Bone Walker's lungs, and as she exhaled, she blinked.

"Are you back?" he asked.

She just looked at him.

Stone Ghost slipped the turquoise necklace from around his throat and handed it to Bone Walker, saying, "The Warriors gave this to my great-great-grandmother many sun cycles before I was born. This turquoise comes from the Warriors' turquoise bodies, their bodies that were turned to stone by the monsters."

The necklace dangled over his gnarled fingers. Bone Walker appeared to want to touch it, but was afraid to. She drew her hands back and clutched them in her lap.

"The Great Warriors said that this necklace would protect whoever wore it from all evil. That's why I am so old. Nothing has been able to harm me," he said, and wished that were really the truth. If she could see the scars on his back from the time he'd been captured by the Fire Dogs, she'd know he was lying.

Bone Walker's eyes widened. "Can I hold it?"

"Better than that, I wish to give it to you."

Stone Ghost very slowly lifted the necklace and slipped it over her head, careful not to touch her. The large chunks of blue stone had a greenish hue in the light.

Bone Walker ran her fingers over the necklace.

"It's very old," Stone Ghost said. "So you must take good care of it. I have restrung the beads at least ten times, and my grandmother restrung them several times during her life."

Bone Walker looked up and whispered, "So my breath-heart soul is safe? It will be able to find its way to the Land of the Dead?"

"Oh, it's very safe." Stone Ghost waved a confident hand. "You—"

"But how will you find your way!" she blurted, and her eyes jerked wide with fear. "Will you be lost? Like Owl?"

"No, no. Don't worry. I'll be fine."

"But if you get lost, the monsters eat you!"

"I know, but I have other ways . . ."

His voice faded as Bone Walker reached into her belt pouch and pulled something out. She clutched it in her dirty fist for a long moment, as though it were a great treasure, then held it out to Stone Ghost.

In a worried voice, she said, "Here, I hope this will help you."

Stone Ghost held out his hand and she dropped the item into his palm. A tiny turquoise wolf gleamed. It had been crudely carved, but he could see the lifted muzzle and long tail. One hundred sun cycles ago, the First People had carved similar charms. They had breathed Spirit into them to turn them into living Spirit Helpers, then given the charms to chosen people, to help guide them to the Land of the Dead. "This is beautiful. Thank you, Bone Walker. Where did you get it?"

She gripped the turquoise necklace in both hands, holding it like a tree trunk in a tornado. All of her attention seemed to be on the stones, but she said, "I made it."

Stone Ghost turned the wolf over in his hand, and his breathing suddenly went shallow. He knew where he'd seen one like it before—he'd pulled it from a hole in a dead woman's skull. At the time, he'd thought it meant that Flame Carrier's murderer had felt remorse. But now . . .

"Bone Walker? Was it your grandfather who told you he'd witch your breath-heart soul?"

She lifted the necklace to her left eye, as though testing to see if the turquoise were transparent. In a bare whisper, she said, "A wolf told me."

It was as though he could hear an earthquake coming. The roar began deep in his souls, grew louder, and louder . . .

Bone Walker whispered, "I don't think it's a skin."

"What? I'm sorry. What did you say?"

"I don't think it's a skin," she repeated. "I think my breath-heart soul lives inside my tears."

As the breeze filtered through the roof, the cobwebs on the ceiling swayed and danced, glittering in the flickering light. Bone Walker watched them.

Stone Ghost looked up. The webs resembled fine golden threads.

He murmured, "You may be right."

# CHAPTER 22

"MAUREEN?" DUSTY'S WHISPER brought Maureen straight up out of a sound sleep.

"Shh!" he hissed and clamped a hard hand over her mouth.

"Whaaf," she mumbled, struggling to get away from him.

"Someone's out there!"

Fear pumped through every muscle in her body. Dusty released her and rolled away.

Her scattered senses slowly collected themselves: She lay on Dusty's bed in the darkened trailer house. The clock glowing on the dresser told her it was 2:17 A.M. The pistol made a hollow clunk as Dusty pulled it off of the nightstand. She could see him moving, a dark shadow in the room. The floor creaked slightly as he stepped into the hallway and vanished.

Frozen, time compressed into the thundering beat of Maureen's heart. A hollow sensation, like falling, possessed her. When had she run out of breath?

In that crystal moment she realized what it meant to be alive. How precious it was, and how much she wanted to keep breathing.

A faint click.

She peered into the blackness, eyes wide.

It might have been the hammer drawn back on Dusty's pistol.

*Is this how Dale felt? So terrified he couldn't breathe?*

The heating system whined, and Maureen gasped. She managed to swallow, and got to her feet.

Light flashed on outside, and in the eternal instant that followed, she cringed, waiting for the sound of a gunshot.

"Hey!" she heard Dusty shout. *"Hey, you!"*

Maureen ran down the hallway. Dusty was leaning out the door, but she could see the pistol in his right hand.

"Dusty, who was it?" she asked as she tried to peer around his broad shoulders.

Up on the road, behind the screen of trees, a car engine roared to life. Wheels spun, popping gravel, and Maureen saw the red glow of taillights as the vehicle accelerated down the hill, over the bridge, and roared away into the night.

Dusty stepped out onto the porch. He played a flashlight beam back and forth across the yard.

"Somebody was over by the Bronco. They ran when I turned the lights on."

"Do you think it was . . . was *him*?"

"I don't know. Stay here. I need to check the Bronco."

He walked a circle around the Bronco, shining his flashlight here and there; then he bent down to study the ground.

"What is it?" Maureen called.

"Just scuffed dirt." He shone the light inside the Bronco, then hurried toward the steps. "My toes are freezing."

Standing in the doorway, Maureen fought a shiver of her own.

Dusty closed the door behind him, laid the flashlight and pistol on the table, and squinted through the kitchen window one last time. "It might have just been an ordinary thief. This place has been broken into before."

She rubbed her arms. "I didn't hear a thing. What woke you?"

He jerked his head toward the rear. "Footsteps. This trailer's so old it predates real insulation."

"Well," Maureen said and sank down on the couch. "We'd better call the police."

Dusty ground his teeth a long moment. "I think I'll call Nichols instead. If it was an ordinary thief, the police aren't going to do anything. Nothing was stolen. But if it wasn't just a thief . . ."

Maureen looked up. "You're right." As the adrenaline surge began to fade, she felt sick to her stomach.

Dusty had just picked up the phone when the tapping started at the door. Not a loud knock, but a hesitant *rap, rap, rap.*

Maureen's first glance went to the pistol an arm's length away.

Dusty moved with the silence of a jungle cat. He reached for the gun and stepped back. His face had gone white, his mouth hard. "Who is it?"

A woman's voice responded from the night. "May I come in?"

Dusty shot Maureen a questioning look.

She nodded, but said, "Be careful."

Steps sounded on the porch. "Please?" the woman called.

Dusty held the pistol muzzle down as he swung the door open.

A woman stood there, face half turned as if against the glare of the light. She froze at the sight of the pistol in Dusty's hand, her blue eyes widening. She looked to be in her mid-sixties, slender, well dressed, although her coat was smudged with dirt and leaves. A scuffed purse hung from her right hand.

"I don't think you really want to shoot me," she said wearily. "At least, not yet. May I come in?"

"Who are you?" Dusty asked.

The woman lifted her chin slightly. She wore her shoulder-length silver hair in a ponytail and held it with a large silver barrette. Her delicate nose and fine bones harked to what must once have been great beauty. She was still a very attractive woman. Her blue eyes tightened.

Maureen lurched to her feet. "Oh, good Lord! Dr. Sullivan, of course, please come in."

Ruth Ann Sullivan stepped inside, and Dusty took a step backward, staring at her with glistening eyes.

Finally, he said, "Forgive me if I don't say welcome home, Mom."

BROWSER LAY ON his belly in a collapsed third-floor room in Kettle Town and watched the predawn glow light the eastern horizon. Charred roof timbers surrounded him. The hulking remains creaked and shifted, as if settling into the new day. In the distance, a solitary eagle sailed out over the canyon rim, cut slow circles across the sky, and spiraled lazily to the west, as though to inspect the silent ruins of Talon Town for an unwary rabbit.

Browser rubbed his tired eyes and, once again, checked the positions of the guards he'd posted along the rim and the roofs of nearby ruins. Rain Crow had said they would attack at dawn, but Browser had seen no sign of approaching warriors, and none of his guards had let out a warning call.

Perhaps Horned Ram or Blue Corn had altered the War Chief's plans?

Browser didn't believe it. Blue Corn respected the advice of her War Chief.

Across the valley, the moldering complex of dwellings known as Corner Canyon Town shone. Browser's eyes focused on them. Only last winter, Made People had lived there. The Katsinas' People had traded with them. He and Springbank had . . .

Browser went still.

Springbank had claimed he had relatives there, members of the Badger Clan.

Browser sat up. Pale blue light fell through the timbers around him, striping his buffalo cape.

The Badger Clan was a Made People clan, but the people in Corner Town had accepted Springbank without question.

Blood started to rush in Browser's ears. He stared at

the low ridge near Corner Canyon Town where the
First People had built their great kiva. Less than a sun
cycle ago, Springbank had told him about the magnificent rituals the First People had performed in that kiva,
rituals that brought to life the First People's climb
through the underworlds and their emergence into the
Fifth World of light. Each of the ceremonials had been
perfectly choreographed, a spectacle of such power that
Springbank said it had stunned the rude and ignorant
farmers who made the pilgrimage to Straight Path
Canyon from the hinterlands.

Browser's thoughts tumbled. How ironic it would be
if the last of the First People had taken refuge there,
on the south side of the wash: in land traditionally set
aside for Made People.

Browser glared at each of the distant buildings, as if
just by looking he might unravel its secret.

Tonight, he would go there.

From below him, Catkin softly called, "Browser?"

"Up here."

She climbed through an opening in the floor and
carefully studied the window before draping a gray
blanket over herself and crawling up next to him. Her
turned-up nose bore a sprinkling of dust, as though
she'd been scrambling through the hive of abandoned
chambers.

"The Mogollon scouts have returned. Two scouts,
Fire Lark and Red Dog, spotted warriors."

"Where?"

"High Sun Town. From the descriptions, I think
they're White Moccasins."

Browser looked at the cliff south of Corner Town.
He remembered the stairway that led to the mesa top,
and the road from there that ran straight to High Sun
Town. Springbank had told him that High Sun Town
had been the center of the First People's summer sol-
stice ceremonies. At midday on that longest day of the
sun cycle, the Blessed Sunwatcher had built a fire on

top of Spider Woman's Butte, and dancers had emerged from High Sun Town to bless Father Sun for his gifts of life and warmth. The ceremonial dancers made their way along the road, descended the stairway cut into the cliff, and feasted at Corner Town. When the feast was over, masked dancers emerged from the Corner Kiva at Sunset Town and led a ceremonial procession north across Straight Path Wash to Kettle Town and finally to Talon Town. Just after dark they held ceremonies in Talon Town, then climbed the stairway to the mesa top road that led north to Center Place. When midnight arrived, another great feast was held, offerings were made, and soul pots were broken by the thousands.

"How fitting," Browser remarked. "Blue Corn's warriors are just above us on the Great North Road, and the White Moccasins are just south of us. One side occupies Center Place, the other High Sun. They've switched sides. The south used to belong to the Made People."

"The problem is that we're in the middle."

Browser fingered his war club and turned his attention back to Corner Canyon Town. "He's there. I just know it."

Catkin glanced suspiciously at him. "Two Hearts?"

"Yes." He gestured toward the cluster of blocky structures that dotted the mouth of Corner Canyon. "We're going to have to search them one by one."

"I want to lead the search party."

He swiveled around to face her and examined her stony expression. The dawn light painted her wide cheekbones, but her eyes remained in shadow. "I have to kill him, Catkin."

"Why?"

"Because—" He leaned back against the crumbling wall and let out a breath. "—he's one of mine."

She turned and stared at him. "Because you are both First People?"

"Yes." He drew up his knees and rested his war club atop them. "Uncle Stone Ghost says that our people are doomed if we do not succeed here. It is my duty to see that we do." Browser bowed his head and smiled forlornly. "Which must be a divine joke of the gods."

She cocked her head. "I don't see the humor."

"The joke is that I don't believe, Catkin. I don't know what's true. The katsinas? The Flute Player? I don't care which god wins this war." He smoothed his hand over his club. "This duty should have fallen to someone like Cloudblower or the Mogollon prophet. Someone who has the truth burning in his heart."

"I would rather put my faith in you."

"Why?"

"Because you see all sides. You grew up believing you were one of the Made People. You know how we think, what we feel, but you're born of the First People. Their blood runs in your veins. You are a man between, Browser. That is your power."

He looked out the window again. The pale blue aura of dawn had swelled to fill half the sky. Father Sun would rise soon.

"Catkin?" he said, and heard the edge of fear in his voice. "Does it bother you that I'm descended from the First People?"

She shifted. "It might if I did not know you, Browser. But I do. I'll bet on that before I bet on blood. I only wish—" Catkin's eyes went wide. She lunged for the window. "Movement! On the cliff behind us!"

Browser scrambled to look. Ten warriors, no eleven, climbed down the staircase cut into the cliff behind Kettle Town. The arrows in their quivers flashed as they moved.

"Time to play weasel and coyote. Quickly, run and tell the others!"

STONE GHOST HUDDLED beneath a pile of ancient, willow-twig mats, but he could see Obsidian where she lay on her belly a short distance away. She had her hands pressed to her breast, terrified. The mats covered everything but a lock of her long black hair, which snaked toward him like a deadly serpent. Stone Ghost had ordered Bone Walker to hide with Catkin, where he knew she would be safer; then he'd come here, seeking out Obsidian. One other person hid in the room with them, the Mogollon woman warrior named Clay Frog. She crouched across the room by the door with her war club clutched in her fist.

In a whisper he knew only Obsidian could hear, Stone Ghost said, "You know the little girl, don't you?"

Obsidian looked at him as though he must be mad to speak at a time like this. "If I were you," she whispered back, "I would keep quiet. Or do you wish to have your throat slit?"

Stone Ghost rattled the mats as he turned to relieve the discomfort of his aching hip. "She looks like you. She has your mouth and nose, but her eyes are different. Larger, more deeply set."

"You are a fool, old man!"

"Well, allow me to explain. You see, she knows that she is one of the First People, and I cannot imagine who would have been foolish enough to tell her. Certainly no one I know. The only people who openly speak about their ancestry are the White Moccasins."

"Hush! I don't care if you get yourself killed, but I do not wish to accompany you to the Land of the Dead!"

Stone Ghost tucked his hands inside his cape for warmth, and listened to the darkness. An owl hooted somewhere in the distance, but inside Kettle Town, Obsidian's rapid breathing was the only sound.

"Was Ten Hawks your husband, or Shadow's?"

She hesitated a long time, then said reluctantly, "Mine."

He whispered, "Since your dead husband, Ten Hawks, was a member of the White Moccasins, I thought you might have seen the girl before. I was hoping you might know her parents."

Obsidian hissed, "I don't know anything about her!"

Stone Ghost moved again, and dust sifted down around him, falling from the mats. "I find it very odd that the two of you go out of your way to avoid each other. If the girl enters a room, you leave. If you walk into a room, she leaves. It seems to me . . ."

Clay Frog shifted. It was a subtle movement, the slightest tightening of her grip on her club.

Then Stone Ghost heard the footsteps in the long hallway outside.

Obsidian squeezed her eyes closed and buried her face in the fabric of her black cape.

Stone Ghost listened to their whispers as they closed in . . . and knew if he lived through this, he must speak with his nephew. He had to tell him the suspicions that were eating holes in his souls.

# CHAPTER 23

RUTH ANN SULLIVAN shoved her gloves into her purse and eyed the battered couch and the telephone peeking out of the shirt pile. A wry ghost of a smile crossed her lips. She walked into the old kitchen and looked at the countertop and the table with its cigarette-scarred plastic surface, then shook her head at the black-and-white TV with its clothes-hanger antenna.

"I don't believe it. It's a goddamned time machine." Her Bostonian accent sounded out of place. She glanced at the big pistol in Dusty's hand, and stepped closer to look into his stunned eyes.

"Dear God," she whispered, "so you're my son."

"I think of myself as Sam's son," Dusty answered curtly.

She pointed a slim white finger at the pistol. "Well, Sam would never have owned a gun. He was too much of a coward." Her eyes narrowed. "Or am I misreading you, William? What does a gun mean to you? Is it a substitute for virility?"

Dusty placed the pistol on the kitchen counter. "What are you doing here?"

Ruth Ann gave him a clinical look. He might have been a subject in one of her experiments: the sort for which she could write another scholarly article.

"*Why* are you here?" Dusty demanded to know.

When his mother didn't answer, Maureen broke the deadlock. She walked closer to Ruth Ann and pointed at the dirt and leaves on her coat. "Is that a new East Coast fashion, or were you crawling around under the trailer?"

Ruth Ann looked down at her dirt-smudged coat. "When the light went on, I dived under your Bronco. It was the closest concealment I could find."

Dusty's jaws ached from clenching his teeth. He forced himself to relax. "Were you afraid of me, or the person in the car?"

Ruth Ann's blue eyes pinned him, as if weighing what to tell him. "That was Carter," she said in a brittle voice.

"Carter? Hawsworth?" Maureen asked.

"I think so," Ruth Ann answered, and carefully scrutinized Maureen. "I don't believe I know you."

"Maureen Cole. We've met, actually. At the American Association of Physical Anthropologists' meeting in Denver."

"Really? Well. Let's meet again. I'm Dr. Ruth Ann Sullivan." She extended her hand.

Maureen crossed her arms. "Curious time of night for a visit, Dr. Sullivan."

"I had my reasons," Ruth Ann answered coldly as she withdrew her hand.

Dusty gripped the back of the chair. "Let's hear them."

Ruth Ann hesitated, betraying a flicker of vulnerability. "I thought I should talk to you, William. Find out what you knew."

"Knew about what?"

Her control wavered. "About Dale. About his death. About Kwewur."

"Kwewur?" Maureen asked. "What's that?"

Dusty bent forward, a sudden gleam had entered his eyes. "The Wolf Katchina? Is that who you mean?"

Ruth Ann nodded. Despite her age, traces of her beauty remained. Not just in her looks, but in the way she carried herself.

"What about the Wolf Katchina?" Maureen asked.

Dusty said, "He's one of the katchinas from Awatovi."

"The Hopi village destroyed by other Hopi because it was full of witches?" Maureen said. "Yes, I read Lomatuway'ma's book last summer. Is Kwewur the same—"

"As the Wolf Witch?" Dusty smiled grimly. "I don't know."

He turned to his mother, battling to keep his emotions in hand. This was the woman who had abandoned him when he was six. How did he handle this? What did he say to her? Dusty took a deep breath. "What do you know about Kwewur?"

"Apparently more than you do." She lifted her purse.

"Coming here was a mistake. A big mistake." She turned and reached for the door latch.

Dusty blocked the door. "You're not leaving. Not yet."

She glared at him. "Let me go, William."

"No, *Mother*." The word sounded alien on his tongue. "Sit down. What's it been? Thirty-one years? I didn't even get a postcard from you, then Dale is murdered by a witch, and you suddenly show up asking me about the Wolf Katchina?" He shook his head. "You're going to sit right here and tell me everything you know."

A cold smile bent her thin lips. He could see the fine wrinkles around her mouth, the age lines that hardened at the corners of her eyes. "I don't owe you a thing, William. And you sure as hell can't make me tell you anything I don't want to." She gestured toward the door. "Now, move out of my way."

Maureen said, "Dr. Sullivan, do you know the FBI is looking for you?"

Dusty saw the ripple of fear before she hid it. His mother said, "I'll talk to them when I'm ready."

Dusty pointed to the phone. "Maureen, please dial Agent Nichols's number."

She took a half step before Ruth Ann raised her hand in defeat. "Wait."

Ruth Ann Sullivan met Dusty's hard stare and said, "All right, William, what do you want to know?"

"Did you kill Dale?"

"No."

"Did you steal his journals?"

He could see the confusion when she said, "What journals?"

"Dale's journals. He kept a record of his life. Someone took them before we could read past 1963. He wrote a great deal about you. And him."

She was calculating again, trying to read his motives. Her stony expression stirred something deep inside

him, as though he remembered that look from a time
when she had actually been his mother. Dusty could
hear a little boy crying inside him, and a memory almost surfaced, of darkness and cold, but then it slipped
away.

"Why would I want to steal his journals?"

Dusty reached over and pulled out one of the chairs.
"Sit down. Maybe we can figure that out."

Maureen walked to the kitchen. "I think I'll make us
coffee. This may be a long night."

Ruth Ann Sullivan seated herself awkwardly on the
old worn kitchen chair and laid her purse to one side.
Then she shrugged out of her coat and threw it over
the back. She wore a gray wool dress belted at her slim
waist. The sterling silver clip holding her ponytail
glimmered. She shook her head as she looked at the
scarred tabletop. "What on earth are you still doing in
this rat trap? What is it, some sort of museum? A monument to Sam?"

"It's my home," Dusty said. He turned a chair
around, sat down, and propped his arms on the chair
back. "The only thing he left me."

"But, my God, it looks the same as it did last time
I was here! Well, the television's new, but I served
breakfast on this same rickety table." She smoothed her
hair back and said, "All right, what do you want from
me, William? Some declaration? What?"

His stomach tightened. "I want to know what happened to Dale. Other than that, I don't give a *damn*
about you."

She smiled then, relaxing. "Thank God for that. All
right, here's what I know. A couple of weeks ago I
received a fax. Just a short note that said something
about the second cycle of the moon coming and we
would dance as we once had, our bodies entwined under the stars."

"What did that mean?"

"I didn't have the foggiest idea. I thought it was a

prank from a colleague or a student. I threw it away. Then, several days later, I received another fax. That one said, 'The cycles are coming full. I have never stopped loving you. This time I shall have your body and soul. This time, I shall devour all of you.' " She frowned down at her hands. "I thought it was a gentleman I had been seeing, but when I joked with him about it, it was apparent that he wasn't the sender."

"That's when you called Dale?" Maureen asked as she set the coffeepot on the burner.

"No. I didn't call Dale until the third fax came in. It read: 'We will meet at the center place where the ancestors climbed from *Shipapu* into this world. In the corner house on the night when the dead live. Two cycles of the moon have come full. It is time to end what the four of you began. On the night of masks, at midnight, you shall make the journey. The wolf returns to its beginning.' "

Dusty massaged his brow. "The wolf returns to its beginning?"

She swallowed hard. "Yes, and it was signed Kwewur. That was my first clue that the faxes were tied to the Southwest—to my past. So I naturally assumed it was Dale. But when I talked to him that night, I could tell he didn't know anything about it."

Dusty frowned. "Who are 'the four of you'?"

She touched the swirled plastic pattern in the tabletop. "I don't know. Well, not for sure. I can only guess, but I think it might be me, Dale, Sam, and Carter."

"With Dale gone, only you and Carter are left," Maureen said thoughtfully. "Just what, exactly, did the four of you start?"

"I beg your pardon?" Ruth Ann looked up at Maureen.

"The fax said it was time to end what the four of you began. So, what did you begin?"

"We began a lot of things." Her smile faded. "Lord knows, look at us. Sam killed himself. Carter and I hate each other's guts. Until recently, Dale and I haven't so much as spoken to each other in thirty years. As to what we did back then that could have led to Dale's murder . . . that eludes me." She looked up, obviously perplexed. "It was such a long time ago. Ancient history. What would it serve to dredge it up now? What would it change?"

"You said that you thought Carter Hawsworth was in the car that left when Dusty turned on the light," Maureen reminded. "Why is he here?"

Ruth Ann made an awkward gesture with her hand. "I think he followed me from the hotel."

"How did you get here?" Dusty asked. "I didn't see a car outside."

"A cab. I had the hotel call one." She shifted uncomfortably. "I wasn't getting anywhere on my own. Just one dead end after another. Imagine my surprise when I looked in the phone book and found William Samuel Stewart living at the same address." She looked around. "I would have thought you'd have hauled this wreck out, junked it, and built a real house. This is a nice piece of property."

"Why would Carter Hawsworth follow you from the hotel?" Dusty asked.

Ruth Ann shrugged. "I'm not sure that was him, but it's the only logical explanation. I've been so careful. I'm registered as Mr. and Mrs. George Davis. I even used George's credit card. He's a good friend, you see. I waited until this ungodly time of the night, sure that anyone watching would have given up and gone to bed."

"But you were wrong."

Her blue eyes had a bright savage glitter. "Apparently." A pause. "You mentioned witchcraft in conjunction with Dale's murder?"

"Yes." Dusty outlined the grisly details, hardening his heart against the ache caused by the telling. To his surprise, Ruth Ann seemed genuinely disturbed. He

ended by asking, "Does that mean anything to you?
The way he was treated?"

She stared into a distance only she could see, then
slowly shook her head. "No, except . . ." She looked
up. "Do you think Casa Rinconada could be the corner
place where the ancestors climbed into this world
through *Shipapu*?"

Dusty glanced at Maureen who waited next to the
perking pot. She lifted a shoulder. Dusty said, "What
happened at Casa Rinconada two cycles of the moon
ago? That's a little over thirty-seven years."

Her lips twitched. "How should I know? You'd just
been conceived. I was pretty busy."

He stared at her. "What's Carter Hawsworth's role
in all of this? I know he's been studying Navajo witchcraft."

She gave him a condescending look. "Carter has always been interested in witchcraft. That's what brought
him here in the first place. He's fascinated by the notion of being able to possess others, to turn their souls
to his bidding. It's a godlike power, and as insecure as
Carter is, that's like heroin to an addict."

Maureen shifted the burbling coffeepot on the stove
and asked, "If that's the case, what did you ever see in
him?"

Ruth Ann narrowed an eye. "I was a great deal
younger then, and not so wise in the ways of the world.
You'd be surprised what a young woman, trapped in a
place like this, would agree to in order to escape."

"Why didn't you just go home." Dusty didn't care
if she heard the venom in his voice.

"I couldn't. But that's another story. My parents had
just been killed in a car accident. I was lost, young,
rotting away, and missing the chance of a lifetime to
use my brain for something besides changing diapers
and washing clothes in dingy Laundromats in Tuba
City. Not only that, I was just starting to hate archaeology. The whole thing was so tedious, kneeling for

months scraping away little layers of soil with a trowel.
Ugh. I finally came to the conclusion that the only form
of archaeology I would ever enjoy was one that involved a bulldozer and a backhoe. I wanted the good
stuff quick, so I could get out of the dirt."

Dusty just stared his disgust at her.

"Well, I shouldn't be surprised that you disapprove,"
Ruth Ann said. "Dale once told me that I'd never sunk
a trowel properly. Anyway, I preferred ethnography.
It's cleaner. So was Carter when he came along. He
didn't smell like sweat and dust. He introduced me to
new opportunities in anthropology. He offered to take
me places I could only dream about."

"No matter the consequences to people who loved
you," Dusty shot back.

Ruth Ann's voice came as a hiss. "Don't you dare!
I did what I had to. And whether you like it or not, it
was the right choice." She shook her head. "God, William, don't you get it? The biggest mistake I made in
my entire life was marrying Sam. If I had stayed with
him, I'd have killed him. Then I would have killed you
and hanged myself with a knotted bedsheet. I had to
get out, and I did. It was the right decision then, and
I've never regretted it."

He didn't know what to say to that.

"I fix my mistakes," she finished.

When she looked at him, it was clear that she meant
he was one of those mistakes, and Dusty's already lac-
erated heart bled more—though he didn't know why it
should.

"It was probably a mistake to come here, but I need
to know. Did Dale tell you who might be behind this?
Did he say who he was going up to Chaco to meet?
Did he tell you anything at all?"

Dusty ran a hand through his blond hair. "We didn't
even know he'd gone up there until Maggie found his
truck and called."

"Did he mention Carter?"

"No."

"Do the police have any clues?"

He shook his head. "They're still chasing down leads."

She looked suddenly weary. "God, what is this about? Why is this happening?"

"You must have done something," Dusty replied woodenly. "You, Dad, Dale, and I guess, Hawsworth."

A frown knit Ruth Ann's forehead. "But what? The past is a big place. A lot of things happened. So many . . ." She seemed at a loss. "I thought maybe you could tell me something, give me a clue."

"Well, I can't."

Ruth Ann knotted a fist. "In the note he said he wanted to devour me. That he still loved me. That has to be Carter. 'No' is a word that has always escaped him."

Maureen poured three cups of coffee and handed them out. Dusty clutched his like a life raft. It gave him something to do with his hands.

Ruth Ann raised her cup to her lips and sipped. "The man who killed Dale actually drilled a hole in his head? My God. Poor Dale."

Dusty grimaced at the floor, reliving Dale's last moments again. "Scary, huh?"

Ruth Ann set the coffee cup on the table, clearly afraid. "I was the one he was trying to lure to Casa Rinconada, William. The killer sent those faxes to me. If I had understood them it would have been me there instead of Dale." Her mouth quirked. "Odd, isn't it? I'm alive and Dale is dead because Kwewur thought I was smarter than Dale."

Dusty sipped his coffee and said, "It means he didn't know either of you very well."

CATKIN TUCKED HER war club to her breast and hugged the wall beside the doorway. Old spiderwebs tickled her face. The room was so black she couldn't see her hand before her face. The only sound was the faint breathing of the little orphan girl. Occasionally fabric rasped on the plastered walls or scraped the packed earth floor. Four Mogollon warriors, the orphan girl, and two of the long-forgotten dead hid with her.

As Rain Crow's warriors filtered through Kettle Town, their soft voices carried along the dark passageways.

"See anything?" a man whispered.

Catkin tightened the grip on her war club, her eyes on the door. Her pulse had started to race.

"Nothing but ghosts and corpses," another voice called. "This is silly. The Fire Dogs wouldn't have hidden here. The ghosts of the First People would be crawling all over them."

Catkin glanced to her left. Though she couldn't see them, she knew the Mogollon warriors huddled soundlessly on the opposite side of the door.

She hadn't considered what they must be feeling, but the enemy warrior was probably correct. Staying here, in the presence of moldering bodies, among the ruins of the First People, must have worried the Mogollon.

She did not know what to make of her reaction to that. On the one hand, she was happy that their souls were squirming. On the other, their bravery elicited her sympathy. Would she have shouldered the burden this well if she'd been hiding in one of their abandoned dwellings, surrounded by the desiccated bodies of their dead?

"I thought I smelled the faint trace of smoke." The first warrior's voice echoed.

"It's just the soot," another answered. "The First People burned thousands of fires in here. The soot on these ceiling poles must be a finger thick. If they're anywhere, they're hiding in Talon Town."

"Talon Town?"

"They rebuilt the kiva there last sun cycle. Browser knows it inside and out."

"Maybe Browser and his fools are there, but I think the Mogollon continued on south," the first warrior replied.

Catkin caught the faintest flicker of light illuminating the doorway of the room beyond.

"I would go home if I were them," the more distant voice agreed. "And may their twisted gods help them if they ever venture into our country again."

The light grew brighter and Catkin tried to shrink into the wall. The smooth handle on her war club reassured her. If he stepped into this last room, she would have to strike quickly, kill him before he could shout the alarm. Then, with the inevitability of discovery, they would have to slip out of Kettle Town, try and make it to the rear, and into one of the cliff-based houses. There they could wait until dark and escape to ... where?

*Anywhere.*

If nothing else, Straight Path Canyon was a warren of hiding places. Not only were there abandoned towns in all directions, but dozens of smaller dwellings, and even old pit houses. There were side canyons, niches and alcoves. Boulders had toppled down from above to form sheltered areas.

As the torch neared, she gave the signal for silence, and motioned the rest back against the wall.

Every sense had heightened—a mixture of thrill and the fear of combat. Blood pulsed through her body as she readied her grip. If Blue Corn's warrior stepped into the room, she would swing her club up to catch him as he was drawing breath to shout, his mind still fumbling to overcome the surprise, to evaluate the danger.

She struggled to control her breathing, to still her racing heart.

*Patience, Catkin. Take your time. Wait.*

Flickering yellow light flooded the next room, dancing off the plaster walls. The age-honeyed roof poles reflected warmly. The floor, scuffed and dusty, was speckled with rodent droppings and long dried corn cobs left behind from the days when this had been a storage room.

Out of sight behind the doorway, Catkin collected herself. In the reflected glow, she could see her companions. The Mogollon crouched against the wall, eyes gleaming with anticipation as they, too, gripped their weapons.

The little girl's huge eyes glittered, as if she were waiting for something only she understood. What was it about her? Even now Catkin could sense the strange power the child possessed. Their eyes met, and Catkin felt a shiver course through her. When she looked into that little girl's eyes, it was like seeing into the underworlds, and all the horrors that lived there.

As the enemy warrior stepped into the next room, his sandals scritched on dirt.

Fear rose in Catkin. Fear that the little girl would give them away. Now was her chance.

Catkin fought to clear her thoughts. Her prey was unprepared, heedless of the death that waited but three paces away. He would step into the room and raise his torch, expecting to find another empty room littered with the First People's trash, but his attention would fix on the two corpses in the rear, their flesh shrunken around the bones, empty eye sockets staring from beneath patches of brittle hair. In that instant, she would brutally hammer the life out of his body.

Torchlight illuminated the pack rat nest on the back wall. The collection of cactus pads, sticks, bits of old cloth, and feathers filled the narrow space between the two mummies.

The warrior muttered uneasily as he stared through the doorway. The mummies' shriveled lips were drawn back in mocking grins that exposed brown teeth. Four spirals tattooed their chins.

The warrior stepped back, calling: "Nothing. I've reached the back wall."

"Then let's move on," the distant voice called.

The light retreated, and Catkin leaned against the wall with her heart in her throat. Sweat drenched her arms, cheeks, and forehead.

"Close," Catkin whispered in Mogollon.

"Perhaps the katsinas favored us," Carved Splinter whispered.

"Or favored him," Catkin whispered back. "After all, he'd have died here today."

She motioned for silence and waited for the last of the light to fade.

They waited for another hand of time, before she heard a soft familiar, "Sssst."

"Here, Browser," Catkin called into the blackness.

A red glow appeared, and she could make out Browser, a barely discernible image advancing behind an exhausted bullrush torch. "They're gone," he called. "They didn't even come within three rooms of us. I don't think their heart was in the search."

"They looked in our chamber," Catkin replied. "The ancestors were watching out for us."

"Ancestors?" Browser asked. Dust coated his thick black brows and flat nose as he peered into the room.

She jerked a thumb over her shoulder at the corpses.

A faint smile curled Browser's lips. "My uncle has sent for me. I wish you to be there. I do not know what he has to say, but—"

"Then let's go. He may have seen things we did not."

# CHAPTER 24

MAUREEN WATCHED RUTH Ann Sullivan walk through the thick wooden doors that led into La Fonda's lobby, and turned to Dusty. He sat behind the idling Bronco's steering wheel.

"What do you think?"

His thoughtful eyes remained on the hotel's historic doors. "In my dreams, she was never like this. I mean, she's hard as nails."

"She's also scared to death."

Dusty lifted an eyebrow. "She should be. The Wolf Witch wants her dead."

Dusty slipped the Bronco into gear and turned right onto San Francisco. "We walked right by her hotel last night. She was there, inside. Probably in the same suite she used to share with Dale."

Maureen watched the galleries pass as they turned onto Canyon Road. "Aren't you glad you didn't shoot her? You'd be in a cell right now, waiting for a lawyer."

Dusty's head tilted, as though he was weighing the merits of that scenario.

Maureen added, "Well, just be glad she didn't raise you. She wasn't cut out to be a mother."

"How's that?" he asked.

Maureen braced her elbow on the armrest. "Dale told me about the time she locked you in a basement and left you bawling down there for an entire day. I think Dale said you were five. If you think you have emotional scars now, imagine what another ten years with her would have done to you."

Dusty shifted into a lower gear and slowed down. "Maybe she did do the right thing when she left us. But poor Dale, he got stuck raising me."

"Dale knew what he was getting into." At Dusty's incredulous look, she said, "What? You bought that macho baloney Dale used to spew. 'There was no one else to take the boy.' " She mocked Dale's deep tones. " 'So I packed up the little urchin and made a home for him.' Dale took you because he wanted to. You made him happy, Dusty. He loved you."

Dusty's eyes glistened, but she didn't know if it was tears, or just the way the lights on the instrument panel lit his face. He pulled into his driveway, turned off the Bronco, and sat in silence. "I miss him. I miss him so much."

She reached out and gripped his hand. "I know."

STONE GHOST STOOD on the second-floor hanging porch behind Kettle Town, gazing up at the cliff. Morning sunlight painted every ledge with a golden glow. The Shadow People had retreated to the crevices, but he could see them peeking out, examining the day. A flock of piñon jays soared high above, trilling to each other.

"Uncle?" Browser called from the door behind Stone Ghost. "Please don't stand out there."

Stone Ghost heaved a sigh and walked into the dimly lit chamber where Browser and Catkin stood. Lines creased Browser's forehead and ran down around his mouth. His bushy black brows had lowered. He carried his war club in his right hand, as though not yet certain the enemy was gone.

"I watched Blue Corn's warriors climb the cliff staircase," Stone Ghost said. "We are safe for the moment,
Nephew."

Browser seemed to relax a little, but Catkin remained
vigilant. She had her fists clenched at her sides, and
the muscles of her tall body bulged through her red
war shirt. Sweat streaked the dust on her wide cheekbones and turned-up nose. Her shorn hair had started
to grow out, hanging down to her chin.

"Straighthorn said you wished to see me, Uncle. I
hope you do not mind that I asked Catkin—"

Stone Ghost waved a hand. "I'm glad Catkin is here,
Nephew. She may have insights that we do not."

Browser nodded and spread his feet, waiting.

Stone Ghost's turkey-feather cape swayed about him
as he hobbled toward the wall and sat down. He leaned
back and extended his aching legs. "The little orphan
girl is one of the First People, and I believe Obsidian
knows her."

Browser frowned. "Why?"

"I spoke with Obsidian."

"And she told you she knew the girl?"

"No. She vehemently denied it, so vehemently that
I'm sure she was lying."

Browser exchanged a glance with Catkin, then came
over and knelt in front of Stone Ghost. In the light
streaming through the doorway, Stone Ghost saw the
rips in Browser's cotton cape. "Why do you think she's
one of the First People?"

"She told me that she is related to Cornsilk."

"Children say many things, Uncle. That doesn't
mean—"

"You are right, but let's say that she *is* one of the
First People. Where do you think she came from?"

Catkin leaned against the door and gazed out at the
sunlit cliff with her eyes squinted. "There are many
First People scattered about, Elder. She might have
come from anywhere. So many villages have been

burned, who can say which was her home?"

Browser let out a breath and glared at the dirty floor. "If Obsidian knows the girl, and the girl is one of the First People—"

"The child also told me that her grandfather had witched her breath-heart soul so that it would never find its way to the Land of the Dead."

Catkin jerked around. *"Her grandfather is a witch?"*

Browser held up a hand, signaling Catkin to hold her judgments. "Uncle, please. When I had seen four summers, your own sister once told me that if I didn't stop beating up on the little girls in the village, she'd sneak into my room while I slept, slip a yucca hoop over my head, and change me into a little girl."

Stone Ghost chuckled. "My sister always had a strange sense of humor."

"Yes, but you see what I mean. I have known many grandparents who resorted to threatening their grandchildren when the children were being rebellious."

"Yes, yes, I know. But let us say the little girl is not mistaken. She is one of the First People and her grandfather is a witch."

Catkin stepped forward with the graceful agility of a hunting cat. Her eyes had gone hard. "Are you saying that you think she's Two Hearts's granddaughter?"

"I'm saying it is possible. And I'm fairly certain, even if she isn't Two Hearts's granddaughter, that her family lives among the White Moccasins."

"Then why is she here? Did they send her to spy on us?" Catkin demanded.

Stone Ghost took a moment to rub the top of his kneecap. The pain was fiery. "I think she ran away."

"Ran away?" Browser asked.

"Yes, and from my conversations with her, I don't think it's the first time it's happened."

Browser rose to his feet and glanced uncertainly at Stone Ghost. He paced back and forth. "This is interesting, Uncle, but I'm not sure why it's important."

"Well, I'm not sure it is. But think on it for a time, Nephew."

Catkin took a step closer and whispered, "If there is any chance she is a member of the White Moccasins, we should kill her. Now! Before she has a chance to 'run away' again and tell them everything she has seen here!"

Browser folded his arms across his broad chest and peered at her from the corner of his eye. "I will not kill a child. I don't care if she is Two Hearts's grand-daughter. She has a right to run away, and if she wishes to stay—"

"You're right." Catkin seemed to wilt. She took a step backward, then turned away in silence.

Stone Ghost bowed his head. The memory of watching children leap from the burning kiva at Longtail village still lived in his heart.

Stone Ghost grunted as he got to his feet. "There is one last thing, Nephew. While you are hunting Two Hearts, I wish you to remember that we may have his granddaughter."

"You mean"—Browser's mouth hung open—"as a hostage?"

Catkin gaped at Stone Ghost.

"I believe the child is here of her own will, Nephew, but Two Hearts may not know this. Do you see what I mean?"

Browser's face slackened in understanding. "Yes, Uncle. I see very clearly."

BROWSER ROLLED TO his side in his blankets and reached for his war club. He had to leave for Corner Canyon Town in less than one finger of time, and worry swelled his heart until it hurt.

He ran his fingers over the wooden handle of the
club. He had come from a rich clan in the Green Mesa
villages, but now he had almost nothing. He contem-
plated that as he studied his club. Years of use had
polished the hard chokecherry, and blood, sweat, and
the oils from his hand had darkened it. He knew every
swirl and pattern in the grain. Since the fire at Longtail
village, his club and his bow were the only possessions
that mattered to him.

*And the turquoise wolf sewn into the hem of my war
shirt.*

He sighed and looked up at the ceiling poles illuminated by the light of his fire. Kettle Town, no matter
its other faults, was rich in fuel for the warming fires.
Old willow matting, collapsed roof poles, corn cobs
and stalks, bits of brush dragged in by pack rats, filled
the chambers.

"Browser?"

He sat up and his blankets coiled around his waist.
"Yes, Obsidian."

She entered his chamber hesitantly, as though afraid
of what he might do or say to her. She looked around,
then silently marched across the floor and knelt before
him. Tangled black hair spilled from the frame of her
hood in an unruly cascade, and her jet ear loops
winked.

"I wish to speak with you."

"Speak."

She glanced at the doorway to make sure they were
alone before she whispered, "What are your plans?"

"I plan to keep us alive long enough to find your
father, Two Hearts."

"Browser, you must listen to me. I want you to kill
him, but it must be done delicately. You do not wish
to turn the remaining First People against you. He has
their trust."

Browser shoved his blanket away. "How would a
witch gain anyone's trust?"

She peered at him though large dark eyes. "One person's witch is another person's Spirit Elder. The First People consider Two Hearts to be a very powerful and charismatic leader."

Obsidian tucked a lock of hair behind her ear and let out a breath. It was such a frail, vulnerable gesture, he found himself backing away, sliding across the floor to lean against the wall.

She said, "Your uncle came to see me earlier, when we were hiding. He thinks the little girl is one of the First People."

"Why does he think that?"

She waved a perfect hand. "Who can say? He wanted to know if I knew her or her parents? He was very offensive."

Browser brushed at a streak of dirt that ran down his arm. "Do you know the girl or her parents?"

"Of course not! Even if I did, what difference would it make?"

"I'm sure my uncle wishes to return the girl safely to her family."

Obsidian gazed at him with scared eyes, then quickly looked away. In the silence, she straightened her pendant. "I do not know her, Browser."

Obsidian sank to the floor and her black cape settled around her like sculpted darkness. "Do you know how this began, Browser? It began more than sixty summers ago. Our people were scattered. Many, like you, hadn't been told their ancestry. Some had to be found, others had to be convinced of the truth. It takes time to ensure that new recruits sincerely believe. He worked very hard to do these things." She glanced at the door again. "I think that's why the White Moccasins have taken to eating human flesh. In the old days, the Blessed Sun used it as a weapon to control the Made People. Today Two Hearts uses it to bind his warriors to him. But only the most dedicated will eat the flesh of another human—even if that human is a Made Person. Many cannot stomach it."

"How many First People are there?"

She lifted her shoulder. "I don't know. Perhaps one hundred. But they are all afraid. Father told them the Katsinas' People would lose faith and fade away, especially after so many kivas had been rebuilt without the fulfillment of Poor Singer's prophecy. But, now, he knows you will not fade. You must be destroyed."

"More and more villages are converting," Browser said, "he can't kill us all."

She rocked slightly, and Browser was painfully aware of the sensual way she moved. What was her power over his body? Why did he always imagine himself loving her? He averted his eyes, angry with himself.

Obsidian said, "But he must try, Browser."

"Why? Why can't we live in peace?"

Her shoulders relaxed, and her hood fell back slightly revealing the turquoise pins that glittered in her hair. "The coughing disease and the way it wastes people really frightens Two Hearts. He believes it comes from the katsinas and, worse, he has never been able to cure it. He is convinced that the katsinas destroyed the First People's power, and if we do not stop them, they will finally destroy the last of us."

Browser dropped another piece of wood into his warming bowl. "He will not stop them."

Obsidian wet her lips and looked at the floor. Browser could sense her fear, and it tugged at his own need to shield and protect.

"Browser, you are one of the First People," she said with the patience a mother would use with a child. "So am I. I have lived in fear and loneliness for sun cycles. I have nowhere to go. My father wants me dead. He wants to cut the beating heart from my body, and put it into his own chest so that he can live forever."

A soft sound, like claws on stone, came from the

passageway. Obsidian swallowed hard and listened. Browser knew it was a pack rat. He'd seen the little animal earlier in the day, but Obsidian waited until she could identify it, too.

She turned back and whispered, "I wish you to think about something. I have talked to White Cone. He says we would be welcome among the Mogollon. The Bow Society would guarantee our safety. You, Catkin, and me."

Browser frowned in confusion.

Obsidian met his eyes, then rose and gracefully walked away. She stood in the far corner, where the shadows lay deepest, her cloak swaying about her.

"I know that you love Catkin, Browser. Unlike many of our people, I don't mind living with Made People." She shifted and the warming bowl's gleam illuminated her face. "And I don't mind being a second wife. Over time, I hope that I might earn some of your love."

Browser felt numb. "Obsidian, I don't think—"

"Don't you understand?" Her hands tightened to fists. "I have no life here! Most of my friends died when Longtail village burned. Men sneak into my chamber in the middle of the night, expecting me to open my legs like some camp bitch, because Shadow lay with them the night before. Do you know what that's like? What I have had to do to protect myself?"

"I'm sure it has been difficult for you, but—"

"Shadow said that she'd had you," Obsidian whispered. "That you had a staff like fire-hardened piñon." She leaned her head back, exposing her perfect throat. "Gods, I'm tired of this. I can't do it any longer, Browser. You know the truth, and I'm glad of it. I only ask one thing. Take me as your wife. If you will do that, I will do anything you ask of me."

Browser watched as she tightened her arms beneath her breasts, causing them to swell over the fabric of her dress. "I need time to consider this, Obsidian."

"I have nothing but myself to offer you, Browser. I

pray that that is enough." She shook her head and her hair tumbled from her hood.

Browser rose unsteadily to his feet. "Obsidian, I will not leave the Katsinas' People. They need me."

"But we could all go!" She spun around and her cape whirled like a summer dust devil. "There aren't very many Katsinas' People. Why can't we all go south?"

Browser tied his war club to his belt and reached for his bow and quiver. "Give me some time to think on this, Obsidian. There are others I must speak with."

"Yes, yes, of course," she said and looked up at him as though he knew more than the gods themselves. "I will wait for your answer."

Browser nodded and left the chamber. His steps echoed down the long hallway, but he barely heard them. As he rounded the corner, he saw Catkin.

She stood guard, looking out the window to the east. Starlight gilded her tall lanky body and glimmered in her short black hair.

"Ready?" he called as he neared her position.

"Yes," she said, and followed him.

But her steps were uneasy, too light, like a woman afraid of being attacked from behind.

DUSTY SIGNED THE last of the forms and slid them across the counter to the uniformed policeman, feeling hollow and sick all the while. The officer carefully checked the signature before he plucked a ring of keys from the Peg-Board behind him. "It's parked in space twelve. Give that other copy to the lot attendant and he'll let you out."

"Thanks." Dusty took Dale's keys.

Maureen said, "Why don't you drive me around to the Bronco, and I'll drive it home."

"It's a deal." Dusty looked down at the keys. Something wasn't right. "Excuse me. Where are the other keys?"

The cop raised an eyebrow. "What do you mean?"

"I mean, he had more keys. Where are they?"

"Those keys were in the vehicle when the FBI wrote the impound request. We checked. If you think there should be more, you'll need to take it up with the officer in charge of the investigation."

Dusty fingered the keys, cataloging each as he touched it. "Right," he said. "Thanks."

He led the way down the hall and through the side door that led to the impound lot.

Once they were outside in the bright sunlight, he turned to Maureen. "I've used these keys a thousand times. His house key, office key, the key to my trailer in Santa Fe, and his UNM office keys are missing."

Maureen's dark eyes narrowed. "We'd better call Agent Nichols right now."

Maureen reached into her purse, fished out her cell phone, and punched in Sam Nichols's number. She spoke for a short time, nodded, and pressed END.

"Nichols is out of the office," she said. "I suspect he's in Santa Fe having a nice chat with Ruth Ann. His secretary said she'd give him the information. Meanwhile, we'd better see to changing the locks."

Dusty frowned. "How could the FBI have missed that?"

"The FBI had no way of knowing how many keys Dale had on his ring."

Dusty handed the paper to the attendant, a Hispanic in overalls who walked across to meet them. He had ORTIZ stenciled above his breast pocket. The man checked the signatures and pointed at the motorized gate. "Go through the gate and turn right."

"Thanks."

As Dusty headed for the familiar red Dodge pickup, his leg muscles seemed to turn to lead. They grew heavier with every step, until he could barely force them to take him to the truck.

He stopped by the driver's door. The truck looked dingy. Road grime and city dust had settled on the vehicle in a gray-brown film.

As he reached for the door handle, a sudden feeling possessed him.

He stopped, unable to touch the truck, and turned to Maureen. "The officer said they'd found Dale's keys in his truck? That can't be right, Maureen."

She propped her arm on the bed. "Why not? It was late at night, he probably figured no one else would be around."

Dusty jangled the keys. "So, Dale gets out of the truck thinking . . . what? He must have been nervous about meeting someone in the dark. He *knew* someone was out there waiting for him. He might not have locked the truck, but he'd have taken his keys. I'm sure of it."

Maureen brushed strands of windblown black hair from her face. "If you're right, someone went through his pockets, found the keys, and put them back in the vehicle."

Dusty shook the keys at her. "And just left the old house key and the keys to the truck?"

He could see understanding dawn in her widening eyes. "My God. You mean he knew which keys to take."

"Yes."

They stared at each other; then Dusty unlocked the truck door and pushed the button to unlock Maureen's door. He climbed into the driver's seat with a queer feeling in his gut. The dash sparkled with faint traces of the powder the police had used to dust for prints.

As he started the engine, he said, "The man who killed Dale has a key to my house, Maureen."

"We'll change the locks. First thing."

Dusty adjusted the mirrors and put the truck in reverse. "That doesn't mean he hasn't already been there—or isn't there now, for that matter."

Maureen made a tense gesture with her hand. "Let's just go, Dusty. We have a lot of things to do. Especially you."

He eased out of the space and headed down the lane, following the EXIT arrows. Every time he blinked an afterimage of Dale's panicked face glowed on the backs of his eyelids. Was Dale trying to tell him something?

He turned down another lane and said, "What do you mean, especially me?"

"It's not important."

"Tell me. Maybe it'll take my mind off the keys."

"Well, it's just that, when all the paperwork is finished, you'll get his house, his possessions. What are you going to do with them?"

"I haven't thought that far ahead." Dusty turned down a new lane, heading for the lot exit. "I'm not sure I'm ready to think about Dale's stuff yet, Maureen."

She braced one hand on the overhead strap. "Well, there's no rush. I left John's things for more than a year before I made the first sort."

"A year?"

"Yes. I needed time to convince myself that I could put his favorite shirt into the Goodwill box. It wasn't easy. My heart needed to heal before I could face throwing away his personal treasures."

"What makes you think I'd throw them away?"

"You can't keep everything, Dusty. Sure, the artifacts are important, but what about all of the birthday cards he's kept for fifty or sixty years, the knickknacks, and faded newspaper articles? What about his clothes, his furniture? Do you want that house? If so, do you want it furnished the way he left it?"

Dusty glared out the window, irritated that the lot attendant was waiting for him at the open gate. He waved as he passed and headed down the street. He stopped beside the Bronco and Maureen climbed out.

"See you soon," she said.

He nodded, and watched her open the Bronco door. Traffic was piling up behind him as he eased the clutch out and headed down the street toward the office.

*The keys. Dear God. Whoever killed Dale must have watched him use the keys. It had to be someone very close to Dale. No wonder I'm a suspect.*

Dusty's fingers tightened around the steering wheel.

*But if the killer was that close to Dale, he's also close to me.*

*COLD SUNLIGHT DRENCHES the tan cliff and shoots like arrows into Piper's eyes.*

*"Did you tell him that I knew you?"*

*Piper tries hard not to cry out as Aunt Obsidian twists her arm.*

*"Answer me!"*

*They stand in a tumbled pile of rocks behind Kettle Town, but on the second-story porch, warriors perch, watching the stairs cut into the cliff behind Piper. They do not see her, but she sees them through the cracks in the rocks.*

*Aunt Obsidian kneels in front of Piper and her eyes are a dead flying squirrel's, huge and bulging, filled with anger. Her black hood waffles around her face in the icy wind.*

*She shakes Piper so hard that Piper's head snaps back and pain flies down her spine. A sharp squeak comes up her throat, but she keeps it locked behind her clenched teeth.*

*"What are you doing here?" Aunt Obsidian's voice*

is a snake's hiss. "Did your mother send you to spy on
me?"

Piper hears, but she doesn't really. She has put her
breath-heart soul in the boulder in front of her, and all
it hears is Wind Baby whistling around the corners of
Kettle Town.

"You are a bad girl!" Aunt Obsidian whispers and
shoves Piper hard into the rocks. Gravel scritches beneath her sandals, and she almost falls. "No wonder
Father hates you!"

Piper tries to live inside the tears of the boulder,
and she feels very old and sad, as though the boulder
thinks it's dying, and is frightened. She peers at the
ground and sees small rocks and sand that have fallen
from the boulder, and she knows why it's scared. It
doesn't want to fall to pieces.

"Wait until that old man finds out who you are. He'll
order his warriors to take you out into the desert and
leave you, without food or water, so you'll die. Do you
hear me?"

Piper sucks her lip.

Aunt Obsidian slaps Piper and her feet go out from
under her. She hits the ground hard and lies on her
belly among the fallen rocks and sand, a piece of the
boulder that is alone now. If she listens very hard, she
can hear the boulder crying.

Aunt Obsidian lifts a finger and stabs it at Piper. "I
have a chance, Piper. One single chance to live like a
normal woman. Go home!"

Tears fill Aunt Obsidian's eyes as she turns and
stamps away through the rocks toward the town.

Piper breathes in the dust from the boulder's skin
and wonders if she has swallowed part of its breath-
heart soul, if right now the boulder is living inside her.

Piper wraps her arms around herself and curls onto
her side, trying to keep the boulder safe and warm.

Up above her . . .

Wings flutter.

*Owl lands on the top of the boulder, cocks his head, and peers down at Piper. He is big and gray.*

*She whispers, "I wish she were dead."*

*Owl fluffs out his feathers as though cold.*

*In a voice like Wind Baby's on a still summer day, she whispers, "Your aunt has tears. Did you try to live inside them?"*

# CHAPTER 25

BROWSER SPLIT HIS forces into four parties and sent each in a different direction to scout Corner Canyon Town. If everything went according to plan, they would all be in the same general area by moonrise. In the absolute worst case, should anyone be discovered and unable to flee, others could cover their retreat.

He took one last look around the huge Kettle Town plaza. The faded images of the katsinas that had once painted the front of the town had cracked and flaked off. He could discern patches of huge eyes, black beaks, and fanged muzzles, but little else.

"This must have been a remarkable place one hundred sun cycles ago," Clay Frog remarked as she followed Browser's gaze. She wore a gray knee-length war shirt.

"Yes," he replied softly. "It must have been."

"Do you think we'll ever build anything like it again?"

Browser shook his head uncertainly and, from behind him, he heard Catkin respond, "How can we? When we killed the First People, we killed their knowledge. Do you know a mason today who can construct a five-story building? I don't."

Sadness filled Browser. The glory was draining out of his people, like water down one of the washes. To stand here, before Kettle Town, and imagine it as it had been, was to feel a hole open in his heart. His people had once raised stunning towns like this, now they spent their time running in fear, desperately searching for their next meal, and thinking up ways to kill each other.

*Were the old gods so bad, Browser? Is Two Hearts right when he says our troubles were brought by the katsinas?*

He trotted away from Kettle Town and onto the broad thoroughfare that had long ago linked Kettle Town and Talon Town to the smaller towns across Straight Path Wash. Now rainwashed and windswept, the road was yet another reminder of his ancestors' greatness.

He could feel Catkin's eyes boring into his back. She had been looking at him strangely, and he knew she must have seen Obsidian enter his chamber.

He would tell her. But not now.

He didn't know what to think about Obsidian's offer. When he'd looked into Obsidian's eyes, he'd seen desperation. He had never had a beautiful woman throw herself on his mercy that way—and he was certain she had an ulterior motive. Was she working with Two Hearts? Trying to get him to abandon the Katsinas' People? Or did she truly wish to marry him?

*You have time. Before you decide anything, you must kill Two Hearts.*

He led the way down into the wash. The inky darkness made the descent tricky, and he had to feel for each foothold.

At the bottom, he reached out and took Catkin's hand, guiding her. She tightened her grip in his, and

for the moment he maintained the contact, leading her
across the gravel bottom of the wash.

He had to release her in order to climb up the other
side, and there, stepping up onto the canyon floor
again, she resumed her position behind him.

He knew this road; he'd taken it many times when
the Katsinas' People had lived in Straight Path Canyon.
It led to the great kiva in Corner Canyon. Had anyone
used the kiva since the Katsinas' People had held their
last ceremonies there? Or had the huge subterranean
ceremonial center been left to the pack rats, mice, and
bats?

Fearing ambush, Browser left the rutted road and
followed a meandering route that wound through tawny
patches of grass. When they had lived in Hillside village, an extended family had eked out an existence in
Pottery House. Browser remembered one of the little
girls, a whip-thin urchin with a curious brown discoloration on her face.

Catkin made a faint click with her tongue, and
Browser immediately sank to his haunches, listening to
the darkness, sniffing the air. True to their training, the
Bow warriors dropped and did the same. The faint hint
of smoke rode the cold breeze that drifted down the
canyon. Perhaps someone still lived in Pottery House?

Browser reached back, tapped her knee twice to indicate an advance, and rose. He could feel Catkin walking close behind him; the Bow Society warriors
followed.

Browser circled downwind of Pottery House, approaching slowly. It wouldn't do for them to be discovered by either turkeys or dogs. But only the musty
scent of decay came to his nostrils. Humans left traces
of boiling food, of cloth and baking corn, and of course
their excrement, on the wind.

He eased up to the western side of the house and
placed an ear to the stone, but heard nothing. He moved
slowly along the wall. Midway down the room block,

a weathered pole ladder sagged against the wall. Browser bent down and touched the soil at the base of the ladder. Bristly weeds met his fingers, not packed earth from the passage of moccasins or sandals.

Catkin tapped his shoulder and pointed up the ladder. He nodded, and she started up.

He and the Fire Dogs waited in silence. He might have passed fifty breaths before Catkin's body darkened the top of the ladder, and she carefully descended.

"Gone," she whispered. "They're long gone. Each of the roof entrances is open. It's blacker than the First World inside. Nothing to smell but mold."

"Then let's move on. Spindle Whorl House is a bow shot to the south."

At Spindle Whorl, the results were the same. The seven irregular rooms, and the solitary kiva on the east side of the structure, had been abandoned for at least a sun cycle. The place lay in disrepair.

Browser led his team past the villages that clustered around the great kiva. Talking Stitch Town stood silent and ghostly in the slanted glow of the rising moon. No evidence of violence could be seen, but two corpses sat outside the northern kiva. They had been there so long that only white bones, many scattered about, were left.

"So many left unburied," Browser whispered as he looked down on the nameless dead.

"It is the times," Catkin answered.

"Let it not be so for us," Clay Frog added. "Death does not frighten me. But being left alone, to wander forever in search of one's ancestors, that is frightening."

Browser toed one of the gleaming bones from the path and led the way to War Club village, a bow shot to the east.

They ran in silence until they saw it. Long and hooked at one end, it was a sprawling place.

A sun cycle ago, six families had lived in War Club

village. True, they hadn't kept the place like it had been in the First People's days, but it had been a community. The people had grown enough to feed their families and to trade for trinkets.

They scuttled into the shadows of the northern wall and looked for a ladder. When they couldn't find one, Catkin and Red Dog boosted Browser to the roof. He had made two steps when he came upon a ladder that had been pulled up and stowed on the roof. He glanced back at the new moon; its white light silhouetted him. Taking a chance, he placed each foot with care, pausing by one smokehole after another and sniffing.

At the third, he caught the dissipated odor of a warming fire, and could hear the faint burr of a sleeping man inside.

Browser crouched and searched the rooftops for the humped shape of a sentry huddled under a blanket. For thirty heartbeats he waited, seeing nothing. Two Hearts was their leader; he would be heavily guarded. Browser checked the other rooms, but found no one else.

He lowered himself over the wall and dropped lightly to the ground.

"One room occupied," he whispered after leading them into the shadows. "I could hear someone sleeping, smell his fire. But he was alone."

"A traveler," Catkin guessed. "Someone passing through. We've checked, the weeds have grown up here, too. The lower kivas haven't been used recently."

"I agree. There was no sentry posted." He leaned back against the wall and studied the moonlit canyon rim.

"There's been no sign of movement." Catkin exhaled and her breath rose in the pale light. "Are you sure he's not up there at High Sun? That's where the White Moccasins are."

Browser frowned, aware of the way Clay Frog and Red Dog watched him. They really expected him to know where Two Hearts was hiding, as though he were some sort of oracle. "He might be there," Browser agreed. "But that's for tomorrow night. I want to be sure that we're not missing something here." He pointed at the staircase, a dark slit in the rock where it hid in the shadows. "It wouldn't do to be caught half-way from the top with warriors above you and more below."

"I agree," Red Dog said with his heavily accented voice. "Like Clay Frog, I want to lose my soul at home, where it can be cared for. Not here, where so many enemy ghosts prowl."

"Let's all stay alive." Catkin playfully tapped his shoulder with her war club. "You have my promise that I will guard your back."

"And I will guard yours," Red Dog responded and grinned.

Catkin had always had a way with the other warriors; they instinctively liked and respected her, whereas he had to earn every warrior's confidence.

"Let's check Scorpion village next." Browser pointed to the blocky buildings four bow shots to the southwest. They gleamed in the moonlight, standing near a pillar of rimrock that had defied the ages.

"Keep low," Catkin reminded. "Move slowly. We don't know how many scouts they have up on the rim."

Browser's leg muscles tensed as he skirted the talus that had tumbled from the rim. The boulders helped to screen them from above.

He knew Scorpion village well. He and the Katsinas' People had lived there before moving across the canyon to repair and reconsecrate the great kiva at Talon Town. When they had lived there, the village consisted of fourteen rooms and five kivas. While the Katsinas' People hadn't built onto the place, they had replastered it and fixed the leaky roofs.

Browser scrambled the last distance into the shadow of the west wall. A small drainage that ran from the rimrock to the southwest cut down close to the town.

In his day, it had watered the corn, bean, and squash fields. From the looks of the place, no one had planted the fields since.

Browser took the ladder to the roof, moving cautiously as he crossed the second story. He paused, listening as he reached his old room. Here he had lived with Ash Girl and his son, Grass Moon. A spear of pain made him catch his breath. He closed his eyes, remembering his sick son. How was he to know that bubbling laughter would soon give way to frothy blood, that the flesh would melt from those strong bones and leave nothing but a weak shell?

*Praise the gods that we cannot see too far into the future.* How would he have borne the knowledge that his little boy would soon be dead? That his wife would betray him for her witch father, and that he would kill her to save Catkin's life?

An owl hooted, high above, to the west. Browser looked up at the rimrock. He could see the bird against the dark sky, its feathers outlined by the ghostly thin light of the moon. On silent wings it flew to the top of the small ridgetop house, screeched, then soared away like a black arrow, heading toward the Corner Canyon kiva.

Browser felt as if an invisible hand had just reached through his chest and stroked his heart.

Yes. There. That's where Springbank had lived. Up on the gray shale ridge in a five-room building, attached to a single kiva. He had insisted on living separately, saying he needed time alone to communicate with the katsinas.

Browser stepped around and stared up at the square-roofed building. Owl House, Springbank had called it, in what most people thought was jest.

Was that Two Hearts's evil lair? Is that where he'd lain with Ash Girl, heedless of the fact that she was his daughter as well as Browser's wife? Is that where he'd broken her so thoroughly that a monster soul had slipped inside her?

"Browser?"

He jumped at the hand that settled on his shoulder, and instinctively swung his war club up, ready to strike.

"Sorry," Catkin whispered. "You were taking too long. We've checked the rest of the town. No one is here tonight, but people camp here with some regularity."

He took a breath, stilling his frantic heart. "Yes," he answered. "I was just . . ."

"Lost in the past," she answered, knowing him too well.

He pointed with his war club. "Did you hear the owl screech? It went to perch up there."

"I heard no owl."

He felt cold, as though a mantle of snow had settled on his shoulders. The chase was coming to its conclusion. His gaze lifted to the rimrock.

"Two Hearts is here, somewhere, Catkin. I know he is."

DUSTY USED THE jack to lower the old Holiday Rambler camp trailer onto the hitch of Dale's Dodge. He'd always think of it that way: Dale's Dodge, the truck he'd finally splurged to buy after years and nearly three hundred thousand miles in the old IH Scout. Would this truck last so long, or go so far? Dale would never have the chance to find out. Dusty blinked and his dry eyes burned, as though longing for tears he could not allow himself to shed.

The hitch thunked onto the ball and Dusty snapped the latch home. He was hooking up the safety chains as a pickup pulled into the office parking lot. Plugging in the lights, Dusty smacked the dust from his hands and straightened.

Rupert stepped out of the green Park Service truck. On the other side, Maggie Walking Hawk Taylor, also in a pale green park uniform, opened the passenger-side door. She clutched a brown paper bag in her right hand.

"Hey, Dusty," Rupert greeted and extended a hand. "Hoped I'd catch you here."

"Hi, Rupert. Welcome to the big city."

"Hello, Dusty." Maggie walked up and hugged Dusty fiercely. Then she stepped back and handed him the bag. "Aunt Sage sent you this."

Dusty opened it and looked in to find fry bread.

"It's her traditional gift to a grieving family. She makes it a little different," Maggie told him. "She uses cinnamon and sugar."

"Tell her how much I appreciate it." He smiled his thanks. "I'll see if I can't get out to see her sometime soon to thank her personally."

"She's not . . . well, she's not receiving visitors these days, Dusty. So don't worry about it. I'll tell her you said thanks."

"The cancer?" Dusty asked, another wound lancing his heart.

Maggie nodded. "She won't go to hospice or even take anything for the pain." Maggie avoided his eyes. "I've been staying out there. We've been discussing things. Things she said I was going to have to know."

Dusty looked down at the sack of fry bread, wondering how long it would be before he would have to reciprocate, sending a gift of food to Maggie. He'd forgotten that Pueblo tradition after Aunt Hail had died. With the tenderness of Dale's death eating into his soul, he promised he'd do better next time.

"You about ready?" Rupert propped his hands on his hips, looking over the trailer.

"I'm pretty well packed." He indicated the stack of

screens in the pickup bed. Shovels and pickaxes were laid out on the bed along with two big army-green footlockers that contained the dig kits: level forms, Ziploc bags, artifact bags, soil sample containers, a camera in an ammo box, a chalkboard for photo notes, north arrows and metric scales, line levels, a collection of pointing and square trowels, string, and the other minutiae of good excavation.

Rupert arched an eyebrow. "Didn't you hear agent whatshisname? You're not digging."

"I know, but Nichols told me I could watch from the sidelines." Dusty opened the passenger door and set the fry bread inside. "Michall talked to me this morning. We're renting her the equipment for her crew. It's a business deal. All aboveboard. She's paying for it with real coin of the realm. Good old U.S. cash, legal tender for all debts public and private. We've even got a contract, signed and sealed."

"Uh-huh." Rupert pulled sunglasses from his pocket, slipped them onto his thin face, and studied Dusty. "How much is she paying?"

"A dollar."

Rupert chuckled. "You don't mention that around the FBI, all right?"

"Right." Dusty nodded.

Rupert's smile faded. "We just came from a meeting with the feds. We're working with them hand in glove. Their ERT team has some pretty strict rules for handling evidence if we find anything. At a moment's notice the archaeologists may have to bail out while the scene is sealed."

Dusty glanced up at the bright midday sun. "What do they think we're going to find down there? A drug lab? It's going to be subtle, Rupert. Something your standard run-of-the-mill FBI white guy would walk right past."

Rupert sighed. "You and I think a lot alike. That's why I insisted that Maggie handle this."

Magpie looked away. "I didn't want to. I mean, God, Dusty, it's Dale. The place they left him." Her expression pinched. "You didn't see him. Not when they brought him out of the ground."

Dusty's hands clenched of their own will. "Did you?"

She hesitated. "Yes, and I swear the very air smelled of evil." She let out a breath. "But I've been talking to Aunt Sage. I'm prepared. I can do this." Her determined eyes met his. "Aunt Sage says I can, and I must."

"You're sure?"

Maggie nodded. "If Michail cuts anything, I'll recognize it. Not only that, if it's as bad as we all think, I'll find someone to handle it."

Dusty said, "I'll help you," but wondered how the FBI ERT guys were going to take having a couple of Keres tribal elders showing up on-site to conduct the kind of rituals necessary to capture and destroy ancient witchery.

"You want to follow us up?" Rupert asked, jerking a thumb at the truck.

"No, I have to get back to Santa Fe. Maureen took the Bronco to my place. We have to buy groceries, lantern fuel, get propane, all that."

"You and Maureen?" Maggie lifted an eyebrow suggestively. "You know, Dale always had hopes for the two of you."

Dusty smiled sadly. "It's not like that. We're friends. That's all. It's just that we were together, you know, when it happened. It's as hard on her as it is on me."

"I doubt that," Maggie said. "But I'm glad she's here, so you don't have to do this alone."

Dusty jammed his hands farther into his pockets. "Yeah, well, I haven't had much of a chance to be alone. It seems I'm very popular these days. I even had a visit from my mother last night."

Rupert straightened, a keenness in his expression.

Dusty wished like hell he could have seen the man's eyes, hidden now by the sunglasses. "Ruth's here? Here? In Albuquerque?"

"No. Santa Fe. She was staying at La Fonda. That is, unless Agent Nichols snapped her up as a witness. We called him immediately. Figured it would do her good to sit in for an FBI grilling."

"You think she had something to do with this?" Maggie asked, incredulous.

"Yeah, something," Dusty admitted. "But not directly. This whole thing goes into the past, something between her, Dale, my dad, and Hawsworth."

Rupert tilted his head and examined Dusty. "I'm surprised. After what she did to you, I never thought she'd have the guts to come back and face you."

Dusty shrugged. "I think she's terrified, Rupert. She had to face me to find out what I knew about Dale's death."

Rupert straightened to his full six feet six inches, and softly asked, "Are you okay?"

Dusty nodded. "Yeah. I'm okay."

They stood in companionable silence for a few seconds; then Rupert looked at his watch.

"Maggie, we've got a hard three hours back to the barn. That, or we'll have to file the paperwork for overtime."

"That's the life of a federal drudge, sir."

Rupert made a face. "I get no respect." He started toward the truck, but stopped and turned back. He had a strange look on his face. "When you get to the canyon, find me. Dale always told me to keep my mouth shut about the past. Especially with you, Dusty. He didn't want me stirring the ashes in fires long dead. I don't know everything, but I know some things."

"*What* things?" Dusty asked.

"When you get to the canyon, we'll talk," Rupert called over his shoulder as he opened the pickup door and slid into the driver's seat. "And if you see your

mother, tell her I've got beer on ice. See what kind of
reaction that gets out of her."

"Beer on ice?"

"Yeah." Rupert backed out of the parking lot. Just
before putting the truck into forward, he called, "I
didn't think much of her back then, Dusty. Maybe she's
changed, huh?"

Dusty watched him drive away, remembering her
from last night. "Then again, maybe she hasn't."

STONE GHOST PULLED a brown fabric bag from
his pack, tugged the laces open, and poured the dried
onions into the boiling pot that hung on the tripod over
his warming bowl. The old pot bore a thick coating of
soot, which almost obscured the gray clay beneath.

Bone Walker crouched across the fire with her arms
folded atop her knees, and her doll in her right hand.
The heavy turquoise necklace he'd given her still
draped her neck.

That morning he'd heard her running through the
hallways, running like a scared rabbit, making soft
pained sounds. He'd called her name, and she'd
climbed the ladder to get to his chamber, then run into
his arms—the first time she'd let him touch her. Stone
Ghost had held her in silence until she'd fallen asleep.
Often throughout the afternoon, she'd awakened from
nightmares, shaking.

"This is not much of a supper," he said. "Onion soup
thickened with a little blue cornmeal. Are you hungry?"

Bone Walker stared at the far wall through wide
empty eyes. The eyes of the old Bone Walker, days
ago, before they'd started talking. Dirt streaked her
pretty face and faded blue dress. She must have slid

her hand through the grime on the floor while she slept, then rubbed her nose.

Stone Ghost wondered what had happened to her.

He added three more twigs to the low fire in the warming bowl and watched the flames lick up around the base of his soup pot. The spicy scent of onions mixed with the sweetness of the blue corn to create a mouth-watering aroma.

Yesterday, he'd thought he might be making headway with Bone Walker, getting her to trust him a little, but for most of today she'd been quiet, hiding in corners, sleeping with her blanket pulled over her head.

"I have some juniper berry tea made. Would you like some, Bone Walker?"

She didn't seem to hear him, but the cornhusk doll was turned as if to peer at the teapot resting beside the warming bowl.

Stone Ghost dipped a cupful from the pot and handed it to her. When she didn't take it, he set the cup on the floor beneath the doll.

Stone Ghost picked up his own teacup. Juniper berry tea had a tangy pungent flavor. He took a long drink before lowering his cup to his lap.

In a tender voice, Stone Ghost asked, "Where do you go, Bone Walker, when you aren't speaking? Do you go to a place inside you or a place outside?"

Bone Walker's head tilted toward him, but she didn't look at him. She looked past him.

"I'm curious because once, when I was a boy, the village bully struck me in the head with a big rock." Stone Ghost used his fingers to part the white hair on the right side of his head so that she could see the scar. "I fell flat on my face and I think my breath-heart soul slipped from my body. I found myself looking down at this bloody-headed boy, but I was floating like a milkweed seed, going higher and higher. My mother told me that she had tried to wake me for two days, but I just lay on my hides staring at nothing. So, I went somewhere outside my body. I . . ."

Bone Walker shuddered and clutched her doll more tightly.

"Bone Walker?"

"Are you going to m-make me go away?"

Stone Ghost's bushy white brows lowered. "Why would I do that? You've been a good girl."

The soup pot bubbled and spat.

"But if my parents were bad, would you make me go away?"

Stone Ghost smoothed his fingers down the warm side of his cup. "No, child. I wouldn't blame you for things your parents did."

Bone Walker blinked and her eyes had a human inside them again. A small shaky breath escaped her mouth. She rose, trotted around the fire, and crawled into his lap. With her free hand, she reached up and grabbed hold of the leather ties of his cape knotted beneath his chin. As though this would keep them together, no matter what.

Stone Ghost patted her back gently.

After a short interval, he asked, "Are your parents bad people, Bone Walker?"

She tucked her head inside his cape, hiding her face, but he heard her whisper, *"I hate them."*

Stone Ghost looked down. The desperate love in those words lanced his heart. Tan dust and old juniper needles filled her tangled hair. He patted her again. "Who are they? What are their names?"

Bone Walker leaned against his chest. It took some time before she said, *"Daybreak beasts."*

Stone Ghost's hand hovered over her back. Where had she heard that? Almost no one these days knew about the daybreak beast. It was very, very old.

"Yes," he said and stroked her tangled hair. "I understand."

Grandfather Snowbird told Stone Ghost the story

when he'd seen five or six summers. When Wolf finally led the First People up through the last underworld into the light, he told them: *"For you it will always be daybreak on the second day of the world, my children. You will forever live suspended between Father Sun's first and second coming. Remember the daybreak beast. You cannot kill him, but you can tame him and use his Power."*

It was on the second day of the world that Father Sun decided the First People needed company, and he'd turned buffaloes, ants, coyotes, and other animals into humans: Made People.

Stone Ghost had always wondered about the final moments of glory when there were just First People walking a shining new world like gods.

Before there was an "us" and a "them."

Before they realized paradise was gone forever, and the daybreak beast was born in their hearts.

# CHAPTER 26

CATKIN, CLAY FROG, Red Dog, and Browser crouched in the shadows of Scorpion Town. Browser kept running his hands up and down the shaft of his war club. Catkin had seen him like this before. When battle was close, he couldn't seem to stay still.

She glanced up at the block of rooms two bow shots above them. Owl House was poorly lit by the fingernail moon. Did Springbank lie up there? She could imagine him, age-wasted, pale, his lungs mottled black with old blood. His skin would be tight, eyes sunken into his skull. Those withered brown lips would be drawn back to expose his peglike incisors. Did the old witch really believe that by taking Obsidian's heart he would be able to prolong his foul life?

Catkin hefted her war club. "How do you wish to do this?"

"The main party of White Moccasins are camped at High Sun, one half-hand's run from here, but there will be guards above us somewhere. We can assume that they haven't seen us yet. Had they, an alarm would have been raised."

"A half-hand isn't much time," Clay Frog reminded. "It is even less when you are involved in a fight for your life. That main party could be here before we know it."

Browser gripped his club tightly. "Let's split into two parties and work up the slope from different directions."

"Or come back tomorrow night with more people," Catkin suggested. Her belly knotted. Something told her they should not do this tonight. "By the time Sister Moon rises tomorrow, we could have the job done."

"And it's possible we'd have cloud cover, like we did at sunset tonight," Clay Frog added, sensing Catkin's hesitance.

Browser's eyes slitted as he studied the ridgetop structure above them. She could feel his need to storm up there, to rush the place, and end it once and for all.

"Tonight," Browser said. "It must be tonight."

Catkin took a deep breath. "All right. Perhaps we should take the rest of the night to slowly get into position, then spring on them as dawn approaches. Men are the most tired then."

Browser did not even look at her. His eyes remained on the dark ruins of Owl House. "Clay Frog, take Red Dog and circle, stick to the shadows next to the cliff and move from boulder to boulder, it will give you a little more protection. Catkin and I will work our way

to the toe of the ridge. From there we will crawl from
bush to bush as we make our way up."

"Yes, War Chief."

But no one moved. Red Dog and Clay Frog exchanged worried glances.

"Let's do this," Catkin said and rose to her feet.

Clay Frog and Red Dog cautiously marched off to
the right; then Browser started up the hill. They had
made less than four paces when a cry carried on the
still night.

From long practice, Catkin dropped to a crouch, her
eyes searching the darkness. Where he walked ahead
of her, Browser was already down, frozen in place in
the trail. Clay Frog and Red Dog had followed their
lead, their figures hunched ten paces away.

"Who was that?" Browser's voice was barely above
a whisper. "One of ours?"

Catkin swallowed hard, whispering, "I thought for a
moment we were discovered, but I think it came from
over by the staircase."

"Agreed," Clay Frog hissed. "That was not a warning cry."

"Follow me," Browser ordered. "No matter who it
was, they are alert up there now. We won't be able to
get to them."

In a low bobbing line they duck-walked back to the
protective shadows of the village walls. No sooner had
Catkin reached the shadows than a piping whistle, the
sound like a night bird's, carried on the still air. Moments later, another responded from the ridge where
Owl House looked ever more impregnable.

"Gods," Browser whispered. "Something has alerted
them. Let us hope it is not our other scouting party."
He hesitated and shook his head. "Back. Let's go
back."

Catkin prayed that Jackrabbit, Straighthorn, Carved
Splinter, and Fire Lark were being equally smart.

As they turned to go, Catkin cast one last glance over

her shoulder, and there, faintly visible atop the roof at
Owl House, she could see a person staring off toward
the staircase to the south. A glittering haze of windblown hair swam around the person. Was it a trick of
the distance, or was it a woman?

MAUREEN SAW THE man as she drove the Bronco
into Dusty's driveway. Sunset cast slanting shadows
through the winter-bare cottonwoods and across his
tall, thin body. He leaned against a white Chevrolet
with his arms crossed nonchalantly. The car sported
New Mexico plates, traces of road grime around the
wheel wells, and a scattering of small dents. He
watched her drive in. In his sixties, he looked lean to
the point of being bony. Despite a receding hairline, he
wore his white hair long, pulled back in a ponytail.
That coupled with the tweed coat, brown Dockers, and
snazzy black turtleneck gave him an upscale cachet.
She would have immediately placed him as trendy
Santa Fe, even without the big silver belt buckle with
the large chunk of turquoise.

When she looked into his cold blue eyes, Maureen
knew him. She'd seen him at Dale's memorial cere-
mony, and again on the photo Agent Nichols had
showed her: *Carter Hawsworth.*

Maureen cut the ignition, gathered her purse, and
slipped a hand inside to push the 911 buttons on her
cellular phone. If necessary, all she'd have to do was
thumb the SEND button and scream out "Upper Canyon
Road."

She kept one hand inside her buffalo purse, a finger
on the button, as she stepped out of the Bronco and
slammed the door. "Hello. May I help you?"

The man straightened, the move oddly graceful. "I

was looking for William Stewart. I understood that this
was his address." He pointed to the pathetic aluminum
trailer hunkering on the creek bank.

"Thought you'd try it in the daylight this time, Dr.
Hawsworth?"

He gave her a speculative look. "Do I know you?"

"No. I'm Dr. Maureen Cole."

He considered her, lips pursed. "I don't remember
having heard of you. You are a colleague of Dale's?"

"I was. Though recently I've been working with the
FBI. In fact, I was just discussing you with FBI Special
Agent Sam Nichols. He's very interested in talking to
you."

To her surprise, Hawsworth sighed and chuckled.
"Yes, I know. My sister has been leaving that message
on my answering machine. I rather suppose that I
should give the agent a call."

"Why did you leave Dale's memorial without intro-
ducing yourself?"

He stared down at the ground. "It was one of those
things I just had to do. You see, in the beginning, I
thought it was Dale."

"What was?"

He stepped away from his car. "About a month ago
I started receiving messages. The first was a sand painting. An image of me that had been done in the middle
of the night on my doorstep. A yucca leaf, like a spear,
was thrust through the image's chest."

"You thought Dale had done that?"

"No. But some of the other things . . . well, suffice it
to say that Dale was among the few people on earth
who would have known the significance a yucca hoop
has for me."

He looked suddenly frightened. Maureen took her
hand off the cell phone and reached for the key to
Dusty's trailer. "I don't suppose you still have this
yucca hoop?"

Evidence. Everything always came down to evidence.

"Bloody hell, do you think I'd have kept such a thing? God no, I immediately burned it. The same with the messages that came in on the fax. As soon as I detected Dale's subtle hand, I called him. Told him to stop it, that I knew it was him."

"Is that why you went to his memorial service?"

"No, no." Hawsworth waved it away irritably. "When I heard he'd been found in Chaco and how he'd died, I knew it was something else."

"Something else? Not someone?"

He studied her, his pale blue eyes prying away as if to determine what she really knew. "If I told you that witchcraft is always more than 'someone,' would you immediately consider me a lunatic? Some New Age fruitcake? Or would you allow me the courtesy of my professional identity as an anthropologist and grant me the benefit of the doubt?"

She gave him a thin smile. "I'd give you the benefit of the doubt, Dr. Hawsworth."

"Thank you, Dr. Cole." He steepled his fingers as though addressing undergraduates in the lecture hall, and started pacing lithely before her. "You see, one need not believe in witchcraft itself. I mean, I don't accept that it works as its practitioners believe, but you must understand that the followers are ardent. That *they* believe is sufficient. As a result, it isn't witchcraft itself that carries power, but their belief and the extent to which they pursue their ends. Thus it is—"

Maureen interrupted, "Dr. Hawsworth, I'm more than passingly familiar with the professional literature. Get to the point."

He seemed slightly off balance, as if by derailing his train of thought, she'd made him lose his place.

"You were telling me why you went to Dale's memorial, and left before it was over."

"Yes, you see, I—I," he stammered, then seemed to

catch himself. He squared his thin shoulders. "I'm sure the witch was there."

"The person who killed Dale?"

His cold blue eyes seemed to enlarge. "That's right. I hoped I would see him. Recognize him. And then, all of a sudden, I saw you looking at me, and I realized immediately that going there was a mistake, because as easily as I might have picked out the witch, so might he have singled me out of the crowd. I had already received his unwelcome attention. I did not wish to solicit more."

"Didn't you keep any of the things he sent you? As evidence?"

"Of course not! Why on earth do you think I would have cared about evidence? I immediately swept the walk after I discovered the sand painting. The faxes I threw away."

She impatiently jangled Dusty's keys. "Who were the faxes from?" *The Wolf Witch?*

He frowned. "When I received my phone bill, I checked. The faxes had all been sent from a hotel. The business office at the Hotel El Dorado, right here in Santa Fe. It seems that anyone can just walk in and have the hotel send a fax. They only make a record if it is charged to a room. The faxes sent to me were paid for in cash. The sender only signed his name as someone called Kwewur. I looked it up, found the reference in Fewkes. It's the name of a Wolf Katchina."

Maureen studied him thoughtfully, wondering what Ruth Ann Sullivan had ever seen in this man. "Why haven't you told all this to the FBI?"

His lips tightened in an expression like a cartoon turtle might have made. "I'm not sure I could adequately relate the serious nature of southwestern witchcraft to American federal agents. They don't believe in it, you see. They would be suspicious, perhaps misinterpret my motives in trying to discover the witch."

"They don't seem to misinterpret much, Dr. Hawsworth."

He looked genuinely pained. "But I doubt they have the facilities to pursue a witch. It's not in their cognitive framework. The witch could be right under their official noses, flipping them the proverbial finger, as it were, and they'd never see him."

"Would you?"

"Absolutely. You see, Dr. Cole, I've been studying witchcraft for the last forty years. It brought me here, to the Southwest. Since then, I've followed it to Australia, Polynesia, and Africa. I have over fifty publications in professional journals. If there is a modern expert on preliterate witchcraft, I fear I am he."

"Why did you follow Dr. Sullivan here last night?"

Hawsworth paused, his frown deepening. "I beg your pardon?"

"You followed Ruth Ann Sullivan here from her hotel at around two A.M. last night, didn't you?"

"Who? Ruth? Last night?" He looked perplexed. "She was here?" He looked around as though the surroundings had suddenly been tainted.

"Someone followed Ruth Ann Sullivan from her hotel to this place last night. She assumed it was you."

He made a distasteful face. "Why would I do that?"

"I haven't the slightest notion. As I said, she assumed it was you. Her reasons for making that assumption are her own, but I would imagine that something must have warranted them."

He folded his arms again. "The knowledge that I would love to drive a stake through her black heart is no doubt part of it. Had I known she was coming here last night, I would indeed have followed her. Did she seem frightened of me?"

Maureen nodded.

"Good!" he exclaimed with true glee, and clapped his hands together. "If you see her again, tell her I'd take great pleasure in flaying her skin from her body."

He smiled. "But slowly, Dr. Cole. Very slowly."

"I take it you and Dr. Sullivan aren't on the best of terms."

"In Africa I was working in the Namibian bush. I met the most fascinating reptile there. The snake is called the black mamba, *Dendroaspis polylepis*, to be precise. It's a beautiful thing, slim and graceful, and it moves through the grass with such sinuous grace. When encountered, it lifts its head up, and being more than ten feet long, it stares at a man at eye level. The only defense is to move your hand back and forth." He made a motion, as if polishing glass. "The reason is that if the snake strikes, it will hit your hand instead of your face or throat. In the intervening two minutes that you have to live, you might be able to amputate your hand or arm in time to save your life."

"Does this have a point?"

"Indeed, Dr. Cole. Mambas reminded me a lot of our dear Ruth. Unlike the snakes, however, she strikes at a man's crotch as well as his face."

She clutched the keys and said, "Weren't you the man who wooed her away from her husband and son once upon a time?"

Hawsworth gave her the same condescending smile a tolerant adult would give a child. "That was more than thirty years ago. She was young, beautiful, and only beginning to develop poison sacs."

"But you were together for two years after she ditched Samuel Stewart."

"Yes." His lips thinned again. "Remarkable, isn't it?"

"What are you doing here? What do you want?"

He pulled himself up, that scholar's frown deepening in his forehead. "I was hoping to find this William Stewart. I hear that everyone calls him Dusty."

"That's right. What did you want with Dusty?"

Carter Hawsworth scowled at her, as if trying to

evaluate her character. "I should probably speak to him."

"I don't think he's anxious to talk to you, Dr. Hawsworth. He associates you with one of the more traumatic moments in his life."

Hawsworth waved it off. "Oh, you should have seen him. A squalling brat in dirty clothes. Most unruly. He was a little monster. I can understand Ruth wanting to leave him and this shabby trailer behind—though they only came here between the field seasons. Sometimes the housing was a great deal rougher than this."

Maureen narrowed her eyes. "If you want to talk to him, he's going to want to know why he should listen instead of breaking your jaw first."

"I beg your pardon?" he said as though stunned. "I'm here to help him."

"Dr. Hawsworth, you ran off with his mother. He's hated you all of his life. Why in the world would you want to help him now?"

Hawsworth blinked, as if he truly didn't understand. "Dr. Cole, that was *thirty years ago!* What difference would it make today? But that's all right"—he pushed out with his hands, as if to ward her off—"if he doesn't want to see me, that's well and fine."

She sighed irritably. "Look, that's his decision. What do you want to tell him? I'll deliver your message and after that it's up to him."

Hawsworth turned, flipped his white ponytail, and stalked to his car. He got in, rolled down the window, and said, "Tell him . . . tell him I have reason to believe that no one from those days is safe. If he wants to know more he can contact me. Assuming he wants to discuss this matter in a mature and sensible way, we will decide what to do about Kwewur."

"Right." Maureen stepped up to the man's car door. "How does he reach you?"

"I'll call him. His number, like this address, is in the

book." Hawsworth twisted the key. The Chevy roared
to life.

Maureen was smiling as Hawsworth backed around,
shifted the transmission into gear, and accelerated
away. The little white tag hanging from his rearview
mirror had said: SANTA FE HILTON PARKING. Better yet,
the expiration was still three days away.

# CHAPTER 27

BROWSER KNELT IN a collapsed room high in Kettle Town and watched the morning glow change from
gray to pink. Jackrabbit and Straighthorn had just returned, and stood behind him, breathing hard, covered
with dust.

"We got separated, War Chief," Jackrabbit said.
Sweat streaked the young warrior's face, cutting dark
lines across his pug nose and around his wide mouth.
"We were taking our time, moving slowly, checking
abandoned houses. We split up to check several old pit
houses. I sent Fire Lark and Straighthorn ahead to War
Club village. We were supposed to meet there. Carved
Splinter was behind me when we left the last pit house.
A moment later, when I looked back, he was gone. I
didn't think too much about it since we were all supposed to meet at War Club village anyway." The young
warrior shook his head. "Carved Splinter wouldn't
have just wandered off." He swallowed hard. "A half-
hand of time later, we heard a cry, like someone being
hurt. Then came whistles, and I knew that something
had gone terribly wrong. We waited for a half-hand of
time, just in case there was something we could do . . .

or in case Carved Splinter showed up. Then the warriors came."

"What warriors?"

"White Moccasins, War Chief. Straighthorn saw them first. At least ten climbed down the stairway, dressed in long white capes. I made the decision to draw back. We took shelter in a drainage and waited. Just before daylight we withdrew and returned here."

Browser carefully searched the approaches to Kettle Town, hoping desperately to see Carved Splinter trotting in. He did not wish to tell old White Cone that he had already lost one of the Bow Society's best warriors.

The plain with its abandoned ditches and cornfields remained empty, but for a slight breeze that whisked a swirl of dust off to the east.

THE THING ABOUT Santa Fe, Maureen had discovered, was that even in early November, the weather could be incredible. With a bright sunny day, and temperatures bumping up against seventy Fahrenheit, the outdoor dining area at Nellie's proved the perfect place for lunch.

Dusty had dropped her off that morning while he ran errands to the bank, the hardware shop, and the place that did lube jobs down on Cerrillos. After promising to meet him at Nellie's at noon—the restaurant attached to the Loretto Hotel—she had drifted in and out of the shops around the plaza.

What was it about the Southwest? She could browse with passionate disinterest through the trendy shops on Queen Street in Toronto and rarely have the craving to do anything extravagant. But in the first fifteen minutes in Santa Fe, she could blow her yearly salary. It wasn't just that it was Indian artwork. She'd seen that at Sainte

Marie Among the Hurons in northern Ontario. The difference was that here, in the Southwest, Native art had made the transition from being quaint relics to something beautifully relevant to the twenty-first century.

Studying the katchinas in their wealth of styles, she couldn't help but wonder why her Iroquoian contemporaries at Six Nations couldn't find a way to share the power and beauty of the Society of Faces. Iroquoian False Face dancers were every bit as delightful as katchinas, and often a great deal more colorful.

She considered that as the midmorning sun warmed the outdoor restaurant. It reflected from the cement and the bright yellow napkins on the table. The historic Loretto chapel stood immediately to the south, guarded by overarching cottonwoods. Behind her a traditional-looking ramada enclosed the server's stations and fireplace. In front of her, the plastered walls of the Hotel Loretto, with its plastic-shrouded luminarias, glowed in the clear morning.

"Excuse me?"

Maureen started from her reverie. The tall woman standing beside her table wore a gray wool suit with matching waist-length cape, opaque white nylons, and brown pumps. Her perfect silver hair was accented by the red silk scarf knotted at her neck.

"Hello, Dr. Sullivan, fancy meeting you here." Maureen felt her happy mood evaporate.

"I was sitting over there." She pointed to the far corner table beside the cement railing. "I thought perhaps you might like company?"

Subduing her first instinct to say no, Maureen moved her bison-hide purse from the other chair. "Be my guest."

Ruth Ann Sullivan seated herself, looking every inch an East Coast matron. She unhooked her cloak and spread it over the chair back. Back straight, posture perfect, she crossed her arms primly and studied Maureen through hard blue eyes. "You're not the sort I would have figured my son would attract."

"How would you know? You don't know anything about your son."

Maureen raised the big yellow coffee cup to signal for a refill. They had marvelous coffee here, rich and black—even better than her favorite Tim Horton's off the QEW back home.

"Just after I escaped the Gestapo treatment of Agent Nichols, I did some research." Ruth Ann smiled coldly.

"Gestapo? Like white lights, a wooden chair, black leather gloves, and rubber hoses?" Maureen asked.

"No, him, me, and my lawyer, in the Santa Fe residency." Ruth Ann arched an eyebrow. "Did you really think I killed Dale?"

"No, but I thought you might know who did." Maureen leaned back as her cup was refilled, and the waitress, a middle-aged woman, asked if they were ready to order.

"Just coffee for me," Ruth Ann said.

"I'll order later, please," Maureen replied and waited until the waitress had stepped out of earshot. "Whoever killed Dale knew enough to make it look like southwestern witchcraft."

"Perhaps the killer read too many Tony Hillerman novels." She loosened the red scarf at her throat. "I wish I had known who you were the other night at the trailer." Ruth Ann smiled wearily. "I really would not have expected someone of your reputation to be with William."

"What sort would you have expected?"

"A field bimbo. The rotating sort we used to call teepee creepers. Usually young, out on their own for the first time, bursting with desire to crawl into the crew chief's bedroll and benefit from his status." She waved a thin hand. "It's not just in archaeological field camps, of course. We train our young women to be that way. It's fascinating. I spent a year at a high school, watching the most popular girls: blond, buxom,

and beautiful, from educated, upper-class households.
They just couldn't wait to pair themselves off with the
football heroes, the boys with expensive cars, and the
track stars."

Maureen sipped her coffee and thought about all of
the problems Dusty had relating to women. Even the
field bimbos would have scared him. "You thought
Dusty would be shacked up with a golden girl?"

"I would have imagined. What we think of as silly
high school girls is really a microcosm of adult female
behavior. We still teach our girls to create their self-
identity through their husbands' status and their husbands' possessions."

"Somewhere along the line, I missed that lecture.
Must have been because of the poor schools on the
Reserve." Maureen watched Ruth Ann across her cof-
fee cup.

"Then you aren't as good a physical anthropologist
as your vitae would indicate. The same behavior is exhibited in a troop of Gelada baboons. Females want to
be bred by alpha males. They gravitate toward them
through an attraction as magnetic now as it was in the
middle of the Pleistocene."

"Much the same way you were attracted to Carter
Hawsworth some thirty years ago?" Maureen asked.

Ruth Ann tipped her face to the sun. "Exactly the
same way. Have you and William been lovers for long?
Or is this just a field affair?"

"Dusty and I are professional colleagues and good
friends," she said, "only."

Ruth Ann's mouth pinched. "Maybe, but the way
you look at him, either you've been in his bed, or will
be soon."

"Would that bother you?"

She laughed. "What sort of relationship do you think
I have with him? I couldn't care less who he screws."

Maureen toyed with her cup. "I've been wondering
why the killer was so certain he could lure you here

through those faxes. What could have happened back then to make you feel you had to come back here—"

"You're fishing," Ruth Ann responded archly.

Maureen sipped her coffee, but her eyes never left Ruth Ann. She said, "Something brought you here. Something as innocent as curiosity or as powerful as guilt. Either way, if you'd cut the ties with the past as cleanly as you would have us believe, you wouldn't be here."

Ruth Ann exhaled, then nodded slightly. "Dr. Cole, why don't you and I just lay our cards on the table? At this stage, I'm not sure where scoring points for being clever will get us."

"Very well, did you have Dale killed?"

For a long moment Ruth Ann's hard eyes bored into Maureen's. Finally she said, "Dale and I hadn't spoken in years. Why on earth would I suddenly place myself and my career at risk to murder him?"

"You used to be lovers. Maybe you hold a grudge."

Ruth Ann laughed and slapped the table. "You're right! There is *always* a reason to kill an ex-lover. What did Dale tell you about me?"

"Not much. He told me a little about Dusty's childhood, and about how you treated him and Sam. He told me about you and Hawsworth. That's all. We didn't know that you and Dale were lovers until we began reading the journals."

"I would appreciate the opportunity to look through those journals," she said stiffly, "especially as they regard me."

Maureen took another drink and savored the rich flavor for a time before she answered, "So would we. Someone broke into Dale's house and stole them while we were up at Chaco."

Ruth Ann leaned back and looked around the airy restaurant while she studied the information. "Rupert?"

"Rupert?" Maureen started. "The park superintendent?"

"Or Carter."

"Why Rupert?"

"Oh, come on. You don't think he's some saintly Indian, do you? He used to pick women up at bars, fuck them, and drop them off at the nearest bus station. That's how he met his wife, Sandy, for God's sake."

"Rupert Brown couldn't have taken the journals. He was at Chaco with us. It would have been impossible for him to be in two places at once. And believe me, he was still there after we left. He couldn't have beaten us home." Maureen leveled a finger, "You, however, have been sight unseen for days, eh?"

"I didn't even know about Dale's journals." The answer sounded lame to Maureen.

"He was a young field archaeologist, living out of his truck. Are you telling me you didn't know he kept a journal while he was in the field?"

She made a dismissive gesture. "Oh, I might have. That was so long ago, how would I remember?"

Maureen let her have it her way. Instead she said, "Tell me about it. Your side, I mean. Just how deeply are you involved in witchcraft?"

"I'm an anthropologist, dear. You don't study human culture without running into witchcraft. The first article I published was on southwestern witchcraft. But I am not 'involved' in it."

"But you know what it means when a man's feet are skinned, his body is buried in a yucca hoop, and a hole is drilled in his head. Someone stuffed another human's muscle tissue into Dale's mouth, and he was buried upside down in an archaeological site."

Sullivan's face remained expressionless as she listened. "The actual methods of witchery were Carter's fascination, not mine. If you look up that article, you'll find he was the senior author. He's the one who got me involved in witchcraft stories in the first place. Him and his witch."

Maureen shifted uneasily. "Was that before you ran out on Samuel?"

Sullivan's mouth hardened. "I wouldn't try to sound so judgmental, Dr. Cole. You weren't there."

"Then inform me, please."

"I don't think so. That was in a different millennium, a different life." She toyed with the tabletop, thoughtfully running her fingers over the surface, then looked up suddenly. Her smile was as sharp as cut glass. "Oh, what the hell. They're dead . . . Sam . . . Dale. I could just wish Carter was. Now there, Dr. Cole, is someone I wouldn't mind going to jail for murdering. It would damn near be worth it."

"If Carter was that bad, how could Samuel Stewart have been worse?"

She snorted. "God, Sam was a crusader. It was the sixties. How do I explain the world then? Most of us truly believed that we would die in thermonuclear explosions. Our friends were dying in Vietnam and our government was lying to us. Samuel was one of those free spirits who thought that by knowing people in the past, we could know our future, avoid the mistakes that kill civilizations and maybe build a better world for ourselves and the whole planet."

"That doesn't sound like justification for desertion."

She glared at Maureen from under lowered eyelids. "Have you ever lived with an idealistic fanatic? In the beginning it's heady stuff, this charging windmills and rewriting the future of man. After a couple of years the endless abrasive enthusiasm begins to wear holes in your soul. After William was born, I was supposed to become some sort of maternal clan-elder earth mother goddess. The pure virgin mother, symbol of fertility, but not sexuality. To hear Samuel tell it in those days, breast milk was to a child as rain was to the Shalako. Motherhood wasn't biology, it became religion."

"You still wanted your career."

"Which I wasn't about to find in a Laundromat in Gallup."

"Did Dale and you . . . I mean, you and Dale were lovers long before you met Samuel. What happened there?"

Ruth Ann cocked her head slightly, trying to read Maureen's reaction. "Have you ever been tied up in a love triangle?"

"Once, a long, long time ago in high school. It wasn't pleasant."

"It's less so when your husband and old lover are best friends. Sam and Dale liked each other in spite of my incendiary presence. Dale might have been the biggest mistake I ever made."

"How is that?"

She smiled at something in the distant past. "He didn't write it in his journals?"

"If he did, we didn't get to it before the thief ripped them off."

She fingered the tabletop. "Dale never married. For that I'm sorry."

"Why?"

"I did that to him." She ran a manicured hand through her silver hair. "Oh, I knew it would break his heart when I showed up with Samuel. I wanted it over with. Samuel was new, exciting, and, I thought, brave. He'd just walked out on a fortune, told his family to go fuck off, that he was going to be a field archaeologist, and they could take their mansion and money and suck eggs."

"So you left Dale?"

"Dale was getting too close." Ruth Ann looked up. "He was a possessive kind of person. Even in his old age. You knew him. A dominant male. When you worked with Dale, there was never any doubt who was in control. Yes, he was a team leader, and always took your input and made it part of the project final report. He wanted your best effort and rewarded you appropriately to the quantity and quality of your work. But he was the boss. Period."

"I think that's what made him one of the greatest anthropologists of the twentieth century," Maureen stated bluntly.

"No doubt that's an accurate assessment. As a lover, however, an independent and self-possessed woman looks for something a bit more egalitarian." Ruth Ann tugged at her red scarf again. "You never had an affair with Dale, I take it?"

Maureen just stared at her.

"Don't looked so shocked that I'd ask. Dale had affairs with lots of women," Ruth Ann continued thoughtfully. "He liked smart, strong, and independent women. He couldn't stand the others, the golden girls we referred to earlier. He called them 'breeding stock' for the species. Absolutely necessary, but not worth his time. So he was always caught on the horns of a dilemma. He wasn't attracted to women who didn't challenge him intellectually, but he always had to have them in an inferior position."

"And as soon as they subordinated themselves," she finished, "Dale lost interest?"

"Yes. Curious, isn't it? Dale knew it, too. Hell, I told him over and over. He just couldn't accept a woman as an equal. Or a man, either."

"Well," Maureen said, and looked down into her coffee cup, "at least in that regard, Dale was an egalitarian."

Ruth Ann shook her head. "What is it about men, always trying to make women into something they're not?"

"So you thought Samuel would be a way of shutting Dale down. Using one man to handle another? Risky. Especially when you end up married."

"And pregnant. That was the biggest mistake of all."

"But one you could correct, eh? You just attached yourself to a man with a plane ticket to London."

Maureen watched the angry red rising in Ruth Ann's cheeks. After several seconds, Maureen added, "It's kind of like stepping-stones to avoid getting wet in the river of responsibility, isn't it? Dale, Samuel, Carter, and Dusty, all left behind on the grander road to fame."

"You should know. You're famous in your field. I wager there were a number of stepping-stones in your life as well."

Maureen picked up her coffee and drank. The sun had warmed the yellow cup, and it felt good against her chilly fingers. "What drew you back here, Dr. Sullivan? You and Carter are the only two left from those times. It's up to you to break this thing open."

"What makes you think it's just us? God, Cole, there were others, too. You don't think we just lived in a vacuum, do you?"

Maureen's fingers tightened around her cup. Nonchalantly, she asked, "What others?"

"Colleagues from that time and place. How should I know? I never kept track. I wanted to forget that part of my life." She lifted a mocking eyebrow. "It might even be my son, for all you know. How did he feel to learn that his adopted father and mentor, the noble Dale Emerson Robertson, had fucked his mother long before his father did? Dale never told him, did he? Surprise me and tell me I'm wrong, that Dale could actually have admitted it to the boy."

"Dusty didn't kill Dale. He was with me."

"Ah, yes, your platonic relationship crops up again." She reorganized the silverware with her long fingers. "Tell me, Doctor, what is it like to be so morally superior that you can't allow yourself to be a woman in the presence of the man who loves you? Or is William his father's son? Afraid to lay a finger on the woman he's in love with?"

She stood and threw a couple of dollars onto the table. "If he ever tries, let me know if he's as impotent as his father was."

Ruth Ann strode purposefully to the low stairs that led down into the Loretto gardens.

Maureen turned back to her yellow coffee cup. In the back of her mind, a voice kept whispering, *"Him and his witch, him and his witch . . ."*

# CHAPTER 28

BROWSER TOSSED IN his sleep, desperate to understand what his dead son was trying to tell him. Grass Moon had come to him right after he'd fallen asleep at dawn, and kept waking him throughout the morning. But Browser couldn't hear the little boy. Each time Grass Moon opened his mouth to speak, he broke into violent coughs that ended with blood on his lips.

"Try again, son," Browser pleaded, seeing the fear in Grass Moon's eyes.

The little boy took a breath and tried to form words, but blood sprayed from his mouth, speckling the soil at his feet. Grass Moon reached out to touch Browser, and gasped, *"owl . . ."*

Browser jerked awake and in the sunlight percolating down through the rifts in the roof, he saw Catkin lying on her belly beside him. He had his arm across her shoulders. Her beautiful oval face and turned-up nose gleamed golden.

Browser inhaled and the scents of moldering wood and dust filled his lungs.

When they had crawled into their blankets, exhausted from the night's activity, they'd been an arm's length apart. When had he curled against her?

He closed his eyes for a moment and let himself

enjoy the yucca soap fragrance of her straight black
hair, then dared to press closer. As the curves of her
body conformed to his, she stirred, but didn't wake. A
soft contented murmur came from her lips.

Browser savored the feel of her, the angles of her
shoulders against his muscular chest, her round bottom
pressed firmly against his groin. The hardening of his
penis sent an insistent tingle through his loins. He
couldn't help himself as he tightened his hold on her.

He knew the moment she woke, felt her move, but
not away, no, closer, pressing against him. Browser
tensed as she reached back, slid her hand under his
blanket, and grasped him.

Catkin opened her eyes and a soft smile turned her
lips.

"I didn't mean to wake you," he said.

"It was a pleasant way to wake up, Browser. But
why are you awake? We've slept barely five hands of
time."

"I had a strange dream. My son, Grass Moon, came
to me. He was trying to tell me something, but I only
understood one word, 'owl.' "

Catkin released him, and her smile drained away.
"Owl House?"

"Maybe. I . . . ," he started, and heard the faint grating of a leather-clad foot on the floor in the next chamber.

By the time Yucca Whip ducked into their doorway,
they were separated, a respectable space between them.

"Yes?" Browser asked, trying to still his rapid
breathing.

"Someone is coming, War Chief. We thought you
should know."

"Who?"

"One man and two dogs."

"Carved Splinter?"

"No. An old man."

Browser threw back his blanket and reached for his

weapons. Thankfully his war shirt hung loosely as he rose. By the time he followed Yucca Whip through the labyrinth of passageways, his ardor had faded to a pleasant memory. Catkin followed quietly behind him, displaying no evidence of the precipice upon which they had just balanced.

Yucca Whip led them up several ladders to the third floor. There, in the doorway, Fire Lark peered out at the midday sunlight.

"Where is he?" Yucca Whip asked.

"He just vanished from view. Down there." Fire Lark pointed to the southeastern wall. "His dogs went with him. I assume he's . . . there."

Browser watched as a man clambered up over the southern room block that restricted access to the plaza. He was old, white-haired, and brown-skinned, but limber and active. The two dogs, one black the other brown, sniffed around at the open doorways as they jumped down from the crumbled walls. The man proceeded to the pilastered front of the building and disappeared out of Browser's sight under the wall.

"Come on," Browser said. "I know the bottom floor. We can trap him inside."

"Perhaps we should avoid him?" Catkin asked.

"If he lives here, he may have information about Two Hearts. If he's just innocently passing through, we may have to take other measures. Or perhaps he is bringing us information about Carved Splinter. Regardless, we must know who he is and why he's here."

Browser led the way back through two rooms to a ladder that poked out of a roof opening. Taking the rungs one at a time, he dropped down into the blackness of Kettle Town. He stayed close to the outside wall, where enough light filtered in to illuminate his passage.

Behind him, Catkin, Yucca Whip, and Fire Lark followed on silent feet. The dilapidated warren that was Kettle Town had survived the sun cycles better than

Talon Town. Perhaps because less fighting had taken place here. Or, maybe the builders who erected the giant town had taken more care in its construction. While the upper floor had collapsed, the spectacular destruction that made travel through Talon Town a risk to life and limb didn't yet apply to Kettle Town.

Browser gestured silence as he crept across a room and hunched over a ladder leading down to the second floor. After listening a time, he climbed down and led his party through three rooms. Again, he stopped and perched over a ladder that led into the room block below.

A low growl came from beneath and Browser made a gesture of futility. He had misjudged the air currents that wafted through the huge town. This one carried the scent down.

"Who's there?" a voice called.

Browser made a quick gesture, sending Catkin and Yucca Whip back the way they had come. He waited for a moment and said calmly, "You are now surrounded. My warriors have gone to block the exits. Who are you and what do you want here?"

"Browser? Is that you?" Steps grated on sand. "It's Old Pigeontail."

Pigeontail? The Trader? What was he doing here? Browser chewed his lip, glancing at Fire Lark, who shrugged in return. Pigeontail was known to practically everyone. For sixty sun cycles he had run the roads, trading from one end of the world to the other. Most people considered him to be a scoundrel. He charged scandalous prices for his goods.

"Where are you?" Pigeontail called up. "I'm alone, but for my dogs."

"I know you're alone. I watched you come in."

"Then why didn't you hail me, War Chief?"

In the gloom Browser could see him, a thin old man with a wrinkled face, his white hair pinned in a bun. He wore what looked like a brown tunic, and carried a pack on his back. Both of the dogs growled.

"Calm your dogs," Browser said. "I heard they almost ripped old Lizard Bone's leg off up in Northern House."

"He shouldn't have been teasing them. Anyone who teases a Trader's dogs gets what he deserves." Pigeontail swung his pack off his back and rested it on the floor. To the dogs, he said, "Lie down and guard."

Both dogs immediately lay down on either side of the pack. Pigeontail's bony brown hands grasped the polished ladder, and he climbed toward Browser.

Browser backed away to allow the old man to climb into the room.

With his strange light brown eyes, Pigeontail studied Fire Lark. "So, it's true. You've take up with the Fire Dogs."

"Circumstance and prophecy, it would seem, have made us allies," Browser said.

Pigeontail scanned the ruined chamber. "Did you know that you're surrounded here?"

Browser nodded. "I know that Blue Corn is on top at Center Place, and the White Moccasins are at High Sun House. Do you know where my warrior is? The one who was taken last night?"

Pigeontail heaved a tired breath. "I imagine that he's dead by now." A pause. "Shadow got him last night, oh, it must have been a hand of time after you checked my room in War Club village."

"That was you?" Browser's eyes narrowed. "The man I checked on didn't wake."

Pigeontail smiled warily. "That's because his dogs alerted him the moment you stepped out onto the roof. He told them to be quiet while he feigned deep sleep. Had you been foolish enough to come creeping down my ladder, I would have brained you from behind, and while the dogs savaged your fallen body, I'd have dealt with the second fool to come down that ladder."

"Why are you here, in the canyon?"

"I'm on my way south, War Chief." He glanced at
Fire Lark and smiled. "You'd be amazed at the wealth
of turquoise, jet, and shell beads I traded for in Flowing
Waters Town. I even have copper bells, but you'd
know a lot more about where they came from than I
would." The old man went silent and looked around
the room again. "War Chief, is there somewhere more
pleasant for us to talk than here in this wrecked room?"

Low growls came from below.

"Your warriors?" Pigeontail asked. "The ones sent
to cut me off?"

"Catkin?" Browser called. "We're up here. It's Old
Pigeontail. He says he wants to talk."

"The dogs won't bother you, Deputy Catkin,"
Pigeontail called down. "So long as you step wide
around the pack."

Within moments Catkin and Yucca Whip climbed
into the chamber. Catkin shot glances up and down
Pigeontail's lean body.

"I don't suppose there's a stew on?" Pigeontail
asked.

"We're a little short on rations," Browser answered.

"Then you're in luck." Pigeontail fingered his chin.
"I just might have a jar filled with cornmeal. Excellent
stuff, milled on Matron Blue Corn's mealing bins by
practiced young maidens. It's even spiced with beew-
eed."

"Are we to be your guests?" Catkin asked, cocking
her head suspiciously.

"No, but I might be induced to trade." Pigeontail
grinned. "It's the times, you see. So many of these bits
and pieces of the First People's wealth are floating
around. A jar of cornmeal for perhaps a couple of those
turquoise frogs? No? Well then, maybe one of those
jet bracelets?"

Browser replied, "We're a war party, not a trading
company, but we'll see what we can come up with to
barter for dinner."

"Any news of Carved Splinter?" Catkin asked Browser.

Browser's gut knotted at the anxious look in Catkin's eyes. "Pigeontail says that Shadow has him."

Her jaw hardened. She could well guess the terrors that had befallen the young warrior. "Is there a chance he's still alive?"

"If he is," Pigeontail said emphatically, "he's in the bottom of the deepest kiva in High Sun House, surrounded by White Moccasins. And you have a reputation for not leaving people behind, War Chief." He shot a meaningful look at Catkin. "So I'm sure the White Moccasins are expecting you."

Pigeontail studied the Fire Dogs again, evaluating, before he continued, "With enough brave warriors, you might fight your way in there, War Chief, but I can promise you, you won't fight your way out."

STONE GHOST EASED up to the door and leaned against the plastered wall to listen. He'd seen Straighthorn enter the chamber fifty heartbeats ago. The scent of pack rat urine burned his nose. He looked up and saw sticky streaks of it flowing down the wall to his left.

"I don't know," Bone Walker said.

Straighthorn's voice had gone low and threatening. "If you know something, you'd better tell me. Right now. That was you, wasn't it? In the rock shelter with Redcrop?"

Feet shuffled and Stone Ghost heard Bone Walker sucking on her lip.

"Do you remember Redcrop?" Straighthorn asked with an ache in his voice.

Redcrop had been killed by White Moccasins right

after the kiva fire in Longtail village. Straighthorn had loved her very much.

Straighthorn said, "Redcrop. She was the girl who was tied up with you in the rock shelter near Longtail village. Do you remember her?"

Bone Walker made a high-pitched sound, as though straining to get away from a hard hand.

Straighthorn heaved an angry sigh and said, "I'm sorry. Maybe you aren't the same girl. Maybe I just want you to be so that I can drive a stiletto through your heart the way the White Moccasins did Redcrop's heart."

Bone Walker's voice was a tiny tremor: *"My heart? You want my heart?"*

"No, I'm sorry. I didn't mean to frighten you. It's just that I—"

In a choking sob, Bone Walker said, "If you kill my heart I won't be able to look inside it!"

"What do you mean, look inside it?"

"I mean first. I have to look in it first."

Stone Ghost squeezed his eyes closed and listened to the blood surge in his ears. He was growing to love this child. It would shred his souls if she—

"Do you know who Two Hearts is?" Straighthorn asked.

Bone Walker didn't answer.

"He's a very powerful witch. We are trying to find him so we can kill him."

A soft suffocating sound filled the chamber, and Stone Ghost realized that Bone Walker must be crying.

"I'm going to kill him myself," Straighthorn assured her. "With this stiletto on my belt. Do you see this?"

Bone Walker sobbed.

Stone Ghost clamped his jaw. He knew he should stop this, but he needed to hear her answers to Straighthorn's questions.

"What about Shadow Woman?" Straighthorn pressed. "Is she your mother? I'm going to kill her, too. She's a monster. A hideous animal disguised as a human."

The little girl stuttered, "S-sometimes she has b-bead days!"

"Bead days? What's that?"

Bone Walker said, "B-bad days."

Straighthorn's cape rustled, as though he'd stood up. "Do you know Shadow Woman? If she's your mother, why hasn't she come to look for you? Maybe she doesn't care about you."

Stone Ghost peered around the door into the room. Bone Walker stood with her head tipped far back, staring up at Straighthorn. She had her tiny fists clenched at her sides.

Straighthorn glared down at her. He'd cut his hair in mourning for Redcrop and the irregular black locks framed his thin face and hooked nose. "Just remember. If you know anything, you'd better come and tell me."

He turned to leave, and his threadbare red cape swung around him.

Stone Ghost backed out of the room.

As Straighthorn passed him, Stone Ghost gripped his arm and motioned for Straighthorn to follow him. Straighthorn's fiery brown eyes tightened, but he nodded and followed Stone Ghost down the hall to a nearby chamber.

When they stood alone in the musty darkness, Stone Ghost said, "Who told you the child might know Two Hearts and Shadow Woman?"

Straighthorn gave Stone Ghost a disgruntled look. "Obsidian. She said that you questioned her about it. That you thought the child might be related to them."

"Did Obsidian say the child was related to them?"

Straighthorn frowned. "No. She just mentioned the possibility."

Stone Ghost smiled in a grandfatherly way and put a hand on Straighthorn's shoulder. "Thank you, Straighthorn. If she tells you anything else, I would appreciate it if you would let me know."

"Of course, Elder."

Straighthorn bowed respectfully and left.

Stone Ghost braced his aching knees and listened to the youth's steps echo down the long hallway.

*So, Obsidian wishes the child dead. Why?*

Obsidian knew how much Straighthorn had loved Redcrop. Just planting the thought that Bone Walker might be related to Redcrop's murderers could have been enough. Fortunately, today, it wasn't. But who knew about tomorrow? Who else had Obsidian told?

Stone Ghost hobbled back down the hall and reentered the room where Bone Walker had been standing. It took him several moments to find her. She lay in the darkest corner, covered with fallen stones she must have collected from the floor. She had her back turned to Stone Ghost.

"Bone Walker?" he called softly. "Are you all right?"

The stones rattled, then one hit the wall, hard.

He walked over and sat down next to her. All he could see beneath the stones was a sliver of her blue dress and a lock of her long black hair.

"Rocks have souls, you know," he repeated her words. "Be careful who you hurt."

The stones rattled again.

Then her dirty hand snaked from beneath the stones and reached for the rock she'd thrown.

She dragged it back and petted it gently.

Stone Ghost smiled.

DUSTY WATCHED MAUREEN thoughtfully poke at her lamb-stuffed poblano pepper, shoving the last bits around her plate with her fork.

The Coyote Café brimmed with patrons. The clatter of silverware and dishes melded with the background murmur of animated conversations. He had led her up the green cement stairs from Water Street and into the tan interior with its rounded fireplace, north-facing windows, and ornate wooden reception desk.

Her eyes fixed on the wooden animals who lived on the hood over the open kitchen. The howling coyotes with their kitsch neckerchiefs seemed to hold her attention.

"Something you'd like to tell me?"

She looked at him. "Actually I was just thinking that you're the luckiest man alive."

He speared his last cube of tenderloin and ate it. "I'd be curious to know how you figure that."

"The greatest stroke of luck in your life occurred when your mother abandoned you."

Dusty leaned back in his chair and wiped his mouth with his napkin. "It didn't feel that way at the time."

"No, I'm sure it didn't. Nonetheless."

Dusty wiped his hands and refolded the napkin. She had a strange, almost angry look in her eyes. "I imagine that Agent Nichols is about finished wringing him out by now. I want my chance next."

"You think Hawsworth did it?"

He placed the folded napkin on the table. "We'll know if Nichols arrests him."

Maureen rested her fork on her plate, as though her hunger had vanished. She wore a pale blue sweater, and her long braid seemed to pick up the hues, glinting azure in the dim café light. She leaned forward to brace her elbows on the table. "Ruth Ann could have done it, too, Dusty. Something about her just isn't right, and she's certainly not telling us everything. Something happened back in the past. Something between her, Dale, and Carter."

"You mean besides a little fornication and frolic?"

Maureen ignored his attempt at humor. "Your

mother said something that's been bothering me. She said that Carter had his own witch."

"You don't *have* a witch, Maureen. They have you."

Maureen picked up her honey-coated blue corn bread, and aimed it at him. "She made it sound like the witch was Carter's private teacher."

Dusty pushed his plate across the marble tabletop. "Well, it's possible. Hawsworth is an expert on the subject. Somebody had to show him the ropes."

"Yes, but let's not forget that Ruth Ann's first article was on witchcraft in the Southwest. Did Carter's witch show her the ropes, as well?"

He thought she was beautiful when her black eyes turned cool and accusing.

"I wouldn't doubt it," he said, wanting to discuss anything but this, and added, "let's order dessert."

All through his cactus mousse custard he pondered what a man would have to do to have his own "private" witch?

He was still thinking of that as he drove out to the trailer.

Maureen silently watched the galleries pass, then as they neared his trailer, said, "You're better than all of them, Dusty. I don't know how, but you came out a better human being."

"I came out fine because of Dale."

"Yes." She nodded. "But Ruth Ann made a good point. She said that Dale could never deal with a woman on an equal basis."

"That's nonsense. Dale dealt with females just fine. He thought you were the finest physical anthropologist in the world."

"But I was part of his team, Dusty. Don't you see? Did you ever know him to work for anyone else? Dale was always the boss. Ruth Ann says that's why he never married. He couldn't maintain a relationship, no matter how much he was attracted to a woman."

"Yeah, well," he said. "I've been called the 'Two-month Wonder' by a number of women—because that's how long they could stand me."

"I've stood you for three months," she noted.

"Yes, but have you enjoyed it?"

She gave him an amused look. "Yes. Very much."

He smiled and pulled into the drive that led to his trailer. Stopping beside Dale's truck, he shut off the engine and looked at her. "That's because we're friends, Maureen. Not lovers. Something changes when you go to bed with a woman."

"I wouldn't know. I've never gone to bed with a woman."

"Well I have, and believe me, something changes. They get crazy."

"You mean you get crazy."

Dusty opened his door. "Yeah, well, maybe."

She got out of the Bronco and closed the door. "The point I was trying to make is that unlike Dale you can work with women as equals."

Dusty watched her march toward the trailer door. "You think *I* treat women as equals?" He walked up behind her, searching for the key. "You're the first female to say so."

He stood behind her, close enough that he could smell her delicate scent on the evening breeze. Finally, he found the shiny new key, unlocked the door, and flicked on the lights. As he headed for the kitchen, he asked, "Coffee?"

She set her purse by the door. The way she was looking at him made his nerves begin to vibrate. The chilly air had brought color to her cheeks and her black eyes seemed to be stirring with some emotion he couldn't understand. Dear God, she was beautiful.

"Can I ask a question?" her voice had lowered, softening.

"Yeah, sure."

"Did you ever hear about your father being impotent?"

That caught him flat-footed, one hand on the refrigerator handle. "What?"

"Did you ever hear that?"

He turned and braced a hand on the kitchen counter. "No, but who would tell me?"

"Ruth Ann claimed Samuel was impotent."

Dusty hesitated, thinking about that, then turned back to the refrigerator. "She hated him, Maureen."

Maureen shrugged out of her coat and went to stand before the picture of Samuel Stewart. "Not at first. From what I can gather, your father was a kind and sensitive idealist. He probably fell head-over-heels for Ruth Ann. She was beautiful, sexy, and available. She must have seemed like a dream come true until she grew tired of him and the Southwest."

"And me," Dusty added pointedly.

Maureen seemed to be lost in the photograph of Sam beside the pickup. "She must have made his life a living hell."

"And everyone else's life who ever knew her."

Maureen walked to the table and slid onto a chair. "When she talked about his impotence this morning, Dusty, she meant it. It wasn't just spite."

Dusty pulled a beer from the refrigerator and pried off the cap. The rich scent of Guinness made him feel better. He took a long drink, then said, "I can understand how a woman like her would make a man impotent."

The lines around Maureen's mouth deepened. "Poor Sam. She broke him, and then she left him in the dust."

Dusty set his Guinness down and reached for the coffee. As he spooned grounds into the basket, he said, "It's more than that—she killed him. Maybe she wasn't in the room when Dad stuffed his finger into the light socket, but she might as well have been."

Maureen turned her level eyes on him. "Maybe she regretted that—and wanted to be there when she killed Dale."

# CHAPTER 29

THE FIRE POPPED and tentative flames licked around the curved bottom of the corrugated cooking pot. Flickering light illuminated the faces of the people crouched anxiously around the walls, their eyes on the pot. The delightful smell of boiling blue corn mixed tauntingly with the antelope bone butter. Catkin's stomach twisted in anticipation.

Stone Ghost sat in the rear of the chamber with the little girl's head in his lap. Half asleep, she had her cornhusk doll clutched in her hands. Stone Ghost had spread his feather cape over the girl. He must have been cold, but he seemed content.

Browser settled himself between Catkin and Old Pigeontail. She was intimately aware of his thigh pressed against hers. She had to fight the urge to reach down and touch him.

"It's an interesting problem, War Chief," Pigeontail said. "You are boxed by two larger parties." He cast his appraising glance across the room to where Obsidian hunched with her back to the wall, speaking with Stone Ghost. She had washed her hair to its usual gloss.

"Are you trying to give me advice, Elder?" Browser asked.

"If it were me, I would wait until nightfall, drop into the drainage, and follow it away. By morning I would be long gone."

Catkin asked suddenly, "Elder, why are you here? You always seem to show up at the most inappropriate times."

Pigeontail smiled. "I'm curious, that's all. I would see the people brave enough to corner Two Hearts in his own lair."

Conversation stopped as all eyes turned to Pigeontail.

Catkin said, "How do you know this is his lair?"

Pigeontail refilled his teacup from the pot at the edge of the coals and swirled the liquid, as though examining it. "The man you knew as Elder Springbank committed terrible crimes at Longtail village. You unmasked him there, but he lived here for many sun cycles before that. Isn't it an odd coincidence that you have come here, to this place, just after Gray Thunder's murder, and just after word has gone out that Two Hearts seeks the heart of the beautiful Obsidian?" He glanced meaningfully across the room.

Obsidian's dark eyes widened.

"How do you know that?" Browser asked.

Pigeontail opened his hands. "I am a Trader, War Chief. I go a great many places and hear a great many things. I have been doing this for more seasons than anyone alive. Oh, I have traded with the White Moccasins for sun cycles, just as I have traded with the Mogollon and the Hohokam. I go everywhere and speak to everyone. I am alive today because I keep people's secrets."

"But not the secret that Elder Springbank wishes Obsidian's heart," Catkin said.

Pigeontail gave her an amused look. "It is not a secret, Deputy Catkin. Besides, the White Moccasins trust me."

"And you were just there," Stone Ghost said from the rear.

Pigeontail turned to smile at him. "Yes. I was." He glanced at Obsidian again. "You will be glad to know, incidentally, that Two Hearts says if he can't get your heart he will have to find another relative to provide the heart."

Obsidian lifted her chin haughtily. "Then he should take Shadow's worm-ridden heart. It would fit him well."

The little girl jerked upright in Stone Ghost's lap. Utter terror twisted her young face. Stone Ghost said something soft to her and stroked her hair.

Catkin glared at Pigeontail. "You just visited the White Moccasins? What's the matter with you? Don't you care that they killed, beheaded, and stripped the meat from the people at Aspen village? Or that Springbank burned half our children to death in Longtail village?"

Catkin started to rise, but Browser's hand stopped her. "Wait," he whispered.

Pigeontail just sipped his tea, apparently unflustered. After a moment of silence he said, "Catkin, I have lived over seventy summers. In that time I have seen atrocity after atrocity." He cocked his head, his eyes, like ambered pine, on hers. "What one people might consider a vicious and evil massacre is considered by the perpetrators as a just and morally correct response to aggression. Look around you. Your people have always considered the Fire Dogs to be cowardly fiends. Yet, here you are, sharing their companionship, fighting side by side, the slights and insults of the past forgotten for the needs of the present. One person's fiend is another's hero."

"Yes, but Two Hearts is a witch, Pigeontail," Browser said. "We've always hunted down witches."

Pigeontail raised his hands. "Yes, you have. You've hunted them because you're not witches yourselves. Listen to me, I can only tell you the rules under which I must live as a Trader. I take no one's side. I tell only what people want told. By following those rules I have stayed alive all these sun cycles. It is not pleasant to deal with friends who murder other friends, but it is how I must live." He paused, holding Catkin's gaze. "Would you have me leave here knowing I could go to Center Place and tell Blue Corn that you are in Kettle Town? Or would you have me go to High Sun, my head full of things to tell the White Moccasins?"

"I would smack your brains out," Catkin said, "before I let you take one step from here."

"Then you understand, Deputy Catkin." Pigeontail smiled disarmingly.

Stone Ghost rose and hobbled forward unsteadily. When he lowered himself to the floor beside Pigeontail, the old Trader winced.

Stone Ghost's thin white hair blazed in the firelight. "But it brings up a good question," Stone Ghost said. "I have known you since you were a boy and have never seen you act brashly."

"Me? Brash?" Pigeontail asked.

Stone Ghost smiled, but it only reached his lips. His eyes remained keen and unamused. "Surely you know that we are in great danger and that by coming here, you are in great danger. Why take the chance?"

Pigeontail's brows arched. "Momentous things are happening, old friend. You are in the middle of them. I would see what happens." He chuckled. "Look at me! Have you ever heard of a Trader who lived as long as I have? On rare occasions, yes, but look at me. I can still run the roads. My old bones and joints continue to carry me on my journeys. Perhaps it is the will of the gods that I have been to so many places and talked to so many people. But I can't go on forever. I feel the stiffness and my back hurts every time I shoulder a pack. I have seen so much in my time, have watched our peoples through the coming of the coughing sickness, and watched them waste into death. I have seen the increasing warfare, the growth of the Katsinas' People, and the rise of the Flute Player warriors. I have walked through the ruins of once thriving towns, kicked the unburied bones of friends to clear my path. I have seen the rebirth of the White Moccasins, and now word that the First People still live is spreading across the land. Gray Thunder, a prophet from the Fire Dogs, has been murdered in Blue Corn's Sunrise House, and Mogollon and Straight Path warriors hunt the old witch Two Hearts in retaliation." His smile was crafty. "I may not live much longer, but what a story I will tell on my deathbed."

Stone Ghost rubbed his hands together. "Then, I take it you have forgiven me for the murder of your brother?"

Catkin started, watching Stone Ghost and Pigeontail with renewed interest.

"My brother did what he thought he had to. As did you, Stone Ghost." Pigeontail seemed to be staring into the past. "I told you, I, too, have to live by the rules. Tell me this: In the same situation, would you do it again?"

Stone Ghost stared down at his hands and nodded his head. "I, too, have had a long life, Trader. His death taught me a great many lessons." Stone Ghost filled his lungs. "You should know, if anything happens to me, that he hangs in the bag—the one made of Hohokam cotton with red stitching—from my roof pole at Smoking Mirror Butte. If I don't get back, find him. Take him home. And tell him I will see him in the afterlife."

Pigeontail's eyes had narrowed and the sudden tension could be felt, straining the air.

The skull in the bag? Catkin remembered with a flash of inspiration. Crooked Nose! She could see Stone Ghost as he had been that night, snow drifting in through the holes in his roof while he cradled a polished skull in his lap. *"Crooked Nose says you saw the Blue God."* The old man's words rolled around her head.

"He knew!" Catkin looked up, aware that all eyes were on her. Had she spoken aloud?

"Knew what?" Browser asked.

"Crooked Nose," she said, and turned her attention to Stone Ghost. "How did he know?"

Pigeontail had shifted, fire in his eyes. "What are you talking about?"

"He told you, Elder. Remember? That night in your house under Smoking Mirror Butte. He told you I had seen the Blue God."

Obsidian couldn't help hissing as she drew in her breath.

"Yes, I remember. You said you didn't believe in her," Stone Ghost reminded gently.

Catkin tightened her fist. "That was a long time ago, Elder. Back when the world was much simpler."

"You only thought so, Catkin." Stone Ghost smiled. "Now it flies around you like a whirlwind."

"Why did you come here now?" Browser asked suddenly. "You could have gone any direction after you left Flowing Waters Town. You carry some of the First People's wealth that you traded for in Flowing Waters Town. Why bring it south? To trade it back to the White Moccasins?"

"That is another reason, yes, but mostly I was curious about Gray Thunder's murder." Pigeontail looked at White Cone, asking in fluent Mogollon, "Bow Elder? Did you do that to stop him from spreading heresy?"

"We had no hand in Gray Thunder's death." White Cone lifted his right hand. "After he prophesied his death, I would have cut off this arm to have taken him alive back to my kiva. His death came from outside."

Stone Ghost said, "Given the manner of it, he was killed by Two Hearts, and most likely Shadow. Two Hearts and Ash Girl killed the warrior Whiproot in the same manner in Talon Town."

"Yes, I remember." Pigeontail nodded.

"Shadow had an ally in Flowing Waters Town," Stone Ghost said. "Someone had to pass her through the sentries."

"We were very closely watched," White Cone said. "A woman approaching Gray Thunder's room would have been seen. When this is finished here, we must go back and question the guard who watched Gray Thunder's room that night."

Pigeontail said, "Whatever he knew, he has taken down to the Land of the Dead. That is why Blue Corn pursues you. Her guard was killed the night you left. She is rabid to find you. To avenge his death."

Stone Ghost bowed his head and stared into the fire. "Then perhaps it was not Shadow Woman who killed the prophet, but someone else."

"But she was there, Elder," Catkin said. "I *saw* her."

"Yes," he murmured. "Fortuitous, wasn't it?"

"I don't understand, Uncle." Browser looked perplexed. "Gray Thunder's body was treated exactly the way my warrior's was at Talon Town. The details were the same right down to the tracks in the blood."

"That only means that the real murderer was cunning."

"Why?" Catkin asked in frustration.

Stone Ghost looked at Pigeontail. "Tell me, when Whiproot was murdered in Talon Town, was it talked about? You were there soon afterward, did you bear the tale?"

"Every Trader in the region did. I, myself, was taken into the room later by Peavine. She showed me how he was found, how his arms and legs were. The bloodstains were all over the walls. I told as many people as I could."

The orphan girl sat up, and Stone Ghost turned to look at her. Her freshly washed face made her huge dark eyes seem even larger, like black bottomless pits.

Stone Ghost didn't take his eyes from her when he said, "I think you had best prepare, Nephew. Given the fact that Pigeontail walked in here in bright daylight, Blue Corn's scouts must know we are here."

"The White Moccasins, too," Catkin reminded and gave Pigeontail a look of sheer loathing.

"I shall say nothing," Pigeontail replied. "You have my word on that."

Catkin said, "It's already too late."

"Yes. It is." Browser nodded wearily. "Which means our quest to corner Two Hearts in his own lair will have to wait."

"Why is that?" Pigeontail asked.

Browser bent his head. "Because very soon we are going to be attacked. You like to carry stories, Trader. Well, tonight, you will either see me defeat two large parties of warriors with my handful of Fire Dogs, or you shall leave here with the story of our deaths."

Pigeontail grinned in a way that turned Catkin's stomach. He said, "Either way, I assure you, it will be heroic."

CONCENTRATION HAD NEVER been a big problem for Dusty. But this morning it was. He'd already overcooked the eggs. He stood over the stove, head wreathed in the aroma of eggs, green chilis, and his homemade Anasazi and black bean refritos. But his mind drifted. He used a spoon to taste, making sure that the right mixture of fresh cilantro, cumin, and chopped white onion had been achieved. With the spatula he eased the eggs onto the corn tortillas, and spooned hot salsa over them. He crumbled cheddar onto the whole and dished refritos onto the side of the plate. There. Done. Even if the eggs were hard as rocks. The coffee had just begun to perk.

The sound of the shower had stopped ten minutes ago, but he'd yet to see Maureen.

He glanced at his foldout couch, his bed from last night already stowed, then turned to study the hallway that led to his bedroom. Would he ever be able to sleep there again without thinking of Maureen's body?

He sighed and poured two hot cups of coffee. He set

them on the kitchen table, then glanced at his watch. Eight-thirty. They'd slept late, and it was a long drive to Chaco, especially pulling a trailer on those roads.

Dusty cupped a hand to his mouth and called, "Maureen? Breakfast is on the table."

"Be there in just a second!"

As Dusty reached for a bottle of hot sauce, he heard a car pull in. Through the louvered kitchen window, he watched Sam Nichols step out of a government Dodge.

"We've got company," he called down the hallway. "Agent Nichols is here."

By the time he opened the door, Nichols was climbing onto his rickety porch. "You're out early," he greeted. "Come on in. Had breakfast?"

Nichols gave him a thin smile and looked curiously around his trailer. The place seemed to shock him.

"Well, it's homey," Dusty defended. "And it was Dad's. And yeah, I know, it's not much."

"Upper Canyon Road," Nichols added. "Driving up here I had, well, a different idea."

Dusty smiled and stepped out of the way to let Nichols into the trailer. "Right. Most people do. So, if you ever get called in to investigate my murder, start with the lawyer next door. He's getting desperate enough to hire a hit man to get me out of here."

Nichols cocked his head, his mind chewing over something that had apparently occurred to him.

"Uh, you didn't say anything about breakfast. I can throw another egg—"

"No, no." Nichols shook his head. "Smells great though. I'd take a cup of coffee."

"You got it." Dusty walked back to the kitchen and poured another cup. As he delivered it, he said, "Have a seat," and pointed to the couch.

Nichols remained standing, but he sipped the coffee. "Have you heard from Rhone?"

"Sylvia? Not today. Why? Should I have?"

Nichols's one good eye missed nothing. "Not necessarily."

Maureen stepped out of the bathroom and made her way down the hall. Her braided hair was still damp and she looked wonderful. Dusty stopped short to enjoy her, skin damp and flushed. She wore blue jeans and a black turtleneck.

"Good morning, Agent Nichols." Maureen shook his hand and turned to the breakfast plates. "My God, that smells wonderful. I'm starving."

"Dig in," Dusty told her. "Don't let it get cold."

Nichols propped an elbow on the file cabinet and sipped. "Good coffee. Go ahead and eat."

"You're sure you don't want some?" Dusty indicated his plate as he sat. "It would just take a minute."

"I ate," Nichols said. "Thanks for the leads on both Dr. Sullivan and Dr. Hawsworth. Sullivan pretty well expected me to drop in on her. She's moved from La Fonda to the Loretto, says it's much nicer. Hawsworth is still at the Hilton. I assume that after our little talk, he's not going anywhere except back to his house in Taos."

"Any arrests?" Maureen asked, trying to be casual as she fished for information.

Nichols scowled down into his coffee. "Look, before we can make an arrest, we have to have a case. So far, we can't build a case on what we have."

Dusty balanced *huevos* on his fork. "Ruth Ann and Carter both say it has something to do with the past." Dusty had noticed that people who knew her forty years ago called her Ruth, but he would always think of her as Ruth Ann. Somehow it sounded more menacing.

"Dr. Sullivan said that Carter had his own witch." Maureen took a drink of coffee. "Maybe he'd tell you who—"

"Way ahead of you, Dr. Cole. The guy's name was Cochiti. He died over a year ago. Kind of mysterious circumstances. Coroner's report said he fell down a canyon slope. They attributed all the bruises and the cranial trauma to the fall."

Dusty lifted his gaze to pin Nichols. "It was out on the reservation, right?"

"Yeah. Place called Tsegi Canyon."

Maureen turned suddenly. "Isn't that traditional?"

"Yes."

"What's traditional?" Nichols asked.

Dusty used a piece of tortilla to scoop up eggs and chili. "The way they take care of witches. In the old days they stoned them to death and buried them. Western law has problems with such doings, so today, suspected witches 'fall' off the rimrock."

"I see." Nichols stared into his coffee. "Hawsworth was in Taos, with witnesses, when it happened. We couldn't find a link."

"What about his calls to Dale?" Maureen asked. "Could he explain them?"

"Hawsworth says he was getting faxes. Threatening messages from someone called Kwewur. He says he thought Dr. Robertson was sending them, and he called him to get him to stop." Nichols sipped the coffee. "We checked the phone records. Nothing conclusive."

"He told me," Maureen said, "that they were sent to his home from a hotel, the El Dorado in Santa Fe."

Nichols blinked. "What else did he tell you?" He set his coffee aside as he pulled out his notebook.

Dusty finished his breakfast and went to wash the plate as Maureen outlined her conversations with Hawsworth and Ruth Ann.

When she was done, Nichols watched Dusty dry his plate and put it in the cupboard. "So, tell me, Stewart, what do you really think they're going to find when they dig up that site out there at Chaco?"

Dusty reached out to Maureen. "Maureen, if you're finished, hand me your plate."

She stood and handed him the plate. As Dusty

washed it, he said, "I think we're going to find the reason Dale was killed. But before you get your hopes up, I want you to prepare yourself."

"What for?"

"I don't think the evidence is going to make any sense to you, Agent Nichols, and I doubt it will be something you can take to a prosecuting attorney."

"Such as?" Nichols asked.

"I think we're going to find a witch." Dusty dried Maureen's plate and stacked it atop his in the cupboard. He'd been finding witches in every archaeological site he'd dug in the past two years. They seemed to be his lot in life. "Alive or dead, he's there."

"We're back to witches again." Nichols sighed. "Put there by Dr. Robertson's killer, I suppose?"

Dusty shook his head. "No, it'll be prehistoric. But he's there."

"How do you know?" Maureen asked.

Dusty gave her a solemn look. "There was an old pot hunter's hole. Do you remember?"

Maureen frowned. "Yes."

"I think the person who killed Dale dug that hole. I think he found something in there that tied him and Dale together, and I think I can—"

"Sylvia Rhone," Nichols said out of the blue. "How long has it been since you've talked to her?"

Dusty shook his head, puzzled by the abrupt shift in conversation. "Yesterday, why?"

Nichols pushed his glasses up on his nose. "How well do you know her?"

"Very well. She's a good friend."

"How long since you've seen her?"

"I saw her at Dale's wake in the office." Dusty leaned across the counter. "What is this about, Nichols?"

"We can't confirm her whereabouts on the weekend of Dr. Robertson's death."

"Well, I can." Dusty straightened up. "She was in Colorado doing a pipeline survey."

Nichols nodded. "That's what she told us. But no one saw her out there."

"Of course not, it was Saturday, and she was in the middle of nowhere."

Nichols seemed to be thinking about that. "She had a gasoline and dinner receipt from Cuba, New Mexico. Does that make sense to you?"

"Sure. It's on the way to the project area."

Nichols lifted a finger and pointed it at Dusty's heart. "It's also the closest town to where Dr. Robertson was killed out at Chaco."

Dusty folded his arms like a shield over his chest. "Coincidence, Nichols. I have a work order in the office from the pipeline company. She was supposed to be up there."

Nichols took a sip of his coffee and his eyes drifted around the trailer as though cataloging every spiderweb that draped the windows. "To your knowledge, did Robertson ever have an affair with Rhone? You know, a field camp fling?"

Dusty's eyes turned to stone. "Dale never had an affair with a student, period. Why?"

"Just wondering. Michall Jefferson hired Rhone to help with the dig, so I did some research. She has an extensive file with the Social Services department office in Idaho."

"Yeah, so what?" Over the years, Sylvia had told him a lot about her childhood. She'd spent the first eight years of her life being shunted from one foster home to another, and not all of her "parents" had been guardians.

Nichols took a few seconds to absorb Dusty's hostile tone, then said, "You think she needs your protection?"

An odd squirming sensation invaded Dusty's chest. "Well, if anyone needs my protection, it's Sylvia. If you're thinking she's a suspect, forget it."

Nichols ran his thumb over the handle of his cup. "You and Rhone seem very close, why?"

"I don't know," he responded defensively, "maybe because we both had screwed-up childhoods. Sometimes I think she knows me better than I know myself."

"Uh-huh. And do you know her better than she knows herself?"

Dusty stared angrily at Nichols. "You'd have to ask her."

"Did you know, for example, that Rhone tried to murder one of her foster fathers in his sleep? She used a pair of scissors. Rhone claimed she didn't even remember the event. The Social Services people jerked her out of the home immediately, of course, but it took a long time before they could find her another home."

"How old was she?" Dusty asked.

"Four."

Dusty nodded, remembering Sylvia telling him a story about one of her "fathers" in Idaho. The man had sneaked into her room every night for months when Sylvia had been four years old. All Sylvia remembered was the feel of his mouth over hers, and his stinking smell, like gin mixed with saltwater, but the description had been enough to turn Dusty's stomach.

Dusty said, "Maybe he deserved it."

Nichols smiled, as though he'd just confirmed one of his pet theories, and it irked Dusty. Especially since he didn't know what the theory was.

Nichols said, "Let's change the subject for a moment. Weren't you ever curious about your father's family?"

Dusty felt oddly as though he was being methodically bludgeoned. Either Nichols was very good at his job, or he was a sadist.

"Sure I was. Dale didn't want to talk about them, but I used to ask. He told me he had called Dad's folks, and they didn't want me. He'd asked if they'd fight his taking custody of me, and they said no. Dale ended up as my legal guardian. End of story."

"But you never called them? Never wrote letters?" Nichols asked.

"What for? Sure, I thought about them sometimes, but my family was Dale. They didn't want me. I didn't want them. What could I possibly have in common with a bunch of Philadelphia rich people?"

"Probably nothing," Nichols said, "but if Dr. Sullivan ever brings them up, tell me about it."

"Right." Dusty frowned. "Why should she? As I understand it, she never even met them."

Nichols glanced at the rolled sleeping bags and bags of food stacked by the door. "I take it you're headed for Chaco Canyon?"

"As soon as we lock up here." Maureen stood.

"I wanted to remind you, Dusty"—Nichols fixed him with his good eye—"that your position is a little delicate out there. You are not to compromise that dig in any way. Do you understand me? If you so much as touch anything, my team will consider it to be obstruction of an investigation. I'll file those charges and slap you in front of a judge's bench before you can whistle."

"I understand."

"See that you don't *forget* in the heat of a discovery."

Dusty turned on the hot water and let it run on his hands while he thought about Sylvia, and the demons that haunted her sleep. As steam curled up around his face, Dusty said, "Tell me something, will you, Nichols? If I can compromise the investigation so easily, why are you allowing me to go out there at all?"

Nichols walked over and stood across the counter from Dusty. The wind outside had blown wisps of his thick black hair over his horn-rimmed glasses. "That's simple, Stewart. Killers really do love to return to the scene of the crime—it gives them some perverted kick—and Hawsworth told me that he believes everyone from that time is in danger."

"Yeah, so?" Dusty asked.

Nichols put his empty coffee cup on the counter, and his eyes glinted. "So, either you're the killer, or you're bait for the killer."

Dusty felt suddenly hollow, floating. He heard his mouth say, "Okay."

"Good. One last question."

"What?"

He could see Nichols's square jaw grinding beneath his shaved cheeks. "You've been on a lot of excavations with Rhone. Does she sleepwalk?"

Dusty didn't answer. He was remembering the time they'd made camp on a mesa top, and she'd almost walked off the cliff at midnight. "Maybe. How should I know?"

Nichols nodded as though he knew Dusty was lying. He turned away and seemed to be looking absently at the door.

Dusty lifted both of his wet hands in a gesture of surrender. "Nichols, listen, I don't care what you think, Sylvia is not capable of murder. I *know* her."

Nichols tucked his notebook back in his coat pocket and shifted as though not certain he should respond to that.

"I'm not accusing her of consciously doing anything wrong, Stewart. Abused children often do things they don't remember. It's as though their young minds were shattered by unendurable pain, and to protect themselves they had to sever the neural pathways to the memories. But the memories are still there, and sometimes, late at night, they peek out. The adult does anything she has to to shove them down and get that door locked again." He opened the door. "I'll see you out at the crime scene."

Nichols left.

Dusty braced his hands on the counter and closed his eyes. In an agonized whisper, he said, "I'm starting to hate that guy."

# CHAPTER 30

BROWSER LAY ON his stomach in the collapsed remains of a fourth-floor room, watching Pigeontail walking south across the flats toward War Club village. His two dogs trotted at his heels.

"Why did you let him go?" Catkin asked from where she crouched under the slanting roof. "He'll tell everyone where we are."

"I let him go because it doesn't matter who he tells."

Catkin frowned. "Why not?"

"Because by now the White Moccasins know exactly where we are. Carved Splinter will have told them."

Catkin's grip tightened on the hilt of her war club. They both knew the effect of torture. A man would shout out anything if his tormentor was cutting the flesh from his body and dropping it into a cooking pot before his eyes.

Catkin whispered, "Then the White Moccasins may have been watching us for some time, probably from the south rim. Pigeontail's visit here was just the final confirmation."

"Yes." Browser nodded. "They will be here just after dusk. As soon as they can approach without being seen. They will want to make sure we don't escape under the cover of darkness."

"What about Blue Corn's warriors?"

"I think Blue Corn will be unsure. All they saw was an old Trader and his dogs walk across the canyon to Kettle Town. Then, after a couple of hands time, he walked back."

He ducked under the sagging roof and walked to the ladder. Climbing down, he led her through the labyrinth of passageways to the main room. There, in the crackling light of the fire, Stone Ghost and White Cone talked. Obsidian was tending the fire. She turned her large eyes on Browser and smiled at him as they entered. Several of the Mogollon lay wrapped in their blankets, sleeping.

"Nephew?" Stone Ghost asked.

Browser glanced around the chamber. "Where's the little girl?" He was accustomed to seeing her with Stone Ghost.

"I don't know," Stone Ghost said, and his wrinkles rearranged into sad lines. "She disappeared right after Pigeontail left. I looked for her, but I haven't found her yet."

Obsidian said, "I thought it was strange that we could be cooking and she wouldn't be hovering over the pot like a starving weasel."

Stone Ghost gave her a murderous look.

Browser said, "If she's not back by the time we have to move, she will have to take her chances."

Stone Ghost bowed his white head and nodded. "I know, Nephew."

Browser turned his attention to White Cone. "Elder? I need your warriors."

White Cone's black eyes tensed. "You've had my warriors at your disposal for days now. That is why Carved Splinter is missing."

"Yes, Elder, I'm sorry. He was a fine warrior. But since he vanished, your people are more leery of my orders. In our present situation I must take some desperate measures to save us. I was hoping you might acknowledge my authority."

"A great War Chief should be able to achieve respect without another's help. You once had a reputation as a great War Chief. Recently, people have said you lost your Power, that the gods abandoned you."

Browser felt the sting of humiliation. "Elder, I cannot always know the ways of the gods. My concern is how to defeat two different enemies at the same time. As to the belief that I have lost my abilities and Power, well, Elder, I'm counting on just that."

"How will you do this?"

Browser knotted his fingers around the hilt of his belted war club. "I have heard that the Society of the Bow produces warriors who can kill with the silence and swiftness of Falcon. Is it true?"

White Cone's eyes were keen and alert. "It is." The old man aimed a finger at the empty mat beside him. "Sit down and tell me *exactly* what you plan."

THE COLEMAN LANTERN illuminated the interior of the battered old camp trailer with soft yellow light. Maureen slid into the booth with a steaming cup of tea, forcing Sylvia Rhone and Michall Jefferson to slide around the table. They didn't even seem to notice. Both were engrossed in discussing how they would open the excavation tomorrow.

Dusty stood in the kitchen, making a lettuce and tomato salad. His blue eyes were a million miles away, probably walking some trail with Dale. Though he'd yet to display any real grief, she could see it in his slow, careful movements, as though if he didn't concentrate, he wouldn't even be able to toss a salad.

Maureen ran her hand over the scarred tabletop and

thought back to other times when she had sat with Dale
in this little booth. He would always fill her memories.
She could see him as he had been at the 10K3 site, and
then at Pueblo Animas: his wiry gray hair matted from
his fedora hat and his bushy mustache curled with his
smile. He was peering at her with knowing brown eyes
from the past. At this little square table, Dale had been
at his imperial best. Some of the most important artifacts in the Southwest had rested upon this vinyl surface. Now it supported a plate of baked beans and
tamales: the canned variety warmed in a skillet. To her
amazement, a boxed chocolate cake sat to her left—
compliments of Dusty's shopping expertise and Safeway.

Sylvia shoved a lock of shoulder-length brown hair
behind her ears, and her green eyes pinched as she
listened to Michall line out the excavation units. "So,
we're going to start digging right on the spot where
Dale was killed?"

"That's what the FBI wants," Michall said. She'd
pinned her red hair on top of her head with bobby pins,
most of which were about to fall out. Red curls drooped
around her ears.

Sylvia sat back in the booth. "Okay, but I'd prefer
to work up on it from the sides. You know, to get in
practice before I have to start worrying about missing
the 'subtle clues' Dusty keeps talking about."

"You'd better not miss anything," Dusty said as he
picked up his Guinness, walked over, and set the salad
bowl on the table next to the chocolate cake. "You're
the one who's been taking all those religious studies
classes. You ought to be able to recognize witchery
before anybody else out there."

Sylvia blinked like he'd just said something truly
astounding. "You bet, boss, absolutely, so long as it
deals with Aboriginal Australian metaphysics, I've got
it covered. My last class delved really deep into that
stuff."

Dusty gave Sylvia a reproving look as he started filling plates and handing them around the table. "Well, just keep your eyes open. There must be similarities between Aboriginal and Puebloan witchcraft."

Sylvia scowled. "Like what? The uses of witchetty grubs and rattlesnakes?"

Maureen smiled. She and Sylvia had become close friends during the excavations at 10K3, and had worked together at Pueblo Animas. Sylvia's keen wit included neither piety nor good taste, but Maureen had watched her work endlessly in the hot sun, muscles rippling under smooth sun-browned skin. She'd had a really tough childhood, much tougher, Maureen suspected, than Agent Nichols knew. After all these years Sylvia still slept with a baseball bat—just in case. Everyone who'd ever worked with her knew you did not surprise Sylvia when she was asleep.

Michall Jefferson, on the other hand, was a new element in the equation. A sober-eyed redhead, she had an Irish phenotype, short in frame, but with the broad shoulders of a swimmer. She had just finished the course work for her Ph.D. and had turned in the first draft of her dissertation. She wore a hooded gray sweatshirt with UNIVERSITY OF COLORADO stenciled across the front.

They ate in silence for a few minutes; then Sylvia said, "Hey, Dusty, what do you really think about all this?"

He looked up from his plate. "What do you mean?"

"Well"—she lifted a shoulder—"I mean, I don't know how to feel about digging this site."

Dusty swallowed another bite of tamale and wiped his mouth on his sleeve. "Don't feel, Sylvia. Don't think. Just dig. Every year dozens of archaeologists excavate murder sites. In places like Bosnia and El Salvador, they have to dig up mass graves, a lot of them filled with recently murdered children. You're just excavating a site, Sylvia. Do it the very best you can."

Sylvia chewed a mouthful of salad and reached for her Coors Light can. She pressed in the sides, then released the pressure so that the aluminum popped out with a *tink*.

"You know, you couldn't do that with a real beer," Dusty said.

"Yeah, but the only difference between Guinness and ninety-weight gear lube," Sylvia responded, "is the price."

"And the creamy fizz." Dusty lifted a bottle of Guinness to the light. "This has fizz, and it's like oatmeal, it'll stick to your innards."

Sylvia *tinked* her Coors can again. "I always knew you were constipated. That's what gives you your peculiar personality."

Dusty pointed at her with his beer bottle. "You'd better be thankful I'm not in charge of this project. I'd make you dig the trash midden."

"Fortunately, this is Michall's project, and she says I have to dig the kiva."

Michall's pale eyebrows lifted. "Yep. It's just me, Sylvia, and the FBI." She shook her head. "God, I can't believe I'm actually doing this, digging the site where Dale was killed." Her face worked, communicating her upset.

In a soft voice, Dusty said, "Well, just do it like he'd have wanted: perfectly. Imagine him looking over your shoulder the whole time."

Michall's expression tightened. "Thanks, Dusty. It's creepy enough as it is."

"It's not the dead that you have to worry about." Maureen held her teacup in both hands. The pleasant aroma of mint was a welcome change. "It's the living."

"Damn right," Sylvia said. "I watch TV. Murderers always return to the scene of the crime. Who knows what sort of monster might come walking up to us out there?"

"I won't even notice," Michall said. "Not when I'm

excavating the place where Dale was murdered."

"I'm glad you're the one digging the site," Dusty told Michall. "Dale would have appreciated the fact that you were in charge. He had a lot of respect for you."

She smiled at that. "God knows where I would have ended up but for Dale. I'd probably be married, with two-point-three kids, a mortgage, a house in the suburbs, and a harried life juggling kids, household, and husband."

"Well," Dusty chimed in, "you do have the SUV."

Michall drove a Dodge Durango, but somehow the blue four-wheel drive Maureen had seen that afternoon with its big meaty rubber-lugged tires, spattered mud, and heavy-duty winch evaded the "soccer-mom" model.

"Yeah," Sylvia said. "I can just see you as a housewife watching *Days of Our Lives* at noon every day."

Michall chuckled. "I came out here four years ago to escape my boyfriend. You know, one last fling with life before I married him. I had my B.A. in hand, and wow, what a rush! I could use my degree and go dig in the Southwest before I moved into a nice house in Chelsea."

"Where?" Dusty gave her a puzzled look.

"Boston. My degree was from Boston College. How was I supposed to know that Dale was waiting for me out here, like a big brooding bird of prey." Michall's voice dropped to mimic Dale's. "Ms. Jefferson, you have a rare sense for archaeology. You are one of the truly gifted. However, if it is your desire to return to Boston and function as a bipedal set of ovaries, that, too, is a noble profession. The species does need to be propagated."

Sylvia smiled appreciatively. "God, Dale had such a way with words."

Michall shrugged. "How do you respond to that? I mean, of all the people on earth there was something about Dale that made you want to do your best. I would have rather crawled across broken glass than have disappointed him."

"As I recall," Dusty said, "he worked things out behind your back."

Michall had a thoughtful look. "Yeah, it was coming up on fall and Dale asked if I wanted to start my M.A. in January. He said Colorado was going to have an opening. He'd even lined up a couple of scholarships for me. There it was, a cut-and-dried decision."

Sylvia cocked her head, asking, "Do you ever regret not marrying that nice young man and having all those rug rats?"

Tears sprang to Michall's eyes. "The only thing I regret is that Dale won't be in Boulder next spring to see me hooded. We had a bet. If I finished my Ph.D. in two years, he bought dinner."

A heavy silence descended. The only sound came from the hissing lantern.

Sylvia tossed off the last of her beer. "Yeah, well, I'm headed for the dormitory room that Rupert assigned us behind the park headquarters. It's going to be a long day tomorrow, and a nasty one if there's frost in the ground. That means swinging a pick." She stood up and slid out of the booth.

"I could always wander over to make sure you get up on time," Dusty offered.

"No, thanks," Sylvia replied. "My eardrums haven't recovered from your last shotgun blast."

"Yeah, thank God there are no guns allowed on national monuments," Michall added.

Sylvia's expression turned suspicious as she eyed Dusty. "You didn't bring one, did you?"

Dusty's blue eyes widened innocently. "With the FBI watching my every move? Come on."

"Yeah, right." Sylvia turned to Michall. "Hey, Mick, you want to follow me back? Just in case my Jeep blows the transmission on the way?"

Michall stood up. "Sure. No problem."

"Good night, all."

Dusty locked the door after they'd stepped out into the night.

Maureen tossed the last of the forks into the dishwater and scrubbed them, then rinsed with hot water from the teapot. The paper plates went into the trash. Dusty used paper towels to wipe out the Teflon-coated pans and stuffed them into the cupboard.

He leaned against the counter, staring down at the floor. Maureen slipped back into the booth to finish her tea. She watched him, seeing the interplay of emotions. As tough as it was going to be on her, it would be harder on him. They would only be spectators, sidelined while others uncovered the soil that held the key to Dale's last hours on earth.

"Michall seems like a sharp woman," Maureen said.

When he looked at her, pain lay behind his eyes. "Dale was right about her. Too good to waste as breeding stock. God, Dale was right about so many things. Michall, Sylvia, Steve, you . . . and me." He smiled at that, and said, "Good night, Maureen."

Caught off guard, she watched him step back and close the door to the small back bedroom. She could hear him as he undressed for bed. The little trailer rocked slightly under his weight.

She sat quietly for a time, finishing her tea, then pulled on her coat and stepped outside to head for the rest room. The campground was empty. She stopped, staring up at the sky. The stars seemed to pulse. Had she ever seen them so clearly?

"Yes, Dale," she said plaintively. "You were right about Dusty and me."

When she finally returned, excited by the chill of the clear night, she found the trailer silent. She folded out the front bench bed and tried to think. Her movements were slow, preoccupied, as she rolled out her sleeping bag, undressed, and turned the knob on the lantern.

The light sputtered, yellowed, and died.

As she rolled onto her side the silence dropped around her like a weight. With only the ticking of the cooling lantern, Dusty's face filled her mind. She could sense him, his presence oozing out from behind that thin door. Was he lying awake, staring into the darkness as she was?

Was he hurting?

Maureen wished she had the courage to go back there and ask, but she was too afraid of what might follow. They were growing closer every day, and she wasn't sure how she felt about it. On the one hand, it soothed something inside her to be close to a man again. On the other, it scared her to death. She still missed John, and deep inside her, she knew she always would. But what did that mean? Did it mean she would never have a normal relationship with a man again?

She punched her pillow to fluff it up, and flopped her head down.

John had been the love of her life. He still filled her dreams. Her greatest fear was that she would never truly love again. And, the way she was going, that was likely to be a self-fulfilling prophecy.

She exhaled hard and tried to go to sleep.

"HOW DID WE miss them?" Horned Ram demanded. "Our warriors searched Kettle Town from top to bottom. All that they found were dead First People, pack rats, and bats."

Blue Corn grimaced. "You're assuming that they really are there."

Horned Ram fingered his chin as he paced back and forth in the room. Rain Crow stood in the corner, his arms crossed as he considered his young scout. The youth had only seen fifteen summers and seemed terrified of Horned Ram. "You're sure it was Pigeontail?"

"Yes, War Chief. He came from War Club village, walking straight for Kettle Town. He and his two dogs. He was inside for at least two hands of time. Then, when he left, it was straight back to War Club village."

Rain Crow arched an eyebrow as he met Blue Corn's eyes. "That isn't exactly proof that Browser is hiding the Mogollon in Kettle Town."

"He's there," Horned Ram insisted. "I can feel him. His presence is like an owl's on the roof. I say we take our force, surround the town, and search it room by room."

"I thought you did that last time?" Blue Corn asked.

"That place is a rat's maze. They could have scurried around behind my warriors."

"Well, this time, make sure you find them. Then when you've driven them into the back, fire the place. Kill anyone who runs out."

"You would burn Kettle Town to get these few Mogollon?" Rain Crow asked. "Some of my ancestors built that place."

"If your ancestors were pawns of the First People, that is not my concern." Horned Ram gave Rain Crow a cold look. "Burning Kettle Town is just another way of stamping out more of the First People's perverted works."

Blue Corn weighed her options, then said, "As soon as our warriors return from scouting the lower canyon, prepare them for an assault on Kettle Town. Let us finish this. The gods alone know what is happening with our Katsinas' People hostages in Flowing Waters Town while I chase phantom Mogollon around Straight Path Canyon."

Rain Crow's ruined face reflected nothing of his thoughts. "Yes, Matron."

Blue Corn studied Horned Ram from the corner of her eye. The Red Rock elder had a grin on his frog face, as though he already smelled blood on the wind. He liked the killing and death. It fed something in his breath-heart soul the way a simmering buffalo stew did a starving man's stomach.

She wondered whether her calculations for the future should include the elder. He was brash, effective, and totally without scruples when it came to the destruction of those who did not share his beliefs. Such a man and his warriors could be utilized as a terrible weapon. Assuming, of course, that they could be controlled. What good was a weapon that was as dangerous to its wielder as it was to her enemies?

Blue Corn chewed on her lip as she considered. This alliance had seemed a golden opportunity when Gray Thunder first appeared, but she now feared it might prove more frightful than she had ever dreamed.

Blue Corn had never been one to turn down an unexpected opportunity, but she hoped this wouldn't be like having a rattlesnake in a pot. You always had to hope you could continue to keep it locked inside.

*A* NEST OF *snakes squirms in Piper's belly as she crawls up Straight Path Wash as fast as she can. Her knees are raw and bleeding, like they've been rubbed with sandstone, but she cannot stop. She must hurry! Hurry!*

*She'd found the trail two hands of time ago. Mother was very careful, her sandals barely scuffing the sand, but Piper knew those steps. She had tracked her mother many times.*

*Was Mother looking for me? Did she try to find me? Tears choke Piper.*

*When the wash cuts deeper, Piper stands up and runs with all her heart, flying down the bottom of the wash. The small rocks scream and shoot out behind her feet.*

*"I'm sorry I ran away, Mother!" she sobs. "I'm sorry!"*

*If Grandfather can't get Aunt Obsidian's heart, he will take Mother's heart. She knows he will.*

*A burning flood gushes up Piper's throat. She stumbles and retches onto the shining sand. She retches until her belly aches and twists, and she can't get enough air.*

*For a few instants she stares at the world through blurry eyes, then Wind Baby blows up the wash and strokes Piper's face with strong icy hands, and she runs again. Fast!*

*Hurry, hurry . . .*

DUSTY STUCK HIS thumbs into the back pockets of his jeans. Three FBI guys stood on the other side of the yellow tape, clipboards in hand. They had just handed out white sheets of paper with the "rules" for handling evidence. Rupert Brown and Michall stood reading the sheets with quizzical expressions.

It wasn't bad enough that the government dictated how even normal archaeology was conducted, but here it was down to directives concerning everything including the sharpening of trowels.

To her credit, Michall took it all in stride.

"So, what do you think, Stewart?" Sam Nichols walked across the site and gave him a penetrating look. He had the collar of his brown canvas coat pulled up, and his horn-rimmed glasses rode low on his nose.

"I think this is bullshit."

Dusty gestured to the pile of rubble beyond the tape, and the cold wind tugged at the brim of his brown western hat. "Very soon, your people are going to realize that this crime scene is also an archaeological site. It has its own special problems and needs that don't fit anybody's rules."

"Maybe, but your people aren't trained in forensic evidence recovery."

"And your people aren't trained in archaeological data recovery," Dusty reminded. "But it's okay, Nichols. They'll be on the same page by the time they get down to the intact levels."

Nichols gave him a disbelieving look. "Intact levels? Anything worth getting is going to be around where Dr. Robertson was buried." Nichols pointed to the frosted dirt, still readily visible where it had been turned.

"I'm sure that's how it works in most modern murder cases, Nichols. I don't think that's what we'll find here."

Rupert Brown left Michall's side and walked toward Dusty and Nichols. He wore a green nylon coat with the Department of the Interior patch on the shoulder.

Nichols said, "You really believe that the person who killed Dr. Robertson buried something here?"

"Or something was already buried here and that's why he picked this spot. Kwewur may be playing with us, Agent Nichols. I think he—"

"Dusty's right." Rupert shoved his hands in his coat pockets. His six-foot-six-inch frame towered over Nichols. Even Dusty, at six feet even, had to look up to meet Rupert's eyes. "I think it's like a turnabout on the old European trick of having illiterate natives sign a treaty they couldn't read. Kwewur is betting you can't decipher the message he left here, Nichols."

Nichols studied Rupert as if just seeing him for the first time. A faint look of hostility lit his eyes. "You seem to know a lot about him."

Rupert shrugged. "You grew up in Baltimore where witches showed up for Halloween. They were make-believe characters. I grew up in the Southwest, where witches were not only real, but you knew who was and was not a witch. You knew people who had died from their evil spells, or someone who almost died, and had to pay the witch to break the spell. Then, lo and behold, they got well. I was attacked by a witch once, Nichols. Because of that, I've spent more than half of my life studying southwestern witchcraft. I know it works and I can tell you, the key to a witch's survival these days is misdirection. He *wants* you to disbelieve."

"You mean he thinks I'm a fool?"

Rupert shook his head. "No. Just the opposite, Agent Nichols. He's playing a game with you. The difference is that he knows that his rules are different from yours. But you think the rules of the game are the same."

"Meaning?"

"Meaning he believes in you, but you don't believe in him."

"But you do?"

Rupert watched the crew preparing to dig.

Nichols's mouth pressed into a tight white line. "You have a Ph.D., Brown. And you really believe that crap?"

"Kwewur believes it, Agent Nichols, and Dale is dead."

"Yeah. Right. That's why I'm in this godforsaken place, Brown."

Rupert gave the agent a small smile. "If you wouldn't mind, I'd appreciate being addressed as either Dr. or Superintendent while I'm in the park."

"Sure, Superintendent Brown." Nichols frowned off into the distance. "That's your grandson out there, isn't it? Driving that pickup?"

"Yes. He's doing rounds. Picking up trash."

"Maybe I'll go down and talk to him." Nichols paused. "Does he believe in witches?"

"Go ask him."

Nichols nodded to Dusty before walking off, a thoughtful slouch to his shoulders.

Dusty gave Rupert an askance look. "Are you okay?"

"God, no."

Rupert shoved his hands more deeply into his pockets. "On top of everything else, he's driving me crazy. Nichols has been throwing his weight around, reorganizing every park employee's schedule, tearing down tape, putting up tape, blocking roads, opening roads, giving orders, pointing his finger. That's what I really don't like. The finger-pointing thing." He shook his finger in Dusty's face to illustrate, then tucked it back in his pocket. "See?"

Dusty smothered a smile. "I think he's just being thorough, Rupert."

"Sure, I know what he's doing. He's got people just sitting, watching to see who does what. For the past couple of nights he's had agents out here, watching the site. The murderer returns to the scene of the crime. Maybe it'll work, but if he wasn't such a *koyemshi*, a clown, with his head stuck in the regulation book, he might have already figured this thing out. He really hates being out here, and it shows."

Dusty pushed windblown blond hair out of his blue eyes and decided he ought to change the subject. "Did you hear that Carter Hawsworth dropped by to see me. I wasn't there, but Maureen was."

Rupert's brows lifted. "Really? Is he still as much of an asshole as he used to be?"

"Well, Maureen wasn't impressed with him."

Rupert shook his head. "Don't get tied up in messes, Dusty. If you and I meet again twenty years from now, I'd like it to be one of those 'good to see you' kinds of meetings rather than the 'you asshole' kind."

"What kind of messes did you have in mind?"

"The kind that gets your friends killed." He used his chin to point to where Michail and Sylvia slipped under the ribbon and began hammering in a datum stake, then setting up the transit to grid the site.

"Speaking of friends, I saw Lupe last time I was here."

"He's making flutes, can you believe it? Good flutes! He's selling them to tourists. He's even got a CD, and sells them in the boutiques up in Taos and over in Durango." Rupert seemed genuinely pleased. "But then there's Reggie. Don't ever have a grandkid, Dusty. The boy's still not talking to his mother. That's bad. I don't care what she did to him, she's still his mother. But Reggie's trying. He's pretty well dried out and cleaned up. He's even been going down to Zuni to attend the sacred rituals. I think he's going to be okay."

"Not everyone has your gumption, Rupert. It's up to Reggie what he makes of himself."

"Yeah, but I have to try to help. He fell apart when Sandy died. She was the only mother he'd ever really known. I swear, Reggie was so high on drugs, he didn't know what he was doing when he broke into all those houses."

"Well," Dusty said, and his eyes tightened, "grief makes you crazy."

Rupert's wife, Sandy, had died from cancer four years ago. She'd been a good, kind woman. Dusty remembered her shaking a spatula at him one very hungover morning at breakfast, and saying, *"Don't let nobody tell you that you're a bad boy, Dusty, 'cause you're not. You're just really stupid sometimes."*

He smiled at the memory. He'd been sixteen and what Dale had called "his worst nightmare."

Rupert watched Nichols reach his car and drive off to intercept Reggie. "You know, sometimes all a kid needs is a chance."

"Yeah, I do know. I hope it all works out for him."

Rupert nodded, then a smile brightened his face. "Reggie's been talking about Maggie. Can you believe it? I guess he's trying to get up the nerve to ask her out."

"She'd be good for him," Dusty said. But deep down inside he wasn't so sure about that. Maggie was a traditional with deep-seated Keres beliefs. Not the hellraiser that young Reggie was. Although, if Reggie really had been trying to get his spiritual life in order down at Zuni, maybe things would work out.

Dusty looked back to watch Maureen drive into the Casa Rinconada parking lot. She parked the blue Bronco beside Michall's Durango and stepped out. Even over the distance, Dusty felt his heart lift as she started down the interpretive path past Tseh So and toward the ridge overlooking the Casa Rinconada great kiva.

"I think maybe she's good for you, too," Rupert said, his brown eyes measuring Dusty's expression.

"She's just a friend." He tried to wave it off.

"I thought you were sharing the trailer?"

" 'Sharing' is the key word, Rupert." Dusty tried not to squirm under that intense gaze.

"Does she know how you feel about her?" Rupert asked.

"How do *you* know how I feel about her?"

"I have this sixth sense. It's an Indian thing, very mystical. All I have to do is see your face light up and, bingo, I can read your mind."

Dusty folded his arms protectively over his heart. "Well, keep it to yourself. I'm not going to turn a nice friendship into a disastrous romantic interlude that will leave us hating each other." He paused. "Besides which, she's still in love with her husband."

"I remember Dale talking about that." Rupert kicked at the cold soil. "How long have we known each other?"

"All of my life. Why?"

"All of your life." Rupert paused and gazed off into the distance. "In many ways, you are like my son,

Dusty. You and Lupe. I remember how the two of you used to play together."

"Yeah. I remember the time Lupe almost knocked me unconscious with a rock. Great fun."

Rupert laughed. "Yeah, well, when I see you and Maureen, I say to myself this looks like the right one. Maybe you should listen to your elder, for once? You don't want to end up like me, old, bitter, and alone."

Dusty studied Sylvia as she walked across rubble with the transit rod. Her freckled face had gone red in the cold wind. Then his gaze shifted back to Maureen. She lifted a hand and smiled.

Dusty said, "I won't, Rupert, I promise you that. If the time is ever right, I'll do everything I can."

"*Make* the time right, Dusty." Rupert paused. "Don't let her get away."

"Yes, Dad."

He studied Dusty thoughtfully. "I'm going to tell you the same story I told Lupe and Reggie when they were involved with good ladies, ladies I knew would make them happy, so you'll really understand. Are you listening to me?"

"Yeah, Rupert. Okay."

"The only woman I ever loved with all my heart left me for another man. I'd like to think it was because I didn't make enough of an effort to let her know how much of my heart and soul she really had. When she went, I came within a whisker of destroying myself. I wrote to her for years, but all my letters came back marked 'Addressee Unknown.' In all of my life, I've never completely recovered from what happened with her. Don't live your life like I've lived mine, wasting away over a woman you didn't do enough to win."

Dusty looked at Rupert from the corner of his eye. "I thought Sandy was the love of your life."

"Sandy was my best friend, Dusty, and I loved her very much. But it took Sandy and me years to learn to love each other. Those first few years, every day was

a fight. We worked through it. We raised a good boy.
I ate out my own heart when she died. But, no, she
wasn't the love of my life."

Rupert smiled faintly as a flock of crows wheeled
over their heads. His eyes had gone tight. "Don't think
you have all the time in the world, my other son. Because you don't."

# CHAPTER 31

POLISHED BONE WATCHED the two shabby elders as they stepped out from behind Kettle Town and
made their slow and laborious way down the road. As
the afternoon sun bore down on his back, the high canyon rim sent its shadow across the crumbled sandstone
below.

"When did they get there?" he wondered.

Surely these were not the tricky Mogollon he'd
heard of from the tortured youth's screaming mouth.
No sane warrior would wander out into the open knowing that he was being observed the entire time.

And then one of the elders fell.

Polished Bone lifted a lip in a sneer. Made People
refugees, no doubt. Perhaps someone Old Pigeontail
had told to flee while he was in talking with Browser
and his warriors.

Browser, now there was a man Polished Bone would
love to meet. Perhaps he'd get his chance tonight, as
soon as the cover of darkness masked their white capes.

Browser couldn't have known that by killing Ten
Hawks and Bear Dancer, he had sealed his fate, and
the fate of the Katsinas' People.

One of the elders was stumbling, leaning on the other as they made their way to the crossing where Straight Path Wash cut into the flat canyon floor.

Polished Bone sharpened his attention. The only place they might be able to escape would be in that wash. If they didn't immediately emerge, then it was a ruse, a party seeking to escape down the sheer-sided arroyo to one of the side canyons.

"Two people," he murmured thoughtfully to himself. Were they really old men? "Or Browser and Catkin? Cowards! Are you running?"

But no, here they came, struggling up out of the arroyo and staggering onward, their ratty clothes whipped by the west wind. It tugged at their loose white hair.

Polished Bone smiled in grim amusement. That was like Browser, no doubt desperate to save two old derelicts so that they wouldn't get hurt in the ensuing battle. Shadow had said he was quick of thought, but vulnerable when it came to those under his protection.

The two elders continued their irregular snail's pace down the road. The journey had taken them nearly a hand of time. Polished Bone shook his head. Fools, they should stop at Talking Stitch village and take cover for the night. If they didn't, the White Moccasins surely weren't going to allow them within the safety of High Sun's walls. Not with what they might learn. And sleeping up on the mesa was brutal this time of the sun cycle.

To his surprise, the two elders didn't make for any of the small houses that dotted the canyon floor under the cliff. Instead they came straight on for the stairway that he guarded.

"Silly old fools!" Polished Bone left his comfortable vantage point in the cleft in the sandstone and took a more open position where he could see down the stairway. Sure enough, here came the elders. He could see them more clearly now: a man and a woman, old and frail, their clothing mere rags. Poor things, they were literally pulling each other up the stairway, panting with effort. The man looked the worse for wear, old and crippled, his back bent. An expression of agony marred his wrinkled face. The wind whipped his white hair.

Polished Bone squatted on his heels, absorbed by their struggle up the stairway. He fought the sudden urge to go down and help them. They were going to be coyote meat anyway. Either the frost would get them, or the wind would freeze them, or they'd collapse from exhaustion by the time morning arrived. Besides, they were Made People. Let them take whatever fate the gods decided.

A third of the way up, they stopped, wheezing and panting. The old woman looked up, seeing him skylined. She waved and called in a feeble voice, "Young warrior! Come help your elders!"

"Make it on your own," he answered. "Unless you'd like to tell me about who is staying in Kettle Town."

The old man looked up, a hand to his heart. Pain filled his eyes, and the set of his mouth betrayed a desperation that Polished Bone could understand. It was the look that came when hope had vanished like dew in a hot summer drought.

One by one, the elders struggled up the stairs carved so long ago by their ancestors. Arms flailing, the old man missed a step, and the woman caught him a hairsbreadth from falling.

Polished Bone shook his head. He needn't worry about them discovering his fellows at High Sun. They'd never make it that far before nightfall.

"Why . . . won't . . . you . . . help?" the old woman gasped between breaths as she neared the top.

"You are not of my clan," Polished Bone answered, the irony of that being his own personal joke. "Ask your ancestors when you see them."

Step by step, they made their way up until the old

man reached the worn sandstone flat. There he seemed to melt, curling into a fetal ball. Wind Baby picked heedlessly at his tattered clothing. It looked dusty and moldy, so old that the patterns had faded from the material. It had been a high quality once, many seasons past.

Polished Bone lifted his eyebrows as he watched the old woman bend down to whisper to the old man. In his bony hand, the elder clutched something as though it were the most precious of possessions.

"Warrior," the old woman said, reaching out to him. "If you will help us, take us to shelter, and feed us, this is yours." When she opened her hand, Polished Bone started. There, in her palm, lay a polished copper bell.

He stood up, nerves tingling. "Where did you get that?"

"It's yours if you will help us," the old woman pleaded.

Polished Bone stepped up and reached for the bell, but she pulled it back in a miserly motion. "Help," she repeated, her old sad eyes on his.

"Give it to me." With his right hand outstretched, he fumbled for the war club on his belt with his left. "If you don't, I'll just take it from your clubbed bodies. You—"

The old man's sudden movement caught him by surprise. The elder's hand whipped up, the clenched fist driving a deer-bone stiletto deep into the hollow under Polished Bone's ribs. He staggered back, stunned by the pain. His terrified reaction was to slap both hands to the wound as though to press the hot gouts of blood back into his ruptured heart.

"Well done," the old woman said, her voice clearer, the accent thicker.

"And with pleasure, White Cone." The old man stood straight now, a smile on his thin brown lips. "Arrogance and foolishness make a poor mixture, don't you agree?"

White Cone tossed the polished copper bell into the air and snatched it away as it fell.

The world jerked as Polished Bone stumbled backward and sat down hard. The pain searing his chest became his world. His blood, so much of it, spilled over his hands and soaked the front of his war shirt. The edges of his vision were going gray, hazy. The world spun sideways, and his cheek was against the cold sandstone.

"Give your ancestors my regards," the accented voice said. "Tell them you are a gift to the Land of the Dead, courtesy of the Bow Society."

"Well, that's one," the old man said. "If you're up to it, we have two more to go."

"Next time, you're the old woman with the bell."

Polished Bone felt them push his quivering body over the edge, but he didn't feel the fall, or the smacking impact he made as he landed on the rocks a bow shot below.

NOT MUCH HAPPENED on the first day of digging, which didn't surprise Maureen. Michall placed her grid over the site and, with the help of the ERT people, got most of the scrubby rabbitbrush and saltbush cleared from the tumbled stone that marked the Bc60 ruin. Surface mapping of the features, the collapsed kiva, and surface artifact recording and collection took the rest of the day.

She watched Dusty pace the perimeter marked by the yellow crime-scene tape, up and back, biting off comments as Michall and her crew followed the instructions of Nichols and the ERT team members.

The next time his path brought him close to her, Maureen said, "It's a good thing they couldn't hire you to do this job, eh?"

"What?" he said, irritated. Wind waffled the brown brim of his cowboy hat and flicked the hem of his denim jacket.

"I mean, if you were in charge, this excavation would take twice as long since you'd be arguing every step of the way with the ERT people."

His blue eyes narrowed. "I'm not that bad. Yet."

Maureen crossed her arms against the wind's bite. "Don't you think Michall's doing a good job?"

"Of course she is. I trained her."

"Then just relax and let her work." She walked up and took his arm, feeling the tension in his swelling muscles. "Let's take a break. I want to see the sites down here. You can tell me all about the Casa Rinconada great kiva, and why it doesn't have a great house attached to it."

Reluctantly, he let her lead him down from the humped shale ridge to the Casa Rinconada kiva. The subterranean ceremonial chamber stretched more than sixty feet across. Snow lined the kiva bottom; it had swirled through the red and black sands to create a beautiful abstract design. Concave drifts scalloped the bench that encircled the structure.

Dusty said nothing. She could see how upset he was; his mind seemed to be locked on some perplexing problem.

"What's wrong?" she asked.

He tugged his gaze away from the kiva, deliberately avoided her eyes, and glared at the rimrock. "Rupert said something this morning that's been bothering me."

"What?"

"I'm not sure I want to tell you."

Maureen shifted. "Then don't."

As he turned to face her, a gust flipped his blond hair around beneath the brim of his hat. He squinted against the onslaught. "He seems to think that we're perfect for each other."

Taken aback, she smiled uncomfortably. "Really? What does he know about us?"

Dusty jammed his hands deeply into his coat pockets. "That's the problem. He doesn't know anything. It's not like Rupert to say something like that. He minds his own business. Always has." His fists strained against his pockets. "Maybe it's Dale's death. We're all strung out."

She nodded, relieved that he hadn't said what she'd expected him to. "That's something we have to watch out for, Dusty. During times of crises people are naturally drawn together. But when the crisis ends . . ."

The lines at the corners of his eyes crinkled. "Right. The Florence Nightingale effect. I only think I'm falling in love with you."

Maureen had to force herself to take a deep breath. "Dusty, I have feelings for you, too, but this isn't the time. Maybe in a few months, when your heart is intact—"

"But not now." He exhaled in relief, smiled, and said, "Thank you, Doctor."

"You were hoping I'd say that, weren't you?"

"Very much."

Maureen laughed and looked across the canyon to the road that led to the Park Service headquarters and Rupert's office. She could see Nichols's car where it had pulled up beside Reggie's green pickup. Strange how memories connected without any apparent rhyme or reason. The feelings stirring within her had reminded her of a phone conversation from long ago. She'd been sitting on the sofa next to John in his tiny apartment in Quebec when he'd called to tell his mother they were going to be married. John had pulled the phone away from his ear when his mother had shouted, "But she's an *Indian*, dear! Why would you do that?"

Maureen said, "I appreciate the compliment, though."

"Well, you earned it. Believe me."

Dusty took his hands from his pockets and crossed his arms over his broad chest, like a barricade. "I'm worried about Rupert. I think this thing may have affected him more than any of us know."

"He said he'd known Dale for more than forty years. It must be hard."

Dusty nodded, as though glad to be speaking of something else. "Dale once told me that Rupert was about the smartest man he'd ever known. That once he got over being Indian and Mexican, and just let himself be Rupert, he'd make something of himself. And look where he is now, Dr. Rupert Brown Horse, park superintendent. About to retire with full pension. And he's been smart, invested wisely. You ought to see the house he has west of Cuba in the foothills. It sits on twenty acres surrounded by timber, has a little creek running through it, and even has a small pueblo that he's going to dig in his retirement."

"Good for him." She stared down at a swirl of snow blowing around the kiva bottom. "Mixed blood is common among my people. We've been intermarrying for four hundred years. We just accept it. But in the West, both the western United States and western Canada, it's different. I think it's because it's still new here."

"We don't think in . . . the . . ." Dusty frowned down at the kiva bottom.

"What's wrong?"

"That's not *right*."

Dusty trotted around to the south and descended the steps down into the kiva. His boots crunched through the snow that filled the hollows of the steps.

Maureen followed him, ducked under the lintel, and stepped onto the kiva floor.

Her first awareness was of the masonry, straight, beautiful, so intricately placed. Each of the small square wall crypts might have been an eye from another world, watching her. The kiva seemed to pulse with the voice of the wind.

She turned around, gazing up at the sky. Her senses seemed to be on fire. There was a presence here. Old and powerful. Across from her, she could see through the T-shaped northern entrance to the bleak anteroom beyond. The stone bench was empty, but for the snow, lonely now where once it had supported dozens of finely dressed people. Their ghosts watched her as she walked past the raised fire box.

Dusty stopped dead center between the foot drums and the four round roof supports and knelt.

"What was the trench for?" Maureen asked, pointing at the shallow circular trench that ran around the end of the exposed tunnel in the kiva floor.

"We don't know. It was Chacoan, filled in by later Mesa Verdean people when they refinished the kiva in the mid-1200s. But this . . . this shouldn't be here."

She looked down. "You mean the sand? Why not?"

"In a kiva cut out of gray shale, where do you get red, black, and white sand?" Dusty stiffened as if stung. "There was a sand painting here."

He lurched to his feet as though he'd just seen a coiled rattlesnake. When Maureen looked, all she saw was a thin green yucca leaf.

"Step back," Dusty said. "Move your shadow."

Maureen carefully retreated and circled. She was looking now, forcing herself to see, to catalog and interpret what lay before her on the ground. The dark stains, weathered and bleached by the melting snow, had a familiar brown—"Oh, God, Dusty."

"What?" He spun around.

She pointed. "That's blood. Blood is delicate, it decomposes rapidly in sunlight and the moisture feeds soil organisms."

Dusty pulled his pen from his pocket and used the tip to whisk multicolored grains from the brown stain.

His hand started to shake. He slowly rose to his feet.

"Maureen, move back." His breathing had gone shallow and rapid. "Step on the tracks you made on the way in. Call Nichols. I want him in here right now."

"What did you find?" She tried to look around him, but his body blocked her view.

"Just go! Now."

Maureen headed toward the stairs; when she reached the top, she looked back.

Dusty stood with his feet braced and his fists clenched at his sides. The shiny black stone he'd uncovered glinted in the light.

# CHAPTER 32

HE SEES HAD watched the old people emerge from Kettle Town and proceed with painful slowness across the canyon. They had provided a grateful distraction from his boring duty. Rain Crow had placed him here, on the stairway just north of Kettle Town, to "keep watch on things," and report back.

He Sees got to do this a great deal. Not everyone, especially in Red Rock country, had eyes like his. He couldn't see very well close up, but far away, he had eyes like Hawk. It seemed as if he had spent his entire life on high lookouts either half frozen from the cold wind, or baked and blistering from the summer sun.

But two old people . . .

They weren't worth the energy to run back to Center Place with a report. A sentry, especially one such as himself, developed a sense for what was important. Why the two would have left in the middle of the afternoon was problematic, but then, who knew what the Trader had said in there? When they began their fumbling ascent up the far stairway, He Sees watched, alarmed when one nearly fell.

He was still watching when, to his surprise, he saw the distant figure of a man step out of a fissure in the rock. The man moved like a warrior, and though he couldn't be sure, He Sees thought the fellow had a war club at his belt.

When the two elders made the summit and the old man collapsed, He Sees waited. Why didn't the warrior help them? The fool, he . . . but then, yes, the man was stepping closer, his hand outstretched.

He Sees frowned when the old man suddenly leaped up, and the warrior backed away, stumbled, then collapsed and fell.

"What is this?" He Sees whispered.

Shading his eyes, he struggled to see, cursing the distance for the first time, and wishing that his eyesight were even better. He stood up, rising from the protection of an old shrine, unable to believe what he saw. The two old people rolled the young warrior's limp body to the side; then they tumbled him off the edge of the cliff.

The body fell, hitting the rock ledges on the way down.

"Ambush!" He Sees said. "They were not . . ."

Sand trickled below him, making a distinctive *shishing* sound. He lowered his hand from his eyes and looked down.

She was no more than fifteen steps from him, a bow in her left hand, an arrow drawn back in her right.

He Sees met her eyes and their souls linked. She was beautiful, tall, with wide cheekbones and an oval face. In a flash, he knew her: Browser's deputy, Catkin. But how had she—? Gods, while he had watched the old people she'd climbed up right under his nose.

A sliver of sunlight flashed down the arrow when she let fly.

The impact was silken. As the sharp point sliced through him, his mouth fell open, and he started to pant as though he'd been running forever. In all of his imaginations of this moment, he had never thought of the cold. The arrow was icy where it lodged inside him.

He stepped back, and turned toward Center Place to cry a warning. The second arrow shocked him. Staggering on his feet, he stared down at the stone point protruding from the middle of his chest. Blood bubbled into the back of his throat and sprayed from his mouth.

His knees buckled.

His last sensation was hearing her feet as she sprinted up the road he was supposed to be guarding.

DUSTY STOOD WITH his back to the wind, the collar of his Levi's coat pulled up to keep his neck warm. Gray clouds scudded out of the northeast, marking the arrival of a cold front dropping out of Utah. He stood at the western lip of Casa Rinconada, just back from the interpretive sign, and watched as the ERT team crawled over the kiva bottom on their hands and knees. They had taken samples of the sand, of the bloodstains, and collected the glittering basilisk. Now they were inspecting every square inch of Casa Rinconada's floor.

Twenty feet away, to Dusty's right, Maureen and Nichols stood. As she talked, Nichols took notes.

He heard Nichols say, "So it may have happened here, and he moved the body?"

"Maybe," Maureen said in her professional voice. "But we need more information. It snowed on the blood; then it warmed up and melted. I hope you can get something, but it's going to be tough."

"And," Nichols said pointedly, "we don't have any tracks down there but yours and Stewart's from today." He peered down into Casa Rinconada. "I can see how you picked that sand out. It is different. But what made you think it had anything to do with Dr. Robertson?"

"I'm an archaeologist," Dusty said as he turned. His tone implied that that explained everything.

"Right. So?"

Dusty shoved his hands into his jeans pockets and walked toward Nichols. "The very first hafted ax head I found was in a Moenkopi sandstone outcrop. It was a crummy thing, battered, and badly weathered. No one in their right mind would have looked twice at it. It lay on the sandstone, in a pile of rocks."

"How'd you know it was an ax head?"

"It was granite, and the nearest granite source was forty miles away. It's the same with the sand down there. When I saw it, I knew someone must have carried it in."

Nichols squinted at him with his one good eye. "Dr. Brown told me that lots of tribes use this kiva for ceremonials. Maybe the Navajo held a Sing here?"

"Maybe," Dusty agreed. "Did Rupert tell you he'd scheduled one? You have to have permission to do that in a national park."

Nichols shook his head. "He didn't say anything, but maybe somebody—like young Reggie out there— didn't want to get permission, and came here anyway."

Dusty knotted his fists in his pockets. "That's possible. I'm not the only one who hates government regulations, but no one—not even Reggie—coming here for a sacred ritual would have a basilisk, Nichols. They're evil. Pure witchery."

"He's a thorny kid, isn't he?" Nichols said. "You interrupted my little talk with him. He's what I'd call a very angry young man with a chip on his shoulder."

"He's had it tough."

"Do you know anyone who hasn't? I'm starting to

think all of your friends are basket cases." Nichols jotted something in his notebook and stared balefully down into the kiva. "It's sure a big thing, isn't it?"

Dusty waited until the gust of wind passed, before answering, "Imagine digging that much soil out of the ground. Hammering down through the sandstone and shale with stone-headed mauls and digging sticks. No backhoes in those days."

"Impressive." Nichols looked around. "What's that? Those ruins over there?"

Dusty looked across the canyon. "That's Pueblo Bonito. An Anasazi road ran right across there"—he pointed—"from Casa Rinconada's northern anteroom over to the southwest corner of Bonito. And the next ruin to the east is Chetro Ketl. If you get time you might want to walk through them. They were built between A.D. 900 and 1150. North America wouldn't have buildings this large again until the 1830s."

Nichols gazed across the canyon, wind-whipped now, and cold. Chaco looked dreary in its winter clothes, the rabbitbrush and grass turned tan to match the soil.

"Why would the Anasazi have come here? This is a barren place." Nichols was shaking his head.

"It was different then," Dusty said. "You're standing in the capital of an empire that covered one hundred thousand square miles. But if you need to put that in perspective, next time you're in Washington, D.C., imagine what it will look like in five hundred years, after the buildings fall down and the trees are growing out of the rubble that's the Capitol building."

Nichols shot him a sober glance. "You think it will come to that?"

"Sure." Dusty shrugged. "It always does. Persepolis, Greece, Ur, Rome, the Maya, the Khmer, the Anasazi, or the Cahokians, they all follow the same pattern: They go through a warm wet climatic episode, overpopulate, build their cities, cut down all the trees, and overuse the soil. Then the climate changes, turns cold and dry, and they can't feed their people. Some critical supply runs out. People feel deprived. Deprivation is the single most powerful human motivation. Someone goes to war to win resources, and the system breaks. It cascades like a house of cards with ethnic hatred, religious war, and crusades. The trade routes are cut and the people fall into barbarism." His gaze drifted over the ruins before him, imagining how glorious they must have been one thousand years ago. "Why should we be any different?"

"Aw, come on. This is the twenty-first century." Nichols examined him like a hawk with prey.

"How much oil do we import from foreign countries? How much wood? You know that plum you had for lunch yesterday? It probably came from South America."

Nichols grunted and flipped through his notebook. "There's something I've been meaning to talk to you about."

"Okay. What is it?"

He ran his finger down the page. "We were doing some background on you." He glanced up to read Dusty's reaction when he said, " 'The Mad Man of New Mexico'? Where does that come from?"

Dusty winced. "I hate that name."

"After what happened to your father, being locked up in an asylum, I can see why."

"For what it's worth," Maureen said, "Dusty's nickname comes from his unorthodox field methods; it has nothing to do with his father's illness. His methods generate some professional jealousy."

"Yeah, I figured that out," Nichols replied. "You, on the other hand, Dr. Cole, are highly thought of by most of your peers."

Maureen spread her feet, as though preparing for a lecture. "Physical anthropology is more of a traditional

science, Nichols. It isn't as bloodthirsty as archaeology."

Nichols returned his attention to the kiva. "Mr. Stewart, why do you keep finding these basilisks?"

Dusty felt light-headed. "I'd never seen one until we
dug 10K3. We found a murder victim with one on her
chest. Our monitor, Hail Walking Hawk, wanted me to
rebury it." Dusty shrugged. "God, I wish I had."

Nichols perked up. "You've still got it?"

"It's cataloged," Dusty told him. "In the collections
at UNM. We also found a second one at Pueblo Animas."

"You found it," Maureen corrected. "Dusty has a
thing for finding them. We've tried curing him twice."
She gave Dusty a hard look. "You're not going to start
having nightmares again, are you?"

"I didn't touch this one."

"Could it be the same one?" Nichols asked. "Or do
these things turn up all the time?"

"It's easy to check whether or not it's the same one,"
Maureen answered. "Get on your phone and call the
curation facility at UNM. They can look up the catalog
number and trot back in the stacks to find it. If it's
there, well, I guess we've answered the question."

Dusty said, "To answer your question about how
common they are, not very. The 10K3 basilisk was the
first pre-Columbian one ever found. They're more
common in modern societies, but still not abundant."

"How many people know about this pre-Columbian
basilisk?"

"Anyone who was on the 10K3 project." Dusty
frowned. "Michall, Steve, Sylvia, Maggie, Dale, Maureen, and me."

"Don't forget," Maureen reminded, "that you de-
scribed the artifact in the final report. Anyone in the
profession could have gotten it through a simple request."

"Anyone?" Nichols had his pen poised to write. "Like Carter Hawsworth?"

"Of course," Dusty said.

"Where is this report?" Nichols asked. "I'd like to see it."

"There's one over in the headquarters building." Dusty pointed across the canyon. "And another in Washington, one at the National Atmospheric and Oceanic Administration in Boulder, Colorado, another on file with the National Park Service in Albuquerque, one on file with the State Historic Preservation Office in Santa Fe, another—"

"Whoa." Nichols put his hand out to stop Dusty. "In other words, there are copies everywhere. So, it wouldn't have been hard for someone like, say, Dr. Hawsworth to have read it."

"All he had to do was drop by the university," Dusty admitted.

"Which he did quite frequently." Nichols seemed to be talking to himself. "Interesting."

"How's that?" Maureen asked.

"Oh, nothing. Ruminating, that's all."

"Nichols!" one of the agents in the kiva called. He held up a piece of paper he'd dug from under the snow. Weathered and soggy, Dusty could see the printing on it even from where he stood.

"What is it? One of the interpretive brochures?" Nichols called.

The agent, holding his prize up with forceps, shook his head. "No, sir. It looks like a fax. It's addressed to Dale and signed by . . . Jesus. How do you pronounce this? Kweee . . . Kaw . . ."

"Kwewur," Dusty said, barely audible.

Nichols stepped to the edge of the kiva and called, "Bring it up here, now! I want to know what it says."

As the agent got to his feet and carefully made his way to the stairs, Dusty looked at Nichols. "So Hawsworth has been a frequent visitor at the university. Have you searched his house?"

"I don't have cause to search his house, Stewart. So far, I can't prove he's done anything wrong. But why? What would I be looking for?"

The agent climbed the stairs and headed toward them.

Dusty said, "Dale's missing journals."

AS HE RAN up the road toward High Sun House, Browser looked down at his white cloak and white moccasins. They flashed silver in the dim evening light. Even at night, he would make a perfect target. He tried not to think about it. He had to have faith that the plan would work, that they would still think him too incompetent to have thought up something this clever and daring. He forced his legs into the distance-eating trot he had developed during the sun cycles of warfare.

High Sun House dominated the southern skyline. He cast a glance over his shoulder and there, a hard hand's run to the north, Center Place projected like a dimple from the mesa north of the canyon. No signal fire yet.

Gods, this wasn't going to be his last run, was it? He reached up to massage the slight ache that lay behind the scar on his forehead. He could feel the dent left by Elder Springbank's war club.

Elder Springbank, in reality, the witch, Two Hearts— he had been coiled in their midst the whole time. That was the trouble with witches, they hid and worked their evil from unsuspected places. Two Hearts had brought him here, to this most desperate gamble of his life.

This was by far the most delicate part of the plan. He had to get close, but not close enough that they could see his face. Then, he had a hard run, at least a hand's worth, in which he could not be caught.

High Sun House was a compact three-story town built on a high point with a view for four days' run to the south. From here the First People had tied their southern empire together. Distant rebellions were reported, and important visitors were heralded days before they could physically arrive.

Browser concentrated on his pace, and thought about the fires that once had been lit, and the mirrors that once had flashed the Blessed Sun's messages to the distant towns and houses. How odd that he, a descendant of the First People, was about to lure his relatives out into the open so that they could be killed.

A secret part of him wondered what his great-great-great-grandmother, the Blessed Night Sun, would have thought. Would she hate him for this?

As he approached High Sun, his skin began to prickle as though swarmed by insects. Where it dominated the heights, High Sun looked like a square bastion of purple against a bluish-yellow evening sky. Browser slowed as he neared the northern wall. Gods, they wouldn't have a guard outside, would they? Some warrior who would rise from one of the piles of stone toppled from old shrines?

To his relief, a voice called from the wall above, "Who comes?"

"Hurry!" Browser cupped his hands. "War Chief Browser, of the Katsinas' People, is searching the towns below the staircase. He and his warriors are tearing Pottery House apart! Two Hearts is at risk. It is only a matter of time before they find him!"

Then Browser turned and ran as he had never run before. His white cape flapped like monstrous wings behind him.

The man yelled, "Wait! How many warriors does he have?"

Over his shoulder, Browser called, "More than we thought!" and ran harder.

The road took him straight north.

How long did he have? Against trained warriors, who had certainly been preparing for a night raid on Kettle Town, he doubted he had one hundred heart-beats before they pelted down the road after him.

*And if Springbank is really there, inside High Sun, they will know this is a ruse.*

Would they still come boiling out after him? Were they even now perched on the high walls, watching his white cloak disappear into the darkness, laughing at the absurdity of a War Chief who could pitch so lame a diversion and then run away?

As if to allay his fears, a distant twinkle of fire blazed to life near Center Place, now nothing more than a dark hump on the distant mesa.

Catkin! He was sure of it. She had done it! Her diversion must be working. It had to be working.

He hadn't had the time to worry about her until now. But as he ran, fear traced fiery lines through his veins. He might die tonight, and if he did, it didn't matter. But if she died, and he lived . . .

Browser shoved the thought away. Fearing for loved ones sapped a warrior's strength. Instead, he forced himself to dream—to dream of what it would be like to run away, just he and Catkin, Uncle Stone Ghost, and maybe some of their trusted friends. Could they find a place with fertile soil, a small supply of water, and live in peace? Gods, was that so much to ask? Not fame, or power, or prestige, just the simple peace to raise corn, love Catkin, and perhaps see a couple of their children live to be adults?

A shout broke the silence, and Browser twisted his head to look back. Dark shapes lined out on the road behind him. He almost laughed with relief. Two Hearts must not be at High Sun House. This desperate scheme might work after all.

If he lived. If Catkin did her part. If . . .

If only they had had time to love each other that afternoon.

With his life balanced by a thread, the world depending on his next actions, why did that one thought lodge between his souls?

The shouts grew louder, and he could hear them coming, their feet pounding out his doom.

Browser ran with all his might.

"HE TOOK IT from me! He . . . took . . . it! Where is he hiding it? I must have it!"

Piper crouches on the dark northern side of the kiva, scratching shapes into the crumbling plaster with her fingernails. The plaster screeches its upset. She scratches harder to cover Grandfather's wheezing voice.

"Piper. Where's . . . your mother? Go find . . . your mother!"

Grandfather thrashes from side to side. His arms are a dying bird's wings, flopping, trying to fly.

She scratches in time with the thumping sounds, making them go away.

Mother was not here when Piper arrived.

But there were three warriors. Grandfather ordered them to pull the ladder up through the rooftop opening, so Piper couldn't climb out again and run away.

She grits her teeth and scratches so hard that her fingernails break and bleed. Red streaks the wall.

She looks at it and thinks how beautiful it is.

Red on white, like the blood on Grandfather's cape.

"Piper! For the sake of the true gods! I need . . . water. Bring me water!"

Piper glances at the canteen leaning against the fire pit stones, then scratches harder and hums, making the *scratching sound with her mouth, making it very loud.*

*Grandfather wheezes and can't seem to catch his breath. Baby bobcat mews are coming up his throat.*

*"Piper I—I'm witching your breath-heart soul . . . putting it in a rock . . . a—a pendant . . . that was buried long ago."*

*Piper's hand freezes. She can feel her heartbeat slowing, and her lungs struggle for air. She reaches down with both hands and holds tight to the turquoise necklace Stone Ghost gave her. He said it would protect her. He said it was very Powerful.*

*"Yes," Grandfather whispers. "You can feel it, can't you? That pendant . . . rests on a dead woman's breast . . . locked in darkness . . . just as your breath-heart soul will be . . . forever. Forever in darkness."*

*Grandfather reaches out to Piper with a clawlike hand. "Bring me water!"*

*But Piper can't.*

*She can't move at all.*

# CHAPTER 33

WHILE MAUREEN CHOPPED up the makings for a salad, Dusty cooked dinner. Pots filled with macaroni and cheese—southwestern style—bubbled on the stove. Dusty's version of the dish contained a large amount of diced Ortega green chilis, and several crumbled chunks of extra sharp cheddar. Additionally, tonight's fare included fried potatoes, sliced thin and cooked in butter in the cast-iron frying pan. He'd sprinkled chili powder instead of salt on top.

A real vegetarian delight.

Sylvia sat in the back corner of the booth, a thoughtful expression on her face. She alternated between munching on cheesy fishes and sipping from her can of Coors Light. Though she'd washed her hands and face after the day's work, dust still coated her brown hair and green T-shirt.

Michall, to her nutritional credit, snacked from a bag of unsalted sunflower seeds. She sat across the booth from Sylvia with her red hair pinned up. A thin line of mud showed just above her brown turtleneck.

"This is so bizarre," Sylvia said. "I mean, I've run bits and pieces of dead people through screens for years. But, I mean, wow. This is Dale's dirt."

"Yes," Dusty added seriously, "and don't forget it."

"I wonder why the UNM field schools didn't dig this site," Michall asked.

"I don't know," Dusty said as he stirred more cheese into the macaroni. "They dug most of the Rincon small sites between 1939 and 1942."

Michall frowned. "As I recall, it caused a lot of problems when they discovered that the small houses were occupied at the same time as the Great Houses, but either by different people, or the same people living differently."

"The first," Sylvia said. She accented her point with a handful of cheesy fishes. "If you buy Steve LeBlanc's warfare theory, and Christy Turner's Chaco hypothesis, then the country bumpkins from the hinterlands came to Casa Rinconada to be impressed by the grand Chaco priests. The priests put them up in the small houses and, after dark, showed them miraculous wonders." She stuffed the cheesy fishes into her mouth and slurred, "Tha's why the trench is in the floor. The priests could rise up out of the underworld right before the hicks' eyes."

"Your mother taught you never to talk with food in your mouth," Dusty said irritably. "Show us some common courtesy."

Sylvia washed it down with Coors and answered, "Courtesy is never common. Especially around you."

"It's the basilisk." Maureen shot her a warning look. "It's eating at Dusty. Me, too."

"I thought you didn't believe in it?" Sylvia studied her fingers, dyed yellow from the crackers. "Or has experience changed your mind?"

"I don't believe in it," Maureen said with certainty. "It's just a carved stone. But it gives Dusty nightmares and I have to consider that."

But as she started to cut up tomatoes for the salad, she wondered why, if she didn't believe, the little fetish worried her so much.

"What's even more weird is the FBI finding the note buried in the snow. I'm never going to feel the same about Casa Rinconada." Sylvia shook her head. "It used to be one of my favorite sites. I mean, you walk down there and you can feel the power, you know? Even after all these years. It still hums."

Dusty slammed his fork down and braced his hands on the counter.

Sylvia jumped. "What did I say?"

"Nothing. It—it's not you. I just keep thinking. Those dark stains on the dirt. The fact that Dale was killed—"

"We don't know that for sure," Maureen cautioned, wondering if Dusty was finally going to shatter into a thousand pieces. "Let's wait for the blood analysis before we come to any conclusions about what happened down there."

"But . . . the note . . ."

Sylvia came to attention. Her green eyes narrowed. "What about it? You haven't told us anything."

Dusty didn't reply for a while; then finally he said, "It said something like: 'Dale. Hello old friend. Almost two cycles of the moon have come and gone since that terrible night. What you took from me cannot be forgiven. On the night of the Masks, when the Dead walk the world, come to the great corner kiva, old friend. I shall be waiting.' " Dusty picked up his stirring fork again and aimed it at the pot like a knife. "It was signed Kwewur."

"Who's Kwewur?" Michall asked with wide eyes.

Dusty said, "A katchina from a dead clan. From Awatovi."

Sylvia nodded. "I read about this. The Hopi burned Awatovi to the ground because they thought the village was filled with witches. Then, at Polacca Wash, they chopped up the captives."

Maureen finished the salad, set the bowl aside, and went to refill her coffee cup from the pot on the stove. She glanced at Dusty, judging his mood, before she asked, "Two cycles of the moon? How long is that?"

"A little more than thirty-seven years," Dusty replied. "But I have no idea what happened at Casa Rinconada in 1964."

"Dale took something from Kwewur. At least that's what the note says. Something that couldn't be forgiven. What could it have been?" Maureen slid into the booth beside Sylvia and set her coffee on the battered old tabletop. "It's all so cryptic."

Headlights flashed through the trailer windows, and Sylvia put her hand against the glass to block the glare. "Hey, it's Magpie!"

Dusty stepped to the door and opened it. "Hi, Maggie. Come on in."

"Hi," Maggie said, but she'd stopped short of the door, and was holding something in her hands. "Losing things already, Stewart? I'm glad this is a report and not a bag full of sacred artifacts."

She handed him a thick booklet, the kind copy places made with plastic binders. It was paper, eight and a half by eleven.

"This isn't mine." Dusty took it, squinting down at it in the lantern light. "Wait a minute. This was just lying outside?"

"Yes, on the ground." Maggie pulled her coat off and hung it on the peg by the door. "Smells great. Was I smart enough to get here in time for dinner."

"This is a joke, right?" Dusty asked, still holding the bound pages. "You didn't really find this on the ground outside."

Maggie lifted an eyebrow, catching the serious tone in Dusty's voice. "I saw it when I pulled up and stopped. I thought it was yours so I picked it up. It was lying right outside the door, on the ground. Want me to go put it back?"

"What is it?" Maureen got to her feet and walked over to Dusty. She read the front sheet and whispered, "Dear God."

Dusty swallowed hard and handed it to her. "Please guard this while I get the pistol and take a look around outside."

Dusty went to the rear of the trailer and came out with his pistol.

"Stewart, that's not what I think it is, is it? You know the rules about firearms."

He gave her a steely look. "You, of all people, know what we're up against. You didn't see a thing, Maggie. And neither did anyone else in this trailer. Right?"

Maggie gave him a worried look, and jerked a nod as he shouldered by and slipped out into the darkness. She took a deep breath, shook her head, and leaned sideways to read over Maureen's shoulders. "What is that? It looks like . . ."

"Dale's handwriting? Yes. This is one of his private journals."

Sylvia came over and took it from Maureen's hand. "How did one of Dale's private journals wind up outside the trailer on the ground?"

Maureen rubbed her arms, a sudden chill in her spine. "More to the point, who left it there? And *why*? What do they want us to read?"

AN ARROW RATTLED in the rocks a body's length from Blue Corn. She ducked and almost lost her precarious footing on the canyon rim. A cold wind blew out of the starry west, teasing her hair and fluttering her dress.

"That way!" Rain Crow pointed with his war club, sending four of his warriors scrambling off to the east. A misstep meant a fall to the canyon, a bow shot below them.

This was madness, trying to fight a running battle in the rimrock above Straight Path Canyon. Boulders jutted from the canted bedrock, and could hide one, two, or no assailants. Three of her warriors had been wounded, perhaps some were even dead by now. When she looked back over her shoulder, she saw the flickering on the rooftop where some thrice-cursed fool had built a fire.

Another arrow hissed into the rocks below her. From instinct, she bent down, despite the pain in her leg, and picked it up.

"There!" Rain Crow cried. "No, you fools, off to your right. Just below the crest of the hill!"

"It's a diversion," Blue Corn said as she inspected the thin wooden shaft. She stumbled painfully in the gloom. "They want us off balance. This is a willow stave. Probably a piece taken out of an old sleeping mat."

"It may be a diversion, but some of those arrows are real. We must run these rats down, before they pick us all off." Rain Crow watched his warriors as they charged forward, bent double to decrease their target area. At the slow rate of their advance, the mysterious archers would have more than enough time to abandon their positions and retreat.

"No, pull back," she ordered. "Rain Crow, this is meant to wear us out, to keep us from the canyon."

He stopped short, and she could feel his eyes on her as he considered the situation. To date they hadn't had a clean shot at one of the darting, weaving targets.

"But, Matron—"

"Fall back!"

Rain Crow called, "Retreat! Regroup at the stairway."

"Gods know, Rain Crow, climbing down that stairway is where we will be the most vulnerable. We need every archer we have."

She turned and picked her way back over the rocks and loose soil. Her aching hip sent fire up her side, but she couldn't limp, not on this rotted slope.

Rain Crow came to offer his hand, and with his help she made her way back to the roadway. The rising sandstone hid Center Place from her view, but below, part of Kettle Town's walls were visible.

"What happened?" Horned Ram stood, guarded by his Red Rock warriors. They had arrows nocked in their bows.

"A diversion," she told him. "Phantoms shot splinters at us, then fled." She offered the willow stave.

Her warriors re-formed, eyes on the eastern edge of the rim where their tormentors had disappeared.

Rain Crow studied the dark rocks warily as he started to say: "I think we—"

They rose from just under the lip of the stairway, four of them, loosing arrows from beneath their white cloaks.

The ambush came as a complete surprise. Blue Corn instinctively dropped to her belly, trying to wiggle down into the worn sandstone. But she could only cover her head and listen to the screams of her warriors.

"By the gods, how did this happen?" Horned Ram bellowed. *"We had to practically step on them!"*

"Rise!" Rain Crow shouted. "There are only four of them! Follow me!"

"Black Stalk is shot through the guts!" someone cried.

"Go!" Blue Corn ordered. "I'll tend to him. Avenge him! In the Flute Player's name, *go!*"

Blue Corn watched her warriors rise, hunched figures with bows, ready to loose deadly arrows as they scampered to the top of the stairway.

Rain Crow's voice carried, "Where did they go?"

"Careful. Watch out."

"I don't see anything!"

Blue Corn crawled over to Black Stalk and rested his head in her lap. The young warrior gripped the arrow shaft that stuck out of his abdomen just below the navel. Despite the darkness she could see the spreading blackness of gut blood as it soaked the panting warrior's shirt. She ran cool hands over his hot face.

"You're going to be all right, Black Stalk," she soothed. "Just hold on."

"Matron?" he asked through clenched teeth. "Blessed Flute Player, it burns like fire."

"It's the gut juice," she said. On the night breeze she could smell the sour stench of punctured intestines.

He shivered, his feet kicking slowly, futilely as his sandals slid across the gritty stone.

"Matron," he whispered. "I would ask a favor?"

"Of course, Black Stalk. Anything within my power."

Sweat trickled down his face to dampen her shirt. With a trembling and bloody hand he unhooked the war club from his belt. Offering it, he said, "Kill me, Matron. Quickly. I've seen wounds like this. I don't want to die slowly. And if you pull this arrow out, you'll take half of me with it."

"Black Stalk, I—"

"Please, Matron. You've seen gut-shot men die before. You *know* what it's like."

At the pleading in his voice, she took the heavy war club, and eased his head down so that he stared up at the glistening Evening People.

"It's a . . . good club, Matron," he said through gritted teeth. "My father . . . made it . . . before he . . . died. Straight . . . and true."

"Yes, a good club," she answered, deadening her heart. Was this the Black Stalk she remembered as a little boy? The one she had watched grow tall and strong? She had seen him on the day he had walked across the plaza, no more than thirteen summers in age. It had been spring, and despite being frightened half out of his wits, as all little boys were, he carried his head high as he went for his first kiva initiation.

*Now I must kill him.* She shifted, rising onto her knees. The shaft of the war club was cool and thick in her hands. The smell of Black Stalk's blood and guts hung like a miasma in the air. *What brought me here, to this place, to do this to such a nice young man?*

She lifted the club, her muscles suddenly rubbery and weak. A constriction, like a tightening band of rawhide pinched her chest. She couldn't find her breath.

"Please, Matron?" Black Stalk whimpered. "You have no idea how this hurts."

Her heart might have been a stone as she raised the war club high and with all of her might brought it down on his head. The impact carried up the wood, into her hands, arms, and shoulders. She heard as well as felt the sickening snap of the bones in his skull. His body spasmed, then went still.

She flung the club away, and couldn't stop the sudden rush of tears. For long moments, she sat there, in the middle of the abandoned road, and sobbed as she hadn't since she was girl.

"Matron?" Rain Crow's gentle voice broke through her misery.

"Yes, War Chief." She ran a sleeve over her hot, wet face and straightened.

"There are four of them. They're headed south, past Kettle Town. I'd say they were heading straight across the canyon."

Blue Corn looked at Black Stalk's crushed skull, and her souls seemed to wither.

"Find them," she ordered. "Kill them. Kill them all, and bring me their heads, War Chief."

"I'll leave a few warriors to keep you—"

"No! Take everyone. No prisoners, War Chief. You have your orders. Go! Just get away! *Leave me alone!*"

She heard the eerie shriek in her voice. Soul sick, she bent double, holding her stomach, hearing Rain Crow barking orders as he and his men clambered down the staircase after the white-caped assailants.

THE ONLY SOUND was the hissing of the Coleman lantern and the flipping of pages as Sylvia read Dale's journal.

"Get a load of this," Sylvia said. Her green eyes widened. "Who was Melissa? A graduate student?"

"That's enough, Sylvia," Dusty said, and held out a hand.

"Why? Don't you want to read it?" Sylvia asked as she handed him the photocopied journal, open to the page.

Dusty shook his head. "No." But his eyes were inevitably drawn to the name:

*"Melissa has been sleeping in my tent for a week. The crew's starting to talk. I have to end this. I should*

*have never started it to begin with. She's so young and
beautiful. And brilliant. She's asked me to oversee her
dissertation research. Do I dare put myself in the position of being close to her for another two years?"*

Sylvia's hand hovered in midair. "Yeah. I thought
you'd want to read it, and you didn't even have time
to get to the juicy stuff?"

Dusty closed the booklet and set it on the kitchen
counter. He couldn't look at Sylvia, couldn't meet her
eyes. So what if Dale had had an affair with one graduate student? That didn't mean he'd made a habit of
it. Field affairs happened. Generally, they didn't mean
a thing.

Dusty said, "Nobody touches this from here on out.
It's evidence."

Maggie and Maureen sat at the rear of the table with
their eyes on Dusty, while Michall craned her neck to
peer out the windows into the darkness.

"Uh, Dusty," Michall said. "You know, right, that
the person who left that is probably the person who
murdered Dale?"

Dusty contemplatively walked into the kitchen and
placed the pages on the counter. "That's the point,
Michall. We're supposed to play along, pick out the
clues."

"Well, if that's so," Michall said as she jerked the
curtains closed, "he's one sick son of a bitch."

"If it's a he." Dusty smoothed his hand over his
beard while he studied the ominous papers. He had the
overwhelming desire to sit down with them right now
and read every word—but, damn it, he hated being led
around by the nose. The diary had been left because
something in it incriminated a specific person, which
meant . . . what? That the incriminated person was *not*
the murderer?

He glanced over at Maureen. She sat with her elbows
braced on the table, staring at him. Dusty said, "What
do you think we should do?"

"Despite all the manhandling you, Maggie, and Sylvia have given it, Nichols might be able to pull fingerprints, fibers, or other incriminating evidence from it." Maureen pulled her cell phone from her shirt pocket. "Nichols might also want to set up roadblocks, have his people scout around the trailer for tracks."

Dusty nodded. "Call him."

The sight of Dale's handwriting brought an ache to his heart.

"Agent Nichols?" Maureen said. "It's Dr. Cole. Someone just dropped a copy of one of Dale's stolen journals at our trailer." A pause. "Yes." Another pause. "We won't move until Rick and Bill are here." Silence. "Maggie Walking Hawk Taylor found it on the step when she arrived for dinner." Maureen frowned. "Yes, somebody did open it. Sylvia." Another pause. Maureen nodded. "Yes, I think you'll find her fingerprints on a number of the pages." And then, "We won't step out until they arrive." Maureen punched the END button on the phone.

Sylvia said, "Oops."

Dusty's stomach twisted. What was Nichols thinking? That Sylvia had just covered her tracks?

Maggie said, "You think the murderer is a woman?"

Dusty slid into the booth, forcing Sylvia to scoot over next to Maureen, and said, "There was a woman at Dale's funeral. Do you remember, Maureen? I didn't see her, but you said—"

"The one who touched Dale's ashes and hurried away? Yes. I remember." Maureen searched Dusty's face. "In her thirties, wearing a black fur hat and dark glasses."

"Maybe just a colleague." Dusty shrugged. "I didn't see her."

Sylvia stared wide-eyed at the windows. "Damn! She's here. Or he's here? In the park. Just watching us?"

"Playing with us, you mean," Dusty said. "How long till the FBI's here?"

"Five minutes," Maureen replied, a distance in her gaze.

"Aunt Sage says that the witch is like Coyote and he's teasing us like he would a family of rabbits trapped under a rock," Maggie said soberly. She poked at her macaroni and potatoes with her fork.

Dusty immediately gave her his full attention. "What else did your aunt tell you?"

Maggie took a bite of macaroni, chewed, and swallowed. "She said that he's powerful. Maybe the most powerful witch in a hundred years."

"Him? As in a man?"

"She didn't say. But it could surely be a woman." Maggie was frowning, hiding something. A terrible confusion lay behind her strained expression.

"Could she find him? Figure out who he is?"

Maggie's voice broke as she said, "Dusty, she's dying."

He took a deep breath and nodded. "I—I'm sorry, Maggie. It seems like the whole world is dying around us. Everyone we love."

"Aunt Sage said that he has to be stopped." Maggie jabbed her fork at her food. "That something is happening, changing in the witch's life. If he isn't caught he's going to keep hunting."

"Not Coyote," Dusty corrected. "Wolf. He's Kwewur, the Wolf Katchina."

"No, Dusty." Maggie gave him a warning look. "He's not the Wolf Katchina. He's the Wolf Witch, who has taken the katchina's name and fouled it, the way witches do. Aunt Sage is worried. She says that Grandma Slumber and Aunt Hail have been talking to her."

Sylvia had turned so pale her freckles stood out like brown dots. "From the Land of the Dead?"

Maureen had narrowed her eyes, but said nothing. For that, Dusty really appreciated her.

"What did they say?" Dusty asked without missing a beat. "Did the elder tell you?"

Maggie nodded. "Aunt Sage told me they were worried, that an old evil had escaped from the past, and was released into this world. That we touched it at 10K3, and at Pueblo Animas, but it is centered here, just like it was in the old days, when the white palaces fell."

"Okay, right," Michall said as she finished off her dinner and laid the fork down. "Ancient witchcraft loose in the modern world, guys?"

Maureen raised a hand. "Michall, before all else, I'm a scientist. You were there for the beginning of the work on 10K3. Whether you believe in the spiritual aspects or not, there is a link between that site and the things that are going on now."

Dusty and Maggie stared at each other. "Did Hail tell you anything at all about 10K3?"

"She told me that the evil was too strong there. She said, 'He's won again.' That's all she'd tell me. That's one of the reasons I made Aunt Sage go to the healing up at Aztec when Washais called."

"Who?" Michall asked.

"Washais is my Seneca name," Maureen told her. "Hail Walking Hawk preferred to think of me that way."

"It means bloody scalping knife," Sylvia said with aplomb.

Maureen's brows lowered. "You Whites are so inventive."

Sylvia grinned.

"Getting back to the witch?" Dusty said, his attention on Maggie.

"He's old," Maggie said. "Aunt Sage said she couldn't really hear what Slumber and Hail were trying to tell her from the other side. Just that the witch had found something here, in the canyon, and it has been growing inside him."

"Or her," Maureen interjected.

"Did Aunt Sage say if it was a woman?" Dusty asked.

"No."

Sylvia whispered. "Did you see *The Blair Witch Project*? If I hear something like popcorn popping outside of the dormitory tonight, I'm going to come looking for you two." She pointed at Dusty and Maggie.

Maureen said, "I don't know much about witches, or witchcraft. I've only just begun studying it. But I do know something about death rituals. For example, my people, the Iroquois, keep our dead close until the Feast of the Dead when we send them to the Village of Souls. The southeastern tribes, the Cherokee, Choctaw, Chickasaw, and Creek, build shrines and keep the corpses of their ancestors literally next door. The Apache and Navajo are dreadfully frightened of the dead. Among the Navajo, you can tell a witch because they dig up corpses and loot graves." She turned her gaze on Maggie. "Among the Pueblo people, witches are known for eating the flesh of the dead, aren't they?"

Maggie nodded. "That's right."

Dusty asked, "Where are you going with this, Maureen?"

Maureen made a face. "I'm not sure, yet. But it has to do with motivation. Like that photocopied journal in front of you. It doesn't make sense. Why is this happening the way that it is?"

"I'll bite," Sylvia said. "Why?"

"That's what we have to figure out." Maureen steepled her fingers, mind knotting around the problem. Dusty thought she looked stunning, her eyes animated in the lantern light.

"So you don't think it's an ancient evil that got let loose?" Maggie asked.

Maureen shrugged. "Maybe that's part of it, but what does a witch want? What are the things that motivate them to do what they do?"

"Power," Maggie answered. "A witch wants to amass wealth and gain status. He wants to be looked up to, to be noticed and feared. He wants to be important."

"So, what's the worst thing you can do to a witch?" Maureen pursued.

"Stone him to death and bury him under a rock," Sylvia supplied.

"I don't mean how do you punish him, I mean how do you really piss off a witch?"

Dusty smoothed his hands over Dale's journal. "Humiliation is the worst thing you can do to a witch."

"Think back to that note that they found in Casa Rinconada today," Maureen reminded. "Something happened in the past that can't be forgiven. Something worth waiting more than thirty-seven years to avenge. Humiliation?"

Dusty's eyes went to the photocopied diary. He exhaled hard. "No matter what, we're supposed to read it. Kwewur wants us to read it."

Lights shone outside.

"We will," Maureen promised. "Just as soon as Bill and Rick dust it for prints and check for fibers." She narrowed her eyes in thought.

"What?"

"Something Rupert said . . . about witches and how they are into misdirection. If I could only . . ." But she shook her head, dashing his hopes.

# CHAPTER 34

BEAR LANCE CHARGED northward along the dark, starlit road. He could see the runner when he crested the high points. The man's white cape flashed. It had to be Polished Bone or Puma Silk, one of the two sentries left to watch over Elder Two Hearts and the canyon.

"But what if it isn't?"

Could this be a ruse? Were they being led into a trap?

"What was that?" Stone Lizard asked between panting breaths.

Bear Lance cast a glance over his shoulder. Eighteen men lined out behind him, running in their distance-eating stride with their white capes flapping like wings.

"I don't like this. I'm worried about being ambushed."

Stone Lizard replied, "Then let us be careful."

Bear Lance had succeeded the great Ten Hawks after his death and become War Chief for the Red Lacewing Clan in Straight Path Canyon. The awesome responsibility had fallen onto his shoulders at the most difficult of times. The existence of the White Moccasins was now openly spoken of among the Made People. Elder Two Hearts, descendant of the Red Lacewing Matrons, lay wounded, slowly dying, and now, if his scout ahead could be believed, was being hunted by War Chief Browser. Not just an enemy, but also one of the First People.

As he ran, Bear Lance couldn't help but feel the

wrongness of this. Why hadn't Polished Bone, if that's
who that was, run inside to deliver his message?

*Maybe because the situation in the canyon is too
critical? He knows he has to get back quickly.*

Bear Lance thought of Two Hearts lying in the lone
small house, guarded only by a warrior and Shadow
Woman. He hadn't liked the idea. No, he hadn't liked
any of it, but the elder had ordered, and as War Chief
to the man he considered the Blessed Sun, that was
enough. But Shadow, even after all these sun cycles,
frightened him.

She had been his lover, his enemy, his greatest desire, and his utter despair. On rare occasions she still
crawled into his blankets and stroked his body into a
throbbing fountain of ecstasy. Then, one hand of time
later, she would shrivel his souls by eating raw flesh
stripped from one of her Made People victims.

"A light." Stone Lizard pointed at the heights in the
north. The tiny flicker came from Center Place.

"A signal fire?"

Stone Lizard said, "Perhaps. But signaling what?"

Bear Lance gripped his war club. "You are sure that
was Polished Bone up there?"

"Blood Ax thought so, but he wasn't absolutely positive."

Bear Lance wet his lips and sucked in a deep breath,
forcing his legs to move faster. "If that is not one of
our warriors, and he gets to the Blessed Elder with so
much as his bare hands, he can end all our dreams."

Night deepened around them as they ran. Bear Lance
passed the familiar shrines and felt the road begin to
slope down to the canyon and the stairway.

"Careful," he called, raising one hand. "I want arrows nocked. I don't want us to be taken in ambush
here. Spread out and keep—"

"About time!" a familiar female voice hissed.

Bear Lance shied away from the shrine at the side

of the road where a dark figure arose, ghostlike in the darkness. Her long black hair shimmered with a silver fire in the starlight.

"I didn't—"

"*Fool!* What took you so long?" Shadow demanded. "A war party is coming! You must hold them, or destroy them."

"The Blessed Sun, is he—?"

"Being moved to a new location. The Blue God curse you for standing here talking while our elder is at risk!" She flung an arm toward the trail. *"Go. Now!"*

AS THE LAST of the White Moccasins charged down the stairway, she slumped to the ground. Her bones shook like sticks. But she had done it. At the last moment, as the warriors slowed, something had risen from deep within her and she had found a part of herself she never knew existed.

Gulping deep breaths to cool her fevered body, Obsidian forced herself to her feet and started down the stairway in the wake of the departed warriors.

Gods, why did it have to be so dark?

Placing her feet, she lowered herself step by step, desperate at the feeling of unseen eyes in the darkness. When she reached the road, she slipped off to the side, making her way through the tumbled boulders below the cliff.

She heard the sudden cry, and then shouts and howls accompanied by the sound of battle.

If she could only make it back to the safety of Kettle Town, she'd never . . .

Silky laughter seemed to seep from the rocks. "Why, *Sister*, what did you just do?"

DUSTY CROUCHED NEXT to Maggie at the edge
of the tape, watching Michall carefully screen the last
of the disturbed fill that had surrounded Dale's body.
Nothing had been recovered from the dirt except several potsherds. "Nothing" was the key word. Just like
nothing had been recovered from the FBI search
around the trailer the night before. Not that that surprised him. Were he Kwewur, he'd have sneaked up
on the pavement, left the diary, and slipped away. Asphalt left no tracks.

The gray November day was cold. Rupert had
thoughtfully provided tarps and straw bales to keep the
excavation from freezing at night.

"Let's go deeper," Michall called as she finished the
last of her notes. "It's kiva fill so I say we take twenty-
centimeter levels until we come down on the roof." She
shot a glance at Dusty, as if seeking his approval. He
nodded, aware that in another time, he'd have instinctively looked to Dale for similar concurrence.

He missed Maureen. She'd been gone for only an
hour, taking the propane bottles to Cuba to get them
refilled, but it seemed like an eternity. He was genuinely worried about her.

Gravel crunched when Maggie shifted to sit down
cross-legged on the frozen soil. "It's odd, isn't it? Being on the outside of the excavation?"

"It's driving me crazy."

In a low voice, Maggie said, "Dusty? I've got to talk
to someone. If I tell you . . ."

"Sure, Maggie. You don't even have to ask."

"Remember that night? Back at 10K3? The night
when you first called me out to the site to tell you
thought you had uncovered a witch?"

"Uh-huh."

"You trusted me."

"Yep. I still do."

She stared thoughtfully at the excavation where Michall's crew was working. Finally she said, "About last night . . . at the trailer. I said that Aunt Sage was telling me those things."

"She's not?"

"Some. The rest of it has been coming to me." She gave him a sidelong glance, as if to measure his response. "Sometimes I catch an image, like a phantom in the half-light. I know it's Grandma Slumber and Aunt Hail. And they're gone, just like that."

"What does your aunt Sage say?"

"That I need to let myself go, allow myself to see."

He considered that. "So do it."

She shivered despite her coat. "I'm afraid I'm going nuts. What if it's schizophrenia?"

"Being nuts isn't so bad. People have called me crazy for years."

"Don't joke."

"Okay. Maggie, I think you need to talk to your aunt. That's what elders do, they help people find their gifts. They guide them down the road to Power."

"Thanks, Dusty." She made a face. "I started talking to Reggie about it, and, God, maybe it was the wind, but I'd have sworn I heard Dale's voice telling me not to."

Dusty studied her, his heart skipping. "You think?"

She shrugged. "I don't know. Maybe it was my subconscious. I got to thinking about it later, and, well, there was something about the way that Reggie was looking at me, almost like he wanted to devour me on the spot. You know what I mean?"

"No. Look, the only advice I can give is that you trust yourself, okay? That, and go talk to Aunt Sage about it."

"As soon as I can. I'm worried sick about her. And

things are so tense here these days, I can't get away."

Dusty picked up a handful of soil and poured it from hand to hand as he watched the white Ford Explorer pull into the parking lot beside the crew vehicles. A tourist? At this time of year? A brave one.

Dusty said, "I thought Nichols had closed the road."

"He did; then he reopened it." She lifted her eyes heavenward in a gesture of exasperation, and added, "You think I'm going crazy. You should have to work with Rupert these days."

Dusty smiled, but wondered about that. Had Nichols reopened the road to allow the murderer to return to the scene of the crime? Were the openings and closings some sort of clever FBI trap?

Maggie scrutinized the woman who got out of the car wearing a thick down coat with the tan hood pulled up and said, "I'll take care of it if she gets too close."

He nodded.

Maggie's brow furrowed as wind tugged at her shoulder-length black hair. "Dusty, the morning I found Dale's truck, I saw an owl. He was sitting in the road. I stopped, and he just vanished." She paused, letting that sink in. "Then, over by Casa Rinconada, I would have sworn that I saw Dale walking up the trail."

Dusty tried to keep his heart from leaping. The wound in his soul opened. "God, I hope you did. Did he look all right? I mean, you know, happy?"

She shivered inside her brown Park Service coat. "He did. He looked just like the old Dale. I think he was telling me he was all right. That he was still with us."

"That makes me feel better."

"I wish I felt so good about it. I'm worried what people will say if this gets out."

Dusty brushed his hands off on his pants. "You just need more time, Maggie. I think your people will accept it. You have to open yourself up, give them a chance."

"Easy for you to say. You don't know the things that are being whispered about Aunt Sage."

"What things?"

The worry in her face couldn't be hidden. "All of my aunts had Power, Dusty. They could see the dead. Sometimes just having the ability scares people, if you know what I mean. They don't understand."

"You mean there's talk that she might be a witch?"

"Shh!" Maggie said, and looked around to make sure no one could overhear them. She murmured, "Yes, now let's talk about something else."

"Okay," he said, but the news stunned him. Maggie's aunts were the only truly holy people he'd ever known. He brushed at the dirt on his pants and looked toward Casa Rinconada. The woman had her back to them, looking down into the kiva. "Where did you see Dale?"

Maggie turned and pointed. "There. He was walking out of the morning, looking just fine, Dusty."

Dusty smiled.

Maggie's gaze rested on the tourist, probably seeing that the woman didn't step onto the ancient walls, or throw trash into the kiva—which tourists were prone to do; it was just a big hole to them. After a long silence, Maggie said, "What do you know of Reggie Brown Horse?"

"Rupert's grandson?"

She nodded. "He seems nice. He's been coming by my place a lot, bringing me things. You know, gifts he's found, pretty stones. Last night, he brought me a single rose."

Dusty shrugged. "He's on probation. Breaking and entering, burglary, fencing stolen goods, I don't know all of it. Maybe he's changed. I'm sure being up here with Rupert has helped."

"He isn't the first kid coming out of that background to get a little off track. Especially since he and his mother don't get along. You know Reggie's father, right?"

"Lupe. Yes. I hear he's making flutes and selling them. I always liked Lupe." Dusty smiled at the memories. "We had a couple of wild times when we were both kids." He hoped she wouldn't ask him to explain that. If she thought the stories about him dancing with strippers and freezing his nether portions to Wyoming trucks were bad . . .

"We're all so fragile," Maggie said. "Reggie most of all."

Thankfully, she turned her attention to the FBI team. They pitched rocks out of the kiva, while Michall and Sylvia shoveled dirt into screens. "What is it about men and women that makes us so dangerous for each other?"

"Bad genes," Dusty said. "It's that X and Y chromosome crap."

Maggie laughed, then carefully asked, "What's happening between you and Maureen?"

"What do you mean? Nothing."

"Why not?"

"God," Dusty said, annoyed, "give us some time."

"The way the two of you look at each other, I'd think your souls were getting sticky."

He laughed softly. "Not yet. Well . . . maybe a little. We'll see what happens after all this is over."

Maggie smiled and tucked her hands into her pockets. "Good."

The tourist climbed from the trail below. She had her head down, and her tan hood waffled around her face, hiding it.

"Here comes your charge," Dusty said. "As the resident tourist herder, maybe you'd better go empty the potsherds from her pockets and send her back to the established trails."

Maggie stood up and called, "Pardon me, ma'am, but this area is closed to the public. You'll have to stay on the prescribed trails."

"Indeed?" she called in that precise New England

accent. "I think your administrator would approve of my being here. I believe he would consider it, well, let's say professional courtesy."

Dusty put a hand out to restrain Maggie. "It's all right. It's Ruth Ann Sullivan."

"Your *mother*?" The note of incredulity and the look on Maggie's face were precious.

"In the flesh. Now, what was it we were just talking about? That thing with men and women?"

"Forget I said it," she muttered. "Want me to go warn Rupert that she's here?"

"He's got papers to shuffle and a park to run. I'll make sure she doesn't flip cigarette butts into the carbon samples and keep her from collapsing the ruin walls."

She gave Ruth Ann a skeptical look, then turned to hug Dusty, as though she thought he might need it. She whispered, "Thanks for listening."

"Yeah, Magpie, anytime. See you." He let her go and watched her give Ruth Ann a wide berth as she headed down the hill.

Ruth Ann Sullivan wore a thick coat, the sort sold by upscale sporting goods stores. Her hiking boots looked brand-new, slightly dusted from the walk up to the site. A knit cap was pulled over her shining silver hair. She looked somehow disheveled, her blue jeans wrinkled.

"You must have risen at four A.M. to make it out here this early."

"I slept in the Explorer last night." A faint smile crossed her lips as she looked back at Maggie, who picked her way down the ridge. "Another one of your women, I take it? You surprise me. You're more of a lothario than I would have thought. What happened with you and the good doctor, the one with the black eyes and the killer figure? Did she finally come to her senses?"

In a curt voice, Dusty asked, "What are you doing out here?"

The wind teased strands of her silver hair as she turned toward the dig. "That's where they found Dale?"

"It is."

"What have you discovered?"

"Nothing yet."

She let out a breath as though relieved, or maybe disappointed, Dusty couldn't tell for sure.

"Slept in the Explorer, huh?" he said and crossed his arms, anticipating an argument. "You didn't, perchance, drop a photocopy of one of Dale's journals by my trailer before you came out here, did you?"

Ruth Ann turned slowly. Her eyes resembled cut diamonds, hard and glittering. "You have a photocopy of one of Dale's journals? I'd very much like to see it."

"Why?"

"Did you read it, William?"

"I will as soon as Agent Nichols gives it back."

She didn't say anything, as though waiting for him to continue, but her gaze affected him like a knife in his belly, carving him apart. "Nichols must have read it by now. And he hasn't found the killer, or the dig would be closed. Oh, come on. You must have sneaked a glance at the pages? What did it say?"

Dusty matched her stare. "He said you were a ruthless bitch who would stop at nothing to get your way."

Ruth Ann's left brow arched. "Amazing, your mouth still quirks when you lie. Just like it did when you were five years old."

She walked away, toward the site.

# CHAPTER 35

BROWSER SLIPPED AND skidded down into Straight Path Wash, his fevered lungs burning for breath. They were still behind him. He'd seen them less than fifty heartbeats ago. He unpinned the white cloak he'd taken from the body of the scout killed by his uncle and let it drop into the dark mud. Then he bent down and stripped the white moccasins from his feet. He quickly replaced them with his own worn brown buffalo-hide pair and slogged downstream through the runoff.

The cold air felt wonderful. It dried the hot sweat on his skin and cooled his lungs.

He heard shouts, but from the north. Browser hesitated only a moment, listened, then ran again. Blessed Gods, was it working?

He trotted forward on unsteady legs and hunkered down beside the roadway. He could hear labored breathing. He lifted himself and peered over the bank. They wore white cloaks, but not the fine cloaks of the White Moccasins; these had been dyed with white clay and ash, but the effect was the same in the darkness.

"Here!" he called.

"War Chief?" Yucca Whip led his party toward Straight Path Wash.

"Yes. Take your cloaks off and toss them into the wash. Then follow me."

As they tossed their capes into the mud, the gasping Yucca Whip managed to say, "You should have seen it! Masterful! They were looking everywhere except at their feet. I'd have never believed it!"

More shouts.

"Quickly, this way." Browser led them westward, then dropped onto his belly on the cold ground. They lay down behind him. "Look!"

There, running northward, they could see the shining cloaks of the White Moccasins. Angry shouts broke out from Blue Corn's warriors when they, too, picked out the bobbing white cloaks.

"Holy Thlatsinas," Yucca Whip whispered. "It's going to work."

"Where's Catkin?" Browser asked, scanning the group.

"I don't know, War Chief. Her party drew the warriors off to the east, but as soon as they figured out it was a diversion, they returned. If the deputy or any of the others was wounded, none of the Straight Path warriors spoke of it."

Browser returned his attention to the closing warriors, but a knot of worry drew tight in his chest.

RUTH ANN SULLIVAN stopped at the edge of the yellow tape and watched Sylvia screening the dirt that Michall shoveled up to her. The FBI team had started to sweat. It beaded their faces and ran down their necks. Sylvia kept giving Ruth Ann questioning looks, obviously wondering who she might be, but Michall barely seemed to notice her. Dusty walked over to stand beside his mother.

"So, this is where they left him?" Ruth Ann said.

Standing there in the wind, Dusty tried to decide what he felt for this woman, but he didn't seem to feel anything. It was as though a big blank hole opened up inside him when he looked at her. "What do you mean, they? You think it was more than one person?"

She shrugged. "Dale was a big man."

"Not that big. He'd lost a lot of weight. He was seventy-three. Bone and muscle mass decreases with age. I'd say he might have weighed one-thirty or one-forty, somewhere in there." He was looking at her, remembering the way she'd walked up the hill—as though she owned the world.

As if reading his mind, she said, "You don't like me, do you? Not that it matters, God knows."

"I don't know you well enough to dislike you. Give me another day."

She laughed, the sound of it dry and brittle. "No wonder you got along with Dale. I must admit, I thought about killing him once upon a time, and I sure as hell would have if he'd been behind those faxes."

Dusty studied her face, and for a moment he could see her as she had been when he was four or five. Ravishingly beautiful, smiling, her long blond hair whipping around her face in the wind. Where had that been? What dig? One of the excavations out at Zuni? A sensation of happiness spread through him.

He marveled at that. All these years he'd believed she'd never really done archaeology—yet he had memories of her on excavations. Memories he'd apparently locked inside himself and forgotten. Or perhaps Dale's words that she'd never "sunk a trowel" had tricked his memories into retreating?

He said, "Why are you still here?"

"Your friends at the FBI asked me not to leave." Her squint wasn't just the wind. "And I'm interested. I thought I'd see where this investigation of yours goes. I've just about come to the conclusion that Carter's at the bottom of this. He always was a vindictive son of a bitch."

"Why would he kill Dale?"

"Envy, William. It's a hideous emotion. Dale was

everything Carter wanted to be: famous, respected, powerful, charming, and virile. He got along with people. All Dale had to do was turn on that charm and even his enemies liked him. He was a big man in every mannerism and aspect. Carter Hawsworth, for all of his show, is small-minded." She shook her head. "It must have come as quite a blow to Carter when he returned here to find just how important Dale had become."

Dusty nodded. "The governor even gave him an award last year, for his contributions to understanding New Mexico's past."

"In Carter's mind, that's reason enough for murder."

Dusty watched Sylvia pick something out of the screen. She examined it, then tossed it aside. Probably a rock. "You're pushing this 'Carter the Murderer' thing pretty hard, aren't you?"

She slipped her gloved hands into her pockets. "The human muscle tissue that you said they found in Dale's mouth—"

"Had been taken from a cadaver; it had preservative in it."

She rubbed the back of her neck, and whispered, "A cadaver," but it sounded like a question. "So, the murderer must have had access to a medical school, anatomy lab, or mortuary."

"Or graveyard. If you know about southwestern witchcraft, you know how important graveyards can be."

"And Dale was killed right here?" She was staring woodenly at the excavation. "But why kill him . . ." She turned slightly as she examined the surrounding canyon. He saw her finger moving, marking off the landmarks, and then she stiffened at some thought in her head.

"What are you thinking about?" Dusty asked.

"Nothing, I just . . . are you *certain* he was killed here?"

"Actually, we just found out yesterday that he was

killed in Casa Rinconada." Dusty was watching her. "The bloodstains are still there, on the kiva floor."

She swiveled around to look back at the great kiva.

Something about her expression, the odd tension in her face, the hardness at the corners of her lips . . .

Dusty said, "But then, you knew that, didn't you? That's the first place you went when you arrived. You stopped there and looked in for a long time. What were you seeing? The way Dale looked in his last moments?"

She swallowed hard. If anyone ever looked guilty, Ruth Ann Sullivan did. He saw the fear in her eyes as she turned away and started down the hill.

"Wait!" Dusty started after her. "How did you know he'd been killed there? Did someone tell you? Or did you—?"

She spun around, panic and tears mixing on her face.

"I *didn't* kill him, you simpering little bastard!" She broke into a hobbling run.

"Wait. Come back!"

When she hit the graveled path, Ruth Ann Sullivan broke into a flat-out run, headed back to her parked vehicle.

Dusty watched her speed away down the dirt road. Only when he happened to glance back at the dig did he notice that Michall, Sylvia, and the FBI guys were watching, wide-eyed and silent.

THE WHITE MOCCASINS boiled up from Straight Path Wash. Rain Crow blocked the first blow with his war club; then the battle disintegrated into a mad chaos of slashing, hacking warriors.

"Kill them! Kill them all!" The cries of the White

Moccasins carried over the grunting pants of men fighting for their lives.

Screams rang out as warriors were battered senseless, or some archer drove a shaft into a sweating body.

"Orphan scum!" "Dirty killer!" "Bastard born of a slave!" Curses were hurled as the melee swirled. "Kill our Blessed Elder, will you? He'll eat your liver!"

"Die, you puss-sucking First worm!"

Rain Crow twisted his ruined face into a grimace and blocked yet another of the raining blows that were being showered upon him. Sun cycles of practice stood him in good stead. He ducked, and his assailant's momentum carried him past. Rain Crow thrust his war club into the man's crotch with enough force to send him howling and reeling. A follow-up stroke crushed the man's ribs. Pivoting on his foot, he split the fellow's skull with a meaty smack.

Somewhere to his right, a man let out a bloodcurdling, eerie scream as he died.

Around him, warriors swirled in a blur. The white cloaks of the enemy mixed with his darker-dressed warriors.

Rain Crow charged headlong into another white-clad warrior. The impact of their bodies thumped hollowly. Rain Crow recovered first, but his enemy skipped back and blocked his savage attack. An eternity passed as they swung at each other. It might have been a macabre dance, each step and movement part of Death's mating ritual.

An arrow whisked past Rain Crow's cheek. The White Moccasin flinched; Rain Crow slammed his club into the man's shoulder and kicked him hard in the belly. The shocked warrior staggered back, and Rain Crow broke his neck with a quick swing of his club.

For a heartbeat, he stared down at the man, surprised to be still alive, his eyes blinking. Then he glimpsed movement to his right—and a brilliant yellow bolt blasted through his vision like lightning on a summer night.

YELLOW LANTERN LIGHT pulsed over the interior of the battered camp trailer, reflecting from the wood veneer walls and the heaping plates of enchiladas on the table. The scents of melted cheese and cumin filled the air. Dusty ate another bite of blue corn enchilada.

"You should have seen it," Michall told Maureen as she tucked a loose strand of red hair behind her ear. "We didn't know who she was. We figured she was cool because Maggie hadn't chased her away. Then she and Dusty started yelling at each other." Michall scooped up a forkful of food, and continued, "Turns out he's reaming Ruth Ann Sullivan. The *real* Dr. Ruth Ann Sullivan, of Harvard fame. Right there in front of us!"

"Yeah." Sylvia thumped her Coors can and squinted at Dusty. "Talk about a dysfunctional family. You guys wouldn't even have made it to the waiting room on *Leave It to Beaver*."

"Sylvia," Dusty warned, "give it a break."

Michall gobbled down a big bite of dinner and continued, "The FBI went crazy, taking notes, talking on their cell phones. The excavation came to a dead halt."

Dusty glanced at Maureen, who gave him a sympathetic look, and kept eating. He'd added whole coriander to the sauce, giving the enchiladas a real tang.

Sylvia took a sip of Coors and thoughtfully changed the subject. "You know that FBI guy, Rick? He's a pretty good hand. Bill, however, is a worthless sack of shit. I can't figure how a guy like that gets by. He doesn't like to get his fingers dirty. How do you think he deals with a bleeding corpse?"

"Lots of rubber gloves," Dusty answered. He didn't feel like talking. The day's activities had left him drained and irritable. He ate another bite and crunched a cumin seed. He should have let the sauce simmer longer, but damn it, he'd been hungry—and in a hurry to be done with the day.

Michall covertly watched Dusty as she finished her enchiladas. He could feel her gaze on him. His mood had put a damper on everyone's spirits.

When they had all finished eating and sat around sipping their drinks, Sylvia gave Dusty a knowing look, and said, "Come on, Mick, let's get out of here. Every bone in my body is crying for sleep, and I still have field notes to finish."

Sylvia slid out of the booth.

Michall opened her mouth to say something, caught Sylvia's look, and said, "Sure. Okay. I'm finished with my beer." She tipped the can and gulped the last ten swallows. "Good night, Dusty. Good night, Maureen."

Michall pulled on her coat. At the door she said, "See you guys tomorrow."

Through the window, Maureen watched them drive away, and stood up. She dropped her paper plate in the trash, washed her fork in the sink, and rinsed it off with hot water from the teapot. Then she set the half-full enchilada pan on the ice block in the cooler. It would be fodder for breakfast in the morning.

While she worked, Dusty walked his fork across his plate in a rocking motion. The tines left patterns in the damp paper—a sort of punctate indented design, just like that found on a lot of ancient pottery.

"She really got to you, eh?" Maureen asked.

Dusty shrugged. "I think I got to her more than she did to me."

"Did you believe her when she said she'd slept out at Chaco in her Explorer?"

"Yeah, she looked it."

"Then she didn't leave the diary."

Dusty's voice softened. "She could have paid someone to leave it for us, Maureen. Who knows what that woman is capable of?"

He put his fork down and started massaging the muscles at the back of his neck. They really ached.

Maureen dried her hands on a paper towel and slid into the booth beside him. "Let me help you with that."

Uneasy, Dusty turned slightly, and Maureen started massaging the muscles.

"Oh, my God, that feels good," he sighed, and leaned into her hands.

"Well, don't get any ideas, I'm just doing this because I can't stand to hear the air crackle."

Dusty could feel his anxiety seeping away, his headache even eased. "You're good at this."

Maureen smoothed away a lock of his blond hair. "I took a massage course in college. The same semester that I had macramé."

"Tough load."

She smiled. "For what it's worth, Ruth Ann had the same effect on me. When she walked away from my table at the Loretto, I would have loved to have run after her and wrung her neck. I didn't because I was surrounded by people, but out here, I might have."

Dusty closed his eyes, and images of Dale flashed through his mind. The grief that he held locked deep inside him wriggled up and shot through his chest like tiny fiery lightning bolts. What had Dale ever seen in his mother? "Ruth Ann called you my girlfriend, the one with the black eyes and killer figure."

"Well, I like the last part."

He reached up to touch her right hand. "I told her we were friends. Only."

Maureen patted his fingers and continued massaging his ironlike muscles. "I doubt that she believed you. She seems to think you're some kind of Casanova."

"She called me a leather rio."

"That's 'lothario.' "

"Whatever." He lowered his hand and wondered what he was going to do. Dale had been the center of his life, the one person he trusted. "I worried about you today. I'm not sure you should be running around alone—even to go to the grocery store. I kept wondering what it would be like if you didn't come back, and it scared me."

Maureen stopped massaging, hesitated, then leaned forward to wrap her arms around his broad shoulders. Dusty was afraid to move, afraid she might let go. "Are you all right?" she asked in a tender voice.

He exhaled the word "No," then shook his head. "I don't think I will be for a long time. I keep hearing Dale's voice."

Maureen tightened her hold. "What is he saying?"

"I can't make out the words, but his tone is angry and frightened, as though I'm missing something right in front of my eyes, and he can't understand why I'm so blind."

Headlights cast white on the trailer windows as a vehicle pulled in beside the Bronco.

Dusty pulled away from Maureen. "If it's Sylvia, I'm going to brain her."

"We both will," Maureen added with a smile.

The motor outside shut off and a door made a soft thump. Seconds later there was a knock at the door.

"William?" Ruth Ann's voice called stridently. "May I come in?"

Dusty squeezed his eyes closed. "Oh, God."

# CHAPTER 36

BROWSER SLID FORWARD on his belly and peered over the low rise at the two dark figures. They walked among the dead and wounded like silent specters.

"Let's go get them," Fire Lark whispered.

"Wait," Browser cautioned. "We have just avoided one trap, let's not walk into another."

"Blessed Thlatsinas," Yucca Whip whispered. "I wish it had been daylight."

Browser hissed, "The losing side would have broken and run, knowing they were beaten. They were fighting in the dark, that's why they slugged it out until only two were left standing."

"But, to have—"

"Shhh!" Browser could barely see the two standing figures now. They had walked to the edge of the battleground and stood talking in low tones, gasping for breath as they turned and slowly began to walk northward toward the lumbering darkness of the cliff. In their wake, occasional groans and moans could be heard among the wounded.

Then a single scream rang out.

"Who's there?" a frightened voice called. "Get away! Don't—" The voice was choked off by the hollow thunk of a war club against a human skull.

Yucca Whip whispered, "Who is that out there? Is he going around killing the—"

Browser clapped a hand over his mouth, barely exhaling, "Silence," as he struggled to see through the night.

They lay like the dead while the evening chill settled on their cold flesh. The wait seemed eternal as the faintest glow built on the eastern horizon and finally surrendered to Sister Moon.

Still, Browser wouldn't allow them to rise. They shivered until their teeth began to chatter. Blow after blow silenced the cries of the wounded. Browser allowed a hand of time to pass before he tapped Yucca Whip on the shoulder and rose. He led them forward. At the edge of the road, he surveyed the dead.

"Who did this?" Fire Lark whispered. "I never saw anyone!"

Browser knelt by one of Blue Corn's warriors. The man lay on his back, his half-open eyes gleaming in the moonlight. The arrow through his guts, though fatal, should have allowed him to linger for at least a day or two. The red stain on his chest, however, betrayed the wound that had killed him.

"Stiletto," Clay Frog said woodenly. "Someone went through and made sure."

The hair at the back of Browser's scalp started to prickle. He spun around, searching. "Yes, and if she's not hunting us now, she will be soon."

"Who, Blue Corn?" Clay Frog asked.

"No," Browser replied. "Keep your eyes open."

Slowly, painstakingly, he led them across the battlefield, weaving between the bodies. He almost tripped over a man who lay sprawled in a narrow drainage. Moonlight bathed the exposed arms and legs, each of which had been sliced open. Cuts of meat had been taken from the bone.

"Blessed Gods," Clay Frog whispered, pointing at the head; like a broken pumpkin, the insides had been scooped out. "The killer took his brain, along with the steaks!"

Browser squinted into the darkness. She was out there, somewhere, maybe looking at him this instant. "She's taking meat back to Two Hearts," he said.

"By the Blue God," Clay Frog whispered, one hand against her flat stomach. Her short black hair glinted in the moonlight. "And I thought that what she had done to Gray Thunder—"

"She didn't need meat that night," Browser replied grimly. "Come. Let's go find the rest of our party."

He hadn't made three steps when he saw the man. Somehow in the darkness, Shadow had missed him. He had crawled away on his hands and knees. Browser could see that much from the scuffed soil and the blood trail he'd left.

Browser kicked the man's foot and got a low groan.

"Watch him." Browser grabbed the man's foot and pulled him backward to see if he held a weapon. His hands were empty. Despite the clotted blood on the man's face, Browser knew him. He knelt at the War Chief's side and called, "Rain Crow? It's Browser. Can you hear me?"

The War Chief murmured, his movements weak and aimless.

"Kill him." Yucca Whip hefted his war club. "It will be a kindness. Sometimes, when men are hit in the head, their breath-heart souls flee."

Browser hesitated and glanced around, unnerved by Shadow's work. "No, we must bring him along. Let's hurry. I don't want to be out here longer than we have to."

Catkin had gone to divert Rain Crow and his warriors. Where was she? Had she escaped the fighting on the cliff top? With a sudden desperation, he bent down, pulled one of Rain Crow's arms over his own shoulders, and lifted.

"Here, War Chief." Red Lark and Yucca Whip stepped forward. "You've done enough for the night. We will carry him."

The memory of the dead warrior with moonlight shining into his empty brain case hovered about him like foul mist.

He tried not to think of Catkin, and what Shadow Woman would do if she caught her.

*MY SOULS DANCE, twining up to spin as the Blue God laughs.*

*The party of warriors walks away, heading north. I lift my head and sniff the cool wind. I cannot smell them. The odors of blood, entrails, and death are too strong.*

*Then I turn back and run a slender finger along the side of his jaw, feeling the chill that has leached into his flesh.*

*"Didn't I tell you I was the Summoning God, Bear Lance?"*

*I reach beneath his war shirt, and my fingernail traces a path around his testicles before I grip his cold penis. Unlike times past, he does not gasp and tense. Reluctantly I withdraw my hand and return to stroking his slack face. My dark hair spills over him.*

*The breath-heart soul lingers near the body after death, so I know he is watching me, hating me, but unable to do anything.*

*"You knew this would happen eventually," I whisper. "Ordinary men cannot touch the flesh of the chosen and survive."*

*I kiss his cold lips, then rise and sling my blood-soaked shirt, heavy with meat, over my shoulder.*

MAUREEN LEANED AGAINST the kitchen counter, watching Ruth Ann and Dusty toy with their coffee cups. They sat on opposite sides of the table, facing each other like predators over the carcass of a fatted calf. Ruth Ann tugged at her gray wool turtle-neck. She appeared to have trouble breathing, and sweat shone on her bladelike nose. Fragments of grass dotted her silver hair. Had she been sleeping on the ground?

"I will make this succinct," Ruth Ann began. "I came here because I did not kill Dale. I knew nothing about it until I heard it on the news. I am here because I was *summoned*."

"What does that mean?" Dusty asked. He held his coffee cup in both hands.

"I'm not entirely sure myself, William. I was half-way to the highway before I turned back." She sipped her coffee, looked surprised, and sipped it again. "There's something I need to ask you."

"Why? What I thought has never mattered to you before."

"No," she said straightforwardly. "It certainly hasn't, but it does now. These messages from Kwewur, Dale's death, the missing journals—they all point to something long ago." She cocked her head. "Are you sure that your father is dead?"

Dusty jerked as though he'd been struck. He stared at her through hard unblinking blue eyes. "He was in a mental institution. I assume they know who occupies each room. He was examined by a coroner. There was a funeral, notices in the newspapers, along with articles about Dale going through the proceedings to be de-clared my legal guardian. If Dad faked his death, he did a damn fine job of it. And I would have heard from him."

"I'm sure your childish mind thought you'd hear from me, too," Ruth Ann countered. She looked around the trailer, as though cataloging every speck of dust. "William, I'm just trying to cover the bases here, that's all."

"Let me get this straight," Dusty said, and leaned across the table. "You think Dad faked his death, then hid out all these years just to kill Dale. Why would he do that?"

"Sam was a very patient man, and Dale took everything Sam had."

"Everything?" Maureen asked. "More than just you?"

Ruth Ann gave her a condescending look. "Everything means everything."

"Ah," Maureen said with a nod, and her stomach turned. "I see. You were married to Samuel, but you were still sleeping with other men, and Sam knew it."

"I knew it, too," Dusty said.

Ruth Ann didn't even blink. "Well, don't blame me. They called it erectile dysfunction, William. Sam was so desperate, he took off one weekend and went to Mexico. There was a surgeon down there. He told Sam that the problem was caused by scar tissue around a nerve, and performed some hocus-pocus procedure."

Maureen closed her eyes. "What happened?"

Ruth Ann jiggled her coffee cup. "Absolutely nothing. I don't know what the surgeon did, but Sam was completely incapable after that. That's when he really went overboard with his archaeology. As if the harder he worked, the more we would have to share professionally, since we had nothing to share personally."

"When did you get pregnant?" Maureen fit the pieces together. "Before or after Mexico?"

Ruth Ann shrugged. "I honestly don't know. Neither did Sam. On occasion I tried things with him. Sad sort that I was, I thought it was partly my fault."

"Wait a minute." Dusty's breathing had gone shallow. Maureen could see the truth sinking in as his blue eyes widened. "What are you saying?"

Ruth Ann held his stare. "You wanted to know why I stopped and looked down into Rinconada today? For all I know, you might have been conceived there. I went there often enough."

"When you weren't at La Fonda," Maureen pointed out.

"We only went there in the beginning." Ruth Ann leaned back. "Santa Fe, especially in those days, was still a small town filled with gossip."

Dusty looked as if someone had just kicked his guts out.

Maureen walked over and slid into the booth beside him.

Dusty stammered, "That's why you think D-Dad might be alive? Because you—"

"If Carter didn't kill Dale, Sam is the only other person who would have had a reason."

Maureen leaned back. "Why have you dropped Hawsworth from the suspect list?"

"Who said I dropped him? Professional jealousy *might* be enough, even for Carter, and"—she lifted a finger—"I've heard him threaten to kill people for less reason than that. Unless he's gone way overboard and begun to believe he really is a witch. In that case, Dale, who's innocent for the most part, just got in the way. It's me that Carter really wants dead."

Maureen thought back to the conversation she'd had with Hawsworth. "But why would he be after you?"

"He has recently discovered that beyond the old reasons, he has ample new ones." Ruth Ann shifted wearily. "Lord knows, he does."

"Did you ever leave a man behind who didn't hate you?" Dusty asked.

"It was the sixties," Ruth Ann said, as if that was sufficient. "I don't make any excuses for what I did or why I did it. I wanted to be an anthropologist, to step outside of the roles I'd been enculturated for. So, I did. I turned the tables on my culture and made my own way."

Maureen returned to the subject at hand. "So Sam

said nothing. He claimed Dusty because not to would have exposed his impotence. But, tell me, did you ever tell Dale that Dusty might be his?"

"Of course not. First, I couldn't be sure. Secondly, I didn't want to. When I heard later that he had taken over legal guardianship of William, I was fairly sure that Dale believed the boy was his son. It made a great many things easier for me."

Dusty's voice was like silk. "You're good at easy, aren't you?"

Stiffly, she answered, "I don't care for the censure in your voice, William."

He burst to his feet, staring down into her startled eyes. "I don't give a *damn* what you care for. You just waltzed in here to tell me that *Dale* was my father? Why?"

Ruth Ann leaned back, frightened by his physical presence. "I thought you'd like to know."

Dusty felt a sudden weakness, as if all the nerves had been cut in his body. He straightened, and stepped away. "Damn it, this is going to take some time to get used to."

"Time?" Ruth Ann asked, and laughed. "I hope you get it."

The knock, when it came, was tentative. Nevertheless, it brought them to a sudden and complete silence. Maureen's stomach knotted, adrenaline surging.

Dusty, the first to recover from the start, called, "Come join the party!"

Maureen was expecting Carter Hawsworth, not the young woman who opened the door and climbed up the aluminum steps.

She stood perhaps five-eight, slender, with ash hair. She wore a black wool coat. Slim black boots—the velveteen type more common to Fifth Avenue—made her feet look delicate. She had a long but pleasant face, and hauntingly familiar dark eyes.

When she spoke, it was with a delightfully modulated English accent. "My, this is the absolute *end* of the earth!"

Ruth Ann's hands clenched to fists on the table. "Why, Yvette, fancy meeting you here."

"I know you," Maureen said, her heart leaping. "You were at the funeral. I saw you reach down and touch Dale's ashes. Who are you?"

"I'm Yvette Hawsworth, Dr. Cole." She turned to Dusty and extended her hand. "Hello, dear brother. If I'd known you existed, I swear I'd have knocked you up for a chat long ago."

Dusty just stared at her.

Yvette said, "Mum didn't tell you about me, did she? No? Pity. It makes my father's reasons a bit more understandable."

"Reasons?" Dusty said. "Reasons for what?"

Yvette removed her gloves. "For wanting to kill her."

STONE GHOST GINGERLY lowered himself to the pile of stones—part of a collapsed third-story wall—and peered out the window at the small party that straggled up the south road from Straight Path Wash. In the hazy moonlight, he had difficulty keeping count, and his eyes were not what they used to be.

"It looks like five walking and a sixth being carried," White Cone told him, the Mogollon elder shading his eyes.

"I think so, too." Stone Ghost sighed. "We will know soon enough."

The sounds of battle had carried to them, though they had seen nothing in the darkness. For long hands of time, worry had eaten at Stone Ghost's stomach.

So many things could have gone wrong. Battle plans

rarely survived the release of the first arrow, and Browser was the only family he had left. Through the hardships of the last two summers, a bond had grown between them that was even stronger than that of blood.

As the staggering party approached, a figure rose from the shadows of the outer wall. Slim and agile, she rushed out toward the leader. For a long moment they clung to each other.

Stone Ghost smiled in the moonlight. His world was still intact. Catkin and Browser were alive.

"Come," Stone Ghost said. "Let's go down and see who is hurt."

White Cone grunted and rose, favoring his left hip. "Do you think they could be carrying Obsidian?"

Stone Ghost hobbled past White Cone and out into the dark hallway. "I pray that's who it is. She should have returned many hands of time ago."

# CHAPTER 37

DUSTY LAY IN his sleeping bag, staring out the window at the moonlit darkness, wondering about Dale. If Ruth Ann had been right—that Dale had taken Dusty into his life because he'd believed Dusty was his son—why hadn't Dale every spoken of it? Obviously, he wouldn't have told Dusty when he was a grief-stricken boy still wounded over his mother's defection and his father's suicide, but what about later? Maybe by putting off the discussion for so many years, it had simply become impossible for Dale.

*And it didn't matter. He was my father, and he knew it.*

Dusty flopped onto his back, trying to find a comfortable position.

As the trailer shook, Maureen called, "Dusty? Are you all right?"

"This is like a bad mescaline hangover."

Her voice returned, "Really? I wouldn't know. Drugs are too scary for me."

"After tonight? Are you kidding? Drugs don't seem scary at all."

To his relief, she chuckled.

He draped an arm across his forehead. "What did you think of sister Yvette? I don't know what to make of her."

"She likes the 'good life,' that's for certain. London, New York, Paris. Her clothes are not made in the good ole USA. They're very expensive."

Dusty turned his head slightly, as though he could see her through the wall. "You mean, like L.L. Bean expensive?"

"No, like Versace or Vuitton expensive."

Dusty's brows raised. The only "labels" he knew were Carhartt, Wrangler, and Levi's.

Dusty tossed to his left side and glared at the wall. "Do you think it's true? That Dale's my father?"

Maureen was silent for a moment. "You don't really look like Samuel Stewart. I don't know. There are ways of finding out. Blood tests. DNA. Things like that."

"It's just so strange. When I was growing up, I used to wish with all my heart that Dale was my father—as though that would have somehow changed our relationship."

"And now?"

"It's going to take some time to come to terms with."

She took a deep breath. "You know, all of this: Dale's death, the investigation, the revelations, the heartache and grief . . . it will pass."

"I know." He paused. "I've been trying to imagine what it must have been like for Dad . . . I mean Sam. There he is, watching Ruth Ann's belly grow, knowing it isn't his, and Dale, his best friend, is slipping away to screw his wife. I feel like I'm in a soap opera."

He heard the cushions on her fold-down bed shift, as though she'd sat up or rolled over. "Well, don't hold it against Dale," she said gently. "The guilt must have nearly killed him. Not only had he betrayed his best friend, he'd also sired a child on the man's wife. Then, after Ruth left, Dale took care of Sam as best he could. Think about how hard it must have been to commit the man he helped destroy. Imagine how he felt after Sam's suicide." Maureen paused. "No wonder he never had a steady woman in his later years."

"Afraid to, eh?"

"Maybe."

Dusty ground his teeth for several seconds, then said, "But it would have helped so much if Dale had just said, 'William, I'm sorry. The man you think was your father couldn't get it up, so I had an affair with your mother. You were the result.' "

The floor creaked as Maureen walked down the hall-way. She appeared in his doorway dressed in a white T-shirt that fell to the middle of her thighs. Her long black braid stood out against that pale background. She leaned against the door frame and said, "Dale was a very good person, Dusty. He loved you. If he hid things from you, it was because, in some way, he thought he was protecting you."

"Protecting me from what? Finding out my mother was a slut? Or that my father was impotent? I might have cared when I was twelve, but when I was thirty, Maureen?"

She folded her arms, as though the night's chill was eating into her flesh. "Personally, I think Dale knew you inside out. Children tend to feel guilty about things that aren't their fault. I suspect he wanted to spare you that."

Dusty sat up and leaned against the cold wall of the trailer. Maureen's eyes glistened in the darkness, watching him.

She said, "Dusty, do you think Samuel Stewart is alive?"

"Good Lord, how do I know?" He lifted a hand uncertainly. "Even if he could have faked his death, why wait until now to deal with Dale? A really pissed husband usually picks up a pistol and settles the dispute immediately."

"Tell me about what happened after your mother left? Did your father hate Dale? Throw him out of the house, shout at him, that kind of thing?"

Dusty shook his head. "No. I don't know how, but they were still friends."

"Do you think he knew that Dale and Ruth Ann were lovers?"

"My guess, and it's only a guess, is that even if he did, he blamed himself. He probably thought his sexual problems had sent her running to Dale."

Maureen came in and sat on the foot of his bed. Her long brown legs shone in the moonlight streaming through the window. She stared at the floor for a time, then turned to Dusty. "May I ask you a tough question?"

"What tough question?"

"At Dale's funeral, Yvette touched Dale's ashes in a very tender way. She ran her fingers across them, looking sad, and then turned and left. It didn't make sense at the time. But, now . . ."

Dusty gave her a quizzical look, then, as her meaning dawned, he blurted, "You mean, you—you think . . ." He searched for the right words.

Maureen nodded. "I'm sure Ruth Ann told Carter Hawsworth the child was his, and he believed it—that's why Yvette carries his name—but I'm not so sure Yvette believes it. She touched Dale's ashes like she was saying good-bye to a father she had never known."

Dusty rubbed a hand over his face, as if to wake himself from a nightmare. "But what could have happened to suddenly make her think Hawsworth was not her father?"

Maureen shrugged. "I assume someone told her."

Dusty's thoughts jumped around, trying to figure out who and, more important, why someone would have done that after all these years. Who would want to stir a thirty-year-old pot?

Dusty said, "I noticed that there was no real love lost between Ruth Ann and Yvette."

"So did I."

Maureen looked out the window and seemed to be examining the moonlight on the cliff. "How old do you think Yvette is?"

"Younger than I am."

"That's what I thought, too." She tilted her head. "After the 10K3 site, I did some research on Ruth Ann. Dale's comments had piqued my interest. There's a sizable body of literature about her, but none of it mentions a daughter. Nor does a daughter appear in the much more limited information on Hawsworth. That's strange, don't you think?"

"Yes."

Maureen grabbed the blanket folded at the foot of Dusty's bed and spread it around her shoulders. "She does look like Dale, don't you think?"

Dusty's brows lowered. "Yes. Especially her eyes."

"If Hawsworth just recently found out he'd raised Dale's child, would he take it out on Dale? Is that motivation for murder?"

"Possibly."

She let out a breath that frosted in the moonlight. "There's another question I'd like to ask you, Dusty, but I've been dreading it."

"Go ahead, it's the perfect night for awful things. What do you want to know?"

She turned and moonlight slivered her face. Her aquiline features—the straight nose, full lips, and dark eyes—gleamed an eerie white. "Dusty, please answer me honestly. Are you *certain* that Dale never had a relationship with Sylvia?"

Dusty's hands turned to fists as he felt his anger rising—and wondered why the very idea coaxed such rage from his heart. "Dale knew about Sylvia's childhood, Maureen. He would never have risked hurting her. I *am* certain of that."

"When Sylvia opened Dale's journal and asked about 'Melissa,' your eyes immediately went to the passage. Who was she, Dusty?"

He ran a hand through his blond hair. "A graduate student he was having an affair with. Dale knew he had to end it, but she had apparently asked him to be on her dissertation committee. He was trying to figure out whether or not he could stand being close to her for another two years."

Maureen's gaze drifted over the bedroom while she absorbed that. "By now, Nichols knows that Dale did have affairs with students. He will be watching Sylvia like a hawk."

"I know."

"Is that what the murderer wanted us to find in the diary? Or is there something else there that only you would understand?"

"I've been waiting for Nichols to return—"

"I don't think he's going to, Dusty. Not until this is over."

Dusty nodded and let his chin rest on his chest while he waded through the morass his insides had become. "Well, he can't trust me. I guess I understand that."

She stood up, pulled the blanket from her shoulders, and spread it over the foot of his bed again. "I think it's time we both got some sleep. Tomorrow is going to be another long day. Good night."

"Good night, Maureen."

She disappeared down the hallway, and he heard her bed groan as she sat down on the old foldout.

But he didn't close his eyes. He stared out the window at the cliff and the stars that gleamed above the rim, and wondered why he had reacted so emotionally to her question about Sylvia. It was as though, just by asking, she had soiled Dale's integrity.

*Which is ridiculous, she did no such thing.*

But somewhere deep inside him, he'd felt she had, and he'd defended Dale. Would he always feel compelled to do that?

Probably.

For despite all the things he had learned about Dale, he could not believe Dale would do anything to deliberately hurt another human being—and certainly not for his own gain. Dale did not use people. Not even Ruth Ann's stories would change Dusty's mind about that. Dale was a decent human being. Period.

Or was it just that Dale had been decent to Dusty?

Did one person ever really know what another person was capable of?

His thoughts returned to Sylvia, and Rupert's words: *"A witch hides by misdirection."* Dusty knew the stories. A really good witch, one filled with power and evil, could stand right beside you, and you'd never know.

Sylvia wouldn't have had any trouble carrying Dale's weight from Casa Rinconada up to Bc60. She was studying witchcraft, for God's sake! And if that deep-seated terror that lived inside her had sneaked out . . .

Dusty bit his lip. *Yes*, he admitted to himself, *Sylvia could kill someone if they hurt her badly enough.*

But then, so could he.

THE FIRE IN the cracked gray bowl had burned down to a red glow. Matron Blue Corn pulled again at the tight cords binding her wrists. Catkin hadn't shown either respect or sympathy when she'd knotted them.

Blue Corn winced as she tried to shift and the pain shot up her leg. The way they'd bound her ankles and run a cord up to the wrists left her in excruciating agony.

"My warriors will be back to rescue us," Horned Ram promised from across the room. He, too, looked like a macaw bound for travel. When traders brought the brightly plumed birds north, they often tied them up into bundles to keep from being bitten and scratched.

"You didn't acquit yourself well. It wouldn't surprise me if they didn't set you free just for the privilege of knocking your brains out of that worthless head of yours."

A smile displaced the pain on Horned Ram's frog face. "My people know my value. And it isn't as a corpse laid out on the ground after some fight."

She grunted, wondering what was happening, how it all could have gone so wrong so quickly. Gods, she'd been sitting there like a wounded goose when they had surrounded her. She had looked up through tear-blurred eyes to see Deputy Catkin and three armed Fire Dogs surrounding her.

She had opened her mouth to scream and stared down an arrow shaft pulled back to its head. Catkin's soft "I wouldn't do that" had carried more threat than a vile shout.

With nothing but death as her lot should she resist, she had meekly let them drag her to her feet, bind her hands and feet, and stuff a rag cut from Black Stalk's bloody garments into her mouth.

Only after darkness masked their movements did they ease her down the stairway, and that process had left her blind with terror. In the charcoal blackness, a misstep would have meant a fall and death.

They had been at the bottom when Horned Ram had run straight into their arms. In his fear and excitement, he just assumed they were allies, crying out, "Quick. The fighting is that way. They are White Moccasins! First People! Hurry so you don't miss the opportunity to kill some!"

The next sound had been Catkin's war club breaking his shoulder.

The journey to Kettle Town had been punctuated by the distant sounds of fighting, the faint clacking of wood, the screams and angry cries.

"What happened out there?" She shook her head.

"They'll be coming for us." Horned Ram winced as he tried to shift. "Gods, this hurts. I'm too old for this."

"Is that why you ran?"

"I was coming for reinforcements."

"All of our unwounded warriors were committed." Blue Corn stared her hatred at him.

"You couldn't tell friend from enemy out there. It was the middle of the night." He moved and his broken shoulder bones grated. Horned Ram shuddered and went white. "It will take them a while. They'll return to Center Place. When they don't find us, or the wounded tell them we didn't come back, they'll come here."

"I wouldn't count on that." Browser stepped into the room. Behind him came a throng of Mogollon warriors followed by Jackrabbit and Catkin. The first thing the deputy did was step over, expression serious, to check Blue Corn's bonds. She tugged them to make sure of their strength.

"What happened?" Blue Corn snapped. She might

be trussed up like a captive bird, but by the Blessed Flute Player, she was still a Matron. Then she saw Rain Crow, his limp and blood-soaked body supported by two Fire Dogs. They laid him carefully by the heating bowl while others ripped apart another of the willow mats and began feeding sticks to the embers.

As the flames leapt up, Blue Corn caught glimpses of Rain Crow. His head looked shiny from the blood in his hair. It had dried into cracklike patterns on his face.

Browser crouched before her. An absent part of her realized that his hands weren't even blood-smeared.

"Matron? They are dead."

"Who won? The White Moccasins?"

Browser's eyes dropped. "No one, except perhaps Shadow Woman. She killed the last two of your warriors."

"But there should still be wounded! Not everyone—"

*"Yes, everyone,"* Browser said, and his voice sounded deeply weary. He took a breath. "Matron, why are you here? Why are you placing yourself at risk?"

She glared up at him. "You, or your friends, killed my warrior. You spat upon my hospitality."

"We killed no one," Stone Ghost said as he hobbled into the room, supporting himself with a juniper walking stick. The dark wells of his shining eyes reflected the firelight.

"Liar! My warriors will be here s-soon!" Horned Ram sputtered. "They'll see what you've done to me. How you've treated me, and they'll take their revenge!"

Browser's response came so softly Blue Corn almost couldn't hear it. "They're dead, Elder. All of them. Dead."

Blue Corn blinked, trying to understand. "Killed by White Moccasins? They're real?"

Browser nodded and let out a tired breath. "You asked for proof once. Upset that I had no dead White

Moccasins to show you. Now I have enough bodies to glut an army of crows. But, Matron, I don't have the will to show them off."

She watched, hearing the truth in his weary voice. The reality left her too stunned to speak as Browser turned to Stone Ghost. The elder knelt beside Rain Crow, examining his wounds.

"How is he?" Browser asked.

Stone Ghost gently felt the bloody matted hair on Rain Crow's head. "The war club crushed a small part of his skull. From the hair that's torn off, I'd say it was a glancing blow." Stone Ghost turned Rain Crow's head and peered into his eyes. "But his pupils are two different sizes. His brain is swelling with evil Spirits. They'll be feeding for days. If he lives through the next quarter moon, his souls might come back."

"He's tough." Blue Corn looked up at Browser. "What are your plans for me, War Chief?"

Browser rose and stared at Horned Ram. The old man squirmed, testing his bonds. "You allied yourself with those who stir hatred, Matron, and look what has become of it." He turned back to Blue Corn. "If you give me your oath that you will not retaliate against me or the Katsinas' People, I will release you. We are not your enemies. We never have been."

"I still have wounded up at Center Place."

Browser nodded. "I will send someone for them at first light. I will not risk my people at night with Shadow prowling around."

"*Your* people?" She arched an ironic eyebrow. "I mostly see Fire Dogs here."

"We are Katsinas' People, Matron. All of us."

She narrowed an eye, taking his measure, seeing the terrible fatigue that weighed his souls. "Come, Browser, do you really believe in the katsinas?"

He smiled. "There is only one thing I am certain of, Matron. If we don't stop killing each other, it won't matter who is right. In the end, we will all be dead."

He gestured toward the south. "The only one left from tonight's battle is a witch. I greatly fear that when all of this fighting is done, witches will be the only survivors."

"The Katsina religion is witchery!" Horned Ram cried. "You are all a vile pollution in the sight of the gods. They will destroy you, you and your—"

"Cut me loose, Browser," Blue Corn interrupted, and held out her hands. "I don't know where we will go or what we will do, but I will not fight you." She glanced at Rain Crow. "If for no other reason than you brought my War Chief back to me."

He pulled the hafted chert knife from his belt and sawed through the cord that bound her ankles and wrists.

As he stood, he looked at the warriors standing around the room and said, "I'll take the first watch."

"No, War Chief," a young Mogollon warrior said, and stepped forward, chest out, eyes level. "Jackrabbit and I will take the watch. Sleep soundly, War Chief, and know that we are alert and watchful."

The Fire Dogs were on their feet, lithe and deadly, hands on their weapons. Blue Corn wouldn't have believed it had she not seen it with her own eyes. Flute Player take her, they worshiped him.

"Shadow is out there," Catkin said. "Never forget that."

Yucca Whip nodded. "Yes, Catkin."

Blue Corn rubbed her wrists, amazed as Catkin led Browser from the room. Horned Ram, still trussed, watched them go, his eyes filled with hatred.

# CHAPTER 38

DUSTY AWAKENED AT the sound of Maureen's voice: "Good morning, Yvette. Care for coffee?"

"Yes! Smashing!" the cultured English voice responded as the trailer rocked with her entry. "I feel bloody beastly! I swear, I'm half frozen and every joint in my body is screaming."

Dusty sat up, yawned, and reached for his jeans. The chill of the morning left his breath frosty in the air. He pulled on a sweatshirt and his boots, stood and studied himself in the mirror. His blond hair stood out at odd angles, and his puffy eyes made it look like he hadn't slept all night, which he hadn't.

He combed his hair with his fingers and headed down the hallway.

"Good morning," Maureen said. She stood at the kitchen stove with a spatula in her hand, turning over eggs and chilis.

Dusty stopped very close behind her and said, "Sorry about last night. I didn't mean to sound—"

"You didn't," she said, and smiled. She wore a blue turtleneck underneath an oversized gray sweatshirt. Her freshly washed and braided hair was still damp and smelled of shampoo. She pointed to the coffeepot. "Have a cup. You'll feel better."

He poured a cup of coffee and stepped over to the table. "Good morning, Sis," he said as he slid into the booth opposite her.

In the morning light, Yvette Hawsworth was an attractive woman, and yes, he could see Dale in her long face, thin nose, and most of all in her eyes. The rest of her, the ash-blond hair, the fine bones, all seemed to be Ruth Ann.

"Ever slept in a truck before?" He smiled, trying to set her at ease.

"No, and I must say, it's a bit of an experience." Her laugh betrayed a sudden insecurity. "But for your blankets, I'm quite sure I would have died."

"You wouldn't have. If it gets too bad you can always turn on the engine and pray you don't asphyxiate before dawn." He took a sip of the coffee and let the rich dark brew soothe him. "I was born in a truck. At the side of the highway south of Tuba City."

She lifted a slim eyebrow, as if trying to determine how much of what he was telling her was bullshit.

He wrapped his fingers around his coffee cup. "Is this as much of a shock to you as it is to me?"

She laughed. "You have no idea. Tell me . . . William? Is that what I should call you?"

"The only person on earth who called me that was Dale. When Ruth Ann does, it makes my nerves grate."

"Dusty?" She placed her palms together in a prim gesture, her eyes searching his. "Did you send me that fax?"

He slowly lowered his cup to the table. He could hear the eggs sizzling in the pan in the kitchen. "What fax?"

"Two weeks ago. The fax telling me that my life was a lie."

He shook his head. "Yvette, until you walked in here last night, I didn't even know you existed."

"No one did," Maureen said as she separated three paper plates. "I take it you're eating with us? There's no other breakfast out here. The closest source of food is the cold locker at the gas station in Crownpoint." She shot a scathing look at Dusty. "And believe me, you don't want to try it."

"I told you," Dusty protested, "I didn't know you then."

"Yeah sure, eh?" Maureen shook the spatula at him. "The enchiladas at the Pink Adobe almost, I said *almost*, make up for that sandwich."

"I feel rather a fool," Yvette said, shifting nervously in the booth. "I followed Mum until she took off on that dirt track. I was just bloody determined to see where she'd got off to, what great secret was hidden out here. A number of times, I thought I'd lost her. It's a good thing I rented that bush vehicle."

"Bush vehicle?" Dusty asked. "Where'd you learn to call a Jeep that?"

"On safari," she told him, and shook hair out of her eyes.

"Hawsworth took you on safari?"

"Oh, God nó." She seemed uncomfortable. "I went to Africa while Carter was working there. But mostly I went with my first husband."

"First?" Dusty asked. "How many have you had?"

"Three. Currently I'm between."

Dusty silently sized her up again. She didn't take after her mother, did she?

"You went on safari and you didn't have any idea about backcountry?" Maureen asked.

"Well, you see, Africa isn't like this, at least not the places I went. People imagine tents and *Out of Africa*, but it's really quite civilized. The lodges have running water and gourmet food."

Maureen scooped eggs onto the paper plates, and brought two to the table, along with forks wrapped in napkins. She set one plate in front of Yvette and the other in front of Dusty. The glorious aroma of cheddar and chilis wafted up to Dusty.

Maureen went back for her plate and said, "You're a real mystery woman. Your name doesn't appear in any of the biographical material about Ruth Ann Sullivan or Carter Hawsworth."

Yvette wet her lips. "No, they were rather Machiavellian about that, weren't they? Believe me, growing up between them wasn't any picnic. I raised myself, bouncing from boarding school to boarding school." She lifted her eyes. "Tell me, did Dale Robertson . . . did he have any idea that I existed?"

Dusty shook his head and toyed with his cup, moving it around the table, remembering what Maureen had said last night. "And he would have told me, Yvette. Why do you ask?"

"Well, I was born in Geneva, Switzerland, in '70. Isn't that a rip? I have dual citizenship, Swiss and British. Right off I was bundled away into a facility while they ran off to the Pacific. Auntie Vi did most of my raising when I wasn't in school."

"Is that why you came here? To find Dale?" Dusty asked as he took his fork from his rolled napkin.

"The fax came two weeks ago. When Mum refused to talk about it, it made me suspicious. Not that we ever talked, but this was worse. She had never been part of my life, and after she and Carter split, he hadn't much of a care for me either." She frowned as she sipped her coffee. "Then a couple of days later a letter arrived with an old newspaper clipping from an Albuquerque paper. There was a picture of Mum, not much more than a girl, and Dale Robertson. They were at an archaeological dig. A note penciled at the bottom read: *'Meet your real father.'* "

Dusty guessed, "Could Hawsworth have sent it?"

Yvette shrugged. "I called Auntie Vi for Carter's address. My father and I hadn't been in touch in years. We don't share much in common, you see. Imagine my surprise when I discovered he was in Taos." She pronounced it Tay-os.

"So, what did he say?" Dusty ate a mouthful of *huevos rancheros* and gave Maureen a thumbs-up sign.

She smiled and slid into the booth beside him with her plate and coffee cup in hand.

"He told me flat out that it was ludicrous, that of course he was my father, but after he said it, he hesitated for a long time, and finally said he'd call me back."

"Did he?"

"No, it was Mum who rang me up, asking where I might have gotten the bright idea that Carter wasn't my father. I told her about the fax and the news article. She was quiet for a moment, and then asked if Carter had returned my call. I told her no."

"Did you talk to Dale?" Maureen asked, and dipped up a forkful of eggs.

She nodded. "I got his answering machine. At the beep I couldn't say anything. Bloody hell, what does one say? 'Hello, are you my father?' "

Dusty sipped his coffee and gave her an askance look. "A newspaper article and a fax don't mean he was your father, Yvette. It just means someone wanted you to think he was."

"Yes, I—I know." She looked at him soberly. "But the letter I received from Carter, FedEx, the following day, informed me most tersely that to his mortification, I was *not* his daughter. Apparently he had received a fax asking how I might have blood type B when Mum and he were both type O."

Maureen's fork hovered over her plate. Her eyes narrowed as she looked at Yvette. "Dale was AB." She turned to Dusty. "And you're type B."

Dusty took another bite of breakfast and around a mouthful said, "Yeah, so?"

"If Ruth Ann and Carter are both type O, they can't have a child who is either type A or B." She scowled at her eggs. "You wouldn't possibly have any idea of Samuel's blood type, would you?"

Dusty blinked. "I'm not sure I ever knew his blood type."

"Then Dusty and I share the same blood?" Yvette looked surprised.

"It's an exclusionary test," Maureen told her. "It only means that if you are type B, Carter Hawsworth cannot be your father, eh? Not if he's an O."

"But Mum is an O."

"Yes, and an O crossed with another O results in type O blood in one hundred percent of the offspring. If Ruth Ann is an O and Dale was an AB, then fifty percent of their children would have been type A and fifty percent would have been type B." She used her fork to point first at Dusty, then at Yvette.

Yvette frowned. "Mum told me she left the U.S. six months before I was born."

Maureen looked at Dusty. "Dale told me that Carter and Ruth Ann were together for two weeks before she left. Does that ring true?"

Dusty nodded. "You thinking what I'm thinking?"

Maureen answered, "It looks like she was pregnant again with Dale's baby, couldn't stand Sam's guilt, and—"

Dusty finished, "Along came Hawsworth, and she was on him like a leech."

Yvette seemed to be stunned by the loathing in Dusty's voice. Her shoulders hunched forward. "But what of Dale Robertson? He just bred Mum like a prize mare, and sod the poor bloke stuck with the child?"

Dusty ate the last of his eggs, wiped his mouth with his napkin, and leaned back. "If he'd known about you, Yvette, he would have done something, and when he did, it would have been classy, up front, and honest. Just like he did with me." Dusty tossed his napkin on the table. "I don't know what our mother or Carter have told you, but you could do a hell of a lot worse than having Dale Robertson as a father."

Maureen's dark eyes fixed on the window, but she didn't seem to be looking at anything outside. She murmured, "Why bring the children into it? Why does the murderer need you and Yvette here?"

Dusty replied, "I didn't get any faxes."

"No," Maureen said, and slowly turned to face him. "He expected you to be here."

*I STARE AT her in wonder. Raising my head, I sniff cautiously, drawing in her scent. She and I are so much the same—and so very different. I search for the odor. Has she been with him? Is he hers now? But my nostrils fail to detect the musk that lingers on a woman after she's coupled with a man.*

*Sister looks at me, distress in her large dark eyes. She has never had my strength. "He is coming for you, Shadow. For you and Father."*

*"Of course he is," I reply. "I am the Summoning God. They all come to me. Some sooner than others." I place a hand to my belly, aware of the glow within. Father's power never ceases to amaze me. Where others leave only the faded memory of pleasure, I am his fertile soil.*

*"Shadow," she says, looking anxiously across the kiva to where Father lays moaning in his blankets, "you have no need of me here."*

*I throw my head back and laugh. Piper lies frozen, her breath-heart soul paralyzed in the air above her. What did Father do to her this time? How did he witch her so completely. Was it the turquoise necklace? When, and where, had she gotten that? Is Piper truly so weak? I expected more from her.*

*"Ah, Sister, I may have great need of you. Tell me, in what should I place more value? In your heart, or your body?"*

*Her face has become a pale mask.*

*"Tell me of Browser."*

*"I think he knows where you are. Were I you, I would leave, Sister. Now, while you can."*

"I see."

"Don't take him lightly."

"Browser?" I smile, remembering the times I have tempted him, fondled him, seen the battle in his eyes as his heart struggled with his manhood. Yes, he desires me. All I need is a little time. "He's the most dangerous man I know, Sister."

"You continue to overestimate him. You should have seen him, worry dripping from his skin like sweat. The desperation in his eyes was overpowering when he asked me to help him."

I watch her, and she squirms, unable to meet my eyes. She is smart not to challenge my stare. I would reel her breath-heart soul out of her the way a hunter does a yucca cord string from a rabbit hole. Instead her eyes are fixed on the fragments of bone littering the kiva. She is particularly fascinated by a section of shinbone. It gleams like shell, stark against the ash-stained earthen floor.

"His name was Carved Splinter," I tell her, gesturing at the length of broken bone. "I sucked the marrow from it for supper last night."

She swallows hard, the color draining from her face.

"He was a Fire Dog. Not a real human like you and me, Sister."

"I know . . ."

She is so weak. I hide my anger, saying, "I am disappointed with you, Sister. But for you, Bear Lance and so many others would still be alive. Perhaps you don't understand, living as you do in the midst of Made People, but we are fewer as a result of your actions last night."

She hears the wrath throttled deep in my throat. She glances at the bloody cloth, heavy with meat where it hangs from one of the pilasters. I watch the shiver pass through her soft flesh. It pleases me. I know what she has been trying to do. But for my appetite, I would seek to take her place. It would not be such a bad life,

*sharing Browser's bed, being his wife. But it is only
fantasy. The Blue God has other plans for me.*

"How will you make this thing you have done right,
Sister?" *I tap my chin with a long finger, and hide a
smile as her gaze slides again to Father where he lies
dying.*

"He wanted your heart from the very beginning, Obsidian. Yours or Piper's. But I had such high hopes for
Piper." *I glance at my daughter again, seeing her
empty eyes, and wonder if indeed, I shouldn't cut her
chest open.*

*My sister swallows as if her throat is too tight.* "I
have something better to offer you, Shadow. If you will
let me speak with Old Pigeontail, I'm sure that I—I
can arrange—"

"Indeed?" *She cannot see the smile that lights my
breath-heart soul.* "You still amaze me, Sister."

CATKIN SIGHED AS she gazed at the morning light
that cast a glow into their room. A warming bowl
rested an arm's length from their bed, the coals cold
and gray.

Browser made one of those male sounds of inde-
scribable contentment and hugged her.

Through the window, he could see the half-moon-
shaped bulk of Talon Town. He stared at it, wondering
at the twists and turns of life.

It had started on the morning of his dead son's funeral, one sun cycle ago, with the discovery of a desecrated grave, with the wounding of his lover,
Hophorn, and his wife's disappearance. It wasn't until
now that he could understand that this cycle had begun
then, on that cold and blustery morning. One after another, each event had unfolded to bring him, the Kat-

sinas' People, and his Mogollon allies to this place at this time. It had brought him here, with Catkin, in love, and craving a future that he could just barely feel with the fingertips of his breath-heart soul.

But it would cost something. What? The gods never granted happiness without a price. As his ancestor, Poor Singer, had known, there was always a payment to be made.

He propped himself on one elbow and gazed down at Catkin with thoughtful eyes. At the feel of the cool air on her sweat-damp chest, she tugged up the blanket, and smiled.

His hand crept to her breast. She slipped one of her long legs over his. "Are you all right?"

He smiled. "I have finally made peace with life. I understand now."

"Understand what?" She toyed with his short-cropped hair.

"That the most important thing isn't clan, or honor, or status, or wealth, or any of the things our people believe. The only things that truly matter are having a full stomach, a soft warm wife, and the knowledge that you'll see the sunset." He tipped his round face and sunlight flashed through his thick black brows. "Catkin, when we are finished here, I want to go south."

She studied the longing in his eyes. "Why south? What's in the south?"

"It's far from the First People's kivas and towns. I'm thinking of the mountains. Maybe a green valley halfway between the Fire Dogs and the Hohokam. A place where a man and woman can build a little house, grow some corn, and love each other."

"Just one soft woman?"

He smoothed a hand over her hair. "I'm not fool enough to put you and Obsidian under the same roof. You'd kill her."

She stared at him with glistening eyes. "You are not

a wise man, Browser, discussing a beautiful woman immediately after sharing my bed."

He studied her with genuine amusement. "I don't love her. I love you." The blanket fell from his muscular brown shoulders, and he tugged it up again. "Do you realize that last night's battle was a miracle?"

"I do."

"A War Chief lives all his life dreaming of conducting a fight like that. We tricked two war parties into fighting each other. We didn't take a single loss. No one was even wounded. We destroyed two enemies and didn't suffer a scratch in the process." His smile turned sad.

"Then why are you sad?" She took his hand and held it to her heart. "You were brilliant. You should be proud."

"I'm more proud of sharing your blankets than of that fight last night. After my wife . . ." Pain tensed his expression. "I wasn't sure I would ever be able to share a woman's blankets again."

Catkin slipped her arms around him and pressed her naked body against his one more time. "My blankets are always open to you."

"And mine to you."

They held each other until Father Sun's light filled the room and their blankets became too hot.

As he rose and reached for his war shirt, Browser gazed out the window. Some of his warriors had gathered on the first-story roof, pointing.

Browser looked out, seeing the lone figure with two dogs trotting stolidly toward Kettle Town. "Old Pigeontail is coming. He seems to be in a hurry."

"Anyone with him?"

"No. Just him. But somehow, I don't think we can take any comfort from that."

# CHAPTER 39

MAUREEN LOOKED OUT the window of the Bronco as Dusty drove past the interpretive signs for Pueblo Bonito and Pueblo del Arroyo and then crossed the bridge over Chaco Wash. In the mirror he could see Yvette's rental Jeep following him.

"Why do you think she wants to see the place Dale died?" Maureen asked.

"She thinks he was her father. That's enough of a reason," Dusty said, and squinted at the road, wondering just where Maggie had seen the owl. The Casa Rinconada parking lot was just ahead, it had to be somewhere in here.

Maureen said, "Have you thought about the actual mechanics of the murder?"

"What do you mean?"

"I mean Ruth Ann couldn't have killed and buried Dale by herself. How would she have gotten his body out of the great kiva and up the hill to the place where he was buried? She doesn't look strong enough."

Dusty parked the Bronco and gazed up the ridge to where Michail, Sylvia, and two FBI men peeled away the black plastic that had covered the site. Yvette pulled in beside them. "I hadn't thought of that."

They got out of the Bronco and met Yvette on the trail. As they walked, Dusty gestured to the great kiva. "Dale was actually killed at the ceremonial chamber in front of us, but he was buried up there where you see the people standing. "Do you think Ruth Ann could have carried a one-hundred-forty-pound body up that slope?"

Yvette's eyes widened. "Perhaps. She goes to the club every week. She used to run in marathons. Finished respectably at Boston a couple of years ago. I wouldn't have known, but Collins was in New York on business."

Dusty pulled his collar up against the wind. "Who's Collins?"

"My third husband. He faxed me the sports page of the *Boston Globe*. It said: 'World-famous anthropologist to run Boston Marathon.' I came to the States straightaway. I wanted to see her."

The wind whistled up the slope and ate into Dusty's exposed face. "Did she know you were coming?"

"Yes, I called first, but it was a terrible trip. The traffic was beastly; they shut down the city for the Marathon, you know. I got to her home just after Mum did, she was still hot and sweaty, wearing her track suit. It didn't go well. I left twenty minutes later."

Dusty decided not to ask what that meant.

"What happened with Collins?" Maureen asked.

"He died," Yvette said evenly. "Killed on the motorway. He crashed his Jaguar." She pronounced it Jagu-waar.

Maureen's expression went from evaluative to concerned in a heartbeat. "How are you doing?"

Yvette replied cautiously, "I'm whole, actually. Life goes on."

In the silence that followed, Dusty led the way past the Tseh So ruins and walked to Casa Rinconada.

He stood at the edge of the kiva, staring down into the sunlit depths. The place had changed. He would never come here again without wondering if Dale's screams had echoed from the cold stone walls.

"You can see some of the sand," he said. "We think it was a sand painting. Maybe used by Kwewur to trap Dale's soul."

Dusty glanced at her. She looked a lot like him. She had his jaw, and he could see his nose on her, scaled down, more feminine. The biggest difference in their faces was her thoughtful brown eyes. Dale's eyes.

"All that was left was the blood?" she asked in a small voice.

"That and a note. The FBI has it. Apparently it was sent to Dale to get him to come here on Halloween night. After the witch killed him and mutilated him"—it surprised him how easily he could say that now—"he carried Dale up there." He pointed to the excavation on the ridge to their south and headed in that direction.

She followed him up the slope, walking carefully in her funky black suede boots with their high heels. She stopped beside him at the police tape.

"Michall, Sylvia," Dusty called, "this is Yvette Hawsworth."

Michall climbed out of the chest-deep kiva and shook hands. Sylvia just leaned on her shovel and waved.

Rick and Bill perked up at the Hawsworth name. They walked around the kiva and eyed her carefully.

"Does Agent Nichols know you're here?" Bill asked after introductions.

"He's scheduled to talk to her later," Dusty said, preempting anything unpleasant. To his relief, Yvette didn't fumble it. She just nodded.

"This is where they found Dale." Dusty pointed. "Buried there. So we're digging. Trying to find out why the killer chose this spot."

"Any clues yet?" she asked.

"Talk to Michall. She's the Principal Investigator here." He stepped around to study the profile where the pit transected the kiva. "Hey, what's that discoloration?"

"The coyote hole where the site was potted." Michall hopped lithely back into the pit and pulled a trowel from her back pocket. Using the point she outlined the intrusive dirt that funneled down and disappeared into the pit floor. "It's been a while, Dusty. But not that long ago."

"How do you know that, Professor Jefferson?"

She walked to the side of the kiva and reached into a brown paper sack to pull out a rusty beer can. "Coors," she said. "Steel. And look at the top." She turned it to expose the characteristic triangular punctures made before pop-tops.

"Late fifties through the sixties," Dusty said.

"Hey, you're good at this. Have you ever thought of doing it for a living?" Sylvia asked.

"Careful," he said. "Your next excavation is going to be a cat box."

Sylvia grinned and used her shovel to start chunking out the next twenty-centimeter level. "I once knew a guy who found a Folsom point in a cat box," she said. "Course it had fallen out of his shirt pocket when he bent over to . . . Whoa!" She laid her shovel to the side and got down on her hands and knees. "We got bone here, boss."

Maureen leaned as far over the police tape as she thought she could get away with, and called, "What kind of bone?"

"Hold on." Sylvia brushed sand from a brown sliver. A white gash marked where the shovel had cut it.

The FBI guys were on her like vultures, staring over her shoulder as Michall bent down to look.

Dusty knotted his fists. He couldn't see anything except a cluster of backs.

"Washais?" Sylvia called. "I think we need you in here."

"Wait a minute." Bill stood up, one hand out. "She's not cleared."

"Right," Sylvia said. "Can you tell me what this is? You've been doing great for a cop. You've actually proved you could learn how to dig like an undergraduate. You haven't torn out the strings, and you haven't collapsed the pit walls. Now, we can shut this down for a week while you guys get an ID, or Washais can tell us in five seconds. Which is it?"

Rick, his dark blue FBI jacket mottled with dust and smeared with dirt, took the bone from Sylvia and studied it for a moment. Then he looked up at Maureen. "Dr. Cole, I'm only asking for an opinion. I'll have this analyzed later to ID it for certain. Do you think you could—"

Maureen was under the tape like a hound after a rabbit. She took the bone from his hand and turned it over and over again.

Yvette shook her head. "My mum did this once upon a time? Mum, who wouldn't take a chance on opening a car's boot for fear of cracking a nail?"

"Well, if it's any consolation, she told me she hated archaeology. The Zuni used to call her The-Woman-With-No-Eyes because she never looked at them, she just looked at her papers," Dusty said. "But that was before she got famous. She wasn't—"

"Human," Maureen said. "What we have here is about fifteen centimeters of the distal portion of the tibia—the shinbone—right side. Probably male from the robusticity of the bone. The spiral fracture was perimortal. It occurred around the time of death." She lifted the fragment to the gray light filtering through the cloudy sky. "I can't tell you here, but from the looks of it, I'd say this was butchered."

"Butchered?" Rick asked. "You mean they cut him apart?"

"Probably," Maureen said.

"Is it prehistoric?" Rick asked. "Or is this one of our unsub's previous victims?"

"Don't be a dork," Sylvia said, leaning on her shovel handle. "Look at it, Rick."

Rick took the bone, slightly cowed by Maureen's

amused expression. He studied it for a moment and said, "Prehistoric, right?"

"Why?" Michall asked. Her red hair blowing about her face in the wind.

"Because if it was modern, you wouldn't be jacking me around like this."

"That's a smart cop." Sylvia nodded, dug another shovelful, and artfully tossed it up into Michall's screen.

"Seriously," Michall responded, "why's it prehistoric?"

Rick scowled as he studied the bone. "Uh, the discoloration?"

"Right." Maureen pointed to the patterns on the dirt. "And what's this?"

"It looks like marks left by roots," Rick guessed.

"Very good, Rick. Acids in roots etch the bone's surface. It takes time. If this was a modern forensic specimen, the roots wouldn't have had time to create this effect on the bone's cortex."

"Hey! Wait a minute," Dusty called. "What's the provenience on that tibia?"

"Pot hole backfill," Sylvia called back. "Disturbed. It's out of context."

"Damn," Dusty said.

"What's that mean?" Yvette asked.

"It's been moved. Probably dug out when the site was potted in the sixties and then shoveled back in when the hole was backfilled." He paused, frowning. "Hey, Michall? You've read all the Parking Service's notes on this site. Did they ever mention backfilling this?"

She looked up from the screen where she was processing the dirt Sylvia had tossed her. "No, Dusty. It's just recorded with its original Bc number."

Dusty shook his head. "That can't be right."

"Why not?" Yvette was watching him with Dale's eyes. It was almost spooky.

"The beer can. The lack of documentation of the backfill, a chunk of human bone that big. It's not the sort of stuff the Chaco Rangers would throw back in a hole." He looked out at the canyon before him. "In the sixties? This isn't the kind of place pot hunters would hit. It's open. You can see this ridge from the entire west end of the loop road."

"Unless it was done at night," Maureen said as she walked up with the precious tibia fragment in her hand. "Maybe it was a summer temp working on his own after hours?"

"Yeah, maybe. It's certainly happened before." Dusty frowned down at the tibial shaft. "You think it was butchered?"

She used a fingernail to trace the thin line incised in the dirt-encrusted bone. "I need to clean it and look at it under the microscope, but yes, I'd say that cut mark was made when someone disarticulated the foot."

"Cannibalism or disarticulation for secondary burial?" Dusty asked.

"If they cut the body apart to make it easier to carry to another place for burial"—Maureen's dark eyes challenged—"how do you explain the spiral fracture?"

"What about the spiral fracture?" Dusty crossed his arm. "The tibia might have gotten broken when the pot hunter dug up the site."

Yvette looked over Dusty's shoulder as Maureen pointed to the dimple where the bone was broken. "Remember? The fracture was perimortal? That dimple marks the hammer impact right there." She turned it over. "And if this was cleaned, we'd see scrubbing from the anvil right here."

"Pueblo Animas all over." Dusty took a deep breath. He turned. "Sylvia?"

"Yo, Boss Man." She looked up.

"When you get to the kiva roof, keep a sharp eye out. I'm betting you a case of Coors we're going to cut

the same McElmo ceramics that we did at 10K3 and
PA. You get my drift?"

Sylvia stopped her shoveling. The wind whipped her
brown hair around her freckled face. "Yeah, Dusty, I
got you."

"She didn't sound happy," Yvette noted. "What did
you mean?"

Dusty shoved his hands into his pocket. "It's hard to
explain unless you—"

"Got charcoal!" Sylvia sang out and knelt in the pit.
"We're coming down on a burned layer."

"Surprise, surprise," Dusty whispered, remembering
the charred ruins and burned bodies at Pueblo Animas.

BROWSER AND STONE Ghost stood with Old
Pigeontail in the room where Horned Ram lay bound.
The Red Rock elder had turned a shade of gray, and
his shoulder, swollen and bruised, looked terrible. Blue
Corn knelt at his side, mopping his face with a damp
cloth.

Pigeontail's faded red cloak swayed around his tall
body as he walked over to Horned Ram to examine his
injuries. His tawny eyes gleamed in his long face.

"If you do not cut his bonds soon," Pigeontail said,
"he will lose this arm. It's already turning purple." He
bent down and gestured to Horned Ram's bad shoulder.

Browser rested his right fist on the hilt of his belted
war club. Casually, he said, "I plan on freeing him
before that happens."

But only just before. Every time he looked at the old
man, anger stung his veins.

Pigeontail straightened up and gave Browser a worried look. "I came to talk with you about Obsidian."

"What about her?"

Stone Ghost gripped Browser's forearm. "I didn't tell you last night," he said softly, "because I thought she still might return, and you needed your sleep desperately, but she is gone."

"Gone?" Browser started. "You mean she never came back?"

Stone Ghost nodded, and his wispy white hair caught the morning sunlight. "Since the battle went as you'd planned, I assumed she had succeeded in luring the White Moccasins down the staircase, but something must have happened after that."

Pigeontail took a deep breath and said, "I don't normally bend my rules, War Chief."

"But you are going to this time," Browser replied stiffly, and his fingers tightened around his club. "If you know something, you had best tell me. *Now.*"

Pigeontail held out both hands in a gesture of surrender. "That's why I came. To tell you. Obsidian apparently climbed down the staircase after the fight, and Shadow captured her when she started across the battleground."

DUSTY SAT ON the Bronco's tailgate, his legs swinging. He, Maureen, and Yvette were lunching on cold enchiladas. Two vehicles down, Michall, Sylvia, and the FBI guys sat in Michall's blue Durango and worked on sandwiches and cans of pop. He looked at Maureen, trying to read the thoughtful expression on her face. She kept glancing curiously at him, probing for his response to the morning's findings. The odd one out, Yvette, stood to one side, chewing thoughtfully on her enchilada. She used copious amounts of Coke to soften the impact of the spices. Evidently jalapeños weren't common fare in London.

"Beer and bones," Yvette said, a perplexed look on her face. "It's just so blinking peculiar." Her gaze took in the canyon, tracing the cold sandstone walls. "All of this is. It's hard to believe that people lived here, let alone that they still do."

"You're just not used to it," Maureen said. "I grew up in Ontario, in the forests. My country is cool and green and I live on one of the largest lakes in the world. The first time I stepped off an airplane in Albuquerque, it was complete culture shock. From Toronto to Chaco in one day, slap, bam."

"But this place, it's so bizarre."

"It's pretty normal to me." Dusty bit off another hunk of enchilada and washed it down with a swig from his soda can.

"But it's so bloody far from anything like civilization!" Yvette cried.

"Hip hip, hooray," Dusty answered. "That's the whole point."

Yvette gave him a blank stare.

A mud-splattered automobile was making the curve on the loop road, its top just visible across the winter brush. He could hear it, slowing, making the right onto the Rinconada road.

"Company." Dusty pointed with his enchilada. "This guy's got guts to do it in a two-wheel drive vehicle that's that low to the ground. From the looks of it, he just hammered the accelerator and blasted his way through the mud puddles on a hope and a prayer."

The Chevrolet pulled into the parking lot, swung wide, and pulled up in front of the interpretive sign. Two semicircular arcs had been left by the wipers as they sloshed the mud from the windshield. The hood, grille, doors, and even the roof were mud-coated. Gunk on the side windows darkened the interior, shadowing the single occupant.

"Heads up," Maureen said cautiously. "If that's who I think it is . . ."

Dusty took another bite of enchilada. At the same time his nerves started to tingle. No, this wasn't going to be some tourist out to see the sites.

The man who opened the door had a beanpole figure, his white hair pulled back in a ponytail and clipped with a silver clasp studded with turquoise. His thin face, long nose, and startling blue eyes gave him a mature look. Dusty figured him for his early sixties. He wore a brown canvas duck coat, the kind sold in places like Eddie Bauer stores where the trendy bought "outdoor" clothes in Santa Fe. A garish silver belt buckle with big chunks of turquoise snugged a woven-leather belt around his slim hips. Expensive ostrich-skin boots were on his feet.

"Bloody hell," Yvette whispered.

"You know him?" Dusty asked.

"Hello, Father," Yvette called. "I fancied you'd show up eventually."

*Her father?* It took a moment for the meaning to sink in.

"Want to go meet Carter Hawsworth?" Maureen asked. "Just promise me you won't do anything dumb—like get yourself thrown in jail for murder, eh?"

Dusty set his half-eaten enchilada down, wiped his fingers with a paper towel, and swung down from the tailgate.

Hawsworth stepped up to Yvette, his head cocked, a pinched expression on his face. His first words were, "I want you to know, I don't hold it against you personally."

Dusty almost recoiled at that familiar English accent. He'd listened to it enough on the answering machine tape. He could still hear that voice saying, *"I'll be your worst nightmare."*

"Thank you, Carter. It's not like I was consulted, you know." Yvette had crossed her arms, the posture something a wounded child might have adopted.

"I know." He studied her with angry blue eyes.

"Over the years you cost me nearly two hundred thousand pounds. Isn't that an incredible amount to lose to fraud? Had your mother swindled that sum through fraudulent FTSE investments, I could have her locked away for life. But since you were a child, I have no real recourse."

Dusty blinked, asking Maureen from the side of his mouth, "What's a pound worth?"

"About a buck fifty, U.S."

Yvette's expression had cooled even more. "Did you come to present me with a bill, Father?"

Hawsworth finally smiled, the expression anything but warm. "In the first place, I'm not your 'father' as we both now know. In the second, I would, if I thought I had a dog's chance in hell of collecting." His eyes narrowed. "But I wouldn't bill you, Yvette, I'd send it to your foul bitch of a mother."

"And have a right jolly time getting her to pay," Yvette replied bitterly.

His eyes seemed to burn as he said, "Oh, fear not, Yvette, your mother shall have her comeuppance. From now on, I'm the cunning spider in her life. And she knows it. No matter what it takes, I *will* destroy her. And, why, yes, you can tell her that. See what sort of expression you get?"

"I couldn't care less what the two of you do to each other. Your squabbles are your own."

"You're not the least bit sorry for poor old Mum?"

"If you recall, we've both been lied to. Very well, what do we do now, you and I?"

"Nothing." Hawsworth stuffed his long fingers into his back pockets. "The nice part is that we don't have to perpetuate the lie anymore, Yvette. Don't you find that liberating?"

"Oh, indeed," she replied stiffly. "In more ways than you could know."

He shook his head. "I must say, it's quite something to discover that you've been a cuckold. I swear, I'd kill

Dale for doing this to me—but some bastard beat me
to it. Were it me, I'd have made him suffer a bit longer
before I put him out of my misery."

Dusty's universe collapsed, funneling itself into the
image of Hawsworth's face. A vague comprehension
of the man's expression imprinted: the transition from
loathing and anger to downright fear . . .

"Dusty! *Dusty!*" Maureen was screaming into one
ear. The words intruded, bringing him back to the here
and now. Her frantic hands were tugging on his arm,
trying to break his hold. He was standing, his fists knotted in the lapels of the thick duck coat, his knuckles
pressing together as he lifted Hawsworth up on his tip-
toes, and half choked the man.

"Dusty, let him down!" Maureen was screaming.

Despite heart-pumping anger, Dusty forced himself
to relax his hold and step back. His hands kept grasping
and knotting in the air. "You son of a bitch," Dusty
whispered. "You'd better be glad I'm not—"

Hawsworth stumbled back, face white, a hand to his
throat. "You *assaulted* me!"

"What's the trouble here?" Bill asked as he advanced
from Michall's Durango. He was still chewing some of
his sandwich as he wiped crumbs from his blue FBI
coat.

"Hey, Bill," Dusty managed through gritted teeth,
"meet Carter Hawsworth, returning to the scene of the
crime . . . just like Agent Nichols figured he would."

Bill was watching them, a hard expression on his
face. Rick had come to back him up. Michall and Sylvia, large-eyed, stood behind them. Sylvia held a handful of cheesy fishes; Dusty could hear them crunching
in her tightening grip.

"Please, don't hurt him, Dusty," Yvette said from
the side. "He may be an ass, but he was fair with me."

"Dusty?" Hawsworth asked, and his mouth dropped
open. "Oh, of course. You're Sam's little snotty-nosed
boy. The one Ruth couldn't wait to be rid of."

Dusty's universe had begun to narrow again, but Maureen reached out, restraining his arm and dragging him back as he started forward.

Carter looked at Dusty as though he were a species of insect. "Yes, breeding will tell. The nasty little boy becomes a burly bully."

"Father"—Yvette stepped in front of Hawsworth—"stop trying to provoke him."

"You grew up with him?" Dusty asked Yvette. "You're lucky you're not a basket case."

"Like you, Mr. Stewart?" Hawsworth asked. "You should have seen yourself as a child, dirty, whining, forever with your finger in your mouth. When I think of you, I associate you with the stench of urine. I do hope you finally grew out of that."

Maureen's grip tightened on his arm. "Leave it be."

Bill stepped up. "What are you doing here, Dr. Hawsworth?"

"I came to see where Dale was killed." Hawsworth shifted his attention to the FBI agent. "This is still public property. I am violating no law."

"Just came for a look-see, huh?" Bill reached into his back pocket and pulled out a notebook. He checked his watch and noted the time, jotting down notes. "It's not exactly an easy place to get to, is it?"

"No. And I have little to say to you. I gave my statement to your Agent Nichols. If you have any other questions, I refer you either to that document or to my lawyer."

"Yeah." Bill cocked his head. "I read your statement. I was fascinated by the fact that you couldn't account for your whereabouts on Halloween night."

"As I told Agent Nichols, I was out on the Navajo Reservation, doing research."

"I read that. On plants." Bill gave him a quizzical look. "I couldn't pronounce the name."

*"Toloache,"* Hawsworth said condescendingly.

Dusty exhaled hard, immediately drawing Bill's attention.

"Tolo—," the agent began.

*"Toloache,"* Dusty finished, his hard gaze on Hawsworth. "I'm sure that poor Agent Nichols, like a good East Coast city cop, had no idea what you were talking about." He reached over and eased Maureen's hand from his sleeve.

"What is it?" Bill asked, his pen poised.

"Sacred datura," Dusty replied. "It's a pretty common plant out here. Normally it's hard to find this time of year, but we hadn't had a freeze up until Halloween. The monsoon season was good and rainy this year. Lots of moisture, lots of blooms. Let me guess, Dr. Hawsworth, when you're not busy seducing other men's wives, you're an ethnobotanist, right?"

Hawsworth crossed his arms, head back. "My, you really are a younger edition of your mother."

"Yeah, that's me," Dusty said, "and I have a very long memory. It goes back to the times when you couldn't keep your hands off Sam Stewart's wife. Along with memories of you, I have a good imagination. I can visualize poor Sam as he crawled up on the sink and stuck his finger into the light socket."

"Well, I didn't make him do it!" Hawsworth replied.

"Maybe not. But you made it a lot easier."

"You *do* have a good imagination." Hawsworth chuckled and waved a hand at Yvette. "Can you also imagine your mother with lots of different men? Even Dale? Yes, the good Dale Robertson, planting the sweet young Yvette in your mother's belly."

Yvette blinked and pain lit her eyes.

Dusty said, "Why did you say that to her?"

"Wait until you're stiffed for two hundred thousand quid and made into a bloody fool before the world. It sours the milk of human kindness."

"While you're feeling sour, I have something else to bring up."

"What would that be?" Hawsworth looked amused.

"A tip for Bill, here. He needs to write it down in his little book. It's interesting that you told him you were out looking for *toloache* Halloween night."

Bill waited for Hawsworth to comment, then said, "I'll bite. Why is that interesting?"

Dusty was watching Hawsworth, their eyes locked in mutual loathing. "Because he could have called it 'sacred datura,' or 'western jimsonweed,' or 'Indian apple,' or even *Datura meteloides*, but he didn't. You see, sacred datura is an interesting plant. The blossoms were used historically to put infants with colic into a drugged sleep. Just the fragrance can make you dizzy, impair your ability to think and walk. Sometimes *curanderas*, medicine women in the backcountry will use it to deaden pain before setting broken bones or pulling teeth. It doesn't take much, fifteen to twenty seeds, to kill an adult. But even a nonlethal overdose can cause permanent insanity."

"But Dr. Robertson wasn't poisoned," Bill reminded.

"That's not the point," Dusty said.

"Then what is?" Bill sounded irritated.

"*Toloache* is the word witches use for the plant, Bill. No one else calls it that."

"That doesn't prove anything," Hawsworth said shortly. "I'm an anthropologist. I know the names!"

"Yes," Dusty agreed. "And the FBI doesn't. You were counting on that, weren't you? What's *toloache* to Agent Nichols? Nothing. Just another weird anthropological word. One he couldn't easily cross-reference. Witches survive through misdirection. They like being clever, thrive on outsmarting their opponents. They like working at night—whether they're collecting *toloache* or sucking a man's soul out through a hole in his head."

This time Hawsworth stepped forward, his bony fist rising to shake under Dusty's nose. "You're just like Dale: an arrogant loudmouth. You don't know the half of it, Stewart. Well this time the trickery is over. The stakes have risen. Kwewur will get you, just like he got Dale, and it will fill my soul with joy when it happens." Hawsworth stalked away.

On impulse, Dusty called, "Too bad about Cochiti! Watch your step around cliffs, Carter. It's a long way down."

Hawsworth gave him a look that would have splintered bone. The tall man folded himself into his Chevrolet, slammed the door, and started the engine. Throwing the car into reverse, he swung around and roared off on the way to the loop road. Tires squealed as he made the turn onto pavement and accelerated.

"Someone ought to tell him the park speed limit is thirty-five," Sylvia noted as she fished more cheesy fishes from the box.

Yvette swallowed hard, struggling to keep her composure. "Excuse me. *Toloache?* Cochiti? Did I just miss something?"

Maureen's expression was thoughtful. "Dusty just accused your father of being a witch—and he didn't exactly deny it, now did he?"

"That is one dangerous man," Dusty whispered.

"I don't think you did yourself any favors here today, Stewart," Bill noted as he scribbled furiously in his notebook. "He doesn't strike me as the forgiving kind."

"That makes two of us," Dusty replied.

BY LATE AFTERNOON, the sun began to break through the clouds, and shafts of golden light lanced the cliffs, but the west wind had a real bite to it. No one complained, because no one even seemed to notice the cold.

Dusty stood beside Yvette, clasping his fleece collar

beneath his chin, as he studied the progressing excavation. The fallen kiva roof lay exposed, the soil black with charcoal. When it had burned, the south side had fallen in first. The northern half, which they were excavating, had hinged, so the roof poles and cribbing sloped downward, disappearing into the unexcavated south half of the kiva. Michall had taken, stabilized, and bagged core samples for tree ring dates; then she'd collected soil samples, and mapped in and photographed the burned beams.

Dusty prowled the rim of the kiva like a hungry coyote, staying just behind the yellow tape. In the center of the rich black earth Michall and Sylvia had excavated from the kiva, a round brown spot marked the location of the old pot hunter's hole.

"Hey, Bill?" Dusty called. "I want you guys to consider something."

"Yeah? What?" The FBI agent looked up from his notebook where he jotted observations.

"Dale was laid in that hole upside down. The person, or people, who buried him didn't dig a new hole, they reopened this old one. I mean, Dale's head was right over that brown intrusion down there in the kiva roof."

"Uh-huh." Bill studied him. "What's your point?"

"If that hole was dug in the sixties, your unsub and the pot hunter may be the same guy."

"Or girl," he added. "Sure, Stewart, maybe. Or it could be wild-assed coincidence. Maybe the dirt was softer here, because it had been dug up before."

"Yeah, well, it would have been, but—"

"But that's the point. If I'd just murdered someone and was looking for the easiest place to bury them, I would not have spent my time stabbing a shovel into sand that's been filtering into the kiva for the last eight hundred years." He offered his hands for evidence. Swollen red blisters dotted his palms. "It's hard as Hades. I would have tested a few places, and dug where it was the softest. Right here." He pointed to the old pot hunter's hole.

Yvette leaned toward Dusty and asked, "Could Dale have done this? Dug this hole back in the sixties? Maybe the person who killed him buried him here as a payback for digging this hole? Or for taking something he found."

Her once immaculate black wool coat was covered with wind-whipped sand. She must have been freezing. She had her arms wrapped around herself, toughing it out.

Dusty shook his head vehemently, then abruptly halted.

That was an interesting idea. Not about Dale, but maybe someone he'd worked with. He turned to look back at the Casa Rinconada kiva and recalled the things Ruth Ann had said, about how often she'd come out here in the sixties. Sunlight blazed from the kiva's perfectly fitted stones. Dale would never have dug a hole in a site unless it had been gridded first, and excavated according to accepted scientific methods—but Ruth Ann was another thing. She'd gotten out of archaeology because she'd hated it: *I wanted the good stuff quick, so I could get out of the dirt.*"

As he turned back, Dusty saw the green Chevy Suburban coming up the road toward them. Dusty had been wondering where Nichols was.

He looked at Yvette. "Dale never potted a site in his life. And this was a pot hunter, a vandal, somebody who wanted the good stuff quick. Even if an archaeologist had dug that hole and the records were lost, it would have been excavated differently. The walls would have been square. Not only that, Dale was immaculate when he dug. He'd never have backfilled it with a beer can and a big chunk of tibia."

Bill had been listening and taking notes. "Okay, Stewart, what's your take on why this hole's dug in the north half of the kiva? Why not smack dab in the center?"

"The center is generally where the roof entry is. The fire pit sits below that, so that the smoke goes straight up and out, right? The only thing pot hunters find in fire pits is charcoal. Prehistoric charcoal doesn't sell for squat on the open market. The best chance for pottery or artifacts is on the north or south next to the wall. That's what our pot hunter was doing."

"Are many pot hunters women?" Yvette asked.

Dusty paused, glancing at Maureen. She inspected some burned fragments of bone that Sylvia had recovered from the screen.

Dusty shook his head. "Not usually. Women pot hunters in the Southwest are generally in their fifties or sixties, and married to men who are the true aficionados. They mostly run the screens and do the surface collecting. They're the types who hand out cups of iced tea and wear fluffy sun hats."

"I daresay you don't much approve of them," Yvette noted.

"Not even slightly." Dusty glared at the hole. "But this wasn't dug by a weekend pot hunter. This is much more to the point. It's focused."

"How can you tell that?" Maureen asked as she looked at the brown soil so perfectly outlined in black. "It's just a hole."

"No, it's not. The pot hunter had some archaeological savvy. He knew where to dig to get to the good stuff the fastest."

"Would Carter Hawsworth have known that?" Maureen asked.

Dusty shot Yvette a sidelong look to catch her reaction. "Yes. He would have."

"Oh, my God, this floor is . . ." Then Sylvia yelled, *"Shit!"*

Dusty jerked his head up in time to see Sylvia drop the shovel and claw at the air as a section of pit floor

collapsed beneath her. A sodden thump followed, and
dust fountained up. The ragged hole had the same
rough diameter as a fifty-five-gallon drum lid.

Dusty screamed, *"Sylvia!"*

# CHAPTER 40

OLD PIGEONTAIL'S LIGHT brown eyes seemed
to peer right through Browser's body as he said, "It's
a bit more difficult than you think, War Chief. You
see, Shadow sent me. She wants you to know that Obsidian has been taken to High Sun House."

To one side, Catkin shifted, her moccasins grating
on the room floor. She had crossed her arms, the fingers
of her left hand tapping a nervous cadence on the
wooden handle of her war club.

Blue Corn and Horned Ram watched in silence from
the rear of the room, their eyes wide.

Browser stroked his chin, glancing at Stone Ghost.
"Why there?"

"I assume," Pigeontail said, "that Shadow is going
to pull Obsidian's heart out there. Two Hearts is convinced that it will save his life."

Browser's gaze sharpened. What was Pigeontail's
hidden motive here? Why was he doing this? And he
recalled something with a start.

In Browser's mind's eye he could see that sunny day
as he, Redcrop, and Uncle Stone Ghost had walked
across Longtail village's plaza to the small fire. There
Matron Ant Woman huddled beside the flames as she
ate corn cakes. It had been the day after Matron Flame
Carrier's funeral, during the Feast of Mourning.

The image was so clear: Ant Woman's age-creased expression, her dark eyes seeing so far into the past. Stone Ghost had asked about Flame Carrier's early life, about the time when she was a young woman. The old woman's reedy voice filtered out of Browser's memory . . .

*"Old Pigeontail was from somewhere near Green Mesa. He frequented our village. He's still around, charging outrageous prices for his trinkets. He may know. And your Matron was married to him for a few summers."* And then she had admitted: *". . . Spider Silk ordered her to marry him. I never knew why."*

Browser felt a cold chill run down his back as he studied the old Trader, noting the bones underlying the loose flesh on his aged face. And suddenly he knew why the Blessed Spider Silk had ordered that long-ago marriage.

"Catkin," Browser said softly, "remove your war club." As she quickly complied, Browser said, "Thank you. Now, at my command, I would like you to break Pigeontail's shoulder."

Catkin said, "Yes, War Chief."

Pigeontail swallowed hard, then asked, "What are you saying, Browser? I have told you the rules under which I must work."

"I think my nephew understands that, Trader," Stone Ghost replied evenly.

"Then what is this about? Why would you have the deputy strike me?" Pigeontail raised his hands in supplication.

"So that it would hurt more when we bound you," Browser answered. "And binding you would be a necessary process before we dangled you upside down over the fire. Not a hot fire, mind you, but rather a bowl of glowing coals. If we do it correctly, we can sear the skin off your skull, and as it blisters, the brain will begin to boil beneath the charring bone. Handled correctly, it doesn't kill, but I've heard that it will leave the survivor mostly demented and in pain."

"You are not frightening me, War Chief." His head high, Pigeontail's nostrils flared with disdain. "If you do this thing, you will reap nothing but trouble. Traders will walk three days out of their way to avoid you and the Katsinas' People. You will be shunned by all good people. It is that threat of retaliation that has protected Traders since the beginning of time."

Browser removed his own club and slid his hand up and down the shaft. "Our world is dying around us. I've seen graves robbed and the bodies butchered as if they were deer. What is one tortured Trader in a time of famine, death, and man-eating White Moccasins? What is your pain compared to entire kivas full of children being incinerated because their parents believe in the wrong gods?"

"War Chief, I don't think—"

"That I care?" Browser inspected the stone war head; the chert cobble that he had lashed there so long ago was nicked along the edges, bits of dark matter in the deep cracks where he'd been unable to clean it. "Tell me, Pigeontail, how many summers were you married to our dead Matron? Two? Three?"

The question seemed to catch Pigeontail by complete surprise. "Married to . . ."

"Our dead Matron," Browser told him. "Flame Carrier. The Blessed Spider Silk ordered you to marry her. As I recall the story, you were younger than our dead Matron, and the two of you fought like beasts."

Pigeontail's expression drooped. "Who told you about that? I've tried to forget it my entire life."

Browser slashed a blinding backhanded blow, the war club whistling through the air, its passage whipping Pigeontail's white hair. *"How many summers?"*

"Three," Pigeontail cried as he flailed backward, only to have the tip of Catkin's club jam hard into his back, propelling him forward with a jolt.

Stone Ghost stepped to one side and said, "Trader,

we do not do this lightly. As you are no doubt aware, my nephew and I are descended from the Blessed Night Sun. You see, since most Traders are Made People, they would not retaliate against the Katsinas' People for murdering a First People's spy—especially one working for the White Moccasins." Stone Ghost stopped, cocking his head to study Pigeontail's reaction. "What does Shadow really want?"

A slight sheen of sweat had broken out on Pigeontail's forehead. "She wants revenge. The destruction of Two Hearts's warriors last night has thrown her into a violent rage. Beyond that, Two Hearts is dying. He is desperate for two things: Obsidian's heart and the turquoise wolf that War Chief Browser stole from him."

"And you?" Browser asked as he swung his club. "What is your place in all of this? That you are the eyes of the White Moccasins, I understand, but—"

"I am *not* their eyes," Pigeontail hissed. "I go where I will and do as I please. I serve no master but myself. They have their own eyes, and believe me, they are everywhere." A faint sneer bent his lips. "What about you, War Chief? Whom do you serve? The Made People? The ones who hunted your ancestors the way they would have had they been but rats or other vermin? Or do you serve the katsinas?"

"I serve my people," Browser said, and thrust his war club into Pigeontail's face to stifle the man's rebuttal, adding, "I'm just trying to find out who my people are, Trader."

"So, tell me, War Chief," Pigeontail demanded despite the club shoved against his lips. "What do you *really* believe?"

"I believe in Poor Singer's prophecy," Browser said truthfully. "I believe the words that Gray Thunder spoke in Flowing Waters Town: That we will only survive if we lay our differences behind us. Myself, I have never seen a katsina. I don't know if they exist or not. But Gray Thunder's words were of hope, of a way to live together. The Made People hunted us down because we made slaves of them and committed terrible atrocities. Maybe the horrible deeds of the past must be paid for, but the ways and means of the White Moccasins, Two Hearts, and Shadow are wrong and I will destroy them."

"You would turn against your own kind?"

*"My kind!"* Browser thundered, bulling forward and pushing the old man back against Catkin's club. "My kind doesn't eat the flesh of men! My kind doesn't murder entire villages of men, women, and children, and most of all, *my* kind doesn't burn kivas filled with children!"

"The gods demand these things, Browser!" Pigeontail roared back. "The Blessed Flute Player, Spider Woman, and the Blue God, like the First People, are in a battle for their lives!"

"Then let the gods fight their own battles," Browser said.

Pigeontail met his glare. Eye to eye, they stood; then, several breaths later, Pigeontail shrugged. "Why should it matter? You are one man. Very well, pack up and go. Take your Fire Dogs and leave. If you won't fight for your people, at least promise me you won't fight against them."

"You think it's that easy? That I can just walk away? That I can forget what Two Hearts and Shadow did to my wife? Forget the friends they have killed? Am I supposed to leave the ghosts of those hideously burned children to wail in lonely pain? To ignore the way they killed my Matron—your onetime wife? What they did to her body? The soul they stole by drilling a hole in her living head? And leave Obsidian for that monster and his misbegotten spawn to murder?"

"If you stay, it will cost you your life, Browser." Pigeontail was watching him, searching his expression . . . for what?

"My life?"

"And that of your party." Pigeontail smiled. "Although Shadow's warriors might want Blue Corn released."

"Blue Corn?" Stone Ghost asked.

Pigeontail gave him a curious look. "She is one of us. I don't think she knows it, but she is. Most of her lineage is descended from the First People. She is not pure, having intermarried with Made People, but enough of the blood remains that it is worth keeping her alive."

"I don't believe it!" Blue Corn blurted.

Pigeontail shrugged. "What you believe doesn't change the way things are. Your great-grandmother made the decision not to tell her children. At the time it seemed prudent. The Made People were at the height of their power. Prospects for our kind were dim. It was a way to maintain control of Flowing Waters Town. The place, as you know, was important to us. It was supposed to be our new beginning, a fresh start after the Blessed Featherstone led us out of Straight Path Canyon."

Blue Corn's eyes slitted as she studied Pigeontail. "I'm supposed to believe that? That I'm descended from First People?"

Pigeontail shrugged again. "I have no care what you believe."

Stone Ghost stepped forward and examined Blue Corn's face. "What is your clan?"

"She is descended from the Red Lacewing Clan," Pigeontail answered. "Of the Blessed Weedblossom's lineage." He gestured around. "Ironically, Kettle Town was once theirs."

"Weedblossom?" Blue Corn whispered, her thoughts knotted around the revelation. And in that instant she looked suddenly unsure, casting an unnerved glance at Pigeontail.

"So my entire party can just leave?" Browser asked. "We can walk out of here without being attacked?"

"That would be permitted . . . provided you turn that little turquoise wolf over to me." Pigeontail's curt nod guaranteed it. "As to your safety, I will make the case to Shadow." A curious amusement lay behind his eyes. "She has a certain, well, softness for you, War Chief."

"Why do we need anyone's permission? I thought the White Moccasins were killed in the ambush last night?" Under Catkin's critical gaze, Pigeontail might have been a mouse beneath Coyote's nose.

Pigeontail lifted an eyebrow. "That is today, Deputy. What do you think will happen tomorrow, or a moon from now? You have dealt the White Moccasins a stinging blow. Had it been your pride that was slapped so ignominiously, would you forget about it? Just let it go?"

Browser made a face against the sinking sensation in his stomach. "What of Obsidian? May she go with us?"

"I told you, War Chief, she's in High Sun House, being prepared for the ritual sacrifice."

Browser read that slight gleam in the Trader's odd eyes, as though he were waging a desperate gamble.

Browser nodded at his deputy. "Break his shoulder, Catkin."

She was well into her swing when Pigeontail ducked away, yelling, "Wait!" He rolled sideways as Catkin's blow sailed through empty air. "Gods! You'd do this thing? Hang me over fire?"

"Deputy," Browser said in chastisement, "you're losing your skill. I told you—"

"Wait!" Pigeontail screamed as he skipped to the side on his old legs. He had his hands up as Catkin circled, preparing for another blow. "Blessed gods, War Chief, are you mad?"

Browser growled, "I'm tired of being made a fool of! Perhaps your death will show them I'm serious!"

Catkin deftly chased the old man back into a corner of the room and lifted her club to strike.

"In the name of the Flute Player!" Pigeontail wailed as he looked into Catkin's implacable eyes, "What do you want to know?"

Browser roared, "I wish to know where Obsidian is!"

Pigeontail wearily slumped in the corner. "Telling you won't make any difference. The rituals are almost finished." Catkin lifted her club again, and Pigeontail rushed to say, "She is in Owl House! In the kiva, bound across from the Blessed Two Hearts!"

"How many warriors does Shadow have?"

Browser's blood ran hot and swift in his veins, eager for the battle. His enemy was just over there, across the canyon, poorly guarded and vulnerable.

"Two. The sentries who had been assigned to guard the elder. They keep watch from the rooftops. There were three, but Shadow sent one of them to Starburst Town for reinforcements."

Browser shot a glance at Catkin. "Then we must hurry." He noticed that Blue Corn had a dazed look, as if she had come adrift from the world, eyes focused on some distance in her head.

Catkin watched Pigeontail with narrowed eyes. "This is a trap, Browser, and you know it. Is one life worth the risk?"

Keen anticipation lit Pigeontail's eyes. Where did that come from? What did it mean? What was he waiting for?

Browser turned to Stone Ghost.

Perspiration had glued his uncle's thin white hair to his wrinkled forehead, but his black eyes blazed. Stone Ghost said, "Catkin is right. This is certainly a trap. Which means you must make certain, Nephew, that you are smarter than Two Hearts, and few have ever been. That's why he's still alive, though we've tried to hunt him down many times." Stone Ghost stepped toward Browser and looked up. "You must also make certain that anyone who chooses to accompany you on this raid knows he is going there for one reason, to kill the most dangerous witch in the land. There is a good chance that all of you will die at Owl House."

Blue Corn added, "There is one more small thing to consider."

Browser turned to face her. She looked suddenly frightened. "Yes, Matron?"

"Two Hearts is a very powerful witch. If there is any chance that Obsidian's heart can extend Two Hearts's wicked life—"

Browser spun around. "Catkin, find Straighthorn and Jackrabbit! The time has come to end this."

# CHAPTER 41

"CAREFUL!" DUSTY CRIED as he leapt the yellow tape and ran. "Stay back! The whole roof can go at any second!"

No one questioned his unexpected authority as he shouldered through the gaping FBI agents to get to Michall and shouted, "Give me your flashlight!"

She pulled it from the sheath on her belt and thrust it into his hand. Dusty dropped to his hands and knees and crawled forward until his head cleared the hole. "Sylvia? Do you hear me?"

"I'm okay!" she called up.

Flipping on the flashlight, he shot the beam around the interior and saw her, sitting about four feet below. Dust covered her from head to toe.

Sylvia coughed and shielded her eyes against the light while she looked around the interior of the kiva. "Oh, Dusty, you're not going to believe this." She lifted a long tan object and pointed to the floor in front of her. They were everywhere.

"What does she see?" Michall asked.

Through the swirling dust, he made out the bones, and a portion of the curving kiva bench that buttressed the north wall. Plaster still clung to the stone in places. Dusty swiveled to look at Maureen. "Sylvia is sitting in the middle of a bone bed."

Maureen hurried toward him, and Dusty slid backward, gave her the flashlight, and said, "Be careful not to collapse the rest of the roof."

"I'll be careful." She took the light, got down on her belly, and slid forward to look. Her long black braid snaked through the dirt at her side.

Yvette and the FBI guys looked wary and uncertain, obviously expectant, but without the feeling of pure ecstasy that shone in Michall's wide eyes.

"It's intact," Dusty said to her unasked question. "The roof hasn't completely collapsed onto the living floor on the north side."

"Dusty?" Maureen twisted her head around to peer at him. "We have . . . let's see . . . one, two, three, at least three femora that I can see. From the looks, it's probably two individuals. Well . . ." She paused, as though confused. "This is strange. You can't have three different sized lefts, and that fourth femur is smaller."

"What does she mean?" Rick asked Dusty as he wiped his brow with his coat sleeve.

"She means there are probably more than two individuals."

Michall said, "Okay, how do you want me to do this? I'm not a physical anthropologist."

Dusty studied the slanting pit floor, and for the first time since Dale's death, he felt whole, excited, happy to be alive. "If we can get Sylvia out without bringing the whole thing down, I think you should drop back. The smart way is to trowel this down to the burned beam." He cocked his head, reading the pit floor, seeing through the soil. "The best entry is right there in the middle of the pot hunter's hole. We have to assume that he fell through, too, just like Sylvia did. And both of them have destroyed the context. Which means we can—"

"Huh?" Rick asked as he photographed Maureen's butt where it hovered over the hole.

"The pot hunter and Sylvia had to put their feet somewhere," Dusty said. "That means that they either crushed or kicked the bones aside."

"That's bad." Bill was holding a tape recorder where he'd been dictating notes. "Sylvia just destroyed evidence."

Dusty said, "But we also have about a third of this kiva floor intact! The pollen, the phytoliths, the artifacts, everything's there."

"Except what the pot hunter took," Michall corrected. "It's not like it's pristine."

"Yeah, but this isn't the thirties, almost-a-doctor Michall. For now, this is pretty spectacular."

"What the *hell* is going on here?" Nichols's unexpected voice demanded harshly. "Stewart! You consider yourself under arrest for interfering with an investigation!" Sam Nichols stood at the edge of the kiva in his brown canvas coat, breathing hard. His thick black hair was sticking out at angles from under his gray knit cap. "Is that Dr. Cole in that hole?"

Dusty smacked dirt from his hands. "Agent Nichols, we've hit the mother lode."

"I hope that means you have a damn good explanation, Stewart!"

Dusty helped Maureen out of the kiva as she crawled back, a glow in her eyes. "I could see two adult skulls, a male and a female."

"Uh, Sam," Bill said, his tape recorder held out in Maureen's direction. "We've had some interesting developments. I wouldn't file charges on Stewart or Dr. Cole yet. We'd probably better take Stewart's advice and excavate as he recommends or we'll collapse the rest of it. Stewart says that—"

*"Hey!"* Sylvia yelled, her arms extended from the hole. "Somebody get me out of here! This is spooky!"

Michall said, "Give me my flashlight, I want to go look."

Dusty handed it to her, and watched Michall slide forward on her belly until she could shine her flashlight down into the hole.

"Hey, swamp rat," Michall greeted. "You look picturesque squatting there amid the bones."

Sylvia replied, "Come on. Get me out. There's something really strange about these bones. It's as though I can feel them crawling all over me."

Michall panned the beam around for a while, then asked, "Is that a wall crypt over there?"

Sylvia answered but Dusty couldn't make out the words.

"All right." Nichols fixed his good eye on Dusty. "Assuming that I'm not dragging you off to Albuquerque and one hell of a stiff fine, what's going on here?"

"We don't know for sure yet," Bill said from behind. "Sam, there's a kiva full of dead people here. You just missed the collapse of the hole in the roof."

Dusty caught movement from the edge of his vision and spun around. "Yvette? Where are you going?"

She was headed downhill, her black coat flapping.

"I'm cold!" she called over her shoulder. "See you later."

"Yvette?" Nichols asked. His horn-rimmed glasses flashed as he whirled to take another look at the woman.

"Yvette Hawsworth," Dusty said. "She just showed up at my trailer last night—"

"And you didn't call me immediately!" Nichols roared. He waved an arm. "Rick, would you kindly run down and detain Ms. Hawsworth. Stewart, Cole, get in my car! Let's find a place to talk."

BROWSER STOOD IN the windswept plaza, the ruins of Kettle Town rising around them. The long-abandoned town felt oddly remote, as if the place watched through the dark windows and doorways, waiting for some great event to unfold.

Rubbing a hand down the back of his neck, Browser could feel the eyes of the old ones—his ancestors—upon him. He addressed his small party: "First, I need two volunteers to make sure that Matron Blue Corn gets safely to Flowing Waters Town."

Two of the Mogollon warriors trotted forward, expressions grim. "Yes, War Chief. Upon our lives, the Matron will be delivered safely."

"You need not do this," Blue Corn said, a grudging respect in her eyes. "Just get me back to Center Place. I left three wounded warriors there. They will be wondering what has happened. They can get me home. Or, rather, we can get each other home."

"See to them, too, if you will," Browser charged the warriors.

"Yes, War Chief."

"I do not think this is smart," White Cone said from the side. "It is not the time to divide our forces."

Browser cast a sidelong glance at Pigeontail, aware that the old Trader seemed to soak up each word like a wadded fabric shirt in a rain puddle. "We must move rapidly, Elder. If not, Shadow's reinforcements will arrive from Starburst Town before we can rescue Obsidian and be on our way south."

Stone Ghost added, "Time, my friend, is the one thing we do not have."

"Those who jump too quickly fall into fires or

floods," White Cone countered. "But, very well, what of Elder Horned Ram? He is failing."

"We'll take him with us." Browser took in Catkin's stunned expression, then turned to Blue Corn. "He wanted us dead, didn't he?"

"He did," a gravelly voice called.

Browser turned to see Rain Crow propped in the doorway, a war club hanging from his hand. He squinted against the daylight, and his expression reflected the terrible agony inside his head. He took a step forward, wobbling, and had to use his war club like a cane to brace himself.

Blue Corn asked, "War Chief? Are you fit to travel? Are you ready to start home?"

Rain Crow swallowed, his negation the faintest shake of the head, as if any more would have split his skull. "No, Matron. I wish to remain here for a time. Browser is going after Two Hearts, correct?"

"I am." Browser nodded.

"Then I am going with you." Rain Crow lifted his ruined face and glared at Browser.

"I need you at home," Blue Corn said shortly. "And beyond that, you're not fit to fight a mouse, let alone White Moccasins. You look like a passing butterfly could blow you over."

Rain Crow smiled. "Matron, while I have been sick, tongues have been loose. The talk is that the White Moccasins were responsible for Gray Thunder's death. None here has let slip, or even hinted, that my guard was killed in retaliation." He almost toppled, jamming his war club down to keep his balance. "I would know who caused my guard's death." He shot a veiled look at Browser. "You, War Chief?"

"No," Browser insisted. "And I doubt that any of the Mogollon did, either. My suspicion is that Shadow did it."

"I share your thoughts." Rain Crow took another step. "And I think you are right to keep Horned Ram close. He is the sort of serpent you are better off keeping in a cage. At least when you can see him you have an idea of what he's up to."

"Why would I want you with me? You look like you're about to fall over dead yourself," Browser said.

The grim smile played about Rain Crow's pain-wracked lips. "I relieve you of any obligation for me, War Chief. I will make my own way. Should I fall behind, you have my leave to abandon me. I have sworn an oath to find and kill the culprit who murdered my guard. It is something I must do, that is all."

Browser nodded, remembering how disoriented he had recently been when Two Hearts had cracked him in the head. The pain had to be like watery fire running through Rain Crow's brain. "Very well, but you are on your own if you come with us, Rain Crow."

"I understand that," the War Chief replied.

Catkin stepped in front of Browser, her back to the others in the room, and whispered, "We can't take an old man and a wounded warrior with us! Are you trying to get us all killed?"

He gazed into her dark panicked eyes and said, "I have reasons. Please—"

"What reasons? They will slow us down to a crawl, and if Horned Ram has the chance, he will scream out our location to our enemies! Have you lost your wits?"

Browser put a hand on her shoulder and felt the bunched muscles. "Not at all. My wits are the only thing I have left. I can't explain right now. You must trust me."

She didn't wish to. He could see it in her expression. The cant of her jaw, the way her nostrils flared. But she nodded and stepped back.

Browser called, "Red Dog? Fire Lark? Please find a ladder and lay Horned Ram on it. I want to be out of here in one half-hand of time."

"What will Straighthorn and I do?" Jackrabbit asked.

"Come with me."

Browser turned toward Old Pigeontail. "Tell me one last thing, Trader? Are you certain Carved Splinter is dead?"

Pigeontail gave Browser a sympathetic look. "Only bones remain of the young warrior. And most of them have been boiled and splintered, if you understand my meaning."

Jackrabbit's throat worked.

Browser looked at the young warrior. "I have special duties for the two of you. Gather your things and meet me at the front entrance of Kettle Town. We will discuss it there."

"Yes, War Chief."

THE CONFERENCE ROOM at the Visitors Center spread about sixteen by twenty feet and had artsy photographs of Chaco Canyon on the pale green walls.

Nichols leaned back in the chair at the head of the long rectangular table and glared at Dusty and Maureen, who sat side by side to his left. Stewart appeared a little insecure, but Cole stared right back at Nichols, as though she'd endured a thousand such interrogations and wasn't intimidated by him at all. Nichols took out his notebook and slapped it on the table.

"This is a criminal investigation, for God's sake. Are you two particularly dense?" He loosened his tie and reached for the cup of weak coffee Rupert Brown had provided; it steamed on the battered government table-top.

"Not at all, Nichols." Maureen crossed her arms. "And neither are your agents. Both of your men are conscientious. They wouldn't allow anyone to compromise evidence."

Nichols squinted at her. "They've assured me of that,

but your involvement *appears* to be a conflict of interest, Dr. Cole. Do you understand that?"

"They needed the input of a professional archaeologist as well as a board certified forensic anthropologist, Nichols. That's all it was. Unofficial Q and A."

Nichols shoved his glasses up on his nose. "Not when those specialists are potential suspects in a federal homicide, Dr. Cole!"

"Oh, come on, Nichols," Maureen said. "We have a dinner receipt from the Pink Adobe the night Dale was killed. I think our server was Maria. We sat in a corner table. She can place us there. You have a telephone log for Dusty's trailer. Or you should have. If you don't, you can subpoena it. You know that we answered Sylvia's call from Albuquerque. Not only that, neither of us would have wanted Dale dead."

Nichols shoved his notebook around the table. "That's the problem. No one does. I have no *real* suspects, folks. Every lead has petered out to nothing, which means *you* are still suspects."

"What about Carter Hawsworth?" she asked.

"I don't have anything I can take to an attorney. The same with Dr. Sullivan. No one in Dr. Robertson's department sticks out. Stewart looks to inherit, but it's not a huge chunk of change, just enough to pay the estate taxes and leave him something comfortable for the future."

Maureen braced her elbows on the table, and her black eyes gleamed. "What about the lab work? The notes? The blood tests? The fax they found in Casa Rinconada?"

He said nothing, frowning. Finally he grudgingly offered, "The fax was printed on Dr. Robertson's machine. The phone company records sent us to the Marriott. The same one we stayed at. At five thirty-seven on Halloween night, someone used the business center to send it. They paid cash for the service. No one remembers what the sender looked like."

"Just like Carter Hawsworth claims happened to him." Maureen frowned.

"Could he have sent them to himself?" Dusty asked. "You know, as a cover?"

Nichols swiveled his chair back around to face them. "The basilisk on the business card from Stewart's office? Same thing. No prints but yours and Stewart's. It was Bic ink." He sipped his coffee. "The diary that was left outside of your camp trailer? Professionally done at a print shop in Albuquerque. We're still following up on that one. Maybe we'll get lucky. But, again, no prints outside of yours, Maggie's, and Sylvia's."

She considered him for a moment. "That in itself says something."

"Enlighten me, Dr. Cole."

"In my part of the world, we call him a 'player,' someone who knows the rules of the game. He's done this before, Nichols. He knows how to hide evidence, and he likes doing it. He's baiting us. He knows what he can get away with. You just have to hope he'll get bored with the easy stuff and take a chance, give you a dare."

Nichols glared at her with his squinted eye. "I thought of that, but you're the only person out here who 'knows the rules.' "

Maureen shook her head. "What's my motive? Why do I want to murder one of my best friends?"

He sat back, dull eyes on his coffee cup.

"No idea, eh?" she asked.

"No, and it pisses me off." A slight tic jerked in his cheek. "I feel like I'm chasing my tail."

Dusty said, "Remember when Rupert said this wasn't a White crime?"

Nichols nodded. "I do."

"You're looking for White motives. That's why you're getting nowhere."

Nichols leaned across the table and almost shouted, "That's anthropological bullshit, Stewart!"

"Then how did you miss *toloache*?"

"What?"

Dusty went on to explain that Hawsworth had used a witch's term. "It went right past you. Just like Hawsworth wanted it to."

"Look, we've put the guy under the microscope. So, he used a term from the Native language. Dr. Cole has flipped out more bone terms in the last couple of hours than I've ever heard. You guys talk that way."

"It's not a White crime," Dusty insisted doggedly.

"Motives are motives. I don't care whether you're Navajo or Hindu. Besides, none of my sources in the traditional community picked up a single red flag. The only Indian suspect I have"—he held out a hand to Maureen—"is sitting here in this room."

Maureen laced her fingers on the tabletop. "Then why haven't you arrested me?"

Nichols felt like throwing his notebook at her. "All of my evidence is circumstantial. I've decided I'm not even going to charge you with interfering with an investigation. Bill and Rick spoke up in your behalf, and Rick said he'd do it in a court of law. Which also pissed me off!"

A knock came at the door, and Rupert Brown leaned in. His gray temples accented his brown hawklike face. "Sorry to interrupt. I thought I'd check to see if you needed anything."

"No, Dr. Brown, we're fine, thanks," Nichols said.

"Okay. Then I'm off for D.C." He lifted a hand to Dusty and Maureen. "See you when I get back."

"D.C.?" Nichols said. "Whoa! As in Washington?"

"Yeah. Big high mucky-muck meetings." Rupert smiled. "It's the annual policy implementation and general bullshit session that the Department of the Interior makes us endure each fiscal year."

"Have a nice trip," Maureen called as Rupert started to shut the door.

"Hold on!" Nichols shouted. "Who said you could leave town?"

Rupert opened the door and leaned against the frame. "I didn't realize I needed your permission, Agent Nichols. But if I do, *please* make me stay here. I beg you. No, I beseech you. I might even forgive you for screwing up my park."

Irritated, Nichols flicked his pen open and closed several times, then said, "No. Go. I'm sure I can find you if I need you."

Rupert smothered a smile, saluted, and shut the door.

"So, getting back to this dig," Nichols said.

"Look, Nichols"—Maureen leaned forward—"you have a kiva littered with human bones. No one out there—not Michall or Sylvia, and certainly not your agents—is prepared for the kind of analysis that will be required over the next few days."

Nichols jotted down a note about her manner: *Dr. Cole is insistent, authoritative, abrasive. Thinks we're incompetent.* He said, "You want to do it, huh?"

"I'd love to. But I think it would be better if you conscripted Sid Malroun from OMI. He's used to bodies in the flesh, but if he needs me, I can crawl over the tape and give him a hand with the cannibalized bone."

In the middle of jotting another note, Nichols's pen stopped. "The what?"

Dusty smoothed his hand over his blond beard and said, "We found a cannibalized leg today. Someone had carved the flesh off the bone. We saw the same treatment of bodies at the 10K3 site and at Pueblo Animas. Believe me, Nichols, there's a relationship between Dale's burial site, the basilisk, and those two sites. Each is rife with witchcraft and cannibalism."

Nichols studied their expressions. Both appeared excited but rational. "Didn't Rhone work on those sites, too?"

Stewart straightened slightly. "Yes. What of it?"

Nichols shook his head and finished his note. "Nothing . . . just correlating."

# CHAPTER 42

THE LINE OF people stretched behind Browser like a slithering snake. As each person exited Kettle Town and came to meet them, Catkin's eyes narrowed more and more. She thought he was mad. And he wasn't so sure she was wrong. He was gambling on legends. A thing no one sane would attempt.

"Clay Frog, please help Rain Crow."

"Yes, War Chief."

She trotted back. Rain Crow limped along behind them, his lopsided face looking worse for the contorted expression he had adopted to grit back the pain.

Clay Frog offered an arm to the burly War Chief from Flowing Waters Town. He took it gladly.

Rain Crow had to be in excruciating agony. Having suffered a similar, if less threatening wound recently, Browser had to admire the man's courage and endurance. Not only did he have a skull-cracking headache, but his balance and coordination were slightly off, as well. Worse, after a blow to the head like that, a man's souls could slip away before he realized it. Nevertheless, Rain Crow doggedly walked forward.

"Why am I still a prisoner?" Old Pigeontail asked from where he stood a half pace ahead of Catkin. "I've told you enough to get myself killed should Shadow or her allies ever find out."

"Then we are your best hope for a long and happy life," Stone Ghost told him. He plodded along on stumpy thin legs, his wrinkled old face set with determination. White Cone walked at his side. "Be content, and keep your mouth closed."

"Where are the two young warriors?" Old Pigeontail asked.

"I sent them back with a message for Matron Cloud-blower." Browser pointed his war club at the withered Trader. "And my uncle told you to be quiet."

Catkin looked at the elders, and her jaw clenched.

Browser could read the tracks of her souls in her eyes. She could not believe he was actually doing this.

Yes, the elders ought to be up on the mesa top with Blue Corn, headed for safety, but it had been impossible to convince either of them. For Stone Ghost, this was the end to a journey he had begun many sun cycles ago, when he'd mistakenly blamed a young warrior for a crime he did not commit. Until Stone Ghost stood over the corpse of Two Hearts, he could not say, "Here, it ends."

Old Pigeontail looked over his shoulder, fully aware that Yucca Whip and Red Dog followed immediately behind him. After Pigeontail's story about Carved Splinter, either warrior would gladly crack his skull open, and he seemed to know it.

Browser glanced back. Badger Dancer and Fire Lark bore old Horned Ram on his litter. They had looted the ladder from a collapsed room on the fourth floor, padded it with blankets, and made a platform to carry the Red Rock elder. Horned Ram looked gray and pale; each step that jolted his broken shoulder reflected in the corners of his constantly tensing mouth. When he met Browser's eyes, it was with a look of loathing.

*Yes, soon you will tell me what you know.*

They headed south onto the road. When they had

gone far enough, Browser turned to stare up at the cliff behind Kettle Town. Blue Corn's party labored up the stairway, climbing for the mesa top. It was the first step on their journey, and the Matron was already lagging behind.

"Do you think she believes it?" Catkin asked. "That she's descended from First People?"

"It doesn't matter," Browser murmured. "So long as she never tells her people."

"You think they will kill her if they find out?"

"I think they might."

Browser looked back at Kettle Town. With the plaster cracked off of its once-pillared portico, the town looked like a squat grinning head with too many teeth. The image wasn't macabre, or sinister, but rather reminded him of a perplexed and exhausted observer.

Blue Corn's party reached the top of the cliff. For a few brief instants, they stood skylined, then one by one, they disappeared.

Well and good. The Matron was out of harm's way.

The flat, washed clay of the canyon bottom ahead reflected the sunlight. A bow shot in front of them, irregular dots marked the roadway where it dived down into the wash.

Browser slipped his fingers along his war club. He and his club had become old companions, survivors of many desperate battles. The touch reassured him.

An ominous silence settled on the party as they approached the battleground where the bodies of the dead warriors lay as they had fallen. Even as they closed, Browser could hear the muffled gurgles and occasional faint hiss as the corpses warmed in the morning sunlight.

"Blessed Gods," Rain Crow muttered as they drew up. "Did no one survive?"

"Only you, War Chief," Browser said. "And that is a miracle. If you hadn't crawled as far as you did, today you'd be a wandering and homeless ghost searching futilely for your ancestors."

They passed the first of the bodies; the blood had dried black. Expressions on the faces of the dead ran the gamut from tranquil, as if blissful in death, to contorted grimaces. Men with dried sunken eyes and receding lips watched them pass.

"Blessed Gods," Fire Lark hissed, pointing with his war club. "That one. Look. He's one of them. A White Moccasin. He's been . . ."

"That's Shadow's work, my young friend." Old Pigeontail smiled back at Fire Lark, enjoying the young warrior's discomfort. "The man you see there is Bear Lance, one of Shadow's old lovers. Sometimes I wonder whom to pity more, her enemies, or those that she takes a special liking for."

The Mogollon and Rain Crow stared at the few dead who showed evidence of butchery. The bones looked oddly thin where they protruded from the thick muscles of a carved leg.

Browser ordered, "Move."

As they started away, White Cone asked, "What sort of monster is she?"

"A monster as terrible as any in the legends of your people or mine," Stone Ghost said.

Browser pointed ahead. "Yucca Whip, check the bottom of the wash before we cross and make sure that no ambush is waiting for us. Then guard the other side of the crossing and ensure our safety."

"Yes, War Chief." Yucca Whip charged forward, smoothly withdrawing a fistful of arrows from his quiver and nocking one.

"I wouldn't believe it," Old Pigeontail said under his breath.

"Believe what?" Catkin asked, sparing him a quick sidelong look before returning her attention to the crossing.

"That Fire Dogs would follow a Straight Path War

Chief. More, that members of the Bow Society—of all the Mogollon—would follow Browser."

"Perhaps Poor Singer's prophecy is more Powerful than you thought it was. Perhaps this alliance is just the beginning," Catkin said.

"And perhaps," he responded, "you are just a small group of fools who think that you are more than you are."

Browser looked down into the vacant eyes of one of the dead White Moccasin warriors. Lightning patterns of blackened blood streaked his face.

Browser said, "We will soon find out, Trader."

As THE SUN dipped toward the western horizon, the cliffs shimmered the color of pure gold. Dusty added another stick to his campfire and looked around the canyon. Clouds filled the eastern sky, slowly heading west. He watched them for a time, seeing how their shapes changed; then he took a deep breath and savored the pungent scent of burning juniper. Maggie leaned back in one of the lawn chairs, her legs out straight, her eyes locked on distant thoughts.

Maureen had gone back to the dig, and said she'd return at sunset with Sylvia and Michall. He'd told her he'd have dinner ready, but it would still be a while before he'd bring out the grill and the buffalo burgers. He wanted a good solid bed of coals to roast them over, slowly, very slowly. It wasn't every day a man had the pleasure of eating rich, succulent buffalo. Maureen had found the burger at a specialty food store in Santa Fe. He'd been saving it, hoping to cook it to celebrate a significant find—like today's intact kiva floor.

Dusty walked back to the trailer, opened the squeaky door, and went to the little closet in the rear, where he pulled out two more folding lawn chairs. He grabbed the small ice chest filled with beer on his way outside.

As he unfolded the chairs before the fire, Maggie said, "Dusty?"

"Yeah?" He heard the worry in her voice.

"Aunt Hail came to me in a dream last night."

"She did?"

"She's worried." Maggie avoided his eyes. "She thinks the danger is closing around us. These words stuck in my mind. 'Can't you see him? He's right there, looking over your shoulder, and laughing as he closes his hoop around you.' "

"Did she say who he is?"

Maggie shook her head, lost in thought. "No. Maybe it was just a dream. I mean, how do you tell the difference?" She looked up then, pleading. "Was it *really* Aunt Hail, or just my imagination?"

"I don't know. You should ask your aunt Sage. Maybe she could help you."

Maggie gestured impotence. "I'd love to. I'd call her, but she won't trust the phone lines when it comes to talking about spirit things. She doesn't trust electricity. What she means by that is that she's unsure if witches can monitor it. It's still so new that no one knows if witches can hear things through telephone lines."

"Yeah, like the FBI. Think there's a similarity?"

Maggie smiled at that. "I'd drive down there, but with Rupert leaving, I can't."

"He gone?"

She nodded. "He left me in charge. I didn't get a complete briefing. He was in his office with Dr. Hawsworth for about an hour. And after Hawsworth left, Rupert didn't look happy at all."

"Yeah, Hawsworth has that effect on people. He's sort of the human form of Kaopectate."

He saw Yvette's Jeep coming, and let out a soft groan. She'd looked like a skewered rabbit ever since seeing Hawsworth. He flopped into the chair and reached into the ice chest for a bottle of Guinness.

She stopped twenty paces away, and dust boiled up behind her Jeep. The instant she got out, she cried, "I can't bloody believe it!" She tramped toward him like a woman on a mission.

"What?" he called sociably.

"First I have to deal with my father, and then the FBI! I'm a suspect! In the death of a man I never even knew! Agent Nichols has been raking me over his own proverbial coals!"

Dusty gestured to the remaining lawn chair. "So, you want a Guinness or a Coors Light?"

"What?" she asked as though startled by the question. Her ash-blond hair looked like it hadn't been combed since dawn, and she'd been sweating. Tiny curls framed her forehead. "Oh. Right! Damn. Set me up, Landlord."

Dusty reached into the ice chest and shared a quizzical look with Maggie. "Who?"

She unfolded the other lawn chair and sat down. "Barkeep? Is that the word you use out here in the wilderness?"

"This isn't a wilderness. That's over by Kayenta."

He popped a top on a bottle of Guinness and handed it to her. The way she upended the bottle and chugged made his brows lift in admiration.

"What a sodding miserable day this turned out to be."

"What did Nichols want?"

She glared at him over the bottle. "Everything! He wanted to know when I entered the bloody country. All about the faxes and E-mails I'd been sent. How I came to know about Dale. What I felt when I found out. Did I hate him for being my mother's lover? What did Fa . . . Carter do? What did he say? Did I have any reason to think Carter would have killed Robertson. And on and on and on!" She shivered and tugged the collar of her black coat closed. "Good Lord, Stewart, what are

you and Maggie doing sitting outside on a night like
this? It's freezing."

"Pull your chair closer to the fire." He threw another
piece of juniper on the flames. "You'll be warm soon
enough."

"And as to me," Maggie said, standing and stretching, "I have a park to run. I'd better get back to the
office. If Agent Nichols is up to his usual tricks, he's
got one of the bathrooms closed off and everyone's in
a panic."

"Good night, Maggie," Dusty and Yvette said in unison, and then turned to stare curiously at each other.

Yvette dragged her chair closer as Maggie got into
her pickup and drove off.

"Maggie seems like a gem." She rubbed her face, as
though massaging the fatigue away.

"Yeah, she is. She's a real special friend." He looked
at her. "You okay? I mean after some of the things
Hawsworth said to you. I can't believe that guy. I
wanted to choke the living daylights out of him."

"That's just Father. I mean, Carter. Bloody hell, this
is going to take getting used to." The firelight cast an
orange gleam over her pretty face.

She did look like Dale.

Dusty lowered his gaze and pretended to study the
Guinness label while he hurt. Flames crackled up
around the new tinder, and sparks spiraled into the cold
air. "Yvette?"

"Right here." She gestured flamboyantly with her
hand. "And going nowhere since that tight-knickered
bastard took my passport."

Dusty met her eyes. "How do you feel about all
this?"

She chugged more of the Guinness, before she replied, "I feel like bloody damned Alice falling through
the looking glass."

Dusty smiled. "Sorry. I'm feeling pretty confused
myself. I can't imagine having someone like Haws-

worth for a father and Ruth Ann for a mother. And then there's Nichols sniffing around like a starving coyote."

"Well, it's not going to be pleasant, you know."

Dusty frowned. "What isn't?"

"What they find out about Collins."

"Your husband? The one who died in the crash?"

She pursed her lips, hesitated, and finally shrugged. "There were questions about the crash, Dusty. The people who saw it said he accelerated like a crazy man. He never even touched the brakes. Just smashed himself under the back of a stalled lorry."

Dusty didn't quite know what to say. He toyed with his beer, then said, "My father committed suicide, too."

"Well, it would be nice if it was all so clear, dear brother. Unfortunately, when the widow collects over a million pounds of insurance, on a policy that was taken out the week before . . ." She gave him a knowing look and handed him her empty Guinness bottle. "I don't suppose I could trouble you for another? This one is quite done, and after the day I've had, all things considered, I think I could stand being a little tight tonight."

Dusty took the empty, set it beside the ice chest, and pulled out a fresh bottle. As he popped the top for her, he said, "Well, why would Nichols care? It's not his jurisdiction."

She looked at him as though he must be joking. "Why would Nichols care that I'm a suspect in another suspicious death? I can't imagine."

MAUREEN AWAKENED AT the graying of dawn, and though they slept in different sleeping bags, she found Dusty comfortably pressed against her on the

foldout couch in the trailer. Her face felt icy, and she
could see frost on the aluminum frame surrounding the
window. Her breath rose in the cold.

At her movements, Dusty opened one blue eye. "Is
it morning?"

"I think you can sleep for another hour if you want.
I'll get breakfast started." She unzipped her bag and
sat up.

"Wake me when Yvette gets up?" he asked.

"If it's before noon, you mean?" she said, and
smiled. "Speaking of which, how are you feeling?"

"Perfectly fine. There's an intact kiva waiting for
me."

Maureen rose, fully dressed in jeans and a black
sweatshirt. As she slipped on her hiking boots, she
peered down the hallway toward the bedroom. Yvette
lay snuggled under the blankets like a caterpillar in a
cocoon. Only her hair protruded. She'd been in no con-
dition to drive, and she certainly could not sleep in her
Jeep. She'd accepted Dusty's offer of a bed without the
slightest hesitation.

Dusty rolled to his side and said, "I wager Yvette is
not going to have a pleasant morning."

"I suspect not."

Maureen stood up, went to the kitchen, and poured
water into the coffeepot, then filled the basket with
coffee. While she worked, she gave serious thought to
the shower in the dormitory behind the park headquarters where Michall and Sylvia were staying. The problem with life in the field, and the one thing she still
could not abide, was the lack of hot water. Maybe tonight she'd take them up on their offer for a hot
shower.

Maureen slipped on her coat and stepped outside into
the shimmering morning. The trucks, the trailer, the
rabbitbrush, and the picnic tables carried a quarter-inch
layer of frost. She walked hurriedly down to the rest
room and, with great stoicism, exposed herself to the

cold. At the same time she reminded herself that her ancestors had withstood colder temperatures than this, for much longer periods of time, and without the benefit of Duofold and Hollofil.

She made her way back to the trailer and found Dusty gone and Yvette sitting at the table.

"Where's Dusty?"

"Went to the loo." Yvette had a pained look on her face. Her hair was mussed, and her white turtleneck looked the worse for wear. Through puffy eyes she watched Maureen check the coffee and unpack eggs from the cooler.

"I feel bloody beastly," she muttered.

"There's orange juice in the cooler," Maureen said sympathetically. "That or a can of Pepsi."

"Pepsi?" Yvette screwed up her face. "That sounds positively sadistic."

"Trust me. It'll help."

"Plenty of experience, Dr. Cole?" She narrowed an eye. "I didn't see you sucking down pint after pint last night."

"No, I don't drink."

"That doesn't mean I'm going to get a lecture, does it?"

Maureen smiled. "I wouldn't dare to lecture anyone, Yvette."

As Maureen melted margarine in the frying pan, she thought about how she'd fallen apart after John's death, and how Yvette didn't seem to show any of the normal signs of grief she would have expected. After everyone had gone to sleep last night, Dusty had told her a few of the details of Yvette's husband's death, and Maureen hadn't been able to get them out of her mind.

Cautiously, Maureen said, "You seem to have survived your husband's death much better than I survived mine."

"Yes, well . . ." Yvette looked down at her hands. "I think Collins and I were together just because we didn't have to be someplace else. The investigators, sod them all, tried every trick to pluck that out of me."

Maureen chopped up the last of the fresh poblano peppers and added them to the pan. "Were you together long?"

"Too long," she said, and looked around at the shabby interior of the trailer. "You'd jolly well never catch me living in a mobile camper like this. Just where the hell are we? Is this Chaco place even on maps?"

While Maureen peeled an onion, she replied, "Chaco Canyon is on lots of maps. This is actually a popular tourist attraction."

"Really, well, good on them." She propped her hands on the table and twisted them, appearing distracted.

"You don't really look like much of an outdoors type. Why did you stay so long yesterday?"

"I just couldn't make myself leave. I kept watching, wondering, and then to see the bone and the burned wood . . ." She smiled. "It was really fascinating. Though, you can be sure, had I known that Father and then your blasted Mr. Nichols were going to arrive, I'd have been long gone." She stood up and groaned. "You don't really expect a girl to walk down to that cold toilet when there's a perfectly good little water closet right behind you?"

"With no running water because the pipes would freeze this time of year." Maureen pointed at the camper door. "I'm afraid your only choice is a tall bush or the rest room down the way. Welcome to the Wild West."

"Bloody hell," she muttered, and pulled on her long black wool coat. "So, how long have you and Dusty been together?"

Maureen used the spatula to dig *refritos* from the can and added them to the simmering pan. "We're not together, Yvette. Just friends."

"Oh, sorry 'bout that. But he's handsome, isn't he?"

"Yes, and he knows it, too. He has quite a reputation as a lady killer."

"Too bad he's my brother." She paused, her hand on the door handle. "Tell me, did he have a lonely childhood?"

Maureen met Yvette's curious eyes. "After his mother left, I think it was pretty tough on him. But, later on, he had Dale, and Dale loved him very much."

Yvette nodded. "We're not that different, he and I. Except I never really had anyone."

Yvette opened the door and stepped out onto the rickety trailer steps.

Maureen watched her pass the window; then she poured herself a cup of coffee and leaned heavily against the counter.

# CHAPTER 43

SUNLIGHT DRENCHED THE rimrock as they stepped out of the Bronco, but shadows still clung to the canyon bottom, creating a well of cold air.

Yvette parked beside them and climbed out of her Jeep.

"Yvette?" Maureen asked as she put on her gloves. "Do you have any other clothes?"

Looking a bit uncomfortable, she said, "I'm afraid everything looks like this."

"Then," Dusty said as he buttoned up his denim coat, "I think you had better take a day and go shop for something more practical. A down coat and some hiking boots for starters."

Yvette sighed, "I suppose I should at that."

When the first gust of wind hit Maureen, she jerked her wool hat from her coat pocket and slipped it on her head. "Michall is going to be very glad that Rupert provided that tarp and those hay bales. That freeze last night went deep. I wish I'd . . ."

Dusty blinked at the hill where the site nestled.

"What is it?" Maureen followed his gaze to the irregular shape on the hilltop. She didn't remember it, but maybe it was just the poor light.

The sound of a truck motor made her turn. Michall and Sylvia's vehicle led the FBI Suburban around the turn from Loop Road onto Rinconada Drive.

"What *is* that?" Dusty whispered, and started up the trail.

Maureen gripped his sleeve to hold him back. "I think we should wait for the FBI to get here."

"Why?"

"If it's something unusual, you want them to find it first. That way it doesn't look like we did it. Understand?"

"Oh. Sure. Okay." Dusty tucked his hands in his coat pockets. His gaze was fixed on the ridgetop site.

"Good morning!" Sylvia called as she climbed out of the truck. Brown hair stuck out from beneath her gray knit cap. She lifted a gloved hand to wave.

Dusty waved back, but he'd started grinding his teeth, obviously eager to be at the site. He folded his arms and gave Maureen an irritated look when the ERT people climbed into the back of the Suburban and began handing out equipment. Dusty leaned sideways to whisper, "If my crew took this long to get to the site in the morning, I'd fire them."

Yvette chuckled. "They're bloody government employees. What do you expect?"

Finally, they started up the trail toward Dusty, Maureen, and Yvette.

Dusty looked at Maureen. "You think it's safe to go up now?"

She took his arm. "Why don't we let them lead the way."

He muttered something unpleasant under his breath, but he waited.

Sylvia climbed the hill first. As she approached, she called, "Hey, Washais. How are you this fine morning?" She had her pack slung over one shoulder and a thermos in her other hand.

Maureen waited until Sylvia came closer, then said, "What's the strange shape at the site?"

Sylvia stopped and squinted, and her expression slackened. "I don't know. Let's go find out."

"Now you're talking," Dusty said, and headed up the hill beside Sylvia.

Everyone else followed.

The black plastic was not as Michall had left it the night before. Two of the straw bales were set neatly side by side on the ground, making the strange shape seen from below.

"Somebody's been here." Michall looked at Bill and Rick. "Did you guys bring Agent Nichols up here last night."

"No." Rick had his camera out. "Don't touch anything. Stewart, you, Dr. Cole, and Ms. Hawsworth just arrived?"

"Five minutes before you did."

"We waited for you," Maureen told him. "We didn't want another tongue-lashing from Nichols."

"Good." Bill knelt to study the black plastic tarp. "Okay, let's take this one step at a time. Rick, you keep shooting as we take this apart. If someone's been dicking with our evidence, I want it thoroughly documented."

"Uh, guys," Sylvia pointed. "Someone has also been in our back-dirt pile. Look at the hole scooped in the side."

The shovel, its handle frosty, still stood, stuck in the hollow that someone had excavated. Bill pulled Mich-

all away and gestured Rick over. "See if you can get
photos of the tracks." He looked back at Dusty and
added, "I want everybody else to stay put. Don't move
an inch. Do you understand me?"

Dusty nodded. "Yeah. I understand."

The two agents donned gloves and carefully peeled
back the black plastic. The kiva depths remained in
shadow, the other straw bales barely visible.

As the light filtered in, a mound of dirt like a cinder
cone appeared in the center of the kiva floor. Rick and
Bill pulled the plastic back farther, and Sylvia's breath
caught. She stumbled backward, hissing, "Oh, Jesus!"

Michall whispered, "Son of a bitch."

Maureen stared, unable to move.

Dusty murmured, "Dear God, don't let it be anybody
we know."

Two human feet, bloody and sand-matted, protruded
from the fresh earth. They looked small. Too small to
be a man's feet.

Maureen closed her eyes, afraid of the worst.

BROWSER LED THE way past Corner Kiva, slowing
only long enough to stick his head inside and ensure
that no party of warriors lurked there to ambush them.
Catkin followed behind him, her war club thrust in Old
Pigeontail's back to keep him moving. As they climbed
the slope, Catkin peered down at the abandoned villages of Pottery House and Spindle Whorl. Fallen
stones and bits of cracked plaster covered the ground.

It had taken them much longer than Browser had
planned to get here. Time was their only advantage.
The elders, Rain Crow and the wounded Horned Ram,
had slowed their pace. Would they have time enough
to rush Owl House, kill Two Hearts and Shadow, and

still make an escape? That *was* what Browser was planning, wasn't it?

A sudden whirlwind sprouted from the washed clay, lurching and dancing as it toyed with the weeds and wavered its way across the canyon floor. Before them, the sandstone rim jutted against the southern horizon. The deeply eroded cliff looked almost tired in the late fall light. How many pairs of eyes watched from up there? Catkin's skin started to crawl. They turned away from Corner Kiva and began the last climb up the ridge toward Owl House.

The small block of rooms stood on the ridgetop. It seemed to waver in the clear light. As they climbed, the cold grew deeper and more bitter, forcing the elders to huddle together with their capes clutched at their throats. Stone Ghost hobbled up the slope behind Pigeontail, grunting softly. His thin white hair whipped around his wrinkled face. White Cone struggled up behind Stone Ghost.

"Fire Lark, break right," Browser ordered. "Red Dog, take the left. Let's make sure we see all sides as we approach."

At his words, the warriors tapped their weapons in acknowledgment and split off from the party, advancing along the slope at a trot.

Catkin walked up to stand less than a handsbreadth away and whispered, "We're just going to walk up the hill to the Owl House?"

"Yes."

"There must be a way around, Browser."

His thick black brows had pulled into a single line over his flat nose. "By now, they already know we're here, Catkin. Being clever isn't going to help us. We must strike before Shadow and her warriors have time to move Two Hearts, or get reinforcements from Starburst Town."

Catkin's gaze lifted to the rim and she searched for

the guards Pigeontail had said would be here. She saw no one. But they must be there.

Owl House had a commanding view of the canyon bottom. Not even a rabbit could have hidden in the flat expanse that stretched from Corner Kiva to Straight Path Wash, much less a war party. The only cover was in the tumbled rimrock that lay beneath along the cliff face several bow shots to the south.

Catkin glanced at Old Pigeontail. Something about him wasn't right. He looked smug and self-confident—as though proud of himself for leading them into this trap.

She looked around the canyon. Nothing, only the deteriorating houses and the pale barren silts of the canyon bottom could be seen. Above, on the rim, nothing moved, no heads rose against the skyline.

It couldn't be this easy, could it? Just walk up and storm the house? Kill Two Hearts and Shadow and set Obsidian free? She stepped closer to Browser, lowering her voice to say, "I'm worried."

"Why?" His eyes searched the single-story structure they approached.

"I don't like the way Pigeontail is taking this. He doesn't seem the slightest bit concerned even though he has betrayed the White Moccasins and Two Hearts."

"That's because he lied to us back at Kettle Town."

"Lied?" Catkin whispered. "You know this to be true?" She shot a hot glance at Pigeontail.

"He gave in too easily. He must have been lying."

She shifted and clutched her club more tightly. "Then he got us to do exactly what Two Hearts and Shadow wished."

Browser nodded. "Yes, but we're ahead of schedule. Ordinarily, I would wait until nightfall to go in, hoping darkness would cover our approach. Two Hearts knows this."

"You are telling me that we're walking into a trap?" she asked, searching his face.

"Of course."

Catkin gripped his sleeve and pulled him back to stare hard into his eyes. "What is your plan?"

Browser smiled at the commanding tone in her voice. "Just promise me: When I give the order, kill Two Hearts. His death and Shadow's are the two most important objectives. Everything else—Obsidian, you, me, the elders, the Mogollon—is secondary." He gave her a look that melted her heart. "Do you understand?"

She twined her fist in his sleeve as though to rip it from his arm and said, "Yes. I understand."

He smiled. "I thank you for you loyalty, Catkin. Because this is a turning point."

"What do you mean?"

"I mean that if we are successful, killing Two Hearts will be the beginning of the end."

"The end of what?"

"Of this war, of clan against clan, of the katsinas against the old gods. It might take generations for all of the hatred to seep out through the people, like rings on a pond, but in the end the waters will be still again, as they were before the katsinas came to Sternlight. Someone must show the world a beginning—that we can all live together: Made People, First People, and Mogollon."

Catkin studied the blocky shape of Owl House on the hilltop. "Who will win, Browser? The old gods, or the new gods?"

"I don't know," he whispered. "But let us go and stamp out this evil now. Let us make a beginning to the end." He walked up the slope.

Catkin reached into the quiver that hung down her back and pulled out two arrows. She thought she caught sight of a head lifting ever so slightly from the rooftop of Owl House.

"They're watching us," she said.

"Good. It is time to spring their trap and see how they plan to kill us."

"THE THREE OF you were together all night?" Agent Nichols asked for the fifth time as he paced up and down the yellow tape in front of the murder scene.

"All night," Maureen said. "We didn't hear anything. There was frost on both our vehicles this morning. So we didn't drive anywhere. We didn't do it."

Nichols had that look in his eye. He wasn't a man a sane person wanted to cross. His fists worked for a moment as he read the truth in Maureen's eyes, then turned away and walked to where Sylvia and Michall sat on a small sandstone ledge. Spooked and cold, they obviously longed to be anywhere but here with a corpse in their dig.

"Jesus," Dusty whispered. "Why is the killer doing this?"

Maureen felt a sudden chill. "He's just taking it to the next level of the game."

"What do you mean?"

"This is the dare," Maureen murmured as she watched Nichols pace. "And Nichols knows it."

Yvette said, "Since I have a good solid alibi, I suppose I'm off the good inspector's list of suspects. But given his mood, I don't fancy asking him for my passport back. At least not in the near future."

Dusty smoothed his hand over his beard. "Who do you think the victim is?" He tipped his blond head toward the hilltop. "Could you see anything?"

Maureen shook her head, not willing to tell him what she'd thought about the size of the feet, because if she was right, Dusty was about to lose someone else. "We're not going to find out until Sid gets here."

"From Albuquerque? That's late afternoon at the earliest. Won't Nichols try to . . ." Dusty turned at the distant chatter of a helicopter.

"I think"—Maureen looked toward the southeast—"that when Agent Nichols gets pissed, things happen."

Dusty's eyes narrowed as he shifted to watch Nichols question Sylvia and Michall. Both women looked like they wanted to throw up. "Think I ought to mosey over there and eavesdrop?"

"Not unless you want to spend the next couple of nights in a cozy little cell learning the intricacies of body-cavity searches, good cop/bad cop interrogations, and the ins and outs of the lawyer-client relationship."

The helicopter cleared the rimrock and settled over the parking lot. Dust whirled as the bird spooled down. Moments later the doors opened and Sid Malroun and four men in blue FBI coats ducked out. In a knot they hurried across the parking lot toward the trail that led up past Casa Rinconada.

"Dusty?" Maureen asked, and gave him a frightened look. "If this site has been disturbed, do you think—?"

It took a second before her meaning dawned and his gaze went to the great kiva where Dale had been killed.

"Oh, my God."

"Nichols just said we weren't supposed to go back to the trucks," she reminded. "And I ought to say hello to Sid. It would look perfectly natural if we walked down to meet him, then you could—"

"I hear trouble in your voices," Yvette said, and leaned closer to join their conversation. "Are we off somewhere?"

Maureen said, "We're just going to take a walk down the hill."

Yvette followed them, tagging along.

They reached the great kiva at the same time Sid Malroun and the FBI men came walking up the interpretive trail. The FBI call must have pulled Sid out of bed. Brown stubble covered his face, and the sparse hair on his mostly bald head stood straight up. His glasses had frosted when he'd stepped out into the cold air so Maureen couldn't see his eyes.

"Good morning, Sid." Maureen walked forward to shake his hand while Dusty stared over the side and into the depths of the kiva.

"Maureen, good Lord, are you still mixed up in this?" Sid asked as he shook.

"Apparently."

"Okay. Tell me what I'm looking at today?"

"I don't know." Maureen frowned up the hill at the displaced straw bales. Everyone, as she'd expected, turned to follow her gaze. "The FBI won't let me near the body. I've been trying to tell them that—"

Dusty turned, cupping hands around his mouth to shout: "Nichols? I think you should see this! The blood down here is already frozen, but it's a safe bet that it matches the corpse on the hill!"

Nichols spun around where he stood on top of the ridge and squinted across the distance to where Dusty pointed into the dawn-shadowed great kiva. He left the ridge at a run. Maureen had to hand it to him. He vaulted the sage and rabbitbrush with grace that belied his age. When he stopped at Dusty's side and stared down at the dark stain on the kiva floor, his face reddened. "Bill? Rick? Get over here and photograph this!"

Maureen and Sid went to stand on the other side of Dusty. Maureen stared down at the large bloodstain on the frosty kiva floor.

"See that sand pattern that's just barely visible through the frost?" Dusty pointed to the left of the blood. "It probably matches the samples you took out of here a few days ago."

"Meaning?" Sid asked.

Dusty said, "I wager he gets it from the same place, Dr. Malroun, probably a sacred place."

Maureen studied the footprints that led from the

stain, across the kiva, and up the stairway. Small prints, like those of a woman, or a diminutive man. The murderer hadn't been so careful this time. Or maybe she couldn't be. Perhaps she hadn't anticipated the frost, or it had happened in the middle of the murder.

"Well, Sid," Maureen said through a long exhalation. "You have your hands full."

"Yes." He nodded. "As of today, our man is a serial killer."

"Brilliant," Yvette said unhappily, "and I was pissed out of my gourd. He could have driven right up, opened the door, and lifted me out with no one the wiser."

She shoved her hands in her coat pockets and stalked up the trail toward the excavation.

Maureen quietly said to Sid, "You really think it's a man?"

Sid rubbed his stubbly jaw and studied the footprints. "Not necessarily, but I think it's prudent to keep saying so in public."

He turned slightly to watch Yvette climb the hill. Then his eyes drifted to Sylvia where she knelt looking down into the excavation. His brows lowered.

In a low voice, he added, "I'm not even sure it's one person we're looking for."

# CHAPTER 44

As THE DAY ground on, Dusty's patience wore thin. Maureen sat on a rock and watched him pace the yellow tape like a caged tiger, watching the FBI team secure the scene, record the evidence, and carefully dig the corpse from the loose sand and the straw bales that the killer had used to prop his victim's body.

Preliminary inspection revealed that the soles of the feet had been skinned, but hastily, as though the killer feared discovery. The toes had been hacked off to make the skinning faster—which is why the feet had looked so small. A yucca hoop encircled the man's body. Then, as the knees were uncovered, Maureen could see the yucca leaves that pierced them. The man's genitals had been sliced from the pubis with a sharp blade.

When the technicians finally lifted the body from the soil, Yvette let out a soft cry and put a hand to her lips. Tears glistened in her wide eyes.

It took Maureen a moment longer. Blood and filth matted the face, and gore ran from the hole that had been sawed in the rear of the skull—but she saw his silver ponytail.

Yvette whispered, "Oh, no. God."

"Who is it?" Dusty asked.

Yvette took an involuntary step backward. She was shaking. "It's . . . I think it's . . . my father. Carter." Her voice broke.

Dusty turned back to scrutinize the body as they carried it across the kiva and said, "Are you sure?"

Yvette nodded. "Yes."

Maureen put a hand on Yvette's shoulder. He may not have been a good father, or even her biological father, but for most of her life she'd thought he was. Softly, Maureen said, "I need to go tell the medical examiner. It will cut the time it takes to verify the ID. Will you be all right?"

In a breathless voice, Yvette said, "Where's my mother? Does anyone know?"

As Maureen walked toward Sid Malroun, she heard Dusty answer, "I suspect Agent Nichols will have her picked up within the hour."

OWL HOUSE CONSISTED of five single-story rooms with a contiguous kiva on the south side. The long axis of the edifice ran northeast-southwest along the ridgetop. To take it, Browser had split his forces, sending Badger Dancer around to the north and west with Split Beam and Clay Frog. Meanwhile, he, Catkin, Yucca Whip, and Fire Lark charged in from the south and east. White Cone and Stone Ghost stood just out of range, guarding Pigeontail and Horned Ram, with orders to kill the Trader should anything go amiss, and make their escape as best they could. Rain Crow, practically wavering on his feet, gripped his war club and staggered forward, his cloudy eyes fixed on Owl House.

Browser zigzagged as he ran. From the corner of his eye he could see Catkin sprinting up the slope, her long legs pumping. Sunlight flashed off the polished wood of her bow. She had never been so beautiful. Gods curse him, why had he wasted so much time mourning the dead when he should have been sharing her blankets?

Heart pounding, he charged up to the wall, more than a little surprised that no arrows darted from above. Catkin flattened herself against the wall beside him, followed a half breath later by Fire Lark.

"Up!" Browser said, raising his right foot.

Catkin and Fire Lark cupped their hands, lifting as Browser straightened. They almost threw him, despite his weight, onto the roof. He caught the lip, nearly falling as the plaster crumbled under his fingers, and flipped himself onto the flat earthen roof. In a split heartbeat he was on his feet, surprised to see . . . nothing. No enemy waited to club his brains out. The only movement was Red Dog being boosted in a similar fashion to the opposite side of the roof. Eyes wide, panting, the warrior scrambled to his feet, his war club up to deflect a blow.

Browser stepped warily to look down at Catkin. "Hold your position, but be on guard. Red Dog and I will check the rooms."

Browser tiptoed lightly to the dark roof opening. The ladder's two weathered gray upright poles stuck up against the sky. He tested the roof near the entryway and quickly pulled his war shirt over his head. Red Dog was watching with a sudden frown, baffled as Browser took a quick wrap of his shirt over the head of his war club. Then he ducked low and shoved the cloth bundle over the lip of the entryway before jerking it back in the manner of a peeking head. Nothing. Again he feinted with the bundled cloth.

Red Dog had finally caught on and pulled off his own blue war shirt, mimicking Browser as he feinted at the next room opening. Generally, if a warrior were waiting in ambush within, their nerves would be pulled as taut as damp rawhide in a hot sun. At the first movement they'd loose an arrow.

Browser circled, grasped the ladder in both hands, and pulled it out of the room. He lowered it over the side of the building and Catkin swiftly climbed up.

"It's too dark to see into any of the rooms," Browser told her as he slipped his war shirt on. "Let's pull up all the ladders. Anyone inside will stay that way until we decide to let them out."

"Or until they knock a hole in the wall," Catkin said. "What about the kiva?"

"That's our next stop."

Catkin whispered, "He's here, Browser. I can feel him, like a cold wind whispering around my souls."

Catkin led the way to the south roof. From there they could look down on the kiva—a round disk raised to knee height above the ridgetop. A faint twist of blue smoke rose from the hole in the kiva roof.

Browser met Catkin's knowing eyes and took a moment to touch her shoulder. That one light touch, the feel of her body, sent warmth through him. Her reassuring smile was just for him. And with that, he squatted, swung his legs over the side of the wall, and dropped lightly to his feet on the kiva roof. Two heartbeats later, Catkin thumped down beside him. Stepping to the side, he motioned to his warriors who waited beside the walls. In single file they trotted along, forming up on either side of the kiva entry.

Browser turned, gesturing to Red Dog to stay on the high rooftop. With his index and middle fingers he pointed to his eyes and made the "keep watch" sign.

Attacking a kiva was a relatively straightforward problem. All an attacker need do was pull out the ladder and drop burning brush down the entry hole. The next move was to throw hides or damp cloth over the hole. The smoke, flames, and heat finished the job without exposing the attacker. If you wanted the occupants out, however, the ladder was left in place as the flaming brush was dropped in. Provided the ladder didn't catch fire too quickly, the defenders would eventually be driven out, crying, coughing, and blinded. It was an easy matter to simply wait at the top of the ladder with war clubs and beat their heads in as they emerged. The problem Browser now faced was how to retrieve Obsidian from the kiva before he set fire to it.

"Browser?" a woman's gentle voice came from the kiva.

He glanced at Catkin and answered, "Obsidian? Is that you?"

"It is." Something about the sensual tones warned him.

"Come out, Obsidian. We're here to take you away." To Catkin, Browser silently mouthed: "Shadow Woman?" and shrugged his shoulders.

Catkin tightened her grip on her war club.

"I'm tied up. Please come and get me!"

A muffled voice rose, like a woman trying to scream with a hand over her mouth. Then a child let out a high-pitched roar of sheer terror, which was abruptly halted by the sound of a fist striking flesh.

*"Bone Walker?"* Stone Ghost cried, his eyes suddenly huge. *"Bone Walker, is that you?"*

He rushed forward, but Rain Crow gripped his arm and held him back. They spoke to each in quiet harsh tones for several moments; then Stone Ghost reluctantly stepped back. But he stood as though poised to run the instant he could.

Browser considered, then said, "Shadow? Do you remember the turquoise wolf? The one Two Hearts lost when he attacked Hophorn outside of Talon Town. The turquoise wolf that belonged to the Blessed Night Sun? I'm setting it here on the kiva roof, and then I'm coming down. If I don't call back to Catkin, she'll take her war club and smash it into dust."

Silence, and then Browser recognized Two Hearts's weak voice. "Don't, Browser." A faint cough and a groan. "We can work this out."

"Yes," Browser agreed. "You send Obsidian up, and I'll send the wolf down. Do we have an agreement?"

He could hear whispering from below.

"Browser!" Red Dog shouted. "War parties! Several of them, White Moccasins, they're boiling out of Straight Path Wash and from War Club village to the east!"

"How many warriors?"

Red Dog straightened. "Five there. Ten, no . . . ten and two there." He turned slightly. "From the west, there are more. Five . . . seven in that band."

Twenty-two at least. Not to mention any that might be down in the kiva with Two Hearts.

"Find the best positions to shoot from—then take cover!" Browser ordered, pointing toward Owl House's roof with his war club. "Make sure that Stone Ghost and White Cone are lying down on the roof, safe. Pull up the ladders. We can hold them here!"

White Cone glanced down from above. "With your permission, War Chief. I will handle the defense from up here."

"I appreciate that, Bow Elder. Now sit down and rest. We have some time before they arrive. Reserve your strength and mind for the challenge to come."

"Browser?" Shadow's sensual voice drifted from the kiva. "It doesn't have to be this way. Let us talk."

They had maneuvered him into coming here, then left the place unguarded. If he did only one thing today, he could kill them. Surely they knew that. Which meant they had risked everything to get him here. Why?

"I'm listening, Shadow," he said as he strode to the edge of the roof. The seven warriors from War Club village ran full tilt to cut off the stairway that led out of the canyon.

"You have us, we have you," she called. "I think we can bargain."

"Red Dog," Browser called, "any activity in the rooms?"

"No, War Chief." The young warrior stood looking worriedly at the closing warriors.

"Good. If this turns against us, kill Pigeontail. In the meantime, find anything that will burn. Pull the roof apart if you have to, and get the kindling to me."

"Yes, War Chief." Red Dog bounded away and Browser could hear the scraping of a ladder.

"Browser?" Shadow called. "If you harm us, neither you nor your Made People friends will leave here alive. You know that, don't you?"

"We came here to die, Shadow. You and Two Hearts have destroyed everything we hold dear. You killed and butchered our friends, killed our Matron. You burned innocent children to death in the Longtail village kiva. The only thing we value now is your deaths!"

"We had our reasons! You are one of us, you should know!"

"Reasons?" he shouted. "You are witches! You—"

*"Browser?"* Red Dog called from above. "The White Moccasins will be in range soon, should we shoot at them? Slow them down?"

Browser shook his head. "Wait, Red Dog. There's no sense in wasting arrows."

Browser took the ladder that Red Dog had lowered and raced to the roof. From the vantage point he could see the closing ring of warriors, taking their time, moving into position.

Cupping his hands to his mouth, he called, "Stop where you are! I am War Chief Browser, of the Katsinas' People. The witches, Two Hearts and Shadow Woman, are in the kiva. If you attack us, we will set fire to the place and burn them with it. If you would see your leaders alive again, you will withdraw."

One of the warriors stepped out, the breeze fluttering his white tunic. "I am Thorn Fox, of the Red Lacewing Clan, War Chief of the Starburst warriors. You are surrounded. Your only hope for survival is to surrender."

"Piece of filth," Rain Crow growled.

Browser called, "War Chief, we will not surrender, and you will not attack."

"Why won't I?"

"Because, I told you, if you do, your elders will be burned to death."

"If you kill them," Thorn Fox warned, "we will kill you—then we will hunt down and kill your families! Your clans will be cursed!"

"Hold your position!" Browser called.

Turning he strode to the kiva opening. "Shadow? Thorn Fox is out here. Tell him to stay back, or I will set fire to your kiva this instant!"

MAGGIE PULLED UP and shifted her green pickup into park. She stepped out as Dusty opened the camp trailer's door. The rimrock on either side of the canyon had turned brown and foreboding beneath the gray clouds that obscured the late afternoon sky.

"Hello, Maggie," he called. His blond hair was mussed, and his blue eyes were red-rimmed.

Nichols had run everyone through the mill that morning, and Dusty looked it. Worse, when she'd called Rupert in Washington that morning, he'd told her that under no circumstances was she to interfere with Nichols's investigation. The FBI agent had had her jumping through bureaucratic hoops all morning.

"Hi, Dusty." She walked over and climbed the aluminum steps. Inside it was warm and the air smelled of coffee and green chili.

Sylvia and Michall sat on the foldout couch up front. Maureen and Yvette were in the booth. Maggie could tell Yvette had been crying. Her eyes were swollen and her face puffy. "Hello," Maggie greeted, taking in the sister who had just magically appeared in Dusty's life. It would never cease to amaze her that Whites treated relatives so cavalierly.

*She has a wounded soul. Be wary until you know what she is.* The words popped into her head, as if whispered from another place. Was that Grandmother Slumber's voice?

Dusty said, "What can I get you to drink, Maggie?"

Maggie looked around, confused by what she had just heard. Maureen and Yvette had coffee. Dusty clutched a half-empty bottle of Guinness and Sylvia had her traditional Coors Light. Michall held a can of cherry soda.

"Coffee would be great." Maggie slid into the booth near Maureen. Her nerves were humming. Was her grandmother trying to warn her from the other world?

"So, are we all under arrest?" Dusty asked as he poured a cup of coffee and set it in front of Maggie.

"Not yet," she told him. "Rupert's on his way back. I called him on his cell phone. Got him out of a life-or-death budget meeting. He said he'd explain the situation to the deputy director and catch the first flight he could."

Maggie turned to Sylvia. "You okay after Agent Nichols put the screws to you?"

Sylvia nodded, her face pale. "Can you believe that guy? God, he took me into that conference room and I thought I was in the hands of the Gestapo. He must have spent every dime the Bureau has to rake up all those nasty things from my childhood. God, you'd think I'd killed Dale, the way he was asking questions."

"It's all right," Michall soothed, reaching out and punching Sylvia's shoulder. "I told him if you'd done it, the skull would have exhibited blunt-force trauma— I also told him where to find your baseball bat."

"Thanks," Sylvia said. "That's all I need. The FBI looking under my pillow."

Michall jiggled her half-empty soda can. "That was a grueling experience, answering all those questions. Nichols kept staring at me with that funny eye of his. I thought my oral exams were tough. After what he put me through this morning, my Ph.D. dissertation defense is going to be a piece of cake."

"What about you?" Dusty asked, and pinned Maggie with tired blue eyes. "Did Nichols take a chunk out of your hide, too?"

She nodded. "I just got out of my 'interview.' Once he established that I didn't know Hawsworth, he seemed to lose interest in me, but he sure quizzed me about you."

Dusty pulled back in mock surprise. "You mean he

thinks I have a motive? Just because Hawsworth ran off with my mother and ruined my life?"

"It always seems to come back to that, doesn't it?" Yvette asked.

Maggie cocked her head. "Are you *really* Dusty's sister?"

She studied Maggie through eyes that looked fragile. "Same mother," she said in a small voice.

"You have my condolences," Maggie said before sipping coffee. Then she added, "The reason I'm here, outside of the good coffee, is that Agent Nichols has a dilemma."

"No shit," Sylvia said. "For one thing, I'm out of here! I have just established new standards for my work. I won't excavate any kiva unless the bodies have been dead for at least a week."

"Damn straight," Michall agreed. "Sylvia and I talked it over. We're leaving tonight."

"That's part of Nichols's dilemma." Maggie cradled her coffee, grateful for the warmth on her fingers. "He's more convinced than ever that the site needs to be dug, that some important clue is there. His problem is that each of you are now potential suspects."

"So," Dusty finished, "where's he going to find a crew?"

Maggie tilted her head uncertainly. "I told him that if he doesn't get it dug in the next couple of weeks, the frost is going to make it impossible for him to finish the excavation before spring." She took a deep breath. "I asked him to call Steve."

Dusty nodded. "Good choice. If Steve can find a crew."

"He's bringing four graduate students, leaving this afternoon from Tucson. He says he'll be here in the morning." She winced. "Dusty, I went out on a limb and told him he could use your equipment. Is that all right?"

"You were worried about that?" Then he nodded,

eyes warming. "Of course you were. I'm not thinking straight. I'll gladly loan him my equipment, unless Nichols thinks my equipment will bias the investigation."

Maggie stared into the depths of her coffee. Her grandmother had once told her that Dreamers could see things in black liquids. "Dusty, I need to check on Aunt Sage, but I'm in charge while Rupert's in Washington. I can't go. I have a terrible favor to ask. Would you mind—?"

"Not at all," he cut her off. "I'll leave as soon as we eat. Are you up for burritos?"

Maggie smiled her relief. "Sure. I haven't eaten since six A.M. I'm starved." She added, "Thank you, Dusty. I've just got a bad feeling, that's all."

The faint voices, barely audible in her mind, whispered in assent.

# CHAPTER 45

CATKIN SPREAD HER feet, her eyes on the rooftop kiva entry.

It took ten heartbeats.

Shadow emerged from the kiva like First Woman from the underworlds. As she climbed onto the roof and looked around, the wind pressed her soft white dress against her perfect body. Turquoise, coral, and jet beads were woven into her shining black hair. An inhuman gleam filled her black eyes. She moved with the grace of a mountain lion in the rocks, sinuous and sure, each motion fluid.

She smiled when she walked up to Browser, and Catkin's arm muscles tensed, ready.

Browser didn't even flinch as Shadow's slim fingers ran along his chin. Gods, how could he do that? Catkin would have been cringing under that witch's faintest touch.

In a soft sensual voice, Shadow said, "Two Hearts has a bargain for you, War Chief."

"What is it?"

Shadow spread her arms to the warriors below and Browser's own warriors on the rooftops. "All of this was orchestrated just for you, War Chief—your journey from Flowing Waters Town, your stay in Kettle Town, your 'attack' on us here at Owl House, everything was designed just to get you here today. Isn't it lovely? Aren't you pleased?"

Browser shook his head. "What are you talking about?"

"You simple fool! Two Hearts brought you here because he wishes *your* heart."

Browser's hand involuntarily went to his chest. "My heart?"

"Of course. You are both descended from the Blessed Night Sun. You are one of his relatives, and you are a strong young man. Your heart is much better than my sister's feeble heart."

Catkin's stomach turned. She took a step forward with the intent of bashing in the woman's skull.

Browser lifted a hand to stop her. To Shadow, he said, "You are a liar."

"I am?" Shadow raised a slim eyebrow.

Browser smiled grimly. "You never planned to sacrifice the White Moccasins in a fruitless battle. Are you trying to tell me that you didn't think it would be easier to simply surround me in Kettle Town, thus saving your warriors and lessening the risk that I might just burn you alive in Owl House and figure on fighting my way out?"

Her eyes had narrowed. "Nevertheless, *we* brought you here and Two Hearts will have your heart."

"What does Two Hearts offer in return?"

Shadow laughed softly as she walked around Browser. Her white dress conformed to each curve of her lithe body and swirled about her sandaled feet. "You are surrounded. If you fight, you will surely all be killed." She aimed a slender finger at Catkin. "Including the woman you love. So think carefully before you give me your answer."

Browser looked at Catkin with his whole heart in his dark eyes.

"Yes," Shadow hissed in Browser's ear. "I will roast her alive and feed her body to my daughter, then—"

"I ask one thing," Browser said a little too quickly.

Shadow stopped. "Name it."

Before he answered, Browser met the eyes of every warrior, and took a long look at Stone Ghost. "If you will allow everyone else to leave, I will willingly lay down my weapons and be your prisoner."

Catkin stared, speechless. A hoarse chuckle, followed by a cough, came from inside the kiva.

Shadow studied Browser with luminous eyes. After a moment, she stepped over to the kiva wall and looked down the slope to where the White Moccasins waited. "Thorn Fox! Most of these people will be leaving. They are to be allowed safe passage up the Great North Road. You will detail one warrior to follow them and make sure it is so."

"Yes, Blessed Shadow," Thorn Fox called back.

The form of address sickened Catkin's souls. *Blessed Shadow?*

Shadow stepped back to Browser's side and said, "You have the wolf? That was not a lie?"

Browser touched the bulge sewn into the hem of his war shirt.

"You will have to give it up," Shadow told him.

"Then he is that close to death?" Browser asked.

"He is." Shadow paused, and a small smile tugged at her lips. "Just in case your heart is not enough to save him, he must have a Spirit Helper to guide him through the underworlds."

"And afterward," Browser asked. "What of the leadership of the White Moccasins?"

Catkin's gaze went from Browser's face to Shadow's, and back again. Had Browser lost his mind? She kept trying to fathom his plan. He must have one. What could it be?

Shadow moved forward until her breasts touched Browser's chest. "Leadership will pass to the man I choose." Then she turned abruptly and climbed down like a serpent into the kiva.

Catkin crossed the space in two strides. "What are you doing—"

Browser's sharp gesture stopped her short. Anger flashed in his eyes. "Take everyone north to Flowing Waters Town and rejoin the Katsinas' People."

Catkin began a protest when Browser shot a meaningful glance toward the kiva entrance. She didn't need to look to understand that Shadow's head must have been just below the roofline, listening.

"War Chief, as your deputy—"

"I'm sorry, Catkin. I can't let you die. And you know that's what will happen."

"Browser, for the sake of the gods, let's fight!"

"No, Catkin. This is best for everyone." His eyes burned into hers, emphasizing his meaning. "You were right earlier. One life is not worth ten."

What in the name of the monsters of the underworlds was he doing? She searched his face.

"Browser? Please, don't do this, I can't—"

"By doing this, I have given you extra time and I expect you to be a better War Chief than I have been. Remember, the roundabout way is often better than a direct assault against superior numbers. Victory goes to those who are swiftest, and allies can appear from the most unexpected places." He smiled, touched her face lightly with a gentle finger, and ordered, "Now go. *Quickly!*"

"No, Browser, please—"

"Do not disgrace me in front of others by disobedience."

Shadow appeared on the ladder a moment before Obsidian did.

In the light, they might have been identical but for the curious sheen in Obsidian's eyes. She wore a tan cotton shift that was loose, smudged, but her glossy hair hung to her waist. She cast a sad look at Browser, a wistful longing in her eyes. She walked up to him, saying, "Don't you wish now that you had taken me away? None of this would have had to happen."

Browser's lips curled. "You didn't have to join them. I would have seen to your safety."

She shrugged. "They are my family, Browser. My People. I made my own bargain with them. Your heart instead of mine. I'm the one who sent Old Pigeontail this morning."

Shadow told Obsidian, "Go down and wait with Thorn Fox's warriors where you will be safe, Sister. I'll call you when we are ready for the ritual feast."

Obsidian gave Browser a seductive smile as she passed, and Catkin took a step, her war club raised.

Browser gripped her shoulder and pulled her back, whispering, "Catkin, go *now*! You may not have much time."

She swallowed hard and met Browser's eyes one last time. Perhaps if she just looked at him long enough, she would understand his plan. Surely he had a plan. Browser would not just offer himself up like a sacrificial deer! She whispered, "I'll be waiting for you at Flowing Waters Town."

He nodded. "All right. Yes, if I can. Now, go. Hurry. And leave Horned Ram."

Catkin gave him one last incredulous look, then gestured to the warriors on the rooftops. "Come. Let's get out of here!"

Her heart hammered like a foot drum on dance night as the Mogollon filed off the roofs and came toward her in a murmuring knot. Disbelief strained their features. White Cone seemed the most baffled of all of them.

"You heard the War Chief," she ordered. "Let's go."

She started down the hill but Stone Ghost's voice stopped her.

The old man called, "I'm staying."

"No!" Browser shouted, and whirled to look at the old white-haired man. "Uncle, please."

To Catkin, Stone Ghost said, "Tell Matron Cloudblower we wish her well in her search for the First People's original kiva."

Rain Crow appeared on the roof above, leaning heavily on his walking stick. Sweat coated his pain-racked face. Through gritted teeth, he said, "I will be staying also, War Chief. I will just slow Catkin down."

Browser hesitated only a moment, and Catkin swore she saw a slight smile on his lips as he waved Catkin away. "Go on! Leave!"

Catkin led the way out of Owl House and down the slope.

They passed unmolested through the ranks of the White Moccasins, and at the last opportunity, she looked back. Browser and Stone Ghost watched from the kiva roof. Shadow and Thorn Fox stood a short distance away, their heads together, as though in deep conversation.

Rain Crow perched on the roof, like a lonely owl waiting for night to fly far away.

*What just happened there? Why don't I understand what Browser's doing?*

"I KNOW IT'S here somewhere," Dusty said as he peered at the weed-filled fence line that bordered the road. He drove slowly on the asphalt, looking for a break that would mark the two-track dirt road leading to Sage Walking Hawk's home.

"I'll take your word for it." Yvette leaned forward anxiously in the backseat. "You say she's dying?"

"Breast cancer," Maureen answered. "I think the gene runs in the family."

"Nasty lot that. Maggie seems like a gem."

"She's a good friend," Dusty said. The glow of the Bronco's instruments seemed dimmer tonight than usual. He probably needed a new battery, as well as a new truck, but both would have to wait. "We've seen a lot of tough times together."

Yvette was silent for a moment. "You've a great many friends, don't you, Dusty?"

"No, not really. A few good friends. I guess I've never thought about it."

"That's a gift, you know."

"You don't have many friends?" Maureen asked.

"I grew up in a different world," Yvette said bitterly. "If you value friends, God help you if come into money. Old companions vanish overnight. Everything changes."

"Yeah, well, I've never had that problem." Dusty pulled over onto the shoulder of the road as a pickup appeared out of the night and sped past them with the engine roaring. It careered down the road in front of them.

"One really pissed Native, I'd say," Yvette commented. "I hope he makes it home."

Dusty pulled onto the asphalt again. Drunk drivers

were common out here, especially right after payday on the first of the month, but he hadn't liked Yvette's tone. It was superior, as though she'd seen too many TV shows about reservation Indians.

Maureen seemed to sense Dusty's discomfort. She turned around to look at Yvette. "You've had a tough day. How are you faring?"

Yvette shook her head and ash-blond hair fell into her eyes. Dusty watched her brush it away through the rearview mirror. She said, "Stunned."

"I'm sure," Maureen said gently. "He was your father."

"Is that what he was?" Yvette said, and when Dusty and Maureen didn't answer right away, she continued, "He was a cold man. Somehow I ended up in no-man's-land between him and Mum." Her face twisted. "But he deserved better than that. Oh, dear, I swore I'd not break down and bawl like a babe."

Dusty said, "There's a roll of toilet paper in the bag under my seat, if you need it."

"Thank you," she said in a slightly stronger voice. "Both of you. For letting me tag along these last couple of days."

Dusty slowed at the break in the fence. In the distance, off to the right, a yard light illuminated the dilapidated old trailer nestled at the mouth of the side canyon. Dusty turned and rattled over the cattle guard onto the track.

Yvette hesitated for a moment, gazing at the rusty car bodies and trash that hunkered in the weeds, then said, "I truly can't believe people live like this. It's barbaric."

"Barbaric?" Dusty asked, and gave her a curious look over his shoulder. "Living in a place where you can hear coyotes howl and eagles cry? Where you can walk for days without seeing another human being? Personally," he said as he shifted gears, "I think city life is barbaric. Hundreds of thousands of people per square mile, living on top of each other? God, how do you live like that? It's not even *human*."

He pulled up in front of the trailer house, shut off the Bronco, and turned off the lights. As he opened the door, he said, "We don't knock on doors in this part of the world, so just do what I do. It's considered polite to give the people inside time to prepare before they open the door."

Maureen walked around to stand beside Dusty. Her gray coat and black hair blended so well with the darkness she was almost invisible.

Yvette stared at the trailer as though in disbelief. Weak yellow light gleamed in the living-room window. The rickety front porch leaned precariously to the right, and rusty tin cans and windblown plastic bottles lay beneath it. "This place is a bloody junkyard," Yvette said.

Dusty shoved his fists in his pockets and replied, "I doubt that Sage Walking Hawk shares your value system, Sister. Her wealth is not in things, but in family and clan, the animal world, and the Spirits."

"Spirits?" Yvette said the word as though she'd never heard it before. "She believes in Spirits? Like ghosts that roam the world haunting people?"

"Like Spirits that live in the stars and trees, and beneath the water. It's a beautiful belief—one I share. I also believe in witches and Buffalo Above." That completely silenced Yvette. Dusty added, "Remember, Sister, Sage Walking Hawk has spent her entire life enriching her soul." He gave her a hard look. "Can you say the same thing?"

"Are you implying, dear brother, that I've spent my life enriching my bank accounts?"

Dusty walked toward the trailer and, from inside, a wavering voice called, "Door's open."

Dusty climbed up the creaking steps and pushed the door ajar. "Elder Walking Hawk? It's Dusty Stewart.

I'm here with Washais, and my sister, Yvette. Magpie wanted me to check on you."

"Come on in, Dusty." Sage coughed and wheezed as though she couldn't get enough air.

Dusty walked in. The trailer smelled of stale urine and old grease. The knickknacks, the trophies of a lifetime, that sat everywhere cast shadows on the shelves. A giant loom covered the wall to his right, the masterpiece rug unfinished.

Sage turned on a lamp. She sat in a worn recliner, her body emaciated; her pain-bright eyes sank deeply in her wrinkled face. Flakes of dandruff dotted her sparse white hair. The faded picture of a uniformed World War II airman lay crooked in her lap, the young white man smiling out from the past. A cane lay out of her reach on the floor next to a fallen plastic drinking glass.

"Elder?" Dusty asked, walking over and kneeling in front of her. "Are you all right?"

Sage's mouth opened in a toothless smile. "The ghosts haven't got you yet?"

"Not yet, but I'm still worried."

Sage chuckled and it sounded like brittle autumn leaves blowing in the wind.

"Have you eaten, Elder?" Dusty took her hand, and it felt cold. The musky smell of urine clung to her. "I packed a pan of leftover enchiladas in the ice chest in my truck. Can I bring them in and warm them in your stove?"

Her faded old eyes slipped off to the side and she gasped. Dusty felt her hand tense, then relax as she smacked dry lips. "Never felt pain like this. It clouds the mind."

Dusty turned to Maureen. "Maureen? Could you bring in the cooler?"

Maureen turned and her quick steps sounded as she trotted down the steps and out to the Bronco.

"I'd drink," Sage whispered. "Could I have water?"

Dusty went into the kitchen, pulled a glass from the cupboard, and filled it. He knelt in front of Sage and held it to the elder's lips. Yvette was standing to the rear, watching with wide brown eyes.

"Thank you," Sage said after sipping half the glass. "I haven't been able to get up. Legs won't work."

Maureen returned with the ice chest and headed directly for the kitchen. Dusty heard her pull the enchilada pan from the chest, then open and close the squeaky oven door. She came back into the living room and pulled a chair up beside Sage's recliner.

Dusty put a hand to the old woman's forehead. "Elder, please let us take you to the hospital. You're dehydrated, and they can give you something for the pain."

"I'm not going nowhere," Sage insisted. "He's close."

"Who is?"

Sage smiled. "That Flute Player in the black shirt with white spirals. He's been calling to me for days. He comes and goes." Her frail hand trembled as she lifted it to her throat. "He's got a pretty necklace, shaped like a turquoise wolf." Sage's hand dropped to rest on Maureen's shoulder. "What do your people call him?"

Maureen seemed to hesitate, as though not certain what Sage meant. Then she said, "Do you mean Shondowekowur? The faceless one?"

Sage chuckled, her mouth falling open to expose a pink tongue. "He's laughing at you, Washais." Her expression tightened as she listened to a voice none of them could hear. "I'll tell them."

"Tell us what?" Dusty asked.

Her crooked fingers waved in the air, pointing. "I see . . . shadows on the kiva wall, running together and pulling apart. His heart is black . . . filled with anger. But he's . . . he's powerful. Close to death, they dance . . ."

"She's delirious," Yvette said. "Wouldn't it be best to call for medical assistance?"

"Shhh." Dusty held up a hand in irritation. "Elder, who is he?"

Sage's eyes began to close. "Yes, yes. I hear you, Slumber."

Dusty's stomach muscles clenched tight. *Her dead sister.*

Sage's neck weakened and her head rolled to the side. "Kwewur's ears are laid back. His sandals crackle in the dry grass."

Dusty asked, "Who is he after?"

Sage's chest barely rose with her breath. "My bones are breaking apart . . . hurts."

"Elder," Dusty said as he brushed white hair from her hot forehead. "Please let us take you to town. If you don't want to go to the hospital, we'll take you to Magpie's house in Chaco Canyon."

She blinked, her eyes glassy, and her mouth opened and closed like a fish out of water. "All I have to do is step through . . . but Kwewur is waiting. He's waiting right there. For Magpie. Can't . . . can't warn her. Sick . . . too sick."

"I'll warn her for you," Dusty said softly.

He released her hand and walked over to the cell phone—probably a gift from Maggie—and ran his finger down the phone list taped to the wall. He saw Maggie's number first, but a nurse's number was listed right below it. Nurse Redhawk. Her number was underlined.

Dusty picked up the phone and dialed.

Sage's old hand trembled in Yvette's direction and she smiled again. "The Shiwana were there," she whispered. "When you were conceived . . . in the kiva . . . in the moonlight." Sage swallowed hard.

Yvette looked shocked, her eyes wide, like a deer in the headlights. "What are Shiwana? Ghosts?"

"No," Maureen whispered. "Spirits."

Yvette backed up, then turned and walked out the door.

Dusty was about to go after her when a voice said, *"Hello?"*

"Hello, this is Dusty Stewart. I'm out at Elder Sage Walking Hawk's house. She's very ill. I'm afraid—"

*"I'm on my way! But it will take me an hour to get there. Keep her warm and give her fluids."*

"We will. Please hurry." He hung up the phone and turned back to Sage. Maureen had a damp cloth and was washing the elder's face. "Someone's coming, Elder."

"Got to . . . go . . ." Sage whispered.

Dusty's heart ached at her pained expression. Sage was looking into the distance, seeing something outside of this world. He could barely hear her when she said, "Shadow's . . . with him . . . *el basilisco* . . . on her breast."

Sage faded again, gasping from the pain.

To Maureen, Dusty murmured, "Can't we do anything for her?"

"Not without drugs." Maureen shook her head.

"Flying," Sage whispered and sounded suddenly happy. She chuckled again. "Flying . . . in a big bomber . . ."

SAGE WALKING HAWK died forty-five long minutes before the nurse from the Indian Health Services arrived.

Dusty carried her to her bed, gently covered her with blankets, and sank onto the foot of the bed.

He stared blindly out the little window to the starlit desert beyond.

Kwewur was hunting again and Maggie was in danger.

# CHAPTER 46

CATKIN'S MIND RACED as she looked back across
Straight Path Wash. What was Browser thinking? What
curious errand had he sent Straighthorn and Jackrabbit
off on, and how had he allowed himself to walk into
a trap?

*Blessed Katsinas, Browser, did you outsmart your-
self this time?*

True to Shadow's word, only one lone scout followed. The White Moccasin's cloak caught the midday
sun as he trotted behind them. Surely Shadow would
not let them off that easily? But no pursuit was in evidence, rather it seemed that Shadow wanted Browser
surrounded by a ring of warriors. Why? Wouldn't it
make more sense to just kill him, take his heart, and
send the rest of the White Moccasins to destroy Catkin's party?

What did Browser know that she didn't?

She led the way past the sprawled corpses of the
battle. It struck her suddenly that all the arrows were
missing, the quivers of the dead completely empty.
When had that happened? Who had taken them?

White Cone began wheezing. They had come such
a short way and already the elder was falling behind.
Sweat trickled down his wrinkled face. Was that what
Shadow was banking on? That they couldn't travel rapidly with an exhausted elder? In that case it would be
easy to run them down long before they could make
the safety of Flowing Waters Town. Shadow was craft-
ier than Catkin had given her credit for.

And following along, just out of bow shot, came the one lone White Moccasin scout, to mark the trail and make sure that her party could be found when the time came.

"I don't like this," Clay Frog growled. "What was the War Chief thinking?"

"About Gray Thunder's prophecy," Catkin said. Memories stirred of the time he'd rescued her from the Fire Dogs. "The prophet was right. This insanity must end somewhere."

"But how will this end it? We should have fought!" Clay Frog's young face betrayed frustration. "He offered his life for ours!"

"Yes," Catkin agreed. "He did."

A chorus of assent rose from behind Catkin. They would all die for Browser now. Not because of the Bow Society's honor, but because Browser had won their hearts and souls by his willingness to sacrifice his life for theirs.

Browser's words echoed in her head: *"By doing this, I have given you extra time, and I expect you to be a better War Chief than I have been. Remember, the roundabout way is often better than a direct assault against superior numbers. Victory goes to those who are swiftest, and allies can appear from the most unexpected places."*

As they neared the hulking mass of Kettle Town, Catkin turned, looking back at the party following her. White Cone's old face twisted in agony. He'd started to stumble and weave on his feet. Three bow shots to the rear, the White Moccasin scout followed in his shuffling trot.

Catkin slowed to match her pace with Fire Lark's. The young warrior looked at Catkin curiously as she remarked, "It is said, Fire Lark, that you are the best bow shot among your party."

"I am, Deputy."

"I want you to do something for me."

"Yes, Deputy?"

"The timing must be just right, do you understand? And then you are going to have to run very hard to catch us. Can you do that?"

"Yes, Deputy."

"Good, because all of our lives are going to be in your hands."

"Then," Fire Lark asked hopefully, "we're not going straight back to Flowing Waters Town?"

"No, warrior, we're not. We're going to see what it's like to have the heart of a cloud. Today, warrior, we are going to make legends."

THE FRINGED END of Nichols's black muffler whipped around his neck as he walked. He had his shoulders hunched against the wind and his hands deep in the pockets of his brown canvas coat. He turned to Dusty as he led him up the trail toward where Maureen stood, overlooking the excavation. "Steve Sanders says two of the burials are still articulated, but that's not the really curious thing."

Dusty thought about that. What Steve had meant was that the bones were still in the exact positions they'd been in at death. Nothing had disturbed the burials. Then what about the scattered bones Sylvia had seen when she'd first fallen into the kiva?

"What is the really curious thing?" Dusty asked. Clouds filled the sky and it felt like snow, but he'd seen no flakes yet.

"There was a beer can and a pack of cigarettes in the northern wall crypt. That pot hunter's hole led right to it."

"Hmm."

Wall crypts traditionally held sacred artifacts, items

left for the gods. Pot hunters, like all vandals, often desecrated such things. "Is that why you brought me out here? To tell me that?"

"No," Nichols said, and wind flipped his thick black hair around his ears. "I'm taking a calculated risk. I brought you out here hoping you might see something that we haven't."

"Okay."

Dusty felt empty. Sage Walking Hawk's funeral had been a wrenching experience. Maggie had stood through the whole thing, smiling and comforting others, but Dusty had known her heart was breaking. To make matters worse, when it was all over, he'd felt obligated to tell Maggie that her aunt had said Kwewur was waiting for her.

Since her return to the canyon, Maggie hadn't stepped out of her office, and Rupert was acting like a protective bear, refusing to allow anyone to disturb her.

Rupert, himself, seemed distracted after his return from Washington. Something was eating at him, something that had turned his brown eyes somber. When Dusty asked him how he was doing, Rupert told a joke in answer. Was it Dusty's imagination, or did Rupert look thinner, as though he'd lost weight over the last couple of days?

Evil was loose on the wind and Dusty could sense the final pieces about to fall into place.

Nichols ducked under the yellow tape and walked toward Maureen and the kiva rim. Dusty followed him. In seven days, Steve's five-person crew had excavated to the floor of the kiva, even the south half that Michall had decided against touching. An aluminum ladder led down to an earthen pedestal. Fragments of human bone scattered the kiva floor and the ground near the fire pit, but Dusty's gaze fixed on the two skeletons. They lay on their backs with their arms and legs spread. Sandstone slabs the size of manhole covers rested beside the skulls. Big stones. Heavy.

*Someone took extra care to make sure those souls stayed locked in the earth.*

Maureen turned when they approached and said, "The body to the left is male; the female is on the right."

Steve, bundled like an Eskimo in a gray knit cap and red down coat, was working with a brush to clean and record bone fragments before removing them for stabilization and collection. Concentration marred his handsome black face.

Dusty thoughtfully examined the bodies, then shifted his gaze to the square hole in the north kiva wall. "That's the crypt where you found the beer can and cigarettes?"

"Yes." Nichols jammed his hands into his pockets.

"Let me guess," Dusty said. "A steel Coors can, the old kind that had to be opened with a can opener?"

"Right, and the cigarettes, Stewart?"

"Now there, you've got me."

"Parliament." Nichols looked annoyed. "My people tell me that that particular package design was manufactured in the mid-sixties."

Dusty nodded. *About the time my mother was taking her lovers to the Casa Rinconada kiva five minutes' walk away.*

"Dr. Sanders," Dusty called. "Who flipped the rocks off the heads of those two skeletons?"

Steve looked up and smiled. He looked like a young Denzel Washington. Handsome and self-confident. "What makes you think I moved the slabs?"

"I can see the indentations and soil discolorations where they originally rested."

"Right." Steve wiped his face with his coat sleeve. "My guess is that the pot hunters moved the slabs. When they potted the site, we figure the roof was another twenty centimeters higher on the north side. So long as they stayed bent over, they could have duck-walked to the bodies. We also recovered several mid-thirteenth-century black-on-white McElmo potsherds, and a stone ax head, maybe for a war club. Last but not least, we found a beautiful ceramic spindle whorl, with a bit of the wooden spindle preserved. Cool, huh?"

"What about the pieces of bone, Sanders?" Nichols asked, kneeling to scrutinize the fragments he could see.

"Lots of partially calcined, cracked, and perimortally disarticulated bone, Agent Nichols. Preliminary analysis, as suggested by Dr. Malroun, indicates 'Turner events'—that the bodies had been 'processed as if for consumption.' "

Nichols squinted. "What the hell does that mean?"

Dusty answered, "That's the politically correct way to say it looks like cannibalism."

"What about the two skeletons?" Maureen asked. "Any evidence they were 'processed'?"

"Not yet, but the man would have been as tough as an old bull. He was ancient. I mean *really* old, by Anasazi standards. Well past sixty. He's got some curious problems with his bones. Sid says he thinks he suffered from treponema."

"Really?" Maureen nodded thoughtfully.

"What's that?" Dusty asked.

"Syphilis," Maureen replied without looking at him. She was staring at the bones as if she might be able to tell that from up here. "Are there any lesions?"

For an answer, Steve carefully tiptoed across the bone bed and picked up the skull. "See what you think, Maureen." He climbed the ladder and presented the skull to her.

She took it and gently turned it over in her hands while she inspected the outer table of the frontal bone, the forehead.

Dusty knelt beside her. Her braid smelled flowery from the shampoo she'd used that morning. "What do you see?"

Nichols stepped forward to listen. The tail of his

black muffler fluttered over Maureen's shoulder.

She ran a finger over the pitted surface of the frontal bone. "I agree with Sid. Classic syphilitic lesions. Given the advanced stage of the disease, he was probably insane." She lifted the delicate skull to the sky. "And see the porosity?"

*"Cribra cranii?"* Dusty guessed.

"My God, Stewart," she said in mock surprise. "You've actually learned something scientific."

"Despite myself, Doctor."

"What's that mean?" Nichols asked.

"Poor diet," Maureen told him. "Generally we associate these kind of holes, this porous look, with iron deficiency."

"But no cut marks?" Dusty asked, studying every line on the skull.

"No," Maureen answered.

"There's more," Steve called up from the bottom of the kiva. "Somebody caved in the old boy's ribs. Sid says they had started to callus, to heal, so the guy took the hit premortally, before he died. But the broken bones probably punctured his lungs."

"He must have been tough," Dusty granted. "He bled to death inside—but not for a while." He looked around. "So, you're in NAGPRA land, where's your Indian monitor?"

Steve grinned. "That's only for archaeology, Boss Man. This is a federal crime scene. Murder overrides the Native American Graves Protection and Repatriation Act."

Under his breath, Dusty sighed, "Thank God."

"What about the woman?" Maureen asked.

Steve shrugged. "Sid does facial reconstructions. He said she would have been a real beauty. We even found a few of her hairs preserved. Sid's going to run some comparisons at the OMI lab. The thing is, her hyoid bone is broken. Sid says someone strangled her."

Dusty pointed to the area above the woman's shoulders, where a forest of pin flags clustered. "What do all the pins mark?"

"Beads," Steve said. "Dozens of them. Turquoise, coral, jet, you name it. The lady was fixed for a night on the town. All she needed was a tuxedoed gent, a limo, and an American Express Platinum Card."

Maureen studied the woman's splayed pelvis. "Steve? Inside the innominates, is that what I think it is?"

"Yes, fetal bone," he said. "Sid figures she was just finishing the first trimester."

"Mom and dad?" Dusty asked.

"Maybe. I doubt we'll ever know," Steve said.

Maureen looked at Nichols. "If Agent Nichols authorizes it, Sid could run some DNA tests on the bones. We might be able to answer that question."

Nichols tilted his head as though considering the idea.

"One last thing," Dusty said, remembering Sage Walking Hawk's last hours. He took a breath to gird himself. "Was the woman wearing a basilisk?"

Steve straightened and his dark eyes glinted. "No. At least not that we've found so far, but the man had one." Steve pointed to the skull in Maureen's hand. "It was underneath him. He may have been wearing it as a pendant, but it wasn't finished yet. He'd carved the snake inside the broken eggshell, but was still working on the inset for the eye. Other than that"—Steve propped his hands on his hips—"it was just like the one you curated from the 10K3 site." As though someone had asked, Steve added, "And yeah, it's still there in the University of New Mexico collections. I called to make sure."

Maureen handed the skull back to Steve and pointed at the northern wall crypt. It was roughly two feet square and another two feet deep. "That crypt looks like it was dug out with a shovel."

"Probably," Nichols said, and crouched down to

stare at the destroyed crypt. "But the guy found something in it. It looks like he pulled a box out, then shoved the beer can and cigarettes in."

"Did you find anything else?" Dusty asked.

"A couple of handprints, nothing we can really use except for palm diameter. Along with the beer can and cigarette pack, there was some cordage."

"Don't forget the butt." Steve was staring down at the skull in his hand, as though he expected the dead man to suddenly comment on their theories.

"Right," Nichols added. "We found a single cigarette butt. The only problem is, it's been lying in the ground for nigh onto forty years. We'll probably never be able to identify the brand."

Steve turned the skull to look into the empty eye sockets. Unlike the hundreds of skulls Dusty had stared into over the years, this one looked eerie, malignant. Dusty shivered involuntarily.

"What about the cordage?" Dusty asked. "Anything interesting?"

"It was knotted in a loop," Steve answered. "You know, just lying there on the stone. It had apparently been around the box that the pot hunters slid out of the crypt."

Dusty closed his eyes.

"What?" everyone seemed to ask in unison.

"Probably a yucca hoop," Dusty said.

"Like the hoops around Robertson's and Hawsworth's bodies?" Nichols asked.

Dusty nodded. "That's why the slabs were left on their heads. Somebody killed two witches here, dropped slabs on top of them to keep their souls locked in the earth forever, and torched the place before they left."

"Then," Steve said uneasily, "a goddamn pot hunter dug them up again around forty years ago."

Maureen pinned Dusty with hard black eyes. "Are

you suggesting Dale was murdered because the pot hunters dug up this site?"

Dusty spread his hands. "Dale must have known about this, Maureen. He came out here all the time in the sixties—usually in the company of my mother." He turned and gazed down at the enormous circle of Casa Rinconada. The beautiful stonework looked bleak under the gray winter sky. "And I wager he wrote about it in his journals."

Nichols stepped between them. "Why would it matter that two witches, murdered over seven hundred years ago, were dug up?"

Dusty looked past Nichols to the rimrock behind the site, and his soul seemed to glimpse something his eyes could not physically see. His heart went cold in his chest. Something terrible had happened here. He could sense it. Softly, he said, "A stone is placed over a witch's head to keep the wicked soul from rising out of the grave and attacking the living, Nichols. You know, spirit possession, sickness, dying screaming. That kind of thing."

"So?"

"So." Dusty looked back at Nichols and their gazes held. "After this site was potted, I suspect someone was attacked."

Nichols made a deep-throated sound of disgust and walked away.

Dusty looked back at the skeletons of the two witches and old Hail Walking Hawk's voice seeped from his memories: *Many years ago, my grandmother told me about two witches who lived over at Zuni Pueblo. They could change themselves into animals by jumping through yucca hoops, and once they turned a man into a woman. Everybody said they were crazy, but people were too scared of them to try and kill them.*

They'd been excavating the 10K3 site, digging up the brutalized bodies of women who'd been dead for almost eight hundred years. One of the women had had a basilisk on her breastbone. Hail had been certain they'd been killed by a witch.

Only now did it occur to Dusty to wonder how many years ago the two witches had lived at Zuni. Were they still alive?

# CHAPTER 47

"DROP YOUR CLUB and climb down," Thorn Fox ordered, and gestured at Browser as his warriors closed in.

Browser tossed his club to the side. "What about Horned Ram?"

The old man lay gasping on the blankets, his swollen shoulder black and mottled. Shadow crouched beside him. Browser kept his eyes on Rain Crow, watching the warrior's expression. His eyes had fixed on Shadow, anticipation there like a flame.

"Cut me loose," Horned Ram said. "This shoulder is killing me."

"Yes, Elder." Shadow reached into her belt pouch for a thin blade of obsidian. "This will only take a moment."

"Blessed gods," Horned Ram managed through gritted teeth, "I thought you'd never bring this to a conclusion."

"One thing you can rely on, Elder"—Shadow smiled down at him—"I always finish what I start." She leaned forward, her black eyes glittering, and her hand flashed.

Horned Ram's scream exploded in a guttering spray

of blood. Shadow leapt away, but blood speckled the
hem of her white dress. A rich red river flowed across
the kiva roof as Horned Ram's severed throat sputtered
and his limbs twitched. Browser watched the Red Rock
elder's eyes dim and the pupils enlarge.

Rain Crow watched in horror. He frowned as
Shadow stepped up to him, her head cocked. "Is there
a problem, War Chief?"

"No," Rain Crow rasped.

"You always finish what you start," Browser repeated. "How did you enlist Horned Ram in the first
place?"

Shadow shrugged and bent down to wipe the blood
from her obsidian blade onto Horned Ram's clothing.
"We have been working with Horned Ram for a long
time. He had a fertile imagination. We always gave him
information that fed his thirst for violence. Two Hearts
actually brought him into our fold sun cycles ago. Fortunately, Horned Ram never asked questions about who
we were, or why we would let him know the things
we did. All he cared was that we were against the katsinas. I'm sure it all came crashing down on him when
your little trick led his warriors into battle against Bear
Lance's warriors."

"So he ran," Stone Ghost said. He stood like a small
hunched animal, his turkey-feather cape flapping in the
wind. "Not only did he discover that the First People
existed, but that he'd also been working with the White
Moccasins for sun cycles."

Shadow stepped up to him, smiling. "Not all of our
adversaries have your dedication to honor and duty."

Old Pigeontail had been leaning against Owl
House's plastered wall. "What about War Chief Rain
Crow?"

Rain Crow propped himself on his war club, his gaze
fixed on the red pool of Horned Ram's blood.

"What about you, War Chief? Are you with me, or
against me?"

Rain Crow blinked hard, from the blow to his head, or from the sudden death of Horned Ram, Browser couldn't tell.

"With you," Rain Crow whispered. "I'm no fool."

"Good." Shadow paused long enough to run a finger down the side of his ruined face. Then she turned. "Browser? Stone Ghost? Would you be so kind as to climb down into the kiva. We have things we need to discuss."

Browser caught the desperate look in Rain Crow's eyes. The Flowing Waters War Chief didn't look as sick as he had. Some subtle communication passed between them, accented by a slight nod of Rain Crow's head. What had the War Chief been trying to tell him?

Tendrils of smoke coiled up past his shoulders, rising from the hearth below, but the air was strangely cold as Browser descended the ladder.

At the bottom he stepped to one side, blinking to help his eyes adjust to the dim interior. Shadow immediately climbed down and stood beside him.

Stone Ghost took the steps down one at a time, his gaze searching the kiva, probably looking for the little girl. When his feet touched the floor, he gripped Browser's sleeve to steady himself.

Rain Crow's stout body blocked the sunlight as he descended. He kept trying to stifle his ragged breathing, but couldn't. The pain in his head must be overwhelming. When his feet touched the floor, he staggered over to collapse on the kiva bench. Then the ladder rattled as Thorn Fox dropped athletically to the floor.

Murals of the old gods painted the kiva walls: the Flute Player, the Blue God, the Hero Twins, and Spider Woman stood to his right. On Browser's left, one huge painting depicted the First People climbing into this world, carrying enormous ceremonial knives in their hands.

"Who—who's there?" a thin reedy voice wheezed.

Browser saw the broken waste of a man lying on a reed mat. His features were recognizable, but just barely. Filthy white hair matted his head, and his skin, old and wrinkled, hung loose, as though insects had eaten the flesh out from inside him. The wall crypt above him held a beautifully painted rawhide box. A pile of wadded blankets lay at the foot of his bedding, as though kicked off when he'd grown too hot.

Browser saw Rain Crow flinch and turned. Rain Crow's mouth gaped. His eyes had fixed on the pile of bones that gleamed around his feet. Human bones. They were scattered across the floor like litter.

When Rain Crow lifted his gaze to Shadow, it was filled with such horror that Browser wondered if he was hearing the screams of his wounded men as she killed them, then cut the flesh from their bodies.

"You didn't know?" Browser asked softly.

Rain Crow just shook his head, but the hardening around his mouth indicated that he'd come to some decision.

Browser turned his attention to Two Hearts and took a step. Thorn Fox moved with catlike quickness to place himself between Two Hearts and Browser.

"Don't be an imbecile. If I had wished the elder dead, he'd be dead by now. I had plenty of opportunity before you and your warriors arrived."

Thorn Fox grinned; several of his teeth were missing on the right side. The broken roots could be seen rotting in pink and inflamed gums. "Killing you will be a pleasure."

Browser shouted in his face, "Move!"

Thorn Fox regripped his club in both hands, but stood his ground.

"Obsidian," Two Hearts hissed. "Where is she?"

Shadow knelt and smoothed hair from Two Hearts's brow. "The warriors are holding her, Father. Like I said they would."

Browser frowned and exchanged a glance with Stone

Ghost. Stone Ghost pursed his lips and shook his head. Not yet. Not until they knew more.

"The turquoise wolf? Where . . . where is it?" Two Hearts extended a skeletal hand and his fingers trembled.

Shadow stood up. "Give it to me. Now!"

Browser pulled open his shirt hem, and the wolf slid out onto his palm. He handed it to Shadow, who put it in Two Hearts's hand and closed his fingers around it. "Here, Father. Feel it?"

The old man clutched the wolf to his heart, and relief slackened his face. His thin brown lips parted to expose toothless gums. He might have been caught in a moment of pure bliss.

As Two Hearts shifted his foot, a terrified squeak came from the wadded blankets, then soft babbling, like that of a demented newborn.

"Bone Walker?" Stone Ghost called and turned to Shadow. "Please, let me go to her."

"Bone Walker? Do you mean my daughter, Piper?" Shadow waved a hand. "Go. But she has lost her souls. She can't speak or even focus her eyes. I don't know what happened to her."

Stone Ghost gently pulled at the blankets until he'd uncovered the little girl, face dirty, her hair a tangled mass. She lay curled on her side. Her huge black eyes stared intently at nothing, as though focused on some terror inside her. She had both hands twisted in a turquoise necklace that Browser had seen Stone Ghost wear a hundred times.

Had he given it to the child, or had she stolen it?

Stone Ghost sat on the floor and pulled the girl into his lap. Her body was limp, as though her muscles had stopped working. Her head rolled back over his arm. Stone Ghost hugged her to his chest, and whispered in her ear in a comforting voice. The only words Browser could make out were, *"I'm here. I'm right here."*

Browser crossed his arms, shooting a look at Thorn

Fox. "Very well, Shadow, I am ready to listen to your proposal."

Two Hearts coughed, and blood speckled his mouth. "Shadow . . . tell him."

Shadow said, "Browser, the Blessed Two Hearts does not wish to kill you. None of us has pure blood anymore, but you are one of only five men left to us whose blood is almost pure. By mating you with several of our purest women—"

"Like you?" Browser interrupted. *Blessed gods. That's why they let me live this long.*

"Yes, like me," Shadow answered, "and a handful of others. It will not be unpleasant for you, I assure you. Because of our blood, we are all attractive and eager to mate with others of our kind."

*Our kind.* The words sickened Browser.

"We are the last," Shadow said as she strode up to Stone Ghost. "We have only ourselves. Two small clans of First People. That's why it's so imperative that Browser live and marry."

Browser said, "Then why were you hunting me at Dry Creek village. You were out there, weren't you?"

Shadow reached out to touch his shoulder. "I was that close to you. But for Stone Ghost's arrival, I would have killed Catkin that night." She cocked her head, the wealth of beads clattering in her long black hair. "How would that have looked, Browser? Your deputy dead within a body's length of you? Perhaps it would have been the impetus for Cloudblower to dismiss you."

He nodded. "You are very clever, Shadow."

"Yes, and patient."

"Why me? There's always Thorn Fox," Browser reminded. "From the number of warriors I've seen recently, it isn't like we're running out of White Moccasins."

A branch broke in the fire and the resulting swirl of sparks reflected in her black eyes. "We need them, yes, but a good deal of Made People blood runs in their veins. To regenerate ourselves, we must strive for purity."

"I don't think I understand," Stone Ghost said as he gently lowered the limp little girl to the floor. "If you wish my nephew to live, what of Two Hearts?"

"We still have Obsidian's heart," Shadow said easily. "And if that fails, he has the Blessed Night Sun's turquoise wolf to guide him through the twists and turns of the afterlife trails."

Through a tense exhalation, Browser asked, "What if I say no?"

"If you say no," she told him, "the woman you love will die. She can't outrun Thorn Fox with that Mogollon elder panting at the rear. After that we will slowly, one by one, kill everyone else you care about, starting with the *kokwimu*, Cloudblower, and Matron Crossbill."

Browser's fists knotted at his sides. Even if Catkin hadn't understood his message, all they had to do was be patient, keep a close watch on her, and someday she would be vulnerable. All of the skill in the world could not save a warrior from treachery. He turned to look at Stone Ghost, and his heart ached.

Shadow folded her arms and her white dress swayed as she walked closer to Browser. "We are not fools, Browser. Just as you used the northern staircase to trap Blue Corn, by now your people are in our trap." She looked up into his eyes and he sensed an unnatural hunger there, like that of a dying animal. "You will either do as we say, or your friends will be stewed bones by the time the sun rises tomorrow."

"What if I want Obsidian?" Browser measured Shadow. "What if I wish to marry her? A woman can't very well bear daughters when her heart has been pulled out of her chest with a spindle."

Shadow stepped over to the bench and lifted a long slender spindle from the plastered stone.

Browser added, "You know she helped to ambush Bear Lance's warriors."

"Then turned on you when I captured her." Shadow twirled the spindle in her hands. "She's always been a disappointment to me."

Browser shook his head. "If you truly wish to save our people there is only one way! Stop all this murdering and destruction. I want Obsidian. Alive. I want Catkin and the Katsinas' People left alone. And I want my turquoise wolf back. It belongs to me. The gods made sure it fell into my possession." He gave her a knowing look. "Do that, Shadow, and I will help you in any way I can."

Shadow's eyes seemed to enlarge, swelling in her face, as if they were peering into his very soul.

YVETTE HEARD THE auto pulling into the parking space outside Dusty's camp trailer, but didn't think much of it. People came and went constantly. It didn't sound like Dusty's Bronco, but that didn't mean anything. He often arrived with other people.

She stared into her coffee cup, trying to sort out her emotions. She should have been prostrate with grief over Carter's murder. But he'd been more of a father in name than fact. They had always had an uneasy relationship, a sort of keep-your-distance-and-spar, instead of the sort of father-daughter intimacy she had always imagined proper. The fact that she still thought of him as Carter proved something.

Through the years, Yvette had analyzed and reanalyzed her relationship with her parents or, rather, the lack of it. Mum had been even more cold and indifferent than Carter. Yvette had always felt guilty around them, as if she were at fault for something terrible and she'd never understood what it was.

Then she had discovered this curious brother who believed in Spirits and witches, and all sorts of things Yvette considered utter nonsense.

"I'm going bloody crazy," she whispered, and absently listened to the vehicle idling outside.

The old Indian woman's voice kept echoing in the back of her mind. Over and over she heard Sage Walking Hawk say: *"The Shiwana were there. When you were conceived . . . in the kiva . . . in the moonlight . . ."*

But what did it mean?

A door slammed outside.

At the knock, Yvette called, "Come in. It's open."

When Mum opened the door and stepped in, her appearance surprised Yvette. She looked ravishing, wearing a full-length camel-hair coat, a wool suit jacket, tailored gray wool pants, and western-style boots. A silver concho belt snugged her waist, and she'd pulled her silver hair back into a ponytail that hung down to her collar. Her blue eyes had a predatory glitter to them.

"Been out stalking the wily male of the species again, Mum?" Yvette asked, reading that look she had grown passingly familiar with.

"I'd forgotten what Taos was like." Mum smiled. "I guess I never realized I'm getting old. It isn't so bad in Boston. I'm part of the society. Men know me. Powerful men, who can provide the things that interest me. Here, well, I'm afraid it's a younger crowd."

"Sorry 'bout that, Mum."

Yvette moved her coffee cup in little circles over the scarred tabletop while Mum looked around the trailer. Finally, Yvette asked, "What are the Shiwana?"

Mum gave her a speculative look. "That's an odd question coming from you. The Keres tribe believe that the Shiwana are spirits of the dead who climbed into the sky to become cloud beings. They bring rain, they watch over people. The Hopi call them Kachinas. The Zuni refer to them as Koko. Why do you ask?"

"Are they gods?"

"Well, that's debatable. Whites categorize them as ancestor spirits with supernatural abilities. What the people actually think is anybody's guess."

Yvette gripped her coffee cup. When she'd worked up the courage, she asked, "What happened the night I was conceived . . . in the kiva . . . in the moonlight? Were the Shiwana there?"

Mum started as though caught completely off guard, but she quickly recovered and leaned against the kitchen counter. "What are you talking about?"

"Just answer the question, Mum."

"I don't know what you're talking about."

"I'm talking about the spirits dancing the night I was conceived."

Mum laughed. "You've lost it, dear. A few days in the Southwest and you're a raving lunatic."

Yvette looked up. "Is that why you killed Carter? Was it the last part of the ritual you performed the night I was conceived? Or just plain witchcraft?"

Her mother's face paled. "Carter's . . ."

"Dead. Yes."

"When?" she asked breathlessly. "How?" She came over to the table and eased down opposite Yvette.

"He was killed a week ago and dumped upside down in the same kiva where they found Dale Robertson. His feet had been skinned. I don't know much more about it. The FBI is still investigating."

Mum's fists clenched on the table. In a strained voice, she whispered, "Oh, my God."

Yvette watched her mother's eyes widen in fear. "Tell me what happened that night, Mum. I've a right to know."

Mum's fear turned to anger in a heartbeat. Her voice

cut like glass: "Do you want to know the whole of it, Yvette, or just the good parts?"

"The whole, please, Mum."

"Well, first of all, daughter of mine, let's get one thing clear: You don't have any rights when it infringes on my privacy. Secondly, I doubt you can stomach the people you'll have to deal with to hear the full story. I'm supposed to rendezvous with one of them in half an hour."

"I can stomach them, Mum. I've managed with you and Carter over the years. Might I go with you?"

Mum gave her the same murderous look she had when Yvette had been seven and accidentally knocked over a prehistoric pot Mum had displayed on her desk, *the careless hateful look of a stranger.*

"You want to know what happened the night you were conceived? No matter how frightening or ugly?"

"I do, Mum."

Ruth Ann shook her head as though disgusted with her. "All right, daughter, I'll make it short and sweet, and then I've got an appointment to keep."

"Fine, Mum. Let's hear it."

Her mother glanced around. "I came to see your brother. Where is he?"

"He and Maureen went out to the site with that charming FBI agent, Sam Nichols."

"Well, too bad for him, then." Mum got to her feet and her necklace fell forward.

"New pendant?" Yvette asked.

Mum lifted the black stone from where it hung on her breast. "An old one, actually. I've had it for what seems an eternity. I used to swing it over Dusty's crib when he was a baby, to hypnotize him to go to sleep."

Mum tucked the pendant back into her jacket, leaving Yvette barely enough time to make out that it was a snake with a glistening red eye.

All in all, Yvette thought it a perfect match for

Mum's personality. "Good, now I want to hear about that night."

"You won't blush, will you?"

"After so many years with you, I rather fancy that as unlikely."

"We'll see," Ruth Ann began. "Dale and I had been . . ."

# CHAPTER 48

SHADOW STARED AT Browser as if across infinity. Finally she nodded. "You will swear to me that you will act as I wish? I am the descendant of the Blessed Night Sun, as are you. We are Red Lacewing Clan. Just as in the days of our ancestors, if I were to choose you, you would become the Blessed Sun, Browser, the ruler of the Straight Path Nation."

"I will do whatever you ask of me." A hollow prickling invaded his chest. How much time had passed? "But what about Two Hearts?"

Shadow looked Browser up and down and smiled as she pulled her white dress over her head and tossed it aside. She stood naked before him, beautiful. Challenge lit her large dark eyes. "His fate is up to the gods. Come. If you wish to seal this bargain, let us do it now. You and I, here, in front of these witnesses." She clasped his hands and drew him to her, pressing her naked body against him.

She was calling his bluff. Any chance Browser might have had to delay had just been denied him.

In a mocking and irreverent tone, Shadow said, "I, Shadow Woman, of the Red Lacewing Clan, choose you, Browser, as my leader, my chief." She spoke the ritual words with curious ease.

Browser's fists tightened at his sides. Those were the words the Blessed Night Sun would have said to the man she had chosen to Join with. To the man she had chosen to become the Blessed Sun.

Browser responded. "I, Browser, of the Red Lacewing Clan, accept the responsibility for our people, Blessed Shadow."

According to the ancient traditions, they had just become husband and wife. Browser's skin crawled when he looked at Shadow. An animal excitement lit her eyes.

"May Spider Woman bless our actions this day," he said, and put his arms around her in an iron grip.

Her lips opened and he saw the pulse beating in her temple. In that instant, she read his souls.

Browser shouted, *"Now, Rain Crow!"*

Browser shoved Shadow off balance, twisted her around, and brought his muscular arm down across her throat.

The speed with which she reacted stunned him. He had no more than gotten hold of her when she sank her teeth into his arm and grabbed his testicles. A scream broke from his lips, and his frantic jerk pulled her teeth loose. She clung to him, trying to twist his scrotum off his body with one hand, while the other reached up and clawed for his eyes.

At the edge of his vision he saw Rain Crow swing his war club into Thorn Fox's stomach. Stone Ghost had stumbled back, dragging the little girl with him.

Browser used his forehead to butt Shadow hard in the face. At the impact, her head rocked backward and she staggered, overbalancing him. Together they crashed to the floor.

In the mad scramble that followed, she scuttled on all fours for the ladder. He clasped a handful of her bead-encrusted hair and punched her in the face. She flipped, catlike, powerful, stronger than any woman he'd ever known. Her knee shot for his throbbing crotch and yellow light blasted his brain.

Her hand flashed up from the side. Like a striking snake, she slammed him in the head with a hearth stone. Browser roared and threw himself on top of her.

To his left, he caught the bizarre image of Stone Ghost bending over Two Hearts with a broken shaft of human leg bone.

Shadow screamed as Browser clamped both hands tightly around her throat. She bashed his shoulder, arm, back, anywhere she could strike with the stone, but he kept his grip on her throat. Bucking like an elk in deep snow, she tried to throw him off. Each blow of the stone thumped hollowly, painfully, through his body, splintering the world. Doggedly he tightened his grip on her throat, hearing the liquid sounds of her protruding tongue against the back of her palate.

The image fixed in his brain: her parted lips and heaving breasts, her hot breath on his cheek as she struggled for air.

When Shadow's flailing arm lost its strength and the stone fell to the floor, he stared down into her widening eyes, vaguely aware of the blood that dripped from his battered head to speckle her smooth skin. Between his knotted hands, he could feel her pulse as it slowed and see her eyes growing vacant. He felt the Blue God as she settled on his shoulders, hovering and expectant.

*My wife. My wife.* The disconnected words repeated in his brain. *I am killing my wife.*

"Browser!" Stone Ghost's voice barely cut through the exaltation. *"Browser! Behind you!"*

Browser's gaze shot up, and he saw Stone Ghost—crimson-spattered—leaning over Two Hearts, a bloody bone in his hands.

*"Behind you!"*

Browser twisted, but not in time. The blow that was meant to crush his skull landed in the corded muscle of his shoulder, just below the neck, stunning him. Then a hard body slammed into him, toppling him to one side. Thick, muscular arms wrapped around his, breaking his hold on Shadow, prying him away from her.

Thorn Fox kicked him in the belly, and the blow of his war club numbed Browser's spine. He collapsed, dazed, to the dirt floor, unable to catch his breath.

As Browser fought to roll over, he caught sight of Rain Crow, lying on his back in the corner, his arms sprawled. Was he dead?

Thorn Fox's club came down again, and Browser saw a tiny form dart at the edge of his vision. Browser blocked the next blow with his left arm, heard the bone crack, and a searing flash of pain shot through him. He lurched up, grabbed the club with his right hand, and jerked with all his strength, pulling Thorn Fox off balance. The man fell, and Browser drove his fingers into Thorn Fox's eye sockets. He felt his fingertips rip through the tissue, and blood gushed out over his right hand and ran down his arm.

The silence that followed Thorn Fox's shocked scream seemed to deafen. Browser shoved the blind man off him and stumbled to his feet.

Thorn Fox, whimpering, crawled away, his hands searching the floor for his lost war club. Rain Crow got to his knees and wavered. With one final swing of his club, he broke Thorn Fox's neck. Then Rain Crow slumped to the floor, panting.

Browser looked down at Shadow. He had made a mistake once before, believing that he'd killed Two Hearts, but not taking the extra moment to make certain. Browser walked to Shadow's blood-smeared naked body and reached out. He touched her wide, dark eye. She did not blink or flinch. When he withdrew his hand, only the bloody fingerprint marred the glassy orb.

"Uncle Stone Ghost, let's—"

An inhuman shriek rose from the little girl's throat.

She raced forward and threw herself over her mother's dead body, clawing at her skin, squealing incoherently.

Browser staggered back, breathing hard. "Uncle, the warriors down below . . . will have heard the screams."

"Yes, but they may have thought they were your screams, Nephew."

Stone Ghost watched the blood pool from the lethal gashes in Two Hearts's throat and chest; then he dropped the spearlike bone onto the kiva floor beside Shadow's spindle.

Browser winced at the ache in his left arm. One bone was broken at least. Since it didn't flop, the other must have been intact, but, gods, it hurt.

The little girl rose and madly skipped around Shadow's body, humming a haunting song. Her filthy black hair bounced as though alive.

Browser went to Rain Crow, pulled the warrior over, and saw he was still breathing. "War Chief?"

Rain Crow whispered, "Gods, my head. I feel strange, Browser. Tingly, and everything's gray. I can't see . . . can't . . ." His eyes were wide, unfocused. "They killed my sister's . . ."

Browser put two fingers to Rain Crow's throat. He knew the instant the man's heart stopped. He shook his head and lowered his hand.

Stone Ghost asked, "What now, Nephew? It won't take long before they figure out . . ."

A shadow blackened the kiva entrance.

"WHERE COULD SHE be?" Dusty asked as he and Maureen walked out into the evening, away from Maggie's cabin. The sound of voices came from the other cabins, soft and happy. Someone laughed. Dusty lifted his gaze to west Chacra Mesa. The fading rays of sunset made the canyon walls gleam like varnished copper.

"We've tried the dormitory. Neither Sylvia nor Michall have seen her. We could try Rupert's," Maureen suggested.

Tired and frustrated, Dusty said, "I'd really like to find her."

"Dusty," Maureen warned. "She has a lot on her mind: her aunt's death, there have been two homicides in her park, Rupert just returned with a thousand questions. She probably needs time alone."

"Probably, but I still have to find her."

"Do you really think she has to immediately hear that Steve found two witches?"

"Yes, I do. Remember 10K3? Remember how Hail Walking Hawk reacted? Maybe a White person wouldn't care, but you can damned well bet that Maggie wants a heads-up. Finding two witches has ramifications for the traditional community."

He led the way through the scrubby sage to the park superintendent's house. For Chaco Canyon standards, it was actually pretty nice. Dusty had been in it many times.

They followed the gravel walk around to the front, and found a man standing at the door. Dusty slowed, half irritated that some stranger had beaten him to Rupert. The man knocked. But no answer came. He knocked again, waited, then turned to leave.

"Hey, Lupe!" Dusty started forward, smiling. "Long time no see!"

"Stewart? Is that you?"

Lupe might have been in his forties but tonight he looked fifty. He wore a leather jacket and a black felt cowboy hat with a huge silver concho band. He took Dusty's hand, grasping it hard. "God damn, man. Good to see you! What's the latest on Dale's murder?"

"The FBI's still working on it. Steve found two Anasazi skeletons in the kiva today. They had stones on their heads. You get my drift."

Lupe's expression went tense. "Yeah. You be careful, huh? That's bad stuff."

"Hey," Dusty said with a sigh and changed the subject. "I hear you're bilking tourists for off-tune flutes these days."

"Yeah, man. I got my stuff in big-time galleries and there are collectors, people with money, buying flutes these days." He glanced at Maureen. "Hey, Maureen, you still can't find a decent guy to hang around with?"

"There's a limited selection out here." She smiled. "How have you been?"

"Better," Lupe replied. "It's a tough time all the way around. But next time you need help getting this *cabron* in a truck, you call me."

Dusty said, "Lupe and I drank our first whiskey together, got in fights, and did all the things teenage boys aren't supposed to do."

"Yeah, God, we had fun. You remember that time we poached that deer up by Chama? Man I thought we was dead when that highway patrol car stopped us."

Dusty playfully punched Lupe in the shoulder. "We had a taillight out. Lupe was cool as ice. He just acted like a perfectly mannered kid. When the cop asked him where he was going to school, he said, 'At the military academy at Roswell, sir. I'm going to start as a lieutenant when I enlist.' The cop told us to get the light fixed, and sent us on our way with our deer safely in the trunk."

Maureen smiled.

"So, you know where Dad is?" Lupe hooked a thumb at the dark house.

"Nope. We're looking for him, too."

Lupe frowned and reached into his leather coat. "Hey, could you do something for me, man? These are for Dad. I gotta go. I gotta reception tomorrow in a gallery in Taos, and the radiologist said that Dad demanded a copy of these test results as soon as they were done. Could you make sure he gets them? And

this"—he lifted a flannel bag—"is a flute I made for
him. It's beautiful. Turquoise inlay. My best yet."

"Yeah. Sure." Dusty smiled and took the bag and
the envelopes. When he saw the return address in the
glow of the yard light, Dusty's head jerked up. He just
stared at Lupe.

Lupe studied him thoughtfully. "He ain't told you?"

"No." Dusty felt sick to his stomach.

"God, that's where he was all last week. One test
after another. It's cancer, man." Lupe scuffed the
ground with his shoe and glanced uneasily at Maureen.
"But you don't tell Dad that I told you."

Dusty tucked the envelopes into his coat pocket.
"Thanks, *amigo*. Really. *¿Cuanto tiempo?*"

"*Seis meses . . . más o menos.* Reggie's taking it really hard. He won't talk to nobody about it, just sits in
his room in the dark with that old painted box that he
found in Dad's basement years ago, the one Dad kept
his letters in."

Dusty reached for Lupe's hand again and held it in
a strong grip. "Drive carefully getting back to Santa
Fe, okay. I don't want to lose you, too."

"Not me, man." Lupe grinned sadly. "Tell Dad I love
him. I'm outta here."

Dusty waited until Lupe got into his car and started
away; then he lifted a hand in farewell. Lupe must have
seen him through the rearview mirror. He waved.

Dusty slowly lowered his hand. "I thought he was
supposed to be in Washington. Cancer? For the love
of God, is the entire world dying around me?"

Just as they turned to leave, a man stuck his head
out of the cabin next door and called, "You looking for
Dr. Brown?"

"Yes, have you seen him?"

"He jumped in his truck and flew out of here spinning gravel about a half hour ago."

Dusty lifted a hand, called, "Thanks! Hey, you don't
know where Maggie is, do you?"

The guy shrugged. "She left to find Reggie about an hour ago. Him and his trash truck didn't check in at quitting time."

"Thanks, again. Good night."

The guy closed his door.

Dusty looked across the canyon. Headlights sparkled on the road leading to Casa Rinconada.

As he watched them moving toward the kiva parking lot, Dusty suddenly felt weak. A rush of information seemed to fall out of his brain. Things that Sage had said, that Lupe had just said, about Rupert and the old painted box, and Reggie being on parole, and working part-time for his grandfather.

Dusty opened the flute bag. The instrument was beautiful, made of red cedar with a turquoise inlay. In the center, just above the finger holes, surrounded by turquoise, a beautifully carved basilisk had been inset. The single coral eye would stare at the player.

An attached note read: *"Dad, here's my best yet. If you need more of the little snakes, give me a call. They don't take but half a day to carve. Hope this flute makes you well. Love, Lupe."*

*A witch survives through misdirection.*

"Dusty?" Maureen asked as she walked up behind him. "Did you hear a word I said?"

He tugged the laces closed on the bag and reached out, steadying himself on her shoulder. "Come on. We have to hurry."

*OWL IS FLYING above Piper, his wings puffing air on her face where she huddles behind Stone Ghost.*

*She stares up, waiting in silence as a man's legs drop into the kiva. Browser shifts, as if a smoky shadow. For an instant she sees the Blue God—as*

*Browser times the swing of his war club. The man coming down the ladder has just seen Mother's naked body, just realized that Grandfather's bedding is soaked in blood.*

*She watches the breath going into his lungs to shout as Browser's war club smacks loudly into the back of the man's neck. His eyes go blank and he falls to the floor.*

*Owl whispers, "You have been born to a time of war, little Bone Walker. Death swirls around you. Listen, listen for its soft footsteps."*

*She knows the sound. Mother's breath-heart soul hisses as it slips away past her tongue, then makes the faintest rasping as it scampers around the kiva, trying to get away from the body.*

*Stone Ghost lifts a heavy grinding stone, grunts, and drops it onto Grandfather's head.*

*As he staggers back, he says, "I need another stone."*

*Piper points to one of the bench slabs that is loose in its setting.*

*As Stone Ghost rocks it free, Browser lifts the dead warrior's body with his good arm and drapes it over his shoulder. Then he begins the hard climb up the ladder.*

*Piper jumps when Stone Ghost drops the big stone on her mother's head. Mother will never look at her again with dead flying squirrel eyes.*

*Voices call from outside.*

*Piper stares up at the hole in the roof.*

*Owl whispers, "The Blue God is feeding."*

*Piper swallows the sourness that rises into her throat. She's dizzy.*

*Owl whispers, "Shh. Shh. Shh."*

OBSIDIAN FOLDED HER arms and looked up at
Owl House. As the twilight deepened, a chill settled
on the canyon. She rubbed her cold skin. The screams
had stopped, but no one had summoned her for the
ritual preparations. Obsidian had no interest in seeing
Browser's torture and death. She didn't want to witness
his heart being extracted from his chest. Until Shadow
had captured her, she had still hoped Browser might be
her way out. She would have taken him for a husband.
A woman could do worse. But now? She looked
around at the White Moccasins, trying to see a future
with any of them.

*How did this go so badly for me?*

What did Shadow think, that Obsidian was going to
stand down here until after dark? It was getting cold
and she was tired of being ogled. She wished the
hungry-eyed warriors would look elsewhere.

"Something is wrong," she said to Old Pigeontail.

The wrinkles that wrapped his fleshy nose deepened
as he frowned. "Perhaps." He was watching her with
an unusual amusement in his eyes.

"Do you know something I do not?"

He shrugged, a smile hidden behind his thin brown
lips. "The preparations took longer than usual, that's
all. Browser was a strong man. He might have withstood the torture longer than anticipated."

"I don't see why they had to torture him at all. They
wanted his heart. That should have been a simple matter of throwing him down, cutting his chest open, and
pulling out his heart." Obsidian rubbed her cold arms
again, then pointed. "You, young warrior, what is your
name?"

The black-haired youth came forward and bowed respectfully, though his gaze was fixed on her breasts. "I am Star Knife, Blessed Obsidian."

"Good. Go up there and see what is happening. By now, Shadow should have Browser's heart boiling in her pot. This is taking too long."

Star Knife continued to stare at her chest as he nodded; then he turned and trotted the short distance up the hill. His white cape swayed with his gait.

Obsidian glanced at the other warriors in irritation.

They were all watching with speculative eyes, probably waiting for their turn to bed her, as they did her sister. Well, they would have a long wait.

Star Knife climbed onto the kiva roof. He cupped a hand to his mouth and called out, but Wind Baby had been gusting ferociously all day, Obsidian couldn't hear his words.

Star Knife climbed down and disappeared into the kiva.

He didn't come back out.

Obsidian had opened her mouth to shout to him when Pigeontail muttered, "Blessed Flute Player, something isn't right about this. Shadow should have had his answer by now, and that youth should have been sent scurrying."

"Answer?" Obsidian asked. "What answer?"

Pigeontail gave her a disgusted look. "You don't think this is just about you, do you? It's about the future. If Shadow can't turn him . . . Oh, never mind. The gods made you to be beautiful, not smart." He raised his voice. "Something is wrong! Half of you, come with me!"

Pigeontail started up the hill toward Owl House with a cluster of warriors following in his wake.

Obsidian frowned. A pale blue finger of smoke rose from the kiva and twisted into the evening sky. Obsidian started forward, but stopped when a body flopped out of the entrance. Then, a moment later, a second body was shoved out, and a man emerged.

"It's Browser!"

The White Moccasins stopped short, suddenly uncertain. Old Pigeontail leapt up on the roof and shouted, "Kill him!"

Warriors surged forward. One young man vaulted to the roof, his war club held high. In less than a heartbeat, an arrow shaft sliced through the youth's chest. It flashed as he staggered, eyes blinking, blood gushing from his mouth.

Obsidian waved both arms at the warriors. "Get up there!"

As the white-caped men dashed around her, she tried to understand. Browser, half hidden by the smoke, helped old Stone Ghost from the kiva, then lifted Piper out. The three of them turned to run for the rocks under the rim, a bow shot south of Owl House.

"Stop them!" Obsidian shouted. The next warrior reached the roof—only to stumble backward, a fletched shaft piercing his abdomen. As he kicked and screamed, hands clasping the arrow that lodged in his guts, the others charged past.

Obsidian stopped short when another warrior, no more than five paces ahead of her, screamed as an arrow lanced his arm. Obsidian leapt to the roof and looked up the ridge to the rimrock.

Jackrabbit and Straighthorn shot their bows from behind the tumbled rocks.

Obsidian grabbed one of the warriors who ran past. "There are only two of them! You can rush them!"

The young warrior gaped at her in panic.

"Go!" Obsidian ordered. "Now! Take them."

Flames crackled wildly inside the kiva. Tongues of fire leapt up the ladder and caught in the dry matting around the entryway.

Obsidian ran past the bodies to the entryway and bent down, waving at the smoke and heat. Someone had piled firewood around the base of the ladder and kicked coals from the hearth into the tinder. In the gaudy flickering glare, Obsidian saw the bodies with huge stones atop their heads.

*Saved! I am saved!*

A laugh came bubbling up from inside her as she backed away, coughing, and stumbled to the edge of the kiva.

It took several instants before she could identify the cluster of warriors charging up the slope from Corner Kiva. A woman ran in front. "Catkin? What are you doing here?"

Obsidian spun around. The White Moccasins ran southward along the rim, ducking arrows, as they chased Browser and his party.

Obsidian pulled herself up and shouted, "Catkin! Hurry! They have Browser trapped! You can still . . ."

Catkin's arrow caught Obsidian squarely in the chest, and the force of the blow knocked her off her feet. She landed hard.

"No!" Obsidian clawed at the ground. When she coughed, blood bubbled from her mouth and soaked into the packed earth of the kiva roof, frothy and bright.

Catkin and several of the Mogollon warriors ran past. Over the shouts and screams, the crackling of the fire, Obsidian heard the impact as Catkin swung her war club and crushed the right side of Pigeontail's skull.

As her vision began to fade, Obsidian saw the White Moccasins break before Catkin's war party. One long shrill shout carried as they fled into the falling evening . . .

# CHAPTER 49

"GOD, I PRAY I'm wrong," Dusty said as he drove maniacally down the loop road.

"About what?" Maureen shouted, and braced her feet for the next curve. "Tell me what you're talking about!"

Dusty pummeled the steering wheel with the palm of his hand. "Do you know what Reggie does? Why he's on parole in El Paso?"

"No, why?"

"He's a burglar, Maureen. Breaking and entering. He broke into houses in El Paso, loaded stuff in his trunk, and fenced it across the line in Juarez."

Dusty slid the Bronco onto the Casa Rinconada drive.

"What does that have to—"

"Reggie stole the diaries! I'm sure of it!"

Not only were two sickly green Park Service pickups parked in the Casa Rinconada lot, but so was a familiar Ford Explorer, as well as Reggie's trash truck. As Dusty pulled up and shut off the ignition, he just stared at the Explorer.

"What's your mother doing here?" Maureen asked.

"I don't know." Dusty opened his door and stepped out.

The moon hung, nearly full, over the canyon walls. The pewter gleam seemed to set the world afire.

Maureen zipped up her coat and cast a nervous glance at Dusty. What was running through his head?

He pulled a flashlight and his pistol from under the

driver's seat. He tucked the pistol into the back of his jeans, then walked over to Ruth Ann's Explorer. With his hand he wiped some of the frozen mud and dust from the rear window and shone the light into the back.

"What are you looking for?"

"Bodies."

He stepped over to the first Park Service truck, opened the door, and reached for the coffee cup sitting on the dash. "Warm. Rupert hasn't been gone long. Come on."

"This is Rupert's truck?"

"Yes. The other truck is Maggie's."

"How do you know?" They looked identical to her.

"I just know, okay?"

Maureen shrugged and walked along behind him, aware of the darkness, the cold, and the silence of Chaco Canyon at night. Her heart had begun to beat a staccato in her chest. She kept sniffing the clear cold air, as if for a hint of Shondowekowur's foul breath.

"Dusty? Damn it, you're scaring me."

"Yeah," he said. "I'm scaring me, too." After a second, he told her: "If anything happens, Maureen, promise me that you'll run straight back to the Bronco and get out of here."

"I will, but it would help if you'd tell me what you're afraid might happen."

"The same thing that happened almost forty years ago."

The electric feeling grew in her heart. She'd never heard such fear in his voice. "Which is?"

"I'm not sure yet. A ritual. Something about witching souls."

They had passed Tseh So, and started up the trail toward Casa Rinconada. The only sound was the gravel under their boots, and the faint rasping of their clothing.

Dusty whispered, "I can't believe this. This is a nightmare."

"What?" Maureen asked.

"Rupert and my mother," Dusty said, voice husky.

Maureen's boot slipped off a rock in the dark trail and she stumbled sideways before she caught her balance. "You think Rupert and your mother—"

"I think she's the woman he loved with all his heart. The woman he lost to another man."

They scrambled up the incline and Dusty shone the flashlight down into the great kiva. There, in the hollow stone box that once supported the foot drum, a bound figure looked up, eyes slitted against the light.

"Maggie?" Maureen called, recognizing her face. Duct tape made a gray smear across her mouth. Maggie struggled to scream and thrashed back and forth against the foot drum.

On the kiva floor stood a wooden box, beautifully painted, measuring about two feet square. Inside were quart-size glass jars filled with different colors of sand, some with their lids removed. In the center of the kiva, a painting spread across the floor, the image indistinct, unfinished.

Dusty wheeled, flashing the light around, its beam revealing nothing but rabbitbrush and chamisa, though the brush could have hidden anyone.

"Come on"—Maureen tugged at him—"we have to cut her loose and call Nichols."

"Where's my mother?" Dusty asked and flashed the light toward the low ridge to the south. "Oh, my God. Is that firelight? You don't think he already has her up there, do you? In the witch kiva?"

Maureen grabbed his arm. "One thing at a time. Let's turn Maggie loose, call Nichols, then we'll go up there and look."

They hurried for the southern stairway that led down into the great kiva. Maureen climbed down, ducked the lintel, and stepped out onto the dirt floor. She ran to Maggie and started untying the ropes on her hands.

Low laughter echoed from the kiva walls, as if issuing from the niches themselves, and a deep voice boomed, *"Get away from her!"*

Maureen whirled, eyes following the wavering flashlight as Dusty played the beam back and forth.

*"Rupert!"* Dusty cried where he stood over Maggie. "It's over!"

More laughter rolled down as if from the star-filled sky, and the voice sounded muffled, somehow inhuman. "Circles come full."

"Where's my mother?" He stared up at the kiva rim.

Maggie was shouting against the tape. Dusty reached down to pull it off.

*"Don't!"* the shout echoed. "If you do, I'll shoot you dead, Dusty. And her, too. The end of it all. Over with. Dale's seed dies here, where it was planted."

Maureen's blood ran cold. Even now he could be drawing a bead, centering a bullet on the middle of her back. She started to shake.

"Put the flashlight down, Dusty!" The hollow voice echoed around the kiva.

When Dusty continued to hold it, the hearth burst into flame as though previously soaked in gasoline.

"Rupert, for God's sake!" Dusty threw the flashlight down. He stood defiantly beside Maggie, one arm up to shield his face from the heat of the roaring fire, while the other hand reached behind him for his own gun. "Let's talk! You're like a father to me. We could always talk!"

A figure moved on the kiva rim twelve feet above Maureen's head. He stood there, illuminated by the firelight, a tall man, wearing what appeared to be an ancient wolf mask, the leather worn and cracked. Matted gray fur still clung to the collar. The eyes, irregular round holes, seemed possessed. The muzzle had been sewn on, the teeth, perhaps real, had cracked, and now hung by threads. The thing might have been brittle and antique, but it projected a menace that froze Maureen's soul. She could feel it, as though an ancient evil walked the kiva around her.

"I am Kwewur," the man slurred the words and weaved on his feet. "I am reborn!"

Maureen could see that something was wrong with him. Drunk? Drugged? That's why the voice didn't sound quite right.

"Come on, Rupert. You don't have to do this. I know about the cancer! Let me help you! I've known you all of my life. That's got to count for something. We can make this work."

"You know nothing!" The wolf figure raised a small black pistol and aimed it at Dusty's chest.

Dusty spread his arms wide and Maureen saw a swallow go down his throat.

Dusty said, "Agent Nichols knows all about this, Rupert. He knows how much you loved my mother. How you wrote to her for years after she left you. He knows about h-how you were attacked by the dead witch after you potted the site up the hill. I'm sure you probably started studying witchcraft to defend yourself. Nichols knows you hired Reggie to steal the diaries. He-he—" Dusty stuttered, as though frantically putting facts together, but not knowing the proper order. "They'll make him talk, you know, and Reggie will roll for them. Yeah, you were here that day, with us, but you damn well knew that Reggie had plenty of time to go in and take the diaries. Damn, you didn't even know they existed until you rode out here with us and saw the one in the backseat! So, you called Reggie and, piece of cake, he used Dale's keys, taken off his body, to drive up, open the front door, pack up the journals, and walk out."

"Nichols knows nothing," Kwewur slurred.

"Sure he does. Your name is on the park rolls. You were working here thirty-seven years ago. You were potting sites at night. Is that where you found the mask? Up the ridge? In the witch kiva? Let me guess, that's what was in the niche where you left the beer can and the cigarettes. What a sight that must have been. Two witches laid out on the floor, and a wolf mask in an old painted box in the wall crypt. Dale had a suspicion, didn't he? That's why he rode up Tsegi Canyon, and why he wouldn't let me come. He was afraid the Wolf Witch would be someone he knew."

"He deserved to die." The wolf extended the pistol again.

Dusty hesitated. "Why did he deserve to die?"

"He took everything!"

"And Hawsworth? What did he do?"

"He *stole*! He—he stole my *secrets* . . . my *woman*!"

Maureen's heart thundered in her chest.

Carter and his witch. Hawsworth had been learning about witchcraft from Rupert.

Maureen edged toward the stairs.

The wolf cast a sharp look in her direction. "Don't try it, Dr. Cole."

Maureen moved back to Maggie and propped her hand on the stone foot drum near Maggie's face.

Dusty's voice broke, "For God's sake, what will this solve? Those things happened almost forty years ago!"

The wolf head tilted back, and the black eyeholes looked like deep dark caverns. "Dale and Hawsworth took everything from me! They *humiliated* me. I loved her with all my heart! I wrote her a hundred letters begging her to come back. They were in that old painted box! That's when I started learning to be a witch. Two crazy old women over at Zuni taught me. I knew someday I'd pay them back for what they did to me! And then the cancer . . . Out of time. I'm out of time."

Dusty slowly walked toward the rim where the Wolf Witch stood. "Rupert, please listen to me. I know—"

"You don't know!" the man sobbed suddenly, and choked it back. "I wouldn't be dying if it wasn't for your mother! She's the one who wanted to pot that kiva. Don't you understand? When I touched those old witches the evil entered me! Your—your mother . . . she knew what I was, who I was becoming. She's the one who told me to take the box with this mask! She was there at the birth of it all!" He desperately sucked in a breath, as though his lungs were starving. "And then, just a few days later, I found them! Here! I heard them." Rupert silently moved around the rim. The wolf mask bobbed and the teeth flashed in the firelight. "There they were. Dale Robertson, my good friend, naked, screwing the woman I loved. Right there!" He pointed with the pistol to the partially finished sand painting.

"I wasn't strong enough to punish them when I first found out. But I was heartbroken. How could anyone have done that? She was screwing four men at once! I'm going to kill all of you. Everyone who ever hurt me. You will all die before I do, and then I—"

*"Grandfather, no!"*

The deep voice came from the darkness up the hill.

Rupert spun around and almost lost his footing. He staggered. "R-Reggie?"

Maureen reached down and quietly pulled the tape from Maggie's mouth and whispered, *"Stay down!"*

# CHAPTER 50

MAGGIE BLINKED. POWER, something ancient and glistening, flowed around her. Maureen's silhouetted body wavered in the firelight, surrounded by silvery traces of light, like a laser show she'd seen once in Santa Fe.

*Toloache*. That's what Rupert had told her was in the orange drink he'd let her sip on the tailgate of his truck before he'd grabbed her and tied her up. *Toloache*, sacred datura, a plant loaded with alkaloids. Atropine was flooding her system. Spirit power, or a drug? Power or science. Indian or White. She felt her soul swell.

Reggie walked into the fire's glow with tears running down his cheeks. His black ponytail shone in the firelight. "Put down the gun, Grandfather."

Rupert regripped the pistol.

Reggie stepped closer. "I wish I'd known why you wanted me to steal those diaries. I thought they contained some tidbit on archaeology that you wanted. Grandfather, please don't do this. You're a good and kind man. You saved me, and I love you more than anything in the world. Stop this!"

The gun in Rupert's hand shook. "Don't stop me, Grandson! You know they all deserve—"

"They do *not* deserve any of this!" Reggie roared; then his voice dropped to a whisper. "I'm sure you're right. The evil in that thing is what caused your cancer! You should have left it in the kiva crypt where you found it!"

Rupert said, "Those two old witches at Zuni told me the mask would make me the most powerful witch alive. That I would be able to make people do anything I wished them to. And look!" He lifted a hand to the people in the firelit kiva below. "I summoned them to me from all over the world, and they came!"

Reggie dared to take another step closer. To Rupert aimed the pistol at Reggie's heart.

Reggie slowly lifted his hands, as though in surrender. In a very tender voice, Reggie said, "You think these people hurt you, Grandfather? Right now, this instant, you are hurting me far more than any of these people ever hurt you!" Reggie extended his hand.

"Give me the gun. Let's stop this now, before anyone else is harmed."

From the darkness behind Reggie another form emerged, tall, half stumbling. She wore a long camel-hair coat and had her hair drawn back in a ponytail. The silver conchos on her belt flashed in the fire's gleam.

Reggie spun at the sound of footsteps.

"Ruth, stay back!" he shouted. "I told you not to come here!"

Rupert stumbled, and his entire body began to shake. *"No! No! How did she get out of the kiva?"* he screamed insanely, and clutched the pistol as though trying to keep hold of a living animal that wanted to be free. The gun seemed to be fighting his grip. *"Help! Help me!"*

"Oh, good Lord, what's happening?" Reggie yelled, and ran forward.

The pistol bucked in Rupert's hand and the foot drum fractured. Stone chips showered the kiva, falling, falling like many-colored feathers.

Maggie shivered.

Maureen hit the ground on her belly and crawled like a madwoman for the safety behind the foot drum.

"Rupert, for God's sake!" Dusty stood defiantly in the middle of the sand painting, one arm up while the other hand reached behind him, clawing for something Maggie couldn't see. "Nichols is on his way! You don't want to do this! They'll put you away forever."

Maureen's hands were working on the ropes at Maggie's feet. With a sudden rush of relief, Maggie heard Grandmother Slumber's voice.

*"Don't worry. We are here, Granddaughter."*

The ropes came loose around her ankles. Maureen? Or Grandmother Slumber?

Maggie climbed out of the foot drum and rose unsteadily to her feet. Her hands remained bound, but she didn't need her hands for this.

"Maggie, get down!" Maureen's voice hissed from this world.

*"No,"* Aunt Hail's voice said from behind her other shoulder. *"We are all here, Niece. Together we are stronger than he is."*

"I am Kwewur!" Rupert proclaimed. "I'm going to kill all of you!"

*"His name is Two Hearts,"* Aunt Sage's soft voice came from behind Maggie. *"Tell him!"*

"You lie!" Maggie shouted, feeling Sister Datura flowing through her veins. "Your name is Two Hearts!"

The Wolf Witch stopped short, staring at her. The black pistol in his hands wavered, then shifted from Reggie to her.

*"We are guarding you,"* Grandma Slumber assured. *"He cannot hurt you."*

Maggie staggered sideways and struggled to stay on her feet. "We are all here, Two Hearts. Come down here! Come talk to the dead!"

"Maggie!" Maureen shouted from the darkness. "For God's sake, get down!"

Dusty said, "Come on, Rupert. You don't have to do this. I know you've had a tough time, but let me help you!"

"You know nothing!" The wolf aimed his pistol at Dusty's chest.

"He knows everything!" Maggie said. She swayed on her feet as she stepped forward to stand beside Dusty.

The world spun, shifting and slipping around her. By force of will, she managed to slow it, stabilize it. Power built in her breast, ebbing and flowing. "Two Hearts, the dead are coming for you! Look, there, beside you. See them?"

Maggie watched as phantoms appeared out of the kiva walls, ghosts of images that barely trapped a reflection in the flickering firelight.

Kwewur cocked his head and glanced around him. *"What—?"*

"They're reaching for you!" Maggie shouted, and her knees went weak. She had to lock them to keep standing. Dusty's hand clamped her arm, steadying her.

"There's no one!" Kwewur shouted back, and the wolf-teeth in his mask clicked together as he whirled to look at Maggie again.

Maggie bent forward. A pounding rush of nausea overwhelmed her, *and she could see him.* His wiry gray hair and mustache glowed in the firelight. He wore his old battered fedora. "Dale? Dale, thank God!"

Dusty's grip on her shoulder tightened, and Maggie was vaguely aware that his eyes had gone huge and wide.

*"Kwewur! Dale is right there. Right there beside you!"*

Dale's voice filtered between the worlds like a mist: "I'm sorry, my old friend, but I can't let you do this."

Maggie didn't know if anyone else heard, but Kwewur turned, looked out at the night, and shrieked, "Who's there? Show yourself!"

"They've come for you!" Maggie shouted. "Look at them, all around you!"

Maggie's stomach heaved. She threw up, and threw up, until she couldn't catch her breath, and she saw the dead dancing in the firelight on the kiva rim. Her grandmother and aunts, young again, moving between the katchinas like wisps of white smoke.

From a great distance, Grandmother Slumber's voice said, *"We're proud of you, Magpie. We love you so much."*

Maggie's soul was coming loose, twining up and out of her body. She surrendered to hot wavelike caresses of Sister Datura's hands and collapsed onto the kiva floor, where her body twitched uncontrollably.

Rupert swung the pistol forward, aimed at Ruth or

Reggie, or the Spirits he saw. The black steel shook wildly in his hand.

*"Oh, my God, what are you!"* Rupert screamed, and his finger tightened on the trigger.

Dusty screamed, *"No!"* and jerked his own pistol out.

Maggie saw Reggie leap in front of Ruth just as Rupert's pistol cracked, and a blinding flash of yellow swallowed the night.

The next muzzle blast, from Dusty's gun, shook the world.

# CHAPTER 51

DUSTY RAN, HIS pistol clutched in his sweating hand. He took the stairs up two at a time. Moonlight and firelight did a macabre dance on the cliff to his right, the old gods dancing. He swerved around the circumference of the kiva and headed for Reggie.

Reggie lay on his side, his chest blasted open, his left arm protectively across Ruth Ann's waist. Rupert lay almost on top of them, sprawled on his back. The black pistol lay six inches beyond his curled fingers.

Dusty's shot had torn through his right lung. Blood bubbled at Rupert's lips.

Ruth Ann sat up, shoved Reggie's arm off her, and peered at Dusty with drugged blue eyes. A basilisk fell from her blouse and rested on her breast. The malignant red eye glared at Dusty. "Is he d-dead?" she stuttered in terror.

High above them an owl circled. It hooted four times.

Rupert jerked. Frothy blood ran from his ruined lungs. He coughed, and stared wide-eyed at the sky. *"Dale, don't . . . don't!"* His fingers crept toward the gun.

Dusty kicked the pistol away and looked up. But he saw only moonlight. Moonlight and glittering stars.

When he looked back, Rupert Brown was dead.

# CHAPTER 52

STONE GHOST HAD to squint into the late spring sunlight to see Browser as he walked out of Streambed Town. His muscular shoulders bulged through the yellow fabric of his shirt. The spring light filled the canyon, painting the sandstone rims that hemmed Straight Path Canyon in hard light. A faint trickle of water ran in the wash just behind the town. A new summer lay just around the corner.

Bone Walker squeezed Stone Ghost's hand, and he looked down. Her unfocused eyes would forever remind him of Shadow Woman's as they'd stared up at him in death. They were the eyes of an animal, huge and black, and empty. Bone Walker hadn't spoken a word in six moons, but he kept talking to her anyway, talking and telling stories, hoping that someday she would peek out of that inner prison where she had locked her breath-heart soul and say something.

"Browser looks rested, doesn't he?" he asked Bone Walker. "It's all the new people flooding in. He doesn't have to stand guard as often now as he used to."

All morning long, he'd been thinking about what had happened at Owl House six moons ago. He could not get the images out of his mind. They had set the kiva afire. When the roof had burned through on the south, it had hinged and fallen in. A shower of sparks had twirled into the night sky.

White Cone sat in the sun at the base of the new tri-walled Kiva of the Worlds they'd built.

As Stone Ghost passed, he said, "Greetings, Bow Elder."

White Cone lifted a hand to shield his eyes from Father Sun's glare. Wispy gray hair framed his thin face. "A pleasant morning to you, Stone Ghost. Are you ready to head south? I've been thinking of the perfect place for us. On the western side of the mountains. Where the rivers head before winding down toward the Hohokam lands."

Stone Ghost didn't answer for a time. There was a task he had to take care of before he could allow himself to rest. Somewhere out there, perhaps still in the rockshelter near Longtail village, a dessicated mummy lay on her side in the dirt. It was his duty to find Night Sun and give her a proper burial. Her soul had wandered the earth alone for long enough.

Stone Ghost nodded to White Cone and said, "As soon as Matron Cloudblower gives the order, the Katsinas' People will be on their way."

They shared a smile, and White Cone leaned his aged head back against the wall and closed his eyes. He seemed to be enjoying the spring sunshine on his wrinkled face.

Stone Ghost continued on toward Browser.

Just before their paths collided, Browser lifted his gaze to the cliff where his wife, Catkin, stood guard. She was tall and beautiful, and her shoulder-length hair blew in the breeze. They were expecting their first child in four moons.

"How are you feeling, Uncle?" Browser asked as Stone Ghost and the little girl came closer.

"Alive," Stone Ghost said with a sigh. "And you, Nephew?"

"Better."

The pain and fear of that terrible day at Owl House had bound them like thongs of dried rawhide. The power of the White Moccasins had been damaged, but not broken. First People had begun to emerge from almost every village to join the White Moccasins. Their attacks on isolated villages had become brutal, inhuman, and frequent. So had the retaliatory raids. To Browser's horror, Matron Crossbill's people had split off, and began raiding Flute Player villages in the north.

But as the warfare escalated, the Katsinas' People grew. Fully one-third of Blue Corn's Flowing Waters Town's people had converted. It seemed that what Flame Carrier's search for the First People's kiva could not accomplish, a Mogollon prophet's death did. The Katsinas' People would survive. Poor Singer's prophecy would live—and somewhere in the future, the katsinas would dance with the old gods.

"I've been thinking about Owl House all morning, Nephew. I've never had a chance to ask how you knew that Rain Crow had been working with Horned Ram?"

"I suspected the night the prophet was killed. But when Rain Crow insisted on coming with us, I was positive. Neither he nor Horned Ram knew they were working for the First People when they allowed Shadow access to Gray Thunder's room. It must have shocked Rain Crow to see Obsidian in the kiva, having just seen her twin sister murder Acorn and Gray Thunder."

"Why did he do it? Do you know?"

"That I cannot answer. I suspect that our defense of the Mogollon made Rain Crow suspicious. Then the reaction of his people to Gray Thunder's death, the prophet's instant popularity and the sudden interest in Poor Singer's prophecy, coupled with Acorn's death,

left him uneasy. Since nothing was working the way it
was supposed to, Rain Crow knew that he had been
used. I think he came here to find out who had turned
him into a puppet, and who had killed his nephew."

Stone Ghost searched his belt pouch, then extended
his hand. "Here, Nephew. I took this from Two
Hearts's hand before we left. I believe it belongs to
you."

Browser reached out. Stone Ghost laid the beautifully carved turquoise wolf onto his palm. It seemed to
radiate a heat all its own. Browser let out a sigh and
clutched it to his heart.

Stone Ghost watched the long line of people coming
up the road from the north. They couldn't remain here.
The soil was so played out, the rain and runoff so
spotty, they couldn't feed this many people in Straight
Path Canyon.

But they couldn't go north. Over and over he'd heard
the same stories from refugees. They said things were
so bad in the Green Mesa country that most of the
people had moved to the Great River in the east. It was
hard to imagine, the cliff towns deserted, nothing but
pack rats living there.

Stone Ghost looked up at Browser. "Cloudblower is
worried."

"Worried?"

"Yes, another twenty people arrived this morning,
mostly Flute Player Believers who came to see the heroes who could kill the most feared witch in the land."

Browser smiled. "I thought you liked all those hands
touching you."

Stone Ghost gave him a disgusted look. "They just
keep coming, either to see me, or you, or to see if we
really can live together, Made People, First People, Fire
Dogs, and all the rest."

"That's the strength of the katsinas, Uncle."

He pointed to the tall round Kiva of the Worlds that
stood behind Streambed Town. They had finished

building it just yesterday. "I thought the dawn dedication was beautiful, with the pure white plaster and painted katsinas."

"Yes," Stone Ghost sighed, "but no opening appeared to the underworld, Nephew. I wonder—"

"Nor will it," White Cone called.

Stone Ghost turned back to look at the old man. "What do you mean?"

"That's not what Poor Singer meant!"

Stone Ghost led Bone Walker back. Browser followed. "Do you know what he meant? Did Gray Thunder tell you his vision?"

White Cone folded his arms across his drawn-up knees. "Gray Thunder told me that the truth is never hidden. It is always right there before our eyes. We are just blind."

Stone Ghost grunted as he lowered himself to a rock beside White Cone. Bone Walker climbed into his lap and leaned her head against his bony old chest. Stone Ghost patted her back gently.

Life moved, as inconstant and fickle as Wind Baby, frolicking, sleeping, weeping, but never truly still. Never solid or finished. Always like water flowing from one place to the next. Seed and fruit. Rain and drought, everything traveled in a gigantic circle, an eternal process of becoming something new. But we rarely saw it. Humans tended to see only frozen moments, not the flow of things. Is that what White Cone meant about being blind?

"What did he tell you?" Stone Ghost asked.

Browser moved to stand behind Stone Ghost, listening. The fringe on the bottom of his yellow shirt danced in the wind.

White Cone smiled. "When Poor Singer said that you had to find the First People's original kiva, he did not mean the hole where they emerged from the underworlds in the Beginning Time."

"But he said we had to reopen the doorway to the

Land of the Dead," Browser said, and propped a hand on his belted war club. "What else could he have meant?"

"The doorway to the dead is not a physical hole in the earth, you young fool. If you wish to seek the advice of the dead you must have the heart of a cloud."

Bone Walker's fists twined in Stone Ghost's shirt. He lifted a hand to silence White Cone, and looked down.

Bone Walker's lips moved, but no sound came out.

Very softly, so as not to frighten her, he said, "What is it, Bone Walker?"

She seemed to be struggling to find words. *"Tears . . . ,"* she whispered. *"You have to live inside the tears of the dead."*

Browser's face slackened and White Cone smiled.

Stone Ghost hugged Bone Walker tightly against him, and she tucked her head against his chest.

Stone Ghost's heart swelled until he feared it might explode. He kissed the top of Bone Walker's head and said, "I told you, didn't I, that if you worked very hard someday you would be a great Singer."

Bone Walker smiled. A little girl's smile, frail and heartwarming. She looked up with sparkling eyes and focused on the cliff where Catkin stood. She looked for a long time.

Finally, she said, *"He's* going to be a really great Singer."

"Who is?" Browser asked, looking up at Catkin and frowning.

Bone Walker sucked her lip for several instants, then whispered, *"That little boy in her belly."*

DUSTY WALKED INTO the candlelit church and looked around. The place was quiet and empty except for one person. Maggie knelt in the second pew, her hands clasped prayerfully before her. Her gaze rested on the crucifix on the wall.

He walked forward, the paper bag crackling in his right hand, and slid into the pew beside her. The church smelled of melted wax and incense, things he found oddly comforting.

Maggie turned to look at him. Her eyes were swollen, and grief strained the lines around her mouth. She wore a white scarf over her black hair, knotted beneath her chin.

"You're not a churchgoing person," Maggie whispered. "What are you doing here?"

"I thought I'd surprise God."

Maggie smiled. "Speaking of God, how are you doing with the owl?"

Dusty gave her a startled look. "How do you know about the owl?"

"I talked to Sylvia this morning. She said you'd been sleeping with your pistol because the owl follows you everywhere you go."

Dusty turned sideways to face her and propped his arm on the pew ahead. "It's the strangest thing. The owl kept me up hooting when I was sleeping in my trailer in Santa Fe, so I moved to Dale's house, and he showed up there. Perched right on the kitchen windowsill and watched me eat breakfast. Gave me the heebie-jeebies."

Maggie let out a disappointed breath. "When a Spirit Helper comes fluttering at your window, you don't close it, Dusty. You open it as wide as you can."

Dusty made a face. He knew that. It was just hard to do in real life. He gripped the smooth wood of the pew and lifted his brows. "Yeah, well, I'm working on it."

They sat in silence for a moment and Dusty absorbed the calm golden glow of the church.

"How are you doing, Maggie? Are you all right?"

"As well as can be expected after the things that have happened." She glanced at him. "I saw it all, Dusty. I was hovering there, above my body, and I saw you and Maureen and Reggie and Rupert." Her brow furrowed.

"Is that a problem?"

Her brown eyes pleaded with him. "I think the datura did something to me, Dusty. I keep seeing between the worlds, and I know"—she swallowed hard—"that datura overdoses can cause insanity."

Dusty laughed, handing her the sack. "You're not insane yet, Maggie. Of course, it's inevitable. Working for the government is bound to get to you sooner or later." He pointed to the sack. "That's in return for the fry bread you brought me that day. Those are my own special recipe super black bean burritos."

Maggie clasped her hands on the sack and squeezed it hard, as though fighting grief. "Aunt Sage used to say that if you wanted to understand death, you had to have the heart of a cloud."

"Hmm," Dusty grunted. "Which meant what?"

Tears filled Maggie's eyes, but she smiled. "That you had to live inside the tears of the dead."

Dusty sank back into the pew and looked up at the crucifix. Jesus' body was emaciated, his face anguished. But his painted eyes seemed to be alive and looking at Dusty with a kind of curious benevolence.

Dusty held that gaze for a long time. It hadn't occurred to him before, but that's what archaeology was all about.

*Living inside the tears of the dead so we can learn from them.*

"Maggie? We have one more thing to do, that is, if you're up to it."

# EPILOGUE

DUSTY SAT ON the kitchen counter in his Santa Fe trailer, his cowboy-booted feet dangling. He sipped a bottle of Guinness while he listened to his mother.

Maureen and Maggie sat at the table across from Ruth Ann. Maureen had worn her long hair loose, combed to a rich sheen. Her white sweater did nice things to Dusty's imagination. Maggie had a strangely serene expression. A small cedar box sat on the table before her. On the couch, Yvette watched them. Over the last couple of weeks, Dusty and Yvette had come to share a warm but curious sort of relationship.

"Rupert said that we needed to talk, that he'd meet me at Casa Rinconada at nightfall." Ruth Ann propped her fists on the table. Her black cashmere sweater accented her silver hair. "I assumed he wished to tell me something about Dale's murder."

"You weren't afraid he was the murderer?" Maureen sipped at a cup of coffee.

"God no. Why would I be? For years he wrote me love letters. I mean, hell, what would it hurt to see him again?" Ruth Ann laced her fingers together primly on the table, intent on her story. "We had taken a walk up to the site you now call Owl House. We were sitting there, looking down into that kiva, and Rupert handed me a candy." She smiled. "Hell, it was like old times. It was the sixties. Rupert and I used to go up on hilltops, drop a little acid, and watch the sun go down."

"You knew it was LSD?" Dusty asked.

"What do you think I am? A blessed virgin? Of course, I knew. I'm telling you the same thing I told your friend, Agent Nichols, in my formal statement."

"So you went down into the kiva?" Maureen asked, disbelief in her voice. "Knowing that Dale and Hawsworth had been murdered there?"

"In my state of mind, what did I care? Rupert and I pulled the tarp back and built a fire in that old hearth," Ruth Ann whispered, seeing it all again, "and I swear something happened. Firelight in that hearth for the first time in over seven hundred years, flickering on those little pieces of bone and those two skeletons. We talked of old times, of things Rupert and I had done, of things Dale and Sam and I did, and people we both knew. Rupert asked me if I had it to do all over again, would I? I said, 'God, yes. I'd sell my soul to be twenty-five again.' "

Ruth Ann paused, a gleam in her eyes. "That's when he tied me up, put on the wolf mask, and left."

Dusty contemplatively scratched off part of the label on his Guinness bottle. "It didn't occur to you that he was Kwewur?"

"No. Why would it have? He sure as hell hadn't made any threatening gestures."

Yvette made a disgusted sound deep in her throat, and Ruth Ann glared at her.

"So, you just sat there?" Dusty demanded to know. "While he turned Casa Rinconada upside down trying to kill us?"

"Have you ever done acid, William?"

"No."

"Well, you can just sit. It's wonderful." Ruth Ann smiled beatifically. "And I sat, feeling the night fall, talking to that young woman and the old man. The light was flickering on their bones. It was quite pleasant."

"What about the gunshots?"

She spread her hands. "They were katchinas clapping their hands, making thunder in the night. You know, a mystical experience. I could have sat there until dawn, just me, and those two people." She looked at Dusty. "I *would* have sat there if Reggie hadn't dragged me out of that kiva and untied me. He said he'd been working late and seen his grandfather's truck parked in the lot beside Maggie's and mine. He'd stopped to check on things, make sure everybody was all right, and that's when he saw the firelight coming from that old kiva." She twisted her hands on the table and regret tightened her mouth. "I wish I'd known why he told me to stay put. I would have."

"But you didn't. You wandered down the hill to Casa Rinconada," Dusty said.

"Oh, come on, William. How was I to know I'd be walking into a maelstrom?"

Dusty ran his thumb down the side of his Guinness bottle. It felt cool and damp. He was so tired, he didn't have the strength to hate her. But he would always wonder what would have happened if she hadn't come walking in out of the night. Would Reggie have been able to talk Rupert out of the gun?

"Did those people tell you who they were?" Yvette asked. "The dead ones?"

"Just a man and his wife." Ruth Ann sighed contentedly. "Delightful people raising a family. She had several children by him. It was his second marriage. His first wife was killed in a fall. From the cliffs just south of Rinconada. It was icy."

Maureen arched an eyebrow as she met Dusty's glance. But it was Yvette who looked ready to reach out and strangle Ruth Ann.

"And that's it. That's my statement." Ruth Ann clapped her hands together. "Agent Nichols, after giving me a lecture about the use of controlled substances, has allowed me to plead guilty to a narcotics charge, a charge of criminal trespass, and a couple of misdemeanors. For that, I get two years of probation to be administered in Boston."

Dusty had no idea what was going to happen to him. Nichols hadn't arrested him. All the witnesses had said it was self-defense. But he'd killed his best friend's father. No matter what the courts did to him, it couldn't possibly be as bad as what Dusty was going to do to himself over the next forty years.

Dusty squinted at his half-peeled label. "But you'd never been there before? In the witch kiva, I mean?"

"No. Why?" Ruth Ann frowned.

Dusty reached across the counter. He handed the photograph to his mother. "I came across this in Dale's file cabinet while we were replacing the journals recovered from Reggie's apartment."

Ruth Ann took it, looked at it with expressionless eyes. "I remember this. The barbecue in Dale's backyard. God, let's see. 'Sixty-six, maybe? We had a sitter for little William. Sam and I were out for a night of big city living. I ended up passed out on Dale's couch. My God, doesn't Rupert look young and handsome." She tossed the photo back to Dusty. "What's your point?"

Dusty lifted the photo. "When did you give up smoking?"

"Early seventies." Ruth Ann cocked her head, as though trying to fathom his meaning.

Dusty took a deep breath. "In the picture Rupert is smoking Lucky Strikes."

Ruth Ann shrugged, but she appeared uncomfortable. "Yes, so? He always smoked Lucky Strikes."

Dusty frowned. "You told me once you liked to get the good stuff fast. You and Rupert opened that site together, didn't you? You rolled the slabs off the witches, and Rupert took the wolf mask. That was your pack of cigarettes, and maybe even your beer can stuffed into the wall crypt. What did you do? Screw him in there, too? Right in front of the mask? In front of those skeletons?"

She watched him from the corner of her eye, thinking, calculating what he could know. After a long pause, she said, "What if I did, William? Are you going to run back to Agent Nichols and have him add antiquities violations to my rap sheet?"

"You were the one who put Hawsworth together with Rupert, weren't you?" Maureen asked. " 'Carter and his witch,' you said at the Loretto that day. But you'd been doing a little studying on your own. After all, you'd been there."

Ruth Ann smiled coldly. "Finding a witch was a rush. So I tried witchcraft. It didn't work. What was the point of sticking with it?"

"What did you do to Dale? Did you use witchcraft to get him to Casa Rinconada that last time in sixty-nine? We read the journal yesterday. He drove out there to tell you that he never wanted to see you again. That he thought you were killing Sam. Dale even called you a witch in his diary. But the next day, the entry was: *'Dear God, what have I done? There she was, standing naked in the firelight. God, forgive me.' "*

Ruth Ann lifted her hands in a gesture of innocence. "Is it my fault that he couldn't resist me? But for that night, Yvette wouldn't be here."

"Alas, Mum, I am," Yvette said as she straightened.

Ruth Ann gazed at her, looking bored. "Well, I should be going."

She started to rise.

" 'Fraid not, Mum." Yvette raised her voice. "Magpie?"

Dusty was watching Ruth Ann's face as Maggie pushed the little cedar box across the table.

Maggie opened the box and said, "Let's have it, Dr. Sullivan."

"Have what?" Ruth Ann pulled away from the box.

"What you took from the female skeleton in Owl House," Maggie told her.

Dusty crossed his arms and said, "Hand it over."

"Hand what over?"

"The basilisk, Mum." Yvette sat up on the couch and

shoved ash-blond hair behind her ears. "The one I saw
in Dusty's trailer."

Maggie shoved the box closer, her eyes burning bril-
liantly, powered by an inner strength Dusty had never
seen before. "Lift it off of your neck and drop it into
the box."

"I will not!"

"Yes, you will," Dusty said. "That thing is filled with
evil. Either the basilisk goes into the box, or you don't
leave this place alive. Think about it."

Ruth Ann, for the first time, glanced fearfully around
the room. "Oh, do be serious! You'd kill me for a silly
pendant?"

Dusty slid off the counter and stood over her with
his fists clenched. "I don't want to rip it off your throat.
But I will."

"Are you threatening me?"

"Dusty," Yvette said, "she's not going to cooperate,
you may as well just kill her."

Ruth Ann met his eyes, saw the resolve, and wavered. "Oh, what the hell." She reached inside her
blouse, lifted out the black stone pendant, and dropped
it into the box.

Maggie snapped the box shut and reeled, as though
in pain.

"What's the matter?" Dusty asked.

"You should have heard it," Maggie whispered
hoarsely. "It screamed when it died."

Ruth Ann Sullivan looked from one person to the
next, then shoved to her feet. "Well, if you're satisfied,
William, I'm going." She marched for the door.

Maggie and Dusty stood side by side on the rickety
porch watching Ruth Ann Sullivan walk to her rental
car. When she drove off into the late fall evening,
Dusty didn't even wave.

Maggie lifted the box and shook it. "Do you think
*el basilisco* had any inkling that Ruth Ann would drop
him into a mirror-lined box?"

Dusty leaned heavily against the door frame. "Thank God, it's over."

Yvette asked, "Is it? What happened to the mask?"

Dusty turned to look at her. He remembered the feel of the wolf mask, warm and tingly, as though it were alive and breathing on his hands. "I threw it in the fire at Casa Rinconada. I'd swear, as it burned, I saw the Shiwana dancing in the shadows it cast on the kiva walls."

Yvette rose to her feet and stretched. "Well, that's enough spooky stuff for me. Good night, all. I'm off to my hotel for a real night's rest. I'll see you in the morning. *Huevos* at eight, right?"

"Right. Good night, Yvette," Dusty said.

"I'm out of here, too." Maggie clutched the cedar box. "I think I might drive by the Rio Grande bridge west of Taos. It's a long way down to the rocks below."

"Take care," Maureen said.

Maggie smiled and walked to her pickup.

As Maggie's truck wound its way up the driveway to Canyon Road, Dusty's stomach muscles suddenly clenched. He bent double and couldn't seem to catch his breath.

"What is it? What's wrong?" Maureen asked as she rushed to his side.

Dusty held up a hand, walked to the table, and eased down. All of the fear and desperation had seeped out of him, leaving a hollow shell. He started trembling for no reason.

"My God," he whispered as he dropped his face in his hands. "Dale is dead, Maureen. Dale is dead."

Maureen inhaled a deep breath. She didn't speak for a time.

Finally, she said, "But we're alive, Dusty. Let's see if we can find the future together."

# BIBLIOGRAPHY

Acatos, Sylvio. *Pueblos: Prehistoric Indian Cultures of the Southwest*, trans. *Die Pueblos* (1989 eds.). New York: Facts on File, 1990.

Adams, E. Charles. *The Origin and Development of the Pueblo Katsina Cult*. Tucson, AZ: University of Arizona Press, 1991.

Adler, Michael A. *The Prehistoric Pueblo World A.D. 1150–1350*. Tucson, AZ: University of Arizona Press, 1996.

Allen, Paula Gunn. *Spider Woman's Granddaughters*. New York: Ballantine Books, 1989.

Arnberger, Leslie P. *Flowers of the Southwest Mountains*. Tucson, AZ: Southwest Parks and Monuments Assoc., 1982.

Aufderheide, Arthur C. *Cambridge Encyclopedia of Human Paleopathology*. Cambridge, UK: Cambridge University Press, 1998.

Baars, Donald L. *Navajo Country: A Geological and Natural History of the Four Corners Region*. Albuquerque, NM: University of New Mexico Press, 1995.

Becket, Patrick H., ed. *Mogollon V*. Report of Fifth Mogollon Conference, Las Cruces, NM: COAS Publishing and Research, 1991.

Boissiere, Robert. *The Return of Pahana: A Hopi Myth*. Santa Fe, NM: Bear & Company, 1990.

Bowers, Janice Emily. *Shrubs and Trees of the Southwest Deserts*. Tucson, AZ: Southwest Parks & Monuments Assoc., 1993.

Brody, J. J. *The Anasazi*. New York: Rizzoli International Publications, 1990.

Brothwell, Don, and A. T. Sandison, *Disease in Antiquity*. Springfield, IL: Charles C. Thomas, 1967.

Bunzel, Ruth L. *Zuni Katcinas*. Reprint of 47th Annual Report

of the Bureau of American Ethnography, 1929–30, Glorieta,
NM: Rio Grande Press, 1984.

Colton, Harold S. *Black Sand: Prehistory in Northern Arizona*.
Albuquerque, NM: University of New Mexico Press, 1960.

Cordell, Linda S. "Predicting Site Abandonment at Wetherill
Mesa." *The Kiva* (1975) 40(3):189–202.

————. *Prehistory of the Southwest*. New York: Academic
Press, 1984.

————. *Ancient Pueblo People*. Smithsonian Exploring the Ancient World Series, Montreal, and Smithsonian Institution,
Washington, DC: St. Rémy Press, 1994.

————. and George J. Gumerman, eds. *Dynamics of Southwest
Prehistory*. Washington, DC: Smithsonian Institution Press,
1989.

Crown, Patricia, and W. James Judge, eds. *Chaco and Hohokam: Prehistoric Regional Systems in the American Southwest*. Santa Fe, NM: School of American Research Press,
1991.

Cummings, Linda Scott. "Anasazi Subsistence Activity Areas
Reflected in the Pollen Records." Paper presented to the So-
ciety for American Archaeology, 45th Annual Meeting, New
Orleans, 1986.

————."Anasazi Diet: Variety in the Hoy House and Lion
House Coprolite Record and Nutritional Analysis," in Kristin
D. Sobolik, ed., *Paleonutrition: The Diet and Health of Pre-
historic Americans*. Occasional Paper No. 22, Carbondale, IL:
Center for Archeological Investigations, Southern Illinois
University, 1994.

Dodge, Natt N. *Flowers of the Southwest Desert*. Tucson, AZ:
Southwest Parks & Monuments Assoc., 1985.

Dooling, D. M., and Paul Jordan-Smith, eds. *I Become Part of
It: Sacred Dimensions in Native American Life*. San Francisco: A Parabola Book, Harpers; New York: Harper Collins,
1989.

Douglas, John E. "Autonomy and Regional Systems in the Late
Prehistoric Southern Southwest." *American Antiquity* (1995)
60:240–57.

Dunmire, William W., and Gail Tierney. *Wild Plants of the*

*Pueblo Province: Exploring Ancient and Enduring Uses.*
Santa Fe, NM: Museum of New Mexico Press, 1995.

Ellis, Florence Hawley. "Patterns of Aggression and the War
Cult in South-western Pueblos." *Southwestern Journal of Anthropology* (1951) 7:177–201.

Elmore, Francis H. *Shrubs and Trees of the Southwest Upland.*
Tucson AZ: Southwest Parks & Monuments Assoc., 1976.

Ericson, Jonathan E., and Timothy G. Baugh, eds. *The American
Southwest and Mesoamerica: Systems of Prehistoric
Exchange.* New York: Plenum Press, 1993.

Fagan, Brian M. *Ancient North America.* New York: Thames &
Hudson, 1991.

Farmer, Malcolm F. "A Suggested Typology of Defensive Systems of the Southwest." *Southwestern Journal of Archeology*
(1957), 13:249–66.

Frank, Larry, and Francis H. Harlow. *Historic Pottery of the
Pueblo Indians: 1600–1880.* West Chester, PA: Schiffler Publishing, 1990.

Frazier, Kendrick. *People of Chaco: A Canyon and its Culture.*
New York: W. W. Norton, 1986.

Gabriel, Kathryn. *Roads to Center Place: A Cultural Atlas of
Chaco Canyon and the Anasazi.* Boulder, CO: Johnson
Books, 1991.

Gumerman, George J., ed. *The Anasazi in a Changing Environment.* School of American Research, New York: Cambridge
University Press, 1988.

———. *Exploring the Hohokam: Prehistoric Peoples of the
American Southwest.* Amerind Foundation, Albuquerque,
NM: University of New Mexico Press, 1991.

———. *Themes in Southwest Prehistory.* Sante Fe, NM: School
of American Research Press, 1994.

Haas, Jonathan. "Warfare and the Evolution of Tribal Polities in
the Prehistoric Southwest," in Haas, ed., *The Anthropology of
War.* Cambridge, UK: Cambridge University Press, 1990.

———, and Winifred Creamer. "A History of Pueblo Warfare."
Paper Presented at the 60th Annual Meeting of the Society of
American Archeology, Minneapolis, 1995.

———. *Stress and Warfare Among the Kayenta Anasazi of the*

*Thirteenth Century A.D.* Field Museum of Natural History, Chicago, 1993.

Haury, Emil. *Mogollon Culture in the Forestdale Valley, East-Central Arizona.* Tucson, AZ: University of Arizona Press, 1985.

Hayes, Alden C., David M. Burgge, and W. James Judge. *Archaeological Surveys of Chaco Canyon, New Mexico.* Reprint of National Park Service Report, Albuquerque, NM: University of New Mexico Press, 1981.

Hultkrantz, Ake. *Native Religions: The Power of Visions and Fertility.* New York: Harper & Row, 1987.

Jacobs, Sue-Ellen, ed. "Continuity and Change in Gender Roles at San Juan Pueblo," in *Women and Power in Native North America.* Norman, OK: University of Oklahoma Press, 1995.

Jernigan, E. Wesley. *Jewelry of the Prehistoric Southwest.* Albuquerque, NM: University of New Mexico Press, 1978.

Jett, Stephen C. "Pueblo Indian Migrations: An Evaluation of the Possible Physical and Cultural Determinants." *American Antiquity* (1964) 29: 281–300.

Komarek, Susan. *Flora of the San Juans: A Field Guide to the Mountain Plants of Southwestern Colorado.* Durango, CO: Kivaki Press, 1994.

Lange, Frederick, et al. *Yellow Jacket: A Four Corners Anasazi Ceremonial Center.* Boulder, CO: Johnson Books, 1988.

LeBlanc, Stephen A. *Prehistoric Warfare in the American Southwest.* Salt Lake City, UT: University of Utah Press, 1999.

Lekson, Stephen H. *The Chaco Meridian.* Walnut Creek, CA: Alta Mira, 1999.

———. *Mimbres Archeology of the Upper Gila, New Mexico.* Anthropological Papers of the University of Arizona, no. 53, Tucson, AZ: University of Arizona Press, 1990.

———, et al. "The Chaco Canyon Community." *Scientific American* (1988) 259(1): 100–109.

Lewis, Dorothy Otnow. *Guilty by Reason of Insanity. A Psychiatrist Explores the Minds of Killers.* New York: Ballantine Books, 1998.

Lipe, W. D., and Michelle Hegemon, eds. *The Architecture of*

*Social Integration in Prehistoric Pueblos*. Occasional Papers of the Crow Canyon Archaeological Center, no. 1, Cortez, CO, 1989.

Lister, Florence C. *In the Shadow of the Rocks: Archaeology of the Chimney Rock District in Southern Colorado*. Niwot, Colorado: University Press of Colorado, 1993.

Lister, Robert H., and Florence C. Lister. *Chaco Canyon*. Albuquerque, NM: University of New Mexico Press, 1981.

Malotki, Ekkehart. *Gullible Coyote: Una'ihu: A Bilingual Collection of Hopi Coyote Stories*. Tucson, AZ: University of Arizona Press, 1985.

————, ed. *Hopi Ruin Legends*. Lincoln, NE: University of Nebraska Press, 1993.

————, and Michaël Lomatuway'ma. *Maasaw: Profile of a Hopi God*. American Tribal Religions, vol. XI, Lincoln, NE: University of Nebraska Press, 1987.

Malville, J. McKimm, and Claudia Putnam. *Prehistoric Astronomy in the Southwest*. Boulder, CO: Johnson Books, 1993.

Mann, Coramae Richey. *When Women Kill*. New York: State University of New York Press, 1996.

Martin, Debra L. "Lives Unlived: The Political Economy of Violence Against Anasazi Women." Paper presented to the Society for American Archeology 60th Annual Meeting, Minneapolis, 1995.

————, et al. *Black Mesa Anasazi Health: Reconstructing Life from Patterns of Death and Disease*. Occasional Paper no. 14. Carbondale, IL: Southern Illinois University, 1991.

Mayes, Vernon O., and Barbara Bayless Lacy. *Nanise: A Navajo Herbal*. Tsaile, AZ: Navajo Community College Press, 1989.

McGuire, Randall H., and Michael Schiffer, eds. *Hohokam and Patayan: Prehistory of Southwestern Arizona*. New York: Academic Press, 1982.

McNitt, Frank. *Richard Wetherill Anasazi*. Albuquerque, NM: University of New Mexico Press, 1966.

Minnis, Paul E., and Charles L. Redman, eds. *Perspectives on Southwestern Prehistory*. Boulder, CO: Westview Press, 1990.

Mullet, G. M. *Spider Woman Stories: Legends of the Hopi In-*

*dians.* Tucson, AZ: University of Arizona Press, 1979.

Nabahan, Gary Paul. *Enduring Seeds: Native American Agriculture and Wild Plant Conservation.* San Francisco: North Point Press, 1989.

Noble, David Grant. *Ancient Ruins of the Southwest: An Archaeological Guide.* Flagstaff, AZ: Northland Publishing, 1991.

Ortiz, Alfonzo, ed. *Handbook of North American Indians.* Washington, DC: Smithsonian Institution, 1983.

Palkovich, Ann M. *The Arroyo Hondo Skeletal and Mortuary Remains.* Arroyo Hondo Archeological Series, vol. 3, Santa Fe, NM: School of American Research Press, 1980.

Parsons, Elsie Clews. *Tewa Tales* (reprint of 1924 edition). Tucson, AZ: University of Arizona Press, 1994.

Pepper, George H. *Pueblo Bonito* (reprint of 1920 edition). Albuquerque, NM: University of New Mexico Press, 1996.

Pike, Donald G., and David Muench. *Anasazi: Ancient People of the Rock.* New York: Crown Publishers, 1974.

Reid, J. Jefferson, and David E. Doyel, eds. *Emil Haury's Prehistory of the American Southwest.* Tucson, AZ: University of Arizona Press, 1992.

Riley, Carroll L. *Rio del Norte: People of the Upper Rio Grande from the Earliest Times to the Pueblo Revolt.* Salt Lake City, UT: University of Utah Press, 1995.

Rocek, Thomas R. "Sedentarization and Agricultural Dependence: Perspectives from the Pithouse-to-Pueblo Transition in the American Southwest." *American Antiquity* (1995) 60: 218–39.

Schaafsma, Polly. *Indian Rock Art of the Southwest.* Albuquerque, NM: University of New Mexico Press, 1980.

Sebastian, Lynne. *The Chaco Anasazi: Sociopolitical Evolution in the Prehistoric Southwest.* Cambridge, UK: Cambridge University Press, 1992.

Simmons, Marc. *Witchcraft in the Southwest* (reprint of 1974 edition, Bison Books). Lincoln, NE: University of Nebraska Press, 1980.

Slifer, Dennis, and James Duffield. *Kokopelli: Flute Player Images in Rock Art.* Santa Fe, NM: Ancient City Press, 1994.

Smith, Watson, with Raymond H. Thompson, ed. *When Is a Kiva: And Other Questions About Southwestern Archaeology.* Tucson, AZ: University of Arizona Press, 1990.

Sobolik, Kristin D., ed. *Paleonutrition: The Diet and Health of Prehistoric Americans.* Occasional Paper no. 22, Center for Archeological Investigations, Carbondale, IL: Southern Illinois University, 1994.

Sullivan, Alan P. "Pinyon Nuts and Other Wild Resources in Western Anasazi Subsistence Economies." *Research in Economic Anthropology, Supplement* (1992) 6: 195–239.

Tedlock, Barbara. *The Beautiful and the Dangerous: Encounters with the Zuni Indians.* New York: Viking Press, 1992.

Trombold, Charles D., ed. *Ancient Road Networks and Settlement Hierarchies in the New World.* Cambridge, UK: Cambridge University Press, 1991.

Turner, Christy G., and Jacqueline A. Turner. *Man Corn. Cannibalism and Violence in the Prehistoric American Southwest.* Salt Lake City, UT: University of Utah Press, 1999.

Tyler, Hamilton A. *Pueblo Gods and Myths.* Norman, OK: University of Oklahoma Press, 1964.

Underhill, Ruth. *Life in the Pueblos* (reprint of 1964 Bureau of Indian Affairs Report). Santa Fe, NM: Ancient City Press, 1991.

Upham, Steadman, Kent G. Lightfoot, and Roberta A. Jewett, eds. *The Sociopolitical Structure of Prehistoric Southwestern Societies.* San Francisco: Westview Press, 1989.

Vivian, Gordon, and Tom W. Mathews. *Kin Kletso: A Pueblo III Community in Chaco Canyon, New Mexico,* vol. 6. Globe, AZ: Southwest Parks & Monuments Association, 1973.

Vivian, Gordon, and Paul Reiter. *The Great Kivas of Chaco Canyon and Their Relationships,* Monograph, no. 22, Santa Fe, NM: School of American Research Press, 1965.

Vivian, R. Gwinn. *The Chacoan Prehistory of the San Juan Basin.* New York: Academic Press, 1990.

Waters, Frank. *Book of the Hopi.* New York: Viking Press, 1963.

Wetterstrom, Wilma. *Food, Diet, and Population at Prehistoric Arroyo Hondo Pueblo, New Mexico.* Arroyo Hondo Archaeological Series, vol. 6. Santa Fe, NM: School of American Research Press, 1986.

White, Tim D. *Prehistoric Cannibalism at Mancos 5MTUMR-2346*. Princeton, NJ: Princeton University Press, 1992.

Williamson, Ray A. *Living the Sky: The Cosmos of the American Indian*. Norman, OK: University of Oklahoma Press, 1984.

Wills, W. H., and Robert D. Leonard, eds. *The Ancient Southwestern Community*. Albuquerque, NM: University of New Mexico Press, 1994.

Woodbury, Richard B. "A Reconsideration of Pueblo Warfare in the Southwestern United States." *Actas del XXXIII Congreso Internacional de Americanistas* (1959) II: 124–33. San Jose, Costa Rica.

———. "Climatic Changes and Prehistoric Agriculture in the Southwestern United States." *New York Academy of Sciences Annals* (1969), vol. 95, art. 1.

Wright, Barton. *Katchinas: The Barry Goldwater Collection at the Heard Museum*. Phoenix, AZ: Heard Museum, 1975.